SWEDEN

DAVID CHRISTIE

Text Copyright © 2016 David Christie

All rights reserved

ISBN: 9781521003572

For Louise, of course

From his childhood, a man may dream like this about great cities and glorious battlefields, but the real, decisive battles for the preservation of his being and the realisation of everything within it, must be fought wherever destiny happens to cast him, in who knows what narrow, nameless space with no splendour or beauty, with no witness or judge.

Ivo Andric, *Time of the Consuls*

CLOWN: My friend, youth's what one needs, of course,
When one
Is in the thick of battle with the foe,
Or when sweet girls are hanging on
One's neck and simply won't let go,
Or when the finish of a race
Beckons far off to victory,
Or when one's danced at furious pace
Then spends the night in revelry:
But boldly, gleefully to play
Upon the lyre, choose one's own goal
And reach it by some charming way
On random motions of the soul –
Such is the older poet's task; and we
Respect you none the less. The proverbs wrong
You see:
Age is no second childhood – age makes plain
Children we were, true children we remain.
Goethe, *Faust: Part One, Prelude on the Stage*

PROLOGUE

The First time he began the dreaming, and ever after he assumed, the trigger for it all, was his first sight of her.

Not her right at the end.

Nor either of the two in between; whoever they may have been,

But her; the first one, the one who started it all.

Maybe.

1. RED AND GREEN BRACES
30.4.1987

Sunlight had been pouring down into the narrow Soho streets all day, superheating the exhaust fumes of the clutch-crawling traffic into a fetid vapour just short of smog. Beneath his feet, the paving stones had risen to the temperature of baker's oven slabs, broiling his feet in his sweat-soaked socks and sending rhythmic pulses of prickly heat racing up from his soles of his shoes. Throttled by his tie, and with his trousers hanging from his hips like drapes, he had negotiated the press of bodies at Oxford Circus dressed like a lagged boiler.

He desperately needed somewhere to sit down and cool off.

Looking round, he spotted a newsagent on the opposite side of the road whose tattered blue awning offered a thin strip of shade. He crossed the street and stepped gratefully into an eddy created behind the boxes of magazines that were strewn around its entrance. In the shade and out of the crush for the first time in hours he perched awkwardly on the shop windowsill with his back pressed up against the hot glass. Dabbing at the sheen of sweat on his forehead with a damp tissue, he picked up a computer magazine from a waist-high stack in front of him and tried to fan some cool air over his face, but its spine was a thick as a museum catalogue and flapping it only made his wrist ache.

He stood up and checked his watch.

Time to go.

He did up his top button, straightened the knot of his tie, and hitching his sagging trousers up over his hips, took three deep breaths. Exhaling slowly on the last breath, he crossed the street and strode purposefully toward the glass doors.

*

At the desk he stepped nervously from to foot while the

immaculately manicured receptionist ran a crimson fingernail down the list in front of her. He had, indeed, been invited back for a second interview. She handed him a visitor's pass and directed him across the lobby to the area reserved for clients, and those, like himself, waiting to go upstairs. He would be called when they were ready for him.

Step One. He had made it out of the group.

Smiling to himself, he stepped out of the rush of couriers, secretaries and mail-room boys for the first time, striding across the floor and up to the next level with a loose-limbed swagger.

The lobby was empty when he arrived, and he stood for a moment to take in his new, elevated, surroundings. Six low-slung, black leather chairs with chrome frames were arranged around a clear glass coffee table that had been lowered to a Japanese height and was propped up at each corner by translucent resin cubes. A grey metal sculpture, as tall as a man and representing something between a bulb and a dead tree, stood in one corner next to a vase containing an arrangement of tall lilies. The veneer of sophistication was somewhat ruined by the lobby sharing one wall with the lift corridor, along which framed posters of the front covers of dull looking computer magazines had been hung. One of them, he noticed, was the same title as the magazine he had fanned himself with under the newsagent's awning.

Perhaps it was fate.

Over-confident, he made to sit without thinking. Letting his full body weight fall unimpeded into the low slung seat, he crash-landed in a heap, his visitor's pass jiggling about on the end of its chain in front of his crotch like a cheap oversized medallion. Slumped in the chair with his knees as high as his chest he struck a posture so abject, and so far from the impression he was hoping to make, that he wondered briefly if perhaps the whole thing was being filmed as some kind of test for new applicants; a test he was clearly in the process of failing. To make matters worse, his damp trousers had stuck to the chair-leather and, rising half way up his calves, exposed a pair of sweaty brown nylon socks that appeared to merge with his Dr Martens like a pair of huge turds on the end of his legs. To rectify the situation, he started frantically bum-shuffling up the chair like a lazy toddler.

He looked up, and there she was.

Hair a jet-black pre-Raphaelite swoon,

Long lashes and dark, soulful eyes,

Petite,

Power-packed and absolutely present.

Honey-skinned.

Hot.

No, more than that

Dynamite,

From tip to toe no more than five foot four of her,

Precious,

Perfect.

It was only a glance. A sudden flash of sunlight directly into his eyes; a vision of the promised land.

The secretary's shrill voice came over the speakers. "Could Mr X head up to the first floor conference room? They are ready for you now."

Shit. He had to go.

In the lift, he briefly cursed himself for not taking a second glance at her, saying something, or at the very least, smiling. But as the elevator rose he consoled himself with the thought that with a woman as beautiful as that, staying cool and aloof was certainly the correct strategy, and he pictured himself sitting behind a large mahogany desk in an office with his name etched in its glass door, beckoning her in for an interview. The time would come. He was certain of it.

*

There were two of them waiting for him.

They were dressed like twins. Both wore white, narrow-collared shirts and silk-print ties that looked like Jackson Pollack had vomited on them. Both wore grey trousers of a light material that pulled tight over their gym-toned, manly thighs and buttocks. The creases of their slacks fell razor-sharp to an abrupt halt above the ankle, identically tailored to reveal an inch of brightly coloured sock. One was blond and one was dark-haired. The blond-haired one was slightly taller and wore green braces. Dark-hair had red braces. Other than that they seemed to differ only in the shape of the buckles on their shiny black shoes.

Green braces lounged casually at the far end of the room, his jacket slung over his shoulder and held in place by a solitary cocked finger. He registered the new arrival's entrance with a yawn that turned into a smile that might have been a sneer, suggesting he would be irritated beyond measure if the interview wasn't, at the very least, entertaining. Red braces advanced toward him, his walk a parody of assertion, a barrow-boy made stockbroker strut; feet placed flat and wide-spread, knees splayed as though he was carrying water-melon sized bollocks between his legs.

He was at him straight away.

"So welcome…" he hesitated theatrically "…X…? What kind of a name is that?"

"It's my name."

There was a long silence.

X understood the purpose of this. The books on negotiation had all emphasised the importance of silence. Embarrassed by the awkwardness, the weak and unprepared tended to say anything to fill the void. They babbled, equivocated, apologised, backed-down, cracked. He stayed quiet and let them ask the question again.

When red braces obliged he was ready for him and counter-attacked, "It's a memorable one", he replied calmly.

"It's a stupid one". Green braces first contribution from the desk.

"But does it matter if it's stupid?" he asked. "You want to make a secretary laugh?" he stretched out his arms expansively, "Have a stupid name! Better still", he continued, "she gets embarrassed about getting your stupid name wrong and puts you through when she's not supposed to do so to make amends…" He paused to let the thought sink in before changing tack, "Hey!", he shouted, one hand cupped around his mouth as though calling across the office, the other miming holding a receiver pressed to his chest. "Which fucking magazine did you want me to put it in, they all look alike to me…what about that bloke with the stupid name at Z publications …X … Call him!"

"Stupid name", he concluded, "Opens doors".

Red braces was straight back at him, "OK, so you've got a trick. But even if I buy that, it's not good enough. Why X?", and giving him no time to reply he continued, sneering, "Do you want me to start guessing? Let me see…Your dad was an illiterate dosser who scratched the only mark he knew on the birth certificate before dumping you on the orphanage steps… Or maybe your mum…?"

X interrupted. "I changed my name at eighteen by deed poll".

"Still not enough".

What to tell? He had wiped the slate clean at eighteen and moved on. The change of name had seemed a vital, necessary act at the time, the past had to be obliterated entirely and X was the perfect expression of that. There had been legal complications about calling himself X, but he'd been passionate enough about his right to name himself as he chose, that he'd been willing to fight for it through the courts for years. Eventually his case had come to the notice of a liberal chambers who considered it sufficiently a footnote in liberty to take on his case pro-bono. By the time the judgement came through in his favour he no longer cared, he was already X by then. It was simply his name.

"How about this then" he replied, reeling his answer off at pace,

"X; the unknown element in an equation. X; the symbol for a kiss at the end of a love letter. X; the location of buried treasure on a desert island. X; something mysterious and unknowable. X; the extra factor that makes one-person superior to all the rest… I could go on all day, but I thought I was here for a sales interview." That was good. He wasn't a pushover. He was back in the game.

"Can you write?" Red braces barked suddenly.

He could only shrug. What was he talking about?

"I mean", Red Braces continued, "You haven't got the same problem as hobo dad have you? Call yourself X because it's the only letter you can write?"

This was just nasty and stupid. What was he supposed to do? Laugh?

Red Braces carried on after only the shortest of pauses, "We only ask because we found your degree certificate very interesting", his voice was now wheedling and sarcastic," very interesting indeed." I have it here…" He reached behind him, picked up the certificate and pretended to examine it carefully.

Shit.

"X, formerly known as…", and he read out X's birth name, enunciating every syllable with a sneering cadence, while they both stared at him for any sign of a reaction.

Thank fuck for that. They were just taunting him about his name.

"You see the thing is…Red Braces used his birth name again. X raised a hand, "I don't answer to that name, my name is X" he said firmly. "But that really isn't the point here is it?"

Oh Shit. They knew.

"It's not even a very good forgery", Red Braces explained, "it's fuzzy. These things are never fuzzy. And the paper's shit. They don't do degree certificates on shit paper." He shook his head slowly as he spoke, an expression of mock solemnity on his face. Green Braces joined in again. "We checked of course, being professionals. And you know what? They *did* have a record of you starting the course in …what was it… English and Spanish Literature!" He stood smiling straight at X as though he was genuinely delighted at the discovery. But it was all theatrics and cruelty, and in a moment his face slid into an expression of befuddled sadness, and in a sorrowful, softened voice regretfully continued, "But no one seems to have *any* recollection of you finishing the course. Not even with such a memorable name."

The game was up. What were they doing? Just fucking with him until the police arrived?

The panic calmed as soon as it had arrived. Was it even a crime to forge a degree certificate? If it was, it was pretty low-level stuff and he couldn't imagine the police being much interested. He wasn't even an employee here, so why should they care? He picked up his jacket and began to rise to feet. It was time to go. What could they do to stop him? They were hardly going to rugby tackle him to the ground over a misdemeanour.

At that moment they both burst out laughing, Red Braces braying hard with his head thrown back and Green Braces sagging forward on his knees, chest heaving and gulping in air between guffaws. X froze as he stood, bewildered.

Red Braces slapped him on the back and guided him back to his seat with a hand on his shoulder "The look on your face!" He said as he wiped the tears from his eyes, "Priceless. We don't give a shit about your forged certificate" he explained between snorts. "Shows initiative. Got your foot in the door here."

"Who gives a fuck about your honesty", Green Braces interjected, "what we need to know is are you a chimp? Some kind of retard who wasn't smart enough to get a degree". Red Braces picked up the thread, "Maybe university was too tough for you, couldn't stand to be away from mummy for so long…."

Not that.

They needed an answer. OK. "I reached a point where I couldn't imagine how knowing any more about Shelly could possibly be of any benefit to me. I met a girl who felt the same and we took off for Berlin looking for some real life". That might do it. He hadn't stayed still. He had acted decisively. They might like it.

It just set Red Braces off on one. "Berlin", his voice an octave higher as he pronounced the word, "Did you hang out with Iggy Pop and David Bowie?" he sneered, and then began singing "Oh You Pretty Things" dancing around the room in kind of mincing wiggle with his hands cupped over his ears and his elbows sticking out like chicken wings.

There seemed no point in mentioning that Iggy and Bowie had left long before he had got there, and that the track he was singing had no relevance at all to Berlin.

And the dancing. This bloke was a special kind of prick.

What to tell them? No good in confessing that the girl he'd left with had liked first other men, and then heroin more than she'd liked him, and that it hadn't been possible for him to carry on in the co-operative café after his partner's hands had clearly been in the till on so many occasions. She wasn't alone in that, he recalled, but the atmosphere was febrile, and hysterical arguments broke out over cleaning rotas and missing muesli. He'd come home no better off than when he left.

"I split up with my girl. Came home. Got shit jobs. Got fed up of having shit jobs. Thought I'd use my brain to get a better one. Look…", X leant forward as he spoke, fixing his eyes directly on Red Braces, "All the others in the group interview were pimply-faced kids who'd spent the last three years getting pissed at the student bar, doing what they were told and getting mummy to do their washing when they got home. Not me. They were all 'having a go' at landing a sales job, and if that didn't work out they'd go inter-railing or do VSO and get daddy to find them a job at the office when they got back. None of that applies to me. I know what it's like to be broke and on your own. I don't just want to make money, I'm hungry for it. You know it, that's why you asked me back."

Red Braces stopped dancing and Green Braces eased himself away desk. "Listen X", he said, using his name without sarcastic inflexion for the first time, "We publish computer magazines in a highly competitive market. We're very good at it…."

Green braces then delivered a homily on the subject of the greatness of the company and the tough world of advertising sales while Red Braces listened with reverence. Their sudden evangelical earnestness was impossible for X to take entirely seriously, it was as though a pair of skinheads had rolled their sleeves down over their tattoos and were pretending to be Mormons.

He kept smiling and nodding without listening until the tone changed again.

"How much do you know about computing?" Red braces asked.

"A little. I'm not an expert". He knew nothing.

Red Braces nodded. "You know the only thing you need to know about computing? Biggest wins. The computer magazine with the most number of pages wins. Think about it. Say you and your Berlin bride are shopping for a bed… And there's one store with 50 beds and another with 150, which do you go in first?

"The biggest." X fed the required line.

"Exactly, top of the pile and its easy street, the money comes pouring in. Drop off the ridge, you're pedalling uphill and the shit's all flowing down on top of you. Biggest wins."

"That's all I have to know about the computing business?"

"Were you thinking about the cutting edge technology?" They both laughed. "Nobody gives a shit about that", Green Braces explained, "Whatever new bit of junk they're making out to be the next big thing, we stick on the front page. Companies pay us to test their latest gizmo, we put it on the inside pages. Why should I have to read it?"

Red Braces chipped in, "some fat bloke in the basement tests all the new kit, he smells like sweaty hamburgers and earns less than my secretary even though his tits are bigger than hers."

"So X, we need people; One. Who aren't easy to put off under pressure. Two. Who can think fast on their feet. And three. People who have got the killer instinct to sell. Two down", he said smiling, "Now sell me something." He made a sweeping gesture with his hands as though he were an emperor demanding sport in the arena, "Anything in this room."

Red Braces made the choice for him, picking up X's newspaper, rolling it into a cosh and slapping it against his thigh before thrusting it in the direction of X's face, "Sell us that – *The Independent*."

Green Braces was back to scoffing, "The Independent" he sneered. "Bloody wishy-washy liberals who don't know where they stand. Had a man in here with a copy of the Socialist Worker last week", he added. "I could respect that, stood his ground well."

Bullshit.

X's mind was suddenly filled with white noise. He could think of nothing to say about the Independent. There was a long silence while he wracked his brains. The wrong kind of silence. At last it came to him.

"One of the cleverest ideas the Independent had, was that the paper is printed using a different kind of ink. A type of ink that uniquely doesn't come off on your hands"

He ran his fingertips across the front page and then raised up his hands with his fingers outstretched. "Clever", he said. He looked like a simpleton begging for change.

Red Braces had run through a range of pantomime faces during X's delivery, and his mouth had now twisted into an expression that suggested he had something bitter stuck between his teeth. Green Braces stretched his arms out and faked a yawn.

X took a breath and pitched again

"I think you should take this paper seriously", he started, "As the only newspaper to be free of the distorting influence of an owner, it is free to report objectively, subject only to the free judgement of its reporters and editorial team. It's a serious attempt to become a paper of record for the UK, and the damage done to the Times in the last few years means there's a genuine gap in the market."

That was better.

It hadn't worked.

Green Braces clapped his hands in delight, while Red Braces turned away, unable even to look at him. "What shit!" Green Braces declared. "Firstly", he went on, "just shit." "Independent! No influence! Just a bunch of old Telegraph hacks that wanted a slice of the big money. Paper of record! Free judgement of reporters! At least it proves you did go to university after all. Or at least prep school. But again? Who gives a shit? Does it look like the enlightenment out there?" He was into his stride now. "What do you think this is, the age of fucking reason? Perhaps you *should* have read some more Shelly."

Despite the onslaught, X drifted away, gnawing over Green Braces' last sentence. Shelly had been a romantic poet, his outlook partly a reaction to the enlightenment, so it could have been a very clever put down, but as hard as he tried he couldn't see how the analogy worked. Even here, Shelly was useless to him.

Green Braces got the final say, "We don't need to discuss it" he pronounced, "We're of the same mind. Suspected it when you walked in dressed like 1984, with your cheap jacket and your broadsheet newspaper tucked under your arm. Don't finish what you've started do you? Too smart to actually do any work for a degree weren't we? We know your type, all detached and above it all, you'd rather say something clever and ironic than get stuck in. No", he shook his head as he said it, "You're no fucking use to us at all."

And that was it.

*

Punch-drunk from the battering he'd taken, he hung from a strap by the doors in the sweltering, soporific heat of the tube, buffeted like a boxer's dummy by the exchange of passengers at every stop. Hanging limply, he half-nodded off in the heat, a thousand clever responses he hadn't made spinning through his mind, a hundred delirious pitches for the Independent interrupted by flashes of his fists smashing repeatedly into Red Braces' face.

He changed trains and fought his way into an empty seat. With his face pressed against the window-glass he closed his eyes and let sleep overtake him.

2. THE RUNNING TRACK

He was standing on one side of a wide, well-lit boulevard, its lanes divided by twin tram tracks running and bordered by an avenue of mature beech trees that separated the roadway from an expanse of parkland beyond. A cool autumn breeze was ruffling the dry leaves all along the length of the esplanade and with almost no traffic on the road, a quiet, peaceful air pervaded the early evening darkness.

He looked to the left before he stepped off the pavement and crossed to the central divide, pausing before crossing the tram tracks.

A solitary car passed by on the other side, travelling almost silently along the smooth surface of the roadway. The car had clean, elegant lines, but although it was low slung, the driver lying almost horizontal behind the wheel, its design was understated, a dulled-silver passenger vehicle, practical, rather than showy. The only sound it made as it passed was a soft swooshing noise, its engine so quiet that the voices of its occupants could be clearly heard above the tyre rush, conversing in the swooping and falling cadence of a Scandinavian language. The harsh yet soft tones of their easy discourse, mingled with gentle laughter: faded into the night air as the car passed by, leaving only faint cries coming from the parkland behind the trees and the persistent yapping of a small dog to break the silence. X watched the car as it receded from view, following its passage under the soft, yellowed light of the streetlamps, each lamp bulbed by the golden penumbra of light it had captured from the moist air, and hanging, seemingly unsupported in the darkness like a chain of giant glow worms. The car passed between a cluster of clapboard houses that lined one side of the road and the plain concrete platform of a deserted tram stop before disappearing from view. In the distance, the houses' painted wooden facades were dimly illuminated by the tram stop sign, their pastel colours washed out, leaving only pale blues and ochre smears like roadside frescos visible in the half-light. Their small front gardens were bound by low, white picket fencing and the dark bushes of their back gardens merged with the parkland behind. The empty tram-stop, marked only by a short row of benches under an arched plastic shelter, looked as though it was never busy, rather than merely temporarily becalmed, an outpost of a municipal transport system at its furthest reach, the bright city centre long distant and the tramlines here running out beyond the suburbs and into the countryside.

X looked in the opposite direction. The silent tram tracks passed swiftly into a dense woodland of birch and pine that straddled the road. He followed its course as far as he could into the trees, the low-hanging crescent moon picking out its first twist into the shadows, birch trunks silvered by the moonlight standing like telegraph poles along its length, the silver strip of road swallowed up after the first bend by the dense forest mass.

X crossed the other half of the road and stepping under the deep shadows of the trees entered the park beyond. Ahead of him a wide expanse of short-cropped grass, its surface smooth and unblemished, stretched away in the moonlight, dark and featureless until it reached a floodlit athletics track in the far distance. He could make out stick men and women circulating its perimeter, and could now connect the cries he had heard earlier to the grunts of javelin throwers at the moment of release, their flung spears toothpick-sized at this distance. An exalted squeal of delight floated across the field in the clear cold air, and X could make out a stick-woman descending to earth from a successful pole vault, the bar, no thicker than dental floss, still held firm in its slots.

He decided to take a closer look at and stepped off the path on to the moonlight grass.

"Hey! Keep off the grass!" A stern voice called out from behind him.

X started and instinctively stepped back onto the path.

He turned to see a portly, middle-aged, dark-skinned man with a carefully trimmed black beard, sitting on a park bench under the shade of the trees behind him. A small dog was tethered by its lead to one of the bench legs. It had begun yapping at X in concert with its master's voice, but without any real malice.

The man rose and approached X with his hand extended and a broad smile on his face. He was apologising as he came over, speaking an impeccable, if slightly old-fashioned English with a strong Nordic accent and a slightly stilted diction. "Sorry Old Chap" he was saying, "I cannot say I did not mean to startle you. It was indeed my intention! Couldn't resist! No. No. Don't worry about the grass. I was only joking!" he continued, "We all have to step off the beaten track from time to time, no?"

The man's manner was so friendly and his greeting so effusive that X recovered his poise quickly and found he bore him no ill will for his little joke. They shook hands clumsily, the man seemingly unsure whether to grasp X's hand or his wrist and ending up grappling awkwardly with both, the result being an awkward stiffened shaking of the full length of their arms in tandem. They quickly exchanged names, the man introducing himself as Tasan, while the little dog jumped and yapped excitedly around their feet.

X found himself falling into step with the older man and they advanced together across the field toward the running track, Tasan's hand resting on his shoulder, a sense of easy comradeship established effortlessly between them. The journey across the grass seemed to pass more quickly than the distance required and Tasan talked continuously, scarcely pausing for breath for the entire duration of their passage. He stopped only once, to scoop up a dog turd that his pet had deposited, using a small plastic device like a hand-held carpet cleaner that enabled him to collect the shit without touching it with his hands. He returned the device to a leather man-bag he carried over one shoulder and continued his monologue. The sky above them was so vast and star-filled that it seemed to X as though he was falling into it as they walked, and floating euphorically through the Milky Way he found it difficult to concentrate on what the old man was saying. He did manage to glean that Tasan regularly sat on that particular bench in the hope that someone would materialise, and, as they rarely did, how fortunate he felt to have the opportunity to make X's acquaintance. He explained that many of his friends were given to taking exercise over at the running track and he was certain they would be as delighted to meet him as he was. Oddly, it was apparent that Tasan was certain that X's visit would only be brief and this lent a distinct urgency to his words and actions and perhaps the distance seemed so quickly covered as a consequence of the fierce pace the old man set.

They stopped just before the running track and Tasan proceeded to explain the novel system of greeting that the people in this part of the world employed. He explained that they did not shake hands with men or kiss women on the cheek, but pressed foreheads together in the same manner for all genders.

"It is not dissimilar to the greeting of the Inuit people", he explained.

The reference meant nothing to X, although he thought that Eskimos had done something like that. Or was that their noses?

They stood waiting while a group of runners made steady progress toward them round the perimeter of the track. Under the floodlights, the whole vista seemed arrayed like a stage set, the colours heightened under the spotlights, their vividness in shocking contrast to the muted tones of the night beyond the scope of their beams. X watched the runners approach. Most were chatting as they jogged, running through the small clouds of condensed vapour they created with their breath. His first thought was that as a group of people they were all remarkably tall and disproportionately good-looking, and as they got closer he felt no need to change his point of view. There was a broad range of ages in the group, from teenagers to men and women past retirement age, but all had the bodies of those habituated to exercise, and moved with the fluid ease of athletes in training. Muffled against the cold with woollen hats and fingerless gloves, only the runners' faces were visible in the cold air, revealing mostly pale, flushed skin, although there was a scattering of other skin colours in the crowd. Amongst those who had chosen to brave the cold hatless there were many blondes and redheads and the fashion for long hair seemed equally common among men and women, and shoulder length manes were tied back by headbands and a number of pony tails bumped against shoulders. As a collective, they oozed a sense of health and vitality, and he briefly felt sorry for Tasan, seemingly the only overweight person in this land of Amazons and supermen, but on closer inspection the old man himself seemed more barrel-chested and stocky than actually fat.

Tasan waved at the approaching group, and a middle-aged woman with long dark hair waved back enthusiastically, detaching herself from the rest and heading to the edge of the track were the two of them stood. As she did so she gestured sharply to a tall young woman who was running just behind her. The young woman broke off her conversation with a square-jawed dark-haired man in a lime green tracksuit and loped across behind the older woman.

The dark- haired woman pressed her forehead against Tasan's and lent into X to repeat the action with a quizzical expression. Tasan introduced her as Erika. X's clumsy attempt to reciprocate left them bumping heads, and the woman stood back, unashamedly staring at him in blunt amazement.

In normal circumstances, X would have paid more attention to Erika. She was undoubtedly a very handsome woman, with an intelligent and alert face where deep hazel eyes were set between high Slavic cheekbones, and although she must have been in her fifties, aside from a few crow's feet around her eyes, her skin was clear and unblemished. But from the moment she had detached herself from the group, X had to fight to stop himself staring at the young woman in the navy tracksuit who had followed her and was now standing a metre or so away, lightly stretching her hamstrings while she waited to be introduced.

She was mesmerizingly beautiful.

As she bent to stretch her calves, her body moved with the

grace and strength of an Olympic gymnast. The white stripe that ran down the outer seam of her tracksuit leggings, encapsulating in its arched curve from heel to hip the essence all women's beauty, as though drawn with a single stroke of an artist's brush.

When she stepped forward to be introduced, X could only look at her face obliquely. It was not merely that he feared he might stare slack-jawed at her like a simpleton, but because he found the effect of her features so powerful that it was like looking directly into the sun. The fine blond down of her eyebrows, the long dark lashes, the high cheekbones, the graceful line of her nose, the fullness of her lower lip. All were perfection, but it was the impossible penetrative beauty of her eyes that overwhelmed him, iris' the colour of forget-me-nots; eyes that turned an already beautiful face into something otherworldly, the eyes of a Nordic goddess, a creature of faerie, beyond human woman's beauty. Unable to look directly at her he looked down, focussing first on the patch of skin exposed at the perfect bow of her clavicle, where she had unzipped her top to cool down, then as that began to feel intrusive he looked up, veering to the side with his gaze and found himself staring at a wisp of blond hair that had escaped the confines of her floppy woollen hat and wavered in the gentle breeze like strands of spun gold. He found himself fighting the urge to lean forward and tuck back into place a solitary strand that had fallen across her forehead and in front of her left eye.

When Erika introduced them they had touched forehead with only the lightest of contacts and she had kept her eyes averted from his as though she were shy. She was introduced as Eva, and when he repeated her name it felt as though he were taking his marriage vows. Neither of them spoke further, and in the awkward silence that followed he became aware he was staring at her again, and he had to force himself to turn his attention back to Erika and Tasan.

The older couple had stood back a pace, the pair of them were beaming at X and Eva with the expressions of proud parents whose darling children had just performed a particularly clever trick.

"How wonderful to meet you", Erika started up as soon as X looked in her direction, "Don't you agree Eva?"

Eva quietly affirmed, without looking up, that it was indeed a pleasure, but her words were hesitant and seemed strangely forced. X was immediately certain that he had already fucked it up, had stared open-mouthed at this beautiful stranger like a drooling imbecile, or worse still leered like a lascivious creep.

"Of course, you must come and see the city", Tasan was saying, "Eva has an apartment that's at the perfect spot, right on the highest ridge by the tramline stop. Flat number 44. Marvellous views."

"What about it Eva?" he continued, "You will give X a tour won't you?"

Eva raised her head to reply, looking him directly in his eyes as she did so. Her bold stare at him seemed to open up for an instant a corridor into the heart of her, a flicker of sadness surfaced, then, beautifully, a sense of deep empathy welled up from her depths, then faded away, dissolving into sadness and finally as she lowered her lids and turned away; sympathy.

"Yes. Sure. I'd be delighted."

He wasn't convinced she meant it.

Erika was speaking again, "I'm sure next time you come we

can all get to know each other much better", she was saying.

X felt bewildered. Why did they all assume he was about to leave? Why would he be in a hurry to depart? He had just met the most beautiful girl he had ever seen in his life and anyway, he had only just arrived.

Arrived where?

He turned to Tasan. "So where exactly are we?" he asked.

FUGUE

He woke up.

The train was stationary with its engine switched off.

It was quiet in the carriage.

His cheek was still pressed against the window glass, a smear of sweat between his cheek and the warm pane. When he opened his eyes his blurred sight was filled by a field of electric green meadow-grass lit golden by bright sunlight.

Where am I now?

The sun passed behind a cloud and the vision of a meadow dissolved, reforming as merely a triangle of scrubland, cut off in the no-man's land between two merging rail tracks and a raised embankment. Flinty concrete pillars, cast in the same crude rubble-concrete as pill boxes, were posted like sentries around the perimeter, and wire mesh, rusted and woven with brambles, sealed off the island like a forgotten internment camp. It had its own beauty. Nettles and swaying, long-stalked blades, formed bridgeheads on the clinker, and feather-topped sprays cut archipelagos of green and purple along unseen fault lines in the arid soil. An Elder's white flowers curtained the length of the embankment, its powdery white florets held up on thin stalks like religious offerings. Swimming to the surface from the depths of the dream, his focus rested on the heads of sticky wheat-grass poking through the wire mesh, each tiny seed crowned by long fine hairs that curved skyward like inverted sputniks.

He drew back from the minutiae, and as his consciousness slipped back with him into the carriage, an intense feeling of unease grew, a gnawing, itching sensation. A feeling of not-rightness. Something was missing.

Sound.

The train was completely silent. How could it be so quiet? It had been rush-hour when he'd got on.

He was fully awake now.

With his back to the length of the carriage he was suddenly afraid to turn around for fear of what he might see. The silence behind him grew more eerie with every passing second, until the feeling that rows of motionless glazed-eyed commuters were staring at the back of his neck became so overwhelming that he had to look.

He swung round sharply.

He was completely alone in the carriage. Across the empty seats of the deserted train, newspapers lay dropped as though they had been abandoned mid-crossword, and litter was strewn across the floor like a crime scene reconstruction. At the foot of one of the seats, a wrap of shrivelled clingfilm, sticky with egg-mayonnaise, lay around a crumpled Wispa wrapper and a half-eaten apple. A McDonald's carton, its plastic lid popped off, drooled sticky liquid into the grooves of the ribbed carriage floor, its straw pointing directly down the train at X like a solitary accusatory finger. Bright sunlight poured in through the windows on the far side of the train, catching dust particles moving in lazy Brownian spirals in the rays, undisturbed by even the slightest motion in the still air. It was like a neutron bomb had gone off in the train and he was the only survivor.

As the silence stretched on panic began to set in. He formed the conception, then the certainty, that the train had crashed and he was now stuck in some kind of way station between worlds, waiting while the final decision on his destination in the after-life was determined. He became convinced that the hyper-real dream he had just woken from had actually been his last thoughts before his heart stopped beating, and he was stuck here in limbo until the life support machine was turned off. He sat, rigid, his muscles vice-clenched as though under the dentist's drill, straining for something, anything to happen, trying to force time to begin moving forward by the sheer power of his will. After seconds, minutes, hours, of desperate yearning, his blood hammering at his temples, he surrendered, willing to accept any judgement as long as it granted him respite from this suffocating no-time.

There were two dull clicks and the electric motor whirred to life.

A guard's gravelly voice burst out from the speakers, brutally, beautifully normal in his delivery. "All Change… `all change please…this train terminates here. All Change…"

The train pulled into a platform surrounded by grey concrete slabs like utilitarian tombs.

Gunnersbury?

What the fuck was he doing in Gunnersbury?

3. MANIFESTO

He got off at Brixton, side-stepped the old lady who sold combs on her knees in the station foyer, swerving as she reached her emaciated arms toward him across her wretched blanket, and weaved through the crowd up the steps, changing direction swiftly to avoid the wide-eyed feral boy with dreds and a styrafoam cup who worked the stairs every evening, largely ignored unless he started shouting. He took a short cut through the market, regretting it when the stench of offal and blood, ripened to sweetness from the heat, billowed out from the butcher's shops as he passed. He ducked, holding his breath, under ranks of trussed, yellowing chickens, hung like executed prisoners under the striped awnings, their plucked breasts the texture of necrotic scrotal sacs. The day's trading done, the butchers were closing up, hosing down their chopping boards into the street drains, and bloodied water splashed across the pavement forcing X to take a wide detour into the street to avoid staining his clothes. Slipping out through the covered market, he exited by the Left Book Shop and emerged into Coldharbour Lane.

He crossed the road, but was forced to cross back to avoid the backswing of an elderly Jamaican man who was wielding his walking-stick with gusto outside the Atlantic. Dressed immaculately in a faun baggy suit, white tie and shiny shoes, he was raising his stick threateningly and shouting at the frosted glass windows as X passed on the other side of the road.

"You *can't* do this…", the old man roared, "You *can't* do this…I'm coming back in… *Right* now… I'm warning you…I'm coming *straight* back in… "You *can't* stop me…"

No one appeared to be attempting to prevent the old man from re-entering the pub, and he himself made no actual advance on the doors, continuing to hold a stance as bow-legged as a sumo-wrestler's while venting his impotent rage at an invisible audience behind the pub's closed doors.

X turned into Railton Road, stepping inside the Wholefoods Co-operative just around the corner. Unbelievably after the day he had already had, he still had a shift to do tonight. He needed something to keep him awake.

"Have you got any other coffee than this?" he asked, waving a gold-foiled packet of 'Freedom Coffee" at the thin nervous man with a hermit's beard and a Greenpeace T-shirt who was sorting through a pile of used plastic bags behind the counter. When the man finally looked up, he rested both elbows on the boxes of browning greens laid out by the till for impulse buyers who hadn't already got enough curly kale, and fixed X with a hostile glare.

When he spoke, his manner was accusative, "Why would you want another one?" he said, jabbing a finger at the label on the packet in X's hand. "It's made with a blend of Nicaraguan and Angolan beans. The money goes to poor farmers facing up to fascist bombs."

X knew that. "But it tastes terrible", he pointed out, "it's like cigarette ash going down and it's got a bitter after taste…..like chicory….."

The thin man was aghast. "Do you want apartheid and the death squads to win? But if you like the taste of chicory", he went on, "we've got plenty of Barley Cup…."

Tucking the coffee in his pocket, he stepped swiftly through the doors and back onto the street. Though the flames had long since died down, there was still something charred about the frontline, as though the ash of the burning still lay draped over the dark Victorian rail bridge and was ground deep in the brickwork of the long terrace row behind him. It wasn't somewhere he ever felt comfortable and so, looking neither left nor right, and fixing his expression neutral and purposeful, he strode under the bridge and set off at a swift pace down Coldharbour Lane. The barrier block ran alongside him most of the long walk home. It had been designed when an elevated dual carriageway had been planned to smash through Brixton in the 1970s, and while the rest of the town had been spared brutalist architectural destruction, the six-storey rib-block had been too far advanced in development to halt when the project was cancelled. The giant estate, crouched forever in defence against the never-built motorway, presented a vast, high wall to the street, its blank face interrupted only by the tiny, soundproofed windows that pock-marked its length, their thickened glass and mean dimensions protecting its occupants from the ghost traffic roar, and giving the estate the look of a maximum security prison or institution for the criminally insane rather than a home for thousands.

Keeping a steady pace, he walked by on the other side of the street, separated from the estate by a dual carriageway's width of wasteland and rough grass. The long slog home was marked at the beginning and end of the rubble and rubbish strip by the rusting frames of two burnt out cars, bracken bursting through their rusted metal chassis and burst black plastic bin bags stacked on their rotted seats like a tramp family's car loaded up for the holidays.

Turning right at the station, he rounded the Green Man pub on the corner that guarded the entrance to the little network of red-bricked terraced houses that contained his home. Relaxed now, he walked with an easier gait on home turf and thought to himself, as he often did at this stage of the walk, how grateful he was that he didn't live on an estate.

Behind him, the Loughborough Estate receded from sight as he walked, until only the tops of its blocks were visible, the tags that raged across it more like shit thrown at the walls than any attempt at art. In the year he had lived in this part of Brixton something had shifted it a notch nastier and more violent over there, tipping it over the threshold from merely run-down and poor into desperate and hostile. It wasn't just the padlock on the vandalised playpark that had muffled the voices of the children, there was something else, an eerie malevolent silence that seemed to have descended on the whole place. Burglaries were up and the off license on the far side had put in thickened glass and served through a hatch now. He didn't know what had happened; estates were always alien territory if you didn't live on them, and he was thoroughly glad not to be any part of its story.

His area, in contrast, was shabby but decent, and although most of the tiny front gardens were little more than weeds, the street itself was quite tidy; the broken glass and rough sleepers confined mostly to the alley behind X's place. There were more houses with scaffolding and skips outside than sealed up with metal fronted doors, and down the street the red paint of the council owned properties, flaked and peeling from the doors and window sills gave the street a cosy air of faded gentility. People even kept an eye out for each other around here, at least the young couples and the Jamaican families did.

None of them were at all sure about squatters.

*

Griff met him at the door of their squat.

X felt his spirit fall at the sight of his flushed face and nervous expression. Something was clearly wrong.

Griff was an Australian punk who had turned up so late for the party that he looked like he was wearing fancy dress. His hair was soap-spiked into an unstable green Mohican and the straps of his bondage trousers flapped between his chubby thighs as he shuffled nervously at the door. He wore a studded denim jacket with band patches carefully sewn on, and the silver buckles on the steel-tipped boots he'd bought in Carnaby Street when he first arrived ran as high as his knees.

Whatever epoch he was supposed to represent, it wasn't 1988.

Conceivably, Griff had looked tough and interesting for a while as a teenager in the Melbourne suburbs, got a few tattoos, hung around with bikers and other outcasts, but he'd clearly been beaten up a lot too. In a way, it had made him authentically punk, persecuted for being different, defying convention and getting up people's noses just for the way he dressed, but by the time he had reached London in the mid-eighties, all the punks were in the media or pantomime dames for tourists in the King's Road and he didn't fit in anywhere. He'd crossed half the globe to carry on the struggle only to discover that not only did no one give a shit, but cultural Chinese whispers had pitched him up in Brixton dressed as the only man in Britain who hadn't understood that 'The Young Ones' was a comedy.

X had ended up with Griff as a flatmate by a series of events entirely beyond his control and he now seemed to have become a permanent, unwanted fixture in his life. He'd vaguely known Griff from work where, just as X had when he got back from Berlin, he had picked up a job as a volunteer in the same hostel in Vauxhall, not through any particular aptitude for the work, but because the only qualifications required were a willingness to come home smelling of old men's piss and a complete lack of ambition. But even then it had been harder for Griff than X. The old drunks had found him hilarious and he'd had to endure months of them collapsing into choking guffaws every time he waddled past them down the corridors and miming buggering each other when his back was turned. They had eventually got used to him and the laughter had died down into sniggers and the occasional wolf whistle, but his appearance continued to scare the schizophrenics witless, and after a particularly florid wild man in Lincoln's Inn Fields, believing him to be a pointy-headed demon, had gone for him with a ladle, he was restricted to duties in the dormitories where he was, at least, a familiar voodoo. X had been only on nodding acquaintance with him until Griff had decided on a scheme to obtain a British passport, and therefore permanent residence in London's slums, by arranging a marriage of convenience with a fellow hostel worker named Alex. From here, it had just got baroque and pathetic at the same time.

Alex was a slender young woman with long dark hair and sad eyes, beautiful in a way, but absent, detached somehow, a vagueness about her as though some early blow had half slapped her out of the world and she was looking back at it through a faint mist. She dressed in the typical fashion of homeless workers, sweatshirt, tight black jeans and Dr Marten boots which she hand-painted in bright colours, and lived in a well-established squat in Camden with a cooking rota adapted for vegans and group time where you could only speak if you were holding the juju stick. They threw regular squat parties where everyone took mushrooms, talked rubbish and stared into the fire in the garden. All her flatmates were in the grip of a variety of new-age delusions, but Alex, displaced an octave lost, rose above and was untouched by all the ego-madness that surrounded her. At work she listened to the most skittish of un-medicated schizophrenics in the same calm, apparently attentive way she listened to the white witches, seers and Aquarian fantasists she shared her home with, trustingly assured of their ultimate good intentions without listening to a word they said.

Alex had agreed to marry Griff without spending any time thinking it through. If she had thought about it at all, X surmised, she would have justified it as some means of sticking it to the man, in a whimsical, two-fingers up behind your back kind of way, and that would have been enough for her. She had hardly noticed Griff before they made the arrangement and remained largely indifferent to him throughout the process and even the ceremony itself.

He, of course, was in love with her.

The period of cohabitation required to fool any unannounced inspection by HMPD was, unsurprisingly in the circumstances, cut drastically short.

X had ample opportunity to piece together how it had unfolded from Griff's later, endless, anguished re-tellings of the story. As far as X could make out, Alex had treated Griff's presence on the futon in her bedroom as she would have anyone else who had crashed down for the night, and from Griff's account there were often other people in his wife's room and sometimes in her bed as well. But Griff, despite all the evidence to the contrary, had deluded himself into believing that his status as husband gave him more than just the right of acquaintanceship with his young bride.

X had been forced to listen as Griff regaled over and over an interminably dull incident where he had shown photographs of his relatives back in Oz to Alex and she had snubbed him completely. X envisaged the smeary prints of red-faced cousins standing with bikes and skateboards in backyards and fat blousy aunts squinting at the camera on porches in the Melbourne suburbs and sympathised wholly with Alex. Who wouldn't yawn? But Griff was dead set on miscommunication on an heroic scale and would repeat Alex's responses *ad nauseum* to X, each word a dagger to his heart. "She would say to me, her *husband*", his big round face a picture of grief as he spoke, "that she was happy to let me share her room, but if I wanted conversation I should go to the kitchen". He always paused here, just as the final insult to his dignity was about to fall, then, "Everyone else understands this, what's the matter with you, are you retarded in some way?"

This had always seemed highly out of character for what X knew of Alex and he strongly suspected that there were elements in the build-up to this statement that Griff had left out, but as at this point Griff was usually reduced to tears of self-pity, he never successfully teased out the details. What had happened over the next few days was also hazy in Griff's account, but reading between the lines it appeared to X that they had been characterised by outbursts of rage and conspicuous sulking as the groom demanded attention, as was his right, and Alex's increasing bewilderment rising to genuine alarm at his incomprehensible behaviour. His tenure was hanging by a thread even before, after a Castlemain 4X too many, he had taken the fateful lurch from futon to double bed in search of his conjugal rights that had left him at X's door in the middle of the night, weeping, his belongings in two black bin-liners, his face that of a desperate clown.

Looking at Griff shuffling on the front step, he recalled the irritating obligation he had felt to admit him that night. In the end, that was the trouble with squatting. If you took the principled argument that houses should not be left empty when there were people without homes to live in, you couldn't hold on to an empty room when you had one, even if the person who needed it worked with you every day and you already knew they got on your nerves. That the spare room that Griff had moved into was really the loft alcove, and that the stepladder up could only be reached by passing through X's room, wasn't a general problem with squats, just this one, but it certainly didn't make cohabitation any easier. But the real problem was Griff himself, cringingly apologetic during the day, X's nights were repeatedly interrupted by his new flatmate's chest-beating remorse and outbursts of impotent anger. Pissed, he would keep X up for hours after shifts, droning on and on, smoking all his cigarettes during his interminable monologues, and leaving X searching for the best looking dog-ends in the morning to go with his coffee.

It had made him quit in the end. At least he owed him that.

At the door, Griff's face was full of consternation, although it was difficult to tell the seriousness of the issue at hand, as his gloopy round face fell naturally into that configuration, and his Billy Whizz hair always seemed to dramatise his emotions like a giant exclamation mark on his head. He was fiddling with a thick, brass-coloured cone piercing he had had done recently to update his appearance. The cone was heavy and the loose skin of his big floppy nose sagged under his weight making the stud inside catch on his skin. He always fiddled with it when he was nervous.

Jesus, What now?

Griff finally summed up the courage to speak, his other new piercing, a silver ring in his lip, causing him to lisp slightly as he spoke. "Kevin and that girl of his are upstairs in your room.'

Fuck. Just what he needed. Although in truth he was slightly relieved, He'd imagined much worse from Griff's expression, but he was still pissed off. "Didn't I make it really clear – let Paul in but not Kevin…."

Griff's face dropped still further, "I got mixed up, I thought you said let Kevin in but not Paul…"

X suppressed an almost overwhelming urge to ask him if he was, indeed, retarded, but resisted the thought. Griff hadn't mixed it up and was merely lying. Kevin, although not physically imposing in any way, entered rooms as though he was storming the Winter Palace. Griff had probably snapped to attention as he passed.

Kevin was, at least ostensibly, X's friend, and although he frightened Griff, X took him to be a fundamentally decent, though odd, man. He was RCP, or at least felt that their interpretation of Trotsky's ideas was the most consistent, but there were schisms in the local branch and he rarely attended meetings. He remained a believer however, and his allergies coupled with the intensity of his gaze giving him the perpetual red-eyed stare of a fanatic, awaiting the inevitability of the revolution with the same surety as an evangelist's patient confidence in the second coming, no matter how long the arrival had been delayed.

Bollocks. He'll be here for hours.

He must have said it out loud because Griff responded, "They've been here an hour already", his voice wavering, but gaining confidence when he realised X wasn't going to shout at him.

"What's he doing?"

"He said something about 'waiting to see how the ruling class had embraced you into their arms. He was reading a book when I left", he added helpfully.

Great.

"Oh and Paul called, but Diana got to the phone first"

X nodded. More hassle. He'd deal with Diana first. Kevin was his opportunity to get kicked from both sides in the same day, and he wanted to put it off as long as he could.

Griff slipped out the front door and hurried away down the street without a backward glance, and X sat down on the front step, fanning air across his face, suddenly feeling the desperate need to cool off and slow down for a moment. He rested his head against the frame of door, delaying before having to confront Diana.

Diana was another aspect of his shitty life, another problem of squatting, or rather the crappy solution to another problem of squatting – that it was infinitely better to have the ground floor occupied by someone, anyone, than to leave it empty.

After Leslie had left, and before the flowers she had planted in the garden had even wilted he'd been burgled while he was out on a night shift. After the fourth time in two months, he'd sat in his stripped bare room a written a note in marker pen and pinned it to the carpet with drawing pins. It read;

BURGLARS

PLEASE STOP ROBBING ME

I MUST BE POORER THAN YOU NOW

THERE'S NOTHING LEFT TO TAKE

PLEASE LEAVE ME ALONE

The fifth set of burglars, finding nothing to steal, ripped the phone off the wall and smashed the downstairs windows on their way out. One of them had paused to deposit a large chocolate coloured turd on the dead centre of his note.

With Diana downstairs, the curtains twitched at the slightest movement in the street or sound in the darkness, and a wooden fence rose around the front garden, high enough to deter entry, but without breaking any of her sight-lines. The burglaries stopped. They grew plants in the front garden again, but it was never the same.

Security came at a price. He couldn't stand Diana and she dealt with him as though she might indeed respond positively to his lascivious desires but was thoroughly repulsed that he dared to entertain such thoughts. He didn't find her attractive in any way. This created an unstable dynamic between them that made any conversation full of miscommunication and odd innuendo, which by now X merely found tiresome. But that wasn't the worst of it. It was the acoustics of their entirely insulation-free home that pushed them into post-it wars, daily sound clashes and occasional vigorous shouting matches.

Diana had told him, early on, that she was a very spiritual person, that she could sense auras and presences, and that because of her finely balanced position between psychic planes, her karma could be easily disturbed by ugly or aggressive emotions. Or noise. She complained every time he walked up and down in his room, and they had had a stand up row when he had dared to go for a shit when he'd come home from work one time at 2am. He in return was forced to listen to her regular arguments with her partner Phil, his mumblings scarcely audible above her shrill protestations which rose to a hysterical screeching, often followed by weeping and always concluded by hours of tantric sex accompanied by world music, her moans and his grunting mixing with the Kora player's notes and rising un-baffled through the floorboards into his room.

He stopped prevaricating, took a deep breath and knocked on Diana's door.

She was there instantly, as though she had been listening to his movements from behind the latch, which she may well have been, but despite the high probability or her standing with her ear pressed to the other side of the door, she opened it only a crack, keeping it tethered on its thick chain as though she was unsure whether he might attempt to storm into her room and overwhelm her virtue with his violent passions. She cocked her head coquettishly on the doorframe with her eyelids lowered, drawing the band of the silk kimono she was wearing tight, and stealing upward glances at him from under her lids like an aging courtesan. She swept a lock of straggly brown hair away from her face before she spoke.

"He's been marching up and down for hours", her first words a complaint before any form of greeting, although for once he was sympathetic. He didn't want Kevin's steel toe caps pounding the floor in his room any more than she did. He promised to deal with it now that he was home and asked about the phone call.

"It was that Paul", she said, her face tightening as she spoke.

She had taken against Paul straight away, identifying him at some tarot reading as a dark force working against her, the 'Page of Wands' apparently.

He knew Paul should never have grown that goatee.

Behind Diana he caught slight of glittering crystals suspended on invisible threads in the folds of the deep red drapes that hung across the windows and could make out the rows of Buddhas and Hindu deities that were arranged at precise intervals along the bookshelves. Phil lay on the floor behind her, surrounded by piles of heavily embroidered cushions covered with Indian motifs, his head propped up against the sofa. He raised a lazy hand in greeting as he caught sight of X through the gap in the door. Diana's cat had the whole of the sofa to itself, stretched out contentedly along its purple velvet cover, its feet twitching as it chased dream mice, the patch of velvet where it lay scratched to ribbons by repeated clawing.

The message in the end was banal. Paul was awake and he should give him a call. He had asked Diana to remind him that he had a shift starting in an hour's time.

He hadn't forgotten.

He thanked Diana and having promised to deal with the noise from upstairs rang Paul from the phone in the corridor. There was no reply and he had to make do with leaving a message on his answerphone begging him to come round as soon as possible to rescue him from the dictatorship of the proletariat, and then headed upstairs to face the music.

Kevin was sitting on the edge of X's bed next to his girlfriend Catherine, reading a John Braine novel he'd picked up from X's shelves; the orange and black Penguin edition with a picture of Laurence Harvey on the cover that X was particularly fond of and one of the few things the burglars hadn't bothered to steal. He could see that Kevin's sticky fingers had softened the edges of the page he was reading, and he watched him drop it disdainfully on the floor as X entered, its pages fluttering like a dying bird as it fell to the floor by his feet.

"Well comrade", he began, 'from the look on your face your act of class betrayal has not delivered the riches you were hoping for."

X felt too exhausted to comment and made no reply, ignoring Kevin as he began a lecture on class solidarity, concentrating instead on squeezing past them and commandeering enough space on his own bed to lie down. He failed, and had to make do with perching awkwardly on the edge of the mattress next to Catherine with his back half propped up against the wall.

It wasn't as though he was unaware of Kevin's lack of tact and sensitivity, but it had been already been a tough day and he had to bite his lower lip to avoid shouting at Kevin to shut up.

But Kevin couldn't shut up. It wasn't in his nature. At work, his fierce determination to show that socialists were at the forefront of social justice was often admirable, and he tackled each task at the hostel with determination and rigour, no matter how mundane. But his impressive zeal was not tempered by fine judgement or any sense of realism, and his wont to argue passionately for lofty, unobtainable goals at team meetings when only the fire alarm system was up for discussion had bored, then alienated, nearly all his colleagues. Worse still, his muscular secularism was so great that he picked fights with the Baptists on the Strand and had once turned over the Krishna's vegetarian curry vat outside the Bullring in a fit of pique. Like Griff, he was now confined to duties inside the hostel itself. "Never forget X", he repeated so often it was almost a mantra, "this is how Hitler lived after he failed to get into the Vienna school of art, it is our duty not to allow the hate to fester".

Maybe he was right about that. Kevin had his qualities, but he really didn't know when to give it a rest.

"No. I didn't get the job and thanks for asking", X said bitterly, talking over Kevin's on-going monologue, and, unable to keep his irritation in check, half-shouted, "and for fuck's sake Kevin, I was planning to sell computer parts, not join the fucking SS. Will you just leave it alone?"

"Hello Cat by the way", he added.

Catherine looked startled to have been directly addressed and nodded her head quickly in acknowledgement before turning her eyes back to Kevin.

They had always seemed an incongruous couple to X, Kevin with his sweaty hair, straggly beard and beer-belly and Cat, a pretty, pale, timid girl with doe eyes, as petite and gentle as Kevin was bombastic and corpulent. All they appeared to have in common was a taste in clothes, Kevin's perpetually worn combat pants and twelve hole Docs matching her knee-length boxing boots and black leather jacket. Cat was as silent as Kevin was verbose, and she sat beside him, as ever, with her gaze affixed to him with a Manson-like devotion that made her seem less his girlfriend and more like the one and only acolyte of his private church.

Kevin had started up again, ignoring X's words completely, "We are nothing if we are not solid..."

He hesitated and X could sense him searching for the right quote from Trotsky, but temporarily lacking inspiration, he had to resort to trotting out the most obvious line from the Communist Manifesto,

"...united the workers have nothing to lose but their chains".

Kevin completed the line with a flourish, and paused for long enough to open an opportunity for X to interrupt, although he was now so vexed that his interjection was largely swearing interrupted by speech, "That's what I'm fucking trying to fucking lose", he spat out, "my fucking chains". He managed to gain some control, hurrying on before Kevin started up again, "So far being chained to the proletariat has got me what exactly? A time share in a shanty town? A job that pays just more than the dole? But do you know what really pisses me off?' he continued jabbing a finger toward Kevin, "it's that the person I'm most likely to bump into in Charing Cross Road isn't some hot actress who kisses both my cheeks before she totters off smelling of sweet perfume. No. It's some old piss-head, who half-remembers me in his drunken haze, and by the time he remembers its 'some other cunt' he's got a grudge against, I've had to dodge a couple of swings and, if I'm lucky, I'll get the full blast his rancid breath right in my face while he hugs me over and over again apologising while crocodile tears roll down his cheeks."

Kevin was undaunted by X's outburst, "So you live like the rest of us. Tough. In countries where the working class have been prevented from organising they die like animals in the mines and on the factory floors…."

'Oh Fuck off Kevin – its England in the late twentieth century. I'm not asking much from the worker's paradise, a flat of my own; enough money to go out once in a while without worrying about the cost. Fuck it, just hot water would be a start."

There had never been hot water in the squat.

"Material wealth is an illusion…" started Kevin, and for some reason that was the final straw for X. He lost it completely, shouting, his face pressed up against Kevin's, flecks of spittle spraying into his beard, "No, bollocks. Forget what I said earlier. I don't give a fuck if it upsets you. I don't just want a bit of it. I want it all".

X proceeded to count off his demands on his fingers, shouting now as he declared his manifesto. "This is what I want Kevin, a nice flat in a smart area with no bars on the windows, a girl who smells fine and looks good on my arm… A hot hatchback…" he thought for a moment with his fourth finger raised before reeling off the rest of his demands, "A platinum credit card…A job title that impresses people… overseas travel on unlimited expenses and…err…and the finest quality cocaine…" He petered to a halt. He didn't really care much about the coke, but he'd begun running out of aspirations after the car. Surely he had more? He hadn't even used all ten fingers.

He started up again, ranting on before Kevin had time to gather himself to reply, "Look. When are you going to get it? The revolution is never going to happen. No one gives a shit about it anymore except you. They're either too busy making money or wishing they were making money to give a fuck." X got to his feet and began pacing up and down, in full flow and oblivious of the impact of his words, "And when the revolution doesn't fucking happen what the fuck will you have Kevin? You live on a sink estate, your flat's got bolts on the door like a nuclear bunker, they'll never give you a paid job at the hostel because you've pissed everybody off, and what do you get at the Left bookshop? Enough for lunch if there's anything in the till? Your life's as shit as mine. Worse, at least I get paid. Tell me Kevin what has being solid with the working-class got you? Without your never-going-to-happen anarcho-syndicalist fantasy what have you actually got?"

It was quiet a moment, the crudeness of his words hanging like a flinch between them.

"I've got Cat", he said quietly.

X saw Cat look at Kevin, a look so tender with love that he felt simultaneously humbled to have witnessed it and ashamed that his cruel words had necessitated its public exposure.

He couldn't take the words back now they had been said, only stutter apologies to their backs as they rose, hand in hand, from the bed and started down the stairs.

"Sorry!" He shouted after them, "I was tired, I didn't mean it… The interview was really tough…and then there were these two women… only one of them was real…"

He sounded like a madman.

He heard the downstairs door slam.

Damage done. There was nothing he could do about it now.

He slumped back onto the bed and closed his eyes just as the first sounds of Diana's victory in her war with Kevin's boots rose like sonic punishment into his room in the form of the booms, swells and twitters of whales communicating incomprehensible trans-Atlantic laments through the floorboards.

*

He had no more than fifteen minutes of normal, dreamless sleep before Paul arrived, and, after splashing cold water from the sink on his face and under his armpits, was sufficiently awake to stumble down the road to the Green Man.

They sat in the corner of the tiny, crowded public bar, Paul nursing a pint of stout while X sipped at his mineral water and shouted over the reggae at his friend. "What's his fucking problem", he declared, jabbing his finger at Paul as though he was the object of his ire, "I'm just going to sell shit over the phone that one set of people make to another set of people that want to buy that kind of shit. What's wrong with that?"

Paul was making calming gestures with his hands while X ranted on. Although they had drunk here before, the rest of the clientele were mostly elderly, Jamaican, and the kind of regulars who treated the space an extension of their front from. They were attracting stares.

X continued unabashed, "and if I have to put on a particular uniform and speak in a particular way to do that, why's that so shocking? Even Griff put on a tie when he got married and you couldn't do outreach work in a pin-stripe suit…"

X was running out of steam, his train of thought interrupted by a loud guffaw from an Indian man with dark leathery skin and a Guyanese accent who was pontificating at the bar, his gut hanging low as he bent double with mirth at his own joke and slapped the counter hard with the flat of his hand. Remembering where he was, he lowered his voice and allowed Paul to placate his rage.

'OK, OK, I get it X. You told me five times already. You want the flat, the fancy car and the girl who loves you for your Paul Smith underpants. I understand. Why not? You didn't take a vow of poverty".

X took a swift, nervous glance behind him. No one was paying them any attention. The skinny Rasta with bad teeth and a turquoise shirt sitting behind them slammed down a domino on the table top with a loud slap, ending his game and shuffling the pieces for the next one. A bald morose-looking man in a Lacoste top at next table continued to stare at his half-finished pint and at the bar, the only white woman in the pub, a middle-aged never-beauty in too much make-up and heels, continued flirting with the old soaks, giggling girlishly and fluttering her lashes at every tired compliment. X glanced down the length of the bar checking, that he handed disturbed the landlord with his outburst, but the proprietor's demeanour was unchanged, impassively leaning on the counter, relaxed but watchful as he guarded the door to the back-room, where blasts of marijuana smoke billowed into the bar each time the door swung open. The boss was treated with an easy familiarity by the regulars, but his bearing and the sheer bulk of him squeezed into his shiny black suit, made it clear he was not someone it would be wise to get on the wrong side of.

He returned his attention to what Paul was saying.

"But X, I don't agree with you saying it makes no difference how you speak. I can't buy the 'it's just the appropriate language for the occasion' argument". Paul was speaking slowly in a manner that seemed more than a little patronising to X, "We speak correctly to people in our job X. We make adjustments according to character, mood and perspective, ignore the most offensive things they say and listen carefully so that we can understand their needs. Agreed?"

X nodded sullenly.

"Paul continued, "by doing this we slowly earn their trust, and then use the information they give us to try to help them to get off the streets. In sales, I imagine", he went on, "you use the same skills more or less, but every time you talk on the phone about *their* needs, you're really thinking about what *you* want. It's not just language."

X didn't reply, keeping his seething resentment bottled up. Everyone seemed to presume the right to give him moral guidance.

Well they could all go fuck themselves.

He looked at Paul with fresh eyes, seeing for the first time that he wore a uniform he couldn't take off. He could cut his long hair and shave off the goatee, even take out the piercings from his lip, nose and his eyebrow; but to strip him so would cost him everything. He imagined him at work in a building society with a nylon tie and nametag, shuffling like a neutered Catweasal to the thickened glass. All of him stripped away to achieve that much. He was as marked as though he were branded in the face. X stiffened. Did he have the mark too?

He diverted his eyes from his friend and checked his watch. It was time to start his shift. He had to go.

As he rose, the music switched from reggae to Dance Hall and the game old bird at the bar began twirling on the arm of the ageing lothario next to her. The old man raised his arm to assist her pirouette, temporarily crumpling his immaculate linen suit and lifted his walking stick in tribute to the acres of oozing cleavage turning like a pale donor kebab in front of him.

X stepped through the door without looking back.

4. DEL

It was quiet down by the embankment.

He checked his watch. Fifteen minutes to one o'clock.

Almost done.

He tried the walkie-talkie again. Still no reply.

Fucking Lars.

He was supposed to pick him up at the end of his shift, swing by in the van and take him back to the hostel. But even-money, Lars had slipped off home early, and if he confronted him about it tomorrow would claim that the radio had stopped functioning like he had the last time.

Lars was working at the hostel to avoid military service at home in Denmark or Germany or wherever it was he came from, and didn't give a shit about homeless people or anyone else other than himself. He treated the staff with the disdain of the spoilt teenager he was, seeing them as old and therefore already losers, and viewed work as an unwanted interruption to his goal of staying permanently stoned with the other draft dodgers from his home country who slipped away early from hospital wards and day care centres to join him on the bong.

It looked like the night bus again.

For a second he felt like crying, he was so shattered with fatigue.

He'd got through the earlier part of the night wired on caffeine, red-eyed and hyper-alert. But the coffee could not quite bring him back from the pounding the day had inflicted, and its events continued to burst in sparks and flashes into his mind, running in confused loops where reality and unreality were often reversed; the tall blond sitting opposite him in the reception area while the real woman jogged around the dream track at night, and Kevin's face sometimes shouted at him from a behind a pair of red braces.

Fortunately, X's job did not require him to be razor sharp and focused and his clientele were hardly in any position to pass judgement on his performance. He had stumbled into the work by accident when he got back from Berlin, moving from volunteer to salaried employee thanks to the natural ease he felt in the company of the lost and an ability to listen without judgement to the stories that his clients needed to tell. He was now an outreach worker; a specialist working exclusively with men over the age of thirty who had lived on the streets for more than a year and were therefore were classified as 'long-term' homeless. His patch was a quadrant of Central London; a square mile or so in the heart of the city that ran east of Charing Cross Road along the river as far as Waterloo Bridge. He had walked the same route each night for over a year now, offering assistance to the same toughened and confused faces, his progress dictated by the rhythm of the city as it wound down and ending only when the last of its most vulnerable citizens were firmly, if not securely, asleep.

It was probably a noble cause.

It was certainly a losing battle.

The bodies ran the full length of the Strand these days, as far down as the Savoy. Long rows of abandoned humanity, put out like garbage bags for collection, filled almost every doorway. By the time the theatre crowd had dispersed and the most lucrative begging opportunities had dried up, the only gaps in the doorways were where the proprietors had hosed down their shop fronts at closing time. Tonight, he noticed, even some of these sorry plots were occupied, late-comers forced to make do with laying piles of rapidly dampening cardboard beneath them on the sodden ground. Despite the river of bodies laid out along the thoroughfare, they represented only a thin slice of the total street population of London, the Salvation Army estimated that there were around 75,000 sleeping in the night-shelters, hostels, streets, parks and underpasses of the capital on any given night.

X could easily believe it.

In Lincoln's Inn Fields, tent and tarpaulin bivouacs filled the entire square, and there was a shantytown just over the river, a shifting semi-permanent cardboard city located under the roundabout at the entrance to the South Bank that was home to more than a hundred souls. During the day, commuters hurried under the concrete overpass, weaving through the passageways cut between the plastic and packaging coffin-homes, stepping quickly in the half-darkness and keeping their eyes focussed firmly ahead. No one passed through at night.

X had waited while everyone bedded down before walking the rows looking for his clients and keeping an eye out for new faces and drowning eyes. He watched a group of four kids settling in for the night in a doorway. A hardened veteran of seventeen with prison tattoos on his hairless forearms organised the weaker kids into defensive positions with him at the centre, posting lookouts and barking orders like a boy-prince marshalling his troops. A stick-thin, dead-eyed girl slumped in one corner next to a pale, drooling, boy and a kid who could have been no more than fourteen. Other organisations dealt with the homeless young people and X was thoroughly glad of that. They were located more around Soho, closer to the sex trade, than on his patch, and X only saw the edges of the ugly street hierarchies and desperate stories of their world. For his clients, the street youth were folk-devils, knife-wielding amoral animals that ran in packs, menaced them on giro day, and would give them a good kicking if they had nothing worth robbing, or perhaps for no reason at all. It wasn't a perspective X could share. He'd inevitably see them later, when he was completing his rounds, abandoned children left to fend for themselves, the look-out having nodded off, their toughened faces gentled by closed lids, laid out on the pavement in the terrifying vulnerability of sleep without walls or barriers for protection. He always took a wide arc around them as he passed, knowing that the sound of an adult's step in the darkness would hold particular fear for at least some of the children.

X's job was to befriend the men most hardened to street life, earn their trust over time and then persuade them to return with him to the hostel, where the staff could begin the process of finding them somewhere to live. While resident, they could shower, de-louse and get themselves some clean clothes, and tucked up in clean sheets and freed from fear of assault, the hostel would be their first step back to a normal life.

That evening he been too shattered to do anybody much good, contenting himself with smiling and pretending to listen, handing out cigarettes like a generous drunk. He had helped Jimmy the Yip at least, the old boy having pissed himself again, and he had guarded his patch while Jimmy shuffled round the corner to put on a fresh pair of pants from X's pack. But that had been about it.

He'd been relieved when at last his rounds took him into the quieter back streets behind Holborn, where the bodies thinned out and he had only to concentrate on placing one foot in front of the other. Finally, he had reached the river and with the rising tide keeping pace with him as he walked, turned back toward home. He knew it was unlikely he'd find anyone down here, the strong winds that built up along the Thames blew damp, chilled air up over the river wall and the drop of several degrees in temperature they caused could be fatal for anyone sleeping unprotected on its banks. Only the most devastated drunk would ever crash down here. But Frank, X's boss, who had run the soup run for twenty years, had drilled it into him that he must complete every inch of his rounds, repeatedly citing the case of Pete the Bike, now in his seventies, who would have choked to death on his own vomit had he not made that last check at Cleopatra's needle. X had proved Frank right twice, coming across men who had stumbled away from the crowds to fall insensate on the slabs by the river. He'd helped bundle the half-conscious, puke-splattered bodies into the back of the van to be tipped into a hostel bed.

Conceivably he had saved a life, maybe two.

So even tonight, despite his fatigue, X had determinedly fulfilled his duty with every leaden-footed stride.

There had been no one to save.

So that was it. Day done. He tried the walkie-talkie again, more in hope than expectation. Only static came through the speaker. It was certain now. Lars was long gone. The night-bus it was then.

Finally heading for home, his fatigue lifted, his head cleared and his footsteps lightened. For the first time since his shift had begun he looked up.

It was a beautiful night.

He stopped, breathing in lungfuls of chilled, briny air. A full moon had risen, turning the dark surface of the river pale, and its gentle white light, falling through the plane trees that lined the embankment, cast maple-patterned moon-shadows on the paving slabs beneath his feet. The city was quiet now, disturbed only by the muffled noise of taxis passing by behind him, their engine notes dampened by the rushing water to low swooshing sounds like gusts of strong wind. The strip by the river, washed immaculate in the light of the moon, seemed like an island, cast adrift from the rest of the city, a sliver of Shangri-La transplanted to the banks of the Thames.

Revitalised, he set off again, and with his footfalls echoing dully back off the concrete, he strolled like a tourist across the silvered slabs, accompanied only by the great globe lamps suspended along the river wall like the illuminations on a seaside promenade.

It was at this solitary moment of contentment in his long day that he spotted a lone figure, lying prone on one of the wrought iron benches under the shade of the trees. The old man lay on his back, perfectly still, his body's length an exact match for the bench, his head pillowed on one arm rest and a pair of neat brown shoes pressed up against the latticed metal at the other end. A broadsheet newspaper covered his whole body, and had been tucked neatly around him like a fitted sheet. The leaf patterns made by the moonlight stood out boldly against the white paper and lay across his bearded face as though he was buried under a carpet of leaves. A single can of Carlsberg Special Brew stood golden against the leg of the bench nearest his head.

As X drew closer, it occurred to him that the blanched white skin of the old man's face was not merely due to the moonlight, but was, almost certainly, the pallor of death. His first thought was that he should just carry on walking. The setting seemed the most fitting burial ground possible for a street drinker, laid out on this moonlit strip by the river like a Viking warrior arrayed in the bow of his funeral longboat for the voyage to Valhalla. His second thought was exactly the same as the first but entirely lacking its animating spirit.

If it was a corpse, he was buggered.

If he called it in there was no chance of him getting home before dawn, and instead of laying his head down on a soft pillow in his comfortable bed, he'd have to suffer hours of blue flashing lights, matey copper's jokes, and laboriously recorded statements to get through.

The police would come soon enough. Dead was dead. There was nothing useful he could do. Let them deal with it. It was their job after all. Just keep on walking.

Then, as he was passing by the stilled form, he realised it was Del.

Please, not Del.

He approached the bench slowly, hoping that he was wrong and that it was only the white light that had made sleep look like death, but the closer he got the more certain he became that his initial assumption had been correct. Del lay absolutely still on the bench, his soft eyelids gently closed and undisturbed by the flickers and twitches of dreams. His broad flabby face wore a contented smile like that of a man who had fallen asleep in his armchair after tiffin, passing out of this life while dreaming pleasantly of his prized hydrangeas. X leant over the body, trying to summon the courage to touch Del's face to see if it was still warm.

Del opened his eyes.

"Evening officer…. I was just laying down for a moment, lovely night isn't it?"

He sat up, tidying away the newspapers that lay over his legs as he did so, tucking them away behind him as though he would be referring to the business section later. Laughing, X sat down on the bench next to him.

"Dear oh dear", Del began, shaking his head slowly, his bulbous lower lip pushed through his grizzly beard as though his whole face was shrugging. "I was fourteen years in the army, and look at me now." Del paused, letting the injustice and absurdity of it all hang in the air for a moment, astonished once more that such a thing had come to pass, although he had been on the streets for at least twenty years.

"I was in for four years…" he continued, warming to his theme.

The dates always varied in Del's stories, and neither he nor X were troubled by the inconsistencies. They differed partly because Del was hazy about the passage of time, and partly because Del was often lying, or at least had long since forgotten what the truth had ever been.

"Monte Casino…Mount Carmel…Haifa… Hacka… the orange groves, right the way through to Jerusalem…

Del paused again, and they sat for a moment in the bright Levantine sunshine of his memory, shaking his head again, but this time as though what he was saying of his own life seemed impossible, even to him.

'They blew up the King David's hotel", he started up again, 'all those years ago… They blew it to bits, those Jews…" He paused, shaking his head once again. "Joe Stern and his crazy gang." "That was a crowd wasn't it!"

X never really got Del's historical references to his time in Palestine, it didn't exactly seem like anti-Semitism, more that Del's grasp of the political subtleties of the situation went no further than astonishment that the only time he'd ever left London there'd been people who wanted to shoot at him.

"Second battalion Middlesex regiment. I was captain of the football team in Fayed and down the Suez Canal. We had some good players…."

During the long pause that followed this declaration and while Del recalled some regimental encounter with the laced, heavy leather ball on a dusty pitch in Egypt, X felt the familiar shift in Del's dialogue begin, the needle slipping into the most worn groove in the record of his memory. From here on in X knew each word and the action associated with it so well that he could have mimed along as Del sounded out each stanza.

"George Kaiser…Bernie Musset…Dai Hopkins, the Welsh international. I played with the lot of them. Fit as a fiddle I was"

"Fancy that!"

And then into his most repeated passages.

"Joe James…he could head a ball as hard as a man could kick it."

X could see Del remembering the ball thumping into the back of the net at Griffin Park.

"Used to drink at the Rose and Crown. Just round the corner from our house in Sandycombe Road. You know the only man that kept him out of the England team?'

X wasn't expected to reply, although he knew the answer.

"Stan Cullis! Joe would have been captain of England if it hadn't have been for Stan Cullis."

Del could never bear Stan Cullis any ill will, despite his thwarting of his hero's national ambitions.

"Wonderful player mind, Stan Cullis." Del paused for a moment of reverence about the abilities of the hard-tackling centre half. "Went on to manage Wolves", he added, as he always did.

X was drowsy now on the bench, Del's recollection of Brentford players he had once known as familiar to him as a lullaby. One time he'd tried to follow up on Del's claim to have played for the club in the wartime cup final at Wembley in order to get free tickets for the hostel residents. He'd received a polite letter back informing him that no one of that name had ever played for the team, but had enclosed some free tickets anyway. He hadn't been able to find Del on the day of the game and had ended up going with a hard-drinking and incontinent idiot from the hostel instead who had shat himself at half time, leading to a hasty exit from the director's box.

"Packed it all in", Del was saying, making a gesture of drinking from a pint glass, his eyebrows raised in mock surprise, shrugging away a decision made so long ago it was as though it had been taken by someone else. "My dad didn't like that". His tone had changed now, and he leant forward with his hands on his knees as though bracing himself for a heavy blow to the chest. "Used to dubbin my boots before a game, my dad."

X knew the inevitable trajectory of this part of Del's story, and stiffened himself on the bench as though he was shoulder to shoulder with him on the pine bench of the funeral parlour.

"Dead now."

"Long dead my dad, just like my dear old mum."

"In the ground the pair of them, side by side in Mortlake cemetery."

"All alone I am"

And then, just as X had been drawn into the depths of Del's heart rendering sadness, wishing he could breach the terrible loneliness expressed by his words, Del switched tack, shrugging it off in an instant. Suddenly he was smiling, impishly, like both the sordid Father Christmas he now was and the young man he had been in the nineteen thirties, playing football down the park and getting into trouble with his trousers down in the privet hedge with Peggy Hill and her mate on the Worton Estate. On his face it was as though the whole of his life since that time had been someone else's story, and that if he knocked on the door of 37 Sandycombe Road it would all be there once again, his football boots hanging by their laces at the door, his dad in the shed at the bottom of the garden and his dear old mum fussing in the kitchen downstairs.

He reached inside his coat and pulled out a carton of pills, handing them over to X, winking as did so, the earlier sadness so completely dissipated that X wondered once again whether he understood Del at all, whether in fact his quiet statements of unbearable pathos were no more than a ruse to soften up the mark before making the hustle he had planned all along.

Del had often, in exactly the same sequence, chosen this moment to try and off-load something he had shop-lifted or some pills he had nicked off someone at the day centre. His thefts were often absurd, a slab of bacon offcuts one week, giant embossed birthday cards with anthropomorphic animals in bright pastel colours the next, preposterous objects somehow squeezed under his jacket in the butchers or WH Smith. He had always been unable to understand that even if X had been interested in the products, he couldn't accept stolen goods from one of his clients, but Del took no umbrage at each failed trade, and continued to offer whatever he had stolen to X at roughly the price of a four pack of Tenants Super.

"What are these?" Del asked.

X read the label. They were amphetamine sulphate.

He opened the carton. There were about fifty yellow capsules inside.

"Where did you get these?' he demanded of Del, but knew before Del replied that he had been over to the East End to visit Dr Badgett again.

X continued to be amazed that Dr Badgett kept his license. Perhaps a third of London's homeless were registered with his practise, a fact that was only partly determined by the good doctor's willingness to have foul smelling tramps clogging up his reception, but was much more readily explained by his willingness to prescribe whatever anyone asked for without asking too many questions. Dr Badgett's methods had created a entire sub-currency of unneeded pharmaceuticals with psychotropic effects that were traded across most of the hostels and day centres in London.

Del was disappointed when X told him what they were.

"Are you sure they're not anti-depressants", he asked hopefully.

It appeared that Badgett had misinterpreted Del's description of drowsiness and weight gain as hints for a different kind of commodity altogether than the one Del had been hoping for.

"I'm not selling to kids" he added, his voice rising indignantly as though X had suggested he should, his aggrieved tone not arising from any moral compunction, but because he was almost certain to get a good kicking if he attempted that kind of trade.

X handed the pills back to Del with a warning to be careful and gathered himself to leave.

It was clear that Del wouldn't be accompanying him back to the hostel, and even had he wanted to, X had no means of getting him there since Lars had absconded with the van hours ago, so he dug an emergency blanket out of his bag and bid him goodnight. He looked back to see Del settling in for the rest of the night on the bench, the shiny bedspread laid over his legs reflecting in the moonlight like a gilded carapace.

*

Trying to get comfortable on the back seat of the night bus, X reached into his jacket pocket to move a blunt object that was digging painfully into his hip.

It was the carton of Dr Badgett's pills.

Del must have slipped it in as he had been handing him the emergency blanket, probably in some form of misplaced recompense for his gift, or perhaps just because he wanted to get rid of the unsellable pills. He moved it to a more comfortable position and lent his head against the glass. Behind him the sound of a man vomiting in the isle was accompanied by the shrieks of the surrounding passengers as regurgitated lager splattered across their shoes under the seats. Whoops of laughter and cheers emerged from his equally pissed companions, and despite the pungent stench of bile that began to fill air of the top deck X closed his eyes and fell instantly asleep.

5. EVA

He was standing on the same boulevard as before. The beech trees were now almost bare of leaves and there was a chill in the air suggesting autumn had almost passed and winter would soon be arriving. Leaf litter had been raked into great piles beside the old trees' trunks and as he watched a strong gust of wind detached more parched leaves from their boughs sending them floating to the ground like gently falling orange snow. Peering into the gloom he could just make out the old clapperboard houses down by the tram stop and then the sun dipped below the horizon, throwing up one last flare of amber light before darkness descended.

He appeared to be entirely alone.

At first, the only sound was that of the wind in the trees, then, faintly at first, but rapidly rising in pitch and volume, he made out the distinctive whirring hum of a tram's electric motor floating out of the wood to his right. In the crystal clear air, he could pick out the rhythmic clacking sound of tram wheel and track groove meshing, heard a sharp rise in pitch as it rounded a hidden bend somewhere in the forest, and then the tram was suddenly roaring out of the trees, a metal tube of light and noise shattering the evening's calm, hurtling down the track toward him its twin headlamps flaring in the dark. Without thinking he began running as fast as he could, sprinting flat out to try and beat the tram to the stop some four hundred metres down the road. Despite his best efforts the tram passed him long before he reached the platform, but was still waiting, its engine idling and its doors open, as he panted up the concrete slope. The last stride of his sprint took him over the threshold and into the rear carriage. He slumped into the nearest seat and sat, head down, fighting to catch his breath. The doors closed with a gentle whoosh of air and the tram slid smoothly out of the station.

He looked up. The carriage was completely empty.

*

By the time he got off, the carriage was half full. A dozen or so commuters had alighted at various stops and sat alone or chatting to each other in small groups, their voices hushed and their words inaudible to X. Both sexes were dressed in strange and almost identical clothing; tight-fitting, long-sleeved, one piece outfits that covered then from neck to ankle as though they had all just attended a dance or exercise class. Over their leotards most wore high-buttoned, narrow lapelled jackets in a variety of colours ranging from olive green to navy blue. The jackets were also near identical in style, differing only in the smallest of details; a fold at the cuff, an extra ribbon of material at the neck or a variation in the size, shape or number of buttons. They all wore flat, soft-soled shoes and carried no baggage other than small shoulder bags, leaving the aisles free and uncluttered. Surprisingly, given that the lighting in the carriage was subdued and it was dark outside the tram, many of them were wearing sunglasses.

When the tram reached the top of a steep hill overlooking the city he disembarked without thinking, somehow aware that this was his destination. He found himself standing in front of a six story apartment block on a wide street bordered by pollarded lime trees. He paused to let an old woman on a tricycle with a large wicker basket peddle by before crossing the road, and once she had turned down a side street and the tram had dropped over the crest of the hill, the street was empty and silent. He entered the apartment building in front of him, took the lift to the fourth floor, rang the bell of apartment 44 and stood waiting patiently in the corridor.

Eva opened the door.

She was just as breathtakingly beautiful as when they had last met, but this time he was prepared for the shock of her, and, determined to make a good impression, set what he hoped was a friendly, easy-going smile on his face and waited for her to recognise him. To his surprise, he found that he was holding a bunch of slightly wilted daffodils in his right hand, their chirpy yellow heads drooping forlornly over his wrist.

Eva stood frozen on the spot, her lilac eyes wide with surprise and, for a time, made no move either to accept the proffered flowers or open the door and admit him. Eventually she lent forward to take the flowers off him, bending down as she did so to press her forehead against his with only the briefest of touches.

She mustered a wan smile. "You'd better come in."

Eva stood back and gestured him into the living room, telling him to make himself comfortable while she put the flowers in some water.

He sat down and looked around the room. At first he was delighted by Eva's apartment, it had a sense of proportion and under-stated elegance that seemed to match her perfectly. The sofa he sat on had an identical chocolate brown companion set at a right angle to it, which combined with two brightly coloured crash cushions made up a seating area in the centre of the room that was clearly designed to allow small groups of people to converse in comfort and ease. The bare walls had only two adornments, a painting of an elderly man with an intelligent face and kind eyes, carefully rendered in thick oils and opposite it, a bronze sculpture of an ice-skater, its form as exquisitely crafted as a Degas, mounted on a low wooden stand. The lack of objects made the room seem larger than it was, and the sense of space was further enhanced by a pair of glass sliding doors that ran from floor to ceiling across one wall and opened out onto a balcony. Despite its simplicity, there was a degree of sumptuousness about the flat. The cream carpet under his feet felt like down to the touch and the sofa's fabric was soft and yielding and seemed to adjust itself around the shape of his body as he sat. The more he examined his surroundings, however, the more surprised he became by what was missing from the room. It wasn't merely furnished with a minimalist aesthetic. There really was hardly anything in it. He was not altogether surprised to find a living room where there was no TV or video recorder, although in the absence of a fireplace he could not recall a room where the television set was not the centre of focus, and he was actively pleased there that there was no Atari consul or Amstrad, making the assumption that their presence would probably have indicated masculine company. But there was no radio, no hi-fi, no record collection, no means of listening to music at all, and most surprising of all, no books. As there were no shelves, cupboards or any kind of storage space in the room, they couldn't have been hidden from view and their absence seemed to suggest to X that Eva did not read. He was still pondering this thought when she returned.

Oddly, she had put on a pair of sunglasses while she was in the kitchen, and only pushed them up onto her forehead as she re-entered, carrying his wilted daffodils in what appeared to be some kind of coffee pot half-filled with water. She looked around the room, and finding no obvious place to set them down, placed the pot on the floor next to the statue of the ice-skater where they looked as natural as a turd in a sweetshop.

She sat down as far away from him as possible on the other sofa, tucking one leg under her as she settled, and pushed a strand of blond hair behind her ear distractedly before turning to face him. She let out a deep breath and gave him a tentative smile. "Would you mind terribly taking your shoes off?" she asked.

It seemed to take him an age to untangle his laces, during which time Eva said nothing, and when he had eventually placed his shoes by the door and returned to his seat the atmosphere felt distinctly uncomfortable.

When Eva broke the silence, she spoke in short, clipped sentences, her delivery interpretable either as challenging to the point of rudeness, or merely forthright and direct. "Tasan was certain that you would …reappear", she began, "and he was certain that when you did, you would be curious. Are you curious X?"

The manner of her questioning made him feel like an undergraduate student at a tutorial for which he was hopelessly underprepared, but another part of his brain was glorying in being the object of this beautiful woman's gaze. He struggled to concentrate on her words, finding himself wondering why the colour of her eyes was so hard to pin down, they seemed ice-blue now, although he was almost sure that had been a different shade when he came in…

She interrupted his reverie, "So X, do you have any questions?"

X refocused. He couldn't ask her how she would describe her eye colour, or whether she was single, so he returned to his earlier half-thought and asked her about the absence of books in her apartment.

The exchange that followed was much more stilted than he had expected. At first it was as though she had not understood what he had said or was perhaps offended by his question, and he immediately regretted having asked it. She fiddled nervously with her sunglasses, even putting them on briefly, before pushing them back onto her forehead and looking directly at him with a serious expression. It appeared it was the word 'book' that had troubled her, although X could not fathom exactly why, and when she began to make her explanation it seemed both tortuous and overcomplicated, her answer divided into a series of sub clauses about data, novels and scientific research that seemed entirely unnecessary. It wasn't until she used the phrase, 'we all have permanent open access to', that it occurred to him that she was talking about libraries, which, in the end, seemed a very mundane answer indeed.

"But don't you sometimes want to own a favourite story?" X interjected, "so you can dip in and out of it whenever you want to...."

This simple sentence bewildered her once more, but by now it was clear that she was beginning to enjoy the challenge, although X was unable to envisage exactly what challenge he had set her.

It was the word 'own' this time that had troubled her.

"It's not that I do not understand possessions X", she said waving her hand to indicate the objects in her flat, "it is in the context of 'book' I am struggling. No one can own knowledge after all! Wait, I have the solution", she exclaimed with a look of satisfaction on her face and waved her arm as though wiping clean a plane of air in front of her. A panel on the wall in front of her slid aside to reveal a flat grey screen.

X couldn't help feeling a little disappointed. So there was a TV after all, albeit a very stylish one.

Eva made another gesture with her hand which brought the screen to life, but before X could focus on the words and pictures on the initial display, Eva began flicking through the channels by making tiny, rapid movements with her fingers and the images shifted too quickly for X to bring them into focus.

"There", she exclaimed triumphantly, "book: novel".

Words were laid out in sentences across the screen in a simple font, their dark letters clear against a white background like a page in a book. For a moment the sentences slid upwards together, then Eva made a final, flat-handed gesture and the page stilled at the opening paragraph of a novel written in English.

X read, 'The house was named 'the cave'. It was a large old-fashioned three-storied building standing in about an acre of ground, and situated about a mile outside the town of Mugsborough. It stood back nearly two-hundred yards from the main road and was reached by means of a by-road or lane, on each side of which was a hedge formed of hawthorn trees and blackberry bushes.'

X stopped reading. The passage seemed vaguely familiar but he couldn't place it, and anyway, it didn't seem all that interesting.

Eva had become quite animated now. One of her gestures

must have deactivated the controls as she was gesticulating vigorously with her long, graceful arms without disturbing the words on the screen, and her whole spirit seemed utterly altered from when he had first entered the room. "So, novels. The library is on, no in, the screen. I can search for whatever I want. Every novel that has ever been written is available at the flick of a wrist". She smiled as spoke the phrase, enjoying the aptness of her metaphor. "Let us test it", she continued, "What book would you like to see?"

Rather than think of a novel he might actually want to read, X wracked his brains for something that might impress Eva, something literary and not too obvious. His mind went instantly blank. Before the silence made him look ignorant, he blurted out the first title that came to him, "*The Mysterious Stranger* by Mark Twain".

That was good, it even sounded appropriate to the occasion.

Eva smiled, made a few quick gestures and a fresh text began to roll across the screen. "There it is", she exclaimed with satisfaction, "complete and unabridged".

It had taken no more than a few seconds.

Every book ever written, he thought. How fantastic. But how would you know which ones to read? He was about to ask, but Eva had already moved on. "OK", she was saying, "That was book: novel. Now book: Research and information. I am not sure the synonym is exact but here you are".

The screen now showed a single column with the titles of various academic disciplines displayed as sub-headings. The list didn't seem to be in any particular order and he only managed to read the first four, anthropology, sociology, psychology and history, before Eva sent the list rolling upwards. "Any subject you interested in and you can access the peer reviewed research data at all times", she explained, adding "and check the citation index if you so wish. It all updates in real time so you can stay completely up to date", she paused then added as an afterthought, "Of course, more general texts and inter-disciplinary studies are also available for the non-specialist"

From the look on Eva's face when she told him this he sensed that academia was where her true passion lay. He had been in danger of seriously misreading her only a few moments ago when he thought she didn't read. It seemed more likely now that she was really quite bookish even if she wasn't exactly clear what books were.

"What would you like to look at?" she asked, and when he didn't reply instantly, she moved her fingers and the screen turned into a display of small boxes each one containing a separate stylised image.

X could make out a fat fruit fly in the box on the far left, a cell undergoing mitosis in the box next to it and the letters ATCG in a third. He felt momentarily proud of himself that he recognised the letters as initials of the four nucleotides that made up DNA, in exactly the same way he felt when he got a solitary answer right on University Challenge, and realising it was his only chance to sound clever before his lack of knowledge was exposed said, "It's not really my area. Are you particularly interested in genetics?"

"Not really", she replied, "but it is so important that you have to make an effort to keep up, don't you think? It is one of the big questions is it not, at least now that Pandora is out of the box!" She smiled directly at him for the first time and he smiled directly back, unsure whether she had deliberately made a joke or not.

But why did she think that Pandora's box had been opened?

Again, he would have asked, but Eva had moved on to the next stage of her lesson.

"OK. Now, Book: Data", she was saying.

The display on the screen changed again and this time a combination of still images, video clips, tables of numerical data, lists and sub-headings, bar graphs and pie charts were laid out over a background of a waterfall tumbling down the steep sides of a fjord.

"This is my first page", she explained, "this is the data I am most interested in at this point, but you can re-arrange and select what you want. Everyone's first page is different. You can see I have…" And she paused before reeling off the screen's contents in rapid succession, "the time, the temperature outside, the weather forecast…" As she recited each item she made a finger-tip gesture which caused that section to zoom into the foreground as though coming up from the bottom of a well, and then dispelled it to the background by another tiny gesture when she was done with it.

"…the status of my boyfriend and five closest friends……"

X's heart sank as images of two men and four women raced to the front of the screen and then slid backwards again, noting despairingly that the image of a square-jawed dark-haired man, as handsome as any matinee idol, had hovered slightly longer in the foreground than the others.

Oh well, he thought, at least she's heterosexual, there's always hope. But he couldn't help feeling deflated, and momentarily lost all concentration on what Eva was showing him.

She had continued her tour oblivious to his sudden shift in mood, "...the voting intentions on the stem cell implant bill... only twenty minutes to go on that one..." A pie graph, roughly evenly divided had risen to the foreground. It was quickly dispelled. "The discussion forum on...on...", she stuttered for a moment as though she too had temporarily lost concentration and X tried to regain focus, worried that she might have noticed his glazed expression. "...from an academic conference..." she continued, quickly dispelling to the background an image of a grey-haired woman standing at a lectern in front of a huge screen on which a naked man with a spear and vivid facial scarring was displayed.

"The feed from the rover on the surface of Europa", she continued, calling up a blurred, jerky video that showed the edge of a muddy white wheel and part of a distended robot arm slowly traversing the rocky surface of one of Jupiter's moons. X watched as the machine nudged its way through puddles of something that looked like water, but could just have easily been liquid methane, or liquid anything as far as X knew, the rover's camera picking out the moon's boulder-strewn landscape through a fuzzy haze of purple gas that looked distinctly corrosive. "Still no life", Eva was saying, "perhaps Titan would have been the better choice after all". The failure of the Jupiter probe to find extra-terrestrial life seemed to temporarily dispirit her and she waved at the screen in a gesture that resembled a curt farewell. The screen went blank.

She soon brightened however, and was quickly back lecturing again. X set his face to an appropriate expression of concentration, pushing the thought of her square-jawed boyfriend as far back as he could manage. Eva was now explaining that they hardly ever used the screens anymore, as all the data was accessible at all times through the optical sets that he had mistaken for sunglasses.

"It's all displayed on the inner surface", she explained, sliding her sunglasses off her forehead and holding them out to him by one stem. "You select what you wish to look at by moving your eyes from point to point behind the lens".

X slipped the glasses on. They sat awkwardly on the bridge of his nose, and he had to tilt them until they were roughly horizontal to make up for the uneven level of his ears. He found that behind the glasses the light in the room was only marginally dimmed, and numbers and images now covered most of his view without obscuring the room itself. The display reminded him of cheap 3d animal cards he had played with as a kid, each image suspended behind the others in a separate plane, as he recalled the savannah bushes being arranged behind the pride of sleeping lions. The layout in front of him seemed to be what Eva had described as her 'first page', and he could make out one of her female friends in his peripheral vision away to the right of the lens. He moved his eyes in that direction, intending to sneak a closer look at her boyfriend, whether to torture himself or size up the opposition, he wasn't sure, but as he moved his eyes the pictures spun past him and he hastily corrected by moving his eyes sharply the other way. Too quickly. A succession of images cascaded past him, rotating with the speed of a slot machine's pinwheel. The effect was instantly disorientating, like being suddenly spun round on a fairground Waltzer. Unable to regain control of the racing numbers and images he felt instantly nauseous and had to jerk the glasses off his eyes to stop himself from throwing up. The room continued spinning for some time after he had removed them.

Eva was laughing, and then apologising for laughing, and then laughing again as he wobbled on the sofa trying to regain his equilibrium. Had he been standing he would certainly have fallen over. Despite the discomfort he was pleased that he had made her laugh, even if the joke was at his expense.

Eva leant forward and touched him gently on the wrist with the long delicate fingers of her left hand. He felt the contact like a small jolt of electricity. She took the glasses off him, still apologising, covering her smile with her other hand as she spoke, "I'm sorry. I should have explained more carefully".

Her tone became measured and instructive once again, "When you first put them on", she directed, "you need to look *through* the data at a fixed point in the real world. I know!" she exclaimed, smiling, "look at me. I will sit absolutely still in front of you and you concentrate on here", and she tapped the centre of her forehead with one perfectly manicured finger, "When you are comfortable with that, just lose focus on me and re-focus on the image immediately in front of you in the lens. Keep steady until you feel ready, and then make only the smallest of movements with your eyes." She indicated a miniscule distance between her thumb and forefinger, "Just tiny fractions".

She leant forward and slipped the glasses over his ears, sliding them into place and pressing one finger on the centre of the bridge to straighten them. A small smile flickered around her lips as she did so. She sat back on the sofa, tucking one leg under her again and sat perfectly still.

"OK, give it a try now."

Under the protection of the shades he was at finally at liberty to look closely at her without fear of being caught leering, and although he tried to maintain his focus on her immaculate brow, he found his gaze inevitably running down the line of her thin straight nose to her lips, soft, full and partly opened in an amused smile. Her immobility, and the translucent barrier of the glasses, lent an air of unreality to the scene, as though he were contemplating an exquisite portrait rather than a living, breathing human being. It was like meditating in front of a religious icon and, for the few seconds it lasted he felt as though he had been transported to a higher plane of being, a place where he needed no sustenance other than her beauty. He would have stayed, happily transfixed in that moment forever, if Eva hadn't brought him out of his trance by enquiring politely about his progress.

With great reluctance he wrenched his focus away from her to concentrate on the image directly in front of his eyes. A coloured weather map showing coils of isobars superimposed on a map of Northern Europe came into focus. The image could scarcely have been of less interest to him and he only dallied long enough to register that an area of high pressure had built up over Denmark, before tracking his eyes to the right.

Too fast.

The images of Eva's friends flickered swiftly past, and he was only able to catch brief glimpses of a dark-haired, pretty woman with bright green eyes and a bob cut, a tousled- haired blond man with a goatee, an Indian girl with deep brown eyes and long lustrous hair, and then, his heart sinking once again, the square-jawed hunk who was probably her boyfriend; each one slipping past too quickly for anything more than the faintest of impressions. He stilled his pupils again, then tried to track back as slowly as he could but once again his movements were too swift and first the weather map, then half a dozen blurred images flashed past, until he managed to bring the kaleidoscope to a halt on the cloying purple clouds of Europa; the robot inching a few feet further forward across the devastated rocky landscape. He closed his eyes and took the glasses off. He was really shit at this.

"Maybe in time", Eva said, her face full of concerned sympathy, but X suspected he would never master it even with a lifetime's practice.

He handed her back the glasses. There was a moment's silence, and X, anxious not to allow the awkward silence of earlier to return and unable to control his curiosity, found himself blurting out the question that was at the forefront of his mind, "So what's your boyfriend like then?"

He had tried to make the enquiry seem casual, but there was a catch in his voice that betrayed an inappropriate urgency to his question, and perhaps it was this that made Eva blush.

"Oh Olaf", she replied with a snort, waving her arm in a dismissive gesture, "I hardly ever get to see him these days. He's always away in the far North taking terrible risks in the name of science. Or so he says!"

Having started in a casual manner, she quickly warmed to her theme giving X even more reason to regret asking, "He undertakes these absurd deep water dives, collecting samples and so forth, always laughing about leaking suits and telling tales about blacking out under the pressure! He has this belief, or so he says", she went on, "that we must accompany the machines or be left behind by evolution. He is even hostile to the unmanned exploration of space! Thinks our pressurised fleshy bodies should be up there in the vacuum or tramping across nitrogen ice in snowshoes!" She leant forward continuing in a confidential tone, "Deep down, I think he just likes the excitement. He can't do anything by half-measures. You should see him play handball!

X tried to find something positive in her words. At least he was away a lot of the time, but not only did he sound intimidatingly impressive, but it was clear that Eva's dismissive tone was a thin camouflage for a powerful attachment to her Nordic superman.

"Goodness!" she suddenly exclaimed, "I have forgotten the time. Excuse me, I must vote on the stem cell bill".

She slipped her glasses on, and X, expecting her to get up and leave, half stood, wondering if she would allow him to accompany her to the polling station, but a moment later she raised her glasses to her forehead again.

"Sorry about that. Now what were we saying?"

It was X's turn to look bewildered. "That was voting?"

It was clear that Eva was delighted to turn the subject away from her boyfriend, and X had no objection either, and he settled back into the comfortable sofa to let Eva educate him.

She started by explaining that the same technology that enabled her to access data and research materials made it possible to create a form of 'Athenian democracy' in her society. She then made a comment about women and slaves getting the vote this time, which went straight over his head, and must have been joke because she laughed, and then she continued with her exposition, explaining that every adult could vote on every issue, "no need for representatives, no need for a parliament X, here the people are truly sovereign".

It was difficult for X to get his head around what she was

saying, and while he was still mulling it over, she went on to address a series of objections that he hadn't yet even conceptualised.

"You are probably thinking, 'how can everybody vote on everything?' Well that is easily answered is it not? You have seen how easy it is for me to...to cast my ballot. No more than a blink of the eye!" she laughed again as she said this, and this time X did get the joke. Eva then rose and began pacing up and down on the soft carpet in front of him, explaining her argument as though she was a barrister impressing the jury on the courtroom floor, "But that is not the major objection, I think. You ask", although X had remained mute, "what expertise do I possess to be able to make such important judgements? And I say to you, firstly, that most important issues are moral or social questions, and am I not as qualified as anyone to make such decisions? Ah, but you may say, how does the ordinary citizen possess the knowledge and even understand the complexities of the issues in front of him or her? Indeed, how could they determine the full consequences of such decisions without the necessary expertise? Well, again, I say to you, what kind of refined judgement ever existed in representative democracy with your white male lawyers and privately educated schoolboys? What did they know?" Eva's speech had risen to a crescendo, but at this point all the energy seemed to suddenly drain out of her and she slumped back down on the sofa, visibly deflated. "No", she said in a subdued voice, "that is not the way to explain it. I'm sorry X, I should not sound so negative - it will become much clearer when Erika arrives - she will explain it so much better than I."

X tried to reassure her that she was doing very well, and was rewarded with a terse smile. She began again, this time remaining seated and with her voice much more modulated. "You see X, it all rests on education. I hope I will be able to show you how important, how...integral education is to us, not just at school, but for the whole of our lives...it is our primary duty and our greatest pleasure..."

She trailed off, and X wondered if she was talking about her society as a whole or just about herself, and to think he had thought she didn't read...

She picked up the thread again, "So we naturally keep ourselves well informed about the most important developments, and if an issue is significant enough to require a vote by the whole populous, it is prefaced by months of documentaries, learned papers and public debate to bring everybody up to speed. If people do not feel they understand the issue well enough, they are obliged to abstain, and if more than 40% of the population feel unable to cast a vote, the measure cannot pass and we start the education and debate cycle once again. But this does not happen often", she added.

At that moment the doorbell rang.

"Ah, good, Erika has arrived. She will explain it all much better."

X couldn't help but be disappointed. He needed no company other than Eva's and had had quite enough political theory for one evening already.

When Eva opened the door, it was not to admit Erika, instead the pretty young woman with the dark bobbed hair from Erika's first page stood in the doorway. She was quite different to Eva, short where Eva was tall and vivacious where Eva was calm and considered. She greeted her by shouting, "Eva!" in a high register that was almost a shriek, and dispensed with pressing foreheads altogether by throwing her arms around her neck and kissing her full on the lips. The way she was dressed was different too, although the components were the same, but the jacket she wore over her leotard was royal blue and its cuffs made of a soft material that looked like ermine. The cuffs were matched by a long scarf of similar material and subtle details in the cut of her jacket enabled the young woman to carry her outfit with the poise of a catwalk model, yet without deviating from the uniform worn by the commuters he had seen on the tram earlier that evening.

There was some whispering between the two women at the door, and as it opened directly into the room where he sat, X caught some of it. "Is that him?" he heard the new arrival ask, and then, as she poked her head around Eva to catch a look at X, he thought he heard her say, "He doesn't *look* like a chimp", before she was loudly shushed by her friend.

It seemed that Eva was reluctant to let her friend enter, and the young woman had to almost push her aside to gain entry to the room. When she had succeeded she stood staring at him from the doorway, with her jacket on and her scarf still wound around her neck as if she didn't intend to be stopping for long. She kept her face fixed in a tight-lipped, challenging expression while they were introduced, Eva referring to her as, "my best friend Xanthia". X stood to quickly press foreheads and immediately sat down again, but Xanthia remained standing in the middle of the room staring at X as though he were an object in a shop window that she found to be in questionable taste.

The atmosphere in the room was completely altered. Xanthia's naked disdain seemed close to hostility and X became convinced that he must have somehow offended Eva, and that her friend had rushed round to protect her honour, although he was unsure what offense it was he was supposed to have committed.

The situation was saved from becoming any more tense by the sound of the doorbell ringing for a second time.

This time, it was the Erika from the running track.

She entered the room briskly, her face flushed pink and breathing heavily as though she had just sprinted up the stairs rather than ascending to the fourth floor in the lift. Having entered, she quickly took control of the situation, and after hastily apologising to Eva for having taken so long to get there, dismissed Xanthia with a single withering glare of contempt. The expression on the younger woman's face left no doubt that the feeling of antipathy was entirely mutual between the two women.

Erika turned her attention to X crossing the short distance between them in two long strides,

"Delighted to meet you again, I......"

DEPOT

He woke up.

Before his sight returned he could smell the puke.

Shit. Had he vomited in his sleep?

He couldn't see a thing. Was it dark? Where the fuck was he?

Sensation began to return in lurching waves. An awareness of his own body returned first. It felt bruised and cold and there were little lumps of something soft and doughy stuck to his skin of his cheek. The smell of stale cigarette ash began to merge with the stench of sick.

His sight came back slowly, and at first it was though he was peering upward through murky water. A row of blurry upright bars stretched away into the distance in front of him. Wherever he was it was gloomy and smelt bad.

By the time he could make out the drone of a vacuum cleaner echoing from some point below him, he had worked it out.

He picked himself up from the floor of the night bus, wiping away the cigarette butts that had stuck to his face with a dead hand. Pins and needles shot through the arm he had been lying on all night, and, too dizzy to stand up at first, he had to content himself with sitting with his forehead pressed against the metal backrest of the seat in front until he had enough strength to get up and leave.

The bus was stationary, parked for the night in its depot; a driver too lazy to check the top deck carefully before clocking off had either missed his prone form or decided it was somebody else's problem and just left him there.

Passing the startled cleaner whose hoovering on the lower deck had woken him, he stumbled past the rows of stationary red machines and walked as briskly as he could out of the shed before anyone could stop and ask him what he was doing there.

It was nearly dawn and he only had to wait an hour or so before the underground started up. He got the first train from Morden back to Brixton and fell like a dead man into his bed, sleeping dreamlessly until long into the next afternoon.

6. SOCIALIST WORKER

He was determined to be better prepared for his second sales interview.

He'd started with the clothes, picking up a pair of brogues and a tie at Camden market for next to nothing. The old shoes were stiff and brittle, but they only pinched a little, and the mesh of hairline cracks on their leather were easily blackened over with polish. The tie was from the jazz era with an art deco motif and might just pass muster. The trousers were more of a problem. Short of cash, he'd had to purchase them from Burtons, and while the fit wasn't bad, they pulled tight across his crotch and stuck to his legs like Sta-Press. The procuring of an appropriate shirt had been a saga in itself.

They'd been a call to the hostel from someone at Hyper-Hyper, the fashion market in Kensington High Street, about an old drunk who was causing problems. When he'd first turned up the women who ran the Pullman café in the market had taken pity on him, and let him have some of their left-over food. As a consequence of the free meals he'd decided to stick around. At first they'd been able to work around his bash in the yard, but he had rapidly become a nuisance, pissed and abusive by mid-morning, he'd begun threatening the drivers and frightening the women who'd fed him.

When X got there, he'd been relieved to see that it was only Davey Ryan. Davey was only a successful bully if you were female, much smaller than him, or if he succeeded in scaring you with his first couple of brays. He had stood his ground, shoulders hunched and avoiding eye contact while Davey paced up and down like a caged animal in front of him. After ten minutes or so of calling X a cunt while waving his arms around as though he was going to punch him, Davey had put on enough of a show to preserve his dignity and allowed himself to be moved on. Decision made, he became fulsomely apologetic, called X a cunt again, but this time with affection, and shouted his remorse at being such a cunt to the women, who kept out of sight until he was safely off the premises. As he'd been leading Davey away, he'd spotted a beautifully tailored, soft-collared white shirt with pale green buttons and embroidered cuffs hanging on a rail in the yard. Before he had given it a second thought, he'd tugged it off its hanger and stuffed it inside his coat.

Payment for services rendered.

Dressed in his new shirt, smart trousers and tie, he'd gone the Boss outlet in Kensington High Street, and sliced a label off a jacket with a razor blade while he was pretending to check the quality of the stitching on the inner seam.

*

Having sewn the new label into the old jacket in the morning, he'd sat in an air conditioned café sipping at a cappuccino until it was time for his interview, arriving fresh and relaxed with a copy of the *Socialist Worker* tucked under his arm.

When the applicants for the group interview were ushered into the conference room, he ensured that he took up a prominent position at the end of the oval table and sat crossed legged with the paper displayed prominently on his lap. The interviewer introduced himself as Graham Johnstone, tapping the ID badge pinned to his left breast pocket with his right hand as though drawing attention to a medal awarded for valorous service. He wore a brown two-piece suit which went some way to muting the shock of his bright ginger hair, and he had a precise, jerky way of moving that suggested a military background. He had arranged his stationary on the table in rank order beside his bottle of Buxton mineral water and glass, the pens lined up parallel to one another and a pile of paper-clipped documents set square beside them. He stood to begin his introductory words and as he did so caught sight of X, sprawled at the end of the table with the bright red banner of *The Socialist Worker* plainly displayed across his knees.

He baulked, the words he had intended to commence with momentarily forgotten, "Are you in the right place?" he asked directing an expression of mild bewilderment in X's direction.

"I hope so", replied X, deliberately adding nothing to ensure that his interlocutor would have to speak again.

"But…" he gestured at the copy of the newspaper on X's legs, and then waved an arm to cover the rest of the candidates in the room all sitting proudly professional around the table, waiting to get on with businesses. "These people have come here to make money…and…and…" he petered out, apparently lost for words.

"It is a sales interview isn't it?" asked X, forming an open, innocent expression on his face.

"Yes of course it's a sales interview", Graham Johnstone continued, more certain in his delivery now, "it's an opportunity to join one of the most successful companies in the UK, one with a growth rate of 37% per annum and nearly 1000 employees. We're looking only for the brightest and best salespeople to maintain that level of performance, but if you believe all that communist clap-trap…firstly you're a fool, and secondly, what the hell are you doing here? He was quite strident in his tone, almost angry, and for a moment X worried that his strategy might backfire.

"It's a prop", he explained. "My view is, that for a salesmen to succeed he needs to be remembered, and to be remembered he needs to be noticed. But in this situation, I'm at a disadvantage before I start. I'd bet my house that you're straight, and as a heterosexual man you'll naturally look at the women first". He paused, to give Graham time to let the reference to his interviewer's manly demeanour sink in. "And I am in a room full of pretty women", he continued, making a gallant gesture across the table as he spoke, eliciting a couple of smiles to which he paid little attention, keeping his focus firmly on Graham. "But I am not pretty and look very much like the other men in the room." He paused again for effect then stood, smiling, and extended his hand toward Graham, "But at the very least, I hope you'll remember X, the fool who turned up at a sales interview with a copy of the Socialist Worker."

They shook hands and Graham, to confirm he had properly understood X's actions, asked, "So you don't believe in all that…"

X explained that he had bought the magazine from a vendor at

Brixton station solely for the purpose of gaining his attention. He added that the seller had asked him to join the party.

Graham snorted, "And did you?" he asked, in on the joke now.

X replied that at 50p the product on offer was either hopelessly undervalued or worth nothing at all. He had declined. He flopped open the paper on the table.

In huge red letters the headline declared, ORGREAVE – STILL NO JUSTICE!

"Orgreave? What's that?" asked Graham.

X shrugged, "The miner's strike"

"Good God!" snapped Graham, "Are they still on about that? Talk about lost causes!"

With a casual flick of the wrist he flung the paper into a bin in the corner and pulled his chair up to the table. Having made his mark he let the other candidates perform, but their efforts only came across as pale imitations of his earlier audacity, and when Graham challenged them to sell him something, he could sense that they were holding back while they waited for him to make his move.

"Sell me this!" Graham declared, holding up a paper clip between his thumb and forefinger before laying it carefully down in the centre of the table like some sort of doll's house gauntlet. He had a look of triumph on his face as he sat back, confident that the sheer blandness of the object would defeat them all, and he would have the distinct pleasure of dismissing them all as not quite up to snuff.

"May I?" X volunteered, leaning over and picking up the clip.

He knew he could do this bullshit. It was like colour by numbers.

"Mr Johnstone", he began, leaning over the table and shaking his hand for the second time. "It's a pleasure to meet you", he said smiling, "I have something of interest to show you, something that will benefit you and your company. But before I start may I confirm a few details about your business?

Graham confirmed that he could.

"Your company has, I believe, nearly a thousand employees working in a wide range of diffuse fields from design to marketing to television, many of them relatively young people?

Graham nodded.

"And would it be fair to say that these employees are often so focussed on their primary tasks of gathering news, selling advertising and producing magazines that they often pay little attention to the stationary budget?"

He could see Graham's eyes light up at his final phrase and knew he had got the measure of the man spot on, he wondered how many times he had raised the very issue to an array of bored faces at team meetings.

"And yet", he continued, confident of his triumph now, "with all those employees involved in largely clerical duties, all those small expenditures add up, don't they?"

Graham was leaning forward now, nodding in agreement.

X heard the door open and a couple of people come into the room behind him, talking softly to each other as they entered. but quietening as X remained focussed on his pitch. "This is where my company comes in. Take this item", he said, picking up the paper clip from the table. "This is no ordinary paper clip." He held it up for some time looking at as though it were a Faberge Egg while he thought of what to say next. When he'd made something up, he carried on, "This paper clip is a typical example of our company's meticulous attention to detail. It is made of a newly developed alloy that has the same prehensile strength as stainless steel but is 30% cheaper to produce. There is currently only one mill in Korea producing this particular alloy, and my company has the sole UK import license. With low labour costs in the country of origin we can write off the shipping expenses, pass two-thirds of the savings on to you and still make a healthy profit for ourselves. For paper clips the savings would be around…." He plucked a figure out of the air, "£2000 per annum…"

He let the imaginary saving hang in the air before closing,

"Look Graham", he said, "let's get the paperwork done over the clips now, and then we can start talking about some of the serious savings you can make across the rest of your stationary. You've no idea what the mark up is like staplers…" They shook hands for the third time, X keeping firm eye contact while they sealed the deal. Behind him he heard a short shriek and the sound of someone bursting into a fit of giggles before the door slammed, only partly muffling the sound of laughter from the corridor outside.

The interview ended in disarray and only X was asked to stay behind.

*

There was no second interview.

He had been called into the publisher's office, and Roger had put him at his ease straight away, beaming as he entered and crossing the room to greet him effusively. His ad-sales manager, Caroline, stood by the side of the desk, dabbing at her smeared eyeliner with the aid of a compact mirror. She looked up as he came in with panda eyes and waved hello from across the room.

Roger made an immediate impression on X. Although he was immaculately dressed in a deep green Valentino suit that was tailored exactly to the length of his long limbs, it was clear that his natural ebullience was at war with his sartorial elegance. The arms of his jacket were indelibly crumpled at the elbows and a cuff-link had popped on his left wrist, which sent his shirt sleeve gaping open every time he waved his arms, which he often did to illustrate a point or just for the sheer joy of doing so.

X had asked what they wanted him to do for the second interview, but Roger had just laughed. "Don't worry dearie", he declared with a flamboyant gesture of his long arms, "You're in!"

"Honestly", he continued, a hand on his chest as though he were out of breath. 'There's no need for more; we couldn't take it! Caroline was in stitches and we both nearly injured ourselves trying not to laugh. By the end neither of us were sure if Graham knew you were role-playing at all. I expect he still hopes that handshake on the paper clip contract was legally binding…. Marvellous darling, simply *marvellous*, how quickly you got our Graham! I wish we'd got to see the *Socialist Worker* bit too. You *are* a clever diamond-in-the-rough, aren't you! Isn't he Caroline", he called out.

Caroline confirmed that he was, and apologised for the undignified circumstances in which he found her, with her make-up halfway down her face and then thanked him for making her laugh so much that such a repair job was necessary.

X allowed himself a broad smile in acknowledgement and gave his new boss a swift examination. She was in her late thirties, probably, but looked older. She had a plump, pretty face, but the make-up was caked on thick, a heavy dose of slap, he thought, to cover up the consequences of too many late nights and bottles of red wine. Where her tears had washed away the layers of foundation, her skin looked as yellow and waxy as any street drinker's. She was short, large breasted and tottered on seven-inch stiletto heels. Below her jacket her belly pulled her short skirt into a taught arc, suggesting that the sexy look she could still just about pull off had a very limited shelf-life. Although there was a toughness in her face, she was instantly kind and welcoming to X, and he felt from that first meeting that not only had he got the job, but that he had joined their gang inside the company, and that Caroline would be telling him tales of her disastrous love-life by the photocopying machine before the first month was out.

"Yes", Roger started up again, "we loved everything about your performance downstairs, except perhaps for the trousers… But that shirt", he continued, "Is it from *'Jones'* on the King's Road? As he pronounced the store's name he raised up his arms like a worshipper welcoming the descent of the Holy Spirit, but then mocking the gesture with a razzmatazz show biz flick of his wrists.

"Hyper-Hyper", X replied.

"Ooooh!" Roger shrieked in mock delight, "Street-chic! Darling, welcome aboard!"

"Aboard what? X asked.

Roger smiled. "You've lucked out", he said, "You've got *us* and *Restaurant and Café Bar News*. A weekly, where all the money is, an editor who knows her stuff and best of all, in this new age of shining cafes and exquisite Thai restaurants, who is our rival? Which great giant do we have to take down?"

X shook his head.

"*The Caterer and Hotel Keeper.*" He sneered the name, "Now doesn't that just *reek* of glamour! We're going to make *lots* of money X", he said, draping a long arm over his shoulder, drink *lots* of champagne and eat the most *fabulous* food."

"Quick check", Roger had asked as he escorted X to the door, "Are you the sort of straight boy who might consider a visit to the other side once in a while?"

X politely responded in the negative.

"Pity".

"Well the women are very glamorous too", he added, "but you'll need to get a better pair of trousers."

In celebration he took a black cab home for the first time in his life, promising the cabby a hefty tip to persuade him to go south of the river. He sat back in the big leather seat, glorying in the luxury of his own personal carriage, and as the taxi edged through the traffic toward Waterloo Bridge he felt both the excitement and the tension of the day ebb away and exhaustion overwhelm him.

He closed his eyes to take a quick forty winks just as the river came into view.

7. FRIENDSHIP

He was stepping out from the shadows of the lime trees, just as the glass door to the apartment building swung open and the three women emerged into the cold night air. Eva was deep in conversation with Erika, her eyes cast downward as she held the door open for her friend. Xanthia lagged a few paces behind them as they walked toward him, her royal blue jacket buttoned up against the cold and her face set in an expression somewhere between haughty disdain and complete boredom.

"Hello again," he said.

When X spoke, Eva looked up, and at the sight of him let out a sharp cry of shock. Rendered momentarily speechless by his sudden apparition she stood, slack-jawed in the street, unable to muster any kind of reply. Erika too, had been startled, but recovered much more quickly, "There you are X", she said with only the slightest quaver in her voice, "We were just heading out to meet a few friends in a neighbourhood café. Would you care to join us?"

X smiled and nodded his confirmation, and after briefly pressing foreheads with both of them, fell into step between the two women. Xanthia ignored him completely, pushing past the three of them, declaring that it was "all just too weird" as she did so, before striding imperiously away down the street ahead of them.

They walked only as far as the first crossroads, before climbing a steel staircase that rose up the outside of the last building in the row. The staircase zigzagged up a curved gantry tower that butted on to the face of the blunt-edged block like a castle turret, and gave an uninterrupted view of the city laid out below. As they rose, X followed the line of the road falling steeply away from the hill top below him, weaving a dimly lit course through the jet black expanse of a city park before being absorbed in the distance by the yellow lights of the city itself. He followed the snake of the streetlamps through the park, their amber beams broken up by the shadows of the ornamental trees that lay across its wide pavements like art nouveau stencils. In the far distance an arc of lights illuminated the long sweep of a bay, the dark water lit only by the red warning lights of navigation buoys marking a channel out into the deep water.

Where was he? Stockholm? Helsinki? Copenhagen? He must remember to ask.

The cityscape beneath the park was quieted as though it was the early hours of the morning, or perhaps just before dawn. Only the fading light of a tram, heading down to the city terminus, and the red rear lights of a pair of bicycles racing down the hill betrayed any sense of activity, but when the automatic doors of the café slid open, the interior disgorged a wave of heat, music and animated conversation.

The night was still young.

The café took up the whole of the top floor of the building. Three of its four walls were glass from floor to ceiling and one opened out on to a balcony through which the yellow lights of the city below could be made out shimmering like candles on the table of a distant nightclub. The overall effect was one of expansiveness and space, but rather than feeling vast and impersonal, a sense of cosy warmth had been preserved by dividing up the room into individual alcoves, each one laid out with a cluster of sofas around a low glass coffee table, and differentiated one from another by subtle shifts in the colour and tone of the screens and furnishings. The lighting was subdued, with candles burning in small glass jars on the table tops and oblong orange floor lamps whose muted beams were set just bright enough to turn the window glass into a wall of mirrors. In the open central area, catering staff, wreathed in steam, tended a row of gleaming stainless steel coffee machines behind a long glass counter. Dressed in the same simple leotards as their customers, they were only distinguishable from their clientele by their labour, working cheerfully and without undue haste or deference, competently dispatching espressos and cappuccinos and deftly balancing laden trays with the poise and confidence of dancers.

As Erika and Eva escorted him to an alcove on the far side of the room, X had an opportunity to look at the food and drink on display at the counter. Piled up beside the coffee machines were pyramids of guavas, papaya, bananas and oranges, each fruit associated with its own specifically designed mechanical juicer. On the shelf below this healthy fare, pyramids of shot glasses matched the fruit towers above them and broke up a row of glass bottles that ran almost the full length of the cabinet. He glanced at the labels as he passed. As far as he could make out the bottles appeared to constitute a more extensive range of flavoured vodkas than he had ever imagined existed. About a third of the main cabinet was given over to a display of mouth-watering pastries and delicately made cakes, another third to salads, olives, pickled fish and crackers, and the final third, bizarrely, to a series of glass tubes of various types that looked to X like crosses between bongs and hash pipes, and seemed utterly out of place beside the Danish pastries and choux buns.

The two women returned with coffees, pastries and a green drink in a tall, ice-filled glass for Erika. They had just settled onto the sofa when Erika spotted Tasan and a short man with wild white hair entering the café and beckoned them over. Eva was dispatched to the counter to get them something to drink and having done so disappeared, leaving X hemmed in on the sofa between Erika and the two men. When Eva returned she was accompanied by a tall, blond man with a goatee, and a dark-skinned Asian woman with a pierced nose, soulful eyes and beautiful long dark hair that swept out behind her like a bridal train as she crossed the room. X was sure he recognised both of them from Eva's first page, but instead of introducing him to her friends, she ignored him completely and the three of them settled into the sofa opposite where they fell instantly into deep conversation.

Instead of Eva's company, X was forced to engage with the old folk. Tasan had introduced his companion as Professor Knut, and never had a man appeared more professorial. He had a big head, so out of proportion to his little body that it appeared positively swollen and a pair of oversized brown eyes that protruded from his face as though the pressure inside his skull could at any moment cause them to pop out of his head. The professor's hair was distributed seemingly at random across his face and head; a neatly trimmed beard covered his chin, and feather boa eyelids draped over his lids, but had receded in long escarpment over his forehead exposing his scalp as far as the top of his cranium. To either side of this bald crest, white hair exploded skyward in every direction as though it had been consciously backcombed rather than merely left unkempt, and crinkly clumps burst from behind his ears like sprouting broccoli. The overall effect was that of meeting a steroid enhanced

Einstein.

Having resigned himself to being cut out of Eva's orbit, and under intense interrogation from the professor, X focussed on trying to think of pertinent and interesting things to say in order to avoid appearing an idiot. He had noticed the absence of church spire silhouettes in the cityscape below, and figured a question about faith might fit the bill. Knut snorted with disdain and was soon expounding on the subject of religion as though delivering a lecture to a particularly recalcitrant student. "Ach", Knut began, "faith has a number of meanings. Some of which are interesting for sure, but Religion! Holy Books! Revealed truth! We have no time for these fairy stories here! Listen to me X, religion was designed to answer a number of questions - One: Why are we here? Two: Where are we going? Three: What are we supposed to do? – All these questions have simple answers although it took us millennia to get there!" The professor proceeded to reel off the answers as quickly as he had stated the questions, "One: A glorious bio-chemical accident. Two: Back into the soil as nutrients. Three: Nothing. A stupid question if we are back with revealed wisdom, an interesting one if we decide to make our own choices, don't you think?"

X nodded. He had no particular objection to the professor's views. He had met some good people who were inspired by faith and some really ignorant ones too and had long since come to the conclusion that it was the people not the faith that mattered.

The professor, however, was not finished. "I say nothing new", he continued, "If I state that what we think of as *Homo sapiens*, like all other species, is no more nor less than the fleshy extrusion of one of the more successful chains of self-replicating molecules, a protein covering designed to protect its DNA until reproductive age is attained. Don't succumb to illusions young man", he concluded, "the sole 'purpose' of humanity is to ensure the endless transmission of our particular strands of nucleotides through time." With this declaration the professor sat back, a contented expression on his face, certain that he had said all that needed to be said and the matter was now firmly put to rest.

The reaction to Knut's speech was mixed. Tasan wore an expression of mild amusement, but Eva seemed to be regarding the professor with an expression that might have been anger, but could just as easily have been pity. Both of them were clearly waiting for X's response and he felt their fixed stares boring into him like lasers. He wasn't sure he had entirely understood the old man's argument but had been taken aback both by his fierce certainty and his cold materialism. Even if it was true it seemed an inordinately miserable view of the human condition, and before he had thought it through he found himself blurting out more stridently than he had intended,

"But what about love?"

He felt embarrassed as soon as the words had left his mouth, but his sense of having made a fool of himself was tempered by the awareness that his outburst had not only forced a smile from Erika, but had quietened Eva's group, who were now listening attentively to his conversation with the professor.

"Love!" exclaimed Knut disdainfully, "always the poet's objection to hard scientific fact! Love, my dear boy", he continued, "is a survival mechanism, a strategy that binds two units together to further the chances of their offspring making it to reproductive age. Who could argue with that? The nucleotide sequence that coded for that particular electrochemical stimulation occurred aeons ago and would have wiped out all the units that didn't have it. I suspect Australopithecines would have had that bit of code. Why not? Gibbons have it. Not much poetry in gibbons." He put an arm around X's shoulder, "No churches here my boy", he said, his tone gentler now the argument was won, "and no dispute about it either. Our citizens are content to build Jerusalem here", he pointed downward to the café floor, "not up in the clouds".

X had said nothing in reply, relieved that he didn't seem to have made a complete fool of himself and half-certain he had made some kind of positive impression on Tasan and Erika, but his pleasure was short-lived. As the night wore on he became increasingly aware that he was missing out on all the fun, stuck in earnest debate with the old people while everyone else in the café was enjoying themselves. The conversation on the other side of the booth grew steadily more animated; rows of shot glasses were lined up and downed, the laughter got louder and coarser and other groups of young people drifted over to join Eva's set. Even the waiters had an opportunity to participate in the party atmosphere, swapping roles with the customers from time to time while members of Eva's group took turns to serve coffee at the counter and help stack the dishwasher. He would have preferred even working at the bar to his position, squeezed between professorial thighs and prevented from moving off the sofa by the sustained rigour of the old people's attention. As the evening progressed he began to feel more and more as though he was trapped inside a glass box.

Erika had even brought reading material for him. At one point she passed him a small hand-held screen and showed him how to track up down on the page. "If you hope to understand our society", she had said dryly as she stuffed the device into X's hands, "you will need to comprehend its economic system."

X had reluctantly done as he was told and began reading,

"The sufficiency of matter had long been solved, unsurprisingly, given the productive power of the global economy, and yet crushing poverty and inequality persisted. The Gordian Knot was only severed by ensuring that the material wealth was distributed according to need and to a sufficiency of being, when the wage labour value was recalibrated and rewards were set in accordance with their contribution to the collective good. It took a fundamental revolution in the meaning of production to...."

X put the device down. It read like a badly translated version of the communist manifesto, and the last thing in the world he wished to do was spend the rest of the evening deconstructing the dialectic or whatever the correct phrase was. That was the trouble. It always seemed like graft in the worker's paradise. Couldn't he just get pissed with Eva and her friends and have some fun for a change? The thought troubled him momentarily, he felt certain he had had exactly the same conception before, but he couldn't exactly remember when.

He looked up from the device and straight into the expressions of eager anticipation on Tasan and Erika's faces, both of them clearly bristling with desire to hear his response and undoubtedly correct his many errors of interpretation. He was rescued from his re-education by a bizarre shift in the collective behaviour of everyone in the café. In response to some unknown signal, and passing like a wave through the assembled company, everyone's glasses slid down from their foreheads and covered their eyes. Eva and her friends were suddenly frozen in mid conversation, the professor sat stock-still and silent and Erika perched like a statue on the arm rest above him. All movement and conversation in the café ceased at once, leaving just the quiet jazzy background music tinkling through the hissing of steam of a single active coffee machine. X was the only individual in the café without glasses and therefore the only person unaffected by the sudden change.

Perhaps they were all reading some vital piece of transmitted data off the inside of their glasses or suddenly compelled to watch an urgent newsreel, or maybe they had all been de-activated like robots in a science fiction film by some remote pulse. X didn't waste much time speculating on the cause of their sudden immobility; instead he seized the moment to escape his interrogators. Moving as quickly as he could, he weaved around the stationary figures as though he were a tourist strolling through Pompeii, and made his way directly to the counter. Perhaps he could acquire a bottle of vodka before everyone woke up.

Then, just as suddenly as it had begun, it ended. The glasses slid up from their wearer's eyes and conversation started up again. It was as though the projectionist had fixed the error in the reel and the whole scene jumped back to life in perfect synchrony as though nothing had happened at all. The only change that had occurred was that he had, at least temporarily, slipped the clutches of Tasan and Erika.

"Hello Chee Chee, escaped your handlers, have you?"

Xanthia had come up beside him. She was accompanied by a gangly young man with a horse-like face tipped by a bright orange beard, whose arms seemed longer than his legs and whose prodigious height had been mitigated by a stoop so pronounced that his body appeared coiled into a permanent human comma.

He was clearly quite pissed.

"Not nice Xanthia", he admonished, slurring his words as he spoke, "The man's a traveller, we should be welcoming and..." he searched for the appropriate word, "open."

Xanthia snorted.

He turned to X, wrapping a long arm around his shoulders, "Welcome, my name is Per", he said, pressing his forehead against X's and bringing his other arm around him so that they stood forehead to forehead like exhausted prize-fighters He continued to hold the pose for far longer than was comfortable before finally standing back, still holding X but now at arm's length, and looking directly into his eyes.

"You're alright", he slurred. "You are from London, Yes?"

X confirmed he was.

"You", he pronounced after as short pause, "Are a fucking wanker!"

He repeated the insult a couple of times.

Strangely, it was clear that he meant this in a friendly manner, as though he was under the impression that this was how Londoner's greeted each other as a matter of course, and X took no offense.

"What you need", Per continued, "Is one of these". He passed X a shot glass of vodka and gestured him to down it in one. When he had, he poured another spilling a good third of it on to the table as he did so, and ensured again that X knocked it back immediately. He lined up a third before pulling one of the glass tubes that X had seen earlier from his jacket pocket. "Let's smoke outside", he commanded, and looping his Orang-utan arms around both X and Xanthia he marched them out on to the balcony.

Xanthia seemed happy enough to be cajoled outside, and swamped by Per's embrace she kept him upright as he stumbled and swayed across the floor, laughing as she did so, "Per, you are a mess."

Per only grinned by way of reply and steered them both over to the far side of the balcony. He leant back against the rail, took a long drag from the glass tube causing it to glow orange at its tip, inhaled deeply, and, exhaling theatrically, sent a cloud of smoke floating out into the cold air over the city below. He handed the pipe to X.

"What is it?" X asked, surprised that a habit as unhealthy as smoking would exist here.

"THC vaporiser", Per replied, "All the good bits without the tars and tannins. Couple of other cannabinoids in there too", he added.

X took a long drag and held it in his lungs. It had no taste and none of the acrid bite of tobacco or grass. He passed the pipe to Xanthia. Thirty seconds later he was really quite high, floaty and happy without the leaden-limbed sensation of being stoned.

Eva and her two friends joined them on the terrace a moment or too later. "Really Xanthia!" Eva's lips were pulled taught in disapproval at her friend as she caught sight of X's glazed expression.

"Don't blame me. It was Per's idea."

"Relax Eva, interjected her blond-haired friend, "if I'd been squeezed on the sofa with Professor Pompous and cut-you-balls-off Erika Hämstrong all evening, I'd be reaching for a pipe too. Give the man a break." Everyone laughed and the pipe was passed round. Only Eva and the Indian girl declined.

Suddenly X was having a fabulous time.

The drug certainly helped, but the star strewn sky above the balcony was the stuff of dreams and the cold night air wildly invigorating. The young people seemed to have accepted him immediately, and even Xanthia's reaction to him had shifted from hostility to something closer to amused contempt, which was progress of sorts. Although he struggled to think of anything clever or witty to say, the crowd didn't make him feel under any pressure to perform, and he felt he could relax and just listen without fear of judgement. Most importantly, even Eva, who had previously seemed to be largely embarrassed by him, now seemed to actively enjoy his association with her, treating him as though he was a foolish but occasionally entertaining younger brother. He leaned back against the balcony rail and scanned the amused faces in front of him, happy to be in their company.

Attempting to join in, he asked the most obvious question he could think of, 'So what do you all do?' but this instantly set off a ripple of confusion. The Indian girl, Pooja, politely asked him to qualify what he meant as they all 'did' a great many things.

Having spent time with Eva he understood that everyone here required absolute precision in language, so unperturbed by her pedantry, he quickly re-phrased and tried again, "What does everyone do for a living?" He asked.

This scarcely seemed to help matters. Pooja, who seemed to be both gentle and patient, explained that they did many things that earned them money, depending on the time of year, how much they had already earned and on many other factors too. Her forehead was creased with concern as she spoke, her eyes willing him to bring just a little more clarity to his question, but he could think of nothing further to add and merely repeated the same phrase.

Either the earnest expression on Pooja's face or perhaps X's idiocy, set Xanthia off into a harsh cackle which in turn forced a laugh from Per. Unfortunately for him, he had been taking a long drag from the pipe at the time and immediately broke into an extended coughing fit. Per's expression of bemused suffering was enough to make Xanthia double up in hysterics and a wave of grins and sniggers passed round the group as Per coughed and accused them all of cruelty as he struggled for air. Ignoring the hilarity, Eva, who was considerably more sober than the rest, stepped in to sort things out, taking charge as if she was the only grown-up present. X listened carefully as she primly explained that she was "primarily a student undertaking..." and here she paused, slipped on her glasses and then continued, "Undertaking post-doctorate studies." Inexplicably this set Xanthia off again and, having just taken a swig of beer she spat the full contents of her mouth over Per. "Oh man", he complained, "I'm going to stink now."

"No more than you ordinarily do", Xanthia slung back at him.

Eva, having shot a disparaging glance at her friend and been rewarded with a poked tongue, continued, explaining that Sven, the blond man with the goatee, designed and built racing bikes more than he did anything else, Pooja's specialism was genetics although she also designed furniture, and Per, when he wasn't working on the farms raced electric cars. And Xanthia...." She turned to address her friend directly, "How would you

describe your occupation Xanthia?"

Xanthia put her index finger to her lips and raised her eyes heavenward in imitation of earnest contemplation, her lips slipping into a grin before answering, "Fashion designer, actress and superstar at your service", she replied, bowing low from the waist as she did so.

Per sniggered.

"Xanthia also works with disadvantaged people", Eva added.

"Oh Eva, please don't try and make me sound worthy, everybody works with disadvantaged people."

"I don't", interjected Per.

"Everyone except for Per", Xanthia corrected herself, giving him a quick kick in the ankles as she spoke.

"Hey, what was that for?" he complained.

"Because I can't kick Eva, she's too nice", she replied.

Everyone except Eva laughed. "But why would you want to kick me?" she asked, a bemused expression crossing her beautiful face.

"Oh Eva", sighed Xanthia, shaking her head, "that's why we love you so."

X hadn't understood all of the conversation, but had caught the underlying affection in all the exchanges. There was something in the ease and confidence of these remarkable people, an acceptance of each other, and, by default; him, that gave him a tremendous sense of peace and well-being. However this world was fashioned, he thought, the 'revolution of the meaning of production' seemed to have created something so much finer than...than what?

He couldn't recall what he was comparing it to.

A sudden wave of anxiety passed through him, setting his heart racing and blurring his vision. Dizzy, he felt a desperate urge to lie down until he could just get his head straight.... To hide his confusion, he turned his back on the group for a moment, leaning out over the balcony rail while he swallowed back a mouthful of bile and fought to regain his balance and composure.

Too many Vodkas.

As his heart rate slowed he looked down at the lights of the city stretched out along the bay and tried to get back to the sense of peace that had enveloped him earlier, but his mind was still reeling, and unbidden thoughts lodged in his mind. Firstly, it was, "where am I?" but that set off the dizziness again and as he forced it from his mind it was replaced by another. 'Where are all the poor people?' The nausea subsided, but the thought got stuck in his mind and he couldn't shake it. He suddenly felt angry. Then sad. Are they all down there, he wondered, the destitute and despairing, sleeping in doorways and under bridges, begging for change and drinking themselves to death just like everywhere else? No different, except that here I'm stood high above them, in the company of all these beautiful people with their wonderful jobs and great lives, feasting and laughing, as disinterested to their suffering as demi-gods looking down from Mount Olympus. suddenly much more sober, he turned back to his companions.

"Look out ", said Xanthia, "here come the thought police."

Tasan and Erika had finally caught up with them and were making their way in rapid strides across the terrace toward them. Tasan still wore the same Buddha-like smile of serenity he had worn all evening, and X wondered briefly if he had been at the THC pipe, but Erika looked livid, every pace she took full of controlled anger. Per shuffled backwards at her approach, positioning himself behind Sven, even in his drunken state still with enough presence of mind to get out of her direct line of sight. Out of the corner of his eye caught Xanthia mime, 'coward', at him and registered Per's sheepish shrug in response.

Erika stopped a few metres short of the group, her fury focussed directly on Eva, her expression that of an outraged parent about to put a badly behaved toddler on the naughty step. Eva visibly blanched under the older woman's gaze, and lowered her eyelids to humbly accept her chastisement. X instinctively stepped a pace closer to her to provide support, suspecting that he was somehow the cause of the older woman's anger and aiming to shield her as best he could from Erika's wrath. Hoping to draw her attention away from Eva, he spoke up, "We were just discussing how your society works...", he started, feeling rather than seeing, the grateful expression on Eva's face at his interjection, and observing that Erika's frown softened slightly at his words. Having got her attention, he was unsure what to say next, but as it was still in the forefront of his mind, he asked the question that had stuck in his craw a few moments earlier, "and I was wondering...where are all the poor people?"

As with so many of his earlier questions, Erika's first response was that of mild confusion, but at least her rage seemed to abate as she processed the meaning of his simple inquiry.

Erika's hesitation gave Tasan the opportunity to take control of the situation.

He quickly stepped forward to answer, "You see X", he said...

.

SOUTH OF THE RIVER

He came round in the back of the taxi, laid slumped across the seat, his cheek wet against the leather with his own drool. As he struggled to raise his head his hearing burst into life before his blurred vision had cleared. A big dog was barking in his face.

No.

Someone shouting.

The cab driver was leaning over him through the opened rear door, shaking his shoulders violently and swearing at him, a fine spray of spittle showering X's upturned face with every expletive. "Thank fuck for that", the cabbie exclaimed when X opened his eyes, "I thought you'd gone and fucking died on me." He stepped back to let X half-fall onto the pavement, continuing to berate him as he struggled to stand upright.

The taxi was pulled up at the end of his road.

X dug into his pockets and stuffed all the money he had into the driver's hands before staggering down the street to his squat without a backward glance.

The meter, of course, had continued running during X's blackout, and unsatisfied with his already enormous fee, the man continued to shout at his back as he walked, calling him a wanker and threatening to set the bill on him. He was still shouting abuse as X closed the door shut behind him and mounted the stairs to his room.

He lay on his mattress staring at the ceiling for a long time

These weird dreams were becoming a serious inconvenience. Although at least this time he hadn't had far to get home, it had still cost him money he didn't have. Then he relaxed, the dream fading from his mind, as the real events of the day unrolled like cine-film in front of his eyes.

He had done it. He had got the job. He was moving up.

8. SQUAT PARTY

He sat down on the sofa, forcing a chubby, dark-haired girl with thick black mascara and fishnets who he vaguely recognised to budge up and let him in. She shuffled along without interrupting her conversation or looking up at him.

That was the last of them sold. Now he could finally relax.

The early part of the evening had passed in the accelerated time of a groom at his wedding reception, half hustling and half greeting friends. He could recall each character's cameo moment in line at the door only in flashes, everyone getting in a clench and a phrase or two before they got too wasted to communicate. Paul had made a short, irritating speech before taking a fistful of mushrooms on top of the amphetamines, the sum of which seemed to be, "Have a good time X – but don't become a prick." He'd repeated it several times before kissing him firmly on the forehead as though he was granting benediction.

X picked him out in the centre of the room, dancing to invisible rhythms while weaving colours with his hands. Incomprehensibly, a stunningly beautiful girl with a bleached blond crop and a leather miniskirt was dancing with him, following his moves as though he was some kind of yogic master. He smiled, Paul appeared to have achieved the impossible, pulling while he was tripping.

He wished him well.

His encounter with Kevin had been less pleasant.

Having taken pills for himself and Cat without offering payment, he'd pushed past X singing, "the working class can kiss my arse, I've got the boss's job at last" to the tune of the red flag, sticking two fingers up behind his back as he entered the fray.

You can't please everyone.

He checked that he had stuffed the wad of notes as deep as he could down the front pocket of his jeans, tapped the bulge a couple of times in satisfaction and then lounged back on the sofa spreading his arms along the backrest and surveying the scene in front of him like a king presiding over his court.

The party was heaving.

Music was pumping out of the speakers, loud and distorted, and the room was packed with bodies jerking around in loose association with the rhythm. A Hi-energy track was hissing and spitting in its worn groove on the turntable, a diva's voice cresting perpetually euphoric waves over tinny keyboards, and most of the crowd were up, pumping away, sweaty and a little glassy-eyed in the crush. The stairs up to the first floor were rammed and the feet of the dancers in the room above transmitted a sound like the thunder of a bowling alley into the room below. Those who weren't dancing were shouting at each other in small groups around its edges and the atmosphere was febrile, the talk around him more like extended rows than conversation, people on all sides talking over each other in rapid staccato bursts, interrupting each other's interruptions and vehemently illustrating arcane points of argument with the hand gestures of fascist dictators.

He was throwing a good party.

The perfect way to end this chapter in his life.

With his first month's salary from *Restaurant and Café Bar News* he'd put down a deposit on a one-bedroom flat in Hammersmith, with a soft double-bed and no bars on the windows, and with the sale of Dr Badgett's supply of amphetamine sulphate he had enough money for the first month's rent in advance as well. He would collect the keys on Monday and say goodbye to Brixton, burglaries, cold showers and arsehole flatmates forever.

Diana had already gone. The sofa he sat on, now shorn of its purple velvet cover, was the only thing she had left behind following her sudden flight to a Buddhist retreat in the Chilterns the week before.

The only thing that is, if you didn't include Phil.

He looked over at Phil, slumped on one of the speakers in the corner. Blasted on vodka and Dr Badgett's pills. He was violently headbanging, jerking his head and shoulders backwards and forwards with such intensity that he could have been undertaking a wild celebration of liberty, but just as equally a violent expression of pent-up rage.

Diana had explained it hastily to X at the door before she left. She'd begun by saying that the positions the planets had moved to in the sky had forced her hand. Venus had been dominating Mercury for months, apparently, and it had unsettled their relationship. X had noticed that there had been fewer moaning Kora symphonies of late, and briefly wondered if she was speaking in euphemisms. But Diana had been too flustered even to flirt, and if Phil's failure to produce quicksilver was the point of issue, she didn't couch it in those terms. Her explanation involved something about yin and yang and a lot about Phil's refusal to try reiki, and then his refusal to accept that it worked even when it did. The conflict between them had begun to upset her delicate karmic balance, she had explained, and with all the negative energy around Phil, she just couldn't risk being near him anymore. At least, not for a while.

X had thought she wouldn't let him escape completely.

Now that he was escaping himself he allowed himself to reminisce nostalgically about the early days, and buffeted by the cacophony of sound around him, thought back to the first time he had seen the squat.

It had just been a fuzzy black and white photograph pinned to the wall in the Squatter's Advisory Service in the Old Kent Road then, but he had known it was the one straight away. An end of terrace two story house in a part of Brixton that he knew already, not that far from the tube. Perfect. The windows were boarded up, a corrugated iron sheet covered the doorway and the brick on one side was blackened from fire, but it looked structurally sound. Even sightless and damaged it still looked homelier than the concrete slabs and walkways of the other flats pinned on the walls of the empties room.

He had taken down the address, carefully copying the details and tips scribbled around its backing sheet,

LAMBETH COUNCIL – fire damage only superficial! – Padlock on inside door – BRING BOLT CUTTERS + CROWBAR. And in a different hand someone had written - THAT door will come off in FIVE minutes max– WATCH OUT! – NOSEY NEIGHBOURS!

As he headed downstairs he'd pulled a tear-off from a strip pinned by the door that said, "Want help getting in? Will work for a pint. Call Karl" and listed a phone number.

He had met Karl in a pub near the house. When he'd rung he'd asked how he would recognise him, and the deep voice on the phone had said flatly that he'd be, "the bloke at the bar with long hair that looks like a builder."

X had picked him out easily. He was wearing a black t-shirt with a silver Hawkwind transfer dulled grey by grime. His overalls were tied round his waist by their sleeves and hung as low as the top of his steel toe-capped boots. His curly black hair hung down to his shoulders, framing a face indistinguishable from a thousand other South London geezers, except for the livid pink scar of a telephone cut, stretching from ear to lip on the left side of his face.

Karl had been wary as he put his pint down in front of X, and the early exchanges were awkward until X worked out that his name had unnerved him, and that Karl was probing to see if calling oneself X wasn't a police trick to avoid accusations of entrapment by concealing the copper's real name. When he'd eventually assured himself that X wasn't CID, he relaxed, and settled into the task of getting X a home with open goodwill, offering the assistance of his skills, time and tools with an easy generosity before X had even had the chance to get another round in.

After he'd established that X had only squatted in Berlin, where the laws were quite different, he patiently explained the basics,

"Squatting isn't illegal in the UK", he'd started, "at least it isn't a *criminal* act. There's no defence in a civil case against you", he added, "but if the property is empty to start with, you've dispossessed no one, so who's to complain? And even when the owner notices you're there it still takes at least three months to get through the courts before you have to find somewhere else. Better still you want to choose a council place, there's hundreds empty all over South London- you've seen that in the empties room – they've no money to maintain the stock and sometimes they forget about them for years if there's no complaints. It's just possible", he went on, "that even if they do find out you're in one of their houses they'll turn a blind eye – occupied buildings decay slower than empty ones you see. But don't expect to get a tenancy or anything – those days are long gone."

X knew that and said so.

"OK", Karl continued, "as you know the catch is that while squatting isn't illegal, breaking and entering is, so for a short period of time we're vulnerable." He paused for a moment then continued, "You said it was damaged by fire – not too badly I hope. No point in getting in if it's uninhabitable."

X had explained that he'd done some snooping around and that it didn't look too serious to him. The top window frames were badly blackened, but it looked like the fire had been set outside, not inside the house.

"Don't suppose you know what happened?"

X had asked someone in the pub at the end of the road, who'd told him it had been used as a half-way house for mentally ill people released from long-term institutions, and that the last occupant had tried to burn it down during some kind of episode. It had been empty for two years apparently.

Karl seemed satisfied with that, "You'll be a better neighbour then – might help. OK", he continued, "we can get that corrugated iron door off in no time with a crowbar. I've got a good pair of bolt cutters in the van for the padlock and we'll just kick in the door behind it and patch up the frame afterwards. I can't see any problems. We'll do it at about ten-thirty tonight. You need to bring a sturdy padlock, a long metal chain and a strong hasp. Once you're in and secure, I'll leave you to it and pop round the next morning to fix you up properly with one of the old Chubb locks I've got knocking around.

X had been immensely grateful, but had been anxious about breaking in at night, "it's a quiet backstreet", he'd said, "won't the noise of wrenching off a metal door wake everyone up and bring the police down on us?"

Karl had agreed that the noise would be loud as fuck, but added that "people never leave their houses after dark around here, and the darkness will keep us hidden- it's better that way - we don't want to be recognised while we're breaking in," he'd explained, adding. "They'll just peer through the curtains and call the filth."

"And that's a good thing?" X had asked.

Karl smiled, "At that time of night the pubs will be starting to close and the pigs will have better things to do than bother with a break-in. By the time they get round to responding, you'll be snug and cosy inside with your section six notice up in the window. Relax, nothing will go wrong. When I'm fixing the lock tomorrow I'll see if I can get the water and electric on for you – mind you – be warned – they sometimes smash up the toilets and that'll be a right hassle if they have, but even then we'll sort something out."

Karl had been right about everything. They'd got in in no more than five minutes flat, and the screeching sound that echoed down the silent street producing no more than a twitch of the curtains in the neighbour's window. He'd been right about the police too. They'd swung round about one o'clock, and he'd stumbled downstairs in T-shirt and shorts, the blue light flashing silently under the half-smashed door as he fiddled with the padlock.

The bored copper had looked at the section six notice, taken in the shiny new padlock and looked the man in his shorts at the door up and down disdainfully.

He'd asked X how long he'd been there. X had said a couple of days.

The copper had scoffed and made the briefest of attempts to investigate, pointing at the sheet of corrugated iron lying by the garden wall, "How did that get there then?"

X had shrugged, "I don't know – kids? Place has been empty for months."

"Over a year", the copper had responded, "The last nutter to live here liked it so much he burnt it down. Sweet dreams", he'd added.

And then he'd left.

That first night, he'd lain on the floor in his sleeping bag, the carpet around him sprinkled with broken glass, the room lit only by the yellowed light of a streetlamp slipping round the edges of the boarded window.

Karl had fitted the lock, levered up the mains cover in the street, got the water on and by-passed the meter by lunchtime the next day.

X was drawn out of his reverie when someone lurched against the sofa knocking his arm off the backrest, and spilling half a can of Tennants down his shoulder.

The party was still in full swing.

He made out Alex and her crowd on the other side of the room and thought about joining them. They were dancing in a tight group with their hands in the air, waving their heads from side to side with the rhythm like nursery school children. They were so tightly pressed together it was though a wall separated them from the rest of the party, and they frequently touched each other as they danced as though for mutual reassurance.

Perhaps not.

He spotted Griff sat on the stairs with Toby, fortunately deep enough in conversation to unaware of Alex's presence in the room. Toby was X's only surviving friend from his time in Berlin, and had just recently come out, to nobody's great surprise. Intimidated by the gay scene and scared of AIDS, Toby had enlisted X as his companion in his first forays into his new world. He had accompanied him down the bar at Brief Encounter, and onto the dance floor at Heaven, but most often to "Daisy Chain" at the Fridge on Thursday nights, from where most of the party tracks so far had been lifted.

Griff and Toby?

It would make some sort of sense if Griff was actually gay, but he wasn't, or at least he didn't think so. But Toby? Surely he could do better than that? He sincerely hoped it didn't happen; he'd presumed he'd stay in touch with Toby after the move to Hammersmith, but he fully intended never to see that fucking idiot Griff again as long as he lived.

He got up from the sofa, suddenly bored with the music. There was only so much Hi-energy he could take before it all sounded like Euro-pop, and it was his party after all, time for a change in tone. Now that the speed was wearing off he thought he'd chance the 'Acid House' records he'd bought on a whim after payday. For the last month he'd been intrigued by the chart that had appeared, hand-written and blu-tacked to the window of the record shop at the top of the steps outside Brixton station, without knowing what 'Acid House' actually was. The titles of the tracks were weird and unfamiliar, and seemed wildly incongruous on display in Brixton's least funky record store, where the faded album covers of soca, calypso and old blues records that no one bought any more gathered dust in the racks. Since he'd had every record he'd owned stolen in the spate of burglaries and he needed some kind of soundtrack for the party he'd gone in, and having no means of discriminating one record from another had simply pulled out the entire top twenty from the chart and paid for the lot in cash. When he'd got home he hadn't been sure he'd made a good call. He quite liked the strange loops, disjointed rhythms, bleeps and samples, but it was entirely possible everybody else would think it was shit.

What the hell, he'd already bought the fucking things. Might as well give it a go.

When 'The Only Way is Up', had finished its fourth spin on the decks, he put on a 12 inch by someone called Locksy D. The track had the same awkward electronic space as the rest, but was driven by a ska beat. If all else went wrong, X figured, pissheads always liked a skank.

The reaction in the room was immediate, some sat down, dazed by the shift, but some of the semi-comatose in the corners struggled to their feet to give it a go. Paul and his beautiful companion, who had drifted into a corner and were both staring at the ceiling, came back into physical realm and the whole party seemed to kick up a gear. The effect was most dramatic on Alex's crowd, who let out a collective whoop of delight and raised their hands even further in the air as soon as the needle hit the groove.

As he stood, nodding along to the track and congratulating himself on his own good taste, Alex separated from her group and danced toward him across the room holding out her hands out in front of her with her palms up as though she was making an offering to a God.

"Thank you', she said, smiling beatifically and looking up into his eyes.

Returning her stare, X saw that her pupils were hugely dilated turning her hazel eyes almost completely black and giving her a child-like, innocent gaze.

She stroked his hair.

"Have one of these", she said, holding out a small white pill with a dove stamped on it like a pharmaceutical company's logo.

He looked at her again. She was very out of it, but in a blissful, strangely serene way. It looked like fun, but he checked himself. He had to be at his desk first thing Monday morning. This was no time to be having acid flashbacks at the coffee machine.

He politely declined.

She appeared deeply saddened for a moment, then turned and danced away with the same lightness to her step as before. He watched her dancing again with her friends, a huge smile on her face, eyes closed, arms raised, her hands stretching out for the notes with her fingers as though she hoped to pluck them out of the air.

Perhaps he should have taken up her offer.

He then began to wonder if the girl in the fishnets who'd been sitting next to him on the sofa was pretty but a little fat, or just fat, and whether he should have a go or not, and it occurred to him that he was really quite pissed and should at least get a breath of fresh air before he made any rash decisions. He put D-mob's 'We call it Acieed', on the turntable, confident now that it would rock the house, and stepped outside swiping someone's half-drunk bottle of beer on the way.

He stood on the porch, looking down the street perhaps for the last time, and tipped up his beer in the gesture Del used when he mimed drinking a pint, giving a silent word of thanks as he did so and wondering where the old boy was tonight.

While he was lost in contemplation someone came out of the door behind him. To his immense surprise, it was Karl. He hadn't seen him since he moved in and somehow missed his appearance at the party.

He was buttoning up his jacket and clearly preparing to leave.

"I was just thinking about you."

"Yeah? Well thanks for the party, I was having a right laugh but can't stand that shit that's playing now, and anyway I've got a job to do tomorrow"

X felt a bit deflated, but effusively thanked Karl for the help he'd given him that day so long ago.

Karl's reaction was strangely muted. He stood in silence a while before responding, "You know, when I first met you, I thought you might be CID?"

X laughed and said he thought he had.

"You're not CID, are you?" Karl was looking directly at him, his face completely deadpan; his facial scar livid and menacing under the light of the streetlamps. When X realised he was serious, he was indignant. The question was just insulting. "No, of course not", he insisted.

Karl expression remained unchanged and his voice was cold and flat when he spoke, "there's something about you that's not right… it's as though you're not really here but looking down on everybody who is…."

Still taken aback, X explained that he'd just got a new job, he was moving on.

"In a suit?" Karl asked

X nodded.

"That explains it."

Explains what?

Instead of explaining himself directly Karl began relaying a parable about Superman, oblivious or uncaring of X's rising ire as he spoke, "The man of steel", he started, "when he is being true to himself, is the most powerful being in the universe, capable of more or less anything. But a terrible transformation overcomes him when he puts on the suit to head off to the Daily Planet. He instantly becomes a bumbling, clumsy fool, he's bullied by his boss, treated with contempt by his co-workers, the one fit girl in the office thinks he's a dickhead, and he ends up having to make friends with the ginger-haired nonce with the bow tie because nobody else will have anything to do with him." He gave X a cold smile and tapped him on the shoulder before walking away down the street, "Don't let that happen to you X," he called over his shoulder without looking back.

X stood alone in the street, scathing replies dying on his lips as he watched Karl's retreating back grow smaller until he turned the corner and was out of sight.

He took a deep breath. Fuck you. Fuck Kevin. Fuck the sanctimonious lot of you. He didn't need any of them anymore, and anyway, they were all just jealous because they couldn't do it. Karl would still be driving his battered old white van when he cut him up at the lights in his GTI.

He let his anger die down. What did he care in the end? This was a goodbye party after all. Time for one last dance, and then good riddance to the lot of them.

Inside he glanced up, noticing that the weight of dancing bodies above was making the downstairs ceiling bow and shake in an alarming way. As he watched, flakes of plaster floated down into the room, settling on to the dancer's heads like snowflakes.

It could easily fall down at any moment.

For a second he thought he should do something; shut down the stereo, kick everybody out of the upstairs room, close down the party.

Then he shrugged. It probably won't come down, and if it did, it really wasn't his problem anymore. He thought of where he'd be in two night's time, lying back on the bed in his new flat, head propped on the soft pillow, watching sunlight fall through unbarred sash windows onto the acres of soft cream carpet on the floor at the foot of his bed.

Fuck the lot of you, he thought, and threw himself one last time into the crush.

THE BULLRING

Having spent most of his first wage packet on the flat deposit, X was pretty much broke.

At the end of the week the rest of the office decamped to the Dog and Duck in Frith Street to gossip, talk neurotically about work and get hammered, but there were only so many times you could get away with not buying a round, and so most Fridays he'd been forced to make excuses and slip off home to his empty flat as soon as the last sales call had been made. He'd met up with Paul once, but their world's now seemed so radically different that they didn't have much to say to each other, and the night spent nursing a pint in the Green Man had been both awkward and boring. It meant that his weekends were long and lonely, and until his Barclaycard application was processed, X had resigned himself to being alone from Friday afternoon to Monday morning.

At least the London galleries were free, and that Saturday he'd spent most of the day in the Tate. He'd found he had to hurry through the Rothko room, the ceiling seeming to suddenly lower as he entered and the paintings throb on the walls like panting lungs as he passed, and after idling through the smudgy Turners, found refuge at the rear of the gallery in front of an Arcadian landscape by Poussin. He'd spent the rest of the afternoon on a bench in front of the huge canvas allowing himself to fall in and out of the painting. Over and over again he'd wound his way down from the high plateau in the foreground, passed under the boughs of the wizened, alien trees that framed the scene, and on through the fields of gently grazing cattle, following the winding river to the city on the far hill, its palaces, spires and temples a blend of the holy land and renaissance Italy that never was, some kind of paradise whose details were tantalisingly indecipherable in the painting's far depths.

He'd only pulled out of his trance when the attendants had warned him that the gallery was closing, and then walked into Soho, sitting as long as he could over an espresso in Bar Italia before spending the last of his change playing *Outran* in an arcade in Dean Street. He'd had just enough money left to take in a Nouvelle Vague double bill at the Lumiere, but had fallen asleep during the second film, a glacially-paced Jean Luc Godard epic in black and white, where the camera rarely moved and nothing seemed to happen at all. Waking, he'd slipped into the toilets until the late-night screening started, but twenty minutes into Russ Meyer's 'Super-Vixens' trilogy, the stupidity and cleavage had seemed less like irony and more like a teenage boy's wank material, and had left before the end of the first reel, shuffling out along the aisle like a dirty old man who had climaxed too early.

Without sufficient money even for the bus, he'd begun the long walk home with a heavy heart and, suddenly aware that he hadn't eaten all day, took a detour via Lincoln's Inn fields to get a free meal off one of the soup vans he knew would be there at that time of night. He had taken his place in the queue for a vegetarian curry from the Hari Krishnas when Frank had spotted him.

For a moment Frank's face was full of concern, "Things haven't gone badly wrong have they X?" he'd asked gently.

Embarrassed to be caught scavenging, X managed to mumble some kind of reply and, suitably reassured, Frank had switched tack, asking X to do him a favour. "I wouldn't normally ask X, but if you're at a loose end, we've still got the bullring to do and….."

Frank looked toward the soup van and X followed his gaze. The queue in front of the van was shorter than usual, and he could see Lars carelessly slopping soup into a line of plastic cups, the gloopy residue spilling over the rims and forming puddles like little pools of vomit on the surface of the trestle table. If it had been Lars turn to make the soup, X thought, the potatoes wouldn't have been peeled, or probably even washed if could have gotten away with it.

He understood why Frank had asked him to help out. Although the Bullring wasn't any more violent than a rough pub at closing time, at night it was a land of the blind where the one-eyed man was king, and the little empires of the underpass were presided over by debased monarchs whose statecraft was mostly measured in their capacity for unpredictable violence. Even Frank's dog collar wasn't guaranteed protection in there. None of the other charities went in at night, and Frank wasn't strictly supposed to either, but he was in earnest determination about his calling, and ran the risk to make sure that the men he had tended for twenty years weren't completely neglected even for one night. Frank was brave, but he wasn't a fool, and only a fool would go in with Lars as his wing man. There had to be somebody there who would at least be bothered to call the police if he wasn't out in half an hour.

So X had reluctantly agreed to help out and sat in silence next to Lars as the van pulled up at the roundabout opposite the entrance to the cardboard city.

"Twenty minutes OK X', said Frank, "then I'll drop you home."

"Fuck that!" interjected Lars, "You can do what you like with him, but not before you have dropped me back at the motherfucking hostel."

Clearly nothing much had changed since he left.

He sat in the van while Lars insulted the few stragglers getting a last lump of warm soup and a cup of tea from the urn before bedding down for the night. He closed his eyes to shut out the sound of Lars' voice and, despite his need to stay vigilant for Frank, nodded off.

9. JORGUND

The sun was high in the sky behind his shoulders as he walked down the grassy slope, its light white-bright, but not scalding hot, as though it were emitted by a paler, more distant star. Beneath his feet the grass was deep green, soft underfoot and scattered with wild flowers. Ahead, an avenue of ornamental pear trees bordering a children's play area brought the meadow to a close and the sound of infants' oxygenated pleasure floated through the still air.

Around him, a group of about twenty young people were also making their way across the park. They were dressed in their customary manner, but had traded their soft shoes for sturdy walking boots, and each member carried a coloured backpack on their shoulders. There was much chatting and laughter among them, and the atmosphere was like that of a youthful hiking expedition on its way to set up camp at the start of a week's vacation.

In response to some unseen signal the troop came to a halt and he scanned the crowd, spotting Pooja, the Indian girl he had met in the café, and then, on the other side of the group and to his great delight; Eva. She was deep in conversation with her friend Sven and a bald-headed man he had never seen before. As he watched, Eva laughed, and, throwing her head back in delight, she seemed momentarily frozen in the white light, cut out from the background with the unearthly clarity of a Van Eyck painting, her pale beauty hovering above the meadow as though she were a portrait hung in a gallery.

He called out, and when Eva caught sight of him she smiled,

and waving enthusiastically, signalled for him to come over and join the three of them. They pressed foreheads and the bald man, introduced to X as Jorgund, greeted him by cupping the back of his head and pulling him down into a firm, sustained press of against his brow, an action that seemed manly, gay and ridiculous, all at the same time. Breaking from his embrace, X took a long look at him. He differed strikingly from his companions; short and completely bald, with buggy, protruding eyes, he wore a sleeveless jacket that revealed a muscly torso with dragon tattoos, carefully inked in red, green and gold on each shoulder. In conversation his eyes fixed the person he was speaking to with an intense gaze, as though he were attempting to penetrate beyond the surface of their skin by an act of supreme will. This alarming characteristic was offset by an otherwise affable and easy going manner and a broad grin that seemed to permanently occupy his open and friendly face. X liked him instantly.

It turned out that Jorgund was the expedition's leader and Eva explained to him that it was not, in fact, a hiking tour but the beginning of an ordinary working day.

She declared delightedly that he had arrived at exactly the right time to answer the question he had asked at the end of his last visit, "I know it was a while ago X, but you do remember don't you….?

As she said this, she pointed over his shoulder back up the hillside behind him. He looked in the direction she had indicated, and squinting into the sunlight, he could just make out the apartment block at the end of Eva's street, the sun glinting off the glass windows of the café on its top floor. "You were a little…." Her voice trailed off.

"You were stoned man", interjected Sven, laughing.

Jorgund, whose bug eyes had been following the dialogue with his characteristic intense concentration, burst out laughing and slapped X on the back in congratulation, as though he had achieved something particularly grand by sharing a spliff on the café balcony.

"Where are all the poor people?" he repeated in order to reassure Eva that he hadn't forgotten.

Eva quickly translated the word 'poor' into 'disadvantaged' and explained what they were doing that day. "Jorgund collected us from the university" she began, indicating an enormous white stone building that dominated the full length of the ridge behind them, the bone-white turret of a monumental clock tower at its centre looming above the city like an actual tower of ivory, "….and we walked down together."

"Yea", interrupted Jorgund, "We could meet down here, but the stroll is so fine, it is much better to do it together, I think."

"You are all university students then?" asked X.

Jorgund laughed, "Me not so much, Eva nearly always, others often or not so often, you know how it is."

"But we are not university students today", interjected Eva, "today we are undertaking social care tasks for the well-being of our community."

X translated, confident that for once he had understood the situation correctly, "So you're doing some voluntary work", he said, thinking that it was exactly what he would have expected of Eva and Pooja and spoke well of Sven.

Everyone looked slightly confused.

"No X, there are really good credits for this kind of work", Sven explained.

He couldn't help feeling slightly disappointed. He had always found the idea of students doing voluntary work to advance their careers or beef up their CVs somewhat distasteful. But he thought he should check that he had fully understood before he jumped to conclusions. "Academic credits?" he asked

Again they all looked confused.

Jorgund put him out of his misery, "No, my friend, there is good money credit in this line of work", he rubbed his thumb and forefinger together to illustrate the point, "Muchos dollars." It seemed somehow an even worse explanation to X, but he suspected there was something he was missing, so he just nodded as though he had fully understood.

At this point Jorgund brought the conversation to a close by stepping forward and addressing the whole group, bringing to X's attention that everyone else in the party had stopped in their tracks while the four of them had been in conversation. He apologised for the brief delay and introduced X to the collected company. "Hello X", the group chorused in unison. Pooja gave him a cheery wave from across the sea of smiling faces. He waved back. Jorgand then signalled them to get moving again and the party resumed its passage down the hill as before.

Soon they had left the park and entered the outskirts of the city itself, coming to a halt in front of a set of four-storey, brightly coloured apartment blocks with small balconies, each block radiating from a central square like the markings on a watch face. Jorgund circulated around his charges, dispersing snippets of necessary information or listening carefully to queries for a while, then, with only a lazily raised hand as a signal, the group broke into pairs, and with the well-ordered discipline of a military platoon, advanced into the surrounding apartment blocks, each pair commandeering a separate stairwell.

X had started off with Sven and Eva, but Eva had waived him away, "No, you must go with Jorgund, it will be much better, I think." Disappointed, he reluctantly following the expedition leader up the stairwell of the nearest block, struggling to keep pace as Jorgund attacked the stairs like a marine yomping up a steep incline. On the top floor Jorgund knocked on the peacock blue door of apartment 8. There was no reply.

"Can we come in Mr Ekstrom?" he called through the closed door.

There was a shout from the other side that sounded as much like a roar of rage as an invitation to enter, but Jorgund was unperturbed. "I'll take that as a yes", he said to X, smiling, and pushed open the unlocked door.

It was nearly midday, but despite the glass windows that ran the full length of the apartment, the day had been almost completely shut out by a line of drawn blinds. The only evidence of the glorious sunlight pouring down outside was in the farthest corner, where a spray of golden beams had crept in through the gap created by a single broken slat and picked out clouds of dust motes suspended motionless in the fetid air. The shuttered room was lifted from total darkness by the light emanating from a flickering screen on one wall, its surface stuck between two blank white pages and laying a dead, cold wash of light over the room's sparse furnishings. X's eyes quickly adjusted to the gloom, and he spotted the room's only occupant, an old man lying prone on a sofa opposite the blank screen, his face a ghostly white in the reflected glare. The old man's leotard had been pulled down to his waist revealing a torso of flaccid, jaundiced skin, the gaps in his sweaty black chest hair filled with moles and liver spots like lichen covering a rotten tree trunk. Two bottles of Vodka, one half-full, the other completely empty, sat on the glass coffee table next to him. The room smelt of shit.

"Good morning Mr Ekstrom!" Jorgund announced cheerfully.

"Fuck off!" came the man's reply.

*

"There's nothing like an old drunk telling you his made up tales of heroism is there!" laughed Jorgund, pulling off his gloves as he closed the brightly painted apartment door behind him. "Really, I haven't heard the one about his rescue of his epileptic uncle's dog more than twenty or thirty times!"

After the initial unpleasantness, the visit had gone remarkably well, and they were leaving a sweet-smelling, tidy, well-stocked flat with at least one of the blinds open and old Ekstrom ready to go another round or two of repetitive rambling in much better spirits than when they had entered.

"Yes, I visit Gnar three or four times a week", Jorgund continued, "and it is always much the same. Mind you", he added, "last time we were talking on the sofa and he shat himself then and there! Too pissed to sort himself out." Jorgund shook his head regretfully. "I tell you though man", he continued, "we should all clean an old man's arsehole from time to time, No? Puts it all into perspective."

He seemed almost jolly in his recollection.

There was one more visit to be made in the block before they could meet up with the others in the square. In stark contrast to their first visit the flat was light, airy and spotlessly clean, but its occupant was clearly in a much worse state than old Gnar upstairs. They were lying flat on their back on some kind of supportive bed-chair. The bed was attached to a pole and cantilevered by a complex hydraulic system that would have enabled it to be turned and repositioned at almost any angle, but was currently laid out horizontally. Only the patient's head was visible at one end of the bed and that was completely encased in some sort of rubber mask, through which a white plastic feeding tube forced open their lips and looped up into a large vat attached to the ceiling. The rest of their body was completely hidden from view under a translucent white plastic cylinder that reminded X of the iron lungs polio victims had been condemned to live out their lives in during the 1950s. The patient made no response to their presence in the room and X wondered what the value was of treating someone in such a terrible condition outside of a hospital. Bizarrely, the horror of their circumstances seemed to be openly mocked by the presence of an exercise bicycle, multi-gym and rowing machine in pristine condition in the unoccupied half the room.

Jorgund remained as cheerful as ever, but even he was perhaps a little rueful, "Immersers", he shrugged, "most of them are up in the mountains, but some...." He let his sentence trail off and commenced checking cables and tubes around the machine.

X was disturbed by the scene, and feeling somewhat queasy, asked if it was OK if he stepped outside to get some fresh air. Jorgund acquiesced readily and suggested they meet back in the square in half an hour or so when he would have finished up here. As he was leaving, he took a backward glance just as Jorgund released a lever at the base of the table and the white cylinder that had covered the patient's torso uncurled in a single smooth motion revealing the body underneath. It was female, completely naked and grotesquely obese.

In the square Eva, Sven and Pooja were sitting on the low brick wall around the fountain, eating sandwiches and chatting merrily. He joined them and sat, only half-listening to them as they talked while he tried to will the image of the hideously bloated body out of his mind. Taking great gulps of clean, sweet air and letting the bright sunlight warm his skin, his sense of peace and contentment slowly recovered. His companions were exchanging accounts of their morning activities. Pooja had apparently helped bathe an old lady and inoculated her cats, for which the old dear had been effusively grateful, whereas Eva and Sven had tended to a couple of elderly junkies, topped up the heroin in their fridge, left a supply of fresh needles, tidied up the flat and listened to a few stories of the bad old days. They all seemed uplifted by the work and gabbled away happily as they polished off their lunch.

Eva returned to her educational mode with X, but he was happy enough to lounge in the sun and listen to her soft voice, letting the water from the fountain run through his fingers while she talked. The words washed over him while he tried once more to identify her eye colour. They seemed almost violet now. Was such a thing possible? "In case you think we are a city of alcoholics and drug addicts", she explained earnestly, her smooth brow creased in her determination to disabuse him of any such thoughts, "these and other dependencies are very rare in our society. I hope you noticed that it is almost exclusively the elderly that have succumbed, and for that modern genetics has played a big part, but..." she hesitated before continuing, "Take alcoholism, we see it not as a moral failing but more as a consequence of unfortunate probability."

Seeing the blank expression of X's face in response to this statement, she recounted an experiment involving rats. The experiment entailed allowing rats access to an inexhaustible supply of alcohol, and under these conditions it had been discovered that about 10% of rats became alcoholic, 10% teetotal and the rest social drinkers. Apparently human beings exhibited surprisingly similar responses to a free supply of alcohol and in roughly the same proportions as rats.

X mused for a while about what constituted social drinking in rats and for much of Eva's speech couldn't shake off an image of tiny martini glasses complete with olives held delicately in little ratty paws.

Eva had, however, carried on, "So we are all made aware if we are genetically at risk of alcohol dependency and those who have the troublesome gene will naturally abstain. But of course, some people make mistakes and bad decisions and for them we have excellent rehabilitation facilities, and for those who are unable or unwilling to stay sober you can see, we provide decent places to live and..."

"...and caring and compassionate social workers to visit", interrupted Sven, sweeping his arm across the four of them sitting by the fountain in the sun. They laughed.

"And it is the same for all dependencies", Eva continued, "drugs, food, exercise, etcetera. For the people with learning disabilities...."

"Enough Eva", Sven interrupted again, "Leave the poor man alone, I'm sure he's got the message by now!"

Eva looked a little hurt, and Pooja directed an angry glance at Sven, who hastily apologised to Eva and then hugged both his friends in a tight squeeze, finishing off by hugging X just in case he felt left out. They were all smiling again by the time their lunch break was over.

As Jorgund began gathering up his team for the afternoon activities, X felt quite dispirited at the prospect of entering any more gloomy apartments on such a beautiful day. If he could accompany Eva, he figured, he could put up with more or less anything, but he had a premonition that a whole day of Jorgund's relentless optimism and he would end up throwing himself off one of the balconies. As soon as he voiced his objection to the afternoon's plan, the look of disappointment on Eva's face made him regret his words. Pooja made a spirited attempt to persuade him to join them, declaring that she was doing kindergarten and crèche work for the rest of the day and if he accompanied her it would all be very jolly, but Sven came to his rescue, suggesting that they all meet up later at his place, and gently defended X's right to explore the city on his own terms.

X was hugely grateful for his intervention and Eva's mood immediately brightened. She quickly pulled a small hand-held device from her backpack, explaining that, like X, many of the older people had never got used to the glasses so she carried one with her whenever she was at work. She made a few gestures at the screen and a map of the city appeared, and after a few more wags of her finger explained that she had marked the location of Sven's flat and a number of art galleries and museums that she thought he would find interesting to look at on the way. All he had to do was follow the arrow on the screen and he couldn't get lost. She demonstrated the impossibility of him losing his way by spinning the screen round in his hands, amazingly, the map re-orientated itself each time and the arrow remained resolutely pointing in the correct direction with the unerring accuracy of a compass. They waved goodbye, and, slightly regretful at their parting but also excited to be alone in a strange city, X set off to explore.

Only a few blocks away, he was crossing a set of tram tracks when he heard someone calling his name. He looked round, wondering why they had come back for him so soon, only to find that it was another of his acquaintances from the café, this time Xanthia's friend Per, waving one of his spider-like arms from a bench by the tram stop he had just passed.

"Great!" Per exclaimed when X told him that he had three hours or so with nothing much to do but wander the city. "I got started late and missed my connection", Per continued, "So I have an hour to kill also. Let's get a drink!"

They found a pavement café half a block down the street and Per ordered beers for both of them. X realised that he didn't have any money at all, and feeling awkward about accepting Per's generosity without being able to reciprocate, hastily apologised to his drinking companion. Per waived his concern away dismissively. "Did you get any credit for this morning's work?" he asked.

X confirmed that he hadn't, but pointed out that he hadn't

exactly done much either.

"More than me", said Per, "I'll get on to Eva to get you a card", he continued, and then corrected himself, "I'll get on to Xanthia, and she'll get on to Eva. She really enjoys getting on to Eva. Sometimes I wonder why they're friends", he added as an afterthought.

They settled into the aluminium seats on the pavement and sat in silence watching the cyclists stream by for a while. Per was no conversationalist, at least not when he was sober, and a long time passed without either of them saying anything at all. To stop the silence become uncomfortable, he asked Per where he was heading to before he missed his connection.

"Out to the farm again", he replied, "That's what I do, mostly, work on the land, drive tractors and stuff."

He didn't seem too thrilled at the prospect and X said so.

Per spoke slowly in reply, as though he was already bored with the sentences he delivered before they had even left his mouth, "It's not bad", he drawled, "keeps me fit and healthy. The pay is OK - not as good as the social care stuff – but I'm shit at that." He shook his head before continuing, "They all get on my nerves, not just the drunks and the junkies, even the old people...especially the old people actually...Not good, I know, but there it is." He lapsed into silence again.

"So you do this *all* of the time?" X asked, "I'm sure there was something else..."

Per suddenly became more animated, rising from the slouch he had slumped into and speaking at a much more rapid pace, "Yeah. I like to drive racing cars fast! Got a little E-racer down by the docks, a JU754, man she's fast, quicker than...how do you Londoners' say it... shit on a shovel!" Having lent forward to deliver his homily he then slumped back down in his seat, throwing a loose arm in a looping, dismissive gesture, "But where's the money in that? He sighed, "We try to argue that it furthers research into the efficiency of electric engines and therefore contributes to the collective good, but everyone knows that's bullshit. So it pays fuck-nothing", he continued, that's why I have to work on the farms nine months a year - Have you any idea how much capacitors cost?" He shook his head ruefully and then lapsed into silence once more.

The conversation was no more scintillating for the rest of the hour, but X had begun to take the silences as companionable rather than as an indication of boredom in his company, and when it was time for Per to catch his tram, leaving with a smile and the phrase, "See you in nine months", X felt almost sad.

Alone again, he strolled contentedly down the tree-lined streets, enjoying the surprising quiet in the centre of such a big city. Apart from the cheering clack and rattle of passing trams, the loudest sounds were the conversations of passers-by and the bleeping of traffic lights, and the freshness of the air, even in the heart of town, seemed miraculous. Several times he sat down on street benches just to revel in the pleasure of taking great gulps of revitalising oxygen while watching the bustle of street life. Being in no particular hurry, he took time to observe the curious shapes of the modernist office and apartment blocks that Eva had marked for his attention and imagined that he was beginning to develop the sophisticated taste of an architect on vacation. After a while he even began to feel like a local, surefooted in his progress toward Sven's with only the occasional glance at his map, remembering to look both ways before crossing the designated cycle lanes, and keeping an ear out for the quiet hum of the electric cars whenever he crossed a road.

Having reached Sven's home an hour or so before the others were due to arrive, he decided to back-track and take in one of the galleries that Eva had marked with glowing stars on his map. He walked past it twice before he found the entrance. He'd been expecting a monumental building of some kind, Corinthian columns, a marble pediment held up by straining caryatids, a sweeping array of stone steps, or something similar. Instead the entrance was a modest red doorway at the bottom of a short row of steps down to a basement, its sign a small copper plaque on the wall like one for a firm of solicitors or an insurance broker. It appeared that there was no charge for entrance, and as there was no one at the front desk anyway, he wandered in, completely unsupervised, feeling for a moment as though he was trespassing and waiting for someone to ask him what the hell he thought he was doing. No one did.

It was clear that the gallery contained very few works of art, and that each piece had been carefully hung in a room specifically tailored to suit its form. The first room was of modest size and tatty, either in the process of decoration or deliberately left to decay, the wallpaper peeling from the walls exposing slabs of untreated plaster that broke up its surface into ugly, uneven mosaic patterns. There were only two portraits on display, both of elderly people, one man and one woman and hung at either end of the long room. Each crevice and mark of their faces was painted with an exquisite tenderness and an unflinching honesty, the images so eerily alive it was as though the sitters themselves were also visitors at the gallery. The second, and largest of the rooms, contained only a huge landscape in oils portraying a bucolic vista that was neither absolutely real nor completely false. At first glance he had taken it to be a renaissance masterpiece, but as he drew closer he could see that figures lounging under the arbours were dressed in the clothing of the contemporary occupants of this city, and the misty cityscape in the far distance was made up of asymmetrical modernist buildings of steel, chrome and glass. An old man and an old woman, mimicking the portraits in the first room, sat at either end of a long leather sofa, staring at the painting in front of them in complete silence. They neither moved nor spoke when X entered and remained so absolutely immobile that as he left the room that he wondered if they too had been part of the exhibition, life-like sculptures perhaps, or maybe performance artists paid to create an otherworldly effect in the gallery.

The third room was cramped, claustrophobic and as cold as a fridge. A solitary painting hung on its bare plaster walls, an almost featureless seascape that reminded him of Lowry. He shuffled out of the room quickly before its loneliness overwhelmed him.

The final room had a series of red warning signs displayed at its entrance, including a symbol that clearly indicated that children were not allowed to enter. It contained only one painting, propped on an easel in the centre of the room with only the back of the canvas visible from the doorway. X walked toward it with some trepidation, unable to envisage what sort of image other than the crudely pornographic, would require such admonitory caution.

When he reached the painted side of the canvas he was momentarily disappointed. That Edvard Munch's 'The Scream', could be displayed without high security seemed more shocking than the image itself. The distorted human visage, pier and swirling, livid orange horizon were far too familiar to be even remotely disturbing. It might as well have been Constable's 'Haywain', he thought, for all its fearful impact. But the more he looked at it, the more it brought back the image of the obscenely fat woman attached to the machine that had lodged in his mind before, and as he tried to shake it out of his head it seemed to merge hideously with the wailing figure in Munch's painting. He began to experience a violent sense of vertigo, as though he was falling into the painting from a great height, somehow clutching at the fat woman's sagging fleshy folds and tearing at the screamer's eyes to prevent being sucked into the painting itself, all three of them swirling together into its vortex, merging into some kind of monstrous symbiote before being dragged into the inescapable black hole that had opened at the heart of the painting. He turned and fled from the room, not stopping until he was back in the street outside the gallery, hands on his knees, gasping for breath.

*

Sven had told him that his door wouldn't be locked and had instructed him to go straight in and make himself at home if he got there before them, but it still felt immensely odd to be sitting on the sofa in Sven's front room on his own. The room was even more featureless than Eva's, and having no idea how to activate the wall screen he sat in silence waiting for them to return. He got up a couple of times and wandered around Sven's workshop at the back of the flat in an attempt to pass the time, but the sleek looking racing machines that hung from the ceiling and the bike components crammed into every crevice on the walls, meant little to him, and he felt much more like a potential thief than an interested admirer. Still recovering from his moment of existential fear in the gallery, and feeling horribly uncomfortable alone in a stranger's house, he was contemplating leaving when they finally showed up.

The three of them burst in all at once, and were clearly delighted to find him there. His mood changed instantly as the two women pressed foreheads and flopped onto the sofa beside him, demanding that Sven fix them all a drink while they swapped their tales of the day with their 'honoured guest'. A few minutes later, the four of them were squeezed together onto the sofa drinking iced tea while Eva regaled them with a story about an old boy they had visited, who, clearly well into his second childhood, had insisted they joined him in a game of hide and seek. The retelling took some time, as Eva was repeatedly overcome by gales of laughter, the central point being that, like all of the flats here, there was hardly enough furniture to make such a game even remotely viable.

"You had to be there", said Sven.

When it came to his turn to his tell his story, his decided not to recount his disturbing experience in the gallery, but brought up his encounter with Per instead. It had the unfortunate effect of returning Eva to her serious mode and, resuming her earnest voice, made one last effort to teach him economics. "OK", she started, "the amount of money paid for any work done is calculated, on a democratically agreed scale, in proportion to its contribution to the collective good."

X was no wiser than before.

"Give him an example", suggested Pooja.

"Good idea. Right. The care of those with dementia", Eva began, "This is clearly very important work for the collective good and is therefore very highly rewarded. Caring for young children, doctors, nurses," she continued, "these are also major contributors to the well-being of our society and are therefore also well paid."

Pooja picked up the thread, "less directly, but just as important, research and development are obviously vital to improve the quality of life for all", she explained, "medical research has the highest value as you would suspect, genetics and biochemistry are clearly related fields and therefore also highly valued, research into electronics, physics and chemistry slightly less so, but are still well remunerated."

X tried to think of those he associated with earning the most money. He didn't imagine that large landowners or people living of inherited wealth really existed here, so he tried to think of other means of earning a lot of cash. "What about actors?" he asked.

They all laughed. "Ask Xanthia", suggested Eva, "Entertainment is not without value, but is way down the list of remuneration. There is very little money for it. But it is fun, No? Acting. Actors must do other things if they want to spend time enjoying themselves." She became even more earnest than before, "Do not misunderstand X, we value creativity highly, and consider it healthy for everyone to have some outlet to express themselves. The ideal would be for it to comprise perhaps one third of your life, but to do so exclusively would just be self-indulgence, No?"

X thought he had got it now, but was still thinking of high earners in his world, "What about professional sportsmen?", he asked.

They all looked at him blankly.

"We are not sure how that would work", ventured Sven, "Everyone takes part in sport here X, of course, it is essential for health and highly gratifying, but no one pays you for doing so..."

"Does no one watch sport?" X persisted.

"Oh yes", piped up Eva, "and people can get very passionate about it. It's certainly a joy to watch really talented athletes. There is sometimes a big crowd when Olaf plays handball".

"Physiotherapists make an important contribution to the collective good", Pooja added helpfully.

It was clear that there was no such thing as highly paid tennis players or basketball stars here.

The system seemed very clever and right-minded and he wondered why no one had thought of it before. He sat awhile trying to think of objections to it, conscious that they were all giving him space to mull it over and waiting for his reply. He came up with two, but was fairly certain they'd have ready answers. "Who decides the scale of payments?" he asked, "And how does it ever change?"

They were all bursting to respond, but Sven got in first, "Well...

SOUP VAN

"He's back!"

It was Lars voice he heard first over the roar and clatter of the soup van's motor. He was propped up on one of the front seats, hanging limp in the belts, flopping like a rag doll each time the van changed direction.

A sharp left turn sent his body lolling across Lars in the seat next to him, the dead weight of his left arm swinging like a nunchaku into Lars' lap and his head crashing into a shoulder blade as he slumped forward. He was pushed back upright with a shove that felt more like a kidney punch.

"You've been out for half an hour X." Frank's voice this time, deep and full of concern.

"Yea", Lars chimed in again, "You fucking flat-lined in the van", his voice was squeaky with the thrill of it, "I tried everything man! Zero response! Nada! – I tell you it was like Christiane F man – you didn't even blink when I slapped you!"

X wondered how long he'd waited before trying that.

"Working too hard", he mumbled the words, his tongue as thick as a soap bar in his mouth.

His vision swam into focus as he spoke and he regained enough control over his limbs to haul himself upright in the seat. He concentrated on staring straight ahead through the windshield in an effort to keep the nausea at bay and to prevent him having to look at Lars' smug face.

He could see Frank shaking his head out of the corner of his eye; "You were too deep under for that X. It looked more like some kind of fugue than ordinary sleep. Is there any history of epilepsy in your family?"

Fugue? Epilepsy?

"Yea, you were drooling man", Lars added gleefully, "great big gloops of it running down your chin."

*

"You should get yourself checked out X, you don't want that happening when you're driving…"

Frank's last words to him when he finally dropped him home in the early hours, might have had made more of a lasting impression on him if he hadn't woken up the next morning feeling so good.

Exceptionally good.

He was sharply awake the moment he opened his eyes, his energy levels completely restored, feeling more fresh and alive than he had done in weeks. He felt cleansed, as though all the toxins in his bloodstream had been flushed out of him while he slept, and he threw back the Egyptian cotton sheets on his big double bed and stood naked in front of the window ready to take on the world.

Falling asleep in inconvenient places was certainly annoying, but it clearly wasn't affecting his health.

He felt great.

What's more, he was enjoying the fantasy world he had created in his head. He liked hanging out with the beautiful dream girl and her friends. If he had one objection to the dreaming, it was the scholarly and serious tone they often had. He didn't seem to mind when he was there, but when he returned to reality it irked him. Who wants to have an earnest, *relevant* fantasy life for fucks sake?

What he needed was a real girlfriend, then, he was certain, the dream girl and all the rest of it was sure to fade away.

10. SELF-ASSESSMENT
25.8.1988

He looked at his watch. It seemed worth recording the exact moment when everything came together exactly as he had dreamt it would. Four fifteen on August the twenty-fifth 1988. It had taken a year and four months.

Surprisingly quick in retrospect.

He was sitting behind the desk in Howard's office, leaning back in the big leather chair, his hands cupped behind his head, elbows out, faking nonchalance as he nodded along with her words. The woman who had sat opposite him on that first heat-soaked failure of a day over a year ago, when he was a scruffy, squat dwelling nobody and she was a vision of the promised land, set as high above him as any goddess, had appeared in front of him once more.

And this time, he was interviewing her.

He took a quick sideways glance, briefly panicked by the thought that his carefully chosen posture of executive ease might instead be presenting twin arcs of armpit sweat to the beautiful woman opposite him in a gesture as charming as a baboon displaying its buttocks to a potential mate.

He relaxed. No unsightly stains visible.

The magazine had only closed for press an hour ago and despite the lack of armpit sweat, he knew he looked a mess. He fought back the thought. Confidence was all that was important in a situation like this. With enough confidence, scruffy and dishevelled would come across as dynamic and interesting. He could do it. All he had to do was stay cool and calm. A woman this stunning, he figured, would have been gauging men by their response to the erotic charge of her appearance the whole of her life. He could envisage the queues of slack-jawed boys lining up in the playground since puberty, taking their turns to be enslaved or dismissed; the scores of full grown men reduced to putty in her hands; barely stifled yawns the only reward for each heartfelt expression of devotion, their expensive gifts binned when their backs were turned; the thousands of construction workers, shouting and clutching their crotches as she passed.

So he concentrated on remaining calm and aloof, allowing himself only to steal surreptitious glances at her; each time storing away small details like a magpie gathering shiny trinkets for its nest; an oblong, red-faced watch with fine gold hands on her slim wrist, a single cut gem stud earing in her left ear, the softness of her lower lip, the way she set her hands across her lap as she spoke, the lilt of her voice…Portuguese? …Moroccan? …Lebanese?

Where was she from? He mused, turning over the possibilities in his mind as she talked on. From the soft honey-brown colour of her skin she could have been from any one of a thousand places - Southern Europe or the Maghreb perhaps… but maybe as far East as Arabia…perhaps even India. But then again she was could just as easily be any one of an infinite number of possible combinations of mixed race…European and African perhaps… Maybe Anglo-Jamaican…? Her nose was soft and wide enough to suggest Africa somewhere in her story, and her eyes were a deep brown… but her cheekbones were sharp and high, and when she emphasised a point – like she did just then - there was something hawk-like about her flashing eyes, maybe somewhere down the Blue Nile or perhaps across the red sea … Yemen maybe or Oman… Her jet-black hair fell in a single wave of silk from the top of her head to the small of her back without the slightest curl or kink. It was hair that would have been a commodity for a poor Indian girl, but could just as easily have been the pride of a Venetian courtesan. He gave up. Her face was as unplaceable as her voice, the beauty of everywhere and therefore of nowhere at all.

He would have to say something decisive soon.

She had got the job of course, he just needed to work out how he could afford her…

*

The first year and four months hadn't all been plain sailing.

In many ways, the job had turned out deeply disappointing. Where X had been hoping for glamour and excitement, he found an environment only marginally less drab than the hostel he'd escaped from, and his daily duties infinitely more tedious than those he'd carried out on the West End streets. His working environment had consisted of a shabby open plan office on the first floor of the building on Poland Street, divided up by brown cardboard screens into the individual fiefdoms of five separate magazines. Each magazine commanded an area of floor space in direct proportion to its turnover, the title's success therefore directly measurable by the number of moulded plastic chairs and laminated tables in each section, and the degree of swagger in its ad manager's walk. And each magazine's area was populated by the same dull pieces of utilitarian furniture, every object seemingly made of the same colourless plastic, the Xerox machines in each corner, the VDU monitors on every secretary's desk, the saucer-sized ashtrays and chunky phones with their dice-sized keys and coiled plastic leads, all bleached of life and yellowed cadaverous by tobacco smoke and stale air. The sales desks were cheap and tacky, littered with screwed up notepaper and sticky file cards, their edges chipped and scarred by cigarette burns. Almost the only colour in the deracinated room was a threadbare green carpet, stuck down over protruding cabling by shiny black duct tape, strips of which crossed the floor in sticky, trip-hazard tramways. With the windows hermetically sealed and the air conditioning maintained at a constant 22°C whatever the weather outside, he had worked in recycled air as stale and acrid as the interior of a National Express coach

And the job itself was as monotonous as any production line.

The daily target for each salesperson on Restaurant and Café Bar News had been set at six effective calls an hour; an effective call being defined as one where 'you get to speak to a decision maker and discuss the product'. If you had a voice that people liked to listen to over the phone, and you kept at it, you could make an effective call once in every ten or so attempts.

Dial. Hold. Speak. Redial.

Fifty times an hour.

Five hundred times a day.

Even the title was a bastard to say.

"Hi, this is X from *Restaurant and Café Bar News*", took a lifetime to get out and got stuck around your tongue after the millionth repetition.

"Hi, I'm X from RCBN", was shorter, but incomprehensible. He had twice got unexpectedly past a particularly hostile receptionist using the shortened version, mistaken once for a hardwood supplier and the other time for an architect's practice, but neither call had landed a sale in the end.

All you could do was keep going until you blundered into someone who was bored enough to pick up the phone and waste five minutes talking to a salesman, and then at least you had a chance, and once in a thousand calls you hit someone at just the right time, when they were actually planning their marketing, and then, if you were good, you could squeeze a little bit more out of them than they had intended to spend.

But most of the time it was:

"Hi, this is X from the sales team at Restaurant and Café-Bar News, is Mr Smedley available!"

. . . .

"Hello?"

"Hi, I'm calling from Restaurant and Café Bar News, is Mr Smedley in?"

"Which Department?"

"Advertising."

. . . .

"Hi, I'm looking for Jack Smedley, is he in?"

"Its X from RCBN."

"Restaurant and Café Business News."

. . . .

Hi, it's X. Is Jack about?"

. . . .

Roger did his best to make it all seem thrilling, leaping on the tables with excitement when someone landed a big sale, setting the weekly target for champagne low, so that there was often a bottle or two to be shared on Friday after work, and bursting back into the office from visits with tales of Italian coffee makers and German kitchenware specialists who were just about to spend big, telling them all that the magazine would be huge, 'like Arena darling'. And, in truth, they had eaten as well as Roger had promised. Dining on editorial's ticket, he had added chicken satay, plum sauce and Singapore Laksa to his list of newly acquired pleasures, their flavours as different to anything he had previously tasted as discovering a new colour in the rainbow. He also developed a taste for saki, the hot rice wine flung back between soup slurps in their regular sessions in the noodle bars round the back of the Regent's Palace hotel. But although there was champagne and black cabs home on Friday night, he still flinched at the meter no matter how pissed he was, and the balance on the credit card he had been so proud of getting, kept growing, the minimum payment eating further into his pay check with every passing month. His rent took such a big bite out of his salary he occasionally regretted giving up the squat.

But not often, and never for long.

But the real problem wasn't the tedium, or the discovery that the job's veneer of glamour was very thin indeed, it was that Roger's vision of the magazine's glorious prospects had proved unfounded. *Restaurant and Café Bar News* was a flop, its plausible business plan holed beneath the waterline even before launch.

It turned out that none of the magazine's target audience needed to spend a penny on recruitment advertising. Applicants were queuing around the block for jobs in the shiny new London café-bars, and the Thai, Malaysian and New Indian cuisine restaurants that the magazine championed needed no help getting in touch with their own communities. The bitter irony was that the businesses that did need to spend money on advertising for staff were country pubs, hotels and golf clubs, whose food offer was becoming an increasingly important part of their income, and for whom it was difficult to hold on to good chefs, and the rapidly growing sectors of event hospitality and outsourced government services, which gave large catering firms a constant requirement for professionals who could get the job done. They were all in the business of Catering and Hotel keeping. Glamour or not.

It didn't matter a jot that the paper's journalism was good, often breaking stories that were picked up by the National press, or that it gained an avid readership among small restaurateurs in London and fashionable café's in Brighton if no one spent any money in the back of the book. The magazine had failed completely in the rest of the country and piles of returns built up in the circulation department like hay bales.

Despite all this, X had done well in his first two months, banging his head against the brick wall harder than everybody else because he was new to it and the relentless monotony of cold calling and rejection had not yet broken his spirit. He'd sold more than anyone else had ever done before, largely because he hadn't known it was impossible, and he'd lucked out a few times when big sales had just fallen into his lap. Roger and Caroline had been delighted with their protégé, and when the slow-speaking posh girl, who'd managed to sell half a page of property into the classified section each week, despite a timid voice and a tendency to capitulate at the slightest sign of resistance, was finally sacked, X got her job.

The next part *had* been plain sailing. He'd sold property in a property boom.

With this lucky break it hadn't been hard for him to build up his reputation in the company. He' done the necessary graft, chased cafes and kebab shops in the Exchange and Mart and contacted the sellers of commercial properties with the appropriate licences by trawling through the local papers. After two months, he had built up the property section to three pages, and as the pages got busier he persuaded the specialists to take larger ads in order to stand out from the crowd. After three months he had added another page and a half, been promoted to 'assistant manager' and had a junior employee doing all the drudge work for him.

But in truth, as he quickly discovered, it wasn't strictly the number of column inches he sold that enabled his advance; much more important to his rise was his status as Roger's protégé. He quickly came to realise that the company functioned like a medieval court, where advancement was based more on the patronage of powerful individuals than any intrinsic merit. Championed by his publisher, X was automatically granted respect by the other members of Roger's faction, considered first as a promising young page then, following his promotion, as a young knight who might go on to great things; his further advance in the company assured as long as his patron's star continued to rise.

All he had to do was fit in.

It wasn't hard.

The other members of Roger's clique were mostly post-glamorous women in their mid-thirties, all in middle ranking positions in the company and all relentlessly jostling to move up. They could broadly be divided into two distinct groups. About half were brittle, thin and steely, their faces toughened by nicotine and late nights. This group tended to rule their sales teams as fierce tyrants and were often sleeping with someone else's husband. The others were softer, the good life showing in the other direction, as gravity worked harder on bigger breasts and buttocks, and figures that would have hit men like thunderbolts a few years previously now rolled over the top of miniskirts and filled fishnet stockings like bags of walnuts. X was invited to join them for white wine spritzers in the Dog and Duck before migrating to the Soho Brasserie in Old Compton Street, where he would squeeze lime into his bottle of Sol while the women fastened their faces to their giant goblets of red wine like snorkels. He listened dutifully to the endless gossip, and as nearly everyone in the company seemed to be fucking someone they weren't supposed to, the permutations were interminable. X only half-listened to their endless double-crosses and exposures, his indifference to each scandalous betrayal taken most commonly for acceptance, and as a consequence received regular deposits of tear-stained confidences from the drowning-waving women. After less than a month in the job he was the holder of many of the women's most intimate confessions, those normally granted only to their closest of friends, and even among them, only to those who could be trusted with keeping secrets.

X was good at that.

From his sessions in the Dog and Duck, he had learnt that Roger's star, which had burnt brightly enough to earn him the command of a lucrative weekly title, was beginning to wane as the magazine floundered, and he had already begun to prepare an exit strategy, aiming to jump ship to a design magazine he had coveted for some time. He would, of course, try to take as many of 'his people' with him if Restaurant and Café Bar News were to fold.

For his part, although X had control of the only part of the magazine that was making any money, he had consistently failed to sell any of the truly big players into its pages. The estate agents and auctioneers, who handled prestigious London restaurants and key Soho real estate, had rebuffed him at every turn. The biggest of them all, Smyth and Turkingtons, had proved entirely obdurate, their secretaries treating him like a peddler selling lucky heather when he called, and the one time he had managed to get through to Mr Turkington himself, his manner had been bored and disdainful to the point of rudeness. He had made it very clear to X that he thought his magazine to be no more than a rag, and considered the glossier pages and thick binding of their rival to be much more suited to a company as venerable as his. Months of short shrift from his PA had been followed by a letter demanding that he ceased pestering the company's secretaries forthwith, and then stated that Turkington and Smyths would not consider taking an advertisement without proof of the magazines effectiveness, and unless he was willing to offer them a free trial any further contact was futile. It added that they would only deign to take an advertisement if it consisted of a full colour ad on the inside back page.

It was a lot of coloured ink for a paper losing money to throw away for no return, so when Roger gave him permission to go ahead, X had suspected that it had been granted more from desperation than hope. Given the rising volume of whispers in the Dog and Duck and the increasing number of meetings conducted behind the closed door of Roger's office, X assumed that at this stage a little more red ink on the bottom line wasn't going to make much difference and that the magazine was already doomed.

The ad had been run, and he'd gone to the follow up meeting at Turkingtons expecting nothing, pleased, at least, that they hadn't cancelled. To X's great surprise, Mr Turkington himself had been present, sat behind an ornate Biedermeier desk in a blue pin-striped suit and flanked by two crepuscular colleagues in identical outfits. The old gentleman's opening address had been delivered in such a droning monotone, as though he were presenting the options on caskets to a grieving widow, that X had assumed that the news was bad, and it had taken X some time to register that the news was actually good, overwhelmingly good. Turkington announced that they would take an advertisement the following week, "the same copy", he added, but we want to change one of the properties. The agency will provide you with the new film."

X suddenly understood. They had sold one straight off the page! None of the properties had been valued at less than £500,000. They had made back a years' advertising costs from a free ad.

Turkington continued droning on in the same tone, "We will be taking the inside back cover, in full colour for the rest of the year, your rate card…" He ran a bony index finger with a surprisingly long nail down the page in the advertising pack he had never before even acknowledged receiving.

X began to sense money, big money, for the first time. His commission was going to be huge.

Turkington tapped the appropriate figure with his long nail, "£2,500 per week × 50. We calculate that as £125,000."

X struggled to contain his excitement. Nobody paid rate card. For a struggling magazine it was just an inflated figure used to discount from, but X began to suspect that Turkington might consider it beneath him to quibble over so small a sum, especially considering the windfall he had just had.

Turkington wasn't finished, moving his finger further down the list he announced, "And the discount for a year's series is 20%"

He would have had to tell them that anyway, but as they seemed to be willing to pay through the nose, he chose the moment to try and squeeze a little more out of them. "Yes", interrupted X, keeping his tone apologetic and deferential, "but as you require 'special placement' on the inside back page, there is an additional 20% charge. It's on the rate card, at the bottom of the next column I think you'll find." Special placement was almost a theoretical charge for RCBN. Only very successful magazines, where there was intense competition for space, could ever charge for it.

Turkington found the correct column and conferred briefly with his colleagues before nodding his reluctant agreement, "Very well, £125,000 it is. If you would care to arrange the appropriate paperwork right away, you may wait in the lobby while we check it over…"

But when he'd got back to the office with the big deal signed and sealed in his hand, it was already too late. The journalists were packing up their stuff and the sales team had already left, told to come back tomorrow to find out whether they had a future at the company.

The magazine had folded.

Roger and Caroline had tried one last appeal to the directors for at least a delay, on the basis that X's coup brought the whole title much closer to break even. The bid failed, and with its failure his fat commission evaporated, but X had made his mark. For the next few weeks, heads turned as he strutted down the corridors, Roger's dashing young prince, the almost messiah of RCBN. He slept with four women in the office in the following couple of months, almost certainly as a result of the kudos gained from the big sale. At least two of them hadn't even appeared to like him very much.

When it all shook out, Roger got his design magazine and took Caroline with him and X was found a place on a monthly magazine, aimed at the computer graphics and post-production industries that were largely based in Soho, called Virtual Television, a name which had always struck X as particularly dumb.

Everyone else got sacked.

Despite surviving the cull, it didn't at first look like the kind of place that anyone could advance from, even someone with X's enhanced reputation. The status of the magazine in the company's hierarchy could be measured by the contempt in which its long-serving publisher, Robert Benedict, was held. Robert was a balding little man in his late forties, with the charisma and dress sense of a minor office clerk, who had been at the company longer than anyone could remember. Roger's faction's view was that Robert was an utterly talentless nobody who had only survived as long as he had because the magazine continued ticking along making a little money each month, but never produced enough revenue for anyone to see it as a prize worth contesting him for. His lowly status was further demonstrated by his conspicuous lack of an office, and the unfortunate man was forced to attempt to maintain his dignity seated at a desk in the middle of the open plan like any common or garden salesman. Worse still for X's prospects, it was immediately apparent that Robert was horribly threatened by his arrival at Virtual TV, speaking to him from their very first meeting as though he had made an obscene gesture to his wife outside church, and thereafter making it a point of issue to disagree with any suggestion X made regardless of whatever value it may have had. Parachuted in to his magazine against his will, Robert was forced to put X at the opposite end of the sales desks from his own precarious position, and therefore obliged to conduct his daily business face to face with his hated rival as though X was a particularly distinguished dinner guest who had been given pride of place at the table.

Despite these difficulties X had, at least, been able to take comfort in another promotion. As a reward for services rendered on the now dead RCBN, he had been graced with a full manager's title, although only of the classified section and with hardly anyone to manage and no more money than before.

Command of the classified section on a dull monthly wasn't much to build a career on, consisting as it did of tiny ads for obscure equipment and incomprehensible services for the post-production industries, and page after page of short directory entries that rolled over year after year like a phone book.

But he'd lucked out again. This time his good fortune was Jeanne.

X worked out her value as soon as he met her. But he liked her too. Everyone did. Jeanne had been recruited to Virtual TV the week before X joined and was the only actual employee he had. She was a pretty Irish girl of twenty-four with red hair, shining blue eyes and a positive disposition. Most importantly, she had a voice men loved to listen to over the phone, something fresh and unsullied in the soft lilt of her West Coast accent seemed to conjure up a vision of County Claire in front of their eyes and they would listen to her sales patter as though they had been transported to its rocky coasts and Atlantic swells. Jeanne's voice was capable of beguiling men into making deals that their companies didn't really need for just the pleasure of having her call them. Her charm worked with women too, harridan secretaries would soften at her opening address, and making the instant assumption that she was the kind of lass who knew how to chat and gossip and keep secrets, would confide their most private intimacies with her. But her most miraculous effect was on a certain type of middle-aged man, the kind of pompous and self-regarding lecher who was normally a nightmare for female salespeople. Undoubtedly her looks were part of it, but she made no attempt to use her attractiveness in a flirtatious way, and her approach was instead innocent, natural and almost completely without guile. She accepted the attention of older men as something entirely to be expected, and in return for allowing them not to feel bad about looking at her, she expected to be treated with an old world courtesy in return. It worked. Instead of trying to wheedle her in to bed, they would offer her an arm to lean on rather than a wandering hand, opening doors and minding their language in her presence as though she were a favourite niece, just returned from university

He and Jeanne had set about the usual grind to begin with, sweating the small stuff, squeezing out a little more revenue from existing clients before chasing any new ones. It was easier than it should have been. It turned out that Robert's record system was inaccurate, hopelessly personalised and out of date. Just by chasing up annual orders that had been forgotten about or allowed to lapse and adding 10% for inflation each time they rebooked, they pushed the revenue up 12% in the first month. It was easy money, and as nobody had recorded a significant increase in profit on the magazine in five years he looked even more like a sales guru than before without having to do anything much at all.

There then followed a series of petty wars with Robert, but with the sales figures in front to him and Roger's patronage behind him, it was a very uneven contest. First there was a brief flurry about letting Jeanne go out on face-to-face visits, which was a clear no-brainer as far as X was concerned. But Robert insisted she wasn't of sufficient grade and didn't have enough experience and adamantly refused to allow it. X had openly defied him, declaring with the full pomposity of the righteous in a petty dispute that he was the manager of the back of the book and it was his right to make such decisions. Robert had complained about his behaviour upstairs but was ignored, and sales in X's section jumped another 15% entirely due to the impact of Jeanne's charm on the little post-production companies of Soho.

There were more, even more trivial arguments, but the final showdown came about over the use of spot blue, the ultimate outcome of which left Robert emasculated in the office and, fairly shortly after, out of a job. Having done the easy stuff and with no fresh ideas of how to increase income further, X had picked up on a comment of Jeanne's about how horrible the thick columns of house blue were in the classified section. He had made the suggestion to Robert as not much more than half a thought, "If we thin the columns", he had proposed, "and turn them black, we'll have more space on the page to sell and without this cheap and nasty spot blue we can sell the colour back on to the page." Robert had become apoplectic in response to this modest suggestion, "But it's the house colour!" he had spluttered, "it's always been the colour of Virtual Television…you've been here five minutes…you arrogant little shit…What else do you want to do? …put a hologram on the front page…? Change the name to X News eh!? Put a picture of your penis as a double page spread!?"

His rant had been wildly disproportionate to X's request, and as ridiculous as an old street drinker swinging punches at the air, but as Robert had no office to conduct his business in, it had been unleashed in full public view. Across the open plan people had put down their phones to listen in, and into the silence that followed his outburst, scarcely suppressed snorts of laughter rose from his own sales team, and a girl on Accountancy World was overcome with a fit of the giggles.

X passed the dispute up to Roger and, unrepresented at court, Robert was overruled. They got rid of the blue columns and X and Jeanne sold colour back onto the page. The classified revenue leapt a further 20%

And then he had been headhunted. A rival company had run into difficulties with their new weekly television magazine and his name had come up.

*

Before his interview at *New Television* had even begun, he knew was going to get the job and immediately began thinking about how far he could push his salary demands. It had only taken one look at Howard, his publisher-to-be, and X had known that the man in front of him was more vacuous, vain and superficial than anyone he had ever previously met in sales, and there had been plenty of contenders. He was a tall man with a stiffly upright posture and skinny, arms and legs that often completely escaped his control, flailing at elbow and knee like an agitated spider when he got excited. The thick rubbery lips on his pudgy face were set in a semi-permanent pout, and his eyes were hidden behind the kind of large dark sunglasses that Don Johnson would have worn to Miami Beach. His highlighted blond hair was swept into a feathered centre parting and lacquered into place by some kind a greasy gel, the residue of which had dripped onto his broad brow, peppering it with tiny red pimples like gnat bites.

X's interview had been delayed while Howard's tailor finished the final adjustment's on his new suit, and as his glass walled office was tiny, X couldn't even enter until his tailor had scuttled out backwards, exiting like a courtier departing from the royal presence.

The timing of the fitting was, of course, a coincidence.

Further evidence of the man's shallow vanity and lack of imagination was revealed in the sheer volume of clichéd status symbols scattered around the diminutive office. A black leather and chrome chair was squeezed behind a desk far too large for the space, and on its otherwise empty surface a Montblanc pen sat next to a silver framed photograph depicting Howard shaking hands with a balding golfer in a diamond check sweater. A pair of skis and an over-stuffed golf bag were propped against the wall, and to cap it all off, three scuffed polo mallets had been leant casually against the desk as though they had been flung down there after a hard chukka or two at Hurlingham.

When his tailor had left, Howard had shrugged a fresh navy jacket over his brightly striped shirt and braces, and taken two galumphing strides across the room in his tight faun slacks to shake X's hand with a manly vigour, looking him straight in the eyes as he did so saying, "Heard good things about you X".

X started wondering if he could get a car with the job.

Howard was certainly playing with a very weak hand. He let X know that he'd been drafted in from a golfing monthly and knew next to nothing about the television industry. He seemed to have little to offer in terms of ideas either, other than some convoluted management speak that he 'slapped on the table' as soon as the interview began. His expression of a determination to 'bash a few a heads together' and of not being concerned if "we have to break a few eggs to get things shaken up around here', gave X the impression that the man was quite close to being a simpleton.

Taking his cue from Howard's opening address, X responded with as many suitably assertive and thrusting phrases as he could muster. He 'cut to the chase' straight away and stressed the necessity of a 'pro-active strategy' and the need to 'gain a stranglehold' on market share and then followed up by bullshitting about his depth of knowledge of the industry from his time on Visual TV, safe in the knowledge that Howard had no means of catching him out. He allowed himself to let rip with the clichés, certain that the more his words sounded like they could have been said in 'Wall Street' the more Howard would like it, trying out phrases such as, 'he knew who was pissing on who', and claiming he 'knew where the bodies were buried', and concluding that it was 'better to be inside the tent, pissing out, than outside pissing in.' He briefly wondered if he might have overdone the urination metaphors, but decided that it would remind Howard of being in the cadets at his public school, and would pass as suitable manly behaviour between two rugged chaps such as themselves.

After he'd been in the room for no more than ten minutes, X knew he had Howard eating out of the palm of his hand and, seeing no need to delay the inevitable, was thinking of a suitably dynamic metaphor to close the deal on, when Howard saved him the trouble by offering him the job in his own inimitable style. He leaned back in his chair and raised both hands, shaping his fingers into twin pistol barrels and levelling them at X. Fixing him with a steely gaze, Howard cocked back his thumbs and then fired, making a clicking noise with the side of his mouth as he did so and miming the pistols' recoil as he released two imaginary bullets across the desk at X. "Click. Click. – You're the man for the job", he declared before blowing away the smoke from his finger pistols.

The performance was so hackneyed and absurd that in most other circumstances X would have burst out laughing, but he was determined to stay as deep in the bullshit zone as his interviewer, and seamlessly stepped up with his own cobblers, leaning forward with his face as square-jawed and serious as he could set it, he extended his hand and said, "You're right Howard, I am. Let's talk the package."

They'd talked the package and he'd got a car, although a Vauxhall Cavalier was hardly the hot hatch he had had in mind, but at least it was a car, and he'd secured a decent basic for the first time by violently exaggerating the wages he'd been getting at the other company. Howard had also been absurdly generous with his bonus arrangements. He'd immediately poached Jeanne from Virtual Television, doubling her wages and making her assistant manager.

Two months into the job, and Jeanne had begun to work her magic, but he didn't rate any of the rest of the sales team he had inherited, who appeared to be made up of the usual combination of failed actresses and middle class boys 'having a crack at sales' that drifted into this kind of work for want of anything better to do. He wasn't going to make any money with them, so he'd arranged the interviews without Howard's permission and without enough money in the budget to pay for any new staff should he find anyone suitable.

And now he had.

He suddenly felt he had listened enough.

"I'm going to stop you there", he said, "That you lasted a year at CNU tells me you can undoubtedly sell, and everything about your presence and the way you present yourself tells me you are absolutely right for the television market. I hope we'll make lots of money together. Just a few questions", he continued, "Why are you leaving CNU?"

She hesitated.

Later he wondered about that hesitation. Had it really been the nervousness before candour, or the pause she needed for a swift switch in her strategy. He'd made no response to her allure, so perhaps damsel in distress was a better gambit.

She was that good.

But if it was a bluff, it was brave one. She could have been labelling herself trouble.

"There was a problem", she explained, eyes lowered, "my line manager began to believe that he had certain…rights…over me. And when it was made clear to him in no uncertain terms that he didn't, I was suddenly getting all the dead end leads and quiet territories, kept away from the phones all day doing his admin…it got difficult."

He'd better not ask her out too quickly then.

He needed to finish this off. "OK, what are you getting as your basic at CNU?"

"£17,500"

None of us are really earning that much money, he thought. "And with bonuses?"

"I was getting another £8,000."

Shit. He didn't have anything like that available.

Then, picking up on the tense a second later he asked, "Was getting?"

"I've already left."

That might help. If she needed money to pay the rent he could probably squeeze her. No. That would be a bad way to start.

He stood up. "If you're willing to accept, I'd be delighted to offer you the job, but I need to check with accounts to see if we can at least match your previous salary. Can you wait in the lobby for about fifteen minutes?" he asked, "I'll get the receptionist to make you a drink – Don't leave the building without a contract!"

They shook on the deal.

He would have to bully Howard into getting him a GTI. There was no way this woman could be wooed in a Vauxhall Cavalier.

After she had left for the lobby he sat for a while until his head had cleared and he could think straight again. He let out a long breath and then pulled the performance review for Jessica out of a draw in Howard's desk. Jessica was a jolly hockey sticks girl, who always wore the same baggy sweatshirt and jeans to work and was characterised by a cheerful determination and indomitable spirit. Although she sometimes blustered her way past intimidated secretaries, she tended to bark at the businessmen she was supposed to be selling to as though she was herding reluctant ponies around a paddock. As time went on she had got put through less and less. Her effective call rate had dropped drastically and her sales figures were poor.

He poked his head out of the door.

"Jessica", he called out, "I'm bringing forward your review. Can you come into Howard's office now please?"

"Now? You want me to come off the phones now?" she called back.

"Yes – and bring the paperwork – you've already filled it in I hope?"

They sat on opposite sides of the desk comparing the scores they had allocated for each of the key indicators on her performance review. Jessica had graded herself good or excellent on every criteria, whereas X had ticked every single box as unsatisfactory, including, he now noticed, for personal hygiene, which was perhaps, a little unfair.

"I thought I was doing well", she pleaded, "I get along with everyone…"

"I'm afraid that's not my assessment", X responded, keeping his head down and his eyes fixed on the desk in front of him now that he could hear the first sobs breaking in the back of her throat. "The sales figures speak for themselves", he continued, keeping his voice deadpan and still without looking up.

She was sobbing a little now.

"They're not much worse than everyone else's." She was almost begging, her voice whiney, then suddenly rising in tone, "Look!" she was pointing at the performance review he had given her, "you've put *very unsatisfactory* for appearance – What's wrong with the way I look!" she was beginning to shriek now. "Tell me!" she demanded, "Say something!"

She was becoming hysterical and he needed to get this over quickly, so he stood, looked directly at her and spoke with blunt brutality, "This is the television business, and the only people who dress like you are gaffers and lighting riggers. If you ever chose this line of work again, and I suggest you don't – Have a think about that."

His change in tone had stopped her in her tracks, and she slumped back into her chair, her voice suddenly timid, and she could only mumble now through her tears, "What happens now?"

"You collect your belongings from your desk and leave. You will be sent a check that covers your wages up to the end of your probationary period."

"I go? Now? Straight away?" She was stunned.

"Yes", he said crossing the room to the door, "You've just been sacked."

The last phrase dragged wrenching sobs out of Jessica, and X swiftly closed the door behind him to give her some time to pull herself together in private and so that her distress wouldn't distract the rest of the sales team.

He ran downstairs and offered the job to Sara, adding an extra £2,000 on her bonus if she doubled sales in the next six months, having comfortably enough money in the budget now that Jessica was gone.

He could clear it all with Howard later.

11. NOTTING HILL PILL

It had seemed the perfect way to celebrate his acquisition of Sara when Paul had called and invited him to go to Carnival with him that weekend. He had hardly seen Paul over the last year, and had half-assumed their friendship was over so it had seemed like the purest synchronicity that his old friend had got in touch with him on that very day. X had been quite moved when he called, but after putting the phone down he had remembered that Paul always went to Carnival with a load of old school friends he hardly knew, and recalling how awkward things had been between them when they last met, he'd rung Toby to ensure he had someone to talk to if it got at all difficult with Paul.

He needn't have worried. Carnival was Carnival after all, and either the general good spirit of the festival had infected him or Paul was truly delighted to see him, and there were tears in his eyes when he'd hugged him in the crush outside Ladbroke Grove station. That Paul had immediately taken charge was no problem for X either; someone needed to, and he had been quite happy to follow in his wake as Paul led his crew through the packed crowds to the sound system he always insisted they went to, one that set up round the back of Trellick tower, and played the kind of reggae that Paul loved. Toby had been happy enough as they had swayed along behind the floats pumping out soca and danced by youth groups banging away at steel drums, but when they had reached their destination he began to look distinctly nervous.

X could understand. He wouldn't ordinarily come on to this estate either, it had a bad reputation, and the tower block, looming above them like a villain's fortress in red sandstone, gave the sensation of a thousand blank eyes staring down at them malevolently from its heights. But everyone had a day pass for carnival, and as long as they were gone before it got dark, when the police tried to shut the systems down and it all got nasty very quickly, there was no cause for alarm, and he said as much to Toby, trying to put him at his ease.

But Toby wasn't convinced. He was sure he'd heard someone

mutter 'batty boy' as he'd pushed passed, and he kept anxiously looking over his shoulder, convinced that at any moment someone was going to slide up to him and slip a knife between his ribs before disappearing into the crowd.

X looked around. Toby just seemed paranoid to him. It was busy where they stood, but not a true carnival crush, and everyone seemed happy and relaxed. A Rasta family was moving to the rhythm in unison beside them; mum, dad and little brother, no more than ten years old, all providing guard for the toddler jittering between their legs. Couples and small groups swayed lazily around them and the air was drenched with the sweet smell of cannabis. They were so close to the canal that when the MC stopped chatting and the bass died down for a moment, he could hear the sound of ducks quacking on its banks. The atmosphere was peaceful and entirely mellow.

One of Paul's mates was handing out pills, and without thinking much about it, he'd handed over a tenner and swallowed one with a gulp of Red Stripe, it tasted bitter and chalky going down.

"What are they?" he asked Paul belatedly.

Paul shrugged, "Dunno, could be MDMA, might be acid," he replied, "Steve said they were good", he added.

Shit, thought X, unsure if taking acid at carnival was a good idea, and not certain what MDMA was. And who the fuck was Steve anyway? He noticed that Toby had declined. Good. At least one of us is straight if things go awry.

Ten minutes after taking the pill he felt a surge of emotion rising in his chest, a sudden overwhelming affection for the people he'd come with that spread out from him in pulse after pulse of joy and love to encompass the whole crowd. They were all so beautiful, he wanted to cry out and tell them so. He looked up to the sky in celebration of the beauty of the world and found that the light was falling from the sun on to his face in thick golden streams like honey, and he licked his lips to taste the sunlight as it fell. Through the beams, the tower block above him was no longer sinister and menacing, but was now revealed to be what it really was, a rocket-ship built to colonise the stars, frozen in place at the exact moment of its lift off. As he looked, the free-standing lift shaft that rose beside the tower began to peel off at the tip, falling away like a gantry at Cape Canaveral, its concrete cracking and crumbling, folding in on itself in a series of explosions of plaster and brick dust down its length. He could feel the giant thrusters beneath its foundations igniting, the deafening roar as the rocket fuel caught fire, the ground shaking beneath his feet…

And then he was gone…

12. EUGENICS

He stepped out of the warm spring day and into the deep shade of the tunnel, crossing the razor-sharp line that divided the light from the darkness. The air was instantly cold. Around him, other people were moving through the passage, each suddenly quickening their pace as they entered, as though the dank chill of the tunnel had made them all collectively late for an appointment. Far ahead, the exit was visible as a shining arch of light, seemingly floating detached from the darkness and as richly coloured as a cathedral's stained glass.

He speeded up and, matching the pace of those around him, was swept through the dark passage and out into the bright sunlight once more. Ahead of him, a white marble fountain, set at the centre of a circular piazza, threw sprays of crystal-clear water up into the bright blue cloudless sky. Cyclists and pedestrians hurried along pathways and groups of picnickers lounged on the electric green grass. He turned around to see where he had just come from, and was shocked to see a bone-white clock tower rising hundreds of feet above him, its gargantuan height making the long tunnel he had just walked through appear no more than the bore hole of a weevil in its base.

He knew where he was now. He had passed through the ivory tower. He was at university.

To either side of the tower, and in the same spirit of gigantism, a vast array of stone steps swept in a shallow arc into the far distance and rose up, tier upon tier, at least twenty metres above where he stood until they reached the palatial building that ran the full length of the terrace at its crest. The building itself resembled half a dozen Winter Palaces laid end to end, each of its six floors fronted by great curved windows that flung back the reflected light of the sun. Despite the immense sweep of the steps and the edifice above, the impression they gave was of something incomplete, a perfectly preserved ruin that represented only a surviving fragment of a much larger amphitheatre that had once completed the full circle of its gradual curve, and must have constituted a structure so large that the colossus of Rhodes would have been merely a piece of decorative statuary on its circumference. Students sat in groups or lay on their backs in the sun on almost every tier, crowding the nearby steps and peppering the terraces full span, receding to mere dots at its furthest reach, where invisible currents and counter-currents washed them up and down the steps in waves like particles of sand stirred up by breakers crashing onto a beach.

X systematically scanned the steps nearest to him until he spotted Eva and Pooja, sitting together about ten rows above him, he waved and started climbing the terrace toward them. Pooja spotted him when he was a few levels below their perch and roused Eva. They were both smiling when he reached them.

He had done little more than press foreheads with the two young women when Eva had brusquely excused herself and headed off down the terrace steps.

Had she left because of him?

Nothing in Pooja's manner seemed to warrant his fear. She greeted him as an old friend, expressing regret that it had been so long since they had last seen him and offered to share her lunch while uttering conventional pleasantries about the weather and the beauty of the day. Seeing the concerned look on his face, Pooja interpreted his anxiety correctly and put him at his ease, "Goodness X, it's not you", she laughed, "it's Erika – look!" She pointed down the terrace in the direction Eva had departed.

X made out Erika in the crowd, working her way determinedly up the steps toward them and then spotted Eva, swerving between bodies as she skipped down the terrace, clearly set on an intercept course with the older woman some thirty or so rows below them.

He allowed himself to relax, assuming that Eva would return once she had completed her business with Erika, and leant back against the cool stone, shading his eyes from the glare of the sun and scanning the view in front of him. They were seated to the right of the central piazza, opposite an open-air swimming pool, and whoops of delight and the splashes of divers tumbling gracefully from the high boards filled the air. It was Pooja who drew his attention back to Eva, shaking her head as she looked down at her friend, "Eva will be really annoyed", she said through pursed lips.

Below, Eva had stopped with her back to them, standing a step higher than Erika. She had drawn herself up to her full height and her hands were planted squarely on her hips. The two women were too far away for X to overhear the exchange but he suspected Pooja was right, Eva's body language certainly looked confrontational.

"I know she'd sorted this out with Tasan", Pooja commented, "Erika is being really naughty here.'

X looked over at her. She was frowning down at the scene below them, "She knows she's in the wrong. She'll back down. See", she exclaimed, clapping her hands in delight. Erika had indeed backed down and was now retreating down the steps toward the piazza. Eva turned and began striding back up the terrace steps toward them.

Pooja was smiling now. "Really X, that Erika Hämstrong must be the pushiest tutor on campus, she just never leaves Eva alone....

"Sorry about that X", Eva said when she had re-joined them, "it's great to see you again". She sat down next to him, slipped her sunglasses down over her eyes once more, and the three of them sat in silence for a while, enjoying the warmth of the sun's rays on their skin. Aware that with her glasses down, Eva could be reading a novel or watching a film, he left her undisturbed and, largely for the sake of making conversation, asked Pooja, if her tutor was as pushy as Erika. Out of the corner of his eye, he thought he saw Eva stiffen at his question, but she seemed to relax as soon as Pooja began to reply,

"No," she replied, "He's actually a rather brilliant man - Just cares about the research - Obsessive really - like Erika in that way, I suppose, but drives himself much harder than he does anyone else. Cares about it much more than I do I'm afraid! Don't get me wrong", she continued, "the work is terribly fascinating and important but...", she looked suddenly embarrassed as she said it, "part of me would much rather be doodling about in a studio making furniture than in a laboratory measuring prions or sequencing nucleotides – and the implications of the work are......well......complicated...."

Eva sat upright, "Its time", she said, and both women got to their feet. "You too X", she commanded, "You are at university now. Come and attend your first lecture…"

*

As they walked out of the lecture hall and down the terrace steps, X's mind was still reeling. It had been like no lecture he had ever attended and he was struggling to get his head round the implications of what he had heard.

At first he had just been surprised that he was enjoying a university lecture at all. The tutor had been articulate and witty and his presentation full of interesting audio- visual feeds, theatrical tricks and practical demonstrations, but it was the students who had amazed him more. The whole event had been remarkably participative, but rather than a series of irritating interruptions where speakers from the floor droned on about their own hobby horses and obsessions as was his experience, the students had effortlessly embraced the key components of the argument, and when they rose to speak asked exactly the question needed answering, or raised precisely the objection that needed to be raised. X felt intellectually enlivened by the experience, privileged to have been there and even a little humbled to have been part of such a cerebral crowd.

And what he had learnt had been astonishing.

The tutor had explained; as background to the rest of the class, but with the power of revelation to X, that as the early stages of human embryonic development now routinely took place *in vitro* before being returned for gestation in the womb it was taken as a given that genetic engineering was the destiny of all future humans. He commented that since the human genome had long since been completely de-coded, and with the rapid advances in stem-cell technology, it was now customary to prevent the development of deleterious genetic conditions before the number of cell divisions had reached five figures. The tutor then reeled off a long list of debilitating conditions that no longer existed, from cystic fibrosis, Spina Bifida, through Parkinson's disease and early onset Alzheimer's. X couldn't remember them all, but he was certain obesity had been listed along with Schizophrenia and Tourette's syndrome. X had been amazed. To his mind this seemed the greatest advance for human kind since *Homo Erectus* had first kindled fire, but the tutor had stopped well short of vainglory and proceeded rapidly to articulate the fears and ethical issues that these advances had generated. X recalled him saying that, un-tempered, this would create a 'god-like assumption for what the correct form of a human being should be', and described the developments as having the potential to "murder the imagination', going on to say that they represented an opportunity to engender a kind of "foetal genocide of all the infinite possibilities of human kind'.

But just as X was mentally backtracking he was shocked forwards again. The tutor had gone on to argue that the conundrum had at least been partly resolved. Given that any gene that had been switched off could potentially be switched back on again, the solution to the problem was already in hand. As they were aware, he continued, every adult was given the right to examine their full genetic inheritance when they came of age, and with the knowledge of which genes from their original inheritance had been activated or supressed, could chose to have any such changes reversed. He had pointed out that few had elected to restore early renal failure, Crohn's disease or lactose intolerance...

X had sat back in his seat at this point, dwelling on this marriage of liberal and scientific principles, but before he could allow any of his comfortable conclusions to embed themselves, an objection was raised from the floor. The speaker's argument was that much of this reversibility was illusory. Embryonic development was interfered with at such an early stage that it ensured the gross development of the body along the engineered lines and only a tinkering at the edges was possible in adulthood. The tutor had acknowledged the validity of the student's argument and then gone on to outline what he called the 'clone-suicide solution'. He explained that anyone wishing to make fundamental changes to their genome could opt for an unaltered clone to be grown. The clone, when it reached adulthood would concomitantly have the right to accept or reject any further engineering. The individual could thus be in total control of their genetic destiny. He pointed out, however, that as multiplication through cloning had rightly been declared inadmissible, the individual concerned would have to commit suicide in order to grant his or her clone the freedom of choice they desired for themselves. The lecture hall had broken out in uproar at this point.

The tutor, once he had regained sufficient control to continue had suggested that there was a lecture tomorrow on the subject in this very theatre, and an undergraduate led debate the following afternoon. He closed up by suggesting a number of useful sources for study, and stayed behind to answer individual questions.

They strolled down the steps and out into the early evening air, the three of them meandering lazily through the birch –

shaded avenues of the campus, light dancing above them as they walked in the tree's flickering shade; Their walk led them out of the university grounds and into a field of long meadow grass bordered by a fast flowing stream that formed the boundary of the campus itself. On the opposite bank, the terrace of a student café sat above the stream, its tables crowded with scholars dining al fresco in the fine evening air. Eva chose patch of grass on the stream's bank and they lay in the long grass watching the bustle of activity on the far bank.

They had been discussing the lecture in fits and starts as they had walked and Eva picked up the thread, "Of course Jorgund", she started, made the active decision to be bald. He said that the males in his family had always lost their hair young and he wanted to keep up the tradition. So they reactivated the male pattern baldness gene for him- he lost his hair quite quickly - I don't think he even shaves the sides now."

"Most men don't chose to reactivate the gene, I suppose", suggested X.

"No", Eva laughed, "all Olaf's male ancestors were completely bald by twenty-four."

X felt quite smug at this small revelation, although in practical terms it didn't benefit him at all.

Eva had continued on a different tack, "That's another aspect", she started, "Once you accept the complete malleability of the genome you can add features, not just replace some missing proteins, but splice in stuff that was never previously there."

X didn't fully understand, "What do you mean?" he asked.

"You want a prehensile tail?"

"Yuk", Pooja interjected.

X thought about it, coming to the conclusion that it might be cool. Perhaps he'd get a furry one, like a lemur's.

"Well if you did, you could have it. Fancy eyesight like an eagle's? Done. A dog's sense of smell? It's yours. All possible. Not here", Eva continued, "but some places have gone much further down that road." She contemplated the thought for a moment, "I don't know", she carried on, "my first thought is repulsion."

"Mine too", Pooja called out.

"But perhaps we are just being narrow-minded, it is a question of aesthetics more than ethics, No?"

All day, X had felt a step behind everyone else. As soon as he felt he'd caught up, they moved on into another area he hadn't even thought about. There was so much he needed to learn just to be able to keep pace. He felt like he had to attend crash courses on philosophy and ethics at least, and maybe ones on microbiology and genetics too, and he voiced his thoughts to the two women.

They responded by laughing and clapping their hands in unison.

"Well said", Pooja had responded, "Welcome to the club!'

Basking in their praise, X felt more confident in his questions, and part of Eva's earlier answer had nagged at him, "You said that some places had gone much further down the road with genetic changes', he asked, adding, "So there are more radically experimental places then?"

"Yes", Eva replied, "and not that far from here X. Maybe we will all go and have a look someday!"

"Count me out", said Pooja.

Eva shrugged, "Who knows", she mused, "Maybe they are closer to Sweden than us…"

So this wasn't Sweden? Where was he then?

The thought was interrupted as Eva suddenly leapt to her feet and begun waving furiously, swinging both her arms around in a windmill fashion. "Hey Olaf!" she shouted, "Over here!"

Eva's cry attracted the attention of a jogger who had been heading toward the café from the open fields across a wooden footbridge at the end of the meadow. He paused in mid-stride, looking for the source of the cry and, catching sight of the leaping blond, waved, reversed direction and quickened his pace, disappearing into a small copse at the meadow end of the bridge. He re-emerged in the field, sprinting towards them, leaping over tussocks of grass with long, confident strides. Eva ran toward him in the opposite direction.

X felt sick. It was like a fucking Mills and Boon novel. The whole scene felt like it should have been shot in soft focus. He turned away at the moment of their embrace.

When he turned back a muscular, sweaty, dark-haired man was advancing across the field towards him with Eva hanging on his arm…

STILL TRIPPING

He could feel the bass pounding in his chest, someone toasting over the rhythm, the noises of the crowd and then a familiar voice nearby.

He was back at Carnival.

"Fucking Olaf."

He must have spoken out loud, because Toby's voice immediately responded.

"Did you say something X?" The voice was worried.

X nodded. It was the best he could manage.

"You haven't said a word for an hour, even when I was talking directly at you." The anxiety in Toby's voice was palpable.

He had managed to stay on his feet this time. That was a first. He wiped his mouth. No drool. That was a first too. "I just tripped out a bit there…" he managed to mumble as Toby's anguished face swam back into view, "…. The pill came on really fast…"

Toby didn't look greatly reassured, and he took advantage of a small surge in the crowd to slip away. He was back from the dream, but if the pill had been acid, he still had a long way to go, and Toby's hyper-anxious presence was like fingernails down a blackboard in his delicate state.

He stumbled away, looking around for Paul, who would at least be in the same state as him, but as he turned his head to scan the crowd, the whole scene whipped around much faster than his head had turned, and everything became bright and blurry as though he were at the centre of a spinning magic lantern, and he was gone again…

13. EDUCATION

He was sitting on a broad terrace overlooking an open meadow of long grass bordered by a fast-flowing stream. On the table in front of him sat a half-drunk cup of coffee and a wafer-thin hand held electronic screen. He picked up the device. It displayed a map of the university and an academic timetable. Moving his hand across it, he brought the timetable into focus. It laid out a concentrated six-week course of lectures and tutorials in philosophy, economics, sociology, history, psychology, computing, microbiology and genetics. It was a tightly packed schedule with lectures beginning at 8 am and running through to the early evening. Any gaps in the academic programme were filled with physical activities ranging from power-walking to gymnastics. He looked up from the screen.

Erika was sitting directly opposite him and broke off her conversation with Eva to acknowledge his arrival. "Ah, there you are", she declared.

At Erika's words Eva looked up, letting out a short shriek of surprise that caused heads on the neighbouring tables to turn in their direction and earned a disapproving glare from Erika. "I'll never get used to that", she mumbled, before rising to greet X warmly, "Welcome back!" she whispered as they pressed foreheads, and he felt his heart skip a beat at her words.

Erika took control immediately. "You have your study programme in front of you X, and Eva will escort to your first lecture" she said tersely, "and as we agreed Eva, I will leave you to it. But understand that I am expecting thorough, focused scholarship and reports written with appropriate rigour this time."

Eva had smiled wanly, "Come on X", she said, "There is much to do."

And there was.

Every day he tore back and forth across the campus, panting up and down the steps of the clock-tower block, racing across the piazza into the sociology building or the philosophy block, or wherever his next lecture was, checking his schedule only to discover he needed to get over to the sports complex on the far side of the campus for gymnastics or handball or athletics practise. Every day he slipped into the back seats of the lecture halls, invariably late, disturbing the other scholars as he squeezed past, carefully taking notes on a hand-held screen. At the end of every day he was so exhausted that he fell instantly into a deep, dreamless sleep, waking in the mornings as though he had only just closed his eyes. The delight he took in learning came as a complete surprise to him. He found himself fascinated by philosophy, sociology and psychology, but he struggled badly in economics and had to be put in a special, kindergarten class for computing. Even in computing he tried his best although his skills were so poor that he often had to seek help from the nine-year boy who sat next to him. His embarrassment was mitigated by the presence of Jorgund, the only other adult in the classroom, the pair of them often breaking into giggles when they caught sight of each other's bewildered expressions before being shushed by the serious pre-teens around them. Only in microbiology did he lose interest completely and was soon skipping the class altogether, idling away the allocated hours in the student café, or watching the ebb and flow of humanity from the clock tower steps.

He was learning at a furious pace, but seemed to forget

everything at a furious pace too. Subjected to regular cross-examinations about his progress by Erika and Tasan, he became quite adept at blending snippets of data with sweeping, generalised statements, giving the appearance of having a much broader grasp of each subject than he actually had. At first he had found the strange paternalism of Eva's tutors both perplexing and intrusive, but as time went on he began to consider it in a different light, imagining their behaviour as akin to that of a girlfriend's parents, nervously checking up on the attitude and achievements of their daughter's beau, and he began to take their Q & A as evidence of his progress with Eva.

And it was going well. He got to spend at least part of every day with her, in lectures, on the sports field and in long evening sessions on the terrace café. He often made her laugh, and she was always highly attentive to whatever he had to say, asking him endless questions and patiently listening to his every reply. As the weeks passed he was certain that the number of times she mentioned Olaf grew less and less.

They weren't together all the time, however, Eva took her education very seriously and was often studying in the glass pyramidal building opposite the sociology block. His programme of lectures never took him into her building and having failed to ask what subject she was majoring in when they'd first met, it became embarrassing to ask her after so much time had lapsed. Neither she nor her tutors ever seemed to offer any useful clues, and the one time he had asked Pooja directly, she had been so vague that it was almost as though she was being deliberately evasive. After much prevarication, Pooja had finally given a description of Eva's work as some form of cultural studies, and X had given up, assigning her lack of clarity to one of the confusions in translation that came up from time to time. After a while he found that it was perfectly possible to avoid the subject altogether in the way that you could hide your forgetting of an old acquaintance's name almost indefinitely provided you were never asked to introduce them to someone else.

In the third week, disaster struck.

It turned out that Olaf had merely been away on some polar expedition rather than forgotten about altogether, or as X had begun to hope, chucked. Now he was back with seemingly nothing to do other than occupy the seat at the café next to Eva that had previously belonged to X, entertaining the crowd while Eva hung off his arm. He found Olaf immensely tedious and extremely irritating, and couldn't understand why Eva was so taken with him. As far as he could see, Olaf was forever talking about himself, either boring on about marine biology or boasting about the perils of deep water dives he had undertaken. But Eva was clearly smitten. In the cafe she listened tirelessly to his repetitive stories, her face turned up to his reverentially as he spoke, laughing uproariously at his tepid witticisms and leaning forward to sweep the curls of his jet black hair away from his face. X had to acknowledge that Olaf was very good-looking, with his romantic poet's curly locks, athlete's body and square-jawed masculinity, but of all people, he would have expected Eva to be more concerned with substance than style. Worse still, Olaf exuded the unflappable self-confidence of the Alpha male, and duly treated X with an unthreatened decency; his conviviality built on what X took to be an unquestioned assumption of his innate superiority.

His animosity to Olaf was brought to a peak during an afternoon on the handball court. A succession of balls in the face, stumbles to the ground and Olaf's, hearty, patronising encouragement, had left X desperate to punch him in the face, and from then on he began to take elaborate precautions to avoid spending time with him, making a swift exit from the café whenever he caught sight of the happy couple at one of the tables.

    From then on, X began spending as much time with Eva's friends as Eva herself. He grew closest to Sven, who was consistently kind, generous and patient in his dealings with him, and it was his company he usually sought out when Eva was with Olaf. It was only Sven who persisted in trying to teach X how to master the sunglasses, approaching the task with the same methodical patience and attention to detail he employed in constructing his racing bikes, hoping that if he could break down the actions into their simplest components, X would eventually be able to grasp this essential tool of their society. During one of these sessions he had explained that the glasses were transmitters as well as receivers, continuously emitting a range of baseline data to anyone close enough to pick up the signal. "We need to get you set up X", he had explained, "Without it, you are invisible to everyone else, like some kind of a ghost!" X was willing to try, as much in gratitude for his friend's persistence as in any hope of success, and with Sven standing motionless in front of him, he had focussed on the red dot that Sven explained contained his personal data transmissions. He blinked to capture the information as he had been taught, and then read through the display on the inside of his glasses. Pleased with his success, and warming to his task, he was able to read off Sven's age, his hobbies and interests and some of his likes and dislikes. Trying to avoid garnering any more information than he cared to know about the manufacture of racing bikes, he moved his eyes a fraction down to a male symbol. It listed Sven's sexuality and some of his preferences in a partner. Sven was gay. No one had even bothered to mention it before.

But why would they when the information was freely available to everyone who had a pair of glasses? Later he had asked Pooja why so much intimate data was made available to complete strangers, but she hadn't really understood his question and his attempts to steer her in the direction he required had led to a long and complicated lecture on the seven genders and nine degrees of intensity that human sexuality was apparently divided into.

He tried the glasses again several times under Sven's guidance but eventually even his friend accepted the inevitable, and X resigned himself to his ghost status, walking amongst these phenomenally open people as the only closed book on the shelf, the one unknowable node in a world where hearts were displayed nakedly on every sleeve.

Despite the kindness of Eva's friends, X was still on his own a great deal. Sven was often busy with his bikes and Pooja was absent at least three times a week, earning her keep as a social worker down in the city. Jorgund turned up from time to time, popping in for short courses in the health and social care department, and X sometimes bumped into him in the café, as ebullient and enthusiastic as ever, knowing everybody and greeting all with high-fives and whoops of joy. But Jorgund got tiresome after a while and by the fifth week X was becoming quite lonely. It was therefore with unbridled delight that he received the news that Olaf had unexpectedly departed on another expedition, this time to the Antarctic. Once more he could spend endless delightful hours under the gaze of Eva's bewitching blue eyes, and he began to believe that her attachment to him was growing into something greater than mere friendship.

*

On the Friday of his sixth week of study, he had skipped microbiology again and was wondering what to do with the hour until his next lecture, when he saw Tasan waving to him from the entrance of his faculty building. Dreading another cross-examination about his academic progress, he trudged reluctantly over to the old man. After they had pressed foreheads Tasan kept hold of his shoulders, scrutinising X's face with a strange intensity, as though he was examining a fascinating artefact behind a glass case in a museum. Seemingly satisfied with what he saw, Tasan broke into his familiar Buddha-like grin, and still smiling, guided him through the sliding glass doors with his arm around his shoulder. X had never crossed the building's threshold before, and as they entered he felt that he was transgressing; trespassing somehow on ground that had been expressly forbidden to him.

Entering Tasan's office on the top floor amplified his sense of unease. The room was claustrophobically small and riotously disordered. Huge African tribal masks leered down from its walls, anthropomorphic animal deities with hideously bulging eyes and twisted orange rope manes hung above a room in such a state of disarray that it resembled a junk shop that had been ransacked during a burglary. Stone jars with the heads of jackals, curved bronze knives and stone axes spilled from the shelves and lay scattered on the carpet in heaps. A man-sized bronze bull pressed it's flanks against the desk and Tasan was obliged to sweep a pile of animal bones off the only chair in the room to enable X to sit, positioning him with a gape-mouthed black and ochre monster hovering only inches above his head.

He closed his eyes and tried to recall what he had studied since his last interrogation. Nothing came to mind.

When he opened his eyes again he found that Erika had entered the room. She was carrying an uncorked bottle of wine and three glasses, and seemed to be in an unusually buoyant mood. She staggered a little as they embraced, slopping some wine on to the floor as she did so, and held the press for a long time, the strong smell of alcohol on her breath making him feel queasy. When they broke, she stood inches from him, a lopsided smile on her face.

"Are you happy here X?" she asked him.

It wasn't the question he had been expecting but when he thought of Eva, Sven and Pooja and the café by the stream the answer was simple, "Yes", he replied "Yes I am."

Erika's response was to pull him into a tight embrace, and with her body pressed up against him she began gently stroking his hair while looking deeply into his eyes. When she spoke again her voice was soft, cooing, almost flirtatious, "And we're very impressed with you", she said.

X was powerfully disturbed once more. What was going on here? Who were these people? What did they want from him? He suddenly felt horribly, hopelessly lost. He didn't even know where he was.

"Am I in Sweden?" he asked, his voice timid and wavering.

As he asked the question he felt dizzy and his vision began to blur. He closed his eyes and when he opened them again, Erika's lascivious smile and Tasan's Cheshire cat grin seemed to have detached themselves from their faces and begun to merge with the distorted countenances on the walls. A loud drumming sound filled his ears and the masks began to advance towards him, opening their gaping mouths to swallow him whole. He stood up and immediately toppled over. The floor hurtled towards him and the room went pitch black.

All that remained in the darkness were his racing thoughts.

But I've never been to Sweden.

How did I get here?

The darkness was swept away by a sudden vivid flashback – the gallery – the easel –the painting. He rounded the back of the canvas. It was his face superimposed on the painting, screaming open-mouthed but silently into the void.

Darkness again, and then a voice in the darkness.

He opened his eyes. Tasan was leaning over him. "My dear boy", he was saying, "Please. There is no need for alarm."

Strong arms reached down and helped him up, and he was gently manoeuvred into a chair. He could feel Erika's hand resting softly on his shoulder and she spoke to him in a soft, slightly slurred voice "You are not in Sweden", she confirmed, "but if you were...that would be no cause for dismay...quite the opposite." He was offered a glass of water. He took a sip., "Sweden is..." her voice trailed off, "but that you must determine for yourself. But we invited you here because we believe that you have begun your journey to Sweden....and we wish to celebrate that with you."

His strength was beginning to return and with it a rising sense of embarrassment at his sudden fainting fit. He started to apologise.

Tasan cut him off. "We cannot be absolutely sure, but all the signs indicate that you are indeed, what we call a 'Seeker of Sweden', it is a high accolade..." He laughed, "But this has all gone completely wrong. We must start again."

Erika put a glass of wine in X's hand, although he hardly had the strength to raise it, let alone the inclination to drink any.

"A toast", she declared, "To a seeker of Sweden!" and they both raised their glasses...

CARNIVAL HANGOVER

He opened his eyes, but for a long time he remained completely blind.

His senses returned in strict order.

First smell.

The stench of rotting food, cigarette butts, puke and dog shit. Without the other senses they encompassed his whole universe, overwhelming him, pouring down his throat with each inhalation of breath, making him gag on his own rising vomit.

Taste.

Bile and sick in his mouth, flavours of rotten food on his tongue either rising from his guts or being forced down his throat.

He began to panic. He had been thrown in a garbage truck, he was buried in landfill; he was drowning in sewage. He couldn't move a muscle.

Then touch.

He wasn't buried.

His head was raised higher than the rest of his body and cushioned by something. His cheek was stuck to its damp plastic surface and his left shoulder and upper arm lay across it as though he was hugging a lumpy bean bag. His lower body was pressed hard and cold against the ground. He was lying on his side with his head on a garbage bag.

He held his breath.

When sound returned it told him little more, a solitary dog barking in the distance, the whoosh of a car passing by perhaps a block away, a siren in the far distance.

Sight.

He lay in a pile of rubbish at the end of a short alleyway. Unable to raise his head above the garbage, his tilted horizontal view revealed only grey concrete walls dimly lit by a streetlamp at the end of the alley.

As soon as he could manage, he struggled to his feet, holding on to a wheelie bin for support, taking care not to slip on the damp cardboard and bottles of stout that lay like skittles on the pavement around him.

He padded himself down. Nothing broken, but every part of him felt stiff and bruised.

Where the fuck was he?

What time was it?

What fucking day was it?

Before he had staggered the full length of the alleyway, he had caught sight of Trellick Tower above the rooftops. He was still in Ladbroke Grove. The street was quiet, almost deserted. Most likely early morning.

He checked his pockets. His wallet was gone. Fuck.

He had no money and stank like an incontinent drunk. Not much chance of a taxi then.

He began the long walk back to Hammersmith, slapping his chest with his arms to restore circulation to his atrophied limbs, his gait as stiff as a scarecrow's and with a volcanic headache pounding at his temples. Muttering as he walked like a lunatic, he alternately cursed Paul for stiffing him with a dodgy pill and himself for being stupid enough to take one.

Passing a newsagent in Goldbourne Road, he checked the date on the top copy of bundle of newly delivered papers outside its closed doors.

Tuesday 30th August.

He'd been out the whole carnival weekend.

14. FIRST DATE?

Three months of working together, and he had got nowhere with her at all. Everything else, on the other hand, was progressing nicely.

Although he had been thinking mostly with his cock when he had recruited Sara, he had had plenty of opportunity since to reflect on the brilliant instincts of his member. Sara was another Jeanne. Better, if anything.

She had established her position in the office hierarchy by 9am on her very first day. Arriving earlier than anyone else, she had selected a desk at the head of the sales team opposite Jeanne, cleared away the ashtray and arranged her notepad and pens neatly in front of her. By the time X had arrived at eight-thirty, she had worked her way through a stack of back issues of New TV, and was adding another to the large pile on the floor by her feet. Poised elegantly on the edge of chair in her sleeveless navy-blue mini-dress, the very electricity of her presence was enough to transform the drab office into somewhere exciting and full of possibilities. She had a mesmeric effect on the rest of the sales team as they dribbled into work that Monday morning, bleary-eyed, sipping strong coffee to kick themselves awake, yawning, already bored by the day ahead and trying to shorten it as much as possible by clocking in at the very last moment. Exiting the lifts in their jeans and trainers, they paused at the sight of the sudden explosion of glamour that had appeared at the head of their table, and instinctively lowered their eyes as though they were serfs doffing their caps in the presence of royalty. Two of the identikit women who sold display advertising, tottering in later like air hostesses with their bleach blond hair and salon tans, stopped dead in their tracks at the sight of her, and when they resumed motion, gave her desk a wide berth as though they trailed phantom wheeled luggage.

X was unsurprised by this establishment of the natural order, but had been concerned how Jeanne would react to another powerful woman's presence in the office, having been the solitary golden girl up to now. His fears proved utterly groundless. From the moment they set eyes on each other, the women were easy in each other's company. X watched as they chatted between effective calls all morning, and by the time he returned to the office after lunch they were making each other giggle and snort with laughter at will by pulling exaggerated facial expressions during long, dull calls with clients. By the end of the day they had developed a private language of hand signals when on interminable holds, and the friendship seemed set.

X had attempted to understand this surprising and entirely felicitous development. He felt certain that the two women had immediately recognised each other as animated by the same vital force, but different enough to be complimentary, their essence enhanced rather than diminished in each other's presence. He'd wasted most of that first afternoon trying to equate the two women to Olympian goddesses, but kept getting his Greeks and Romans mixed up.

Aphrodite and Athena?

There had been a third goddess.

Diana? The thought made him shudder, a picture of Phil blasted off his head on Badgett's pills at the squat party flashed into his mind from another life.

No.

Two goddesses were enough. It always led to trouble when Diana showed up, he seemed to recall, although he couldn't quite remember clearly how it went in the ancient myths.

Sara was worth her weight in gold. With the rest of the sales team he had to earn his keep, egging them along to keep picking up the phone by a combination of petty rewards and the same kind of tawdry razzmatazz that Roger had practised; strutting like a TV evangelist over desks and chairs while delivering praise or closing a deal, breaking the monotony by forcing them to make calls standing on one leg or in comedy accents and always keeping the weekly champagne target low. Sara required none of that nonsense to keep her motivated. She arrived early each day, giving herself an hour before she started on the phones to read the trades. When she had finished with Campaign, Media Week, Magazine Week and some of the marketing titles she would work her way through the television industry mags, determinedly plodding through every line of the turgid soup that Virtual Television put out as copy. She read everything, even a strange little satirical rag, 'The Dean Street Runner', that was printed privately on cheap paper and was full of industry in-jokes that X didn't understand. She often spent her lunchtimes deep in conversation with the New TV journalist that covered finance, or sat taking notes as the overweight fool who wrote the technology column gassed on. By the end of her first month, she had worked out the fundamental problem with the magazine.

She had been flicking through a pile of back-issues, her hair still wet from her lunchtime swim in Marshall Street baths, sucking on a juice drink she had picked up at Cranks. Jeanne sat opposite her, leaning back in her chair with her feet on the desk. The magazine had closed the day before, and Friday afternoons were a bad time to do business anyway, so there was no real pressure to get quickly back on the phones.

Sara let the copy she was holding fall to the floor with a sigh.

X looked up.

"You know", she had said in a resigned but matter-of-fact voice, shrugging as she spoke, "I just don't think the business model's viable."

She picked up the copy she had dropped and flicked through the advertising pages, tapping some of the individual ads with the tip of the long, immaculately curved nail of her index finger as she did so. "The magazine only makes money when there's some kind of..." She searched momentarily for the correct phrase. "...seismic shift in the industry. Look – Breakfast TV", she tapped a big spread of TV AM ads in the issue she was holding, and then picked up another copy from a few months later, "but when they're up and running, it dies away and we're in the red again", she tapped the only TV AM ad in the copy she held, a quarter page in the left hand corner. Taking another copy from the pile she repeated the exercise, this time tapping half-page ads from BSB and Sky, "Satellite TV", she declared, "and even then....", she flicked the pages of a later copies, the squarial ads got smaller and smaller and then disappeared altogether.

He could only agree.

But that isn't even the main problem", she continued, "All the independent production companies were going to be the Great White Hope weren't they? But look!" She thumbed through page after page of advertising, "They don't spend a penny. They're too small to part with the cash, but more than that, they recruit people they already know, ones they've worked with for years and trust to get the job done. They just pick up the phone and call their chums when they need someone – they don't need us." She concluded, "and they won't be big enough to spend real money for five…maybe ten years…" she shrugged again, "no magazine can carry losses for that long".

Sara was clearly right, it was Restaurant and Café Bar News all over again, another good idea for a magazine that wasn't quite on the money. X responded by switching her and Jeanne from recruitment to the classified section straight away and divided the country up between them, giving London to Sara and allocating the rest of the UK to Jeanne.

Sara was a perfect match for the geeks and technicians who had set up post-production companies in the backstreets between Oxford Circus and Charing Cross Road. Taking advantage of developments in computer graphics technology that nobody else understood, their little companies were now beginning to make serious money, and took Sara's dazzling presence among them as just reward for their entrepreneurial zeal. They liked to talk business with her as publicly as possible, ensuring they were in full view of their rivals by conducting their meetings behind the glass windows of their expensively upgraded reception areas. Here, framed by abstract art and sat on uncomfortable, experimental furniture, she persuaded them to take unnecessary advertisements in New TV while sipping Jasmine tea from porcelain cups with easy grace. Behind the sheen of the fancy receptions, their companies' real work took place in darkened rooms, where the machines that earned the money laboriously rendered each individual image at a glacial pace in near silence, progressing in jerking frame clicks like time-lapse photography. To relieve the crushing boredom of waiting for the next sequence to complete, they had squeezed snooker tables, table football and pinball machines into their back office space, and as they all had time to kill while the machines whirred on, they had got into the habit of drifting in and out of each other's facilities. The owners of rival companies would often pop round the corner to shoot a few frames on the opposition's table, and techies from across the road could be found sharing a spliff out on the fire escape.

It suited Sara perfectly. She could roll up her sleeves and shoot a great rack of pool. She whooped with delight as she spun the paddles at bar football, and she was well practised in letting stoned young men ramble on about their dreams without making them feel foolish. They loved her. She was one of the boys. She was absolutely not one of the boys. And she was untouchable. None of them would have dared. By the end of her first month she had an access all areas VIP pass across the whole of Soho. The money poured in.

There was business to be had in the rest of the country that no one had really chased before and Jeanne set about it with gusto. When she'd made enough contacts over the phone, X handed over his car and sent her out on the road. The gesture earned him a reputation in the company as an exceptionally generous manager, but he had hated the car, and had given it to her largely in the hope that it would put pressure on Howard to finally get him a GTI. Jeanne, however, returned from her long circuits complaining about the shit-bucket he had dumped on her. Having spent her youth fixing the crankshafts and polishing the walnut fascias of her father's collection of vintage Jags and Aston Martins, a Vauxhall Cavalier was some distance from her dream car and she never stopped bitching to X about its failings. Nonetheless, the car allowed Jeanne's talent to be planted in the most fertile soil possible, and the men in brown suits at Anglia and Yorkshire TV who fell hard for her, were joined by a swath of middle-aged divorcees across the country who looked forward to her sales pitches like devotees awaiting the arrival of their sensi. Back in the office after each tour, she picked up bookings every time she lifted the receiver. They went from one page of classified to three in the first three months. Recruitment revenue was flat and the magazine was still making a loss but he had made his mark in the company and picked up a fat bonus from Howard to boot.

X followed up this small success with a pitch directed upward in the form of a memo he sent to Mike Verne, the director responsible for the company's media division. In it he began by pointing out the 300% growth in classified advertising under his tenure, going on to claim that the pace of this rapid growth *may* have been accelerated by an induction training programme of his own devising. The memo went on to outline a schedule of intensive immersion in both the advertising and television businesses, beginning with a required reading list of the trades and rival magazines, weekly discussion sessions, regular meetings with the editorial team and supervised visits to selected companies. He had signed off the memo by suggesting that similar programmes might be useful for other magazines. He had not, of course, developed any such scheme, merely taking credit for Sara's regimen. He personally knew very little about the TV business, relying on Jeanne to provide him with the necessary technical terms if he ever needed them. It was all just stuff to be sold as far as he could see, and no more fundamentally interesting than selling refrigeration parts or plumbing supplies. Mind you, people were always impressed when he told them he worked in television. He liked that.

The best thing about the whole set up at New TV was that X could do pretty much what he liked. Howard was largely absent, spending most afternoons in long meetings on the golf course. These, Howard explained, without revealing any details at all, such things being strictly hush-hush and on a need-to-know basis, related to certain long-term strategies he was working on. Despite the cogs always being 'just about to fall into place', Howard's meetings had so far delivered no more than an improvement in his handicap. He really only turned up in the office for the weekly team meetings where he delivered a long pep talk, largely consisting of a series of upbeat clichés without any discernible thread connecting them.

Howard had a set of affectations and mannerisms that he used in varying combinations during these performances. He would often start with the firm declaration that he 'didn't want them just to drive around the multi-storey looking for a place to park', or similar, delivering the words standing and with his face set thunderous with determination. He would then sit and, leaning back in his chair, extend his wide braces forward from his chest with his thumbs like a proud and satisfied burgermeister, allowing a wide self-confident smile to play around his lips for a while. Then, face clouding over once again, he would warn against complacency before suddenly leaning forward across the table, his voice now stentorious, announcing that he didn't want them to 'merely host a variety of flags up poles and decide which one to salute', "No!", he would shout, usually rising suddenly to his feet as though pulled upward by some unseen force and demanding from them 'blue sky thinking – way above the clouds." Invariably at this point he would begin to pace up and down beside the desks for a while, deep in thought, head down and hands behind his back as though wrestling with his conscience like Boethius in his cell, before returning to the table to deliver the finale, often with a mixed metaphor and always with a thunderous fist on the table, exhorting them to think 'so far outside the envelope that the whole damn box explodes!" Having finished his speech, and leaning forward with his fist still clenched above the table's surface, he would scan the faces of each member of his team, probing for any sign of weakness of lack of verve.

The young people treated him like an eccentric and occasionally benevolent uncle, who would set their bonus targets low if they could keep him happy. They smiled dutifully at his jokes and did their best to look inspired and excited during his weekly address, occasionally cheering if it seemed called for and they could do it without appearing overly sarcastic. Howard was always absurdly pleased with himself after his team talk, and they tried not to notice him pacing up and down behind the glass windows of his tiny office, his mouth opening and closing as he repeated a few phrases he was particularly proud of, advancing up and down in a kind of cockney chicken strut with his elbows out, like a parody of a pearly king's celebratory dance.

They could have sold tickets.

Best of all, with Howard out the way X didn't even have to work the phones much anymore. Jeanne and Sara undertook the labour for him, relentlessly raising and lowering their receivers like Bangladeshi garment workers, they sustained a constant rhythm of charmed exchanges and tinkling laughter, their velvet determination keeping money falling into the magazine like a one arm bandit on frequent pay out.

He only stepped in when Sara needed a male voice to get past one of the protective secretaries who treated her as they would a home wrecking mistress at the door with her bastard offspring. That type of women usually flipped instantly at the sound of a confident male's voice, and X's easy banter was often good enough to get passed through and then he would simply hand back the phone to Sara and, "Sorry Jack, X has been called away, you don't mind talking to me do you...?"

Sometimes he had to work harder, "It's a little difficult to say this, but Sara's very upset by the way you spoke to her..."

- - - - - - - - - - - - - - - - - - -

"Yes, I'm sure you meant no harm...but as her line manager I felt I had to let you know... She was in tears...she wouldn't let you know herself......"

- - - - - - - - - - - - - - - - -

"I understand, perhaps it's only because she's pregnant..."

Sara would ring back a week later in a timid voice and get put through straight away.

The only other time he'd get on the phones was when it afforded him an opportunity to show off. The last time he had done it, it had come off so perfectly that he felt he should have able to retire on the spot like an unbeaten heavyweight champion. It had been a slack afternoon and a call had come through to Kajira, who X had signed up the week before and showed signs of not being as completely useless as the rest. X was listening in to her call as part of her training when he heard a tinny, nasal voice coming out of the speakers raising the standard objection to advertising in a weekly rather than a monthly magazine; that they had no shelf life. "You see", the voice drawled, sounding almost stoned in its delivery, "We use Virtual Television to advertise. It lasts. We've got a pile of them stacked up, flick through them from time to time. But yours...it just flops all over the place, you read it once then throw it away..."

Sensing a sucker, he had got her to switch the call to speakerphone, and signalling to the rest of the sales time to get off the phones and listen in, he picked up the receiver, "Hi Tom", he'd started, "This is X. I know you were talking to Kajira, but I was passing and couldn't help overhearing what you were saying – You read New TV then?"

"Bits, headlines and some of the business news, but there's not much about post-production in it." His voice was bored but not resentful.

At this point X jumped on to the desk and, holding the receiver in one hand and stretching the coiled wire to its maximum, began pacing up and down over the desks, stepping over in-trays and Max-Pac coffee cartons as he strode. "OK, you only read part of it, but do you know who reads New Television cover to cover every week?"

"No", the voice slightly sullen now, "Why don't you tell me...."

Perfect.

"The top 500 independent production companies in the UK Tom - New companies starting up, companies getting bigger with more money to spend, all of whom need title sequences, computer graphics..." He looked at Jeanne for what other services Tom's company provided, she mouthed, 'Telecine'. "Telecine", he added, still having no idea what it actually was, "Your market Tom. Exactly your market. *Everyone* who buys what you sell, reads New TV every week!"

"Yea ...But as I said... it doesn't last..." The voice was losing confidence.

There were various ways to play from here, but X felt he had the right picture of his mark in front of him now, so he gambled that an aggressive approach would work with this one and altered his tone accordingly, "Look Tom, if you've got a pile of Virtual Televisions stacked up in the bogs, and every time a hairy-arsed techie goes for a shit, he takes a squint at one between strains – it does fuck-all for your business".

X paused for dramatic effect.

"He isn't a customer Tom, all he buys is software and porn videos. But when you put an ad in New TV the production company director's secretary delivers it to his desk every Monday morning on a tray with his coffee and croissant... and you know what Tom?.........He *never* shits at work." X stopped speaking, he could have fucked it up completely but he didn't think so.

Laughter came out of the speakers, "Fair point!" the nasal voice said, "bit brutally put, but fair point", adding, "Hey X, have you been over to our place?"

"No."

"You got it to a T man!"

X laughed into the receiver while making a yawning gesture to the watching sales team as he did so. "OK", he began closing, "so you pull all your ads from Virtual TV where we've agreed your wasting your money and, shit, do it now, and we'll book you in for what you're paying there for the first three months - but after that you're back on rate card for the rest of the year." He didn't wait for a reply this time saying "I'll pass you back to Kajira so you can sort out the paperwork..."

There was a brief hesitation, "OK – What the Fuck!"

He handed back the phone to Kajira, who sheltered the mouthpiece to shield the sounds of claps and cheers from his team, some additional applause rippling over the screens from neighbouring magazines sales teams who had paused in their work to take in the show. He had bowed from the waist to all four corners of the room before leaping down off the table. His star was rising.

Howard, blissfully unaware of the contempt in which X held him, was a relentless booster of his protégé, ccing X in on memos he had passed upwards that gushed about the talents of his classified manager, recommending him for accelerated management training and hinting at un-tapped potential of stratospheric proportions. Although this was useful for X in the short term, to have his only source of patronage a man who was pretty much an imbecile had drastic limitations. Mike Verne had never even acknowledged receipt of his memo, and the only time he had met the man he had fluffed it completely. Finding himself stood beside the director at the urinals in the staff toilets, he had been unable to piss, obliged to stand with his flaccid cock in his hands, hovering like a hopeful cottager, until the other man had finished up and was washing his hands at the sink. No. If he was going to get any further, he'd have to forget Howard and maybe Verne too. He needed to build his own faction at this company's court, one with him at its head.

The tools were at hand as soon as Jeanne and Sara were on board.

His early attempts to attract a coterie had backfired completely. When he'd strolled, cock-sure and affable, into other sales teams' turf to introduce himself, he'd been met with a suspicion bordering on hostility. He'd tried blagging it as best he could, greeting publishers in their offices as though they were old friends and squatting, spread-legged and uninvited, on the desks of ad managers while he passed comment on their salespeople's performance. But after one night of cold shoulders and awkward conversation in the company pub, he knew all he'd achieved was to get people's backs up. In truth, before the women had arrived, everyone had thought he was a cunt.

Then it had all changed. His induction journey with Jeanne and Sara around the company levels was like a royal tour, all smiling faces, double kissing and firm handshakes, and when he was seen regularly at a table in the Hen and Chickens with the same two outstanding women, he was suddenly someone everyone wanted to know. Keeping their company made him attractive to other women. Suspicious looks were transformed into sly appraisals and, after a vodka and orange or two in the pub, straightforward propositions. He declined, determined not to jeopardise his pursuit of Sara, but was happy to let the rumour that he was sleeping with both of them circulate freely around the company. Opinions changed instantly. No wonder he was so cocky.

The men who had sneered at him when his back was turned, were now desperate to befriend him, and he forgive them their transgressions with magnanimity inviting them join him at the Hen, where Jeanne and Sara held court in the far corner. Within a month, Sara's knowledge of intrigues and scandals in the company was encyclopaedic, and her sage advice was often called upon in the most intractable cases. X presided at the apex of their two concentric circles, leaning back, detached, nodding and half listening to the conversation around him, kept informed by his ladies-in waiting of only the most salacious tit-bits of gossip. He lounged, aloof and superior, ready to be a duke, but still, at this stage, no more than a contender at the tournament. And he still hadn't got anywhere with Sara.

*

Tonight, at last, he'd managed to get her on her own. Roger was having a celebration of some kind at the Dog and Duck round the corner, and he'd said he'd drop by. Relations between X and his old company had remained cordial since he'd left. Roger blamed himself for failing to find X a better position than the one at Virtual TV, and rather than harbouring any resentment at his defection to one of their rivals, treated him as the prodigal son whenever he put in an appearance at his old haunt.

Jeanne had been deep in conversation with a lad from the post room who owned an MG, and had refused to be drawn from her discussion on the problem of rusty exhaust manifolds, so it was just the two of them who stepped out into the night together. It was scarcely a date at that stage. Their relationship had developed no further than a mutually beneficial arrangement, and the short journey round the corner was more of the same. For X, entering with such a glamorous escort would further enhance his status as goldenballs at his old company, and for Sara, networking was as instinctive as breathing. Some of X's cachet at his old firm might rub off on her too.

Roger was, of course, delighted to meet her, and they immediately settled into the bar together, Roger drawing her close and exclaiming, "Now tell me all the gossip, starting with who X is sleeping with!" He heard her laugh, almost choking on her spritzer, as Roger changed tack, "but before all that", he almost shrieked, "We *must* start with those shoes!"

X had tuned out at that point, and spent the rest of the time in the pub chatting to other familiar faces from Roger's clique. They were all pleasant to him, if a little more distant than before, but only Caroline was welcoming to Sara, the rest keeping their distance and casting occasional glances and sneers in her direction, like startled grazing animals keeping an eye on a new predator near the flock.

*

They were both a bit pissed when they staggered away from the pub and he led her, stumbling, through the back streets. They cut through the alley past Raymond's Review Bar, and as they squeezed between the strip clubs and clip joints, she reached for his hand. The contact was merely the lightest touch of fingertips, the curl of her ice-cold digits meshing with no more than the tips of his, but as they weaved between the bouncers in tuxedos and hookers in G-strings and pink nylon negligées touting for business in the doorways, she tightened her grip. She kept hold of his hand for nearly the full length of Brewer Street, not relinquishing it until they had passed the last of the shops with fly-splattered action movies and Carry On film cases displayed with the cobwebs in the windows. He knew it wasn't from affection, but as protection against the attention she drew from the men who stripped her from under hooded eyes before darting swiftly through the ribbon strip doorways to get to the hard-core porn on sale downstairs, but it still made him feel strong, brave and excited at the same time.

He had hoped to drift with her through the city, half-drunken, catching random beautiful moments by accident, but when, at Piccadilly Circus, he was willing to imagine they had been swept into Times Square or back to VE day 1945 in the light of the glowing neon, she had declared that she was starving hungry, and they had spent the next twenty minutes queuing for a burger in the giant Wimpey on the corner. He had refused to sit amongst the plastic cups and dropped onion slices on the plastic seats, and she had followed him, chewing messily on her burger, wiping tomato sauce away from her mouth with the back of her hand as she tottered after him down the steps past the Duke of York's statue and into St James' Park.

He was back on track now.

He guided her down through the unlit park, the pathway moon-grey beneath their feet and the grass dark as coal behind the low iron railings and led her onto the footbridge over the lake. Here, the city magically disappeared, hidden from sight by the plane trees that lined the Mall as though they had wandered into a secret wood. In the distance Horse Guards Parade was lit up like a grand stately home preparing for a ball, the lamplight casting shimmering gold reflections on the water beneath the lake-side willows, and just visible above the canopies of ancient oak trees the flag above Buckingham Palace fluttered in the breeze. He had brought two other women here, and it had proved the perfect spot to supply a tender opening kiss. Sara just looked bored. She began to shiver in her sleeveless dress. He didn't offer her his jacket. Perhaps she'd step closer to him if she got cold.

The silence was dragging a bit, and in the end he had to ruin the moment by prompting, "Do you like the view?"

"Yea, it's nice I suppose…I like the ducks."

Beneath the bough of the bridge, the waterfowl had settled in for the night in shuffling downy bunches along the banks. X recalled that the banks there were reduced to wastes of grey mud paste and duck shit, but he supposed they did look quite cosy down there now.

The romance of the view having failed, he changed tack and started asking her questions. He could do that. Most men struggled to stop talking about themselves, feeling they had to keep saying interesting things to make an impression, but he knew that what most women wanted was someone who listened to them. He was good at keeping quiet and listening to women. Or at least pretending to listen.

Family was often a good place to start. "I've worked with you for three months now", he'd begun, "and I really don't know much about you. Where are you from? What did your parents do?"

She had immediately pulled him up short. "As someone called X, I assume you'll be cool if I don't talk about my parents."

X was fine, obviously, but he was momentarily taken aback by her curt response and it must have shown on his face.

She had felt obliged to expand, at least a little, "Look, it's not that they were horrible or anything, my adoptive parents that is – and I don't know and I don't care who my birth parents were before you ask. There just came a point when they made no more sense in my life than if we'd met by chance on a railway station platform – which in a way was how it was."

There was no more conversation on the bridge, and as they drifted back through Green Park toward Mayfair, their mood was subdued. He made one last attempt to salvage the evening, hailing a cab to Edgware Road and taking Sara into one of the cafes that sold sticky black coffee and baklava out front and had shisha pipes around the back. She hesitated at the entrance, but he tugged at her hand and she followed him in, sitting down in one of the high-backed wicker seats as he ordered a plug of lemon-flavoured tobacco. What he thought would be a masterstroke, an introduction to a pleasure that she had probably never experienced and a chance to sit and talk late into the night didn't seem to be working. Sara looked ill at ease, and he began to become irritated with her for the first time that evening.

What would it take to please this woman?

But his ire quickly evaporated. Little ripples of displeasure were emanating from the men in white jellabiyas and keffiyeh around them, and X was certain he heard old boy at the rear of the patio mutter 'haram'. He suddenly felt foolish. He had forgotten that with Sara's skin colour she could easily have been a Muslim girl, and even if not, he had brought her into exclusively male company, both of them still slightly pissed and with the woman's arms completely bared. He took off his jacket and put it over Sara's shoulders.

They were unable to get comfortable after that, and left before his pipe arrived, scurrying a few doors down to a Lebanese juice bar, where they sat on stools drinking guava juice and nibbling at a selection of super sweet cakes chosen at random.

For the first time since they left the pub he had hit the right note.

"It's been great working with you X", she said suddenly, sucking juice through her straw with a loud rasping noise like a child at play as she spoke – "This is lovely by the way", indicating the juice and the sweets with a wave of her arm, "thank-you for bringing me here. You know", she continued, "You're the only boss I've ever had who hasn't made a pass at me in the first week." She laughed. "It's weird - I can control any old letch of a client, but bosses get this ownership mentality…as though I've got to put out to keep my job. But you don't make me feel like that – Thanks!" She raised her juice in tribute.

He thought he'd chance it, "So if I didn't presume you had to put out in order to keep your job?" he asked.

She looked stunned for a second and then laughed, stopped, looked at him again and, tears welling up in the corners of her deep brown eyes and laughed whole-heartedly. "Very good X", she said when she had recovered enough to speak, "that's the sweetest pass any of my bosses has ever made to me." She laughed again, bright and short this time like a small bark, then cocked her head slightly to one side, apparently appraising him with a serious expression that turned into a slow smile, "But you *are* my boss …if you weren't…who knows…?" She flashed her eyes and laughed once again, taking another bite of baklava, a flake of almond sticking to her lower lip as she did so "Really this stuff is great…"

He had insisted in accompanying her on the long taxi ride home to Tooting, saying he would take the same cab back to Hammersmith, claiming he would enjoy the tour of the city, and that he wanted to ensure she got home safely. She fell asleep on his shoulder at Lambeth Bridge, and he spent the journey staring at her body while she slept.

Her dress had risen up from her knees as she had slid down on the leather seat, and a strip of the soft flesh of her upper thighs was exposed between the hem and the top of her black silk hold ups. The fabric of her dress was pulled taught across her hips, and her breasts pushed hard against the thin cotton, the soft mounds rising and falling with each breath, their perfect globes gently shaded under the lapels of his jacket. She was so fecund, so lithe and soft and powerful-fleshed against him, that it seemed to him that the force of her sexuality could scarcely be contained by her clothing, and at any moment she would burst out of them, stiches ripping apart up the seam of her skirt from thigh to hip, the taut fabric that covered her breasts tearing apart leaving her gasping and open to him in her lingerie and soft sweet flesh on the black leather seat.

She woke only when the cab had arrived outside her flat, and staggered out, bleary–eyed and with only a loose hand-wave over her retreating shoulder, swayed away down the street, leaving him with an erection and a long, expensive journey home.

He closed his eyes. He might as well sleep, it would stop him staring at the meter and anyway; he could always dream.

15. FUN

He was sitting at a table on the student café terrace with the heat of the sun beating down on his shoulders from a cloudless blue sky. Below him, the stream meandered lazily between moss covered rocks, trickling through the thick clumps of bull rushes that had taken root in the shallow water. On the opposite bank, the meadow grass, grown tall since he was last here, was set ablaze with the blooms of red and purple wild flowers. Summer had arrived.

Eva and Pooja were sat across the table from him deep in conversation. When Eva caught sight of him, she started upward in alarm, knocking over a glass of mineral water with a flailing arm as she did so. She embraced him warmly, "I'll never get used to that", she said laughing.

The two young women were in a buoyant, excitable mood, and they talked over each other in their rush to explain to X that the timing of his arrival was perfect. He had, apparently, returned on the very last day of term, just as the long summer vacation was about to begin. Pooja explained breathlessly that this far north the sun barely dipped below the horizon during high summer, and people hardly slept, and that at times it was as though the whole country was lying on their backs in the parks, staring up at the heavens and soaking up the sun's rays. Eva added that it was, of course, necessary to get at least some sleep, but that you could get by taking little catnaps that felt more like daydreams, but nonetheless did the trick, the important point being that you must sleep properly at least once a day. Pooja interrupted, laughing, to point out that not everybody took that advice and started on a confused rendition of a story involving Per, a Belgian girl and a plank of wood that was so interrupted by bursts of laughter that it remained largely incomprehensible to X, but involved some apparently hilarious misunderstandings after Per had remained awake for a full fortnight the previous midsummer. When they had recovered from the hilarity, Eva informed him that they were all meeting up for a picnic tomorrow to celebrate the start of the holidays and lend encouragement to Sven who was hoping to top out his new studio-apartment that day. He was, of course, invited, if he was still around... In the meantime, she suggested, they should check out the festival of student bands that was taking place on campus that afternoon.

The short walk took them past the concert hall, whose huge doors had been swung wide open to let in the breeze, revealing a tiny wooden stage at its heart like a doll's house miniature, before turning down a series of shallow steps into the upper tier of a sunken stadium. The stadium's bowl had been carved out of the landscape and terraces of grass banking, arranged in concentric circles around a small temporary stage, were covered in the bodies of students dozing in the bright sunshine.

Eva and Pooja slumped down on the nearest free patch of grass on the upper terrace and were soon chatting away, detoxing from their year's intense study, their conversation pitted with in-jokes about faculty members and academic controversies that meant little to him. He turned his attention to the stage. A band were working through an arrhythmic instrumental on keyboards and flute largely ignored by the crowd. The band's set came to an abrupt end, and the bearded keyboardist thanked the crowd effusively while a modest ripple of applause passed round the stadium. A few shouts of "Yaah" rose up from a group of hairy young men down the front who had either had a few beers too many or were friends of the band. It was somewhat less than a clamour for an encore, and the band shuffled off stage, the PA starting up with cover versions of sixties hits while the crew packed their instruments away.

Eva and Pooja had soon talked themselves out, and under the sun's soporific effect they passed quickly from over-exuberance to mellow drowsiness, nodding off together with Eva's head resting on her friend's lap. Left alone, X wandered down toward the stage, meandering through the sleepy, picnicking crowds. On the stage four enthusiastic boys with brightly coloured, spiky hair performed a short, fast paced set of technically competent, upbeat punk. There was some boisterous leaping about by a dozen or so young men at the front but the majority of the crowd remained as stoically unmoved as they had by the earlier prog rock ensemble. The band were very tight and they all seemed to be having a great time on stage, but as their delighted grins burst out at each chord change, X couldn't help thinking that happy, well-executed punk was pretty much the definition of completely missing the point. The boys didn't have many tunes and with the performance soon over, X strolled back up to his friends. They were still sleeping, and looking down on their softened, blissfully contented faces he concluded that he probably didn't have the right to wake them. Sitting beside them while they slept, he had nothing to do, and by the time the next band took the stage he was really quite bored. When the first chords of non-threatening rock boomed out of the PA he yawned and stood up to stretch his legs.

Over the lip of the arena, he could just make out a thin

sliver of the sea through the haze and as he looked a shaft of sunlight, glaring off the surface of the water like a camera flare on celluloid, temporarily blinded him. He blinked to cut out the sharp light.

*

He was sitting on the raised bank overlooking the bay. In front of him Pooja was laying out the contents of a wicker picnic hamper on a white cotton sheet. A bottle of sparkling wine sat cooling in an ice bucket surrounded by six champagne flutes. Sprawled on the grass beside Pooja, lay Eva, Per, Xanthia and Erika.

How had he got here?

He glanced down the bank in front of him. The shoreline cut a majestic arc below him, capped at either end by the pine-covered hills that cradled the city in a natural bowl. Out on the crystal-clear waters of the bay, only the slow, balletic movement of a pair of sailing dinghies and the frothy wake of a silver-coated motorboat disturbed the water's smooth surface. But the panorama's tranquil beauty was fatally disrupted by the dust and clamour of a building site situated immediately below them. A row of three storey houses were under construction, and the air was full of the whine of electric motors, the clanking of levers and the rhythmic hammering of metal The calls of the workers below drifted upward like the cries of gulls feeding on landfill. It seemed like a strange place to choose for a picnic.

Per saw him first, "Look everybody, X is back!" he shouted in an excited high-pitched yelp, and held him in a vice-like embrace as though X was an old army buddy he had never expected to see alive again. It was a wonderful, if slightly overwhelming way to be welcomed, and the feeling seemed to flow over the rest of the group, even Xanthia giving him a wave of greeting although she didn't bother to get up. He settled happily onto the grass next to Eva, with Per still slapping him on the back, shaking his head and repeating, "Seeker of Sweden", over and over again as though he was delighted, but just couldn't get his head round the concept.

Eva explained why they were there and pointed out Sven down below them, unrecognisable in a hard hat and overalls, on the roof of the nearest building, balancing with the confidence of a stilt-walker on a cross-beam, while he completed the final turns on a bolt that secured the roof strut into place. As though he had somehow sensed their attention, he chose that moment to look up and wave at them. They all waved back, Per whistling encouragement with two fingers stuffed in his mouth, a sound piercingly loud where X sat, but almost certainly drowned out by the clamour of the machines long before it could have reached Sven.

The party were intent on watching the construction below, and although it still seemed bizarre to X to be picnicking above a building site, he was soon drawn in. The buildings were rising at a phenomenal pace, the rate of construction so rapid that watching them grow seemed like time-lapse photography. This extraordinary speed was made possible by teams of silver insect-like robots, each about the size of a small child, that swarmed over the buildings like a nest of disturbed beetles. The robots scuttled up and down the timber frames, ferrying small parts to their human overseers and fixing components in place using their spidery metal limbs like fists or drills. A large crane lowered larger, pre-fabricated parts into position with an impossible precision. Sven presided over his dwelling from the rooftop with supreme confidence. Acting as the foreman to his own beetle-robot crew, he summoned the parts he needed with a wave of his hand, halted the robot's work while he checked the fine margins and deftly provided the finishing touches with his own hands.

It occurred to X that Sven must be very well off. His house looked pretty substantial, and its position directly facing the bay surely must be prime real estate. Erica disabused him of the thought. She explained that the necessary credit was raised collectively by the Co-operative of which Sven was a member, and costs were kept to a minimum by the members doing much of the work themselves including the fabrication of components at the factory as well as the assembly on site. "Nearly everyone you see down there will live in these buildings", she continued, "except for a few craftsmen and women who will make the finishing touches.'

X looked sceptical. He had trouble putting shelves up straight and couldn't imagine building a whole house.

"Most of the skills aren't so difficult you know X", Eva said, "Anyone can lay a grass roof..."

Erika felt obliged to add in her most declamatory tone, "You must remember, X, that the right to decent quality housing, to have a home of your own, is the most basic and fundamental of all human rights, and we naturally take it with due seriousness, both for ourselves and for others. Just as we expend energy on our education in order to be able to be active and informed citizens, so too do we develop the skills necessary to build our own dwellings." She paused at this point and then began again, unbidden, and in a mocking tone as though X had suggested something absurd, although he hadn't spoken at all, "What would be the point, after all, of providing health care if you had no sanitary accommodation to abide in?" she added laughing, "What would be the point of education? Would you give Latin lessons to people sleeping in the streets?"

And that was how much of the afternoon passed, as they watched the buildings rise below them, an extension of campus life but better, an open-air tutorial, accompanied with a little champagne and without any pressure. He didn't remember much of it afterwards, like so many of the lectures he had attended at college that had seemed so enlightening at the time but fogged over as soon as he left the room. Later, from the whole balmy afternoon he could recall only fragments of conversation and snippets of data mixed up with other memories more like short cuts of cine-film. A loose strand of Eva's long blond hair falling across her forehead, the movement of her long delicate fingers through the air as she absentmindedly tucked it away behind her ear. Per's broad, idiot grin, Pooja passing him a serviette with a kind, compassionate expression, and through it all, the warm sunshine mingling with the hammering, crashing and grinding from below....

Per on the farms,

"Well it's all GM of course... What's wrong with that? ...the food's a little bland?...only in your imagination...anyway, what are spices for?..."

Erika on ecology,

"Hah! Like that wasn't easy to solve. Once you stop believing that the person who owns the most toys is somehow the winner, and men stopped imagining that driving fast cars was the only way to prove they had a penis, it wasn't particularly hard to protect enough habitat to preserve biodiversity...."

"What! – Why are you laughing? – I haven't said anything funny."

Per's single raised finger behind her head. Erika's pantomime turn behind her, met only by Per's blinking expression of angelic innocence.

Afterwards, X seemed to have remembered the exchanges that had jarred most clearly, although they were not at all typical of the day.

Erika expounding on art; bored expressions around her, "You see X, we recognise the talents of the wild individualists here, but see no reason to revere them..."

Xanthia's snort of disgust, "Oh give me strength!"

Or later, when X had asked why the clothes they wore were so tight. Erika had put him down flat, "Please X - this isn't anthropology."

Xanthia in response; open contempt in her voice, "Oh really Erika – have you no shame?"

That sharp exchange had brought the mutual antipathy between the two women so clearly to the surface that it temporarily soured the atmosphere, and seemed to have sucked all the warmth out of the day until Per cracked a joke about a famous female javelin thrower that was in such bad taste that everyone forgot the tension and started pelting him with food.

The long afternoon meandered along and by the time Sven,

his blond hair covered in dust from the site below, joined them on the bank, Eva had already slipped away, suddenly anxious, explaining that she had to practise for her concert that night. It had been the first time X had heard about any concert, and he suddenly felt left out, wondering if he was even invited, and while he did his best to smile appropriately as they raised a toast to Sven's new home, he was aware that inside he was actually sulking. In Eva's absence it all seemed flat and scarcely worth the effort. He stepped away from the group, suddenly sad and exhausted by the endless daylight, he closed his eyes.

*

He was sitting in the third row of the concert hall. In front of him, the stage was set up for the performance of a string quartet, with the cello, viola and violins propped up on their stands their varnish gleaming bright umber in the stage lights. Pooja was sat next to him alongside Sven. He just had time to nod quick greetings to them both when the chatter in the concert hall died down and Eva and the other musicians emerged from the wings. As she took her seat behind the cello, Pooja grabbed hold of his hand and squeezed it tightly, continuing to hold on while the musicians drew off-key screeches from their instruments and made minor adjustments to the tension in their strings. A shy looking violinist with eyes that appeared to be looking out from deep underwater behind his thick glasses, coughed and then spoke hesitantly into a microphone, explaining that they would be performing a series of pieces by Mahler, and went on to give some biographical details about the composer.

X switched off. He knew nothing about classical music and had never been interested enough even to attend a concert before. All his attention was focussed on Eva. She had pulled her hair back tight across her scalp and coiled it up on the top of her head in a tight bun, revealing the grace of her long neck, and making her face seem both harsh and solemn. Her eyes, a blue so pale as to be almost completely devoid of colour, were darting around in their sockets like those of a small, frightened animal cornered by much larger prey. In the sudden silence in the auditorium, her anxiety seemed to flow directly into him, and when Pooja grabbed his hand again, squeezing so hard that her nails dug into the soft flesh of his palms like a row of tacks in putty, X squeezed back, grateful for the distraction the pain gave him.

From the moment she began to play Eva was possessed by the music. Her eyes half-closed, she made no reference to the score or any acknowledgment of the audience, rising from the depths only to nod to her fellow musicians, before descending again into the melancholy currents of the piece. Although much of the music was slow and punctuated by doleful notes and near silences, when the pace quickened the quartet sawed away furiously and Eva's grace was allied to a hitherto unknown, almost frightening, intensity, the blood rising in her cheeks and beads of sweat breaking out on her brow as she tenderly garrotted the instrument held between her thighs. When the music ended the sharp burst of applause brought Eva back to the surface as though climbing up out of a well, flushed and blushing, surprised to find that she had not been alone in the room the whole time.

When they met up in the bar afterwards, Eva's was still high from the experience, greeting him with a long embrace, her rapid speech interrupted by starts of shrill laughter and extravagant hand gestures. She accepted their compliments with a genuine modesty, wincing as she mentioned a few errors she had made, but was easily mollified by their effusive praise and obvious delight in her performance. To X she looked even more beautiful than before. Her eyes had changed colour again, now an impossible sparkling blue, the colour of sapphires, and lit by an inner glow that seemed to emanate from her whole being.

"We must celebrate", implored Pooja, "let's go clubbing – I'm in the mood to strut my funky stuff!"

X had to refrain from snorting like Xanthia, thinking to himself that, lovely as Pooja was, he had never met anybody less funky, but with the contemptuous laugh stifled in his throat he allowed himself to become excited. Perhaps he would finally get to go out and have some fun with Eva. After all this time in her company at last he might get to see her really let her hair down and enjoy herself, and then who knew what might happen...

It was all quickly agreed. There was a club night in the student building and they would 'dance until they couldn't stand up anymore' as Eva had put it.

While they were waiting outside the concert hall for Pooja to return from the cloakroom, disaster struck. The first X knew of it was when he felt a hearty slap between his shoulder blades that knocked him forward half a pace, and before he could turn to identify who had struck the blow, Eva had leapt past him and into his assailant's arms. "Olaf!" she squealed delightedly, mussing his curly black hair and kissing him repeatedly on his cheek as she spoke, "I wasn't expecting you back until next week..."

"I'm sorry darling. I tried to get back for your concert as a surprise, but I missed a connection and nearly ended up spending the night on a bench on the station platform. Fortunately, this really helpful chap picked me up..."

X turned away in disgust as Olaf told the story of his heroic journey. Back thirty seconds and already he was talking about himself.

He was forced to follow in their wake, unable to disguise his sudden collapse in mood, from Pooja, who kept casting concerned glances in his direction, although Eva was, naturally; totally oblivious. He walked beside Pooja in sullen silence behind the happily reunited couple, forced to watch Eva hanging off Olaf's shoulder, kissing his stubbly cheeks and pushing curlicues of his now shoulder-length hair away from his ears to do so, "Where did all this come from?" he heard her ask him playfully.

"There are no barbers in the Arctic Circle", he joshed, "which reminds me..."

And so it went on.

The whole evening was slipping away from him.

No. Fuck it. He wouldn't let the smug shit ruin his night. He linked arms with Pooja, forced a smile on to his face and announced that they would 'strut their funky stuff together', and marched off after the retreating couple.

By the time they arrived, the club was already packed. Men and women of all ages, gay couples, straight couples, old couples and singles crowded its under-lit dance floor, or sat at its edge on tall stools around raised circular tables. The music was loud in the immediate vicinity of the dance floor, but quiet enough in the rest of the club to hold a conversation without having to raise your voice more than a fraction. The queues at the bar were short. The music varied, during the course of an increasingly interminable night for X, from a mellifluous jazz-fusion, with an emphasis on rhythms rung out on a xylophone, to a slightly harder but still tepid funk, and drifted in and out of the most unchallenging Latin rhythms from salsa to calypso. Everyone danced, young and old, alone or together and no one cared if they were any good or not. The men weren't intimidated by the hip-swaying requirements of the Latin beats, and gay and straight men danced together, touching each other if the moves required it. The conversations around the tables were invigorating and lively, people flirted and paired up, but no one got boorish or messily drunk. The toilets were clean and smelt of pine. On three occasions the tunes were interrupted by a live act, a solo singer with a forked beard and a high plaintive voice, who sang maudlin folk tunes while accompanying himself on a harmonium. The crowd would often join in the chorus of these pieces, singing along lustily and applauding vigorously when the minstrel's short sets were over, many discretely wiping a tear from their eyes as the flute-funk started up again and the dance floor filled. Every second hour they turned the music off and everyone sat on the floor holding hands, while volunteers raised and lowered a huge tarpaulin above them until they had all cooled down and the music could start up again.

It was, all told, a really nice atmosphere and everyone was having a really good time.

Everyone; that is, except for X.

X's determination to enjoy himself despite Olaf's return had not lasted much longer than the time it took to cross from the entrance to the dance floor. Attempting to exhibit the necessary spirit of mindless cheerfulness the occasion demanded, he had allowed himself to be cajoled straight on to the centre of the room, with Pooja ahead of him and Olaf holding his hips from behind in a kind of conga. Once there, he had danced listlessly to the first few tracks with a fixed smile on his face, firmly resolved to focus solely on the women and shut Olaf's presence from his mind completely.

It was a doomed strategy right from the start.

Eva herself was no great dancer, but any moderately attractive woman who moves her hips from side to side and occasionally raises her hands in the air can look like a goddess in a nightclub, and Eva was beautiful beyond compare, but watching her move was to X an achingly bitter reminder of the night that could have been. Pooja too, he had to acknowledge, could indeed, strut her funky stuff. She had let her long dark hair fall freely down the full length of her back, and each time she shook her head it swept about her body in an arc of jet-black silk like a Bollywood superstar. On another occasion, X would have been honoured to be the companion of two such gorgeous women, but not tonight. He could take no pleasure in Pooja's beauty when the true focus of all his desire was revelling in delight at another's company. Every glance at Eva's ecstatic face, reminded him that her joy was not for him and he could scarcely bring himself to look at the sparkling sapphire eyes that shone so brightly for someone else. And there he was, Olaf, a smug half-grin on his face, twirling Eva as if the music playing was ballroom or rock and roll, deigning to accept the kisses that she flung at him from her upturned, smiling face. The only pleasure that X could genuinely gain from the never-ending evening was the discovery that Olaf really couldn't dance at all. He either stepped from side to side to an uneven disco beat that was almost never playing, or stood flat-footed while performing a strange kind of dip from his hips that splayed his knees outward as though Charlie Chaplin had accidently wandered into a reggae club.

Pitiful.

But it was no real compensation, and X had quickly tired of shuffling around beside the canoodling couple like Eva's little brother who had been invited along only because there was no one to babysit him at home, and had retreated from the dance floor to a stool at its edge, where he sat, a lone scowling figure in a room full of people as high on life as evangelical Christians in the grip of the Holy Spirit.

He was nursing a beer and contemplating whether he could drag Olaf to the toilets and strangle him with his bare hands when Eva came over to speak to him. His mood was so black that there was no hope of disguising his unhappiness, and she immediately asked him what the matter was, her face full of tender concern as she spoke. Unable to answer truthfully, X turned his bile on the club, its clientele, the music and its cosy, unchallenging, edgeless atmosphere. Making no attempt to disguise the contempt in his voice he pointed out that there was another, bigger world out there, beyond this 'cosy little campus and all its smug certainties' "I mean", he went on, his voice increasingly bitter, "what do you do around here if you want to take some risks? What do you do when you're angry?" and before she could reply added, "No, better still, what do you ever do that's actually exciting?" He was suddenly aware that he had come close to calling her boring, and wished he could take back the accusation as soon as the words had left his mouth.

But Eva didn't seem at all upset. Rather than being wounded by his words she ignored the implied insult and was laughing as she replied, "Oh X, you will have to stop hanging around with me! Ask Xanthia - I *never* do anything exciting!"

There was no malice in her reply, but perhaps he had touched a raw nerve somewhere, as she added, her voice now sounding disappointed, as though he were a promising schoolboy who had just let his teacher down, "But is that what you are really interested in X? Hedonism? ... And I had begun to believe you were genuinely seeking Sweden..."

HAMMERSMITH BROADWAY

He was jerked awake as the taxi pulled up abruptly at a set of traffic lights by Hammersmith Broadway.

Coming up from the dream, and before his sight had returned, he recognised the distinctive shuddering and rattling of an idling bus engine. Then the bus itself emerged as a big red blur of colour, then the traffic lights themselves, hovering in the air and surrounded by a penumbra of green light.

He felt the taxi pull away. He blinked twice and was fully awake.

He wiped at his mouth with his fingers. Only the tiniest amount of spittle dampened his hand.

He looked at the meter. The figure was shocking but at least this time the dreaming hadn't had anything to do with it.

For the remainder of the journey home he ran the dream over in his mind. On the one hand, its length had been more like an ordinary daydream, and for once there were no untoward consequences from being so totally out of it while he was under. But in every other way it had been as weird as all the previous ones, more like a hyper-real acid-flashback or an out of body experience than an ordinary dream. But the strangest thing about the dreams, he thought, was the way he stepped in and out of the narrative so consistently. He could recall no other dream that he had ever returned to, and certainly none with such continuity of story or cast of characters.

No scratch that, the strangest thing about his fucking dreams was that he had such a shit time in them. It was all very well inventing some Scandinavian Barbie to fall in love with, but what kind of an arse dreams up their own personal Ken to go with her?

It was fucking ridiculous.

No. It was time to knock these dreams on the head once and for all. After all, he now had a real Über-babe to chase down.

16. PARIS

As soon as he'd got the car, he knew that Paris was the answer. If Paris didn't do it, nothing fucking would.

The GTI had finally fallen into his lap through a stroke of pure good fortune. The display manager on New TV, who was in the office so rarely that even some of his own team didn't recognise him when he showed up, was caught fiddling his expenses. Not content with passing the occasional bogus lunch receipt, exaggerating his company-conducted mileage and hand-writing a taxi chit or two if he was short at the end of the month, he had been sufficiently greedy and sloppy in his petty theft to put in a claim large enough to draw attention to himself. When a series of receipts depicting an intense period of business entertaining were found to coincide with the dates of his annual leave, and consisted entirely of meals in cafes and restaurants in Dorset he was out the door without compensation, almost entirely unmissed.

A GTI came with the display manager's job.

He had immediately formulated a plan to ensure not only a firm grip on the 5-speed gearbox for himself, but appropriate advancement for both his protégés into the bargain. He would take the display manager's job, and, of course, the car, bringing Sara with him to the big glossy pages as his assistant manager. Jeanne would be promoted to his old job as classified manager. When he'd called them into Howard's office, it had been to outline his proposed redistribution of wealth and consult on the best way to pitch the idea to Howard. He hadn't been expecting any opposition.

Sara, however, was far from grateful.

She had reacted with barely contained anger, her eyes flashing as she stood in front of him, her hands planted square on her hips, leaning forward as she spoke, "Let me get this right. You two are managers and I'm only an assistant?"

The gaze she had fixed him with as she spoke was suddenly street-fighter tough, and he struggled to meet her eyes. In Howard's tiny office, they were separated by no more than a few feet and the effect was bludgeoning. He would have physically retreated under the power of her stare, but there was nowhere to step back to, and he was able to stand his ground only thanks to the pressure of the rim of Howard's desk against the back of his thighs. Having not anticipated any need for toughness he had prepared no response for her hostility, and, thrown completely off balance, found himself pleading with her to accept the favour he was granting her, "I can't see what the problem is – they're all promotions…No one remotely competent has sold display since the magazine's launch – you'll destroy all your targets…You'll make more money than both of us put together …"

She had remained adamantly opposed.

"Make me display manager or forget it", she insisted.

But she couldn't win this argument. It didn't make sense. He spelt it out to her, "But if you're display manager and Jeanne's classified manager…What am I doing?"

"Good question", she replied tartly, then laughed.

The laughter broke the tension.

She sat down next to Jeanne, the air still charged from the confrontation in the confined space, a single silent shrill note seemingly hovering above the sudden quiet.

Still standing while the women were seated below him, X calmed down, and as he re-ran the incident in his mind's eye, he found it charged with crackling sexual tension. Close enough to feel her breath on his cheek as the laser-flare of her eyes had cut into him, he'd been the object of the brilliant flash of beauty-enraged. For that moment, the Vogue cover model had glared out of the page from under her long eyelashes, proud, angry and defiant and *he* had been the man with enough sheer balls to dare to snatch her attention away from her own self-regard. He had to summon up an image of Margaret Thatcher to prevent himself from getting an erection.

He was brought back to focus when Sara began speaking again,

"This would be better', she began, pretending to be speaking off the cuff, but clearly outlining a pre-prepared plan.

It was only then that it occurred to him that Sara would have had plenty of time to consider the implications of the display manager's larceny. Her network of contacts ran everywhere in the company, almost certainly even into the accounts department. She had probably known about it before the man's wife.

"Jeanne gets classified. I'm the new display manager, but you really luck out X", she pitched, "you get a brand new post with a grand title and overall responsibility for both teams – half-way to publisher if you like."

He was listening.

She was quiet a moment while she pretended to run over possible job titles in her mind, one of her sharp white incisors biting gently on her soft lower lip as she did so, as though she was really lost in thought. "Got it!" she declared, her smile bright enough for truth, "Group Advertising Manager!"

'Group Advertising Manager'. He rolled it over on his tongue a few times. He liked the sound of it. It sounded like something. "Jeanne?" he asked.

"Howard will like it", she'd replied, "No, cancel that, Howard will love it. It sounds innovative… He loves innovative… it may even be…" And at this point she threw her arms in the air and assumed the dazed expression of joy of a worshipper at the Holy Sepulchre, "it may even be…blue skies!"

He'd accepted the superior merits of Sara's plan and switching tack instantly, agreed to pitch it to Howard provided Sara accepted a few conditions first, "First off", he'd begun, "I get to keep the display manager's car and secondly, you have to triple the number of pages to get any kind of bonus at all." He had done his best to sound commanding.

Sara was ready for him, "Triple the pages *in my area* for a bonus."

"Your area?"

"I'm sticking with London. The bimbettes can do all the mileage, they're better suited for it. And you can keep the damn car."

Jeanne had, of course been right. Howard had lapped it up. It hadn't quite been blue skies, but it was certainly out of the box.

Group Advertising Manager he was.

A memo was duly dispatched upstairs to accompany his promotion. In Howard's hand it declared absolute confidence in the upward progress of New TV, expressing certainty that there was even more to come now the 'bad blood' had been flushed out. It praised his young protégé as responsible, once more, for thinking outside the envelope, and how the new innovation was sure to liberate the 'startling talents' of Jeanne and Sara. X was unsure of the wisdom of this. If Nick was protected by his own holy naivety, there was no certainty that Mike Verne had the same myopia. What Howard had entirely failed to see was that he had either created a totally unnecessary extra tier of management or called directly into question the very purpose of his own job. He would have to raise the magazine's income rapidly now, it wouldn't be long before the finance director started to question the wisdom of paying both his salary and Howard's.

But for now he had the car, and Paris beckoned. If he could just get her to come away with him, the city itself would do the rest of the work for him.

He'd made his move on the Thursday, after the magazine had been put to bed, and although the title was still in the red, it had been the fattest issue yet, and the atmosphere in the office had been buzzy. Everyone else had left for the Hen and Chickens to celebrate, leaving just the two of them in the office finishing up the last bits of paperwork from the day's sales. He'd come over and sat on the edge her desk, eyes downcast and speaking in a mock solemn voice had pitched the idea in a tone he had hoped was humble and yet a little gallant at the same time,

"Here am I", he'd begun, "Newly promoted and enriched accordingly, with both the means and a yearning to spend a weekend in

Paris, but...", he raised his hands in a Howard-like gesture of appeal for divine inspiration..., "Alas! Paris without a beautiful woman as a companion is an impossibility!" He dropped his shoulders and held his hands out toward her in a gesture of despair, "What can I do?"

It hadn't gone quite as planned.

Her voice had been cold and emotionless when she spoke. "Just to be clear from the start", she'd replied, "I'll come with you if you understand that the payment for taking me on a magical mystery tour is my company. No more." Then she'd spelt it out, although she hadn't needed to. "I won't be fucking you in gratitude X'.

He winced at the phrase but maintained his cool, "*Charmant!*" he'd replied, "Terms understood."

"And separate rooms"

"And separate rooms. Adjoining?"

"Only if necessary."

"We'll have to work on extracting the full romance of the city, but OK. If we get out of the office sharply tomorrow afternoon...

"Really -this Friday? It's a bit short notice." There was a pause while she thought about it. "Why not!" She was beaming now, a richer smile than he could ever have expected, "Paris – how exciting!"

He turned the corner in the corridor before punching the air with his fist.

*

It had started well.

They'd slipped away from the office about 3 o'clock, apparently on separate appointments, and had got out of London before the traffic snarled up completely. The GTI was beautiful under him, bursts of grip shooting them through amber lights, roundabouts slipping past like chicanes, torque present whenever he needed it, the power kicking in like a mule when he stabbed the throttle. He had put it over the ton on a straight stretch of the A20, and would have gone faster still if Sara hadn't told him to calm down.

Girl next to him, car under him, top down, sun high up above them, on the way to Paris.

That whole afternoon.

Clover.

They had talked easily for the length of the journey to the coast, rolling over their familiar subjects, the prospects of the magazine, the most stupid and significant company gossip, Howard. They had laughed a lot. For the whole stretch between Maidstone and Ashford they had challenged each other to communicate only by trading Howardisms, their increasingly tortured metaphors sending them repeatedly into fits of uncontrollable laughter and culminating in X's 'you've got to take the hamster by the horns and spin it round the wheel", which had them laughing so hard he nearly lost control completely and put the car in a ditch.

Things started to go wrong when they reached Folkestone.

The wait for the ferry to load had taken an age, and once on board, although the sea was scarcely even choppy, Sara had felt immediately sick. She could only cope with the swaying motion of the boat by lying horizontal on one of the benches on the forward deck, the fresh sea air helping her stomach settle except when a swirl of wind swung a plume of ship diesel over her. He'd sat by her a while as she concentrated on keeping the nausea at bay with her eyes closed, shielding them from the sun with the back of a limply held wrist. Having brought over a weak, sweet tea in a plastic cup, and feeling there was nothing else he could do, he'd left to change some sterling into francs and spent the rest of the passage putting his change into the slot machines.

It was a short voyage, and X had thought the worst was over as they settled back into the comfort of the GTI's leather seats on the car deck. They'd had to wait a while for the bow doors to open, and there was a false start, everyone starting their engines although there was no sign of any movement ahead. The delay was for no more than a few minutes, but the effect of all the idling engines in a confined space was enough to push Sara over the edge.

"I'm going to be sick!"

"Shit...puke out the window."

He pressed the button and let the passenger window slide down fully. The petrol fumes rolled in unchecked.

She vomited over her knees and into the footwell, a spray of half-digested tomato slices and cucumber pebble-dashing the instruments beside him.

"Oh fuck No..."

Not on his brand new car.

He looked down at the damage only briefly, before having to concentrate on engaging gear and negotiating the down ramp, and didn't look again until they were weaving their way through coned lanes on the dockyard toward customs. She was completely drenched in vomit. Her purple knee-length velvet skirt was splattered with chunks of regurgitated food as though she had dropped a plate of goulash on her lap. In the footwell her stockinged feet and the heels she had kicked off for comfort earlier lay in a sloshing pool of watery vomit. She seemed to have emptied the entire contents of her guts in one go, and the rising stench of bile was already unbearable. And she was on the point of freaking out.

"Stop the car!" she screamed. "Stop the fucking car!"

"I can't just stop the fucking car", he'd shouted back, "We haven't got through customs yet."

"Stop the fucking car!"

He weaved out of the cones and came to a screeching halt just before the customs post.

This looked really suspicious. A wave of paranoia rolled over him. Shit, did he accidently have some draw on him? He began checking his pockets frantically, digging his fingers deep into the corners to feel for any fragments that might have lodged there.

Sara got out of the car.

She must have had the same thought as X, as, even in her distress, she stood a moment to display her sick-splattered legs to the glass customs booth, before heading round the back of the car and beginning to strip off on the roadside. She responded to the first honks from cars coming off the ramp with a flick of the Vs over her shoulder. By the time she was bare foot and leaning into the boot in only her knickers and bra, the blare of horns from the passing cars was a continuous wail.

When she returned, she had slipped into a pair of tight blue jeans and a t-shirt and sat in the back, refusing adamantly to come anywhere near the puke drenched front seat.

He had entered France as though he was her taxi driver.

*

Fifty kilometres along the road to Paris and he had had enough.

Only with the top down and the windows wide open could they drive without being overwhelmed by the putrid stench, and as the sun dipped toward the horizon it began to get uncomfortably cold in the car.

And Sara was still in the back seat.

He'd pulled up at the first service station they had passed to try and rescue the situation. Dropping Sara of at the cafeteria to freshen up and get something to drink, he'd hosed out the vomit at best he could by the pumps, and bought two beach towels and the strongest air-freshener he could find in the garage shop. When he returned he'd found Sara sitting at a bench in the picnic park around the back of the services. She was taking great bites out of a ham roll and slurping on a large carton of Sprite as he approached, her constitution apparently completely restored. She unwrapped the cellophane on a second roll, "D' ya want some?" she asked with her mouth full, a sweaty pink slice of ham poking out of the limp white bread like a severed tongue.

He declined.

She shrugged and started on the second sandwich, gulping it down with the same gusto as the first.

*

It was a long drive to Paris in a car that smelled like a badly maintained hospital. They drove wearing jumpers and coats, with the top down and with Sara sitting on folded beach towels in the front seat. The pine air-freshener was completely defeated by the stench of puke, succeeding only in adding a sweetened edge to the rancid fumes, a mixing of odours which was, if anything, worse than the smell of bile alone. They had to take frequent stops for respite along the route, standing at the roadside gulping great lungfuls of the fresh night air, hopping about and slapping their arms across their chests to stay warm, as they were buffeted by the vortexes of passing lorries. But the mood inside the car gradually improved as the miles of open fields and chestnut trees rolled by in the dusk light, and by the time the view was reduced to the abstract language of the road at night, red and white smudges and flares rushing toward them in the darkness, they were laughing once more.

After they'd left the service station Sara's had started fiddling with radio dial. Each station seemed to broadcast the same garbage; endless incomprehensible dialogue, conducted by the excitable presenters in a French far too rapid for either of them to understand; the news reportage and interviews blending seamlessly with ecstatic testimonials for furniture salesrooms and bathroom accessories. In between the chatter the DJs played a mixture of ambling jazz, soupy French ballads, and the tiniest trans-Atlantic imports possible. Sara kept optimistically trying to find something better, but after the thousandth burst of static and garbled station interference, his patience had snapped and he had barked at her to 'leave the fucking thing alone for God's sake!"

"Haven't you worked it out yet?" he'd gone on, "They're all the fucking same. You won't find anything better" he'd concluded, "French radio is universally shit." Finding something to moan about that wasn't her ruining his brand new car lifted his mood, and speaking in an exaggerated French accent, he mimicked a French radio executive arranging the station playlist with his fellow executives, "We are agreeeed then Messieurs", he hammered, if it has no discernible bass and as little sincérité as possible, and eet was both big in America and really, really sheet last year we play it. OK!" Suddenly cheerful, he laid down a challenge to Sara, "Go on test it out. Stay on this station and I'll bet you every single track will fit the criteria – I'm telling you, shit tunes are a legal requirement for French broadcasters."

"Meubles! Cinquante pour cent! Fantastique!" faded away followed by a weak, vaguely soulful dirge neither of them recognised.

"Wet, Wet, Wet", the announcer declared orgasmically as the tune faded away, "de l'album 'Popped in and Sold Out'"

"Did they really call an album that?" asked X pausing before adding, "You've got to admire their honesty –add one to the shit column."

"I quite liked it."

He raised an eyebrow in response and said nothing.

There was a mournful torch song in French accompanied by something as painful to the ear as a zither and then, 'Fools heaven is a place on Earth' rang out from the radio.

Sara sang along with the chorus of Belinda Carlyle's big hit.

"Shit", said X.

"It's a classic", argued Sara. He couldn't tell if she was joking.

There was a long stretch of rapid speech followed by portentous chords which was probably the news and then, "It's got to beeeeee perfect."

Sara sang along to that one too.

Four session musicians with pony tails and the cliché level racked up to ten, cash in on a one hit wonder", opined X. "Shit."

Sara hadn't argued.

Then they came thick and fast.

"I could be so lucky, lucky, lucky, lucky…."

"Perfect", exclaimed X laughing triumphantly, "Stock, Aitken and Waterman and an Australian soap actress, could it get any more banal? Has Jason Donovan conquered France too or just Kyle? Will we get Jive Bunny too?"

Then in quick succession,

'Nothing's going to change my love for you.'

"Shit."

Then "Always on my mind', by the Pet Shop Boys, which X actually rather liked, having danced to it a hundred times with Toby.

Sara sensed weakness. "Why would you let that one of the hook, It's just as tinny as any of the others", she'd argued.

X had wanted to defend it even though it meant he would lose his hypothetical bet, and had babbled about how it was 'sad lyrics over uplifting tunes like Northern Soul' and "anyway its knowing…"

"You don't think Bros know what they are doing?", she'd argued, and again he wasn't sure if she was teasing him or actually arguing the case, so he allowed her to win the battle and therefore still stand a chance of victory in the war, and assigned the Pet Shop Boys to the shit category.

They had a disagreement over Terence Trent D'Arby, Sara claiming that 'Sign your name across my heart', was a timeless classic, and X arguing that it was only a hit because everybody fancied him and it would be completely forgotten within a year.

Victory was his when the next track, 'Get out of my dreams and into my car' came over the speakers.

Sara was in fits, "The sex attacker's theme tune, brought to you by the sweet, soulful tones of Billy Ocean. You're right X", she conceded, "They're all shit."

She turned off the radio when U2 came on and by that time it was nearly midnight and they had reached the outskirts of Paris.

*

They had bickered over where to stay.

"It's just practical X", Sara had argued, "We should book in at a Hilton or a Sheraton – we could even get a place by the airport and come into the city tomorrow, they'll have plenty of rooms and are used to people turning up at strange hours…"

There were no circumstances in which X was going to start a romantic weekend in Paris in a chain hotel at the airport, and he drove into the labyrinth of quietened Parisian streets as though he had been suddenly struck stone deaf, letting her carry on talking until he had found an appropriate place to park. He squeezed the GTI into the only vacant slot left by the Citroens, Peugeots and Renaults that ran bumper to bumper along a narrow tree-lined street. Hotel signs with a variety of stars hung above rusting metal balconies along its length, there was a a pavement café at the corner, and a Bar-Tabac halfway down the street and its graffitied shutter pulled down for the night.

It looked about right.

*

Only the last of the four hotels they had tried had any vacancies.

The sign over this one also showed three stars, but it was shabbier than all the others. Two weeping figs grew up either side of the desk, their dusty stems and lifeless green foliage merging with the plastic vine leaves that ran below the light fittings to create a sort of tawdry grotto, the purple carpet at its entrance was threadbare, and a light layer of dust filmed every ornament in the lobby. X had commenced the humiliating ritual of requesting a room with little hope of success, leaning through the plastic fronds to attract the attention of the hotel's elderly proprietor who appeared to have nodded off behind the counter. The old man roused himself and stood, peering at X through lenses as thick as lemonade bottles.

"Je voudrais deux chambres, s'il vous plait", he asked wearily.

On each previous occasion this had been met by, "*Deux chambres monsieur?*" expressed in a tone of appalled surprise and coupled with a look over his shoulder at Sara, young, wild and beautiful, perched stony faced on her luggage behind him, her full breasts outlined against her t-shirt and her tight jeans guiding the proprietor's eyes over her hips to the perfect v at her crotch.

"Oui monsieur, deux chambres", he'd been forced to reply each time.

Each time he had been met with shrugged shoulders and expressions of commiseration both for the lack of room and for his failed conquest. During each shuffling exit, the grey-haired proprietor or stubbled night porter would take his unmanning as license to let his eyes linger lasciviously over Sara's arse as they headed for the door. At each consecutive humiliation Sara had been unable to prevent herself from reminding him that there would certainly have been plenty of room at the Sheraton and that the rooms were clean and comfortable.

But here, for the first time, the proprietor paid no attention to Sara at all, perhaps unable to see her across the lobby through his thick lenses. He reached behind him and laid two keys with wooden fobs the size of paddles on the counter between a bouquet of plastic pansies and a strange Betty Boop figurine, whose enlarged head nodded in time with the hotelier as he recorded their passport details.

To get to the fourth floor they entered a tiny clanking metal lift, and rose slowly, pressed face to face in a space the size of a telephone booth. He handled it as though he was on a crowded tube train, keeping his focus at some abstract point in the middle distance as though he was unaware of her breath against his neck and the brush of her nipples against his chest, allowing himself only glances of her dark hair and shadowed eyes in the flickering light that fell in bands of gold and shade through the metal grill as they rose. He made sure he kept his bag in front of him to hide his erection.

Their rooms were on the same floor, three doors down from each other with a communal bathroom on the other side of the hallway. The first one they tried was lit by a dim ceiling bulb under a pale blue shade, its light so weak that X was forced to trail his hand along the wall for guidance, tracing the wallpaper's embossed floral pattern like brail as he entered. Feeling his way toward the double bed in the centre of the room, he sat on its mattress with a squeak of iron springs and turned on the bedside lamp. The room brightened only a little. He got up and raised the sash window, small flakes of dried paint floating onto the sill as he forced it open. Leaning out as far as he could, he caught a glimpse of the Eiffel Tower over the tops of the roofs in the far distance. He was going to point it out to Sara but she had already turned and wheeled her luggage back into the corridor.

The other room was worse. It had only a single bed and the view out of its window was into a narrow courtyard full of television aerials and air conditioning units covered in thick black grime.

Sara didn't even turn round as she bid him goodnight, waving him off with a tired hand gesture and asking him to wake her in the morning.

He had a desultory wank in his single bed and fell fast asleep.

*

He woke around eight-thirty and scuttled across the corridor for a shower. He had wrapped the thin, scratchy white hand towel the hotel provided around his hips but it was only capable of covering either his cock and balls or his arse, but not both at the same time, and he crossed the hallway as quickly as he could, as exposed as a patient dressed for surgery. At nine, he'd knocked on her door for the first time, shouting through it that he would be in the café on the corner and she should come and join him when she got up. By ten he had finished his second café au lait and sat checking his watch and swirling the soggy flakes from his dunked croissant in the milky residue at the bottom of his cup. By eleven he had given up banging on her door, and with the aid of an Anglo-French dictionary was working his way through a long article in 'Le Monde'. The piece appeared to be about something the Minister of Agriculture either had or hadn't done, but he couldn't make out exactly what it was the minister had been accused of or why he should care, and, giving up he sat staring out the window at the TV aerials and wondering whether she had gone out without him.

At eleven-thirty, she knocked on his door, stepping in quickly when he opened it. He had never seen her so natural and defenceless.

She was still groggy from sleep and, swaying slightly, lent against the wall for support. Standing in her bare feet on the thin carpet, it was as though everything about her had been softened, her face somehow plumper, her curves more rounded and gentle, and her very presence less commanding, more delicate and vulnerable. Her hair was sleep-messed, tousled at the crown into short, fluffy clumps, and thousands of fine strands, static-rich and back-combed by sleep, spun out from her head like the cloud mist formed at a waterfall's edge. She had on a baggy t-shirt and had wrapped one of the tiny hotel handtowels around her waist. She looked up at him from under heavy eyelids, through dark lashes just as long and even more perfect without mascara, and when she spoke, it was through lips swollen puffy by sleep,

"Where's the bathroom", she mumbled.

He guided her out and across the corridor, steering her sleep-befuddled passage with a gentle hand between her shoulder blades. Her T-shirt had got bunched up in the towel behind her back, lifting it up above her waist and ensuring that what she wore give her no more cover than if she were dressed in a high-slit micro mini-skirt. As he walked behind her the short distance across the corridor, he had to fight to restrain himself from reaching out to touch the soft, honey-coloured skin of her upper thigh and the swell of her left buttock that exposed itself in front of him with each alternate stride.

*

By one o'clock he was bored out of his mind in yet another department store.

It hadn't started out that way. When they had finally left the hotel, X had been forced to accept that it had been worth the wait. She looked fantastic.

Sara had put on a collared blouse under a thin lapelled, three-buttoned jacket above a pencil skirt, black stockings and four-inch heels. She had done something with clasps in her hair and subtle changes to her make-up that made her seem both Parisian and yet exotically different at the same time. The effect was mesmerising. The modesty and restraint of the clothing she had chosen was resisted at every seam by the curves of her body, as though Sophia Loren had been cast in Audrey Hepburn's role in 'Breakfast at Tiffany's'. Sara, in a city full of pretty women, turned heads as she walked beside him.

He should have been glorying in the circumstances. But instead he was monumentally bored. The luxury goods and corporate chain stores of the Champs-Elysees seemed as familiar and dull to X as Oxford Street, and even the pavement cafes on its wide boulevard were pastiche. Sara, in contrast, was completely in her element. To her, each high ceilinged hall in each department store was a cathedral, a site of worship to the goddess of good taste. She approached the sculpted, perfectly coiffured women in the makeup department with such élan, that their joyful response to her gesticulations and pigeon French seemed genuine, and hours seem to pass in gesture, counter gesture, smiles and laughter.

When they entered the first perfumery Sara had grabbed his arm declaring, "Heaven", as she sniffed the air. Already bored he had snorted his disdain. "Come on X', she had chided him gently, "after the journey we had yesterday you can't pretend this isn't smell nirvana!" He'd done his best, but had quickly exhausted what small pleasure was to be gained by dabbing sandalwood scents on his wrist and ended up sitting on a shoe plinth in the neighbouring section, tapping his foot and checking and rechecking his watch.

On the third of many floors devoted to women's clothing he had cracked, switching from the suave and debonair man he had hoped to present to her, into a spoilt and petulant child. She had ignored his whining for some time, but he had persisted, finally managing to tear her away from the racks by arguing in that as they were in Paris they really out to do 'something cultural', otherwise, "what was the point in coming…" It had sounded as sulky as he felt.

She had given him a withering look, but had ultimately been willing to agree to a visit to the Louvre. She had brought a guidebook before setting off and it was on one of the pages she had folded over as a 'must see'. They took another taxi. X would have preferred to be transported around the city like a Parisian, descending under the Art Nouveau metalwork of the Metro signs, to be swooshed beneath the surface on rubber wheels, or better still, to experience the city on foot, walking at random through the streets as the surrealists had suggested, chancing on the city without looking for it at all. But Sara had chosen four-inch heels as her footwear and even the short walk from taxi to Louvre was a stumbling lurch over the cobblestones. Before they had even reached the gallery, Sara had been forced to take off her shoes, and tucking them under her arm, had entered the building on stockinged feet like a penitent pilgrim approaching a shrine.

X took an instant dislike to the Louvre. The palace was so out of any human scale that the only conceivable explanation for its existence here on the banks of the Seine, he felt, was if some careless God had jettisoned it by flinging it down wholesale from the sky. It seemed to him that the stone fortress of a gallery squatted in the beautiful city of Paris as ugly and imposing as the Bank of England in Threadneedle Street. His mood didn't improve when it became clear that Sara had no interest in art. Her sole purpose in coming to the Louvre was to see just one painting; the Mona Lisa.

So they marched for an hour through miles of soft-carpeted hallways, paintings, hung in overwhelming gilded frames, crammed onto every square inch of the endless corridor walls. They passed thousands of Madonnas holding distorted infants on their laps, uncountable numbers of last suppers presided over by a mournful Jesus, and an emaciated Christ was tortured time and time again on his cross. Craftsmanship that had seemed astonishing for the first fifty metres was rendered commonplace by endless repetition. After a while he stopped looking at the paintings altogether, and concentrated on negotiating their way through the crush of bodies in pursuit of their goal. But it was difficult to move fast, the bored tourists who clogged the passages moved slowly, drifting along like old people on the edge of dementia at a garden centre, enjoying the experience but not at all sure why they were there. They'd made a wrong turn somewhere and, stuck in a cul-de-sac of still lifes, surrounded by dead pheasants and never-spoiling fruit on pewter platters, he'd lost his temper and dared to suggest that they abandon their quest to see the famous painting.

"Why is it so bloody important to see the Mona Lisa?' he'd snapped.

She looked at him, dumfounded, replying, "Because it's the Mona Lisa", as if no other explanation was required.

But X was irked now and began to argue with her, "But you know what it looks like already. What's the point in seeing it? I'm not giving anything away here but it's a painting of a woman. She has brown eyes and chubby cheeks if I remember rightly. Why don't we look at some paintings we *don't* already know?"

But Sara was not going to be defeated by logic, and they trudged on, eventually joining the correct queue and traipsed with the crowd past the picture, hustled forward by the guards posted in front of the boundary rope. He tried to get something out of the experience as they passed the canvas at the pace of a funeral cortege, but he couldn't summon any emotion at all in response to the picture. Da Vinci was undoubtedly important, he thought, but he was no Caravaggio.

Things had started to look up at Notre Dame. They had entered the church in the middle of a service, with rainbow-coloured light pouring into the nave through the stained glass high above them and with the choir's voices rising through thick clouds of incense, she had been enchanted and, for a moment taken hold of his arm. With rising confidence, he had guided her to the Pont-Neuf to attempt a romantic set piece.

It hadn't worked.

She'd perched beside him on the thick bridge wall as he had instructed her to, facing back into the city while he'd uncorked a bottle of red wine and begun breaking up the baguette, lining it up on the wall next to the ham, camembert, cucumber and fat lumpy tomatoes he'd picked up from a street stall on the way.

"Have you got any butter?' she'd asked.

He hadn't.

She had sniffed at the cheese disdainfully and sat picking of the succulent fat from the ham with the tips of her fingers, dropping it in the river below as though she was removing bird shit from her clothes.

"The bread's a bit crispy."

It was supposed to be fucking crispy.

The traffic crossing the bridge buffeted them with hot exhaust fumes and the wind whipped little bits of grit into their sandwiches.

"So what are we doing here", she'd asked.

He hadn't known how to reply.

It had been a wonderful moment in his life the last time he'd been here, but he realised it had been frankly stupid to attempt to replicate it. He'd come to Paris from Berlin with Nadia, before all the drugs and the nastiness. Some friend of hers had had an apartment in the Sixième Arrondissement that she needed flat sitting for a fortnight while she was on holiday. Stepping out of the Gar du Nord they had scored some weed and had decided to celebrate their arrival in Paris by heading down to the river, picking up a picnic on the way. When they had unwrapped it from the cellophane the grass had been weird-looking, orangey, flaky, and had a strange smell. Assuming they'd been ripped off they'd laughed about it, put it away and concentrated on the red wine instead. They'd ripped the baguette in half, stuffed chunks of cheese and ham inside, and sat chewing and grinning high on the bridge wall, the water rushing far below them as though they were suspended above a ravine. When Nadia had remembered the weed, she'd stacked the joint on the assumption that it was going to be rubbish, but after a couple of tokes they had been knocked senseless by the spliff's unexpected potency. For hours, or so it seemed, they were trapped on the bridge, unable to stand, and confined to their stone cornice they had sat giggling hysterical giggles at the sheer absurdity of their situation. When they had finally got straight enough to walk, they'd staggered off the bridge in each other's arms and falling into her friend's big bed they'd fucked like bunnies until dawn.

That wasn't going to happen this time.

So it was back to the Champs-Elysees again. This time, however, X knew that he would be unable to fake even the faintest enthusiasm for another pair of shoes or a polar-necked cashmere sweater and, leaving Sara to it, arranged to meet her in a café in a couple of hours' time.

He drifted as far as possible from the main thoroughfare eventually finding a network of smaller streets, with bookshops, restaurants, hair salons, and little boutiques. He bought Sara a fine silk scarf in a deep green he thought would match her eyes and then spent an hour selecting some lingerie in a small shop full of white boxes, shelves and glass drawers under the guidance of an elegant Frenchwoman in her forties who carried herself like Catherine Deneuve. She had been charmed by his choice of fine black silk translucent panties and bra embroidered with a bird motif and responded to his choice of garter belt as though he had surprised her with an eye for detail that she would only have expected from a French gentleman of considerable sophistication. She had laid the tissue paper in the box, bound the ribbon with the delicacy of a surgeon's fingers, and presented him with a delightfully wrapped package, a smile, a 'voila!' and a surprisingly large bill.

Sara had been so late at their meeting point that by the time they arrived at the Eiffel Tower, the tour was just being ushered into the lifts. X rushed to join the queue for tickets, but Sara sauntered away toward one of the tower's feet and stood peering up the tower from its base. He had to let go his place in the queue to follow her.

"I'm not going up", she'd said when he'd caught up with her.

X was aghast. "What do you mean you're not going up? The whole point of the Eiffel Tower is that you go up and look out over the beautiful city from above."

"I'm not going up in these shoes", she was adamant, "Anyway, I'll fly over the city someday – I'll see it from above then."

"You have to see the Mona Lisa, but you don't have to climb the Eiffel Tower?" X's delivery was both tense and sarcastic.

Sara responded in kind, a shortness in her tone as though his persistent failure to see the obvious was beginning to get on her nerves. "But I have seen it – We're here aren't we? And anyway, I think it looks more impressive from down here, don't you?"

She had made him take a photograph of her by the huge metal span of one of the feet. She'd posed with one hand held against the sun, maintaining the exquisite artificiality of a fashion shoot for long enough for him to get a couple of shots off.

In the taxi back from the tower, X had an epiphany.

He'd been on completely the wrong track with his whimsical romantic scenarios and felt annoyed with himself for being so stupid. Sara was a different kind of girl altogether; to woo this woman he needed to provide a thick dollop of glamour. There was no alternative. He would have to throw the chequebook at it.

He got the taxi to pull up when he spotted the first up-market, old-fashioned French restaurant they passed. It had the appropriate Art Nouveaux styling with high curved glass windows and beech wood panelling, and through the glass he could make out wide circular tables laid with clean white linen, fine crockery and silver service, the waiters moving between tables with the grace and speed of ballet dancers.

Perfect.

He held open the door for her and they stepped in, entering, flanked on either side by tall glass cabinets set with tiers of delicate cakes and pastries, and were guided swiftly to a table at the back of the restaurant next to a large, bubbling tank, where live lobsters with bound claws shuffled uneasily around its gravel bed.

Neither of them had much French and the menu was hugely complicated and largely incomprehensible. There were twenty pages to the wine folder. With both of them uncomfortable in the unfamiliar surroundings, X chose the moment to take command. With a wave of his hand he sat back in his chair, laying his napkin on his lap and began pontificating. "We are on holiday", he said, "Celebrating. In these circumstances, and faced with a menu we don't understand, the best course of action is simply to order the most expensive item and then eat together whatever emerges from the kitchens." He'd spoken in the most off-hand, man-of-the-world manner he could muster, and Sara offered no resistance so they went with his plan. He was paying after all.

X chose the "Grande Plats de Fruits de Mer", none of the contents of which were familiar to him but knowing that 'fruit de mer' meant shellfish, felt it was the perfect choice to appear sophisticated and he began to look forward to tucking in to steaming mussels and lobster,

Sara could not be persuaded to share a bottle of wine with him, and to his great disappointment insisted on ordering a lemonade. It would be much harder to get her into bed if she wasn't at least a bit pissed. She'd even been disappointed with her lemonade when it arrived, baulking at its sharp taste and asking him if it was supposed to be this cloudy. She put it to one side and ordered a coke instead.

When the dish arrived it consisted of a silver platter the size of a dustbin lid packed with crushed ice and was lowered onto its own silver plinth in the centre of the table with great ceremony by the deferential waiter. The shellfish displayed on it were all cold, raw, or soaked in vinegar. Most prominent were three huge sea snails, their edible parts extending from their shells like thin pale dog turds, half pushed through the animal's anus and onto the bed of crushed ice. There were rubbery balls of chewy whelks, clams in herb-soaked vinegar, cold slabs of Oyster and mussels, four beady-eyed crayfish, a dressed crab and something with big glutinous suckers that might have been squid but was probably octopus. On either side of their plates the waiter laid a complex set of shiny implements that looked more like gynaecological instruments than cutlery. Sara didn't even pretend to try to eat any, but X had to fake pleasure in his grand gesture, eating his way through the least repulsive fare in front of him. But even the oysters slid down like mucus, and by the time he was braving one of the giant snails he could feel the rubbery little cockles he'd picked from their shells with a silver pin earlier bubbling on top of his gastric juices like polystyrene at a weir.

Sara waited him out before ordering a crème caramel. Then there was an extended period where she made her selection from the cake trolley, during which X largely concentrated on not throwing-up. While Sara charmed the waiter with her exquisite choices of pastries, he sat gulping the bile back down, taking sips of water when it seemed safe to do so.

*

It was no later than ten thirty on Saturday night in Paris before X had closed his hotel room door behind him, and another hour before he'd given up and put two fingers down his throat over the toilet bowl, sleeping soundlessly alone in the single bed after his purge.

*

They left for England shortly after breakfast. He felt, and looked, dreadful. Sara was radiant. She was carrying a new clutch bag with a metal clasp and had changed the make up around her eyes to a Parisian style that suited her perfectly. Loading her Chanel carrier bag carefully into the boot she explained with delight that she had picked it up at less than a third of its true price, despite only the faintest of fading from window display. She accepted his present with a smile, saying she would open it when she was back in London, reassuring him that she was sure to find it delightful, "As long as it isn't lingerie", she added, "Men are always buying me lingerie and it never fits."

The journey back was just as long, but passed much more quickly and pleasantly then the outward one. The beach towels were now in a Parisian street bin, and although the car still smelt a bit, they were used it and driving with the top down, the spring air soon flushed out the worst of the odours. The sun was bright and hung above them in a cloudless blue sky for the whole journey back and, muffled in a thick jumper, it was warm enough for Sara to doze off in the leather seat, cat napping through much of France and only waking up as their neared Boulogne. X began to feel that, despite the dashing of his high hopes for the trip, there were hints of a new intimacy between them that hadn't existed before.

When he dropped her off in Tooting, she looked fresh and reinvigorated from the trip, while X was so shattered that he didn't even try to get himself invited in for coffee, and his only thoughts at their parting were of crawling into his own bed and closing his eyes.

"Thanks X", she'd said cheerfully. "That was fun…. But really, you know, we should have flown!"

*

He stripped off as he walked through his flat, stumbling like a zombie in the direction of his bed, leaving a trail of clothes behind him from doorway to mattress. With his last once of energy he pulled his socks off before falling naked, face down on the bed, dragging the sheet over his back with one arm, he wrapped himself in the Egyptian cotton's softness like a moth in a cocoon.

As soon as he closed his eyes the dreaming began.

17. MORE FUN

There was a moment's calm, enough to take in the pale blue sky, the frozen stream and the breath from his lungs condensing in the cold air. Then his feet slid out from underneath him. Instantly his arms were flailing wildly, violently, windmilling as he fought to stay upright while his legs kicked up and out in front of him in a kind of maniacal goose-step. If a firm hand hadn't grabbed his shoulder from behind he would certainly have fallen, painfully, flat on his back on to the hard ice. Propped up by the unknown hand, he gradually regained a semblance of balance and with both feet planted directly beneath him, inched his body vertical until he was able to stand upright on his skates with only a little wobbling at the ankles. He turned his head to thank his saviour, but the lateral motion sent his feet skittering again, and before he was able to express his gratitude fully, he was clinging on tightly to his rescuer's torso, grabbing fistfuls of his jacket and with his head pressed firmly into his chest.

Jorgund accepted his thanks dismissively, greeted him warmly and, once X had reassured him he was OK to stand on his own two feet, let him be, taking two steps away before executing an ice-hockey player's spin turn and joining a group of young men huddled together a few metres away, coming to a halt, effortlessly, in a small arc of sprayed ice.

Left alone, X surveyed the scene cautiously, moving only his eyes to avoid upsetting his precarious balance. Winter had fallen since his last visit and it was bitterly cold. The birch trees in the copse by the bank were now stripped of all their leaves, leaving their thin bare branches shivering in the icy blast of wind that skimmed across the tufted sugar-ice surface of the field, kicking up flurries of snow in wave-ridges as it passed. On the frozen stream itself, about thirty people had gathered below the bridge wearing thick jackets woollen hats and scarves and fidgeting in the cold, the moisture from their collective breath hanging in mist clouds in the air around them. The crowd was growing rapidly as he stood, rigid, on the edge of the throng, new arrivals swooping downstream into the pack or scrambling down the frozen mud banks onto the ice. The biggest group of skaters had coalesced around Jorgund, a broad-shouldered voluble mix of padded men and women, pressed together in a loud, back-slapping cluster of camaraderie. Periodically, individuals would wheel away from the group in stiff, arm-waving pirouettes to re-heat their frozen muscles before re-joining the mass, their movement creating an air of anticipation like the jostling for position of sailing boats at the start of a regatta.

He spotted Eva, gathered in a huddle with Pooja and Sven on the other side of the stream. The three of them sharing a flask of some hot drink, its moist steam escaping sluggishly in the cold air. Eva had her scarf wound about her neck and having pulled her woollen hat low over the bridge of her nose she was recognisable only by the brilliance of her eyes which seemed to flash across the ice toward him like the mirrors of a lighthouse.

X crossed over to them, progressing in clumsy step-stumbles and by using whatever passing body was available to give him some kind of purchase. He was greeted delightedly by his friends, but each attempt to press foreheads undermined his precarious equilibrium, sending his legs into a frantic running on the spot motion followed by a desperate clutching.

His friend's faces bore a mixture of amusement and concern. "Can you skate at all?" asked Sven, after X's feet had performed an involuntary moonwalk, this time with no apparent stimulus at all.

X had actually had lessons as a kid, he seemed to recall, and boldly claimed that 'it would all come back to him', once they got going. His companions accepted his words with sceptical expressions. Pooja offered him some soup, holding on to his spare elbow as he supped from the flask with the same care she would have granted one of the elderly clients she visited in her capacity as a social worker. He'd only managed to get a few delightfully warming sips of the soup down his throat when, in response to a whistle, shout and wave from Jorgund, the whole group began to move off en masse, and the ice was packed with shuffling bodies, brushing shoulders as they swayed up into stride. Eva and Pooja linked their arms through his and pulled him along with the rest of the mob. Their momentum carrying him forward over the ice with his legs held mostly rigid. Escorted in this way by the two women, he was swept, a willing prisoner under guard, down the gently falling frozen stream toward the city, gliding effortless between the snow-covered banks as though propelled through a dream.

The frictionless falling through the wintry landscape continued for long enough that X was lulled into a state of contented stupefaction, and as his progress did not require any real effort on his part, he was able to look around in delight at the beauty of the frozen riverbank. Reeds had been turned into crystalline skeleton armies and small waterfalls into delicate ice sculptures as though time itself had suddenly frozen, and smooth banks of snow swept down to the stream as white as the surface of the moon.

After an hour or so the skaters ahead of them came to an abrupt halt, causing those behind to bash into them as they braked, and sharp cries followed by laughter broke out in the cold clear air. They had reached the point where the stream joined the city's great river, frozen into a broad ice raceway, a quarter of a mile wide, that swept majestically down into the city below. It was like arriving at a motorway junction from a small country road.

On the far side of the river, as though occupying an invisible fast lane, individual skaters, heads down in skin-tight suits, shot by like bob-sleigh racers, while close to the bank families and groups of kids drifted by in clumps, gliding past at an easy pace like lorries on a long haul. Eva and Pooja, didn't leave him much time for contemplation, towing him out into the slow lane with their arms still linked with his like two kind granddaughters escorting a geriatric relative on his daily constitutional, and then gently releasing him into the flow. Sven followed behind, prepared to catch him if he fell backwards.

He began to make slow, ungraceful but upright progress along the river's edge. At first, out of loyalty to the group they had come with, even Jorgund's friends hung back, circulating their quartet like friendly predators, but after a few minutes they grew bored and began to slip away, taking one -two-three steps before slipping across into the fast lane, gliding away like seagulls on a coastal breeze. Jorgund himself stayed close by for longer, concerned and attentive, but as his friends disappeared one by one, X could sense how much he was itching to join them and sought to release him from any sense of obligation. His attempt to wave him away, upsetting his balance again, and Jorgund steadied him one last time before pushing away into the fast lane with wave of farewell, a shrug and an apologetic smile. X heard him whoop with delight as he gathered speed into the first bend. This left only X and his three companions, hobbled to his lumbering pace, all feeling obliged to attend to his trip-stumbling descent. After five minutes or so, he had gained enough confidence to shoo them away, agreeing to meet them at the bottom under 'the green arrow sign on the wharf – you can't miss it", as Sven had explained. Even then Eva remained reluctant to leave him, hanging back after Sven and Pooja had both waved goodbye. She lingered, hovering anxiously around her charge, touching him lightly when he looked likely to fall, as attentive as a parent watching the progress of a newly walking toddler.

X had to insist she leave him be, and despite her protestations, he remained adamant, "Honestly Eva, I'm fine – Go! – Really, it'll be more fun for both of us."

She gave him one last check, touched him gently on the shoulder, and then, her conscience sufficiently satisfied, crossed one slow, long leg over the other and swooped away, gliding across the frozen river bed with the grace and economy of motion of a swan in flight.

Although the highway seemed to dip slowly down to the city, the sensation, to X, was that of standing at the top of a ski-slope and he suspected that the odds of a hurtling rush of pleasure and those of a cartwheeling crash of twisted ankles and broken bones were about even. Still, there was no choice. So he took a deep breath and pushed off. Alone in the cold air, he quickly began to rejoice in his freedom from observation. With each stumble now unwitnessed, there were fewer of them, and he could finally relax his shoulders, let his movements become more fluid, and began moving across the ice less jerkily, starting to sway with a swimmer's motion in a controlled wave down the ice flow. He was mostly alone on the ice in his descent, lost in reverie as he made his slide down the hill. Occasionally he would be startled by the swoosh as a shark peloton of speed-skaters sling-shot by in the outside lane, the blast of wind that followed their sudden assault on the air temporarily unbalancing him in their wake. On two occasions he was overtaken by large groups of young men and women heading down into the city. The first passed around him in a loose swirling pack, many skating backwards as they chatted to one another, they briefly absorbed him in their churning mass of laughter and conversation before spitting him out behind. The second group shot through at speed, their faces set firmly to the wind, advancing at pace in a v formation like geese, their arrow point leader sliding slowly back into the pack as they passed, her replacement inching calmly forward to take their place in the head of the wind. The disruption of their passing caused the first of many falls onto the hard cold ice.

He was rarely joined in the slow lane, and then only for as long as it took a skater to smoothly side step his lumbering passage and glide by. A five-year-old boy with a satchel kept pace for a while, his hands clasped behind his back, before politely stepping past and pulling away into the distance. Later two-pre-teen girls caught up with him, interrupting their continuous stream of chatter only to nod hello as they slid by. After half an hour's descent, he had largely ceased falling over and, enjoying himself, had begun to feel that his fears of catastrophic injury had been entirely unwarranted. His confidence proved premature. As the river neared the heart of the city, its easy curves began to tighten, and, bound now by stone embankments and brick bridge ramparts, it grew narrower and steeper and his speed over the ice grew quicker and quicker. X began scrabbling and stumbling down the ice slip, forced to make sudden desperate changes of direction to avoid wiping out in the bends, his journey now a kind of frantic slalom between high stone walls. Faster and faster he fell, towers and spires, twisted at oblique angles, rotated above his head as the river's course snapped violently from side to side, flinging him under bridge spans and toward jetty walls. In the monochrome of white ice and dark stone, X's jagged passage felt as though he was falling through the chiselled knife marks of a medieval woodcut. The river hurled him on, steepening and splitting around islands of bouldered stone, forever threatening to throw him into bruising contact with its walls or fling him up over its stone ramparts to land in a shattering of bones on the quayside. And then, suddenly, it was over, the river slowed and widened out into the bay, shooting him out on to an arctic ice flow, heading out to sea and into the pale blue sky and white birds beyond.

    Across the bay he could see a giant arrow, glowing neon green against the dark harbour wall and he steered toward it. As he neared he could make out his friends waiting for him on a slipway in the shadow of the high harbour wall, leaping up and down, shouting and waving when they spotted him across the ice. He slid over to them, both hands raised above his head in triumph, his friends cheering ecstatically as though they were villagers rejoicing in the return of a fishing boat long since thought lost at sea.

They clambered up to the top to join the crowds gathered there and weaved their way to a good viewpoint, high on the back wall with a view of the whole sweep of the bay. Below them the frozen harbour had been laid out as a race track, an ice circuit that started between black barricades and high walls, then wound out into the bay itself, completing a long clean sweep before plunging back through the harbour mouth in a series of coiled sinewy curves beneath the gaze of the watching crowds. He made out Xanthia, lower down on the wall but closer to the UV lit track, leaning out over the barrier and shouting incomprehensible encouragement to the cars below.

The race had begun just before they reached their vantage point, and X's first sight was of a procession of bright coloured cars snaking their way out of the harbour mouth. At first he was disappointed, there was almost no sound and the pace was slow. It seemed more like a pageant than a race, and the little cars like child's toys, some sort of flattened dodgems sliding by on the ice.

Sven pointed out Per's car to him as they made their second pass around the circuit. It was about half-way down the field, its shiny livery mostly white, but with a thick orange band running the full length from nose to rear wing with the number twenty-seven breaking up the band in a white circle in the centre of the roof. The second circuit was faster, but still it was all a bit slow and X said as much to Sven.

"Just watch", he replied.

The cars got faster and faster with each circuit until they reached their maximum velocity around the fourth lap, by which time it seemed impossible to sustain such blistering speeds without destroying themselves against the barriers. From this point on the driver's task was to maintain as much momentum as possible around the whole course of a lap, a skill requiring the pilot to execute what amounted to a perfectly controlled power slide across the ice, travelling in a kind of suspended crash, where minute corrections of the wheel, made in long anticipation of the onrushing corners, delivered just enough change of direction to miss the barriers by millimetres. In the harbour section, a sequence of fast corners were laid out, wide enough for two cars to run side by side, and, by allowing two different angles of attack into each corner, overtaking moves were possible here if the chasing driver timed every action to perfection. The layout enabled both cars to maintain impossibly high velocities through the curves and set up a terrifying drag race beneath the cheering spectators. The car with its nose ahead at a certain trigger point, set off a flashing alarm and a klaxon wail and obliged the loser of the drag race to yield, slotting back in line centimetres behind the lead car at the very last moment before a collision was inevitable, nose to stern in line but now compromised for speed throughout the rest of the lap. It was a breath-taking, almost silent, ballet under the lights. The cars, orange, sky-blue, yellow, olive green, shooting like ice hockey pucks across the bay. Spins were rare, but when they happened were endless spiralling ice dances across the track. Most ended in shivers to a halt against the barriers in a spray of ice dust, but in the hands of the most-skilled, neck-snapping gyrations along the ice course were righted with scarcely any loss of speed and to huge cheers from the crowd. As the race progressed and with margins so fine, more and more of the cars showed damaged bodywork from long grinds against the barriers and crumpled corners from being spat back across the track following high-speed collisions.

Per stayed out of the walls and rose slowly up the order. He made two fantastic passing moves below them while they bellowed their support but he was just short of the trigger point on two other occasions and had to drop back in line, his progress up the field stalled.

The last third of the race had a different character. By then the studs and blades on the car wheels had churned the track's smooth surface into ridges and furrows of ploughed ice, and each passing car flung up a spray of meltwater and ice chunks into the windscreens of the following car and left a thick mist of frozen vapour in its wake that hung over the track and was whipped into fractal storm by each passing car.

Sven lent X his glasses so he could get a view of the race from inside the cockpit of Per's car. It seemed impossible that anyone could drive at all in such poor visibility, let alone at such speeds. Chunks of snow and ice spray, smashing on to the windshield repeatedly rendered the driver completely blind, and even when the wipers cleared the debris from the screen, the view from the cab was that of an onrush into a blizzard, a blind lunge into a white out that had to be navigated more by feel and memory than sight. Everyone had slowed, but Per had slowed less than everyone else, and it seemed that every lap they were cheering themselves hoarse as he picked off another competitor.

Sven Shouted through the cheers of the crowd as Per claimed another scalp, "See – when it requires as much bravery as skill, our Sven is, as you say, 'the dog's bollocks'." It wasn't something X ever said, but Sven was right. Under the most hazardous conditions, Per was the fastest man out there. There weren't enough laps remaining for him to get to the very front, but it was a hugely impressive showing nonetheless, and they hugged each other and whooped with wild delight as he crossed the line in fifth place.

Their party split up at the end of the race. Sven, anxious to join Per in the pits, dashed off with a hurried goodbye, shouting down to Xanthia to wait for him. Pooja too had somewhere else to be, so X and Eva strolled up together from the harbour and into a quayside coffee shop. The atmosphere inside was upbeat and the busy café was full of rapid dialogue and clear laughter.

"Is today exciting enough for you?' Eva asked as she put down their coffees and settled in to the sofa next to him.

X could only agree that it was. It seemed incredible that the ice descent was now almost a distant memory. It had been a very exciting day indeed and he said so.

She smiled, triumphantly but without rancour. "And I owe you an apology too X", she said, "last time, when I was so pleased to see Olaf and you were so critical of everything...."

He had thought she hadn't noticed.

"It wasn't right of me to question your values", she continued, "it was...... It was mean. I'm sorry."

He knew she was being too kind, he remembered he'd been almost spiteful that night. She had nothing to apologise for. He tried to explain, but she dismissed his words, "Forget it. Anyway – you were probably right, maybe I do spend too much time on campus."

"You do spend too much time on campus". It was Xanthia joining them at the table. She nodded to X and slumped onto the sofa beside Eva.

"That didn't take long", he said, slightly disappointed that his time alone with Eva had been so quickly cut short.

"Yes, it's very predictable", she explained, "The only bit I like after a race is the champagne and shouting phase. As soon as Per stops swinging you around and laughing he switches into wired lunatic with bulging eyes, either explaining some move you've completely forgotten or ranting about missing torque or whatever." She acted out a maniacal Per talking technical gobbledegook. They both laughed. "So what are we up to later?" she asked Eva.

Eva was a little hesitant in her reply and spoke softly when she did, "We're going clubbing with Jorgund's friends…"

"No!" Xanthia interrupted, clapping her hands and laughing raucously, "Eva and Chee chee go to Mash! I won't tell Olaf if you don't!" and she laughed again, this time a loud, dirty cackle.

"You know it's not like that', said Eva, blushing, "Do you want to come along…?"

"No way. I've already completed my Neanderthal activity for the day. And anyway, I'd rather eat my own excrement ", she added as an afterthought. "Honestly Eva, I'm not even sure that *pan troglodytes* here will enjoy it. Why don't you come out with me instead?"

X suddenly felt dizzy. He blinked. Time seemed to be jumping. Sven and Per were suddenly with them, and the café seemed much more busy than it had only a moment before. Per's hair was sticking upright in sweaty clumps as though he had taken his helmet off just before pushing through the café doors, still adrenaline-wired from the race, his skin waxy pale and his blood-shot eyes darting like a hawk's in their sockets. They remained standing, too rapt in conversation about the merits of different developmental engines to join the others. When X stood to give Per a congratulatory embrace, he got only a quick flash of a smile in response, returning immediately to his debate with Sven.

Xanthia raised her eyebrows to X when he sat down, "See", she said. It was the closest they had ever come to intimacy.

Any hope he had of a private moment with Eva was broken up by the arrival of Jorgund and half a dozen of his friends, who, crashing into the coffee house in a mass of shouting and whooping and squeezed themselves onto the sofa alongside Xanthia and X. Even when they had removed their padded jackets they were as bulky as marines, and as they were all to some degree drunk, they struggled to keep their voices down to the coffee shops' level of trill. A hearty, round-faced lad with a handlebar moustache put his arm around X, "Come with us", he was saying, his beery breath on X's face making him feel faintly nauseous, "We'll take you out – show you a good time!"

When X explained that he thought they were indeed intending to join them at the club, the young man looked initially amazed and then overwhelmed with delight. He immediately shared the good news around the group in a booming voice, and Eva and X were subjected to a round of huge bear-hugs, back-slaps and high-fives. A few minutes later that they were then pulled to their feet and dragged out of the coffee shop like elderly wedding guests pulled onto the dance floor by a group of pissed younger relatives. Xanthia remained seated, one flash of her eyes enough to keep walrus-moustache boy at bay.

"Ach – forget her – she's no fun."

Xanthia waved a dismissive gesture of farewell to X and blew Eva a kiss as they were bundled out of the café by the cheering throng. Walrus moustache and another of Jorgund's friends escorted them up the hill from the café with their arms held in a tight grip on either side like a friendly police escort. It was only a short walk as the club was nearby, its neon sign hanging between the marzipan turrets of an old Victorian music hall at the hill's crest and they were both propelled up the steps and through the doors in the centre of a scrum of bodies with their feet scarcely touching the ground. Inside, they were released from their tight embrace and unceremoniously dumped on to a long wooden bench that ran in front of one of the tiers of dented lockers that had transformed the theatre's baroque lobby into something like a gym changing room. The smell of sweat and beer suds hung heavily in the air.

Eva, for the first time since he had met her, looked as confused and out of place as him. She had taken a moment or two to recover her poise, and, smiling wanly at X had slipped out of her jacket and deposited it in one of the lockers. X followed suit, spending several minutes looking for a key, before realising that there wasn't even a lock on the door. By the time he had finished faffing around, the rest of Jorgund's party had stripped down to bare chests or sports bras and were charging through the big double doors into the auditorium, pumping their fists into the air and shouting out warrior cries as they entered the darkened space beyond. The sound of a band crashed through the doors as they swung open, some kind of fast paced rock with rhythmic shouting over the top, the sound horribly distorted by the lumpy acoustics of the hall.

He looked at Eva. She returned his gaze, head bowed, looking up at him through her eyelashes with a shy, nervous expression and, reaching out her hand, her long thin fingers entwined with his for the very first time. She squeezed his hand tight, and together they stepped forwards through the entrance.

BED

Shit.

That was the wrong fucking moment to wake up.

Perhaps not.

From the warmth of the sunlight on his face, he knew it must be morning, and when his sense of sight returned he could see the golden streams pouring in through his unbarred windows.

It was just after dawn.

He stretched out his arms and legs as though making a snow angel in the soft sheets.

No barking dogs or angry cabbies. No garbage in his face.

Definitely a much better way to wake up.

Normal.

Perhaps they were just dreams after all.

18. POSSESSION

Sara had insisted that they tell no one in the office about their excursion to Paris, as there was no need to start unnecessary gossip, and for the first week back, the existence of their shared secret created an illicit intimacy between them that the events of the trip itself scarcely warranted. But the frisson soon faded.

Then, out of the blue, one of Howard's long-heralded, hush-hush, golf-course negotiations, that they had all assumed were entirely fictitious; actually came off. He'd brought a new magazine into the expanding media division, *Commercial Director*, 'a plum ripe to pluck', as Howard described it, salivating heavily as he spoke and stumbling over the accidental tongue-twister in his metaphor.

Sara had a different perspective. "It's complete nonsense X", she had stated unequivocally as soon as she'd heard about Howard's new acquisition. "It's a vanity publication", she'd gone on, "How many commercials directors are there in the UK? …Ten? …Twelve? They spend a lot of money, sure, but a target audience of twelve? They're not the Gettys."

She had picked up a back issue from the pile by her desk and laid it open in her lap, but the out-sized floppy pages were too glossy to gain any purchase on the sheer fabric of her stocking tops, and the magazine kept sliding over her knees, eventually forcing her to lay it out on the desk in front of her instead. To demonstrate her point, she displayed three full page, full colour ads in turn. Each one showed images of men of similar age and appearance in a variety of dynamic settings, and the pages themselves were large enough to use as wall posters for anyone inclined to do so. It wasn't at all clear what they were actually advertising.

Sara paraphrased the copy as she showed him each image. In the first, a man was beaming from the behind the wheel of a Jeep Cherokee, the machine drawn up at a jaunty angle relative to the page, one wheel balanced on the ridge of a rut in a deeply furrowed trail, a dense forest fuzzily visible in the background. "Hi, Barry Bollocks wants all his rivals to know he is happy as a pig in shit with his new deal for Cadbury's chocolate bananas", translated Sara.

In the second, a pony-tailed man with a balding pate was captured pulling hard against the bow-whip of rod and line from the back of a charter boat in the Florida Keys, poised like a camp version of Hemingway in the sea spray. "Although Grant Testicles is gay, he has made shed loads of cash from a well-known manufacturer of sugary soft drinks, and is as much of a man as the rest of you put together"

In the third a bearded clone of the other two was staring directly into the camera with a self-satisfied smirk, seated behind a large mahogany desk with a huge unlit cigar in one corner of his mouth, Californian palm trees clearly visible through the window behind. "Big Brian buttocks has made a lot of money this year and want's you all to know that his thirty second commercial for stout was worthy of an Oscar and cost more to make than you'll earn in a lifetime."

"The only source of revenue for this title is twelve of these chumps waving their cocks at each other", she went on, "It can't last X, they'll either go bust, or merge, or suddenly decide it's beneath them to waste any more money on people they've already left behind. Mind you", she paused a moment while she contemplated the possibilities, "We might be able to squeeze some money out of it in the short term – but you'd have to be prepared to jump ship sharpish before it crashed, and it will crash – the whole concept's ludicrous."

Sara got the job as *Commercial Director's* Ad Manager.

They were equals now, almost. And he still hadn't fucked her.

Not quite equals, however. Ironically, as 'Group Advertising Manager', X had oversight of *Commercial Director's* revenue as well as the advertising in New TV.

Sara put him firmly to rights when he had attempted to remind her that he was still technically her boss. "Listen X. As we both know, this magazine has a short shelf-life. To make it work at all, you need someone who can make easy company with very rich, very arrogant men. Someone who can flatter them and flirt with them and gently stoke up the rivalry between them without seeming to do so. Someone who can convince them to demonstrate their virility through the pages of ego monthly. Does that sound like you?"

X had to concede that it didn't. They'd hate him.

"Anyway X", she'd continued, "this is classic project Howard. You don't want to be too closely associated with something that's destined to fail do you?"

She had a point there.

"But in the short term", she went on, "I get an insight into how some of the really big money moves about, on an expense account that befits my new status", she laughed as she spoke, and the delight in her eyes sparkled directly at him. "Face it X, you're not my boss any more - I'm two floors away - get to pick my own team…"

He had a flash of panic. "You can't take Jeanne", he blurted out. He could just about cope with losing one of them but if he lost both Sara and Jeanne he was completely fucked. He'd have to start selling again, and he wasn't at all sure he could stand to do that. The only alternative would be to find another Sara or Jeanne and that was near enough impossible. To have stuck the Klondike twice was in itself a near miracle, he couldn't expect to be that lucky again.

Sara put him at ease immediately, laughing gently at his distress, "Oh X!" she exclaimed, "I wouldn't dream of it!"

"Wouldn't work anyway." She went on, "this is a one-woman mission. I can take along a girl Friday and that's about it." She paused in thought a moment, "Give me Kajira" she suggested, and when he looked aghast, changed it to, "OK, one of the others then, one who's not yet completely brain dead. Hey! You can pretend its evidence of the great opportunities the company can offer ambitious young people and - who knows?", she shrugged, "Perhaps it is!"

"It's a new era X", she concluded, "I'm moving up. I'll let you know how the other half live!"

And with that, she was gone.

Except.

She had smiled when she spoke, and it still hung on her as she turned from him, a smile that wasn't just a message of triumph and farewell, a smile he'd seen before, the one she used when she had resolved some complex conundrum to her own satisfaction in a way she thought was both elegant and economical.

Something about him.

*

The informal celebration that followed the magazine's formal launch took place in the Hen and Chickens the same evening. He'd arrived late and the pub was already packed, Sara's popularity and influence across the whole company evident in the crush of bodies at the bar. Everyone was there, journalists and sub-editors, rival sales teams from up and down the floors, people from accounts who he only met when he handed over his monthly expenses, receptionists and secretaries, mail room boys who fancied her, even a few clients had taken the time to turn up and wish her well.

He couldn't see her over the crowd when he'd arrived, but he knew she was somewhere over in their corner, surrounded by an honour guard of excitable young women and gay men, chattering away at ten to the dozen, all seeking to get as close as possible in the hope that some of her sheen would rub off on them. It would have required some undignified pushing and shoving even to get near her, so he stopped at the bar, shaking hands and double kissing other late arrivals, responding to their gestures that he should join them as they made their way over to Sara by saying that 'it was her night' and 'he'd prefer to just admire her from afar for once', reasonably confident that he came across as magnanimous rather than merely sulky.

Arriving late, he'd missed the tab behind the bar, and had to purchase his own champagne at an absurd price, his discomfort further increased by the unwanted attention of a very drunk boy from a marketing magazine whose name he couldn't remember and who insisted on repeatedly apologising for some slight he felt he had once given X, expressing his remorse for the long forgotten insult over and over again until X felt like breaking his champagne flute over his skull.

He kept looking over the crowd's shoulders to see if he could catch sight of Jeanne, but knew that she too would be right at the centre of the throng, genuinely delighted for Sara and almost certainly flushed pink from a couple of Vodka Martinis. Someone in the crowd began banging on a metal tray, and then a deep voice shouted 'Order', followed by some loud laughter and as the crowd began to quieten, Sara's voice calling everyone to attention. To gain height over the crowd, she had stood up on the leatherette sofa at the far end of the pub, choosing the exact spot where he usually sat to address her gathering of well-wishers. He could only make out her head and shoulders from where he stood, just enough to see her raise a half-empty champagne flute toward the ceiling. There was a cry of 'shame', followed by the sound of a cork popping and she temporarily disappeared from view before reappearing this time with her glass filled.

"Thanks for coming everybody!" she declared to a chorus of drunken cheers. "As you know", she went on, placing both hands on her heart and looking wistfully at the ceiling as she spoke, "Thanks to hard work and exceptional brilliance...." There were more cheers and bursts of laughter, "As you all know - I've got my own magazine!" She waved her hands in the air in child-like delight as she delivered the line, beaming and slopping champagne down her dress as she did so and drinking up the raucous applause, cheers and whoops that broke like a sonic boom across the whole pub.

X looked around. All attention was focussed on her, and every face seemed to mirror her own delight. It was an impressive display.

When he looked back, Sara was holding up a poster-sized framed print of the front cover of Commercial's director, where her face had been superimposed on Madonna's body and the headline NEW AD MANAGER printed in bold block type displayed across the bottom half.

She hushed everyone in the crowd again, announcing that she must thank everyone who had helped her and blew kisses at every corner of the room before declaring in a kind of screech, "Where's Jeanne?" and scanning the room like a sailor in the crow's nest looking for land until someone tugged at her arm to reveal that Jeanne was standing right next to her behind a couple of tall lads from an Accountancy magazine. Laughing, she beckoned Jeanne forward, and as the crowd parted a little to let her through, X could make out that Sara was wearing the sleeveless royal blue mini-dress with the low cut back she had worn in Paris, and like all the other heterosexual men in the room allowed himself to enjoy the way it ran like a soft cotton glove over her curves as she bent down to kiss Jeanne.

Jeanne was bullied up on to the sofa next to Sara, and the two women embraced to cheers and wolf whistles from around the pub.

Sara quietened the crowd again, only half-successfully, and announced, "As anyone who has ever worked with her knows, the most helpful, cleverest, kindest most fun person in the company to work with…" she held Jeanne at arm's length while she looked at her, and having seemed to dab away a tear from the corner of her eye added, "we've been a great team!" choking a little as she said.

X raised his glass in a silent toast. There was no denying that.

There were cheers and a short burst of clapping and Jeanne waved shyly to the crowd before stepping back down into the throng.

It seemed like it was over, but Sara quietened the room once again, this time with a serious expression on her face and under her gaze the pub became almost deathly quiet. "But there's one person I want to thank more than any other', she announced into the silence, "He gave me an opportunity here after I'd been through a difficult time elsewhere and needed a break. He's always believed in me, looked out for me and supported me all the way. My mentor, my friend, my ex-boss. Where is he? Where's X?"

As Sara peered over the heads of the crowd looking for him, people who stood between them began to step aside, nudging others to get out the way, until a thin corridor had opened up right the way across the pub from the far corner to where he stood at the bar. He could see all of her now, from head to toe, her hair wild and loose, a light sheen of sweat on the smooth skin over her clavicle in the low cut dress, the perfect heft of her breasts, the curve of her hip. She had kicked off her heels to stand on the sofa, and between the hem of her mini-dress and the top of her sheer black stockings, he could make out an inch of honey brown skin broken only by the twin black bands of her suspender belt, each one marked with a delicately embroidered bird motif above each seam.

And……

There she was.

Hair a jet-black pre-Raphaelite swoon,

Long lashes and dark, soulful eyes,

Petite,

Power-packed and absolutely present.

Honey-skinned.

Hot.

No, more than that

Dynamite,

From tip to toe no more than five foot four of her,

Precious,

Perfect.

And looking directly at him.

"To X!" she declared, her eyes boring into his as she spoke, and raising her glass declared, "To X. No longer my boss!"

The cheers and applause were mixed with laughter at the slightly odd toast, but Sara kept her gaze completely straight, holding his eyes even as she downed her champagne glass in a single draught, still smiling knowingly as she jumped down off her pedestal and re-joined the party.

*

Above him, back arched, she gripped his ankles as she rode him, head thrown back, gasping, the twin sinews of her throat taut with the effort, rising again and again on him, her full, soft breasts spilling out of his hands. He ran his fingers over the two black brush strokes of her suspender belt following the curve of her hips and thighs, feeling the texture change under his fingertips as she rose and fell, honey flesh, black silk, honey flesh, black silk. She leant forward, stretching her soft skin the length of his chest, her lips falling to his, pushing her tongue hard down into his mouth and holding him there, his arms now pinned behind his head, her hands at his wrists as she moved on him. Slowing the pace, she inched the smoothness of his cock down from head to base, rooting him deep inside her and, sleeved in her tight velvet embrace, the downward push taking him to the brink, but before he let go she rose swiftly again, holding him right at the tip, a millimetre short of explosion, quivering on the edge. Her whole being, his whole being; focussed on the same exact point as she stared deep, defiant, into his eyes. She played with him, leaning back again and riding hard and fast, then stopping, rocking back and forth, cooing with pleasure, running her hands over his chest as she moved, pinching one of his nipples, smiling, wicked, dirty, delighted, before riding him hard again, crying out as she came, pounding him until he could resist no longer, spasms shaking his body as everything burst to silence in a blast of pure white light.

He had climaxed with her on top of him, dressed as he had always dreamed she would be, in the lingerie he had bought her in Paris.

*

She lay there, beside him on her back in his big wide bed, spent from lovemaking, her head propped on the soft pillows over which her hair spread like an aureole, her eyelids dropping heavy in languor, her long dark lashes veiling her sex-softened deep brown eyes, a lazy smile playing around the edge of her lower lip.

Perfect.

It was absolutely the right moment. He was certain of it.

Determined not to disturb how she lay by even the slightest fraction, he carefully stretched his left arm round to the bedside cabinet, scrabbling for the book of poetry without turning his head from the vision of her beside him. The book secured, he propped himself up on one arm, opened the slim volume at the marked page and began to read to her in the best Spanish accent he could muster, translating the words after each line.

"*Cuerpo de mujer, blancas colinas, muslos blancos*"

She looked up at him from under heavy lids, a faint smile forming as he read.

But he was in trouble immediately. The translation, 'Body of woman, white hills, white thighs', didn't fit the colour of her skin at all so he was forced to read it merely as "Body of a woman, hills and thighs' which just sounded lame.

Her forehead crinkled into a quizzical frown, but he persisted anyway, "*Te pareces al mundo en tu actitud de entrega*", a fantastic line he had always thought, but his translation as "you encompass the world in your position of surrender", only made her frown deepen and her nose twitch.

The next line, "*Mi cuerpo de labriego, salvaje te socava*", fared even worse, his translation of it as "my rough peasant's body, ploughs into you", produced a snigger in response.

Undeterred, although already sensing disaster, X persisted with the second verse of Pablo Neruda's poem, hoping she would understand how much he had yearned for the moment they had just shared,

"*Fui solo como un tunel. Di mi hulan los pajeros*

Y en mi la noche entraba su invasion ponderosa."

"I was alone like a tunnel", he translated, "even the birds fled from me, and darkness overwhelmed me with its crushing embrace"

"Alone like a tunnel?" she hadn't moved from her position on her back in his bed or fully opened her eyes but her voice was distinctly mocking, "what birds fled from you? Pigeons?"

He carried on bravely, anticipating failure but still hopeful, but by the time he translated the next lines,

"*Para sobrevivirme, te forje como un arma,*

como una flecha en mi arco, como una piedra en mi honda."

Lines he thought both powerful and beautiful, but she was openly laughing.

"To survive you forged me like what? A stone in your sling', come on X!"

He persisted, in the vain hope that the key line of the poem which came next would redeem the whole exercise, but as he saw her brow crinkle into a frown at the line,

"*Pero cae la hora de la venganza*

It wasn't her reaction that stilled him.

It was his.

For following '*Pero cae la hora de la venganza*' were the three short words, *y te amo*.

As he reached them he realised that the moment when it should have been a beautiful truth to utter those three short sounds, it would have been only a terrible, unforgivable lie to even speak them out loud. He knew at that precise moment, for the first time and with absolute certainty that he didn't, never had, and probably never would, love her.

He was stunned into silence.

Sara didn't notice, merely turning away from him, still chuckling quietly at his foolish failed romantic gesture, "Well that didn't work", she said with a snort, but not unkindly, "Now leave me alone will you X, I need to get some sleep. It's been a long day."

He lay on his back beside her, listening to her breathing in the darkness, unable to sleep, his mind racing. He had got everything he wanted, hadn't he? He had possessed the beautiful woman who lay next to him. She had fucked him like a porn star. He had made her come. What was the matter with him? He should be puffed up like a peacock, strutting around the flat, nursing his swollen balls with pride, ringing his mates, bragging, howling like a wolf through the open window, thumping his chest. Yet, in the aftermath of his triumphant conquest he felt only utterly alone and deeply sad.

The last lines of the poem ran over and over in his mind as he lay there, their meaning fully apparent to him for the first time, and as though they had been written only for him and for this moment, he lay, trapped in the poet's *oscuros cauces* where

la sed eternal sigue, y la fatiga sigue, the eternal thirst and the everlasting fatigue, played through him fated to suffer forever, alone in the world as the poet had warned with only *el dolor infinito* for company.

*

With Sara now officially his girlfriend, his star had never been higher in the company. They were the office glamour couple with their good looks, big jobs and stratospheric prospects, and the general consensus was that the world lay prostrate at their feet. He could feel the waves of envy breaking over his shoulder with almost physical force when they promenaded though the building, and when she had stayed over at his, the farewell kiss in the lobby came over like a photograph by Doisneau in the eyes of the awed receptionists. In the Hen and Chickens they presided over flocks of acolytes and sycophants, laughing at their jokes and treating each of his bon mots as though it was a pearl dropped from Voltaire's lips. Even the digs and insults muttered under the breath of the jealous mailroom boys were a compliment of sorts.

For all the pleasure it gave him to be the corporation's coming man, there were drawbacks. He quickly grew irritated by the constant attention and increasingly sought out ways to escape the intense scrutiny. To that end, he had begun to sneak off to an amusement arcade on Dean Street immediately after work when everyone else, including his lover, were already getting their first round in at the pub.

It was one particular game that had drawn him in, a machine so at odds with the rest of blinking, caterwauling, bleeping and roaring machines, and so rarely played, that its very existence in the arcade was a completely mystery to X. While everyone else was killing zombies or kick- boxing or racing cars around the Daytona banking, he had got into the habit of settling into to the plastic seat of a machine built like the cabin of a Tokyo Metro train. It was located right at the back of the arcade, beside the toilets, and X had never seen anyone else playing it. The instructions were entirely in Japanese and he had had to work out the rules himself by trial and error. The aim, he had deduced, was to pull away smoothly from each station without disturbing the standing passengers, and, by travelling at the correct pace, arrive at the next stop exactly on schedule, bringing the train to a halt at precisely at the correct position on the platform. The train itself was driven by a combination of releasing a heavy metal brake handle with one hand while applying slow and even pressure to the long grey bar that controlled the electric motor at the same time. This, he had discovered, was easier said than done, and salary men and sailor-suited schoolgirls were jerked from their hand rails many times before he mastered the art of a smooth exit from the first station, their speech-bubbled outrage filling the screen in incomprehensible Japanese characters each time. If the commuters were actually knocked off their feet the game ended straight away, such incompetence clearly intolerable for any Japanese public servant. After fistfuls of coins and false starts X had finally mastered the departure, allowing him to enjoy the wonderfully peaceful phase where for anything up to five minutes at a time the train trundled serenely through the rice fields and wooden houses of the Japanese countryside and the only requirement was to press sufficiently hard on the bar to retain a constant velocity. During this time he would float away on the peaceful pastoral scene, watching the ducked heads in the rice paddies and the volcanic mountains on the horizon in a state of stupefied contentment, entirely oblivious to the splattering brains of the undead, the slaps and shrieks and gun blasts and the squealing of tortured engines emanating from the rest of the room.

Sometimes he would sit back at the controls and look out from the booth at the rest of the punters in the arcade. Part of his pleasure in the whole experience, he suspected, was the arcade's existence as a kind of nexus point between his old life and his new, a zone where his new world of advertising, publishing and TV co-existed with the homeless world he had known before he stepped up, both groups sharing the same physical space without touching. While young graphic designers and Soho runners splattered brains across the screens, and stony faced Chinese men resolutely stuffed coins in slots beside the roulette and black jack tumbrils for no obvious return in either money or pleasure, half the arcade had no interest in the games whatsoever. The rough sleepers and hostel dwellers who hung about the entrance were a younger crowd than his old charges, but one or two of the faces were familiar from Strand doorways. Some were loitering by the consuls merely for warmth, others doing little deals, and when he looked carefully enough X could see crumpled up notes, tin foil and clingfilm wrap changing hands all around him. Others were scanning the room for those sufficiently engrossed in their game to have let a wallet poke invitingly out of a pocket, or deposited a handbag where a couple of paces and a swift grab could enable a rapid redistribution of wealth. Over by the doors, pretty boys taking a rest from the rough trade round the back of the Regents Park Hotel, stood sharing fags at the open street entrance, all keeping an eye out for the Chinese owners and undercover bill. Bizarrely, the low grade hustles and rat boy faces helped him relax, putting into perspective his minor office gripes and the fears of bursting bubbles that had beset him more and more since Sara had moved on, or perhaps it was a merely comforting to know that it all had nothing to do with him anymore and all their suffering had joined the huge expanse of someone else's problem.

    He sighed and returned to the game, easing into the station only three seconds off schedule, with only a single shaking fist and hieroglyphic bubble from his salaryman in a grey suit. He released the break lever easily and leant forward on the bar, a gentle hum rose from the machine and he left the platform behind and slipped back into the greenery of the Japanese countryside…

19. HEROIC ACT

He was holding Eva's hand as they passed through the big swing doors and into the auditorium. On the stage at the far end, a five-piece band, all as bald as Jorgund, belted out a Motörhead meets the Ramones set at a deafening volume, the lyrics roared out incomprehensibly fast over driving bass. On the dance floor, a sea of semi-naked bodies rose and fell with the music, bouncing off each other's sweaty torsos in arm clinches and elbow clashes, thrashing together like muscular maggots in waves of ecstatic delight.

Still holding her hand, X tugged at Eva's fingers and gently guided her toward a wide stairwell that led up to the balcony overlooking the pit, their fingertips only separating as they took the first upward steps. At the top of the stairs the balcony widened out, becoming as broad as the deck of a ship and ran in a horseshoe shape around the hall. They stood side by side looking down over the rail at the packed auditorium. He made out Jorgund in the crowd, leaping upward, rising out of the seething mass, his fist raised, his face locked in a great grimace of joy. He lifted himself briefly above the crowd before being sucked down only to reappear a few metres away, this time spread-eagled on his back, crowd surfing across the room with his face turned upwards toward them, his expression that of a religious ecstatic in the grip of the holy spirit.

"Jorgund's certainly having a good time", X said to Eva, pointing out their companion's passage across the dance floor below.

He had to step closer to her to make himself heard above

the noise, his mouth only millimetres from her skin as he spoke, and when she replied her exhaled breath caressed his ear like a touch of her fingertips. This close, he felt as though he could sense the subtleties of her mood in the tiny inflections of her voice and read her very soul in the ripples made by her breath in the fine hairs at his neck. He could feel the tremor of apprehension in every word she spoke, a shiver of anxiety, he was certain, caused not by his presence but elicited by the testosterone roars bursting up from the pit below, the cacophony crashing over them like the punishment of the damned.

When she spoke in the shouted whisper necessary to be heard above the noise, it sounded hoarse, deep, and tender, "So, 'Seeker of Sweden'", she said, the title half-mocking on her lips, "An answer to that question you asked?"

He could scarcely remember asking one, but recalled that an age ago in another, very different, nightclub he had bitterly asked her what she did for fun, "Not my form of entertainment", he shouted back, "but I get your point."

She smiled, a flicker at the edge of her lips, "Ah, but that was not the question! You have forgotten asking "Where are all the poor people?"

He hadn't but had thought it had long since been answered.

"There is your answer", she continued, indicating the dance floor below, "Jorgund."

"Jorgund?"

"Yes." She was earnest now, her voice slipping back into the tone of impersonal clarity she employed when educating him, "Jorgund has no higher qualifications. Indeed, academically he is slow to learn – you know this from computing I think?" She continued without waiting for his confirmation, although now he thought about it, it was certainly true, although he's assumed that it was *only* in computing that Jorgund had found it as difficult as he had to learn. "He struggles to resolve analytical problems that you or I would find simple", she continued, "His primary employment is in the administration of simple and repetitive tasks required for the care of sick or elderly people." She paused waiting for his confirmation and then continued, "In your society he would have a minimum wage job at best, barely enough to pay his bills and eat, No? Jorgund would be at the bottom of the...how do you say it ...right at the bottom of the stack".

X didn't correct her. There was no minimum wage in his society that he was aware of, except where there were strong trade unions, but her point seemed true enough.

"But", she continued, "Jorgund is also highly empathic, serious in his commitment to social duties, patient, and happy to undertake menial and unpleasant jobs in cheerful good spirits. He is a kind man. In our society, these qualities are highly valued and well rewarded, so not only is he comfortably off, he holds the respect of his peers and has a good life I think."

X was about to express his agreement when she started up again, "Ah, it makes me so mad X, this argument that some advance, that it would be a more just society if intellectually challenging work was rewarded more generously because of the rarity of its expression and therefore its higher net worth to society. Hah!" she exclaimed angrily as though X had advanced the argument, "Isn't it obvious that meritocracy is also tyranny! – What kind of society do we want? A clever one or a kind one?"

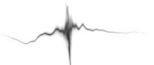

The question was rhetorical, but X answered her anyway, "Both?" he proposed tentatively.

She laughed, "Of course you are right. Forget it. Sorry to be so moody - come on let's have a drink at the bar."

"And then a dance", he deadpanned.

It took her a moment or two before she understood he was kidding.

Three rounds of schnapps later, the band's set was over and the auditorium below them fell abruptly quiet. Tables and chairs were brought in and arranged around the edges of the room and a DJ began playing a mix of electric blues and heavy soul. Eva ordered one more round of schnapps and then suggested they find somewhere to eat.

The boulevard was surprisingly busy despite the lateness of the hour. Cyclists shot by, their heads down against the cold wind, trams clattered past disgorging gaggles of elated passengers outside neon-lit nightclubs, and every restaurant was packed to the rafters behind its steamed up windows. They hadn't drunk that much alcohol, but it had fallen on stomachs protected only by bar-olives and pretzels, and as they weaved their way down the street it was clear that they were both quite pissed. Eva led them down the road, looking for a restaurant she had been recommended; her pale cheeks flushed pink, her eyes sparkling, both of them light-headed in the sharp air, nicely disassociated, floating out into the night together. They walked, not hand-in-hand, but shoulder-to-shoulder, brushing together and apart in a fluid stumble down the street.

He was euphorically happy.

A glass-walled building quite different from the others caught his eye. It was set back from the road behind a row of ornamental pines and lit by a large rotating sign bearing the image of a snake coiled round a staff. He was about to ask Eva what the slightly sinister sign represented when, having finally spotted the restaurant she had been searching for, she gave out a little cry of delight and stepped, without looking, into the road.

Slow motion in the adrenalin rush.

The onrushing car.

His leap in front of the vehicle.

A desperate grasping at her waist for purchase, a heave from the shoulders to shove her forward, flinging her beyond the impact, twisting his body to take the bulk of the blow himself. Looking up at her as they fell, her hair billowing out behind her, her face turning toward him frozen in shock, her arms involuntarily flung out in front of her like a superhero in flight.

Slam. Impact.

Her hip against the roadway and then, in the next freeze frame, her cheek smashing against the kerb, jerking her neck upward, surprise obliterated from her face, her expression instantly transformed into agony. The full weight of his body smashing into her upper thigh, his elbow and face slamming into the ground.

Silence.

All around him everything stilled, either because he was still functioning at mouse-life speed or because everyone had, indeed, stopped and was staring at him. A tall graceful woman with a poodle on a leash, a blond teenager in a bobble-hat, a row of cyclists pulled up at the kerb. All staring at him, the man lying on top of the girl in the middle of the street.

The car had stopped a metre away from them, somehow programmed to come to an immediate halt with faster than human reflexes and impossible brakes, or perhaps just not travelling as fast as the pissed bloke thought it was. It had pulled up comfortably shy of a collision, as insubstantial a threat to Eva's well-being as a toddler on a pedal car.

He lay on top of her in the road. Her face pushed down into the floor, his face pressed square against the cheeks of her buttocks, her left leg bent up under her at an impossible angle.

She was unconscious.

ARCADE

What the fuck?

The first sensation on return was searing pain. His nose felt like it was broken and his elbow smarted like he'd slammed it in a train door.

That couldn't be right. He'd hurt himself in the dream, not in real life. What the hell was going on?

When his vision returned he realised what had happened.

He must have fallen unconscious in the arcade game in a sudden swoon, and, pitching forward in the booth, the full dead weight of his body had smashed him face-first into the lever that powered the Tokyo tube train. Judging by the pain, his nose had slammed into the metal bar and he must have caught his elbow a nasty blow on something, probably the brake lever, on the way down.

Damn! It really hurt. He could hardly move his arm and when he felt for his face his nose and upper lip were sticky with blood.

What was that? Someone tugging at his bruised elbow, trying to pull him out of the booth, "For fuck's sake mate just give me a second will you", he swung round shouting.

"Get Out! Don't want drunk in here! Get out! This no place to go to sleep!"

It was the manager of the arcade.

X struggled to his feet, wiping his bleeding nose on the sleeve of his suit. Shit. This was an expensive mess. No dry cleaner would be getting that stain out in a hurry.

He checked his pockets.

Perfect. Of course he'd been dipped too.

His wallet and his car keys were gone.

20. HARLESDEN DOCTOR

The fucking clock tower again. How the hell had he ended up here?

It was the third time round the Harlesden one-way system and he still hadn't found the doctor's surgery or seen anywhere that seemed remotely safe enough to park the GTI.

When he'd first got back from Berlin, he'd crashed for no more than a fortnight at a friend's house in Harlesden. During that time a nasty looking rash had appeared on his scrotum, and fearing the worst after Nadia's serial infidelities, he'd registered with a local GP. The rash had cleared up on its own, and it was only when he'd decided he needed to get himself checked out after smashing his face up in the video booth, that he realised he was still registered with a surgery he'd never been to in a part of town that always made him nervous.

Deep breath. It was probably worth it.

Smashing up his face had made him wonder if perhaps Frank had been right after all. If it was epilepsy he probably needed to know. If one of these fugues happened while he was driving...

He was driving now.

Deep breath.

On the third tour he began to relax. Once you stopped trying to get through Harlesden, he concluded, you could begin to appreciate what its people had achieved. Faced with an arterial North-South road that ran through the heart of the town and could easily have left its population spectators on either side of an urban motorway, they had simply refused to acknowledge the existence of the road at all. Instead, the people from the Caribbean and West Africa who had settled here, knowing what a village should look like, had simply created one without asking anybody's permission to do so. The rush of vehicles through the high street had been slowed by a kind of rolling road block, cars permanently double parked along its length, others stopping at random, oblivious to horns and flashing lights behind, leaning out of rolled down windows to shout over at friends or harass passing girls. Old men leaned on half-opened car doors in the middle of the jam, shooting the breeze, while young mothers crossed the road chatting to each other as though pushing their buggies across a parking lot. The wide pavements were crowded and loud, young men shouting out the open doorways of barber shops, tired-eyed shop assistants weighing out plantains and yams from the fronts of fluorescent lit 24-hour grocery stores, and every second store selling hair extensions or jerk chicken. The town had survived. Commuters trying to get to Acton or Hanger Lane, sat cursing under their breath at the wheel of their log-jammed cars, forced to wait until the double-parked conversation was over before they could select first gear, reminding themselves to take another route to the A40 next time. It took forever to get through Harlesden.

But the place still made him nervous. Although the Stonebridge estate was cut off on the other side of the North Circular, some of the sheer nastiness of whatever was going on in that labyrinth of grey concrete seemed to seep into the town like cholera, infecting the people with red rapid eye movements and filling the fag butt and dog piss alleyways with furtive deals and sudden inexplicable bursts of rage.

And where the fuck did you park a Golf GTI around here?

*

He had finally found Dr Sookram's practice.

The receptionist, sat behind thickened glass in a booth as drab as any mini-cab office, pointed to a ticket machine on his side of the counter. He tore of a triangular chit of paper like those issued in the dole queue and asked how long the wait would be. She pointed one big-ringed, swollen finger up at the electronic counter above the booth and returned to her magazine.

It displayed number seventy-five He looked at the number on his chit. Eighty-one. Not bad, only six in front of him.

The reception area had all the charm of a veal crate. A row of benches were lined up below a wall-mounted TV that blasted out a continuous loop of advertorials for pharmaceutical products, the volume set loud enough to ensure the even hard of hearing could appreciate the sponsor's full message. The orange plastic coating on the seats shimmered under the strip lighting as though the sweat of their previous occupants had left a thin film on its surface. Taking a seat as far as possible from the TV monitor, he found that the plastic was too slippery to provide any grip for the material of his suit trousers and he had to brace himself at the knees like a sumo wrestler to stop himself sliding off the seat altogether.

Squatting uncomfortably, he looked around. On the next row along, an elderly, leathery-skinned woman, her bulky blue anorak buttoned up over her sari, coughed continuously into the white handkerchief she held in front of her face like a veil. Beside her a morbidly obese woman in sweat shirt and leggings stared at the TV screen while sucking absent-mindedly on her ventilator. In one corner a plastic milk crate held a range of broken plastic toys. A toddler sitting on the lino in front of the box, hit a receiver-less phone on wheels with the torso of an armless Cindy with a remorseless dedication as though he was determined to finish the vandalism an unknown predecessor had begun. Next to him his mum rocked a wailing infant on her knee, its cries only partly drowned out by the booming TV.

 Fortunately, turnover was brisk, and after the obese woman had shuffled out, his number came up.

He went through into the doctor's consulting room. A dark-skinned Chinese man was sat taking notes behind a violently disordered desk covered with crumpled flyers for medical products, ripped open cardboard boxes and plastic vials in cellophane wrappers. An unstable pile of back issues of *The Lancet* tottered at one corner. Above his head, a single framed medical certificate hung on a wall mottled by blu-tack stains, as though a multitude of other qualifications had been recently revoked.

X sat down opposite the desk.

Without looking up, the doctor desk pointed up at the clock mounted on the wall above him, and speaking in a clipped English accent said, "You got four minute."

X was taken aback. It seemed an absurdly abrupt way to begin a conversation, "But what if I'm dying?" he blurted out indignantly.

Dr Sookram looked up, "You dying?" he asked.

"No."

"OK", he looked up at the clock, "then you got three minutes and forty-five seconds."

He smiled without humour and wasting no further time came straight to the point barking, "So. What's wrong with you?"

Suddenly X didn't know what to say, he felt under pressure and suddenly wasn't sure if he even wanted to start telling this man about what had been happening to him. He began to stutter something about experiencing very deep repetitive dreams.

"Dreams?" Sookram interrupted, "what kind of dreams? What happens in these dreams?"

X wasn't sure where to begin and found himself saying, "Well there's a girl – it always the same girl –the dreams are very vivid and…"

The doctor interrupted him again, "This girl", he asked, "she horrible ugly, in your face girl? She got cuts and gashes on her like zombie or witch? She got your mum's face on little girl's body?"

"No", exclaimed X, "she's very beautiful…"

He would have said more but Sookram spoke up again, "and what you do with this girl in your dreams? You kill her? Rape her? Sit up all night talking to her corpse? Put head on end of stick and run round streets? What you do?"

X rushed to disabuse him, "No, we…we hang out together and do enjoyable things…

He intended to say more but was interrupted again, Sookram raising his hand to silence him. "Listen! You worry about too many nice dreams with beautiful girl." He paused, fixing X in the eyes before continuing, "Stop worrying! You boy! You heterosexual boy." He raised his hands to the sky in celebration. "Congratulations! You OK. All normal, no need to worry."

He stopped abruptly. There was a moment's silence in the room.

"What now?" X asked.

"You want anti-depressants. You not getting anti-depressants. You not sad." He was silent again.

"That's it?"

"You got one minute thirty-five seconds."

X hadn't needed them.

21. NIGHT AT THE OPERA

He couldn't honestly say he was looking forward to the double date with Sara and the man who might, or might not be, Toby's new boyfriend.

Toby had given him a call to tell him that he had met an older man who he thought was quite wonderful, and, after he had finished telling X, at great length, the exact circumstances of their meeting, the expression on his face when they had been introduced, the fine brown hair on his head above his smooth forehead, 'like down', the twin crows-feet by his 'twinkling brown eyes' and a thousand other minute details about the man's appearance and deportment, Toby had explained that Stuart had invited him to come to the opera with him that weekend. Apparently he had a box, or access to a box, at the Royal Opera House and had invited Toby along.

"...and he said bring some friends. There's two spare tickets so I thought of you and Sara" Toby had concluded.

X was unsure this was wise, "Let me get this straight", he'd queried, "this is your first date ....and you want us tagging along? Why?"

"I don't know. He said bring some friends. Does that still make it a date?" Toby asked, adding, "I don't even know for certain he's gay."

"He's invited you to his box at the opera", replied X, "you can relax. He's gay."

X had accepted the offer despite his reservations, knowing that Toby would inevitably get hyper-anxious about the event and even if he declined, he would be inundated with phone calls about what he should wear, and how he should act, and what scent was appropriate for a first date, and should he bring condoms or would that be presumptive and crude, and a hundred other queries to which X had no idea what the correct answer should be. By involving Sara, he could side step all the tedium and leave her to deliver all the fussing and reassuring Toby needed, certain that she would do a better job at it anyway. The bigger problem was, he suspected, that, although he knew almost nothing about it, he was fairly certain he wasn't going to like opera at all.

Sara, on the other hand, had been delighted. Like X she had never been to an opera before but knew that it was the kind of occasion where you got a chance to really dress up, and took it as an opportunity to make a suitably glamorous addition to her wardrobe. They arranged to meet outside the Opera House that evening with enough time to get a drink in before the performance started.

Sara looked fantastic of course, in a white silk, knee length dress topped by a matching wide-shouldered short jacket and satin clutch bag. She clacked up the steps on white stiletto heels to kiss X in greeting, the silk clinging across her curves and her dress riding up her thighs as she mounted each step, its low cut décolletage displaying a necklace of black pearls nestled into her cleavage like love beads. It was always a pleasure being seen in public with Sara, and even now, when they seemed to argue with each other most of the time, he still got a massive rush when she walked toward him. As he double kissed her on the steps he was already imagining running the silk of that dress up over her hips when he'd got her home after the tedious part of the evening.

Stuart turned out to be a smartly dressed balding man, neither attractive nor ugly, but terrifically well presented. His pale blue suit was crisp and thin lapelled, his tie secured with a gold tie-pin and his upright posture and firm handshake the perfect match for his fine cologne.

X had disliked him instantly.

Sara already knew him. It turned out he was the director of a Soho computer graphics company and she had met him on numerous occasions while she still worked for X on New TV. When he'd arrived, they'd greeted each other each other with great shrieks of delighted laughter, both of them exclaiming "Oh it's you…" and "I didn't know you knew Toby", and had immediately fallen into an intense discussion of the latest Soho gossip. Toby and X had trudged into the theatre side by side, trailing up the grand staircase and into the crush bar behind Sara and Stuart's unbroken conversation as though they were the couple on their first date.

X looked around. Huge crystal chandeliers hung above them and the walls were covered with giant oil paintings of big-hipped, half naked women and cherubs, hung in gilded baroque frames.

Sara and Stuart were stood with their heads pressed together sharing some private joke as he stood at the bar trying to attract the bartender's attention.

"Maybe he isn't gay", Toby said dolefully.

X had finally caught the bartender's eye and handed Toby a glass of champagne. "This place is grand though isn't it?" he commented, "look at all these taffeta frocks and grey-haired patriarchs in tuxedos." Toby made no response, so X carried on trying to distract him, "Did you see how much fur was being deposited in the cloakrooms -it was like 'The Lion the Witch and the Wardrobe' in there, I was half expecting a satyr to give us the ticket".

Toby just shrugged.

"Come on", X persisted, "this place is dripping with camp - shouldn't you be more excited about it than me? - Maybe it's you that isn't really gay?

"Oh Fuck off X", snapped Toby, "You're not helping".

X was quite enjoying himself, but that all came to an abrupt end when they'd settled into Stuart's box and the performance started. He'd been right. He really didn't like opera. He didn't get it at all. The sets looked like pantomime props and the performers body-shapes were all weirdly compressed as though they had been adapted to bear the weight of gravity on Jupiter; the men beefy and bearded, their great barrel chests squeezed out in front of them like personal grand pianos, and the woman were grotesque galumphing maidens, dragonous harpies pretending to be nymphs, caked in a macabre stage paint as thick as Turner's oils, thumping around the stage like pantomime dames. And while he could cope with the deep bass of the foghorn hero, every time the soprano hit a note and Stuart, Toby and Sara lent forward simultaneously or gasped in unison, he wanted to cover his ears, the terrible wail cutting straight through him like a scream of compulsion blasting out from a tyrannical mother.

It was murder just staying in his seat.

To make matters worse, his moments of greatest discomfort were the emotional peaks for his companions. When he had sat wincing as the chip shop lady on stage below had wailed her last gasp, Sara, wiping a tear from her eye, had turned away from him toward Stuart, who, rheumy eyed from his own sobbing, gave her hand a quick sympathetic squeeze. The melodrama seemed to go on endlessly, but having managed to survive the soprano's sonic attack as far as half-time, he got out of his seat like Lynford Christie from the blocks, and was ordering his second gin and tonic before the rest of them had got to the bar.

When Sara arrived he dragged her to one side, "For fuck's sake babe", he berated her, "It's supposed to be Toby's date and you haven't let him get a word in edgeways with Stuart. Back off will you and give him a chance."

Sara just stared him down.

"Seriously X, are you giving me advice on how to be a fag hag?" she demanded. "Trust me, Stuart's really nice", she went on, "He's just a bit nervous with Toby that's why he's talking so much to me. Anyway, they're doing fine. Didn't you notice they were holding hands during the part where the gypsy girl died?"

He hadn't.

"Let's face it X, everyone else is having a great time. It's only you that thinks its shit. If you want to improve Toby's night, you can stop having a go at me and try cheering the fuck up yourself."

The second half lasted forever.

When it finally ended the three of them had hugged each other and gushed about how beautiful and moving it had been and it had taken him an age to hustle them back down the stairs and out into the cold night air. He was still joshing them along as they came down the steps, and, half turning to see if they'd followed him down, he was caught off balance by an obstruction at his feet and had to make a quick skip-step over it to avoid falling. What he thought had been a rubbish sack that had spilled over the pavement turned out to be a man wrapped in a filthy great coat lying face down in the street. X bent down to try and help him up but only succeeded in turning him over onto his back, leaving him lying at X's feet staring up at him through bruised and swollen eyes.

It was Del.

His nose was clearly badly broken, sitting at an unnatural angle to the rest of his face and his grazed left cheek was gouged with livid red welts as though he had been dragged forcibly through a thorn bush. His grizzly beard was caked in matted blood, and a trail of mucus ran down to his chin where chunks of half-digested food were cradled in its coarse hairs as though in a baby's bib. A strong smell of shit came off him in waves.

"Oh that's disgusting", he heard Stuart exclaim as X searched Del's half-opened eyes for any sign of recognition. Only one eye was open, the other swollen shut by bruising. There seemed to be no light in his pupils at all.

Stuart had stepped forward in front of Sara, using his half-turned body to protect her from the apparition in front of her, holding out an arm as though he was shielding her delicate eyes from such a distasteful sight.

X crouched down next to Del, "Can you hear me Del", he asked trying not to let his voice crack as he spoke, "It's me, X. Are you OK Del?"

It was a stupid question. Del was clearly anything but OK.

"You know him?" Stuart exclaimed, the note of disgust still audible in his voice.

X ignored him, and concentrated on getting an arm around the back of Del's shoulders so he could get him up to a sitting position. He got very little help from Del, but Toby had stepped forward and between them they managed to lever him up, half dragging him over to the wall by the steps when it became clear he was unable to keep himself propped up without support.

"Del, are you alright mate?"

The same stupid question. It didn't need an answer. Del had either been nastily beaten up or taken a serious fall, but although his face looked bad, the injuries X could see weren't all that serious, it was the lack of response that worried him. Was he just very pissed or was it worse than that?

"Del. can hear me mate? Give me a nod if you can hear me."

Del nodded.

Thank fuck for that.

Del tried to speak, blowing little bubbles of saliva at his lips but hardly any sound emerged.

X leant forward pressing his ear up to his lips to hear what he was saying. He could just make it out. "Oh dear, oh dear, oh dear", he whispered into X's ear, "just look at me now…"

X squeezed him on the shoulder, 'Don't worry Del. Nothing that can't be fixed. We'll get you sorted out."

Del grabbed him with his free hand, holding X's wrist in a surprisingly firm grip, "No hospitals", he whispered.

"Alright Del. No hospitals."

Toby placed a hand on his shoulder and asked the same stupid question X had put Del, "Is he going to be alright?"

No. Probably not.

He looked over at Sara. She had begun to shiver uncontrollably. Shock probably. Stuart took off his jacket and draped it over her shoulders. She looked up at him in thanks.

"I've got to call the hostel", X explained, addressing the three of them without making eye contact. He should really call an ambulance, but Frank would be here just as quick and he could make that decision.

If Del knew he was going to hospital he'd try and fight his way out of the van, and if he was strong enough to fight his way out of the van he didn't need to go to hospital. He needed a phone box. "You keep an eye on him for a minute while I make a call, OK."

Stuart's face took on a horrified expression as though X had suddenly asked him if he could take a shit in his living room.

He really didn't like Stuart.

When he got back, Toby was crouched beside Del, and Stuart was standing where he had left him in a protective huddle around Sara. She had pulled his jacket tighter around her bare arms but was still shivering. At the sight of him, she handed the jacket back to Stuart and approached X. Reaching up and cupping the back of his neck she gave him a swift kiss on the cheek. 'I'm off', she said, "You do your thing darling. Give me a call if you need to, even if it's late." And with that she stepped back quickly and in one smooth motion had raised an arm, hailed a cab, and was gone.

Stuart, startled to be suddenly left alone without anyone to protect, suddenly looked nervous himself, and embarrassed by his first reaction to the bedraggled figure in front of him, tried to make amends by asking X irritating questions about Del's welfare and how long it would be until someone got there.

X only grunted in reply.

It made no sense for the three of them to hang around waiting for the van to come, so he waved the pair of them off, kissing Toby and shaking Stuart's hand. He watched them head off down the street, grateful to be able to return to their interrupted date, and now with an exciting story and a shared experience to give their evening some extra frisson. Toby would probably score now. He hoped he'd brought the condoms.

There was nothing much he could do for Del until Frank got here. He didn't even have anything to clean him up with, so he just squeezed down alongside him by the theatre steps and sat shoulder to shoulder with the old man; the pair of them propped up like old soldiers frozen in the trenches at Ypres or Mons.

"Dear or dear, if my old dad…"

X let the tears run unchecked down his face as Del repeated the same words over and over. He desperately wanted Del to suddenly switch, tell him about Stan Cullis or Palestine or Sandycombe Road or better still even, give him a wink, and then try to sell him some rubbish he'd nicked, a giant slab of Cadbury's chocolate or a stack of pornographic magazines, anything.

But he didn't.

He just kept on repeating the same lines,

"Dear oh dear, if my old dad…."

"Dear oh dear, if my old dad…",

over and over until Frank arrived with the van.

*

He'd shaken Frank's hand after they'd helped Del into the back. There hadn't been need to say much. It had been a struggle lifting Del's dead weight into the seat and it was clear to both of them that he desperately needed medical attention.

By any estimation, it didn't look good for Del at all.

Frank would certainly have to take him to hospital, and for a moment he felt he wanted to go along and help them with that, and then; equally quickly; he really didn't.

After they'd pulled away he hadn't known what to do with himself, and had just started walking without any clear sense of where he was going or why, but, inevitably, he found himself where he must always have been headed, down by the embankment where he seen Del that night, silvered under the trees on the bench overlooking the moonlit river. There was no moon tonight. A sharp cold wind blew up off the water, and the concrete slabs of the bank looked grey, lifeless and barren. The dark river rolled by, as utterly oblivious to human suffering as ever, the weight of the rushing water under the bridge ready to suck any boatman without enough strength in his limbs down into its depths.

He sat down on the bench, took three deep breaths and, exhaling slowly on the last breath, closed his eyes

.

22. HOSPITAL

He was standing outside the glass-fronted building with the snake and staff sign rotating at its entrance. He held a bunch of wilting daffodils in his left hand.

Staring up at the sign, the symbol seemed familiar to him from some half-remembered history lesson.... That was it. It was the motif of the Greek god of healing. What was his name? Ass something...Asclepius...That was it, Asclepius, father of hygenia... It was a hospital sign. The snake had looked sinister on the night of the accident, and now it chilled him to the bone for a different reason. Eva was in there. He was certain of it. He'd have to go in there and face the woman he'd badly hurt when he was last here. He took three deep breaths, and exhaling on the last breath, crossed the road and entered the lobby.

The brightly lit reception desk was tended efficiently by a polite woman in a white jacket with the air of concierge at an upmarket hotel. Behind her a reception area was laid out with clusters of small sofas in muted colours, the room part-lit by the light of an aquarium that rose from floor to ceiling along the length of one wall, a thin sliver of oxygenated water housing flattened tropical fish that darted around the bubble streams in cheerful multi-coloured spirals. He was directed up from the lobby to a room on the first floor. The corridors had a faintly nautical trim, white walls lined by navy borders, and the air was alpine-mountain fresh and invigorating. It was a hospital entirely lacking the smell of disinfectant.

The door to her room was ajar, and, too nervous to enter,

he coughed loudly before announcing himself and then remained hidden from view while he waited to see if he would be admitted, prepared to walk away without seeing her if he was rebuffed.

She called him in.

The room was dimly lit. An upturned desk lamp providing the only light, its soft white beam directed to the ceiling and casting long shadows across the bed. She lay in the half-darkness, propped up against the headrest by four fat pillows. There were cards and flowers around the bed, and Pooja was just putting some roses in water as he entered. She cast a quick glance at Eva and a shy smile toward X before removing herself from the room. He crossed over to the bed and sat awkwardly on the chair by its side.

Unable to look at directly at her, and stole a quick glance.

A large purple bruise had mottled to yellow around her swollen left eye and her forehead was covered in livid red scratches. She looked like she had been beaten up.

"I'm so sorry." It was all he could muster. "I hurt you."

"Yes you did."

There was a long silence and X wondered if he should just get up and leave.

Eventually she broke the silence, "But I also think I understand what you thought you were doing, and that makes it complicated." She paused. "It is my understanding that you thought I was in mortal danger?"

X nodded.

"And your reaction under these circumstances was..." and again she paused, briefly gulping for breath as though an unwanted emotion was rising to the back of her throat like a balloon of gas "...your reaction was to risk sacrificing your own life to save mine?"

X nodded again.

She leant forwards in the bed, throwing her arms upward and outward as if praying to the heavens, "I have seen the footage from a number of angles', she exclaimed, "it is clear that you actively attempt to turn in the air to put your body between me and the car like some monstrous human airbag". She collapsed back on to the pillows letting out an exhausted sigh of exasperation.

There was a long silence.

"You hurt me heroically X. You understand that's a little complicated to process. It makes you..." she searched for the word. "...noble; noble but...dangerous... It will certainly take me a while to get used to whatever that combination implies."

There was silence again.

"Nice flowers", she said.

X was unable to reply, the switch in tone sounded like forgiveness but he didn't trust himself to say the right thing.

"Nice flowers", she repeated, "Where did you get them?"

He had no idea.

"Weird", she said.

Pooja came back in, this time with Sven, and their greetings were warm and forgiving and, after they had fussed over Eva, plumped up her pillows and freshened her water, they had sat awhile on the edge of Eva's bed without saying much, occasionally shaking their heads at X

Letting out a short snort of laughter, Sven eventually spoke up, "You're a mad fool X", he said, and even Eva smiled a little.

Just as he was beginning to feel forgiven, Xanthia arrived. Her reaction was different, but consistent with the way she had always been toward him; hostile, contemptuous and protective of her friend. "I'm not coming in while the gorillas in there", she said from the doorway, looking straight through X at Eva. "I just don't buy this narrative", she went on, her voice taut with anger, 'You're lying there with your face smashed up and the brute who did it is looking all sorrowful at the end of your bed and that makes it all alright?"

She glared at X and then looked back at Eva.

"Because he's a 'Seeker of Sweden'!" she began again, "and how likely is it that for bonobo-boy here? Really? Him? But oh no, he's the chosen one and therefore all the normal rules don't apply.... It's all upside down Eva. Erika and Tasan are out there canonising him and you're lying here in a hospital bed." She took a half-step forward into the room and ensured she was looking directly into Eva's eyes as she delivered her final pronouncement, "Listen to me Eva. WAKE UP! One: Those two do *not* have your best interests at heart, and, Two: he", she pointed at X as she spoke, "is primitive and dangerous and ...and absolutely not worth it at all - he's not even good-looking, clever or particularly interesting for fuck's sake."

"Xanthia!" Eva exclaimed.

"OK, OK, I'm going".

Xanthia retreated out of the room, her hands raised as though she was being pushed out the door by an invisible force field, stopping before she was fully back in the corridor, her voice now resigned, dead pan and bitter, "Listen", she began, "I understand that while you insist on playing Fay Wray in this love-in with King Kong I have no influence whatsoever. But Eva", she paused, "Don't ever say you weren't warned."

And with that she was gone.

In the quiet that followed her departure, it was some time before X felt he had the right to speak, and when he did, it was partly to divert attention from the harsher parts of Xanthia's parting address that he asked what she had meant by saying that Erika and Tasan had 'canonised' him.

Sven looked at Eva, and she nodded her consent. Sven was brief and to the point. "They've got a very distinct take on what happened", he began, "They emphasise the heroic self-sacrifice interpretation of your actions at the expense of the 'pointlessly assaulting a defenceless young woman' argument that Xanthia has just so eloquently advanced. They think it's a clear sign that you are, indeed, a 'Seeker of Sweden'.

"They're very excited about it", said Eva wearily, 'they want us to go on a journey now."

"Where?" he asked.

"To Sweden, maybe. At least that's the idea."

"When?" he asked, conscious that his rehabilitation was recent, tentative and incomplete, and trying not to sound too excited at the prospect of a long vacation with Eva for company.

"The spring probably." she replied wearily, "we'd go by

boat if we went, so we need to wait until the weather's improved."

"Do you want to go?" He had to ask.

She hesitated before replying, "At this moment X, I really don't know."

And then they were there, Erika and Tasan, bursting into the room together, their sudden loud greetings and sense of bonhomie out of keeping with the sombre exchange that had preceded their arrival. It was clear they could scarcely restrain themselves from slapping X on the back as he sat at the bedside of the battered woman, and kept beaming at him as though they were the proud parents of the school bully. Erika pressed foreheads quickly, leaning in to ask Eva how she was bearing up. She had hardly begun her reply before Erika started talking over her, expressing her delight at how quickly she had recovered and commenting on how trivial her injuries had turned out to be. She turned her back on Eva to explain to X that all adults in their society were trained to a high standard as paramedics and medikits were available at all major junctions, thus ensuring that Eva had received immediate attention and instant pain relief from the first passer-by at the scene. In addition, she explained, in a world with so little disease, the treatment of trauma had become the most important part of medicine once more, and skills had developed accordingly. She ended by pronouncing triumphantly, that not only would the facial bruising be gone by the end of the week, and that the damage to Eva's leg that had looked so serious had only been a strained ligament and not an actual break after all. 'Fortunately", she added as an afterthought.

She turned back to Eva, "Have you told him?" She asked breathlessly.

"Told him what?"

"About the journey. Of course."

Eva confirmed that she had just mentioned it, and Erika flashed her an angry look, the pleasure she had anticipated as the bearer of good news now quite spoiled. She quickly recovered her poise, "It's all settled, we will set sail in the spring", she announced, 'It is a great opportunity for Eva."

"To Sweden?" he asked.

Maybe.

THE BENCH

He heard Scandinavian accents as he woke.

No.

The cadence was different.

Dutch.

He was sitting on the bench exactly as he had been when he'd closed his eyes.

He let out a long, deep sigh, settling back into his body on the down breath, a sense of forgiveness washing over him like mother-love.

The river rolled by in front of him its dark surface lit shimmering by the globes strung along its banks, timeless, peaceful, and utterly content in its endless course.

A party of six Dutch tourists were gathered around one of the wrought iron lampstands on the river wall. They were in their forties and all dressed in anoraks made of the same material and cut to the same utilitarian design, differing only in colour, ranging from salmon to turquoise and including two differing shades of fawn. One of them was tracing with his fingers the outline of the fish cast in its base, an open-jawed leviathan in sculpted metal that encircled the post in a joyful death-whip of its tail. Their speech floated through the air toward X as gentle and incomprehensible as though the clangers were politely debating some point of principle with the soup dragon.

Their soft voices rose and fell in different patterns to Eva's speech, but somehow in the same comforting key.

He felt completely at peace.

23. TRACKER

Things were slipping at work. Despite his best efforts, the salaries of a big editorial team and the overheads of putting out a glossy weekly title vastly outweighed what he could pull in to the pages, leaving the magazine haemorrhaging money. He needed to double the income to bring it into profit and he had absolutely no idea how to go about it.

It was just after he had put the magazine to bed on yet another desultory Thursday with house ads and testimonials plastering over the gaps of unsold space like scar tissue, that he'd got a letter from the board. He'd opened the envelope with trepidation, expecting the first sentence to begin, 'we regret to inform you…" and he'd held his breath as he read, only letting out a long sigh of relief when he had finished the last word.

It was going to be alright after all. Better than all right.

He'd been selected for the elite management training programme. Only the very highest flyers in the company were ever chosen.

Maybe that memo to Mike Verne had paid off after all.

He ran down the other eight names on the list. Six of them were publishers and one was the director of finance. There was only one other ad manager's name on the list.

It was Sara's.

His first reaction to her selection was irritation that she'd made the list too. It would have looked better if he'd been the only one on his grade to make it, and her elevation seemed for a moment to take the shine of his success. But on reflection he allowed himself to take some pride in his protégé's rise, after all, that they had both managed to get out from under Howard, whose name was conspicuous by its absence. They were both on the way up again. It was worth celebrating. Who knows? It might even help get them back on track.

They certainly needed something. Since the night at the opera their relationship had gone into serious decline. Their estrangement was mostly, but not entirely, due to work. Commercials Director had, as she had intended it to do, taken her into a different world, and she was now often swept across the horizon to New York or LA, bringing back not only the shopping bags emblazoned with designer logos that littered the hallway of her flat in Pimlico, but a new, more intolerant attitude toward him. Now the tiniest cracks in an otherwise perfect evening seemed to open into great fissures in their relationship whenever they ventured out.

He had taken her to see Kieslowski's *Blind Chance* at the BFI, walking down from Waterloo Bridge to avoid bumping into anyone he knew at the Bullring. She had fallen asleep soon after it began and, waking when the film was two thirds over was utterly unable to make any sense of the alternate time lines that were the whole point of the movie. He'd got so irate at her constant stream of irritating and irrelevant questions disturbing his viewing that he'd put his hand over her mouth to shut her up.

She had bit his palm.

Hard.

They'd fought with silence all the way home. The entire journey conducted without making eye contact, her clacking off ahead of him down the street without a word.

All the way back to *his* flat.

The sex was fucking fantastic. Probably the best they ever had.

But that seemed to more or less the only thing they could do well anymore, the sex, and there was increasingly less and less of that. They'd been a few drunken fucks on Fridays after sessions in the Hen and Chickens, but their Saturday mornings together now lasted less time than their hangovers. She soon got bored hanging around his flat on Sundays, and the times when they'd abandon the whole day to pleasuring each other, getting out of bed only to go to the bathroom or grab food out of the fridge, picnicking between the sheets before making love again and again, occurred less and less frequently, and then stopped all together. Now she never stayed past eleven and was always back into business mode before he had downed a paracetamol with his orange juice or stuck his head under the shower.

"It's work X". Was the mantra she most commonly used when he complained that she was always dashing off for some jolly with the nouveau riche, ignoring his calls to slide back into bed. "Its work X", she explained disdainfully while buckling up her heels and straightening her skirt as he lay still unwashed in the crumpled sheets. "It's not easy dealing with insecure 'masters of the universe' each time you step, jet-lagged, off a plane", she'd gone on, "they don't give a shit if you're exhausted or cranky - you've got to keep beaming sunshine smiles 'twenty-four- seven' as they say. Particularly in LA", she added, "where they're knee-deep in beautiful, biddable women. I can only pull it off because over there I'm like their pal, some familiar London face against all the plastic perfection, and they relax around someone they don't have to explain what 'wanker' means and who can moan along with them about being unable to get a decent cup of tea – but that's as far as it goes. I'm not making friends X. Its work." He still hadn't looked placated so she'd carried on, almost apologetically, "and they love you when you're there, darling, when they're not double kissing and looking over your shoulder - but forget about you the instant you've stepped out the door. And you know the only call you're going to get after you've left is a round of fucks if you haven't got their best side in the ad, or the border surrounds not exactly the thickness they required. Trust me X," she concluded, "its work."

Sometimes she lectured him when she should have been sucking his cock, her favourite theme being his complacency. "I spend as much time planning my exit strategy as I do actually doing my job X, and so should you – if you don't plan you're next move soon you'll be tied to the mast with Howard as the ship goes down." She had swept a lock of hair away from his forehead before bending to kiss him. "Sorry X, flight to catch."

The phrase seemed to have become the leitmotif of their affair.

But if she had less and less time for him, she always seemed to have space for Stuart in her diary.

It hadn't worked out between him and Toby, but Sara had stayed in touch, becoming his regular companion at the opera and some kind of confidant, endlessly engaged in half-hushed conversations of the phone. She even went on the fucking march with Stuart. When did Sara ever march about anything?

*

He'd been dragged along by Toby.

Toby had become livid about some legislation the government had imposed, apparently, that made saying positive things about homosexuals a criminal offence, clause something or other… It had seemed implausible to X that there really could be such a law and assumed Toby was exaggerating, but he'd been surprisingly insistent about it over the phone and X had felt obliged to come.

He'd found the whole thing mostly awkward.

He'd ended up marching alongside Toby at the edge of a big group of young gay men in bomber jackets and tight jeans, who'd sung all the way down the closed off streets and through the bewildered, blank-faced crowds from Trafalgar Square to Kennington Park chanting, "We're here. We're queer. We won't go away. We're here. We're queer. We won't go away", over and over in a kind of confrontation-celebration, interrupting their chant only to flirt with the coppers lining the route, sometimes breaking into choruses of "Who's the poofter in the hat?" hoping to catch a policeman turning his head at the cry, cheering and wolf whistling his reddening neck as he turned back to guard duty. X kept feeling he wanted to let the spectators know that, although he supported the cause, he was himself, actually straight, fully aware that it was missing the point entirely.

He'd caught sight of Sara with Stuart over by one of the organic food stalls in Kennington Park, just after Toby had met two of his friends, both exquisitely mannered posh boys, one with heavy dark make-up around his doe eyes.

"Are we boring you?" the doe-eyed one asked, as X had peered beyond him at Sara and Stuart's backs disappearing into the crowd.

"No, sorry", he said half-turning in response, "I thought I saw my girlfriend over there."

Doe eyes fixed his gaze directly on him and batted his lashes, "Oh Dear", he said, sucking his lips and raising the flat of one perfectly manicured hand against a cheek in mock shock, "I know that expression dearie." He propped one arm on his hip and wagged the index finger of his other hand under X's chin, "I know that expression", he repeated, "that's jealousy darling!"

X winced in response.

"Oh Yes – you've got it bad! Here Christian!" he called across to his friend, "lover-boy here is jealous because he's seen his girlfriend with another man at a poof's march!"

They both laughed.

"Oh Fuck off", said X.

"Ooooooooh" they both exclaimed in delight.

But Stuart was gay wasn't he?

*

The high flyers scheme consisted of a series of weekend residential courses at a country house hotel in the Chilterns. Sara hadn't been nearly as excited as X about it, and her ambivalence had got on his nerves, "What's not good about it?" he'd demanded, "You're the one always going on about sinking ships and exit strategies – well this is it our way up and out - we've been selected for fast-track management – we're going to be running the show. We've fucking made it!"

She'd put him down swiftly. "Firstly, we haven't made it. This isn't the victory parade X, at best it's the finals – and in this business you're still only as good as last week sales –what are you hoping for? Making publisher is no guarantee of anything – look at Howard."

"Howard's a prick."

"True, but all I'm saying is that however much you impress them – you're only as lucky as the publication you've got, and even then you're way down the food chain in a big company like this- still making money for someone else and getting tossed some change if it all goes right and your desk cleared by the end of the day if it doesn't. Think about it X. This residential awayday, it's not just a sauna and a chance to fuck me in a big hotel bed, it's a cut-throat competition. They'll be watching us and reporting back on our leadership potential the whole time - it's going to be a Darwinian struggle and relentlessly networking at the same time – You'd better be prepared."

She seemed to put the dampener on everything these days.

*

On the first night after they'd checked in, they sat around the conference room table while the course leader stood above them, his tall, slim, broad shouldered frame held impeccably upright in a navy pin-stripe suit. From his creaseless white shirt and the Windsor knot in his tie, to the faint hint of lemon exuded by his eau de cologne and his white, even and perfect teeth, everything about him was crisply laundered and manly. He was almost completely bald, but the lower half of his head gave the impression of hair with a soft fuzz that thickened above his ears into faint tufts of grey at his temples. His manner was both rigidly upright and military in bearing, but also loose and relaxed as though he had just left the massage table or done a few rounds in the gym.

"Hello and welcome", he began, "My names Martin Walker, and I'm going to take total charge of your lives for the next two days."

He had a slight lisp.

He paused and appraised them all with a thin self-satisfied smile, his expression somewhere between a trendy vicar with a personal message from Jesus and that of a man being sucked off by his secretary beneath the desk. "You'll be tested in ways you haven't been tested before", he continued, "and some of you may struggle to come up to the mark", he paused, then resumed, "I can't deny it isn't going to be tough going at times, but I promise you it's also a chance to shine and gain new skills, to develop and grow as both businessmen and people. He smiled again before concluding, "This is the first of twelve of these meetings and we'll get to know each other well. As I said, my name is Martin Walker, but until you know me better, and as I will be your guide throughout the next year, I want you to address me simply as 'Tracker'."

Fuck, this bloke was serious. To succeed here he'd have to impress him.

The Finance Director raised his hand, requesting permission to speak, "Can we call you *wanker?*" he asked.

X somehow managed to keep a straight face until he and Sara were safely behind the door to her room. She had ruined the sex that night by crying, "Take me Twacker" as he had entered her and when they had eventually stopped laughing the moment had passed completely.

The Finance Director wasn't there the next morning.

The eight of them sat in chairs arranged in a wide circle in the otherwise empty room. They were each given a transcript of a scenario and ten minutes to prepare their response and then Tracker turned on the video camera and left the room.

X read:

Your spacecraft had crashed on the moon. All eight of you and a pet dog had survived the impact but two of you were injured and cannot walk. Your craft was permanently incapacitated and there is only sufficient oxygen available to keep you alive for eighteen hours. The nearest moon base is eight hours of exhausting slog across the powdery surface away, the suits will provide no more than ten hours of oxygen and it is not certain that all of you are physically tough enough to make the journey. The moon base has rescue craft that could reach you in three hours, but only if they know where to look, and the last weather report indicated that a dust storm is due in six to eight hours' time. No rescue craft can fly during a dust storm. The dust storm's likely duration is unknown.

They had to decide whether to stay put or make the trek to the base. If they undertook the journey they needed to prioritise which objects, scavenged from the wreck, they should take with them. He scanned the list, water canisters, salt, sheets of durable plastic, medical kits, concentrated food packs, a pistol, a radio, a transmitting beacon, flares, bottles of sodium hydroxide, an electric megaphone, three two-man storm tents, a pack of playing cards.

They had an hour to come to agreement on what action and which objects to take.

So that was it.

Camera rolling.

*

When they showed the film back afterward, it was like watching a car crash in slow motion.

From the very beginning of the debate, he had advanced his rapidly formulated views with an aggressive certainty, trampling over any objections to his scheme with proprietary might. He had determined that they should make for the moonbase without delay, dragging the wounded on the plastic sheeting which could also be used to shield them from the incoming sandstorm if they didn't make it to the base before it hit. They should travel light to ensure maximum speed, taking only the transmitting beacon, sufficient water for the journey and the electric megaphone to keep them together on the lunar wastes. When he had thought he was being discursive and inclusive, leaning forward to invite others into the debate, the camera revealed that he was merely dominating the discussion and pissing everybody off.

Sub-debates raged about whether they should take the Sodium Hydroxide. Perhaps it could be poured onto the sand to harden it for more rapid walking.

X cut it off.

He brought in the publisher of *Off-Shore Accountancy Age*, who argued that the first thing they should do was shoot the dog.

X nodded along while the argument raged and then cut it off peremptorily with a raised hand.

In the awkward silence that followed, Sara had finally got a word in, "I think we should stay put", she'd stated clearly, "keep calm, conserve our oxygen, switch on the transmitting beacon and wait to be rescued. The probability is much greater…."

He'd interrupted her, standing up to make his point. The camera, positioned behind his left shoulder showed him looming above her, exclaiming in what he had thought was a clam and measured voice, but which the tape revealed to be dripping with condescension, "but the sandstorm is coming in, they won't be able to launch any rescue craft, by the time they can we'll all be dead…."

"But…." The tape showed her trying to interrupt.

He'd talked over her.

The publisher of *PR Today* suggested they should head off with the storm tents and all the food and water they could carry. They could set up a base camp and last out the storm if necessary.

X interrupted him too. He was hell bent on a glory dash for safety with minimum burdens and would brook no argument. On his feet again he'd exclaimed, "we'd be forced to watch the wounded die in the tents", with passion, facing down his opponent as though he was wilfully determined to murder the most vulnerable of them.

He'd looked a complete prick.

He'd taken it upon himself to do the final round up at the end of the hour, although the body language of the others made it clear that no one was at all delighted that he had elected himself chairman. When he'd granted Sara her turn to speak, she'd begun, visibly cross although he hadn't noticed it at the time, "All this boyish enthusiasm for a heroic trek across the wastes is foolhardy. We'd be better off staying put, keeping calm and waiting for rescue. Other than the transmitting beacon and the water," she'd continued, "the most important item is the pack of playing cards. We could preserve oxygen and pass the time by playing…."

"OK. OK. We've got the idea. Do we stay put and die slowly, or give ourselves a chance by making the trek to the moonbase. Shall we vote on that?"

Sara's enraged expression was caught full on in the camera lens, and his high-handed tone provided the soundtrack for the next few frames where she switched to eye-rolling contempt. Only one timid hand went up with Sara's in favour of staying with the crashed ship.

The camera showed him up again, puffed up like a chicken, strutting like Howard after a team meeting as he bullied the others to accept his proposal wholesale, and punching the air as his original plan was adopted, largely unmodified from his very first conception.

When the video was over, Tracker addressed the group. "The correct solution is, of course", he began, a smile flickering around his lips as though he was pulling love beads out of his anus as he spoke, "is to stay put at the crash site and set up the beacon. By far the highest probability for survival rests in staying put..." He reeled off statistics from air crashes to prove his point, "...and in this scenario the only other vital criteria is to stay calm and preserve oxygen..."

X kept his eyes to the ground the whole length of the debrief.

"Now what can we learn about negotiating skills and teamwork from this exercise?' Tracker asked.

The publisher of *PR Today* raised his hand, "that one individual shouldn't dominate the group?" he suggested.

The rest of the afternoon was torture for X.

Sara didn't make eye contact once.

When he was finally alone in his hotel room at last he took a long, hot shower, flinching every time images from the video flashed involuntarily in front of his eyes. He lay down on the big wide bed and stared at the ceiling his arms spread and legs together as though he had been crucified. He shivered each time an unbidden memory of the day's humiliation coursed through him.

Fuck it.

He slipped between the soft cotton sheets, a smile flickering on his face for the first time since the day started.

All he had to do was dream.

He closed his eyes.

24. BOAT

Shielding his eyes from the slanting sun, he could make her out in the haze, not far above him along the harbour wall. She was lounging in a deck chair with her head tilted back and her sunglasses on, one long leg hung loosely over the arm of the chair, a wide-brimmed straw hat shielding her eyes, soaking up the heat of the day in a posture of perfect repose. She greeted him warmly, rising with a sleepy half-smile that was almost a yawn, and stood, stretching her back and shoulders carefully for a while, absent-mindedly attentive to his presence while she loosened up.

He was, as ever, instantly mesmerised by her beauty.

She had undergone a tonal shift with the seasons since he last saw her. The sun had bleached her blond hair almost white, tanned her skin honey brown and laid a scattering of ghost freckles across the bridge of her nose. She seemed completely healed from the winter's disaster, rejuvenated and bursting with health now that spring was here. Watching her stretch, he noticed that she had really stiffened up, and it occurred to him that she might have been waiting in the same position for some time.

"It's only the second day", she'd explained. "I was just getting into it X, you turned up too soon!" she laughed. "I'd got it all sorted for today, hat, novel, sunshine...Don't worry X, I'm stretching because I got *too* comfortable."

"How did you know when I would arrive?"

"Tasan's pretty accurate about these things. He said it

would be today, but I came down here yesterday anyway just in case. It's all quite scheduled. We have to wait for you, and then when you arrive we have to leave straight away. Which reminds me", she continued, "I'm giving us five minutes before I call Erika and Tasan, but if they ask you – say I called you immediately OK?"

He agreed.

"They'll be here as soon as I call, I just wanted to a little time alone with you before all the...fussing...starts." She waved away the thought and then signalled to him, "Do you wish to come on board?"

Until that point his attention had been so focussed on her that he hadn't noticed the sleek yacht bobbing along on the quay next to them. The boat was both modern and venerable at the same time, somehow both a yacht from the Kennedy era, with varnished wooden decking and graceful lines, and a sleek precision- engineered machine. Around the boat's thickened waist, solar panels were rolled up and lashed to the sides like the nets of a trawler. A single turbine sail blade towered high above them, as grey and vast as an Easter Island statue. The bridge sat at the sail's base, the controls hidden behind curved dark glass windows.

There was a moment's unsteadiness as he stepped aboard, and he lurched sideways with the lilt of the boat, then the deck steadied under him and he found himself moving sure-footedly over the boards. He followed Eva down the wooden steps into the cabin, stepping into a sunken circular lounge where red velvet sofas curved around an oval glass table. Eva sat down, folded her long legs under her and settled back into the cushions. He sat opposite her, relaxing into the soft cushions and watched ripples of reflected light play gently across the walls.

"Don't get too comfortable", she warned him, "I've called Erika, and we've got...", she checked her sunglasses, "30-40 seconds before her and Tasan get here. "Listen X", she continued in a serious tone, "One rule for this voyage. If, at any stage you start to form the idea that I am in danger... no matter how overwhelming the urge to protect me may become..." she held his gaze as she spoke, "Don't.

He nodded his assent solemnly.

"Good! That's settled." She stood and led X out of the cabin, counting down as she walked, "five...four...three....two...." reaching one just as they stepped onto the sunlit deck. Sure enough, two dark figures could be made out a couple of hundred metres apart scurrying towards them round the long curve of the harbour wall. Both were advancing at a rapid walk, as fast as it was possible to move while still appearing business-like, a jerky, stiff-limbed motion that, from a distance, made their scurrying in the shadow of the harbour wall like a pair of multi-legged insects. Closer, the effect was more comic. Erika, the lead figure, occasionally burst into short trots before calming herself to a walk, and gradually out-distanced Tasan, who pursued her as though he were chasing an errant wife.

When she reached the boat, Erika was wasted no time on pleasantries, "You called straight away?" she asked Eva.

She said she had and X nodded in confirmation behind her.

"Good." She stepped past them and disappeared into the cabin.

Tasan arrived, out of breath behind her, greeted them quickly and waved to the bridge. A dot of green light on the blacked-out windows acknowledged his signal, the ropes began to automatically unwind from their moorings and the gangplank unfolded from the shore and slid seamlessly into the side of the ship.

He stood with Eva at the prow as the yacht began to glide slowly out of the harbour, moving silently across the still water. Beyond the harbour mouth, X could see that, despite the bright sunlight, the open water was covered with a heavy low-lying sea-mist, bright white in the sunlight and lying in dense clouds across the water from horizon to horizon.

As they passed the twin beacons at the harbour entrance, the ship's solar panels began to deploy along their frames, smoothly unfolding in a silver ripple as though the yacht was a great bird opening its wings for flight.

They slid into the mist and all was hidden from view.

BIG WIDE BED

No. Surely not so soon, he'd only just got there.

He closed his eyes hard, trying to will himself back into the dream, to carry on gliding out of the harbour mouth with Eva on the super yacht, floating off to some new adventure together. It didn't work. The dream was lost.

Bollocks. Why had he woken up then? Nothing had happened.

He looked over at the alarm clock on the bedside table. The digital clock showed 11:15. Hardly any time had passed at all.

What was that?

Knocking. Someone was knocking on the hotel room door.

He rose and opened it. It was Sara. For a second his hopes soared. They would go to bed together and fuck and it would all be alright again.

Her expression was fixed and serious. "Sit down X." she commanded as he stretched to embrace her. This wasn't reconciliation.

"Don't say a word", she ordered, sitting down on the opposite corner of the bed from him, gathering herself before continuing, "This isn't about today", she began, dismissing the events of the morning with a flick of the wrist, her face momentarily mirroring the expression of astonished dismay she had held on camera. "It's not about that X. It's something else, and now seems a good a time to tell you as any."

Shit. She *was* fucking Stuart.

"I'm leaving the company X", she began, her voice cold and monotone, "I'm handing in my notice on Monday. I'm going into business with Stuart, we've been planning it for months. We're setting up our own computer graphics company, I'm going to sell it and he's going to design the programmes. We'll be fifty-fifty shareholders even though he's stumped up most of the cash. I was waiting until it was confirmed that we'd got the lease on an office in Beak Street before I let you know and it came through this morning. We'll formally launch in two months' time."

She'd started her speech still buoyed by suppressed rage at him, but her excitement at her new venture began to get the better of her and she forgot about being angry and began pouring out the details of her company in a rush of pent-up enthusiasm, "Stuart's certain and I agree that there's this niche between TV and computer game graphics that's just going to get wider and wider, and we're in on the ground floor…"

He tuned out during her self-pitch, one question still nagging at him. He couldn't help himself, he had to ask, "So you're not fucking Stuart then?"

The question stopped her in her tracks.

Her face took on an expression of utter bewilderment and she was unable to speak for quite some time. When she could finally move her lips again the only word that came out was, "What!?"

"What!" she repeated.

When she had regained control she began, "One. I'm not fucking Stuart. I am not fucking anyone other than you because I'm your girlfriend. Two. Stuart is gay", she announced, accompanying the words with shrugged shoulders and a mouth drawn down into a clown's frown. Despite her outraged expression, in the end she couldn't help herself, and for the next five minutes her body was wracked by huge guffaws of laughter, at one point braying like a donkey in her mirth, the tears streaming from her eyes leaving mascara trails across her cheeks.

"For fuck's sake X", she finally mustered.

When she had at last stopped laughing at him, he took the opportunity to congratulate her on her new business. It wasn't hard. Despite her mocking and his further embarrassment in what had proved to be a spectacularly crap day, he actually felt uplifted, relieved that the long phone conversations had been only strategy meetings and not arrangements for lover's trysts. He leant toward her, intending to pull her forward and congratulate her properly, but she raised the palm of her hand firmly to halt his advance.

"Don't. I came here to say that I'm off. I'm going home. I'm not staying for the second day and I wanted you to know that I wasn't leaving in a huff because you're a dickhead, although that didn't help, it's because there's no point in my being here – it's almost dishonest – I'm not interested in their crappy management scheme. In truth I don't know why I came at all, unless it was to fuck you in a big hotel bed, and you fucked up any chance of that happening this morning, didn't you?"

She turned just before she opened the door to leave

"And don't do any of that asking me where we stand OK? Right now I think you're a shit, but that's not exactly news is it? I'll give you a call when I've calmed down."

When the door had closed behind her, he closed his eyes again. But as hard as he tried he couldn't will himself back on to the boat.

25. LONG DAY

With Sara gone, he'd redeemed himself somewhat on the second day. In the long run, a salesman who could persuade everybody that he was right even when he was wrong was still some kind of an asset to a company.

All was not lost therefore, and he had set about Sunday's activities suitably contrite, listening attentively to instruction and taking every opportunity to fake an interest in other people's opinions. In the afternoon he had doggedly performed the role of constructive team player under Tracker's benign tutelage. As his team of three built a raft from oil drums, planking and lengths of rope, he'd nodded sagely in agreement with whatever plan his peers had suggested, offering a willing arm and cheerful camaraderie as the device was assembled. When their construction had gradually unbound itself mid-stream, and his partners were cursing and flinging accusations at each other as they slid into the chilled water, he had smiled through gritted teeth and offered only commiserations and a hand up onto the opposite bank. He had even had the foresight to stand and cheer when the glum-faced team led by the publisher of *Off Shore Accountancy Age* paddled home, their unbalanced Kon Tiki only kept upright by using two of the lesser members as below-the-water-line ballast. He had flung towels and sympathetic looks at the victims as they had struggled ashore to stand beside him, dripping with resentment while their leader accepted Tracker's congratulations.

By the evening, his transgressions on the first day were already ancient history, and he hung about long enough at the close of play to stand a couple of rounds of whiskey at the bar while the others bitched about the 'Off Shore Shit' and what a waste of time the whole exercise had been.

He hadn't exactly made friends, but his crimes appeared forgotten in their parting backslaps, and he felt quite good as he settled, unsteadily, back behind the wheel of the GTI.

*

His optimism had evaporated completely by the following Friday.

The magazine had gone out the day before at 24 pages, more flimsy than ever, and even then only after a day of distressing discounting and bad deals, each one more ruinous to the bottom line than the one before. He'd had to run the "Free John McCarthy" copy as a full page for the fourth week running to keep the pagination up. The first time it had looked like a benign act of generosity on his part and had earned him some kudos with the NUJ, but the hostage's weekly appearance now seemed to reveal that the magazine was trapped in an equally desperate predicament, where nothing changed from one week to the next and the most likely outcome to it all was oblivion. But that wasn't even the major reason for his despair. He had a tough morning to look forward to, and a truly miserable afternoon to round off the week.

Del had died.

He'd lasted longer than X had expected, lingering on in a hospital bed but never really recovering from the stroke that had pitched him face forward on to the hard concrete that night. He'd meant to visit, but somehow never got round to it, and he had taken the call from Alex knowing exactly what she was going to say before he'd even put his ear to the receiver. He had managed to dodge the dying, but felt obliged to attend the funeral. He wasn't sure why.

With the funeral at Mortlake Cemetery already booked for the afternoon, he'd decided he might as well stuff the whole day with shit, and had arranged the appointment with Morgan Productions he'd been putting off for months.

He'd driven out to their warehouse just off the North Circular Road thinking about Del, and it wasn't until he'd parked the Golf between a pair of BMWs in the car park that he paid any thought to the visit itself. Morgan Productions were the biggest advertiser in New TV, but it wasn't something he wanted to shout about. They sold videotape in bulk to the industry, and their business model was of the pile-them-high and sell-them-cheap variety. Their great glaring ads announced a never-ending sale in bright red letters, the text broken up by crude starbursts announcing one-time-only deals and offers of redundant stock at low-low prices, their cheap and nasty copy spread throughout the magazine like an unsightly rash on the flanks of a thoroughbred. What was more, each ad had been sold into the mag at a ruinous discount, generous opening offers that had never been renegotiated and last minute space fillers that brought in hardly more than Beirut hostage appeals and had somehow been allowed to become permanent features. They took four half pages every week, but at the rates they were paying he didn't have a hope in hell of the magazine ever turning a profit. To drag it into the black he needed them to keep the same volume of ads but pay more money for the privilege. 'Pay more money for what you are already getting or the magazine goes bust'. It wasn't even a weak hand. It was no hand at all.

He'd have sent Jeanne, but the two partners at Morgan productions, Brian and Neil, were, it seemed, the only two men in England immune to her charms, and she had adamantly refused to go.

It had gone badly from the start.

Brian had sat opposite him on the other side of the big desk in their bleak office above the warehouse, scarcely listening to him while he pitched. The phone rang constantly, and without acknowledging X's presence, he would pick up the receiver and speak in short curt sentences before slamming it down, pressing a button on the intercom and barking instructions at his secretary. He left the room twice, both times waving chits he'd pulled out from between the great piles of invoices, receipts and stock-lists that covered the entire surface of the desk, bellowing as he walked until a woman with nicotine skin and pursed lips appeared at the doorway and snatched it off him. Neil didn't even give him the courtesy of staying in the room long enough to listen to a word he said, thumping up and down the stairs, carrying boxes and orders, his jeans slipped down over his gut to show the top of his arse crack, his baggy Lonsdale sweatshirt mired with grime and sweat and great tufts of ginger hair sprouting from his mutton-flabby forearms as though an orang-utan had been crossed with a football casual in some unholy science experiment.

X talked on, his confidence draining away with each interruption.

His mauve suit and electric blue tie, that had seemed so stylish in Soho, looked hopelessly out of place here, far too bright for the drab grey office. Here, he was an absurd popinjay, a parrot scrapping with the seagulls on the landfill site, doomed to leave with nothing other than his feathers tarnished by coffee grounds and nappy shit.

Gary took the phone of the hook and raised his hand to quieten him. He signalled to Neil who put down the box he was holding and leaned his back against the window overlooking the car park. "So let me get this right, you're proposing that we get exactly the same amount of advertising space in your rag as we're getting now, but we pay 2/3 more than we currently do?" He let out a short, derisory snort, his face twisted into a sneer and turned to Neil, who snorted by way of reply and shrugged his shoulders. He turned back to X. "I haven't noticed your magazine being 2/3 more successful. In fact, it's thinner than fucking ever." He leant down and picked the last issue of New TV off the floor where it had lain next to an overflowing waste-paper bin, and held it pinched between his thumb and forefinger, waving it backwards and forwards above the desk, "Light as a feather – not exactly a stampede into your pages is it?" He turned back to Neil again, "What do we get back from New TV?" he asked, "2/3 more sales than we used to? His voice was thin and sarcastic.

"Nah", Neil replied, the single grunt amounting to his sole contribution to the discussion so far.

"No mate", Brian turned back to X leaning on his elbows, his face suddenly hard and serious, "You can fuck right off back to where you came from with that fucking offer. We don't need you one bit, but I reckon you really do need us. And you, sonny, haven't worked it out *at all* have you? We only took all that space because that sales girl of yours was so hot. We couldn't resist, when she batted her eyelashes and pouted, could we Neil?" He turned to his partner for confirmation and was rewarded with a raised forearm, clenched fist and a leer that was positively sinister in its aggression. "Yea, Neil thought he might be in at one point she was so *attentive*. So fuck it. We threw a few ponies at it didn't we? Maybe we'd have got a lap dance for a full page eh? Few hundred quid didn't make much difference to us either way. And then you mince in, all done up in your purple fucking clown pants, asking us to pay money for what? For the privilege of having you pop round to see us every couple of weeks? Nah, that's not going work. We don't swing that way. I'd rather pull all the ads from you and stick them with the other lot than have you in here again. They've got some boy salesman too, but at least he's not a total tosser, and people actually *pay* to read his fucking magazine."

"Here's the deal Z", Brian pronounced and Neil sniggered in the background, "We're going to carry on paying *exactly* what we're paying now and unless you guarantee we never have to see your queer-arse face again and you send round a decent bit of totty to keep us happy next time, we'll pull the whole fucking lot. OK?" He leant further forward, making a shoving gesture with the back of his hand as though he were flicking a spider of his desk,

"Go on" he said, "fuck off now."

X tripped over the carpet as he stumbled out the door and could still hear them laughing when he'd reached the bottom of the stairwell.

He dropped the clutch too fast when he was reversing out of the parking space, and smashed the rear light of the Golf against the door panel of the BMW with the personalised number plate G325 BRI. It left a dent in the centre of the panel the size and shape of a videocassette. He looked up at the office window above the warehouse entrance. He could see no movement behind the glass, so he put the gear stick into first and gunned it, wheel-spinning across the car park and out into the main road.

*

He'd arrived at Mortlake cemetery just as the meagre remnants of Del's life were about to be ushered into the crematorium chapel. He hadn't had time to change.

They were standing in four distinct groups. Closest to him and huddled round the priest, stood Oedipa and Ruth, two elderly do-gooders who did voluntary work every second Sunday at the day centre and were particularly self-righteous in their piety. Neither Oedipa, a very fat woman who favoured giant floral smocks like bedspreads as her customary form of dress, nor Ruth, a tiny owlish woman with a simpleton's smile who accompanied Oedipa like a witch's familiar, had any particular connection to Del. Their presence here being more concerned with earning a few days off from their future tenure in purgatory than any question of saying farewell to the man himself. They were both standing so close to the tips of the vicar's black leather shoes that he had to keep taking short steps backward to recover his personal space, only for Oedipa to step forward each time. With Ruth shuffling after, the three of them were gradually retreating toward the chapel entrance as though partaking in a slow-paced three-handed foxtrot. The vicar himself was unknown to X, a weak-chinned young celibate, fresh from the seminary, whose dog collar seemed to throttle his prominent Adam's apple and whose vestibule lay over his grey polyester suit like an outsized doily. Cornered by the elderly women at the chapel steps, and crippled by politeness and shame, he cringed back and forth on his heels under the intensity of Oedipa's gaze, his smooth, pale cheeks, blossoming pink as though he were asphyxiating.

Beyond them, Pete the Bike and Davy Ryan had turned up to pay their last respects. Pete had been a mate of Del's, if Del could have been said to have had any mates; but Davey's presence was a surprise. X couldn't remember him liking Del at all.

Del certainly hadn't liked *him*.

They were both in conversation with Penelope, the grey-haired day centre manager whose slight frame was clad in the timeless uniform of the blue-stockinged daughter of privilege who had dedicated her life to good works, a cast off ragged cardigan over a plain cotton dress and grey woollen tights. Her fragile frame and nodding head held a smile that looked both kindly and simple, but she was, in fact, a woman of remarkable resolve who was widely respected by the homeless men she tended and worshipped as a secular saint by Oedipa and her kind. Her head was bowed attentively as she leant forward to listen. Pete had made an effort to look respectable. He must have picked up a clean jacket and tie from the day centre that morning, but as X drew closer he could see that the shirt he was wearing was blackened like a miner's overalls by grime and sweat, almost certainly the one he had slept rough in the night before. His hands were shaking hard, and he kept clenching and unclenching them while stepping backwards and forwards on the spot in little jerky skip-steps as though he desperately needed a piss. X suspected he was making a heroic effort to stay sober out of respect for Del.

Davey had shown no such restraint.

He had clearly had two or three cans on the way to the cemetery and was boisterous and high-spirited if not yet completely pissed. It must have been his giro day, as the navy blue metal heads of unopened cans of Tennants Super poked like clusters of grenades out of both pockets of his great coat. Davey's voice boomed loud over the quietened scene and as X approached he heard him say, "Ah fuck it", then apologise profusely to Penelope before adding, "Del eh? Fucking Del eh?" before apologising again. Pete grunted at him like a farmer herding cattle and he quietened down. Davey was scared of Pete. Pete's rages came on unpredictably and suddenly when he was pissed, his anger dropping from a clear sky with no apparent provocation and absolutely no warning and he when he swung his fists he landed blows like a club hammer. In the end Davey was a shitter. He only really hit women. Pete lowered his head, his eyes jerking involuntarily to the unopened cans in Davey's pockets. Davey grinned but stayed quiet.

Beyond them Frank and Griff stood apart from Paul and Alex. Griff huddled close to Frank, his careful positioning of the priest between himself and Alex suggested that his relationship with his estranged wife had not improved since X had last seen them. Frank had taken off his dog collar for the occasion so as not to pull rank on the young vicar, and he stepped forward to shake X's hand firmly, his face grave.

There seemed little to say.

Griff had made some kind of an effort for the day, his mohican jelled carefully upright, and he had chosen mottled combat pants rather than bondage trousers for the occasion. His new facial jewellery rattled as he leant forward to press shoulders with X.

X nodded hello to Pete and Penelope and shuffled over to Alex and Paul, standing opposite them awkwardly, suddenly aware how long it had been since they had last met and painfully conscious that he had turned up at a funeral dressed as Beau Brummel. In contrast they had made the minimal effort necessary for a funeral. Alex had selected a black sweatshirt to wear over her black jeans and Paul had put on a thin black over a white polyester shirt. He looked dreadful.

After standing awkwardly in silence for a few minutes, Paul, stepped toward him, placed one of his hands on X's shoulder and drew him toward him speaking in a quiet, solemn voice as though imparting some important intimacy. "I hate to tell you this X", he began, looking into X's eyes for the first time since he had arrived, "Electric blue really doesn't go with purple at all. That combination, well…", he paused again, "I'm sorry to be the one to tell you, but it makes you look a complete prick".

"Nice to see you too."

"Someone had to tell you", he went on, "If not at a funeral, when?"

He heard Alex fail to supress a snort of laughter, and when he looked up both of them were grinning.

For a moment they felt like friends.

It was time to go in and they shuffled into the pews as the vicar took up his position at the lectern with Del-in-a-box beside him.

Oedipa and Ruth sat a little apart from Penelope in the front row, their faces set appropriately heavenward, their prayer cushions already on the floor by their feet in their anxiety to get some quality penance in on their knees as soon as possible. The four hostel workers occupied the row behind, and Davey and Pete stood behind them in the back row and as close to the exit as possible.

At least Del had made three rows. He'd been to plenty that hadn't.

The vicar, in his short moment in the spotlight, managed to offend nearly everybody in the tiny chapel. Rather than sticking to the standard script, citing Corinthians 13 and laying Del down in green pastures, he chose the occasion to try out an experimental sermon, a parable about the early Christian church with Del's name slotted into the blanks in the script. He began by describing how the faithful had been truly tested in their labours in the fields under the harsh rays of the sun, through droughts and floods, long cold winters, and untold agonies on the treeless plains, but more sorely still, he asserted, they had been tested by those in their community who wouldn't contribute to the harvest yet felt they had a right to the bread and barley that had been sowed, reaped and gathered by the others. Those who had laboured hardest in the fields had cried out, the vicar intoned, "Why should we suffer in the sun, whilst those that labour only in debauchery drink and eat as we do and reap what we have sown through no effort of their own? But", the vicar continued, leaning forward on his elbows on the lectern and focussing on some distant desert horizon in the midst of the long dead faithful of his tale, "But those who were wisest among them, said 'No! Do not begrudge them, for no man is truly wretched in God's eyes, no matter how degraded and useless he may appear to us."

The boy- priest's words were addressed foursquare at the women on the front row, his milky eyes softening on the florid fat bulk of Oedipa and the tweedy primness of Ruth, their faces upturned to his and their eyes moist in contemplation of their own righteous compassion.

A noise behind him caused X to turn round.

Davey was pretending to steal a prayer cushion by stuffing it inside his great coat, his rotten-toothed grin swiftly extinguished by a sharp bark of command from Pete and the pair of them briefly struggled in the aisle until a glance from Penelope brought them back to order.

X didn't object to Davey's actions. A theft from a church seemed a more fitting tribute to Del's life than any of the priest's words. He stole a sideways glance at Paul before returning to face the front. His friend was red eyed and staring down the vicar with both his fists clenched, his face contorted with supressed rage. The boy-parson remained oblivious, too wrapped in his own godly condescension to notice the waves of hostility breaking over him from the second row. It was lucky that Kevin had been laid low by one of his allergies. He'd have punched him in the face if he'd been here.

He saw Alex touch Paul's hand gently and heard her whisper "Stan Cullis…he could head a ball as hard as a man could kick it". The words and gesture snapped Paul out of his fixed stare, and he returned a small smile of thanks and squeezed her hand back. X felt an overwhelming need to interrupt their exchange to point out that it hadn't been Stan Cullis' neck strength with the leather ball that had impressed Del, it had been… What was his name…? Joe someone… It suddenly seemed very important to remember his name.

And then it didn't.

It was all over. The priest had reached his redemptive conclusion, and after reminding them that the returned sinner, no matter how worthless their life may have been, was as precious to God as that of any other Christian, had made the signal that set the coffin lurching on its short, final, journey to oblivion.

Ashes to ashes, dust to dust.

Always the same.

The heartbeat skip when the coffin made its first jerk forward on the conveyor belt.

The wrenched breath when the curtain closed fully and the box disappeared from sight.

Forever gone.

All over.

Full stop.

*

Afterwards, there was some shuffling around outside, everyone doing their best not to think about the deceased's body going up in flames behind them. He'd let out a sudden sharp sob when Alex hugged him outside the doors, and was even grateful for Griff's embrace, the crest of his Mohawk catching him in the eye as they clenched briefly, giving him a different excuse for the tears that leaked out of his eyes. Oedipa had soon waddled away without a backward glance, Ruth tripping along in her wake. Penelope too, hadn't lingered, pausing only to obliquely apologise for the sermon as though it had been her fault, 'young vicars – you know how it is….", and having thanked them all for coming, she had straddled her bicycle and cycled away through the graves.

Pete and Davey didn't hang around for long either. Having stepped a few paces away from the chapel and popped open one of Davey's cans behind a tomb mounted with a statute of a winged angel, Pete had dallied long enough to say a few words to X. He'd glanced him up and down, taking in his shiny brightly coloured suit and his silk tie and shook his hand, his grip strong and firm now he had the first drink of the day inside him. Slapping a mutton fingered hand on his shoulder, Pete had congratulated him like a proud parent on making something of himself. "Not like these other wasters", he said, a sweeping hand gesture encompassing Griff, Paul and Alex, "Well done lad!" he added, before hurrying after Davey and his extra-strength lager.

When it was just X and the hostel workers left, a tall, lugubrious looking man in a black suit and tie, headed over the gravel toward him, advancing with a strange loping gait, as though the soles of his shoes scarcely made contact with the ground. "Would you be the party responsible for the deceased's remains?" he asked.

Not Really. But who else would be? Del didn't have any living relatives. He'd repeated *ad naseum* that his dad and his dear old mum were, long dead now, side by side in…

He had a thought. Why not?

"Yes, I can be responsible"

"There's a small charge sir", the man added, a regretful expression pulling his visage downward into a bloodhound's jowly droop as he spoke.

Of course there was. That's why he had approached him. In his suit he looked like the only person present who was liable to have any money.

"For the Urn."

"I *have* to pay?"

"No Sir. Only if you wish to collect the ashes in person. We could sprinkle the remains in the garden of remembrance for you without any supplementary charge."

"How much?"

"It depends on the type of Urn you require sir."

Of course. It was the perfect moment for a sales pitch. Who would want to look cheap now?

"Give me a mid-range urn."

"That'll be just under £50 sir."

"£50!" It seemed very pricey. But the man stayed long-faced and silent, unmoved by his exclamation.

X found himself unable to haggle. "Do you take cards?" he asked.

*

They'd had to wait an hour for the ashes to be delivered, presumably it took that long for the oven to cool down enough to scrape Del's charred remains into the copper urn, although it occurred to X that there was no way of telling that the ashes they handed over did not contain at least parts of the previous corpse that had perhaps got stuck in the oven grate. It was equally possible they were just random cinders and had nothing to do with Del at all. But why would they bother to lie?

When he'd mentioned that Del's parents were buried somewhere in the graveyard and that he hoped to scatter his ashes on his mother and father's grave as Del would surely have wished, he'd been met with a look of horrified indignation, followed by a jobsworth's determination not to aid him in his quest to locate the grave. He was informed in a tone that brooked no dissention, that it was only permissible to spread the ashes within the confines of the garden of remembrance. No, they could not inform him of the location of Mr and Mrs Tallet's grave, and any attempt to distribute human remains on said grave would constitute both a serious breach of health and safety and a criminal offence. The specific legislation of the appropriate act was recited in full with a gravitas that suggests the words had been cast in stone on Mount Sinai by the lords anointed himself.

Paul had been ready to start a fight over the matter, but sensing the futility of it, X had signalled him to let it go, and, declaring that he wasn't yet ready to part with the remains of his dear old friend, he had gone back into the GTI, storing Del's ashes in the glove compartment and had driven out of the cemetery behind the soup van, the convoy departing under the suspicious gaze of the crematorium staff.

Frank pulled up at the gate to let Alex and Paul out. He pulled the Golf up at the kerb and the three of them headed back into the cemetery, peeling away from the roadway as quickly as possible, and carefully reading the name off each gravestone they passed. Griff had stayed in the van. It "wasn't really his thing", and "he hadn't really known Del all that well", but they all knew that it would have been deeply unpleasant for him to spend so much time in the company of his beloved, untouchable wife's palpable disinterest. X bore him no malice and waved him out of his life with an emotion that was almost that of comradeship.

They walked for hours.

At first it had been like taking a pleasurable stroll with old friends with the additional thrill of defying authority. Their petty rebellion against municipal regulations seemed an apt commentary on Del's life, and their collective spirits were high as they searched for the Tallet family tomb. Walking along parallel rows, they called out the most absurd surnames or obscure inscriptions on the graves they passed, or broke the silence trading Del quotes. Shouts of "Dear oh dear" and "caught with me trousers down with Peggy Hill on the Worton Estate" were answered with cries of "Escaped one there!" and the words "Stan

Cullis" were echoed by "Dai Hopkins – the Welsh International", the phrases bouncing back and forth between them like the calls of birds.

But the cemetery was endless, and as dusk began to fall and the true probability of stumbling across the correct grave in the vast ocean of the dead became apparent, their spirits dipped. X felt exhausted. It had been a long and troublesome day and as the shadows lengthened and the light faded, he started to slip and stumble more and more on the uneven ground, the leather soles of his shoes found little purchase on the smooth grass and twice he tripped and bashed his knees against tombstones. If this carried on much longer his expensive suit would be completely fucked.

Paul called them to a halt, declaring that he would be on duty in a couple of hours and would have to start heading for the exit if he was going to stand any chance of getting there on time. Alex slumped gratefully to the ground, stretching out on a fallen moss covered tombstone and easing off one of her boots to wiggle her toes and pull up her socks. X stood, leaning against another headstone, reluctant to sit down despite his fatigue for fear of grass stains on his suit.

Having paused for breath, X felt he wasn't quite ready to give up on the wild goose chase they had embarked on, and as Alex wasn't on rota for a couple of days she elected to stay with him for one final push.

"I know you two will do alright by the old boy", Paul said as he bid them farewell, hugging both of them before turning away into the gathering gloom.

So it was just of the two of them, marching on largely in silence for an hour or so more, until the last rays of the sun were just beginning to dip over the horizon and it was clear that any further searching would be completely futile. It was not completely dark however, as a full moon had risen, its silvered light turning the cemetery into an ethereal landscape like a painting by Casper David Friedrich. They stopped in front of a silver birch tree, its trunk a shining pillar in the moonlight and its leaves shimmering in the gentle breeze. It seemed as good a place as any to lay Del to rest.

Alex pulled out a ready-rolled spliff. "Should have been a can of Special Brew really", she said, lighting the joint, "but it seems appropriate to be in some kind of altered state to say goodbye to Del".

X took a toke and they walked together to the silver birch. He lifted the lid and emptied the urn's contents on the ground at the base of the tree. The ashes shone a phosphorescent white in the moonlight, a little mound of chalk dust on the dark ground, as bright white as cocaine powder on a mirror. They both knelt down to take a closer look. X put his fingers into the ashes and picked up a pinch of all that was left of the old man, and rolled it about in his palm. The powder wasn't as smooth as he had expected it to be, but instead had a lumpy texture that reminded him, oddly, of powdered milk, and contained larger, stony fragments like seashells chippings that crumbled and broke apart as he pressed them between thumb and forefinger. Alex picked up a pinch too. She put a little bit of it on her tongue. He did the same. It had no flavour, no taste of anything, just dry and chalky.

Nothing.

They sat back on the grass mound a few feet from the tree.

Sitting in silence, staring at the tree and the phosphorescent ash at its base, time passed without any scale of measurement and the more he stared at the tree the more it seemed to detach itself from the background, becoming a hovering white stem floating away in the darkness. As his eyes began to blur, he became convinced he saw something moving at the base of the tree. An insect, a huge, fat-bellied moth, began crawling out of the ashes and laboriously dragging itself up the tree trunk, its grey outstretched wings scarcely visible, camouflaged against the night by their pale colour and the mottled birth-mark leaf patterns on its swollen white-grey abdomen.

He turned to Alex. "Do you see that?"

She was staring wide eyed at the tree.

"The huge ghost moth climbing the trunk?" she replied in a whisper after a long pause, "I'm so glad you can see it too. I thought it was just me freaking out."

They sat, unable to move, as the moth inched it's way painfully slowly up the full length of the trunk before eventually disappearing from sight as it entered the lower branches.

They'd said goodbye shortly after the moth's ascent, X heading in the opposite direction to Alex, striding across the cemetery toward Chiswick Bridge and the GTI, secretly pleased that she had turned down his offer of a lift home. He blundered through the half-darkness paying little attention to where he was heading, contrary thoughts rushing through his mind without gaining any firm purchase, feeling confused and scared, glad only that he was alone with his thoughts.

What had Del's life been about anyway?

Maybe the vicar had been right and it had all been completely pointless unless there was a God up there who gave some kind of a shit. Of the few people left to mourn him at the end of it all, he doubted that Del could even have recalled their names. Fat white spirit moth or not, it didn't seem to add up to very much.

X stopped. He hadn't been paying any attention to where he was going and was now completely lost. He sat down on the ground, resting his back against a lichen-covered mausoleum, slumped on the damp grass at its base, heedless of staining his suit. It was probably ruined by now anyway.

He was suddenly overwhelmed with fatigue. Might as well grab some sleep here and wait for dawn before moving on. There seemed little point in charging around a cemetery lost in the dark.

He closed his eyes.

26. THE ISLAND

He was standing at the prow of the boat.

Ahead, in the early dawn light, the view was obscured by a thick blanket of white mist that hung, strangely still, over the choppy blue-black water despite the sharp breeze. Spray kicked up from the crests by the wind, stung his face and ears as he stood, facing forward and braced to the wind. He was wearing a warm, padded jacket and scarf, but his head was bare and as the wind whipped needles of fine spray into his face, he felt like he had dived head first into a plunge pool after a sauna, shocked instantly awake alive by the cold. He was holding a mug of steaming coffee in each gloved hand.

Hearing a noise behind him, he turned just as Eva was climbing the steps up from the cabin below, her back to him as she rose, wrapped in a thick wool jacket, bobble hat and scarf. At the top of the steps she turned to face him and he saw her eyes flash from sleep-swollen and drowsy to startled-bright in an instant as the cold wind slapped her wide awake. She laughed at the shock and faced him smiling, radiant and alive, her skin still sun-kissed and her eyes now an impossible blue-green, a feline turquoise colour that shined almost fluorescent against the expanse of muted grey sky behind her.

"For me?" she asked

He handed her one of the mugs of coffee and she thanked him, smiling as she sipped at the scalding liquid.

"There wouldn't be any point in asking you where you got the coffee I assume?"

X had no idea.

"Still weird", she said, shaking her head.

She shivered, "Fresh this morning No?"

They sipped their coffees in silence for a moment.

"Where are we now?" he asked.

"We should be arriving at *The Island*, or as I should say, *The Ship*, very shortly", she replied cryptically.

"Not Sweden then?"

"Not yet."

"But we're on the way to Sweden?"

"Who can say?" she replied, mumbling the words into her scarf before turning away to look out to sea.

"There! Look!" she cried out, pointing ahead over the prow, "We are getting close".

The mist was lifting and he began to make out dark shapes on the surface of the water a few hundred metres ahead. At first he thought they were a cluster of low, flat rocks, just cresting the surface of some offshore outcrop, but as they neared, it was clear that the reef was artificial, a man-made, low-lying barrier, that lay like an undulating plastic road over the water, tracing the counters of a coastline still hidden from view by the mist.

The ship altered course to run alongside the barrier.

Peering over the side, X could make out a chain of grey, oblong coffin-boxes, bound together by cables to form a lattice beneath the water, their flat tops jointing together at the surface to form a continuous sheet hundreds of metres wide rising and falling on the turbulent grey water like tethered mechanical seals.

Erika and Tasan had joined them on the deck, and he asked Erika what they were. "Wave electricity generators", she explained, "they ring the entire coast – all cabled to the shore. Crude but effective", she added.

After ten minutes of sailing in parallel to the barrier, they turned into a narrow passage cut like a gash in the grey ribbon around the island and flanked on either side of its entrance by two large, fortified lighthouses. The mist was beginning to lift with the rising day and as it did so, the line of another, more massive barrier was revealed. Ahead, across the water, rank after rank of huge while concrete pillars crossed from horizon to horizon, the windmill blades each one supported spinning in glacially slow arcs like synchronized razor-wire above the water.

As they neared this second barrier, the pharaonic size of the structures became apparent. High above them the columns rose endlessly into the sky like windowless watchtowers, their tops lost from view in the haze, and falling through the air around them, blades, the size of aircraft wings and as thin as scimitars, cut the air into wafer thin slices. The drone of giant turbine motors turning slowly over hummed like a swarm of angry bees over the rushing of the wind. In the channel cut between the ranks of the silent giants, their craft was buffeted like a toy in swells and eddies of agitated water as waves crashed and rebounded in futile rage against the massive, barnacle encrusted bases, and sea-birds, startled from their nesting sites as they passed, took flight, wheeling and screeching into the air like heralds sending advance warning of an approaching enemy. X felt he was aboard the Argo, the threat of the crashing rocks replaced by the great rotor blades themselves, and he had to fight the sensation that at any moment one of them would lazily extend the circumference of its swing, casually slice the ship in half sending them all tumbling into a watery grave, before resuming its upward arc without losing a fraction of its momentum.

After an hour's sailing through phalanx after phalanx of these enormous sentinels, there was an enormous sense of relief when they had passed the last of them and drifting into the coastal lagoon beyond, cast anchor. The mist had lifted completely now, a blue sky was beginning to force its way into the day, and sunlight broke through the clouds in golden patches on the water as rode at their mooring.

The customs official arrived just after breakfast.

He was a middle-aged, officious man, with sharp, angular features, a clipped manner of speaking and a very smart uniform. A thin moustache sat on his upper lip like a sneer, and his tautly-erect bearing made the occupants of the boat feel instantly slovenly. He nodded perfunctory in greeting, took their fingerprints and retinal data with a minimal of physical contact, and regarded them with an expression of suspicion, bordering on outright hostility, while he waited for the data to be processed and security checked. When all the appropriate documentation was found to have been properly presented, and the security checks duly completed, his manner softened to one of high-handed diplomatic disdain. He made a short speech, intoning in the manner of a bishop addressing his congregation, "On behalf of his majesty King Richard the fourth and fifth, I welcome you on board. Your visa is for one day only. No overnight stay is possible. You must return to your departure point by 10:30 pm. You are not permitted to travel beyond the boundary. If you approach within one hundred yards of the fence you will receive a clear warning. Stop. Immediately retrace your steps. There will be no second warning."

Erika interrupted, "but what if...."

He stopped her with a raised hand. "Don't worry madam. We never make mistakes."

He went on to inform them that his majesty's government took no responsibility whatsoever for their health and well-being. If they become unwell, they must return to their ship immediately. If they became incapacitated or were killed, the authorities would ensure that they would be transported, alive or dead, as swiftly as possible, to their ship. He then welcomed them once again, expressed his hope that they would enjoy the day and walked to the centre of the boat and began hoisting a series of pennant flags up main mast.

Erika, who had been silenced so effectively earlier, was simmering with anger, "What an odious little man", she hissed when he was out of earshot. "Unbearably smug", she muttered, "We never make mistakes... Show me a human being that never make mistakes..."

There was a short delay and X was about to ask someone what was going to happen next, when he noticed two that small sailing dinghies that had been plying the bay, had altered course toward them in response to the customs official's flags. The sailors pulled up alongside, and expertly bound their boats to the larger craft while their loosened sails flapped wildly in the breeze, snapping like intermittent gunshots when they were caught by the stronger gusts blowing off the shore. They were all called forward by the customs official and climbed cautiously over the side into the two waiting boats, while the official thanked the pilots for their positive response to a call to civic duty, "No need to waste tax-payer's money", he declared with a satisfied air, adding, "and it's a nice run into the cove with this wind!"

X and Eva settled cautiously into the second of the boats, this one steered by a rangy, loose-limbed young man with an unkempt appearance. His long greasy hair was partly stuffed under a large floppy hat, and, pressed close to him in the tiny boat, the odour of his unwashed body was rank and strong enough to rise above the smell of salt spray. He clearly knew what he was about on the water however, and they were swept swiftly to the shore leaving the craft carrying the official, Tasan and Erika behind. Their pilot was almost the polar opposite of X and Eva's, a neatly attired older man with delicate features and a slight build, whose skin, a deep walnut brown in tone, suggested an origin somewhere on the horn of Africa. The custom's official stood bolt upright at the mast, resplendent in his smart uniform, perhaps forced into the posture by lack of space, but from where X sat he appeared to be undertaking a re-enactment of some moment of imperial glory; Cook approaching the beach at Tahiti perhaps; or maybe Botany Bay.

They sailed into a pretty little cove, its steep sides covered in dense layers of bracken, which ran up from the waterline almost to the cliff top, where jagged outcrops of granite broke out of the brilliant green and formed silhouettes like battlements against the blue sky. The only path out of the bay was a dusty brown trail that wound its way up the narrow gorge and wound round the cliff edge via a cantilevered wooden walkway above the sheer drop before terminating in a glass building, half built into the cliff itself and most resembling the conservatory of an old seaside town hotel.

They passed up from the bay in single file and cleared the last stages of customs relatively quickly. As the only arrivals, they had to wait no more than a few moments in the empty cliff-side conservatory before moving on, pausing just long enough to be slightly dispirited by the musty blandness of the waiting area. A few plants had been placed in the cornices and between rows of empty seats, presumably to add colour to the beige fittings, but they appeared to have been left untended and the Yukkas and Spider Plants had browned horribly and the leaves of several desiccated Weeping Figs lay on the carpet like forest litter. A bored teenage girl waved them past her desk and under a Beachwood veneer frame that hid the mechanism of the metal detector, ensuring that they entered the country as though passing through the main doors of a slightly tawdry stately home.

After this, they were ushered, politely but firmly, into a small, dimly lit room and informed that they were obliged to watch a fifteen-minute information film before being allowed to proceed any further.

The four of them were the only members of the audience and the room was obviously rarely used, a thin film of dust lay over the fittings and the air was stale and dry. X tried to make himself comfortable, but the moulded plastic chairs were strangely ribbed and shaped for a different size of buttock altogether than his, and he was already shuffling awkwardly when the screen flickered to life. The reel had clearly been used many times before and its dark screen was flecked at the edges with rows of rising white dots and dashes and the soundtrack hissed and crackled as it got going.

The first image on screen was that of a balding, middle-aged man speaking into a forest of microphones. "I am proud to declare", he intoned in a highly distinct manner, with long, deliberate pauses between clauses to add emphasis, "That on this day, and with the sovereign consent of the people, our island has been formally recognised in international law as a ship, moored off the coast of a continental landmass and with all the legal attendances thereby due."

The camera swung round to scenes of wildly cheering crowds gathered in a large square beneath an ornate balcony.

It then switched to an image of the island in cartoon form, portrayed as a ship, heading North through choppy waters, animated waves breaking on its northernmost headland as she made her passage through the swelling waves, the string of islands beyond her prow acting like a carved figurehead on the liberated vessel.

The screen went blank and was then filled with the slogan

WE ARE A SHIP

Then went blank again, followed by,

AND THE SHIP HAS SAILED

And then once more,

WE ARE ALL ON BOARD

The screen went blank, and then, in the bottom corner of the screen, portrait shots began to appear one after another in a continuous stream, flashing up a new image every few seconds. Every kind of face was displayed for an instant, old, young, white, black, fat, skinny, ginger, grey. Some wore naval uniform, most were in civilian dress and all were smiling happily at the camera. Then the succession of faces ceased and another message appeared in bold type on the screen stating;

WE ARE THE CREW

The screen went blank again and then switched to a shot of a middle-aged man with a kindly earnest face and a professorial bearing who was walking toward the camera on a rough track through an oak wood. "When the departure date was declared", he said in a calm, gentle soft-spoken voice, "for some, there were tough choices to make." He paused, and faced the camera directly, his fingers bridged and his face momentarily full of tortured anguish, as if he was personally reliving the moment. "You see", he continued, "the terms of the declaration were quite clear. You had to be on the ship when it sailed, or lose your chance forever. There was to be no dual nationality or seasonal visitors. You were either on the crew or not, and furthermore…", he paused, briefly saddened, before continuing, "…visiting would not be encouraged. In the future, visas would be granted for no more than a single day and would only permit access to certain designated coastal zones." He stopped walking and looked gravely into the camera,

"Decisions had to be made."

The screen switched to grainy black and white footage of departing liners at the dockside, crowds massed on the quayside, seas of white handkerchiefs waving frantically from the decks of the ships at the people filling every crevice along the whole length of the wharf. As the big ships pulled away from the quay, figures could be made out leaning recklessly over the rails, keening back to port at departed loved ones, themselves weeping in unison on the quays.

"There was some sadness", the presenters voice declared solemnly over the plaintive brass soundtrack, the footage now switching to colour shots of huge crowds at airport terminals. It paused briefly on the anguished expressions of separated families giving final tearful backward glances as they dragged luggage to the departure gates. The footage faded out with a lingering still shot of an old Indian woman in a blue sari weeping as she sat alone on a long row of empty departure lounge chairs.

The footage then became a montage; the setting sun on the fuselage of a silver aeroplane taking off and turning into the sky, the lights switching off in banks in the terminal building, piles of litter blowing along the deserted dockside. The music stopped and the presenter spoke into the silence as the sun began to rise again over the dark coastal water,

"But when the ship had sailed......" Images flashed onto the screen of people stepping out of their homes into streets, cul-de-sacs, and balconies, stretching their limbs and smiling as the fresh morning air of the new day filled their lungs, then cut to slow moving machines hoovering the rubbish off the quayside, then red buses and black taxis in a crowded shopping street, children playing in a park, a high-spirited Collie catching a thrown ball in mid-flight, and, he intoned triumphantly;

"...we were all on board."

The images changed to crowds gathering in town squares and village greens across the country, in small numbers at first, but rapidly swelling, a carnival atmosphere developing as crews held rickety ladders aloft to hang colourful bunting from streetlamps and trees, stages were assembled and bands set up their instruments to play. The screen jump-cut from town to town, village to village, city to city. Everywhere smiling crowds were dancing in the streets as spontaneous parties jumped to dubla and bass drum, rock and roll, jit, reggae, ska, funk, punk and metal blasted out over huge PAs on street corners. The film soundtrack somehow blended all these disparate sounds together into soaring sweet soul music and the camera began to ascend upward, rising with a balloon released from a child's hand, looking down first on the little girl's upwardly-lifted trusting face, then the heads of the revellers in the square, catching the smiling faces of the dancing adults around her, then just the tops of their heads in the crowd, a flash of scarlet red beside a stone monument as it rose, and then up, above the church spire, the whole town laid out like a map, stick figures rushing from side streets to join the throng.

The screen went blank again and then cut to a shot of a lanky, mixed-race boy with tousled hair in a white T-shirt and jeans who was leaning against a brick wall while he intently scribbled something on a mini-white board with a marker pen. When he had finished he turned the board to face the camera. The camera panned in. He had written,

I AM THE CREW!

The boy grinned gave a thumbs up directly into the frame, and the innumerable wall of faces began to flicker past this time at an even faster pace so that all the images blurred into one hybrid countenance before the screen finally went blank once more.

They sat in the darkness for long enough for X to think that the screening was over, but just as he was about to rise and make for the exit, it flickered back into life again. A symbol of a ship with a lion rampant beneath it appeared in the corner of the screen, and a middle-aged woman in a gingham two-piece and thick glasses, took up the narrative. She too, was walking toward the camera as she spoke, this time over a busy, traffic-clogged river-bridge. "We then set about the tasks in hand in keeping with the traditions of national character and historic precedent' she explained. "It was established straight away… "she began, her voice trailing out as the image switched to the green benches of a voluminous debating chamber built like a gothic cathedral, where an ancient white-haired man in a wig and red gown was speaking to a hushed room. He was pronouncing, in a clam and measured way that, "not only was it abundantly clear that the ship's crew had an equal responsibility for the smooth running of the ship, it was also entirely evident that they had a concomitant and inalienable right to an equal share in the very fabric of the ship itself." The chamber rose as one to applaud the elder statesman's address.

The presenter, still walking across the bridge, began explaining the origins of 'The venerable precedent', as she called it, and the screen switched back to a portrait of a man in a bedraggled white wig, leaning on a printing press as he examined a freshly -inked sheet with great intensity.

X was distracted by an itch in his back at this point and lost the thread completely during the long following sequence, where five men in big hats and swords overacted some kind of debate in a church. He caught only the phrase "I think that the poorest he has a life to live as the greatest he", which the presenter explained, provided an unchallengeable precedent for all of the ship's government's subsequent actions. "It was determined therefore", the presenter continued, that all the land and wealth acquired by the monarchy or divested by royal grant since the usurpation of the republic in 1649, was to be returned to its rightful owners – as the birth-right of the people themselves."

A sound of soaring trumpets over a succession of images flashed by, each held on screen only for a few seconds, a picture of deer grazing beneath free standing oaks, huge manor houses in their extensive grounds, castles, long stretches of coastline, wide expanses of purple-heathered moorland, luxury apartment blocks, street after street of Georgian terraced houses, yachts, art collections, fitness centres and five star hotels. In the top corner, above the flashing images, a bar graph indicated steadily accumulating wealth, its scale constantly adjusting to keep pace with the value of the appropriated assets rushing across the screen's lower half. Next to it a graphic of the island as a ship flashed with a coloured light each time a new asset was added to the lot of the people. Soon pin-pricks of light garlanded the South and South East and huge washes of a single colour repainted much of the Northernmost third and the South Western archipelago. As more lights twinkled on the entire surface of the island became a glowing patchwork of colour.

Back at the bridge, her face a picture of matronly concern, the presenter acknowledged that, "there was some disagreement about the direction the ship was taking at first."

The view cut to show two burly, red-faced men arguing heatedly across a garden fence, the same brightly coloured flag displayed on poles in both their immaculate lawns.

The presenter spoke over the footage, "First we ensured that those most disadvantaged by the restoration were treated with dignity".

The image switched to a bewildered odd-looking old man with big ears being helped up some shallow steps toward a red-brick cottage surrounded by potted geraniums. On the top step the old man stumbled, but the Asian woman in a nurse's uniform who stood beside him steadied him on her arm and he bent his head, thanking her with a wan smile.

"And when the proceeds of wealth were spent on schools, hospitals, old people's havens, sports facilities and public transport", the presenter continued in a jaunty tone, "tempers cooled."

The film showed the same two burly men from earlier, no longer red-faced, sitting side by side as a sleek steam train pulled out of a whistle-clean station and stayed with them as they marched side-by-side into as shiny new football stadium, the camera honing in on the symbol of a leaping lion embroidered in gilt on each of their jacket lapels.

There then followed a lengthy explanation of the ship's

economics, over shots of smokestacks, mines and gleaming factories, and X struggled to retain his focus. The government had apparently taken controlling stakes in industries and services it considered to be in the national interest and had invested heavily in green technology and clean coal, whatever that might have been. By the time the presenter was droning on about co-operatives, employee share ownership and boardroom representation, X was solely concerned with finding a comfortable position on the moulded chairs.

But it was still not over.

The presenter, now standing in front of a stone statue of a dark-age warrior on a roundabout surrounded by traffic, shouted over the roar, "But of course, our proud tradition of monarchy was retained."

The story was now taken up by a third presenter, this one a very learned looking man, with a shock of white hair and rheumy, bulging eyes. He explained with great care, how the new arrangements were not really new at all, but really the old traditions restored to their rightful place. The old man was so impassioned, his whole body jerking excitedly upward each time he made an important point, that X wanted to believe him, but he found he couldn't make head or tail of his argument. Apparently the new method of choosing the monarch was related to an older system of succession, some kind of 'elective kingship' that had pre-dated primogeniture. X was still struggling to remember what primogeniture was long after the old man had moved on to other themes, and by the time he appeared to mention the Norse god Odin in the line of succession of kings, X knew he was hopelessly lost.

The old man carried on, now gently caressing an intricately patterned gold amulet as he spoke. He explained that the traditional role of the king had always been that of 'the ring giver or the gold-giver' to his people, that the king, from time immemorial had dispensed his wealth to his subjects as part of the very essence of kingship. He indicated the authenticity of the practice by sweeping his arm across the large display cabinet behind him, where similar gold fragments were carefully laid out on row after row of purple velvet cloth, explaining that these had been the king's bands freely given gifts to his followers. The old professor turned to face the camera, his eyes popping with the conclusion of his exposition and triumphantly concluded that the system of 'ritual impoverisation' adopted on board the ship was not innovative in any way, but was, in fact, the restoration of the old ways from before the time of the Frankish yoke.

The shot then switched to a completely bald man in a long white lab coat who explained how the system worked by drawing graphs on a blackboard with coloured chalk. He explained that each year, on the dragon slayer's day, the person in possession of the most wealth in the kingdom was elected as monarch. Their tenure lasted just one year, he continued, explaining that during this time the king or queen would be the living embodiment of the nation's spirit, and in return for the ceremonial glory attendant to their position, were obliged to spend all of their wealth until they were as poor as any ordinary member of the crew. As he pronounced this he lopped the head of the steadily rising curve on his blackboard and shaded in the liberated capital with red chalk to demonstrate the king's gift to his people.

The screen switched to an elderly Sikh man in a purple

turban, waving from the windows of a golden carriage as it passed through the cheering crowds on the streets of a Northern city. The announcer declared that King Sangeev I's rule had been a happy and prosperous one and his subjects were delighted with his gifts and the regalness of his bearing. Then, in an abrupt edit, the film lurched into a brand new full colour print, clumsily spliced onto the old footage. A new announcer's voice, slightly nasal and high-pitched, began speaking over footage of a similar carriage weaving its slow passage through streets lined with flag waving crowds. Breathily, the announcer explained that King Richard IV and V's coronation represented a unique moment in non-constitutional history, becoming the first time anyone had achieved two ascensions to the position of richest person in the kingdom and therefore risen to become a twice-crowned monarch. As the old man was helped from his carriage on screen, the announcer explained in hushed awed tones, how Richard, now in his nineties, had been compelled by his love of money and munificent gesture, to build a second, enormously profitable empire from scratch having redistributed the entirety of his first fortune during his previous reign. The footage showed people openly weeping as the doddery but noble old man was helped up a series of crimson-carpeted steps.

The film abruptly ended and they all sat in the dark for several minutes before the lights came back on.

When they emerged, the custom's officer was standing outside the door. He had changed out of his uniform and was now dressed in a pale green jacket, white shirt and cuffs and a pair of cream slacks with razor-sharp creases. He was making minute adjustments to his appearance by brushing imaginary lint off his lapels and tightening the knot of his regimental tie. He nodded a brief greeting to them before heading off down the path that wound down the hill ahead of him, setting a brisk pace and whistling jauntily to himself as he strode away. They followed, taking pleasure in the sea breeze and the warm sun as they wandered down to the small seaside town below.

*

X and Eva had a moment alone on the beach, licking rapidly melting ice-creams while the sun beat down on the back of their necks. Tasan had retired to a Turkish café on the pier, and X could just make him out, sitting on the terrace, his white panama hat shimmering in the heat haze above the guardrail. Erika, soon tiring of the sand, had headed into town, leaving them alone for the first time since they had arrived. X relaxed, letting the sounds of waves, gulls and children's cries wash away the after-taste of the strange propaganda they had been subjected to on arrival. Despite the hostility to outsiders implied by the information film, there seemed no animosity toward them among the families on the beach, and everyone they had spoken to had been polite and welcoming. The little town seemed entirely at peace with itself.

They were seated in the zone of the beach that was largely reserved for old people and the storage of push chairs, and lining the sea wall next to them, elderly couples in flower print dresses and baggy shorts dozed contentedly in the sun or pottered at the doorways of their well-maintained brightly coloured beach huts. Across the strip of seaweed and driftwood that marked the level of high tide, lay a long stretch of golden sand. Here, the children had built vast interconnected sand castle cities, linking family to family along the beach in a network of turrets and moats and sea-shell pathways. The sand had dried out as the tide receded, and the crumbling sand empires had been largely abandoned by the children who had moved further down the beach for games of football, Frisbee or beach tennis. An Indian family had invited all-comers to their game of beach cricket, and, as X watched, a grandfatherly figure was bowling underarm to a very small boy holding a bat slightly larger than himself. The boy's wild swing made an unexpectedly firm contact with the ball and dropping the bat to the ground, he pelted across the sand like it was burning accompanied by cheers and shouts of encouragement of the other players. Down at the water's edge, X could make out little kids jumping delightedly over the timid waves and splashing in the shallows under the watchful gaze of their mums and dads who had rolled their trousers up to their knees and tucked skirts into knickers to join in the fun. X, was reminded of a poem of Larkin's that ended

> *"It may be through habit these do best,*
>
> *Coming to the water clumsily undressed*
>
> *Yearly: teaching their children by a sort*
>
> *Of clowning: helping the old, too, as they ought."*

He was about to relate it to Eva, but a vague recollection of a disastrous attempt at poetry and romance surfaced in his mind and he shivered at the thought and left the words unsaid.

Later, they wandered up from the beach to the Portuguese café on the seafront where they had arranged to meet the others, and sat drinking coffee and eating custard cakes under the cool air of a rotating fan, while the smell of grilled chicken floated through the door from the Jamaican restaurant next door. There were no more than half-a-dozen people in the café, most of them men, gathered around a large TV screen watching a football match; occasional cheers or groans rising and falling in tune with the rhythms of the game. When Tasan arrived, he and X joined them in front of the screen.

"Who's playing?" Tasan asked, and a young, dark-skinned man in a T-shirt, tailored shorts and deck shoes was nominated by his companions to explain. "It's a big game", he said, keeping his eyes firmly focussed on the screen and talking to them over his shoulder, "The stern derby."

This explained nothing to X, and the man offered no further comment until the ball went out for a throw in and he could give them more attention. He turned to greet them, shaking hands quickly and firmly and introducing himself as Jorge. "Not the biggest", he said, qualifying his earlier comment, "Since we sailed the Auld enemy v Southern capital clashes are much bigger than this, but these sides..." he shrugged.

X concentrated on the match. The quality of football was certainly high, the players clearly fit and well coached and the stadium packed to the rafters. During lulls in the game the camera panned across the tightly packed terraces, where fans wearing the same green or red and white stripes as their teams were arrayed at either end of the ground in great heaving masses of clashing colour. X thought he had worked out what was meant by 'the stern derby', but he was surprised to see the size of the crowd and its mixed ethnicity. Half the players and at least a third of the crowd were of all shades of mixed race, many of Caribbean or African origin. He couldn't remember that many people of colour living in that part of the country and he raised the question with Jorge.

Absorbed in the game, he delayed his reply. A long cross-field pass had been deftly brought under control by the red and white team's centre forward, just inside the opposition's half and on the shoulder of the last defender. As he set off for goal half the men in the café stood up. The number nine skinned the centre back and then, without breaking stride, effortlessly chipped the onrushing goalkeeper from the edge of the penalty box. While the ball was still in flight he turned his back on the goal to face the home supporters, standing with his arms raised aloft as the ball dropped into the net behind him, the crowd's roar breaking over him like a wave. When the cheering in the café was over, Jorge turned to X to answered his question. "As you know", he began, "when the ship sailed many things changed. Perhaps the most obvious – but then again nobody saw it coming", Was that it was *our* ship now. We were the crew – and the crew can go anywhere on the boat – right?"

X nodded.

"So everyone did", he continued, "at first it was just people stretching their legs and looking around, you know, cars, bicycles and caravans all over the roads, tents everywhere, and then with all the wandering, people started thinking that maybe they'd stop some place different to where their families had pitched up in the first place." As he spoke, he leaned back in his chair, as though expressing the collective ease of the ship's crew in the relaxation of his own limbs, "and there was all that land to be redistributed… People could settle wherever they liked…"

He trailed off and X thought he had finished, but he spoke up again with a short laugh, "and you know, if you like palm trees, but you can't get to Freetown or Trinidad no more, where else are you going to go! There are patterns", he said warming to his theme, "it's not absolute, of course, and Cesar..." he indicated the man sitting next to him with a gesture that both identified him and dismissed his opinions at the same time, "rubbishes my views... but I believe there's a sort of ...cultural memory at work...."

Cesar had tuned in, a player was injured and there was a lull in the game while he received treatment. X heard him loudly mutter, "here he goes again..." as his friend began expounding his theory, "look - there are lots of Kurds and Kashmiris in the mountains in the North and West now, and Bangladeshi families living in little villages all over the flat lowlands in the East...and can you be surprised that Jamaicans and Australians ended up on the beach?" he implored, raising his hands heavenward.

"And Portuguese!" someone shouted from the group.

"And Portuguese", Jorge echoed, his expression suggesting the final proof of his thesis had been confirmed.

Cesar stepped in, his voice mocking, "Bangladeshi families in villages in the flat lands! Can you hear yourself Jorge? It's all hopeless generalisation. What about that mad Zambian that lived upstairs and couldn't wait to start mining when the pits reopened in the valleys?"

Jorge was quick to reply, "Copper mining, it's in the blood..."

Cesar laughed, "OK. What about that Moroccan and his family, what was his name...? Went up to live on the figurehead, as far north and as cold as you can get..."

Jorge's response was instantaneous, "It's the open spaces", he argued, "His family was Berber......."

"Berber! Open spaces!"" exclaimed Cesar, howling with derision, "His dad's from the East End!" And with that, he turned away from the conversation and returned to the game, dismissing his friend with a smile and a derisory flick of the wrist.

Jorge was undaunted, and had been explaining how the 'tug-boat' as he called it, the little island just off the stern by the old port city, was a kind of 'little Cyprus now', all coffee shops and backgammon on the sea front', when X had interrupted him to ask if there hadn't been any hostility to all this rapid change.

There was a pause before he replied, and again X worried that he had offended him, but when he spoke he was measured and serious in his reply. "A little at first, perhaps", he said, "but when you've nowhere else to go, you've got to get along with your neighbours, haven't you? And there's enough for everyone", he added, "We know that now. We are all on board after all."

"So it worked out well for everyone?" asked X.

"Mostly", he replied, "I'm not so sure about the West Celts".

X hadn't considered that dimension.

Jorge explained that the view on the ship was that the Western Island was another vessel on the same sea and that they were welcome to join them once they had solved their own difficulties. But the Southern government had elected to stay tethered to the continent and the Western Angles in the North of the island had simply felt angry and abandoned. He added that many of the Celts who had stayed on board had moved to the port side of the ship so that they could stare out to sea at the lost land. "But", he added quickly, "of course that's not the whole picture".

The match was suddenly over. The team in red and white stripes had won, and their companion had to leave immediately, he worked in the fish market, the boats were on their way back in with a good catch apparently, and he had hung on far longer than he should to catch the end of the game. Tasan was keen to see the fishing boats bring in their haul, suggesting to X that it would be quite a spectacle to see the shining herring and cod catches disgorged from bulging nets onto the quayside, but Jorge interrupted him, apologising, saying that as the port was around the next headland and therefore on the other side of the barrier and it would not, therefore, be permitted. He added that the fresh fish would be sold and served in restaurants all along the seafront this evening, and recommended the best places to eat seafood on this side of the barrier. He shook their hands firmly and bid them farewell.

*

As soon as they left the café, Erika took firm charge of proceedings. She had acquired a guidebook and had mapped out a programme that followed the recommended tourist trail to the letter, and if they were to complete the full itinerary they had to stick to a tight schedule. So they duly ran for the double-decker bus, jumping onto the rear platform just as it was pulling away from the stop. The bus swung up from the shore, quickly leaving the cafes and beachfront bars behind and swept them up through short stretches of pine-shaded bungalows on the rising hills above the town and through flashes of wooded glades and meadows before smoothly pulling up on the edge of a village green.

The crossed to-a tearoom on the edge of the green, taking seats on the patio and Erika ordered them all cream teas. X glanced over at the bus, now parked up at the corner of the green. He was momentarily puzzled. It sides were now painted the colour of the grass it stood next to, yet he was certain it had been pillar-box red when they had left the town.

The tearoom Erika had chosen, was according to her guidebook "matched only in its immaculate cleanliness, by the immaculate manners of the staff, it's fine presentation, and its generous portions." The book's claims were accurate, but when the food came, X found he couldn't face eating it; the blood livid strawberry jam and shaving foam tower of cream seemed like a mad child's idea of side dishes for a fruit bun, and no more what he wanted to eat now than if he had been offered trifle for breakfast. Erika and Eva were similarly inclined, nibbling at the edges of their scones and pushing currants around their plates with the little silver spoons. Tasan rescued them from the potential embarrassment of sending untouched food back to the impeccable waitress, by finishing off everyone's portions. He ate with surprising grace given the speed with which he demolished the food, declaring that "they didn't know what they were missing", and smacking his lips in satisfaction as he devoured the last quivering scoop of cream.

X was sat with his back to the café, facing out across the broad village green, and let the calm of the evening wash over him as he contemplated the peaceful view. The green was bordered on its far side by an avenue of Elms, under the shade of which a cricket match was taking place, the long shadows of the stately trees falling across a white wooden pavilion and its painted green roof. At the opposite end, behind a small cluster of houses, two of them thatched, the land rose steeply to a manor house, whose crenelated turret was visible above the trees. A Norman church sat behind the red brick school hall, shaded into darkness by old yews.

They left the tearooms and strolled across the green heading toward the castle, pausing a while at the boundary to watch the cricket match unfold. There were a few other spectators, scattered around in deck chairs with picnic hampers by their sides, and across the field, people had spilled out of the little pavilion and lounged on the steps in small clusters, drinking wine and chatting, their attention only half-focused on the game itself. The batsman in when they arrived was a powerfully built Nigerian man whose long tenure at the crease was characterised by some prodigious strikes. Each true contact with the ball was met with a roar of delight, which broke over the birdsong and restrained applause each time like a thunderclap on a cloudless still day. He hit several sixes, and when he was finally caught at the boundary having completed his half-century, he was loudly applauded from the field, diverting his path back to the pavilion to bear hug the young man who had caught him, his laugh booming in waves across the field and fading away only when he entered the pavilion itself. Another batsman came into the crease. Nothing much seemed to happen and then they changed ends.

They moved on toward the castle.

The path led up round the old church, and passing under the shade of the yews it became open countryside that rolled away softly down a shallow valley, its fields separated from their path only by a low hedge. In the neighbouring fields, a steam fair was in progress and they had an unimpeded view of the show.

Although it was late in the day, the crowds were clearly enjoying themselves and the fair was still in full swing as they passed by. Across the fields, people were milling around the machinery on display in scattered clumps, or lay in deck chairs around a roped central area, soaking up the late afternoon sun while steam-powered trucks in smart liveries queued in a stop-start traffic jam around the centre circle. Just the other side of the hedge from where they walked, a row of old men carefully tended scaled-down steam pumps and miniature engines with a tenderness usually reserved for brides. A young girl with thick glasses was listening to one of the most crepuscular of the exhibitors, taking careful notes on a pad as he pointed out key aspects of his machines mechanism. Further along Eva and X stopped for a while to watch three teams of young men and women, apprentices of some type, compete to strip and reassemble a steam pump while a large fairground stop clock wound down behind them. Beyond the apprentices, a long queue of kids waited their turn for a ride around the field in a sleek yellow steam tractor. On the last stretch, before the path turned away from the field, a quarter scale model of a steam train ran alongside the path, blood-red, arrow-pointed and as futuristic as though it had been designed for Dan Dare. A sign in carnival lettering on dark lacquered wood declared it 'The Hibernian II – World Steam Record Holder'. A cluster of boys, slack jawed, were staring at its pistons with reverent awe as they passed. As they made their way up through the trees, the notes of a pipe organ accompanied them, floating in sweet broken harmonies through the branches, gradually fading away, until the silence was broken only by the intermittent blasts of a steam whistle and the cries of birds.

*

The castle itself turned out to be an eighteenth century manor house of no particular architectural merit, and despite the guide's sycophantic delight in every detail of the family's history, it seemed to X that they had achieved astonishingly little despite three centuries of remarkable privilege and prosperity. There had been a moment in 1890, apparently, when her ladyship Margaret Ann had been considered for the position of maid-in-waiting to the great monarch herself, and the old queen had indeed visited, but in the end, another, far less suitable, rival had been selected. And that seemed to be the full total of the dynasty's modest record of achievement, as far as X could see. He was looking for a way out of the tour even before she began gushing about the seventeenth baroness' pottery collection. explaining that, "Over a lifetime's exercise of the most exquisite good taste, her ladyship had amassed one of the world's most important collection of glazed china dogs", and, blinking with admiration for the baroness' monumental achievements, explained how, "Her fascination with ceramics had led her to have her own kiln installed in the grounds in order to produce her own sculptures. Sadly, when the baroness had first exhibited her challenging work in pottery otters she had been met with ridicule, and, reviled by a politically hostile press, it was only now her work was beginning to be truly understood".

As they were being ushered through a narrow passageway towards the baroness' studio, a door on the left marked 'PRIVATE' crashed open. An old man, topless, scratching at an emaciated chest yellowed the colour of nicotine with his long, dirty fingernails, shuffled into the corridor in a pair of threadbare slippers. Ignoring the tour party completely, he crossed the corridor and stepped into a small bathroom on the other side. Without closing the door behind him he dropped his pants and began pissing into the toilet bowl, his bony arse checks tightly clenched as he emptied his bladder with a sigh of satisfaction. He turned his head as he shook the last drops off, acknowledging the existence of the intruders for the first time.

"Fuck off!" he commanded.

"Yes, of course, your lordship", the tour guide replied, executing a small curtsey as she did so before hurrying the rest of the group past his lordships baleful glare, as he calmly resorted his flaccid penis to its place in his saggy Y-fronts and zipped up his pants.

X skipped out before the ceramic dogs.

He had time to walk along the edge of the ha-ha while the others were still inside. From its brink it commanded a view of the grassy field beyond, where men in ill-fitting cassocks were teaching kids archery using medieval bows. Turning the other way, he took in the panorama of wooded hills beyond the manor house grounds. His eye was drawn to a red danger sign on a post in front of the line of trees ahead of him. Although it was some distance away it must have been quite large as he could distinctly read the words,

'WARNING 200 YARDS – TURN BACK NOW'

X couldn't see 200 yards beyond the sign as a plantation of pines obscured the view, but he peered for some time into their midst to try and catch a glimpse of the barrier. He caught a flash of reflected light bouncing of something metallic above the treeline and stared harder to try and make it out, wondering for a moment if it was a watchtower, but concluded that it was probably nothing more sinister than an electricity pylon.

*

They strolled back to town through a park constructed in the last century, with neat borders, a stone bridge over the duck pond and a grotto where a nymph endlessly poured water from her amphora over glass mosaic tiles. They emerged at a cliff-top with a charming view across the bay and were whisked back to sea level on the leather seats of a vernacular railway, descending in the fin de siècle style of its interior like passengers on the Orient Express.

Erika informed them that at this stage of the tour they had a choice. They could either try out the lido, which the guide described as, 'charming and refreshing', or the 'Red-Tape Free zone', which it described as 'must see'. Tasan was adamant that the zone was the only possible choice and badgered X into joining him. Both of the women elected for a swim.

Tasan set off at a furious pace leaving X trailing along behind him, and he had only just caught up when they entered the zone, stepping straight into the crowded fun fair inside. Hundreds of stalls, from coconut shies to rifle ranges to hook a duck stands were pressed tight against each other under wooden framed canopies. The narrow passages between stalls were crammed with beaming children and fractious parents, every kid laden with cheap plastic guns or tacky anthropomorphic soft toys in bright primary colours, their faces smeared pink with crystallised sugar from candyfloss and toffee apples. Balloons bobbed above its crowded pathways like lanterns on Chinese New Year.

The first attraction they passed was a fun house. Only one

of the metal escalators was still functioning, cracked mirrors hung at lurid angles from its walls, and Gaffer tape was peeling off the razor-sharp edges of the metal slide. On the upper floor, some kids had constructed a defensible redoubt from bean bags and broken wall mirrors, and were resisting the advance of another a troop of boys wearing pirate bandanas who were fighting their way up the stalled treadmill under a barrage of plastic bottles.

Next to the funhouse, the dodgems had a hard funk soundtrack blaring out, complete with the guttural thrusts of simulated intercourse and panting, whose rhythms bore no relation to the slowly circulating electric buggies. Some of the cars were scarcely capable of any movement at all, their snail's progress from one side of the arena to the other interrupted only by the repeated buffeting of those fortunate enough to have chosen better functioning vehicles. Customer dissatisfaction was high, and the two men in puffer jackets who were shouting abuse at the attendant behind the glass windowed ticket booth were in the process of being joined by a third irate punter. On his way to the booth the third man was knocked flat on his back by a grinning eight-year-old joyrider, and he was still chasing the kid around the ring with his fists raised as they passed by.

They skirted an old Coney Island rollercoaster, rattling around its rickety wooden trackway, clacking like a Wild West freight train, children's hands raised in delight in every carriage as it swept by. As they came closer, X heard the operator shouting at the kids each time they hurtled, squealing, past:

"Keep your hands in!"

"Keep your fucking hands in!"

"You'll lose your fucking hands in you don't keep them in!"

His imprecations seemed only to add to the children's delight and despite paying him no heed, they all trooped off the ride at its conclusion with both hands still attached to their wrists.

Against his better judgement, X was persuaded by Tasan to take a ride with him on the big wheel that loomed ominously above the fair. He regretted it almost immediately. Clamped uncomfortably under the thick metal bar they had risen about five metres before lurching to an abrupt halt, an action that sent their carriage tilting violently back and forward on its pinion. There was a delay, during which X wondered if it was still possible to squeeze himself over the restraint and jump to the ground, but concluded that he would at least break an ankle in the fall and was therefore forced to stay put. Eventually, a man in overalls so drenched with grease that they stood stiffly away from his body like a beetle's carapace, stepped over the wheel struts below them; sprayed some oil onto the central axis before hitting it three times with a club hammer using as much force as he could muster. He clambered back out and gave a thumbs-up to the operator. The machine clanked back into life and they rotated upward once more. The wheel made one smooth full rotation before coming, once again, to a sudden jerking halt, this time, inevitably, when they were at the very peak of the rotation, some 100 feet above the ground.

X involuntarily closed his eyes when their carriage began pitching about at the zenith and now found himself unable to open them again. The fear-induced sweat that had rushed over his body at the sudden halt in the ride, began to cool in the chill breeze blowing off the sea and he felt himself start to shiver violently.

"Isn't this marvellous?" he heard Tasan declare beside him.

X risked opening his eyes a fraction and squinted under his lashes at the older man. Tasan was laid back in his seat, arms folded behind his neck, his legs hanging loosely over the void, as relaxed as though he was lounging in a deck chair on his own front lawn.

"Isn't it marvellous", Tasan repeated, "This perfect moment. The air. The view; this perfect stillness brought about by its opposite intention, that of motion. Marvellous, don't you think", he continued, "that the attainment of the opposite of one's goal is often the most entrancing?"

X made himself open his eyes. The town lay displayed beneath them, the illuminations flickering on as the sun dipped below the horizon while they hovered in the cool air. Coloured baubles had been strung cheerfully along the promenade and a strip of white neon light ran out into the sea along the length of the pier, where the pavilion at its end, garlanded in white bulbs, glowed like a Vegas Baptist chapel above the dark sand. He looked down, but found the swirling lights of the rides below him disorientating and he shut his eyes again to prevent himself from being overwhelmed by vertigo. Opening them once more he just had time to catch Tasan beaming at him like a proud father, before the wheel, jerked sharply into motion once more, sent their carriage lurching violently forward on its pivot. Finding himself staring straight down as the chair kicked up behind him, his stomach rose in his throat and he fought to prevent himself emptying its contents on the couple happily swinging their feet in the carriage below.

The wheel conducted a smooth arc and deposited the pair

of them safely back down on the ground.

*

They met up with Eva and Erika on the seafront. The women looked healthy and refreshed after their swim and the faint odours of chlorine and carbolic soap came off them as they pressed foreheads in greeting. Eva seemed pleased to see him, and when he suggested they had fish and chips for supper rather than dine at the seafront fish restaurant Erika had selected from her guidebook, she agreed and the pair of them slipped away.

They had sat on a bench on the pier to eat their battered cod, and having licked their fingers clean, they dawdled out to sea along the rail, strolling side by side past the closed fortune teller's booths, donut making machines and lucky dips.

The ornate pavilion at the pier's end displayed a banner declaring that a 'Spectacular Music Hall Variety Show' was underway inside. X ran his eyes over the bill. It seemed to consist largely of overweight singers, child prodigies, clowns, and dogs dressed in a variety of brightly coloured outfits performing tricks. Eva asked what he thought of line-up and he replied truthfully that they weren't to his taste, pointing out one of the judges, prominently displayed on the banner with his arm rammed up to the shoulder in a large fluffy hamster, whose startled eyes seemed to confirm that he had, indeed, just been brutally assaulted by the broadly smiling waxy-skinned ventriloquist, who was raising the thumb on his free hand cheerfully toward the camera. "There's something not right there", he'd said.

They drifted further down to the end of the pier and lent on

the railing looking out at the moonlit sea. As Eva stood beside him in the dimmed light, her shoulder briefly brushed against his as she settled into position along the rail. The touch caressed his mind for much longer than the brief second the contact had actually lasted. X was acutely aware that Eva's relationship with him had changed since the accident, and he had managed to partly adjust himself to their new dynamic. They were, he understood, once again what they were always supposed to have been; friends.

Yet...

In her friends' company, Eva would readily accept a hug from Xanthia or Per, or lay her head on Pooja's lap or Sven's shoulders, and X had briefly been part of that intimacy. But now Eva never touched him, except for formalities, and maintained, however confined the space they were obliged to share, a constant, exact distance, whose very maintenance required an intensity of focus, that was, at the very least, nothing to do with friendship. That brief touch of the shoulder had changed all that once more. Which way? Relaxed, into true friendship, or...

Eva turned away from him along the rail, looking inshore as he stared in the opposite direction out to sea, the finally calibrated gap between them restored once more to its customary distance. His skin was super-sensitised to the tiny breach, his body forever reaching to stem the gap without moving, yearning desperately for another involuntary slip in her vigilance that would let him in. Saddened, he watched the blinking red light of a fishing boat cross the horizon, its solitary passage across the water seemed an echo of his loneliness. He felt the touch of Eva's hand on his shoulder. The touch, given his thoughts only the moment before, hit him like an electric shock, and, dazed and bewildered, he stumbled after her across the boardwalk as she led him to a rusty iron stairwell that zig-zagged down the outside of the pier to the beach below.

The tide was coming in now, and small waves lapped around the stairwell's base as they stepped out onto the rubble-strewn wet sand. The air was rank with the smell of rotting seaweed and brine, and large clumps of slimy green algae hung from the criss-cross metal bars under the pier like roadkill in window boxes. Eva weaved a confident passage into the stinking shadows under the pier and X followed her blindly, scrambling over the slippery struts as he struggled to keep pace. In the darkness he was utterly unable to suppress his rising sense of excitement. Perhaps, just perhaps, he had read the situation all wrong earlier. Eva hadn't touched him by accident. It had been shyness not disinterest that had held her back. She had sought out the darkness under the pier to be alone with him, certain that here she was free from the prying eyes of Erika and Tasan...

He slipped on some slime and stepped into a pool of rank water, soaking his foot up to the ankle and catching an elbow hard on one of the girders as he fell. He fought himself to stop daydreaming and concentrated hard for the rest of the passage in order to prevent himself falling and losing his dignity completely.

Eva stopped, just before they emerged on the other side of the pier, her face momentarily bisected by the moonlight and the pier's deep shadow, one perfect severed half luminescent, her eyes washed completely of colour by its cold light, leaving her beautiful but dead, as lifeless and perfect as a Greek statue. She took a step back into the darkness, gesturing for him to step forward as she did so. For the briefest fraction of a second he thought she was drawing him to her for a kiss.

No. She just wanted to show him something.

She was pointing toward the shore, "There", she said, "I thought it would be easier to see down here without the pavilion lights".

He looked. At first he couldn't see anything remarkable. The bay was laid out prettily enough, the Christmas-every-day illuminations twinkled cheerfully, and light blazed out of the beachfront cafes and bars.

"No. Look higher", Eva commanded.

Above the promenade, the patterns of lit windows and streetlamps dwindled to darkness as the hills rose behind the town.

And then he saw.

The barrier swept across the hilltops, running the full length of the ridge around the bay as far as the coastal cliffs in the distance. Its wire mesh glimmered in the arc lights suspended above each section, and watchtowers, evenly spaced along its length, were clearly visible in their beams. Emanating in slow sweeps from each of the towers, searchlights picked out the strands of razor-wire strung from the topmost part of the fence, making it shine prettily as though the barrier had been topped out with tinsel. On the length of the barrier immediately above the town, each section of the fence had been sprayed with a single huge block capital letter. The message was clearly picked out by the arc lights and hung like a banner unfurled over the town. It spelt out;

KEEP CALM – AND FUCK OFF

They were picked up from the end of the pier at 10:30pm precisely and a steam-powered skiff took them back to their boat. The ship set off as soon as they had boarded, pulling away from the shore as the first few tendrils of mist formed in the rapidly cooling air over the surface of the dark water.

GRAVEYARD

He woke shivering.

His returning sight revealed the first rays of dawn breaking over the horizon, and he raised a shaking, lifeless arm to shield his eyes from the slanting beams. His back was still pressed up against the tomb, and the cold of the stone had seeped through his shoulder blades leaving him frozen in place like a stiffened corpse on the dew soaked grass.

His suit was ruined.

The pants were sodden, smeared all over with mud and grass stains, and when he inspected the jacket it was clear that flakes of orange lichen had ground themselves into the fabric overnight, turning its purple silk into a tie-dyed soup of colour that he suspected even the toughest dry cleaning would fail to shift.

When he was able to stand, he spent several minutes jumping stiffly about to try and restore some warmth to his frozen limbs, jerking about on the grass like a broken marionette performing a macabre graveside dance as blood painfully returned to his toes and fingers.

Before he left, he checked the inscription on the tomb he had spent the night propped up against, checking whether an act of fate had guided his blind wanderings directly to the grave of Del's parents.

It hadn't.

27. THE IVY

First thing Monday morning he got a telephone call from Mike Verne asking him to join him for lunch that day at the Ivy.

This was it. His big break had finally arrived.

They'd done little more than shake hands and sit down before Mike came straight to the point. "Tell me X, do you think New TV has any possibility of succeeding?"

X was taken aback. He'd assumed he'd been invited to discuss his promotion to publisher in place of Howard. To give himself time to gather his thoughts, he signalled to a passing waiter and ordered a white wine spritzer.

Mike selected a Jameson's with ice.

Even in his state of mild panic he noted the director's choice. It would be useful to remember come Christmas.

By the time the waiter had delivered the drinks, he was ready. "In answer to your question…No. I don't think it can succeed."

"Expand."

"I think we were too early to market," he began…

*

It had just been a matter of rolling out Sara's argument. She had worked it out in her first week, and he largely regurgitated it with a few theatrical flourishes thrown in. Mind you, he'd had to choose his words carefully. Mike had, after all been responsible for the magazine's conception, so he'd had to make sure he praised his original vision, and pinned the blame for its failure on someone else. To ensure his back was covered he'd stitched up the editor, a man he hardly knew. "I assume we're talking off the record?" he'd asked.

Mike had grunted his assent.

Leaning forward across the table as he spoke, he'd speared an olive with a cocktail stick, raising it up like a severed head to emphasis his point, "Editorial's weak. We run pictures on the front page instead of news, which makes us look like a Sunday colour supplement rather than a hard-hitting paper – we're giving them fluff pieces when we should be hitting them over the head with scoops, and… There's no getting away from it…" he leant back, raising his hands in a sympathetic, but condemnatory gesture, "We've got an editor who's a once-was-never-been. He may well know everybody in the business, but it's my distinct impression he's not highly regarded by many, and what's more he's got no balls or business sense…and it shows…" It was time to sum up. "I'm sorry to be so negative, Mike", he said ruefully, "and I'll be back at my desk boosting away this afternoon, but in truth, I think the money's at least five years down the line, and that's a lot of red ink to carry on a weekly…."

X sat back. That was a decent pitch for publisher if ever there was one. Only when he had finished did it occur to him that he had probably just got the magazine closed down.

Mike sat in silence a while, gently stroking his beard with his left hand while he digested X's views.

"And this MIPCOM venture", he said, after he had ordered his third whiskey, "Should I pull the plug on that?"

Oh Fuck. He might have blown Cannes too.

MIPCOM, the annual television festival in Cannes, was to be his crowning glory. The French Riviera on an unlimited expense account. He'd wasted hours organising the trip; booked the New TV delegation into the smartest hotel he could get past accounts, secured a table at the Carlton for the final night and even arranged a helicopter transit from the airport into town. He'd never thought they'd make any money out of it. He'd only managed to blag it because it was so easy to bullshit Howard. He wasn't going to let it slip away.

"It's worth a punt", he started, "True, we're a tiny publication by International standards, and most of the really big money will be spent in the pages of giants like *The Hollywood Reporter* and *Variety*. We can't begin to compete with them, and we scarcely even register on the big studios' radar. But if we can convince the US production companies that we are the key to the British market and snatch…" He hesitated, having no idea of any of the figures, continuing with a number he had plucked randomly out of the air, "…5% of their European budgets, we'll come out of it with a big fat full colour blockbuster of an issue, and who knows, maybe kick some life into the whole project…"

X was fairly certain that he'd done enough to convince Mike of the trip's virtues, so he slipped in another bid for the publisher's job, "Not sure it can be done without editorial support though", he added, "We'd need some news print on the front page - a bit of leverage I could use to flatter the big egos into the pages…"

*

Everything had changed at New TV since his meeting with Mike Verne. A memo had come down from the director's office that he was to be sit in on all future editorial meetings. It didn't sound like much, but presiding over editorial was the publisher's job, if X was coming to the meetings, what exactly *was* Howard's doing?

Even Howard's now realised he had raised a cuckoo in the nest, and his exchanges with X were now laced with a degree of fear. Howard avoided him as much as he could, and when he was obliged to address him directly, he fiddled nervously with his glasses, stumbled over his metaphors and often stuttered to halt mid-sentence. He was off the golf course and in the building more often now, but after a few days of frantic memo writing he clearly didn't know what to do with himself, and sat in his tiny office reading polo magazines or staring into space.

*

His first editorial meeting didn't go well.

"Just put a story on the front page!' he said for the second time, "How controversial is that - it's a newspaper!"

The editor sat opposite him, utterly astonished once more, staring open mouthed as X spoke.

"Look, all I'm asking you to do is run with something like - The Deals of Cannes 1989 – Who are the big players this year? What programmes are hot properties? Which studio stands to make the most money? These are the biggest stories in our business during MIPCOM aren't they?"

The editor ignored X, and, looking directly at Howard asked, "Why is he here?"

Howard mumbled something about the up-coming MIPCOM project and how X was leading on it.

X let the editor splutter on for a while about the sanctity of editorial impartiality, and the sheer presumption of the tail attempting to wag the dog, occasionally interrupted by Howard's attempts to ameliorate the situation with interjections of uplifting non-sequiturs.

When it had run on long enough, he brought it to a close, regaining the floor by talking over the others in a loud, steady voice, "Please record in the minutes of this meeting that it was the Group Advertising manager's strong belief that a story covering the major event in television broadcasting taking place this week was placed on the front page. I would also like it minuted", he continued, "That this should be a non-contentious statement, but instead of dealing with it, the editor's only response was to challenge the legitimacy of the questioner. The questioner being the person, I would like to remind you, who is responsible for raising the entire revenue of the magazine and therefore for paying everyone's wages, including the editor's.

The editor spluttered with rage at his impertinence, and turned again to Howard, "Who is running this magazine?' he demanded.

There was silence.

He couldn't resist. "At this moment", he suggested, pausing for dramatic effect, "I would say it was the Women's Institute."

*

He might as well not have bothered. When he'd opened up the

Cannes edition of the magazine before he'd left the office for Heathrow, instead of a news story on the front page, the editor had chosen to print a huge picture of Daffy Duck. He checked the list of programming that Warners were taking to the festival. Daffy Duck was not on it. They hadn't made a new series since the late 1960s. The editor might as well have spat in his face. He'd made a difficult pitch almost impossible and probably cost them all their jobs into the bargain.

*

His troubles rose out of his body as the helicopter took off as though they had been miraculously lifted out of his body by the sudden weightlessness of flight. Fuck it. He was in Cannes. The sun was shining. He had Jeanne for company.

Jeanne. On reflection, the only true friend he had made in the business. They'd have fun. It was always fun with Jeanne. And lest they forgot, he was taking them to the French Riviera on an unlimited expense account, with a ringside seat right where all the action was. They would sup champagne using somebody else's money and do deals in a grand hotel framed by palm trees on the seafront. He would have a slice of *real* glamour for once. Wasn't that what it was all about? All he needed to do was sit back and enjoy the ride and who knows? Maybe if he played it like James Bond, they might even make some money.

The ground was suddenly a lunar distance beneath him, the helicopter's rapid ascent turning the planes on the runway into children's toys, and when the pilot shifted the angle of the rota blades and swept them out across the bay, the azure sea below seemed to rush away as though the water was hurtling down a chasm.

The sensation reminded him being on the big wheel with Tasan and to stem the sudden sensation of vertigo, he closed his eyes.

28. THE DNA GAMES

The sun had just cut the brim of the horizon, and although a thick band of mist still lay on the surface of the water the air was already hot. As the sun rose, the mist evaporated, revealing that the ship was afloat on a vast aquamarine sea, gliding smoothly over the surface of the crystal-clear water toward a small volcanic island in the far distance. Eva stood beside him on the deck. Her skin had been tanned a deep honey brown by the sun and her eyes had changed to a green the colour of emeralds. The colour match of eye and skin was electric, revealing a new aspect of her beauty, an energised solar radiance of health and vitality that emanated from her like refracted heat. She looked like a golden-girl Olympic swimmer from the Antipodes at the peak of her powers.

But it was too startling a change to be natural.

"Your eyes!' he blurted out.

"Do you like the colour?" she asked, "I thought it matched the tan."

It took Eva a while to understand X's confused expression, and when she did she laughed at him. "X! For a 'Seeker of Sweden' you are amazingly unobservant! Tell me -what colour are Xanthia's eyes?"

He couldn't recall. He hadn't spent a lot of time looking into Xanthia's eyes.

Eva snorted. "You don't know, of course, because she changes it every day!" exclaiming, as though it was utterly self-evident, "Altering the colour of your iris requires no more than a few drops from a vial. I change my eye colour often to suit my mood. Have you never looked into my eyes?"

The question was either so pregnant with meaning that it was only answerable by seizing her waist and pressing her mouth firmly to his lips, or so absent in the faintest comprehension of him that he would have been obliterated to even acknowledge it. He'd thought her constantly changing eye colour was part of an indescribable shifting beauty that was marvellously unique to her. Now he felt that he had been seeing her through a prism, and that however elegantly executed the design had been, the windows of her soul had always been veiled to him.

"So what colour are your eyes?" he asked.

"Ah", she replied, her voice almost arch in its delivery, "That *would* be telling".

So they did hold on to some privacy after all.

As they drew closer, the volcanic island seemed to raise itself from the sea-bed to greet them until hundred-foot high cliffs towered above the ship's mast. The wall of rock, thrown up the volcano's ancient eruption, rose sheer from the waterline, and where the lava had cooled unevenly, ragged turrets had formed on its puckered brim like a medieval castle's battlements. From one of the crests, a still active vent released jets of sulphurous gas and steam into the still air, the yellowed vapour sent swirling above the island by the rotor blades of the helicopters that were descending on the island like bees returning to a hive.

They circumnavigated the island in search of a berth on one of the mile-long jetties that fanned out from the island in a frozen starburst, and gliding into the crowded waterway, they passed huge liners as big as floating hotels and enormous luxury yachts before finding a spot among the thousands of smaller sail boats closer to shore. They moored in front of the only breach in the walls, where a ramshackle town had squeezed itself into the fissure above a thin strip of grey sand, its clapperboard shacks suspended on wooden stilts above banks of scree at the water's edge. All around them, people were disembarking from the ships in huge numbers and joining a giant colourful throng advancing in unison toward the crack in the wall above.

Erika and Tasan had joined them on deck, and X asked where they were.

"An abomination of a place", Erika replied.

In contrast to Erika, who was clearly in a foul mood, Tasan's spirits were high. With a captain's peaked cap perched rakishly askew on his head, his skin darkened to the colour of teak, and salt bleach streaks in his neatly-trimmed beard, it was clear that the sea-journey had thoroughly agreed with him, and he skipped up and down with scarcely contained excitement on the deck, staring at the island as though he could draw it closer through sheer force of will.

When X repeated his question, Tasan replied cryptically saying that, "It was not so much where, dear boy, as when?"

At that moment a slow moving airship crept across the sky high above the island, trailing a huge banner that declared:

WELCOME TO THE DNA GAMES!!!

And then a few moments later the banner's message changed to:

THE SPECIES IS STEPPING UP!

Tasan leapt out of the boat as soon as it reached the jetty and before it had fully moored, beckoning the other's to join him. "No time to waste", he urged, "We have very good seats." Eva and X followed his lead, but Erika refused to budge, brushing off their entreaties to join them by declaring that 'the whole filthy place disagreed with her' and that she would be staying on board until they returned.

Tasan attempted to persuade her, grinning broadly and speaking in a gently mocking tone, "You never know Erika," he'd said, "you might see something better than you imagined". But his words only seemed to make her mood more disagreeable and, disembarking without her, they were swept upward with the excited crowd toward the gap in the lava-cliffs.

X had staggered as they entered the volcano crater, temporarily disorientated by the sheer scale of the spectacle. The whole of the caldera had been turned into an enormous stadium, and tier upon tier of terraces rose from the sunken bowl to the top of the cliff wall and flowed round its contours in undulating stone curves like the steps of a ziggurat. A crowd as big as a large city were perched on the terraces like a giant colony of nesting sea-birds. High above, huge fans, turning slowly in the active vent, blew its sulphurous fumes out to sea, occasional backdrafts of yellow smoke drifting slowly down over the upper tiers.

Tasan guided them down to their seats, and as there was no action taking place on the track below, X scanned the crowd. There was something strange about the audience. At first he couldn't make it out, but as looked closer, he began to notice strange transformations in the crowd's physiognomy. Many of the women's bodies seemed unnaturally exaggerated; faces with swollen lips, and mouths set in a permanent pout were common, and hugely augmented breasts sat above hour-glass waists. As he looked closer still, he noticed that many of them had extruding incisors, like the teeth of wildcats, set in their upper jaws, and then; as a woman he was looking at blinked, he was shocked to see that her brightly coloured iris opened sideways like a cat's. The men were similarly altered, transformed into giants with jaws as prominent and square as half-bricks, and sporting bull necks and impossible washboard stomachs. Like the women, many of the men also had enlarged canines, theirs often as large as sabre-toothed tigers'. He couldn't help but notice that a giant two rows down from where they sat had an enormous cock strapped to his inner thigh like a huge cosh, it's outline clearly visible under his tight shorts. It turned out that this adaptation too was commonplace, and every third man seemed to have a penis anatomically possible only in equestrian animals. Once the initial shock had passed he began to enjoy spotting the rarer transmogrifications, particularly liking the look of the delicate young couple two rows down whose prehensile tails, like those of ring tailed lemurs, curled and uncurled around each other as they sat.

    The announcer's voice burst out like a cannonade around the bowl declaring that the next event, the shot put, was about to begin. It was met with huge cheers around the stadium. X was surprised that what had always been a minority event in athletics could command such an occasion, but the expectancy levels in the crowd were clearly high, and roars and chants began to break out around the stadium as the fans grew impatient for the action to begin. As the last stragglers hurried up the isles, three huge trumpet blasts blew out, and when their echoes had stopped reverberating around the cauldron, the competitors entered the arena.

Now X understood the excitement. The Athletes were gargantuan. None were less than seven feet tall, and many much bigger than that, and across their backs, shoulders, upper arms and thighs, herculean banks of fat-veined muscles bulged well beyond the range of human possibility. Some of the competitors were smooth-skinned, and had hair only on their heads, but many had elected to take the gorilla's pelt along with its musculature and many heads, backs and shoulders bristled with blue-grey and silvered hair. The athletes began loosening up, jostling and shoulder charging each other, breaking into short knuckle-walks, or raising their thunderous arms in handclaps to get the crowd going.

"The gorilla gene was very easy to splice", Tasan informed him. "No other species has really been tried for strength", he added, sounding slightly disappointed.

Below them the first of the competitors got ready to take his throw by raising one of his swollen arms to full stretch hefting a shot the size of a bowling ball in fist. X asked Tasan how much it weighed. "25 Kg", he replied, 'they had to keep increasing the weight to stop them throwing it into the crowd."

The first competitor was human-skinned, and seemed strangely naked in front of his hairier competitors. His anatomically impossible muscles squeezed out like a pink cartoon body builder as he braced to throw. Letting go, the huge cannonball flew high in the air travelling a distance of at least40m before smacking into the turf like a meteorite falling from space. X was hugely impressed, but the crowd's response was muted, and remained so until the biggest of all the silverbacks took up his turn to throw. The gorilla-man crouched at the furthest edge of the circle, his great forearm rammed under his neck, cradling the giant shot in the palm of his hand. Bent down low over his enormous thigh muscles, coiled and compressed for maximum thrust across the circle, he formed a statute of barbarous power, as though he had been carved out of rock by Rodin. He uncoiled suddenly with surprising grace and exquisite balance in an explosion of lightening power and strength and with a roar that opened up the lungs of the crowd let fly, standing screaming the shot's flight all the way out to 70 metres. He had broken his own world record with his first throw, and cries of 'Stepping Up" burst out around the stadium. The competition was his. He pulled out another mighty one for his final throw to set the crowd roaring again, and left with the whole stadium chanting his name.

After the quick medals ceremony, where the flags of the pharmaceutical companies most associated with the winning athletes were raised while xylophone music played, the big screens flashed to an interview with the victor, the words of their exchange crashing out over the arena. X had no choice but listen.

The interviewer had asked the champion what victory meant to him and he replied that, "to know my clip is going to play forever in the Hall of Eternity on Victory Island is a dream come true for me, Jack."

"And what will you do now?"

"We'll first I'll be resting up!"

They both laughed.

"You should all visit Victory Island", he declared turning to face directly into the camera, "I first went when I was just a boy of twelve and it inspired me to follow my dream. I'll be staying with my wife in one of the luxury Thanatos apartments, some of which are surprisingly affordable", he added.

The interviewer laughed again as though he had said something funny. "And what else will you do?' he asked.

"I'll find time for a little wine,"

The interviewer laughed again before asking, "What kind of wine?"

"Oh Yes, thanks." He quickly pulled on a brand new baseball cap with a corporate logo from a cellophane packet at his feet, and placing it on his head, said, "Yes, Zantorini wine! It tastes great and I love the way it's packed with humming-bird mitochondria!"

Both of them seemed to relax once their sponsor duties were over, and the victor spoke softly into the mike, "But that's it for me now Jack," he said "the wife and I ..." he stopped speaking and leaning away from the mike, beckoned his wife up beside him. "Here Joan!" he called, waving a gargantuan arm, until a brown pelted woman, enormous by ordinary proportions but dwarfed by her husband, came reluctantly into camera shot. She had a bronze medal on a ribbon around her neck. "Joan and I are dropping out for good. Don't get me wrong, I think there's plenty left in the gorilla genes and you'll see some great champions throwing heavier weights tremendous distances, but we think we've got the best out of the mix at this stage; lots of strength, with good flexibility and hell! We like the look!"

There were huge roars from the crowd in response.

X was sure his wife was blushing, but it was a little hard to tell behind the hair.

The victor was in earnest now, "You know Jack, that the difficulty in harnessing gorilla-power isn't in the muscles, but the skeletal changes necessary to anchor all that generated torque. We've spoken of this before I know, but for me to create this frame required extensive painful surgery. They had to break my back in nine places before rebuilding my shoulders, vertebra and pelvis in the right shape and then letting the gorilla stems form new bone tissue around them. I was in recovery from bone grafts for six months then another six months immobilised in a cast with a skeleton as soft as marshmallows. It took another year to get the muscle strength back again.

The stadium was quiet out of respect for his dedication and suffering.

"But you see", he went on, "Our children won't have to go through that. We know from what was done to my body the amount of architecture we need to import from the gorilla genes and now we can splice it in right from the start – Their skeletons will grow with them, and by the time they get all big and strong around puberty, the frame will be there. My wife's got some gibbon", he added, "and we plan to keep that on the X chromosome so that some, but not all, of the girls will to be more slender and flexible than the boys....at a cost of a little strength", he added.

There were whoops and cheers from the crowd.

"In vitro?" asked the commentator.

"Do I look like a guy who would go in vitro?" The gorilla-man replied suddenly stern, fixing the interviewer with a hard stare under his low brows, the muscles in his shoulders suddenly tense with energy.

The interviewer looked suddenly nervous.

"Just kidding`', he laughed.

The interviewer looked quite relieved, although it may have been an act.

"No we're going the whole way, gametes up, natural childbirth..."

"With gas and air...", interrupted his wife.

He nodded. "And if it works we'll reach out to other simian men and women to join us... Hell!" he exclaimed loudly, "We can all become ancestors together!"

The crowd howled its delight, and when they had quietened enough to hear him again, he spoke in a tone that was both humble and proud at the same time, saying, "Who knows? Maybe our descendants will be the first humans strong enough to work on Jupiter." He paused smiling before suddenly calling out,"To the stars!" and punching the air with one mammoth fist.

The crowd chanted his cry back over and over again.

The interview was almost over.

They shook hands and the interviewer leant in, "Stepping up?" He asked.

"Damn right, stepping up!" the victor declared, holding his wife's hand above their heads and beaming at the crowd from below his prominent brow ridge, the camera caught the broadest of loose lipped grins.

The chant echoed around the arena and then became intermingled with cries of "Eve! Eve! Eve!"

X asked Tasan why they were chanting, 'Eve', when he was certain that the victor's wife's name had been Joan. Tasan explained that it was a tribute to her, equating her with Mitochondrial Eve, the first mother of *Homo sapiens*, hailing her as the all-mother of a new species of hominid. "I do wish Erika could be here to see this", he added.

The screens flickered back to advertising and they sat back down in their seats. The man in the seat next to them, having screamed his lungs out with the crowd, now lay slumped exhausted on his seat. He declared, "I'm so glad I witnessed that", three times in succession to no one in particular, before collapsing into silent contemplation with his eyes closed.

*

The arena was then re-jigged for the next event; the high jump. A huge circular tarpaulin with a red, white and blue target pattern was stretched across half the stadium like a giant circus safety net. At its centre, a bar was raised on a frame to an extraordinary height, at least twice that of any pole vault X had ever seen. He couldn't help but be curious to see what kind of creatures could scale such heights.

Above the waist, the competitors appeared to be merely handsome men and women, with strong and clearly defined muscles like those of swimmers, but below their navels, the athletes had ceased to be flesh and blood altogether. Their thighs were made of thin, curved, blades of metal, which, flexing with each stride, acted as suspension for the upper body and were pivot-jointed to the lower limbs at the knees. Below the knee, hydraulic pistons ran like sinews down to their ankles where flattened blades, that curved at their tips like Turkish slippers, had replaced their feet. Their walk was balletic and graceful, and they crossed the running track together, rising and falling in their elongated gait like tall wading birds.

Eva began to relax, she let out a deep sigh. "So this is for disabled people?' she asked.

Tasan hesitated. "Not all of them", he eventually replied.

Eva's face held an expression of frozen horror, "...Then some of them chose..."

Tasan gentled chided her, "Suspend your judgement for a moment, my dear", he urged. "Watch!"

The competition was a tremendous spectacle.

Each competitor, having rocked back and forwards on their spring heels while the crowd clapped in rhythm, launched themselves down the runway in three long, loping strides, each one a bound of lunar gravity distance. On the final stride, the athlete took a great leap in the air, deforming their springs on landing to their maximum extent, and compressing the hydraulics in their lower legs. It required total commitment, and when planted with absolute precision, shot the competitor high into the air like a circus acrobat shot from a canon. In flight their heavy lower body was an encumbrance, and much of the skill of the leap involved controlling their aerodynamically compromised shape in the air. At the highest level, when the best were leaping twice the height that X had thought impossible at the beginning, their movements were fluid and graceful, flicking their metal legs over the bar at the last second, like dolphins changing tack in water. But misjudgements were punished severely. Several failed launches Catherine-wheeled across the huge tarpaulin, and others tumbled from the air, metres from the crowd, crashing down on the rim of the target, out of bounds and whipped about like puppets as their springs made contact with the taut matting. Limbs were undoubtedly broken in these falls, and the victims were swiftly stretchered off by teams of medics.

The winning jump was executed with seemingly effortless grace, and waving to the crowd in her long descent, the woman's jubilant face was reflected all around the arena on the giant screens. They all hung with her in her joy as she fell back to earth and a deafening roar broke out across the stadium as she hit the canvas. She turned a perfect somersault on the rebounce and stood still, arms outstretched, soaking up the applause.

Even at that moment Eva had to ask, "Was *she* born disabled?"

"No", Tasan replied, hastily adding, "before you recoil away in horror again, consider this: Look at her expression, does she not seem happy to you? She is the champion of the world – an amazing athlete. She is, at this moment, fulfilled. Will you ever be?"

"But the price..." Eva stuttered out.

Tasan replied calmly, "Let me put it to you, that instead of your disdain, you should instead be applauding her. Her choice to live a life entirely of her own choosing and the liberty that enables her to do so are both surely worthy of your highest regard. Look further. She competes in a spirit of respect and absolute equality with her 'disabled' competitors. She clearly does not see them as maimed, broken things, as you do, but as another aspect of human possibility, and one that has brought her great rewards. Reconsider Eva", he suggested gently but firmly, "Perhaps it is not so simple."

Eva excused herself, saying she needed to get some fresh air.

While they waited for the start of the next race, X struck up a conversation with Robert, their neighbour, a slight, balding man who dressed like an accountant on vacation and was clearly some kind of super-fan He had the habit of perpetually drumming his fingers against his knees in nervous excitement as he spoke, a habit which X found distinctly irritating. He wondered why a man who was so determinedly ordinary in appearance as Robert would have such a passionate commitment to a genetically enhanced games until he noticed something strange about the movement of his fingers over his thighs. Sensing X's scrutiny Robert declared "Ah, you noticed!" proudly, splaying his hands and waggling all twelve fingers at the same time sending a ripple like a tarantula's passage across his lap. "Got it done years ago", he informed X, "Keep thinking I should go for fourteen, but always feel I should get my feet done first."

Eva returned, looking drawn and tired and she kept her eyes lowered as she sat down beside him. The sun had dipped below the crater's lip, and into the darkness, accompanied by *Carmina Burana* blasting out from the speakers, the finalists of the 100 metres, (All species- unrestricted), entered the arena, releasing an explosion of noise that thundered up and down the terraces.

Their heads were hidden by bulbous insect-like helmets and they wore long, richly coloured robes that dragged along the ground behind them, lending them the illusion of gliding, rather than walking, across the surface of the track. Waving to the crowd they sat in chairs behind their neon-lit lanes, sweeping their robes around their feet like a row of alien emperors on their thrones.

"Why the helmets?" X asked Tasan.

"Inhalers", he replied, just charging themselves up before the race. They'll keep them on until the last possible second. And sound-proofing", he added, "They're operant conditioned. The starting pistol triggers an automatic response. They shield their ears to prevent a noise in the crowd accidentally triggering the response.

"Charging with what?"

I won't bore with the chemistry", replied Tasan dismissively.

The music shut off abruptly and the crowd went instantly silent as though their voices had been turned off with a switch. The competitors took of their helmets. X was shocked backwards in his seat. Although the runners were still recognisably human, drastic rhinoplastic changes had been made to their faces. Their noses had been hugely enlarged, turned into long beaks that ran down as low as their chins. When they ducked their heads, they had the aerodynamic profiles of missiles.

"Peregrine falcon", Robert informed them, "300miles per hour in free-falling flight...."

Tasan interrupted his neighbour, pointing out to X that the profile of the nose was least important aspect, and although it looked impressive, was only plastic surgery. "The most important changes", he argued, "are the ones you can't see. "Hummingbird DNA, that's the key", he explained. "In order for those tiny birds to maintain their preposterous flight, their muscle tissue is packed with mitochondria. Splice that into every twitch muscle cell of the sprinter's body and ….BANG!…He clapped his hands together to emphasise his point, "Straight up to speed from a standing start". He went on to explain that the biggest problem was in sustaining that explosive pace throughout the race, "Without supplies of energy and buckets of ATPase", he said, "all those mitochondria blazing away would empty the tanks in a matter of seconds, and the athlete would grind to a halt long before he reached the finishing tape. So the nose is the delivery system to get the necessary substrates into the muscles for the duration of the race. Its entire length is honeycombed with a dense network of capillaries…"

"Mouse placenta", chipped in Robert who had been listening intently to Tasan waiting for his moment to get a word in.

Tasan gave a cursory nod of acknowledgement and carried on, "and the necessary chemical soup is stored in little pouches scattered along the capillaries like liver spots - the DNA's from some kind of vole. The pouches secrete the serum into the capillaries at precisely defined pressures, so by carefully controlling their breathing during the race, the athletes can release exactly the right level of nutrients directly into the mouse placenta, hummingbird charged bloodstream at exactly the right time. Problem solved." He concluded, "Straight up to speed- energy to stay there - lightening on the track!"

X hadn't entirely understood Tasan's but found it fascinating nonetheless.

The athletes stood as one and all gracefully de-robed to their waists, revealing powerful upper bodies. "A touch of gibbon" X thought, beginning to feel like a connoisseur and then laughing at himself. He turned to Eva thinking he'd share his becoming an instant expert with her. She was sitting with her body locked rigid, staring down into the arena, with the thousand-yard stare of a shell-shocked soldier. She didn't look in the mood for a joke.

He looked down again, the athletes had fully disrobed now. Below their waists they were all cat. Covered by pelts of mottled brown fur, their lower limbs were made up of curved sinews, raised haunches and powerful upper thighs, and their feet were long and flat, their claws gripping the track like running spikes. While they waited to be called to their blocks, they paced up and down in their lanes, with a fluid, loping grace.

Tasan quietly continued with X's education.

"You can still see the early cheetah", he said, "it seemed the obvious way to go, given the animal's reputation for speed. But there are all sorts of reasons why the cheetah doesn't work with human anatomy – too light boned – just can't carry the weight necessary to get the power down...and they run too hot... So its heading more leopard now...bit of Jaguar... Of course ", he added, 'if they didn't insist on the 51% rule then the cheetah would have worked fine."

"The 51% Rule?' X asked.

Tasan sighed, "They insist the DNA must always be at least 51% human. Cowards!" he called out as though he were suddenly angry.

Robert sat forward in seat, fixing Tasan with a quizzical stare that bordered on disgust. "We must stay in control", he insisted.

"So you say", he said, shaking his head and chuckling to himself "So you say!".

The race was about to begin. With their feline lower limbs coiled into a frozen pounce and their falcon heads lowered they looked like an army of Egyptian gods arrayed for a battle charge. The gunshot released them, and bounding forward like a pride in pursuit of antelope, they streaked down the track in a breath-taking display of controlled power and grace, the winner crossing the line 5.7 seconds after the gun had sounded.

The screens announced that it was a world record and the stadium erupted, Robert was screaming and leaping up and down and Tasan squeezed X in a tight embrace, "Let Erika call *that* second rate!' he shouted over the roar.

The ceremony followed almost as soon as the race had finished. After being released by the medical team the winner stood wobbly legged on the podium taking frequent pulls from a cylinder attached to his nostrils. The victor was so spent he could scarcely raise a hand to wave back at the adulation of the crowd, but beneath his beak-nose an exhausted and yet triumphant smile could be seen flickering around his thin lips. Concerned at the champions visible frailty, X asked Tasan if he would be OK.

Tasan was reassuring, but did go on to explain that they had introduced a rule that the competitor had to alive to receive his medal. If not, the display in Hall of Eternity on Victory Island would show only the still image of a funeral urn rather than the ever-looping clip of his moment of triumph.

"Has it happened often?" X asked, "The winner dying so fast?"

Tasan nodded, "Four years ago and two years before that, that's when they brought in the rule. Heart attacks. Cheetahs, as I told you – can't take the power. Doesn't happen now."

Eva wanted to leave. Her face was ashen and her legs wobbled as she stood. She informed them in a wavering voice that she was heading back to the boat to check on Erika. As he stood up to join her, Tasan tried to persuade him to stay, "But the All-Body Modifications are the fastest", he argued "The ABM's the Blue Riband event!"

Robert interjected, "and in the self-power generation class they sometimes overheat dramatically – there are often explosions..."

*

They were obliged to exit through the gift shop, an air-hanger sized store in whose maze of aisles they wandered, to a soundtrack that seemed to consist entirely of covers of Elton John's, "This is Your Song", run in an endless loop tape. They meandered past racks of protein shakes and home gyms, T-shirts with, STEPPING UP stamped on the chest, row upon row of bottles of Zantorini wine and acres of merchandise from Frisbees to egg cups to personal massagers stamped with the twin helix DNA Games logo.

Eva's spirits rose in the soporific atmosphere of the store, although she blanched as they passed a floppy-eared black and white rabbit-badger sat on a rotating plinth beside a low-slung sports car. A bored girl with ears like a lynx gave them a leaflet explaining that you could win the car if you guessed how many species made up the genome of the animal.

They wandered out of the store and down through the town to the harbour. With the grand finale underway in the stadium, they strolled past mostly empty cafes, bars and souvenir stalls. Paths no wider than alleyways branched off the main drag on either side, crammed with tiny storefronts, their pavements hidden in dark shadow by the neighbouring buildings. Neon signs crowded over each other at their entrances, advertising strange promises and unlimited possibilities, genetic makeovers, plastic surgery, prosthetic enhancement and inter-species sex clubs. The labyrinth of darkened alleyways unnerved him, and he was relieved that Eva showed no inclination to explore.

They met Erika on the waterside, and although she pretended she had merely been stretching her legs, it was soon clear that she had given the town a thorough examination during their absence.

"Did you find anything of interest?" Eva asked.

Erika's mood seemed to have risen only a little, "No, just cheap knock-offs and things executed in very bad taste…"

X was happy to be back in the ordered calm of the ship, and sat in the central lounge listening to the waves lapping against the hull while Eva dozed. He was startled out of his reverie by an argument that broke out on deck when Tasan returned. He was unable to make what he and Erika were fighting about, only hearing the final exchange with clarity; Erika shouting "You dare to declare your abominations equal to the creation!" and Tasan responding, "Pompous as ever, your holiness; not equal, I declare them superior!". The argument ended with Erika stomping down the steps while Tasan's mocking laughter drifted down behind her through the opened hatch.

The games must have ended at the moment Erika slammed her cabin door behind her, as the sky was suddenly full of departing helicopters, the sound of their blades whirling above him like a swarm of locusts bursting into flight.

FLIGHT

Helicopter blades were still roaring above him, and he floated, weightless in the air, until his sight returned.

He blinked.

His vision cleared instantly.

It had never done that before.

Through the window the same turquoise blue sea lay hundreds of feet below him, its low rolling waves, swelling and breaking in lazy slip-crests across the bay.

All that bizarre fantasy in the blink of an eye?

How could that be possible?

29. MIPCOM

Due to circumstances beyond their control, the manager regretfully informed him, the suite of rooms that X had reserved for himself, Jeanne and Kajira some three months earlier, had been cancelled without notice. Smoothing his silk tie and straightening his silver tie-clip, the manager expressed his deepest regret, his eyes downcast and as sorrowful as an old family retainer obliged to inform X of the death of an elderly relative. He too, seemed genuinely saddened that X's party had been deprived of the opportunity to enjoy the view from the gracefully curved balconies of his magnificent five-star, belle époque hotel. He shook his head, distressed that such an unfortunate conjunction of the stars could have let such a thing come to pass.

The 'circumstances beyond their control', didn't seem beyond anyone's control to X.

And certainly not the fucking manager's.

It was clear as day to X that the hotel had received a last-minute call from an important patron, or someone waving fistfuls of cash, and had thumbed down their list of guests, selecting the one with the least influence or value to discard. But such vulgar accusations of venality slid over the carapace of the manager's impenetrable decorum without gaining the slightest traction and X's increasingly expletive laden tirade quickly reached complete incoherence. He only backed off when he realised he was contemplating reaching across the desk and stabbing the man repeatedly in the throat with his own tie pin. Allowing himself to yield to Jeanne's desperate entreaties, he stormed out of the lobby to pace up and down in the street, leaving Jeanne to smooth things over as best she could.

The hotel had arranged alternative accommodation, but at this late notice, apparently, it had been impossible to find anywhere of equivalent quality. They would, of course, be provided with a full refund.

Maybe it hadn't turned out so bad after all.

*

They only knew how badly they'd been shafted when the taxi had left them outside a modernist six storey block in the foothills miles out of town. A leaking pipe on the hostel's third floor had sent a skein of water running down its façade, leaving green moss hanging in syrupy clumps from the guttering. Above the second floor all the windows had been crudely boarded up with unpainted chipboard.

It would have looked rough choice in the back streets of Amsterdam.

Buzzed in through the fly-splattered plate glass door, they took their keys from the greasy hand of the porter, whose booth, the size of a lottery ticket seller's stall, smelt of stale tobacco and cat's piss. The porter didn't look up as he handed them the keys; maintaining his forensic examination of the centrefold in the magazine laid out in front of him where a large breasted woman wearing only a shiny red thong, lay with her legs spread over the leather seat of a Harley-Davidson. Unsure where to go, they stood in front of the desk as he turned over the page, appearing to forget about them altogether. When he finally noticed they hadn't moved, he grunted, and waved them toward a set of steep, lino-covered steps to the right of the booth, before turning back to his magazine.

They struggled up the steep stairwell, dragging their luggage behind them, and emerged through an unpainted fire door and into a rabbit warren of corridors and cubicle rooms that had been created by nailing thin sheets of orange-stained plywood together. The only ornament on the corridor walls was a blue sticker with a symbol indicating that the use of hypodermic needles was forbidden.

Dodging eye-contact with Jeanne and Kajira, he shuffled into his room. A single bed, covered by a ribbed blue nylon bedspread, took up nearly the whole of the interior, leaving just enough space to stand upright on one side. The orange walls made the room feel less like a hotel bedroom and more like being stored in a packing-crate for shipment overseas. He put his luggage down on the bed and stepped into the bathroom to empty his bladder. The bathroom was so small it was only just possible to close the door behind him, and standing with his calves pressed up against the toilet bowl, he was too close to hit the pan, succeeding only in spraying urine over the cistern. Forced to take a step back into the bedroom mid-flow, he completed his toilet by pissing back through the open bathroom door. With the stench of urine floating in the air he slumped disconsolately down on the bed, propping his head up against the back wall with a pillow as lumpy as if it had been stuffed with chickpeas. He pressed a button to turn on the TV hanging above the doorframe on a hinged metal bracket. When the menu screen appeared it displayed a choice of seven porn channels and CNN.

Great.

This was the life.

*

It didn't get any better at the conference centre itself.

Despite its location on the French Riviera, there was nothing glamorous about the event whatsoever. Miles of coffin-stalls ran along endless corridors, broken up only by booming video screens displaying spinning corporate logos, looped clips of cop dramas and incomprehensible Japanese cartoons. Behind the stands, teams of square-jawed, firm handshaking executives manned the stalls like linebackers, and in the corridors, PR girls with rictus grins handed out leaflets to passers-by, their faces hidden behind caked orange foundation and mascara as thick as tar, like low-rent geishas touting for business. Under the fluorescent lighting, everyone's skin looked pale and waxy and the delegates shuffled slowly down the corridors like reanimated corpses in a cheap zombie movie.

And he had miscalculated in every way.

Firstly, he had brought only the one suit, a lime green, imitation Valentino number that he was certain had looked funky and cutting edge with a dry martini on a stool in the Groucho club. But here in Cannes it was apparent that only women were permitted to wear bold colours, the canary yellow jackets, orange scarfs and blood-red shoulder-padded two-pieces of the few female executives on the stands standing out like neon against the grey and brown of the junior executives. In the world of International Television sales, it transpired, a modest blue pin-stripe was considered a rakishly wild option that only the most senior of executives would even attempt to carry off.

He looked like Coco the clown.

When he managed to catch the attention of a decision maker, which happened rarely, their first response was to involuntary run their eyes up and down his suit with a barely disguised sneer. Conversations that began with a derisory snort were unlikely ever to get any better. But more importantly, and entirely obvious on reflection; the event was a seller's market, and he had nothing to sell. Here, even the production companies with a half-decent product to flog struggled to gain the attention of the distributers and TV channels they needed to meet, and the few familiar faces he bumped into shrugged and bitched about failing to get more than five minutes of anyone's time. So why the fuck would you want to talk to an unheard of British magazine? An unheard of British magazine that had run a front cover of Daffy Duck.

"So why the duck on the front cover? I thought you said you were a newspaper?" The first exchange had been typical of the second and the third.

He didn't really have an answer, "The news is on the inside front page"

"Why?"

X had no cogent explanation, it was just the way it was, but he tried bullshitting. In England, he'd explained, newsprint on the front cover was considered rather vulgar, a full colour picture caught the eye and looked classy, "You know how snobby the British can be".

The vice presidents had all looked suspicious and slightly aggrieved as though he had already offended them by suggesting they lacked class. "I don't get it, *Variety* has newsprint on the front page, *The Hollywood Reporter* has newsprint on the front page, if it's good enough for them..."

Already the exec was looking over X's shoulder, "And why Daffy? Are Warners making a new series?"

The first three had all asked that question. As soon as they did he knew he was fucked. "No", he had been forced to reply, each time trying to spin a line about the magazine using Daffy as a symbol of the great commercial transactions that would be made in animated features and cartoon series at this year's MIPCOM.

To a man they had just looked at him bewildered.

"So why not show one of the series that's *actually* being sold?"

He didn't have an explanation.

"It's like Monty Python", he'd tried on the second stand, making up some nonsense about irony and British taste while peering over the junior exec's shoulder to see if he could attract the attention of Mike Martins, the European budget holder, who was over by the coffee machine.

A puzzled frown wrinkled the forehead of his interlocutor. "I don't get it."

"You don't need to get it", X had suggested, "The British do, and that's the market your selling into – is that Mike Martins over there? I spoke to him on the phone last week and said I'd look him up when I got here."

"He's very busy. Just give me your card and I'll make sure he gets back to you."

There was no point in protesting. He was right not to get it. It wasn't irony. It was just bullshit, and if American's had trouble understanding irony, they had no problems in recognising bullshit.

He couldn't even get close.

By early afternoon he had given up trying to make eye-contact with anyone and had resorted to gathering freebees and pamphlets from the stands and shuffling down the aisles laden down with sheets of shiny paper like a bag lady with a trash-filled shopping trolley. His feet ached in his shoes, his socks were drenched with sweat, and despite the chill of the recycled air, his armpits had begun to exude a stale, musty odour that he knew, given the absence of any kind of shower in his hotel room, would only get worse as the weekend dragged on.

By three o'clock he had to escape, and leaving Jeanne and Kajira to man their deserted stand, had slipped away, stumbling down the steps and into the fresh air and staggering away from the conference centre along the beach. After lying uncomfortably on the scratchy white sand in his suit, beads of sweat breaking on his brow and his trousers rolled up above his ankles like an old codger on Margate sands, he'd bought a pair of baggy shorts and a towel off a marabout, and had taken a swim, determined to wash the stench of stale sweat off him as best he could. Itchy from the salt and with his suit irredeemably crumpled, by four-thirty he felt sufficiently refreshed to face the exhibition hall again, ready to throw his last, almost certainly futile, and definitely tawdry, gambit into the ring.

He'd spent most of the budget on securing a table at the Carlton Hotel for Saturday night and the plan had been to invite sixteen specifically targeted senior executives from mid-ranking US distributors and ply them with sufficient champagne and bonhomie to pick their pockets a little before they sobered up. Three or four sales and the trip would break even; successfully flatter and bamboozle all sixteen and he would return a hero and the publisher's job would be in the bag. He'd asked a design company to 'sex up' the invitation to make it look like a club flyer, but the firm had taken him too literally, laying a slim-waisted Bond-girl in long black boots on the downward slope of the N of New TV, with the same girl bending over at the waist to form the final, lower case n. The W of New was curved into the shape of a woman's buttocks, and the final O of Television was winking suggestively under a lowered lid. He'd been so embarrassed at the crudity of the final product that he had kept its existence secret, hoping that they could stay that way, but his manifest failure to get even within earshot of a single one of his targets had left him with no alternative.

When he showed the cards to the girls, it was only the

desperate expression on his face that had persuaded Jeanne to agree to help him. "You owe me one X", she'd said, as she stepped into the taxi back to the hotel to freshen up, giving him a withering look when he tried to suggest that something sexy might be appropriate.

Jeanne returned. She looked stunning.

She had put on a green dress that ran tightly down her body to just below her knees, its deep emerald velvet an exact match for her green eyes and setting off her strawberry blond hair. She wore her hair up, in a way he had never seen her do before, sculpted into bun and secured in place by a single diamante clasp. Her shoulders were bare and she wore long black gloves that sheathed her arms in silk as high as her elbows. To complete the picture, she tottered on four-inch heels, the arch of each foot secured by a single black strap. She looked delicate, vulnerable and indomitable. She was beaming.

"Come on then", she said, snatching the cards out of X's hand.

"You look amazing!"

"Don't sound so bloody surprised!"

She shuffled the invitations with a croupier's skill, and having found the one she was looking for, tottered down the pale pink carpet like a starlet from the film festival who had got the dates on the calendar mixed up but was determined to brave it out for the cameras anyway. When she approached the WorldVision stand the defensive line parted like tall wheat blown by a strong wind and she strode straight through to the quarterback they had been protecting. Mike Martins broke off his conversation mid-sentence and turned at her approach. She stopped a pace short, and, half curtsied, bringing out one of the silver backed invitations from behind her back, and holding it out at arms-length, like a young peacenik handing a soldier guarding a nuclear facility a flower

"New Television UK invites you to a party at the Carlton tonight", she said, "I hope you'll come".

X thought the man was going to kiss her hand, but instead he made do with a small bow assuring her that he would most definitely be there.

She thanked him from under lowered lids and then spun on a single heel. The crowded parted momentarily and then closed again and she was lost from sight in the press of bodies. X hurried after her, galumphing like an overweight lady-in-waiting in his big green pantaloons, catching up with her at cafe serving cappuccinos and stale croissant to a scattering of customers behind a rope barrier. Laughing hard, she leant on a bollard for support. It toppled over, and X had to grab her round the waist to stop her from falling. A woman at one of the tables steadied her coffee, giving them a furious glance as though they had just made an unsuccessful attempt to snatch her purse.

"Thanks X", she said as she regained her balance. "That was fun!" She shook her head, still smiling, and gave X a mock-baleful look before adjusting the broach in her hair, smoothing her dress down and selecting the next of the cards from the deck; setting off once more with X trailing in her wake.

*

By the time he was ordering the second round of champagne at the bar in the Carlton Hotel, the crush of bodies was so great that it had taken him twenty minutes to press through the scrum, and squeezed between two braying suits, he had just enough space to slip through an outstretched arm, holding out the company credit card like a trader in the pit. He finally caught the bartender's eye. The man nodded, lightly dusting the marble counter in front of him with a fresh cotton towel before leaning in to take X's order. Reflected in the gilt framed mirror behind him, he towered over X like a vengeful barrister bullying an unreliable witness. "No more glasses - only bottles", he hissed, in response to X's order.

"How many do I need bottles for thirty people?"

"Permit me to ask, how many men in the party?"

"Fifteen."

"Quinze bottles then monsieur."

"That many?"

"Oui monsieur", the bartender explained, leaning forward confidentially, oblivious to all the clamour around them, "Every man wants to pop his own cork. Otherwise…It is like…" He made a small gesture with his thumb and forefinger.

"Fifteen then."

"Very good Monsieur".

"One moment", X called back the barman He had almost forgotten, he'd had a request from Anthony What's-his-name, some big shot that had Jeanne said was worth buttering up. He'd 'Had a good MIPCOM' as they said, brokering the sale of a blind TV cop show into most of the networks in Europe, and might be feeling generous. He'd told her he only drank a particular brand. He read off note he'd been given, "And one bottle of Krug Clos de Mesnil too."

"Oui Monsieur- which year?"

Who gives a shit? "Was last year's good?"

"Very good Sir."

"One of those then". He could look at the bill when he got back. Too late to start worrying now.

*

Jeanne's magic had worked. Fourteen of the sixteen on the list had showed up, drifting in out of the sun in the same rumpled suits they had worn all day, ties off, top buttons rakishly undone. Taken together they were remarkably similar, and although there were a couple of bears among them, giants with broad shoulders and hair protruding at the cuffs, the remainder were all short, bullish little men with thinning hair, pot-bellies and too-tight pants. Each stood wide-legged as though they held permanent title to the ground they stood on and expounded their views over their pot-bellies with the bombastic certainty of street-pulpit preachers.

They hadn't come alone. Each middle-aged gnome had arrived with a young, pretty woman on his arm. The women were universally tall, and, taller still in stiletto heels, they towered above their chaperones. Leggy and thin-waisted, their bodies were either squeezed into figure-hugging cocktail dresses with tiny belted waists or sequined mini-dresses cut to the thigh. Their thin, sinewy arms, garlanded by bangles at the wrist, were appended by hands that looked older than the rest of their bodies, each bony finger mounted by a big sparkly ring. With bright red lipstick and cheekbones cut out by rouge, their individual faces had been obliterated by thick make-up, and striking seductive postures with arm and hip they set about admiring the wild wit of their escorts, laughing and lowering their eyes on cue.

Hookers, probably.

They certainly weren't wives.

On the first champagne run he had followed Jeanne as she cut her way imperiously through the crowd, protecting the tray of jittering flutes like a mother shielding a new born infant from harm. He'd managed to shake hands and received a few back-slaps as he handed out the bubbly, but that was about it; they couldn't have had less interested in him if he had been the waiter, and some of them probably thought he was. Jeanne, however, was received quite differently. One of them, quite lubricated already, even bent to kiss her hand as she was introduced, and her easy laughter in response turned it into an amusing act of gallantry; she curtsied, and the other half-cut executives repeated the gesture as she passed down the line. The escorts, who had ignored X completely, bristled at Jeanne's approach, and leaning more heavily on their John's shoulders, stared at her back, silently hissing like cats protecting their territory. Jeanne was soon seated at the centre of a circle of admirers leaving X free to return to the bar for the next round.

But by the time he returned, the masters of the universe had begun to run out of lame jokes and things to boast about to their tricks, and the mood had begun to sour. Jeanne greeted him like a weary front line soldier desperately in need of home leave. He gave her the company credit card and sent her to the bar.

"About goddam time", one of the bears growled at him, but the champagne did the trick. Every man popped his cork. There was a lot of shrieking. X was pulled into the group, and forced to join endless rounds of toasts; first to figures in the industry he'd never heard of, and then to men with made up names that ended in 'cock'. He'd been desperate to escape even before he'd had to belly laugh for the second time in response to the same racist joke about Michael Jackson, and when the men began groping the women's asses, he wrestled his way out from their clinch with the minimum of courtesy.

The rush at the bar had died down and Jeanne had secured a stool. She was talking to an elderly executive who was well into his cups, listening with exaggerated intensity while Jeanne talked at him, waving her arms around as she spoke. The next round of champagne was stacked up on the bar in front of her and ready to go. He wasn't sure he had the strength.

He found an empty stool half a dozen seats along the bar from her and slumped into it. She spotted him and waved, pointing at the champagne. He ran a finger across his throat as though he were slitting it, intending to indicate that he would rather commit suicide than go back.

She looked bemused.

He mimed hanging himself on a short rope. She laughed. He waved his hand to indicate he'd pick up the champagne later. She gave him a thumbs up and sympathetic pout and turned back to her conversation.

Anthony, the executive who'd 'had a good MIPCOM', slid onto the stool next to him. He was better tailored then the rest, in his early fifties but perfectly preserved, with a square jaw, greying temples and a the perma-tan of a prime-time newscaster. He raised his bottle of Krug, "Thank you for the champagne and double thank you for choosing the '88, it was such a fine year!" he said.

Shit. How much had it cost him? At least he'd only bought the one.

"Would you like to try some?" he asked.

X declined. Staying sober seemed very important right now.

"That girl over there" Anthony went on, nodding in Jeanne's direction.

"Jeanne?"

"Jeanne", he seemed to roll her name around his tongue for a moment, "Get me a blow job off her and I'll give you a DPS".

X was dumbfounded.

The man's expression was deadly serious, he didn't seem to be joking at all. "Look", X spluttered out, "She's not a prostitute you know".

"I know, if I'd have wanted a hooker I'd have bought one", he replied calmly, "but I do so much miss English girls in LA, nothing so fresh, you understand."

"She's Irish actually", X fought to contain his anger. The man's tone made his skin crawl, "If you want to talk to Jeanne, that's your business, it's a free country, but don't ask me to pimp her".

There was a pause and when Anthony spoke again his voice was more circumspect, "I'm sorry, you are angered. I was too crude - she's a work colleague of yours and you respect her. My apologies", he bowed a little as he said it, "But it is not impossible for a man of my age and wealth to wish to woo a young beautiful woman. Why not? We are in glorious Cannes after all".

X supposed he should wish him good luck, he was handsome enough, in a pickled Gregory Peck kind of way, but he didn't fancy his chances. What was he 50? 55? Jeanne was twenty-one.

"You know her well?" he asked, "Outside of work?"

X confirmed that he did, adding suddenly and hastily that it was not in a romantic way, and then felt cheap, as though he was opening the way for this creepy bloke's advances.

"I would like to know what she likes and what she hates, that kind of thing", he went on.

"I'm not going to tell you anything"

"But you already have, you've told me that her name's Jeanne and that she's Irish, not English, that's an important detail, don't you think? Tell me - what might she be surprised to find we had in common?"

X kept quiet.

"Is she fond of animals?"

He couldn't remember her being so. She had a cat but didn't make a fuss over it.

"Horses?"

Not as far as he knew.

"Fur", he declared, "Is she in favour, loves to rub it up against her skin? Or anti? Must get these details right. We don't want any blood on the catwalk!" He smiled at his own witticism.

X didn't think she had a view either way.

"What about yachts, lingerie, couture, cars...."

X felt his cheek twitch like a poker tell at the mention of cars.

"Limousine or fast?" Anthony honed in.

X was suddenly fed up with the twenty questions game. "She grew up around vintage cars, restored them with her dad, she can talk about camshafts for hours? OK! Satisfied?"

"What kind of vintage cars?

He wouldn't let up. X could never remember "Old Jags I think, or maybe it was Aston Martins?" He wasn't sure.

Anthony, seemed satisfied enough, and smiling, he hefted the champagne bottle by its neck, swept up two clean flutes from the bar and rose to his feet. "Two DPS if she lets me fuck her", he said, slapping X on the shoulder before heading off toward Jeanne.

X watched him move in. He saw him introduce himself to

Jeanne, and shake hands firmly with the old man she had been talking to, bending low to hear what he was mumbling.

He couldn't watch.

He ferried the next freight of champagne over to the braying pack. Things had got nastier. Most of them were pissed now, and a small group was demanding that he get them some coke. He had no fucking idea how to get hold of coke in Cannes. But that didn't stop one of the bears, big Rab, who had clearly had a skinful, from getting lairy; rearing up and shouting in his face, "What kind of a fucking party is it without coke?" He then turned to his audience, arms outstretched, neck extended, head cocked back, chest out, "What the fuck are we doing with this useless punk?" he declared. One of the bald ones, who was very pissed, got stirred up by Rab's declaration, started forward from the crowd demanding to know "Where our fucking coke was?" over and over again, as though they had paid X to score and he was now trying to rip them off.

The girls knew where to get coke of course, and let it be known, discreetly, that one of the girls might know where they could get some, but they would all have to take a taxi over there. The atmosphere calmed instantly; there was a plan that involved coke and girls, so all was suddenly well in the world again. Even Big Rab's attitude toward X was transformed, and he gave him a big man-hug at the door before stepping back a pace, delivering a drunken knuckle-punch to his shoulder and declaring him "A good guy", before stumbling out into the night.

X returned to the bar.

It was now nearly empty, everybody who had somewhere to go having moved on to a party, or dinner, or a brothel, and Jeanne and Anthony were almost alone at the bar. Anthony was sat with his back to X, his jacket slung over the rail and his manner comfortable and assured. Jeanne had propped her head up with one elbow, and was listening to him with rapt attention, smiling in agreement with what he was saying, her face turned up to his. When she caught sight of X, she called him over excitedly. "Oh my god X", she exclaimed, "you'll never believe it", it turns out that Mr Q here…"

He interrupted, "Please Jeanne, I insist you call me Anthony".

"*Anthony* here has the most amazing collection of vintage cars".

X looked non-plussed but he was also relieved, Jeanne would bore him away now by talking about exhaust manifolds.

"No X - I mean a *really* amazing collection". She reeled off a list of cars. They meant nothing to him whatsoever. "But that's not the best bit!" she exclaimed, more excited than he could ever remember seeing her, and unable to contain the news, "He has access to a dealer's showroom in Cannes with the most amazing machines. You're certain he has an E-type?" She beseeched Anthony.

"He always has an E-type', he reassured her, "and almost certainly a DB5. But the one I want you to have a look at is the Austin-Healy 3000, and I *know* he has one of those."

"But that's *still* not the best bit", Jeanne burst out, "You tell him…"

"As an old customer, I have an open arrangement with the dealership to be able to test-drive the cars whenever I am in town."

"At one o'clock in the morning?"

"The proprietor is aware I keep irregular hours and will send his man round to open up."

"I'm going to be swept round Cannes in an E-type Jag", she declared, beaming with delight.

"I'm afraid you won't be swept round", Anthony interjected, and Jeanne looked temporarily crestfallen, "I've had two much of this…." He tapped the upturned champagne bottle in the ice bucket next to him, "You'll have to drive!" It took a second for it to sink in and then Jeanne leapt to her feet and hugged him, they both laughed.

X felt sick.

"Right!" Jeanne commanded, "No need to waste any time, get me behind the wheel of my Jag!"

Anthony stood and offered his arm, "You'll have to try the Austin-Healy too, you know".

"How terrible!" she gasped, and linking arms with him, they strode together out of the room, Jeanne turned back once, blew him a kiss over Anthony's shoulder, and then she was gone.

He sat alone at the bar desultorily working his way through the champagne until the waiters told him to leave. Jeanne did not return.

Back at the hotel, he slipped under the sheets, and tried to get comfortable on the misshapen pillows, but was unable to sleep. The resident of the next cubicle was watching one of the porn channels with the sound up, and cries of "Ja, Fick Mir, Fick Mir" passed barely muffled through the thin walls. Eventually he gave up on sleep and selected a porn channel on the TV at random, getting a French hard-core film. A stringy prostitute was taking on two bored sex-pros in a mock-up of a motorcycle garage.

He couldn't raise the slightest interest. It just made feel even sadder.

*

They hardly spoke on the flight home.

Jeanne wore dark glasses and sat in the window seat silently staring out the clouds for the whole flight, not once making eye contact with X. They parted at Heathrow without even saying goodbye. Just before she got into her taxi, he had started to run after her, knowing he had to say something. Then stopped. There was nothing to say.

Back in the office he stared at the flashing red light on the answerphone filled with a sense of dread and irredeemable loss. It took him twenty minutes to summon the courage to press the button.

He had only two messages.

At the sound of the voice on the first message, he breathed a sigh of relief, it was only Rab, the one who'd called him a useless punk, apologising for his behaviour and booking a full colour page.

Perhaps the trip had been worthwhile after all.

The machine beeped again and then delivered the second message.

It was Anthony's secretary. The Character Cop Channel would be taking two Double Page Spreads, where should they send the copy?

*

The journey home passed in a blur, and once he was back in his flat he locked the door behind him, turned the answerphone to mute, pulled down the blinds, and started working his way through a bottle Jack Daniels. Drinking straight out of the bottle, he sat on the edge of his bed, flicking aimlessly between channels on the TV until the alcohol had reduced his racing thoughts to incoherent smears and bursts of static.

Lying back on his bed with the ceiling rotating slowly above him, he knew what he needed.

Eva would make it all right somehow.

All he had to do was dream.

He closed his eyes as tight as he could, and then let go.

30. THE FACILITY

He heard the lapping of waves, the dry creaking of a rope and the piping whistles of a solitary wading-bird. The briny scent of sea-air entered his nostrils and he breathed deeply, filling his lungs with the cool, fresh air. He became aware that he was lying down, laid out almost horizontally on some kind of firm, yielding material that matched the exact contours of his body and was exquisitely comfortable. His head had lolled back lazily, and when he opened his eyes he was looking upward at the rising sun whose rays' revealed the opening of a day of pitch-perfect beauty. The sky above was the colour of a child's party balloon, a vast, implausible blue dome that stretched across the vault of heaven undisturbed by even the slightest wisp of cloud. He watched the sun rise fully above the mountain tops, illuminating the moored silver ship, the grey slats of the jetty, the green tufts of tall marsh grass and the deep blue water, all aligned as perfectly as a photographer's composition. He felt completely at ease.

Eva was in the driver's seat next to him.

"Hello X. See!" she said proudly, "I was not startled this time!"

She turned toward him, a flicker of a smile at the edges of her lips. "Tasan was certain you would arrive at dawn. Like clockwork!" she shook her head in amazement, "They've gone ahead", she added with a short laugh, "In separate cars, of course; neither trusts the other enough to let them drive!" Eva turned away from him to concentrate on the controls of the car and, steering from a prone position through the front video screen, negotiated the first few twists and turns away from the jetty, handling the wheel and pedals with calm assurance.

"You might as well just relax", she said, having dealt the narrow lanes around the quay, "We won't get there for quite some time."

Good. No Tasan or Erika. And quite some time with Eva.

He sat back in his seat and let Eva steer them clear of the dock through a ring of vegetable plots, apple orchards and thick-green hedgerows up into the forest above the bay. The bright sun was now partly hidden behind the forest canopy, and the light that burst through its lattice of leaves and branches flickered like a deep-green stroboscope as it slid over the windshield. He stretched his arm out the window, letting his hand trail in the vapour vortices billowing around the curves of the car. It felt as though he was slipping his hands through the cool water of a lake, while an accomplished rower ferried him leisurely to the bank on the other side. The forest gave way to a patchwork of lime-green fields and white sheep and then up through a rocky gorge, where petrified crashes of purple-grey rock hung like flying buttresses above them, and a narrow, ice-crack stream twisted below. Then all at once they had negotiated the last twist of the gorge and were suddenly at the top of the mountain ridge. Eva pulled over, stopping the car on a small promontory with the whole panorama laid out beneath them. The view was breath-taking; the royal blue of the sea stretching to the horizon, and the great green expanse of forest and field like a painted backdrop to a stage set. The boat itself was too small to identify at this distance, but the motion of the waves must have caused it to bob at its mooring, and when its panels caught the angle of the sun, it sent out sharp flares of light like an emergency beacon warning of danger.

They sat without speaking, sharing the moment's beauty in silence.

X felt himself holding his breath.

Eva set the car in motion again.

He exhaled and turned to her. She had been taking a last look at the view below, and turned toward him at the same moment. Their eyes met. Eva's eyes held the distant gaze of a mountain climber, fresh- faced and satisfied at the successful completion of a difficult pitch and full of certainty that the summit ahead would soon be conquered.

She smiled.

His smile echoing hers or hers his, he couldn't say, but he replayed the moment over and over in his mind as they travelled on.

They now crossed a flatter and more arid landscape, passing over a vast undulating plain of red-brown earth, bleach-white boulders and green scrub grass. The heat rose, and with the car running largely on autopilot, they drove on in silence, each of them lost in their own thoughts. The longer they went without speaking the more difficult breaking the silence became. X began to feel gagged, desperate to say something, but afraid that to utter a single word would somehow break the spell, shattering the clear surface of their companionship like casting a stone into the still water of an enchanted pool.

Instead of speaking he looked at Eva.

Hypnotised by the road and lost in her own thoughts, she was completely oblivious to his presence, driving with one hand on the wheel, the other stretched out lazily, fingers catching in the airstream flowing past the car. He had meant only to glance, but unobserved, he allowed his gaze to linger. Her athlete's body was fully displayed before him as though she sat for him on a painter's divan. Slim waist, sweet curve of hip and breast, her long legs stretching gracefully down to slippered feet. He lingered over her delicate ankles and watched mesmerised as she softly rubbed one foot over the other, loosening an ankle by slowly rotating one of her feet like a ballerina limbering up at the bar. She had removed her Alice band, and letting the wind blow freely through her hair, uncontrolled stands licked at her forehead, and wisps spun behind her head in the draft. Her skin was paler now than it had been in the tropical heat of the games, as though she had been re-set to neutral since he had last seen her, with a brush of freckles across her nose and a soft brown tone under fine blond hairs on her arms. Unselfconscious and relaxed, her whole being had softened, the cheekbones and shadows that lent beauty to the fine sculptured architecture of her face were gone – smoothed and rounded out into easier curves. Even the pale blue iris of her eyes seemed gentler.

Perhaps they were closer to her real eye colour.

Perhaps not.

Seeing something on the road ahead on her side, she leant forward momentarily, and, in that dip and bend, with the breeze whipping at her hair, the nape of her neck was clearly visible to him, its modulated softness between arcs of sinew shockingly intimate, a place meant to be felt only with a lover's touch, violated by his uninvited intrusion. Feeling like a voyeur, he began to look away, but not before she had become aware of his gaze upon her. There was an awkward moment, the guilt in his expression disproportionate to the offence, but leading her to suspect that his stare had been lengthy and lascivious.

"We really ought to close the side doors", she barked abruptly, breaking the silence of the journey with an irritated and managerial tone, the first ripple of sound shattering the day like breaking glass. "It increases aerodynamic drag. It's not energy efficient." Her voice was cold.

They drove for a few miles in the chilled, ion-balanced air inside the car, shut in like goldfish in the new kind of silence between them.

When Eva opened the windows, they exhaled in unison. "OK. I will drive 10km per hour slower to compensate, but it will take longer to get there."

"Where are we going?" he asked.

"You'll see."

Eva still seemed to be a little sulky, but X felt he could manoeuver her out of it without too much difficulty. He pressed her again, "Tell me, where *are* we going?"

She relented, and although her tone had returned to her educational default once more, he could hear no anger in her voice. "It's a facility. No it's *the* facility", she began.

X was none the wiser.

"It's a place for…" she hesitated, searching for the right approximation of the word, '…role-playing". She sounded uncomfortable with both the pronunciation and the synonym.

He felt deflated, envisioning first, a battle re-enactment by the sealed knot; overweight middle-aged men and boys drawn up like the New Model Army, with pikes and muskets and tabards, and then, worse still, a vast room with teenage boys and aging geeks with *Star Wars* T-shirts rolling multi-faceted dice as they rose up imaginary elf orders.

"No, that's not right", she said when he expressed his doubts, "It's more like a video game, but a video game you get inside of", she said and looking satisfied with her analogy concluded, 'a role-playing video game.'"

His heart didn't exactly soar.

While he would happily shoot zombies in an arcade, it was really only when he was bored at other people's family events that he'd pick up a younger brother's consul. Role playing games were really poor as he recalled, lots of typing and then almost inevitably elves and wizards were turning up, this time in clunky square pixels. It would all be a lot better than that here of course, and if he and Eva were going to play a little… It couldn't be all bad.

"Not far now." She said.

They turned off the track and the road now followed the contours of a broad steep-sided valley above a lazily flowing river and dusty fields of lavender and maize. A mile or so ahead of them a vast chalk promontory stoppered up the valley as though it were an advancing glacier. At the very bottom of the chalk cliff-face, X could make out an oblong building; reflected sunlight glaring in bursts off its glass walls. He assumed this must be the facility. It seemed a long way to come for something so unimpressive.

Then he realised the scale of his miscalculation. The glass box was only the atrium. The mountain itself was the building.

As they swept closer he could see that what he had taken to be a chalk cliff face, was instead the side of a monolithic building that filled the valley mouth like a beached cruise-liner built on the scale of the Olympian gods, and what he had thought were ridges in the rock wall, were white balconies as long as sea-side promenades running the full width of the valley. Each balcony-strata, he could now see, was marked by a strip of blue oblong windows, marching in an ordered pulsation along the face of the rock. He suppressed a momentary shudder; a sense of malevolence seemed to emanate from the building, as though it was a giant pupating insect or a bloated ant queen, crouching in the valley while it waited to gorge itself on its next meal. The thought passed as quickly as it had come, and as they approached, the building took on a much more benign aspect. Soon they were winding their way through an elegantly laid out formal gardens and he could hear the shouts and exultations of tennis players, and the occasional splash of someone diving into a pool. They crossed a stream where a Japanese garden had been built into the bank, and swept up into the courtyard opposite the entrance.

They entered the green-glass light of the atrium and were greeted by Erika and Tasan and a small, dapper man with a broad forehead, who exuded a sense of exactness and focus. He introduced himself as Svenbrenner and they touched foreheads in a formal, yet strangely tentative way; Svenbrenner leaning forward on his toes and barely making connection with X's forehead, as though he would rather bow formally than take the liberty of physical contact. As soon as the formalities were over, Svenbrenner detached X from the rest of the group and with an arm around his waist guided him across the foyer at a swift stride, leaving Eva, Erika and Tasan following in their wake.

"It's always a pleasure to greet someone on the way to Sweden."

X never knew what to say when people said this kind of thing, so he merely inclined his head respectfully.

"We are very proud of our work here', Svenbrenner continued, "Although sometimes – the responsibility!" He made a gesture that acknowledged and then dismissed the burdens of life, raising his hands, palms out like Atlas holding up the weight of the world, and then relaxed his shoulders and flicking out his wrists, cast away the cares with a Sisyphean shrug.

Unsure of what their work here was, X tried to elicit an explanation that he could understand, but his attempt was a failure. Although Svenbrenner's delivery was clear and precise, his language was so peppered with terms such as 'fully immersive', 'holistically interactive', 'ingested nanodata' and 'non-linear time', that he couldn't make out a thing. Without pausing for breath, Svenbrenner guided them through groups of men and women, some clutching rackets and swimsuits and in a hurry to head out into the day and others dawdling in, tousled haired and red-faced, towels around their shoulders as they strolled toward the showers. His patient monologue continued until they had crossed the full breadth of the lobby and arrived at the reception desk. The others caught up, and Svenbrenner helped each of them into a booth to have their vocal imprints and full body scans recorded. Formalities over, he advised them of their room numbers, saying that their doors would open at their spoken request, and said that he would meet them again later that afternoon, ending by advising X to have a good hearty meal in the meantime.

The rooms they had been allocated were spacious and comfortable, and he had a hot shower before re-joining Eva and the others for lunch. The restaurant was on a broad slatted terrace, with a view across the bright blue water of one of the swimming pools and an exercise circuit in wood-chip laid out through the trees below. Mixed groups of men and women sat around clear glass tables or perched on brightly coloured stools at breakfast bars, many dressed in sports gear, conversing avidly over frothy coffee and juice drinks and taking bites from thinly spread crispbreads and green-leaf salads. There were also larger groups of men, with the air of soldiers on the way to a new posting. They ate vigorously, ladling large helpings of stew from a common pot, dunking big chunks of doughy bread in the sticky mass and quenching their thirst by drinking brightly coloured fruit juices from tall glasses. Women with a similarly expectant air sat supping from huge bowls of ramen noodles and methodically swallowing small pills that were lined up on the tables in rows and could have been sweets, medication or vitamin capsules.

Food had been ordered for X; a heavy stew with thick gravy and onions. It wasn't exactly what he would have chosen for lunch on a sunny afternoon. He fancied a swim in one of the pools and a lazy afternoon chatting on the balcony, and felt it would sit heavy in his stomach. When he said this, they all laughed.

"You go for a swim afterwards", explained Eva, and once again tried to make clear what this immersive thing would be like, but it still made little sense to him.

He stared down at his stew, stirring it around with a fork, reluctant to load up his stomach with stodge, but as soon as he had forced himself to take the first mouthful, he was pleasantly surprised at how delicious it was and discovering that he had a healthy appetite after all, rapidly polished off the whole bowl and two thick trenchers of bread, washing it down with a two glasses of water.

Eva had ordered a salad and juice drink and was pushing the lettuce around on her plate with her fork, occasionally picking at a small piece of green-leaf in silence.

X noticed a degree of unspoken tension amongst his companions and when Erika spoke, her words seemed like the continuation of an argument that had been interrupted by his arrival. "But Eva", Erika insisted, "While you are correct, of course, to say that the balance between objectivity and directly influencing events is a fine one, field work must, however, be immersive, how can it be otherwise?"

He tuned out. They could have been talking about art, or musical performance or critical theory. It reminded X of lectures he'd half-listened to in the great halls of the university so long ago.

How long ago was it? He couldn't recall.

He looked out across the pool. A long-legged woman in a one-piece swimsuit dived from a high board, her body arching gracefully through the air and cutting into the water with a splash. A small ripple of applause drifted up from the poolside.

"But does the *subject* know that!" Eva suddenly exclaimed, the pitch of her voice angry and terse, a tone X had never heard from her before.

What subject could possibly elicit such vehemence from Eva, who was normally so controlled?

Tasan, who seemed to have had no part in the argument so far, stepped in, and speaking sternly and with surprising authority to Erika, stated, "Whatever the merits of your argument Erika, Eva is clearly the one to be the judge of this. You know this. It must be her decision."

The argument was interrupted by the return of Svenbrenner. He was carrying four blackcurrant-coloured juice drinks on a silver tray and handed them a glass each, explaining that it was 'the finest nanojuice' adding that it was, of course, a mixture of both nanobites and vitamin supplements and had been precisely prepared for their individual needs. Suspecting that to ask what nanobites were, would set off a long and incomprehensible explanation, X merely thanked him and drank the juice. It was fresh and deliciously cool after the stew and he gulped it down in a few drafts.

"OK. Good." Svenbrenner concluded, "I gather we are all playing?" Expecting assent, he motioned for them to rise from their seats, but nobody moved, and Erika interjected, "No, only X and Eva. We will compare notes later."

X saw Eva stiffen for a moment, but she stood up as commanded and Svenbrenner, in the manner of a skilled diplomat, instantly adjusted his programme to take in the new arrangement without missing a beat.

"So X, Eva, follow me please."

They were swept back across the atrium Svenbrenner's and entered a long corridor lined by saunas, steam rooms and plunge baths. A huge glass-walled exercise suite ran alongside for several hundred metres, athletic young people rowing, jumping and spinning in padded metal machines behind the glass. Beyond the fitness suite, the corridor came to an end in a tall window that gave a view of one of the balconies that ran along the outside of the building. The balcony was lined with apartments, and in the nearest, couples and families were moving in and out of their rooms to chat with neighbours, or stood leaning over the rail to take in the view. In the first five or six dwellings, window boxes with bright orange geraniums and purple pansies provided the backdrop for little scenes of al fresco dining, but further along the rail the balcony was deserted, the doors closed and the flats apparently unoccupied, the smooth line of the rail running unblemished until it faded from sight in the far distance. They took a right turn at the window, away from the natural light and deeper into the facility itself. The corridor was smaller now and largely empty, only the occasional straggler passing them by from time to time. On one side, a series of identical opaque glass doors were set at regular five metre intervals, and X had counted fifty before one of them opened. A young man with sweaty skin and an unkempt beard stumbled out into the corridor in front of them and stood, seemingly disorientated, with the door propped open at his back to steady himself as they passed. Behind him, X got a brief glimpse of an endless, empty white-walled corridor that swept away with the curve of the mountain itself into the distance, featureless and antiseptically clean. The man gathered himself and headed away down the corridor, the door closing behind him on smooth hydraulics. Fifty more identical doors and then they had arrived.

Svenbrenner stepped forward as they reached their

destination and, holding the door open, he motioned for X to enter with a sweep of his arm. "Here we are!" he declared, "You have a private room of course."

The room they entered was plain, with a medical feel, containing a sink, a cabinet and what X took to be a giant dentist's chair, but as he looked closer, he could see that it was more than that, and whatever it was, it was a very serious piece of kit indeed. Anchored floor to ceiling by a huge shiny metal tube, it was clear that the chair could rotate both around its pole and cantilever up and down, spinning in any direction round its own axis independent of the central shaft. The seat was jet black and made from a soft rubberised substance that looked soft and welcoming to the touch.

A young man was already in the room, waving his hands across a monitor. He had a broad, welcoming face, brown skin and a neatly trimmed beard. He raised a pair of crenelated goggles from his eyes as he stood, saying "OK, that's set up", and with a last glance at the screen, greeted them in a warm and effusive manner, introducing himself as Karl. When it came to touching foreheads with X, he applied more pressure than was customary and held it for a long time, making the contact feel like a cross between a tight embrace and a high-five. He took half a pace back, and running his fingers over his beard absent-mindedly, stared intently at X, maintaining eye-contact for long enough to make X feel thoroughly uncomfortable under his gaze.

Svenbrenner coughed in order to break the awkward silence and explained that Karl was X's personal technician, 'one of their top men, of course', and that he would take him through the next steps. Having said his piece, he stepped backwards and was silently gone from the room.

"Seeker of Sweden huh!" Karl declared, "Great. We've set up just the right one for you I hope." He paused, rubbing the back of his head thoughtfully, "We'll get you suited up later', he started, "but what you need is the basics".

Karl turned out to be as competent as he was easy-going, and when he explained, with clarity and without undue complication, what 'totally immersive' meant; for the first time, X understood.

"So the game will feel absolutely real?" X asked.

"Yes." Think of it this way. Imagine your five senses. Which one do you rely on the most?"

"Sight." It was an obvious answer.

"OK", Karl began, "Your eyes are closed, but we send signals directly to the visual cortex in your brain. Everything you see in the game will look completely real." He paused, then sensing the need to say more, in simpler terms, he went on, "It will be completely three-dimensional. You look wherever you like, up, down, forwards, backwards, you will see what you see. Better actually, you will have 20-20 vision in the game, why not! We have bi-passed any faults in your lens! Your neo-cortex would make up any small jumps in the game's continuity, but with this programme, there's no need, its super smooth..."

"Give me another sense", he demanded.

"Smell."

"Sure" Karl shrugged, "Smell is relatively easy to do and tonally important, but as a species we don't rely on it much. A rose will smell like a rose; shit will smell like shit..." He trailed off. "Another."

"Taste."

Karl shook his head. "Not so good", he admitted, "Eating anything in the game gets complicated. By masticating on food that isn't really there, you stimulate gastric juices that have nothing to digest... it sort of cascades...If you're down for a long time you can be fed on command" he added, shaking his head as he spoke, "but that adaptation's a serious business, more like surgery. That's why you eat a big meal before you go in. You get all the energy you'll need in one go, and you'll feel full so you won't want to eat. There were appetite suppressants in the blackcurrant juice too. Best to not eat anything at all in the game if you can avoid it", he added.

"What about drinking?" X asked.

"That's fine, drink as much as you like, there's a tube in the mask. But go on, give me another sense - one that really matters..."

"Touch" X suggested as he was running out of options, and Karl was delighted that he'd finally given the right answer

"Yea Touch!" he exclaimed, "That's the killer sensation. BANG – you're there, with touch", he made the gesture of an explosion with his fingers. "You press foreheads and they're there, pressing back at you, their skin warm and soft and human." Then, miming breast-stoke with his arms, he went on "You swim in water", he ran his fingers in waves up and down his arms, "that's how it feels, water on skin. The quality of touch you get in this 'video-game - All of it - wind in your hair, sun on your face, sand between your toes. Perfect. Trust me. You'll forget you ever had another body."

Karl paused, elated.

X shared his sense of excitement. He couldn't wait to get started. Then suddenly it occurred to him, "if I can feel every sensation, then I can feel pain."

Karl nodded enthusiastically, "Good point- it takes some people longer to ask that. Yes, of course you can feel pain. It is fundamental to sensation. You would be numb to the world without pain. But we set a maximum threshold, one blast of searing agony and you're automatically ejected from the game. And no real tissue damage", he added quickly, "pain is only electrical impulses after all."

"As is pleasure"

"Quite right".

They were silent for the briefest of moments then Karl pulled himself up to his full height, saying as he stretched "But to make either pleasure or pain, we need to get you into a suit."

It was suddenly time for Eva to leave. He barely had time to say goodbye.

After she had gone he was full of regret. He had let her slip through his fingers. Over her beauty, and the beauty of their day together, he had chosen, like some teenage boy, an arcade game to be played in an underground bunker. The whole drift of the day, seemed suddenly lost to him, a postcard from someone else's memory.

He would have to find her in the game.

The thought pleased him. It felt like a quest.

His mood lightened and he followed Karl willingly into a

small back room to get kitted out. The suit was laid out on a massage table, looking at first sight like the eviscerated skin of a bloated seal, but on closer inspection appeared to be no more than a strange kind of wet-suit, its surface blue-black and flecked with specs of golden mica, rubbery in texture, but made of a lighter, more flimsy material. Karl helped X into the suit with a practised ease, guiding him in from the toes up, and dealing deftly with the trickier seals. The suit had to be careful rolled up his legs like stockings, and then ran in a continuous sheath over his torso, shoulders, and up to the crown of his head, leaving only his face free. Karl's manner was relaxed and cheerful, but X felt distinctly uncomfortable under his professional scrutiny. "Should have shaved your pubic hair", he commented, as X fitted his penis and scrotum into the pocket of the suit that had been sculpted to fit them. "It'll probably itch", Karl added, running his finger down the seal to secure the fit over his testicles, "never mind, too late now!" Fully fitted, the suit was merciless in its anatomical accuracy and dressed like a cat-burglar in latex, X was belatedly glad that glad that Eva had left.

Telling him to lie back onto the table, Karl made a finger gesture over the monitor, and the suit tightened across every inch of his body. The sudden contraction was alarming but brief, and was followed by the feeling that the suit had liquefied on contact, somehow bonding with his skin like a layer of fast setting glue. Karl let him get comfortable with that for a while, instructing him to stretch out on the massage table, relax and wiggle his fingers and toes until he got use to the feel. When X had got accustomed to the sensation Karl began to explain the game. "First you need some background", he said, tossing X a screen about the size and weight of a tabloid newspaper, advising, "If you want to read more text just wave your hand down the screen".

He knew that.

He looked at the screen.

BAKHUNINLAND

On September 4th, Globotech, the corporation that had controlled the monopoly of the West Eurasia region for the preceding 12 years, undertook an accountancy revolution that shocked the world to its core.

X felt a wave of disappointment. An accountancy revolution? He would have preferred elves.

He had to force himself to read on.

The Finance division had determined that two-thirds of the population in the urban conurbations represented a permanent drain on the bottom line, and therefore must be unloaded. On that fateful day the board passed the Enclosure Act without a single dissenting voice.

X waved his hand up the screen, revealing more and more text in the same tone. There seemed to be reams of it. He signalled to Karl, who raised his goggles in response, "I just need a summary."

"I thought so. But it's always best to read the manual first..."

Karl began to lay down the essential parts of the narrative

as quickly as he could. He explained that he could skip much of the detail, as when X was in the game he would simply *know* much of this without any effort of recall. "OK", he started, "The basic premise is that the ruling class have decided that the people in the cities are a drain on the economy, but rather than going through the trouble and expense of exterminating them, have instead sealed the major cities under impenetrable force-field domes and left them to rot."

X interrupted Karl, "I'm not sure this is the game for me."

"Relax", Karl responded laughing, "That's just the set up. All the bad times are over now. You come in thirty years after the domes went up. New societies have formed inside the sealed cities. It's peaceful now."

Reassured he signalled to Karl to continue.

"You can play this game in any city in the world pretty much", he explained, "but I suspect for you it should be London?"

X confirmed, he was, indeed, from London.

"Which part? North? East? South?"

"West." It came out of him like a lurch from his guts.

Strange.

Karl flipped down his goggles, "West London it is."

He flipped them up again, continuing, "Major features. One. The domes have had a major effect on the environment; it's hotter, more moist, and everything's very green inside the cities. It'll be similar to how you remember it but also very different. You'll see. Major feature two. It has a communication system based on music."

X struggled for comprehension.

Seeing his confusion, Karl explained further, "Yes, it's quirky", he acknowledged, "One of the fundamentals of the...game..." he hesitated over the word, "game-*world* is better I think. Anyway, one of the fundamentals of the game-world is that each of the big cities in a territory is individually domed and perpetually separated from the others. OK?"

X nodded.

"But although all communications in voice or text are jammed, music is not. To get around the isolation imposed on them, a musical form without words developed in each of the cities" he explained, "it's made up of regular harmonies, complex rhythms and repetitive beats and loops of sound, that form a kind of musical representation of the collective consciousness of its people, if you like. It's transmitted all over the cities by primitive radio transmitters set up on tower blocks and cathedral spires and out through the dome's walls from beacons on the highest points."

X thought about it, "Why was it set up that way?"

"I'm not sure", Karl replied, "It was in the original set up and people liked it, I guess. You'll see when you get there."

Although X didn't feel any more enlightened about how he was supposed to actually *play* this game, he felt more relaxed, knowing that he wasn't going to be dropped into a war zone. "How long will it last?" he asked.

Karl put his goggles on. "OK, the game-speed in this one is usually 'standard'. So twelve hours here is twenty-four there, but..." he paused for a second while he found the correct data", OK, it's set at 'fast' now. Makes sense", he added, it being the solstice."

"The solstice?" X asked. "Is that important in the game-world?"

Karl waived the mini screen at him, "You can always read the manual", he suggested.

X demurred.

"You'll be down for about twelve hours", he went on, "...and with the speed set at four times the usual rate ...it'll run as four, no...five days. The maths isn't quite as simple as I made out".

Five days. Even twelve hours seemed like a long time.

Karl reassured him. "I'm sure you'll enjoy it. When you come back you'll have enough time for a massage and a dip in one of the pools at dusk. You'll be fine."

"But what if I want to leave earlier?" He asked.

Karl nodded, "Let's set up a safe word now. You say it out loud and you immediately exit from the game. Obviously you don't want to choose something you're liable to use in ordinary conversation."

X thought a while. "Can I have *Flame On?*" He asked, wondering if it would work with two words. Karl was happy with his choice and recorded X saying the phrase three times until he was sure that he had got a consistent voice match. The Human Torch's cry had seemed a good choice when he'd thought of it, easy to remember and he couldn't imagine any circumstance where he would shout "Flame On!" in conversation, but as soon as he had selected it, the phrase turned over and over in X's mind and he could see him blurting it out like he suffered from Tourette's Syndrome the first time he caught sight of Eva in the game. While he was dwelling on this, Karl asked him what kind of specialist skill he wanted.

He got a specialist skill? Great.

Karl prompted him, "It could be something that you've always wanted to be an expert in, like karate, or carpentry...

Neither of those.

"Cycling", he suggested, thinking they'd be lots of cycle paths he could race down.

"OK, said Karl, I can give you that, but not much call for it in Bakhuninland. Anything else?

It took him some time to think of anything else until finally, "Climber – rock climber." He declared. He'd always fancied being good at that.

"OK, cycling and rock climbing it is, I'll throw in pot holing and mountaineering as well. There. Set at expert." Job done, Karl sat shaking his head, "Cycling and rock-climbing? Not the choices I guess I'd have thought a Seeker of Sweden would have made. Wow!"

Just as X was getting excited about the prospect of scaling sheer walls like Spiderman, a wave of despair broke over him. "How will I know what's going on in the game?" he asked, his voice suddenly a little hoarse.

Karl was matter-of-fact, explaining that 'he would have access to all the data, on demand and in real time."

"I can't do it." X forced himself to say, deeply disappointed, but obliged to admit the truth. He explained to Karl about the glasses, all that data, how it just made him dizzy and meant he'd just fall over and crash into things if he wore them. "I can't even control my eyes well enough to stand upright' he admitted, "It won't work." "I'm sorry to have wasted your time."

Karl had tried to interrupt and when X's was finished he patiently explained that he had been made aware of X's problem with glasses, but that it didn't matter anyway as no one in the game-world wore glasses. He made it clear that at this level of tech they simply weren't needed, explaining that the blackcurrant juice he had drunk was packed with nanotechnology, and although X got lost at that point, it seemed that, even now, a swarm of engineered microbots were swimming through his nervous system and setting up way-stations in his cerebral cortex. The embedded nanotech would deliver background data on any object he rested his eyes on, instantaneously, perceived as memory by his consciousness.

The thought of metal spermicelli in his spinal cord was uncomfortable, if it meant no blobs of data floating like sunspots in his peripheral vision and no sudden disorientating shifts of perspective when he moved his eyes; good.

He could do it.

Karl led him back into the main room and settled him into the suspensor chair. The rubberised material of the seat instantly moulded itself to the shape of X's body and he lay supported upright, like a king on his throne. Karl warned him that the final phases would be a little uncomfortable.

X tensed involuntarily as a sudden shower burst of pin-pricks coursed simultaneously across every surface of his skin. The sensation was most pronounced, almost painful, around his fingertips and the head of penis, which at first stung and then became briefly tumescent. The discomfort subsided and he declared himself ready for the final stage. Karl had warned him that even those familiar with immersing often found the last part, the securing of the mask, unsettling, but reassured him that the claustrophobic sensation would pass in a matter of seconds if he stayed calm. As he carefully positioned the mask on his face Karl impressed on him that even if it felt like it wasn't, his mouth would always remain open, and he could therefore always take a clean breath when he wanted to. Karl waved his hands over his monitor and the mask spread in a viscous sludge across his face, spreading over his lips like a heavy greasy lip-stick before drying tight over his skin. It felt like immolation, a voluntary mummification, and he had to count backwards from a hundred and take deep breaths prevent himself panicking. When he was comfortable again, Karl released the electrical pin-prick storm once more. His lips stung and he felt like he had been smacked in the face by a snowball. It was soon over. He was ready.

    He gave Karl a thumbs up and closed his eyes.

BOOK 2

BAKUNINLAND

31. HOME IN THE GREEN

He was cycling uphill. It was hot. Beads of sweat were streaming down his forehead and he had to wipe the back of his hand across his face to clear the stinging salt water from his eyes. To gain traction, he stood up on the pedals, using his full bodyweight to maintain momentum up the incline. His leg muscles took the strain without complaint and he rose smoothly, breathing like an accomplished swimmer on his stroke. Just before the crest, he had to work harder, and leaning forward over the front wheel, tucked his head down like a road racer on the Tour de France. Looking down at the pot-holed tarmac, he noticed how lean and deeply tanned his lower body was, stripped of excess body fat like the limbs of a middle-distance runner and stretched somehow, as though he had grown a couple of inches taller. He raised his head as he reached the top of the hill and immediately slammed on the brakes, bringing the bike to a skidding halt.

A green city lay shimmering in the heat below him

He was standing on an elevated stretch of dual carriageway looking out over the city from the height of its church spires. He was completely alone on the overpass and it was clear that it had been decades, at least, since any traffic had passed this way. The blistered tarmac was broken up by potholes as though it had been blasted by mortar fire; rough grasses and nettles grew in clumps beside the guardrail and a small copse of thorn trees had taken root around the central divide. A dense mass of tightly coiled brambles had sealed off one of the carriageways completely. To his left, the flat roofs of the tower blocks had been colonised by hawthorn and guelder rose, and purple buddleia stems waved like ostrich feathers in the crosswinds. A row of glass office blocks to his right had been smeared into faceless monoliths by pelts of deep green moss, and branches of ivy as thick as tree trunks ripped into a Sport Centre's ventilation tower, sealing off its brick turret like an enchanted castle in a fairy-tale.

He knew this view. Where was he?

The answer appeared in his mind as soon as he had the thought.

The WESTWAY

The Westway! He'd driven across it a thousand times, sweeping into the city at speed, soaring with the tyre wall rush as he flew above the streets, alive to the endless possibilities of the night ahead.

He looked around. The road was as silent as a canal towpath.

Those days were clearly long gone.

He walked to the edge and looked down. Below him, the urban landscape had been replaced by a patchwork of small fields; wheat, barley, maize, lavender, and sunflowers growing where rows of terraced Victorian houses had once stood. Narrow dirt tracks had replaced the roads, and rows of golden wheat pressed up against the front doors of the few remaining buildings. In the changed landscape, the houses had turned into neat little farmsteads, their plots divided up by dry-stone walls made of street curbing and rusty iron railings formed the frames of spindly hedgerows. A few derelict houses still stood among the tilled fields, their brickwork covered in orange lichen like a moth's wings, and dandelions, thistles and red poppies sprouted from the rubble of demolished buildings. All along the guardrail, vines cascaded down to the street, and swept along by the expressway, a seaweed green curtain hid the rest of the city from view. It was all astonishingly beautiful, as though a Pre-Raphaelite cloak had been flung over the concrete, stone and grime, setting the land ablaze with colour and light.

He felt the need to empty his bladder and unzipping his fly, began pissing in a satisfactory stream onto the side of the road, battering the heads of a clump of Michaelmas daisies that had taken root under the guardrail. Concentrating on his relief, he didn't notice the approach of another cyclist until he was alongside him. The man waved good-naturedly as he swished by, shouting, "Save it for the crops!" X waved back awkwardly, one hand still holding his penis.

When he was done, he turned his bike round and without paying any attention to where he was going, freewheeled down the off-ramp and parked his bike up against a railing. Behind him, the pot-holed tarmac began its long descent to Shepherds Bush roundabout, its length broken into sections by scree, clumps of hawthorn and sprays of tall nettles. He hopped over the barrier at a stretch of cleared vines and climbed swiftly hand over hand down the ladder. When he reached the ladder's base, he turned back toward the great vine sweep of the overpass and gave a slow satisfied sigh.

HOME

It was good to be back.

He set off down the red dirt track between the rows of potato plants on either side of him, the path cutting the shortest distance across the little triangle of fields to the shack at its apex. The hut poked out from under the roadway in front of a tumbling fall of deep green vines which, studded by bright florets of the flowering creepers that ran through its weave, leant it a backdrop as magnificent as an opera house curtain,

He stood for a moment, hands on hips contemplating his home.

His mind inventoried the shack as he looked at it. A single story building with a grass and solar-panelled roof, a lounge, a bedroom, a small kitchen and a bathroom. A sequence of figures flashed into his mind - he seemed to have memorised the rooms exact dimensions! He shook his head and stepped forward, passing the little herb garden out front, with its tarragon and thyme spilling out onto the path, and then onto a large porch scattered with a few well-worn easy chairs. Tall cannabis plants cast their distinctive leaf-shadows over pots of chives and rosemary. He ducked his head as he stepped over the threshold and into the lounge. Crash cushions, disorderly but clean, were strewn over the low-slung sofas and worn divans. Books lay everywhere, stacked in tottering towers in the corners, and, piled up, spines broken, on the sofas with coloured post-its marking individual passages. He kicked off his shoes, walked barefoot back out on to the porch, and sat looking out across the potato fields. He leant over and plucked a bud from on one of the plants next to him, crumbled it into a wooden pipe, lit up, and picked up a book that was lying face-down below the chair. It was something by J.G.Ballard. He sat back to read, the chair moulded to his body by old familiarity, and let himself be drawn into the tale.

The day floated away.

Later in the afternoon, after he'd checked that the drainage pipes from the overpass, done some weeding in the potato rows, and had a shower, he'd pulled out a chair, lit his pipe, and sat staring at the cascade of vines at the back of the shack. Mesmerised by the complexity of their green traces, his whole attention had been focussed on a random patch of vine-fall some ten metres above him in the sward. As he stared at the fractal beauty of this tiny patch, the nose of a small furry brown and white creature with huge eyes became visible at the edge the frame. The animal extended a long, down-soft, furred arm toward the next vine-stem moving with a glacial slowness. It took an age for the little spindly limb to cross the tiny divide and X held his breath as it finally closed on its target, afraid that the exertion might have been too much for the little beast. As it grasped the stem the creature extended five soft-padded fingers and spread them, froglike in their breadth, to curl round the leaf-stalk with the same geriatric pace as before.

He blinked. His point of focus was broken and the creature was re-absorbed into the camouflage of green like a hallucination.

32. BREAKING BREAD

Some hours later, when the shadows had begun to lengthen, and the sun dip toward the concrete line, he grew tired of being alone and went in search of human company.

Who was closest?

GARY. Gary was his friend. He could trust Gary.

The image of Gary's broad, open face flashed across his mind's eye and made him smile. As he thought of him, he recalled Gary's history as though a loop of film had suddenly unrolled in his mind. Gary had been a heroin addict before the domes went up, but when the supply of smack into the city had been ended by the barrier's sudden appearance, Gary had undergone a hard cold turkey, followed by a gathering of himself. It would be good to see him.

He dug up a dozen good-sized spuds, and throwing them into his knapsack with some chives and a small bag of weed, stepped into the dark shadows beneath the overpass. Making his way carefully past the moss-covered pillars in the gloom, he emerged into the moonscape of white concrete and rubble that was White City. In the distance, the frames of warehouses squatted like the skeletons of giant beasts, roasting and clicking as their girders expanded in the heat. Gary's shack, no more than a rough canvas sheet hung over scaffolding poles, squatted at the furthest edge of three small fields that had carved out a green promontory in the concrete ocean.

He caught sight of a figure rattling an empty wheelbarrow across the concrete toward the shack with a labourer's easy gait, and caught up with him as he was leaning the wheelbarrow upright against a scaffolding pole. It was Gary. He was wearing ragged jeans, flip-flops and a grubby white T-shirt with "Dirk Wears White Sox" written jaggedly across it. Close up, X could see how strong and vital Gary was, his eyes gleaming like a healthy dog's and his posture square-set against the world, but his face still bore the marks of the once long-suffering junkie with creases like tribal scars etching an archaeology of sorrow across his broad simple face. For a second Gary didn't seem to know who he was, but then recognition dawned suddenly. "Great to see you X!" he declared, and beaming, flung his arms round X's shoulders, slapped him on the back and ushered him around the shack, urging him to sit in one of the tatty camping chairs laid out in a circle around a wood stove.

X picked up a chopping board from a bench beside him, emptied out his bag, and having quartered the potatoes, lifted the lid off the pan that was simmering on the stove and tipped them into the stew. He sat back down and started chopping up the chives. As he worked a radio was playing a wordless trance-like tune; swoops of sound and fat, soft harmonics, looping in and out of complex rhythms, in slow, elliptical pulses, samba-soul sounds rising and falling endlessly in the gaps. It was very soothing.

Levi arrived.

Levi is always immaculately dressed. Levi can find anything that you need in the city.

Levi was a striking man by any standards, with the build of a heavyweight boxer, and skin so dark it was almost blue-black. He wore a waistcoat over a white high-buttoned shirt, slacks with sharp creases and a felt hat, giving him the appearance of an old-time preacher from the Mid-West. He sat down and began slicing up the papaya he had brought, moving his long delicate fingers expertly as he worked, carefully placing the seeds he extracted in a small ceramic pot.

As he worked he talked about his day, "Kew", he began, "I LOVE IT down there."

He went on to describe how the tulip trees in the gardens spread their seeds, throwing up imaginary dust from his hands, then spreading his fingers to demonstrate the sprouting of flowers, "The blooms!" he declared, his face pulled into a grimace of joyful bewilderment, "Bright purple things. Huge!" He cupped his huge hands, encompassing a space as large as a basketball to demonstrate, and swinging his arms in a huge arc, "Beautiful!" he laughed, shaking his head back and forth in astonishment.

X said he'd like to see that

Levi nodded, "You'd like the work that's going on down there too", he continued," doesn't look so pretty, but there's little plots laid out everywhere growing everything from rare crops to hobby projects - Tomatoes, tobacco, turmeric seeds, medicinal plants... They've had great results with cacti down there", he added, "all sorts of uses for those. Tanoop was getting excited about the possibility of tequila!"

"Tanoop was there?" Gary asked, surprised.

TANOOP. Everybody's friend. DJ. Flat on Hammersmith riverbank. Holds great parties. Must see him tomorrow and get hooked up.

"He drops by", shrugged Levi.

"What do you do at Kew?" X asked.

"I'm in the greenhouses mostly", he replied, "keeping the old Victorian boilers going. Bit of metal-bashing. Bit of basic plumbing. Someone's got to do it and I've got the skills", he shrugged. "That's a special place ", he continued, sweeping his arms across the room to conjure up the imaginary glasshouse ceiling of Kew, "The steam", he said, half-standing to mime the vapour bursting through the foliage, "I tell you, it feels pale when you step outside!" He laughed, chuckling deeply for some time at the thought. "Extra bonus!" he then declared. "When the fruit is ripe, we share it out amongst those of us working there. People only take what they need. I had my eye on a pineapple, but when did you last eat papaya?"

He passed a slice to X. He scooped out a piece of the pink flesh, it felt cool on his lips, but as bland as cold potato on his tongue. He swallowed, but the segment felt like lumpy porridge going down and he put down the plate with the rest of the fruit untouched. In contrast, Gary and Levi, cooing with delight at each mouthful, polished off their slices with barely a pause for breath. X offered them his barely eaten portion, "Please. I'm not really hungry."

The both looked up at him, momentarily bewildered at his

reaction, shrugged and then devoured off his too.

At that moment a naked man walked around the corner of the shack. He nodded hallo to Gary and Levi.

"Hi John", they chorused.

JOHN. John is always naked.

John probably wouldn't have been great to look at clothed. He was a short, wiry man, with a mean pinched face and a weak chin largely hidden beneath a straggly beard. Naked he was truly awful. His skin, somehow pale despite the sun, was covered in coarse brown hair. Sprouting from his neck and shoulders like the unkempt pelt of a gorilla, it lay in matted clumps on his chest, two dark curlicues ringing his prominent pink nipples, and ran seamlessly into the forest of curly pubic hairs around his shrivelled penis. He was barefoot and each toe sprouted black bristle-tufts like giant untended mole hairs. He emptied some chopped turnips and sweet potato into the pot and sat down.

Before he had considered whether it was wise, X found himself blurting out, "So why are you always naked John?"

The naked man bristled, his voice an octave up on his earlier greeting. "Why are you always clothed?" he replied forcibly. Before X had even begun to formulate an answer John was on the attack, making his point by jabbing an extended finger at X in time with his words. "You", he jabbed, "are wearing clothes because you have been taught to believe that certain parts of your body...", he listed them as a mantra, "the parts in involved in sexual reproduction, urination, defecation, and, in women, the organs of lactation during pregnancy are sinful, dirty, shameful, awful things that must be hidden from view at all cost. You!" he declared, fixing his eyes directly on X's as he spoke, "Would feel ashamed, would you not, to be naked here with me now. To have parts of your own body revealed to others. Ashamed!" He threw his hands in the air, "Of what?" and then pushing his face up to X he hissed, "Is your dick really so special? The obscenity is in your mind", he concluded, lowering himself into one of the garden chairs. "It's just the body of an animal of our species. No more, no less. But I suspect you knew that already".

It seemed that John had made his point well and X was about to say so, when John leapt to his feet again, "Or am I wrong? Is it *my* cock that's the problem? Is it that the overwhelming power, released by the exposure of my penis, will induce uncontrollable erotic desires in those around me, ending in an orgiastic chaos that, let loose on the world, would bring down civilization like the decadence of Caligula destroyed Rome?" John ceased talking, and ignoring X, leaned over the pot to reach for the ladle, his balls swinging so close to the rim that the fine black hairs on his scrotum kissed its edge as he stirred the stew. X accepted the gesture as the last word on the issue and stayed quiet.

KATE and RHIANNON arrived at the same time.

Kate and Rhiannon are a couple. They like being together, long walks in the fields, and building their home together.

X couldn't seem to remember anything else about them, and what he did recall sounded to him like a lonely-hearts ad. He wondered if they'd met through the columns of a newspaper and that was why he remembered it that way.

They were very different. Kate entered first, bullishly erect as she barrelled in, her slab shoulders and broad chest creating a commanding physical presence in the room although she could have been no more than five foot four. After nodding a brusque hallo to the four of them she stood silently with her arms folded, standing sharply erect but completely at ease like a career soldier on leave. Rhiannon, who had slipped in after her lover, was a slight, pretty young woman, who stepped softly into the space on a wispy frame. Her intelligent face held deep brown soulful eyes, that sparkled brightly in the lamplight but were also somehow sad at the same time, and although her skin shone with the health and vitality of a young woman in her twenties, the delicate tracings of lines around her eyes suggested sorrow of a much older vintage. As she raised her arms to adjust her hair, her bracelets slid down her forearms revealing pink scars at her wrists like scribbled out games of noughts and crosses.

Rhiannon scanned the faces around her before she spoke, blinking nervously as she did so. She looked closely at John who sat with pursed lips, rocking backwards and forwards on his seat, his body still held in tension following his contretemps with X, and then over at X, giving him a short, shy smile. The smile was full of understanding and sympathy and seemed to acknowledge silently that they all knew John could be a bit difficult and he shouldn't worry about it at all. She sat down and started chatting to John, listening carefully to everything he said with her head cocked to one side, asking short questions and smiling at his replies. Within a few minutes they were chopping the green salad the women had brought with them, and the little tension that had rippled across the group had dissipated entirely.

The sun set, and Gary fumbled around the back of his shed in the darkness until he found the switch and a bright white light burst out from above the shack. They all cheered. X had got talking to Kate, and listening intently to what she was saying, he didn't notice the arrival of a new guest until they had already stepped into the circle. When he looked up, the new arrival's face was so strongly back-lit by the arc lamp on the shack's roof that her face was completely obscured and he could only make the glowing silhouette of a woman mounted by golden penumbra of hair, each delicate strand caught and held separate by the harsh light.

The outline of her body, the way she moved.

Eva. She had found him the game.

And as the thought burst upon he was suddenly bewildered, a rush of images of somewhere else, somewhere very different than here cascaded across his mind's eye. She would have had plenty of time to put on a suit and join the game by now.

Game?

He shaded his eyes to see her better against the bright light. Her face was still indistinct to him, but he could see that her body was athletic, a runner's shape. A little more curved at breast and hip than he remembered, and although it was hard to tell as she was stooping a little, she seemed slightly shorter, still tall, but perhaps a couple of inches shy of her old height. When she stepped out of the light he could see that her hair was chestnut brown, rather than fair, and framed a different face, although one with the same fundamental symmetry as Eva's. Her nose was shorter and less aquiline, her lips softer, her eyes hazel rather than blue. But what did that mean? What did all the small changes amount to? Nothing. After all, if he looked a little different in Bakhuninland, so could Eva. She was magnetically beautiful.

It was Eva.

"Hi Clara", Rhiannon called out.

CLARA. Ecologist. Photographer. Apartment by the river.

He immediately recalled its location and interior.

She came over to introduce herself, her lips curved into a curious smile as she shook his hand.

"Hi", he stuttered at her greeting.

What had he just been thinking about?

She settled into the circle opposite X and the conversation around the stove drifted into a discussion about crops. X struggled to pay attention; his whole centre of his being had shifted in Clara's presence, his entire consciousness pulled toward her as though by gravity. He sat transfixed at her shape in space, her legs; her eyes; the quick movement of her hands... As he watched her talk it was as though another form, a milky-white astral projection, seemed to hover around her frame, merging fluidly with her body with each familiar gesture, slipping away in a ghostly after-trail with an unfamiliar one. The person he seemed to have known forever alternating with someone warmer, more relaxed and open who he had only just met.

He only caught individual words and short phrases from the conversation... 'big pharma'... 'got lucky'... 'self-replicating GM seed'... 'Nitrogen-fixing wheat'...

Clara raised her arms and yawned theatrically, "That's the

trouble with bloody farmers", she declared, pouring out glasses of cider from a canister she'd brought, releasing the tart smell of fermented apples into the night air "It's always vegetables and crops. What else has happened in Bakhuninland?"

There was silence for a moment.

"I saw a red panda this morning", piped up Rhiannon. "It was sitting in one of the trees in Shepherds Bush Green, happily munching away and looking out across the meadow. I sat for ages and just watched it chew.'

"That's more like it", said Clara, and went on to argue that as everyone was so focussed on their crops they hadn't considered the ecosystem as a whole at all. "The fauna has developed in amazing ways", she said, "but nobody is paying any attention."

This was contested. John talked about the number of llama herds that were being used as pack animals. Kate mentioned the ostriches they were farming in Camden. Rhiannon shuddered, "Something weird about the eggs", she said, "Too big. All that yoke. Yuk!" She made a face. Gary began moaning about the wallabies that had spread out from Battersea Park, "Pests", he muttered.

"See!" said Clara, bursting in triumphantly, "Farmers! You only notice the animals that came out of the city parks and farms, and you only care about them if they're useful as livestock or represent a threat to your cabbages!"

She ignored their waved entreaties. "Now the red pandas, on the other hand, are really interesting", she declared, "They're examples of some kind of mass jailbreak from London zoo back in the bad old days", she reflected for a moment, "Actually it's much more likely their keepers let them out when they realised they couldn't feed them anymore, but I like the idea of a jailbreak. They didn't all make it of course" she mused, "And I'm glad we don't have to deal with tigers or bears or anacondas." She shivered at the thought.

Gary interrupted, "I wonder what it would have been like if any of the apes had survived?"

Clara acknowledged his words but returned to her theme, "Anyway, some of the small mammals have thrived, particularly the nocturnal ones – and there's always the lemurs of course."

"Lemurs", blurted out X, "There's lemurs?"

They all laughed.

"You need to get out more X", said Levi, "They're everywhere, go for a walk and you're tripping over their damn furry tails."

"We'll have to take you out X, show you the town", said Clara, smiling.

His heart raced.

At this moment, X recalled the strange creature above his shack, and knowing she would be interested, he retold the story. He was rewarded by her rapt attention and he struggled to remember the details, distracted by the awareness of Clara's hazel eyes upon him. She smiled at the end of his rendition, and although she turned away to talk to the others quick enough, she cast occasional glances in his direction for as she talked on, an amused smile hovering around her lips.

The night grew on, and more and more of Clara's cider was shared out until they were all soon pissed, so when Clara announced that they should undertake an expedition to find X's mysterious creature, it seemed like a good idea, at least to half the party. Rhiannon and Kate, however, chose that moment to head home and John made an excuse to leave.

X suspected he was cold.

Clara, Gary and Levi happily stumbled out into the dark with him, in good spirits, torches lighting the way through the fields and their voices ringing out cheerfully to each other across the night air. Defying the pitch-black gloom of the underpass, they burst into drunken nonsense songs as they crossed under the concrete, laughing as their shouts echoed back from the invisible vault above them. At the shack, he brought a chair out for Clara, who wanted to sit in the exact spot where he had seen the creature earlier, and stood with her a while she methodically scanned the wall of vines with her torch, working systematically from point to point, briefly illuminating blocks of green foliage with its yellow glare. She was very focussed on the task, and X stood with her a while in silence until he grew bored and went in to talk to Gary and Levi who had settled comfortably on the porch.

Levi was laughing heartily when they heard Clara shout, "Be quiet back there! You'll frighten it away." They tried to quieten down but were soon guffawing about something or other when Clara shouted for them to shut up for a second time. Gary and Levi took the hint and went indoors, but X picked up a jacket that was lying over the back of his chair and went back out to join Clara. He slid his jacket over her shoulders as she sat, trying not to disturb her concentration on the vines while he did so. She looked up anyway, shivered then smiled. "Thanks", she said, pulling the jacket closer to her, "I hadn't noticed I was cold." She returned to scanning the vine wall, and just at that moment; in the foliage about five metres from where he had seen the creature earlier, Clara's torchlight reflected off the animal's big soft-toy button eyes and the animal froze like a statue in the yellow cone of light.

They watched in silence together. He could hear the sound of her breath in the night air, the faint scent of her skin.

And then the moment was over.

She stretched. "Yup." She said, "Thought so. Slow Loris, that's what it is. Your description was very good. The Slow Loris", she repeated, shaking her head and smiling at the thought. "Fantastic" With that she rose, "I must be off", she said, pecking him on the cheek and stepping back before he had a chance to react, "It was lovely seeing you, I'll come back with my camera another night and get a shot if that's alright."

He nodded his assent.

She waved goodbye with her fingers and a smile, and stepped away, turning her head over her shoulder, "Sorry, I almost forgot. Can

I borrow your jacket?"

It was still wrapped around her shoulders. He had forgotten.

"Of course.'

She thanked him and raising her hand in a final wave, strode steadily down the path, picking her way through the dark with her torch. He watched until the little circle of light was swallowed up in the darkness.

Sweetly melancholic, he drifted back his shack. Levi must have slipped away earlier, but Gary was still there, half-dozing in one of the porch chairs. X sat in the chair next to him skinned up a spliff, took a couple of tokes and passed it to Gary.

"How are you feeling?" Gary asked.

X thought a moment. "Free", he said, "free, elated and waiting for the adventure to begin."

Gary replied slowly, "Well, I agree with the first two, but adventure? See...How can I put this? Take this", he gestured at the joint, "I only smoke this in company, it's good to be in the same place as your host, it's ...civilised. But I'm quite happy to see the world straight the rest of the time. See it for what it really is, rather go through life wanting an orchestral score to strike up every time I light a match - but that's the thing with you dreamers", he nodded at X, "You always want it to be more than it is. You always want a narrative." Gary paused, "But there is no narrative. There's only the heat of the sun, the ripening of the crops, watching the green soak through the concrete, nightfall and daybreak, sowing and harvest...."

"For ever and ever amen", interrupted X.

Gary laughed. "Sorry X...Preaching!" He laughed again, "You win one hand at poker and you want to tell everyone else how to play", he said, "But this is it X – the winning hand. Don't go dreaming of adventures that might never happen", he warned, "Just enjoy it as it is."

They were quiet for a while.

"That was it wasn't it", Gary said, "the last word"

X nodded.

"At least I got it", Gary pointed out, gathering up his belongings and stepping off the porch into the murk, "Don't forget", his voice called back from the darkness, "stone-breaking tomorrow afternoon, I need all the muscle I can get!"

And the night was done.

BAKHUNINLAND DAY 2

33. BREAKING STONES

He couldn't remember sleeping, and seemed to wake to the day with his rucksack packed, already well on the way to Tanoop's.

He'd turned off the dirt track that had once been the Goldhawk Road to cut through Ravenscourt Park. The entrance had been part-blocked by a fallen Horse Chestnut tree, its roots ripped into the air and covered in clods of pale dry earth, and he scrambled over it into a dense woodland where the narrow track squeezed between bramble bushes and sprays of bracken. Oddly, the old playing fields at the heart of the park were still intact, their close-cropped grass maintained by of a small herd of sheep, whose grazing now performed the role of the long-departed groundsmen. The paddling pool was still there too, and exited kids splashed and shrieked in the sky-blue shallows just as he remembered it. Passing under the old railway bridge, now as forgotten and redundant as a Roman aqueduct, he cut across a wide ribbon of wheat where the Great West Road had been, and, having caught a brief glimpse of the river sparkling in the sun beneath Hammersmith bridge, X was soon skipping up the back steps into Tanoop's house.

Tanoop was lounging in a big leather chair behind a mixing desk at the rear of his open plan apartment when X entered. He had headphones on and indicated that X should make himself comfortable while he finished up what he was doing. While Tanoop made minute adjustments to the dials on the instrument panel in front of him, X strolled over to the fridge and popped himself a beer. He sat down on one of the sofas and looked out over the river, daydreaming pleasantly while he waited. Eventually Tanoop pulled off his headphones, "Hey X!" he called across the room, good to see you man!" Tanoop raised his palm to silence him, "Don't say anything. Just pick up the headphones and listen. I'll give you a tour. Try a pill if you feel like it", he added, indicating a bowl half-filled with capsules by the sofa, "the white ones with the little bird on them are very nice."

X declined the pill, but slipped the headphones on and settled back into the sofa. The music wasn't completely unfamiliar to him, he thought of Pink Floyd, then Tangerine Dream, and then he stopped trying to categorise it and allowed it to take him away. The music rose and fell in complex intertwined rhythms, and was composed of a textured pattern of sounds that were somehow broader and more colourful than ordinary instruments. Rising to the surface and falling away to the depths, a deep rhythmic baseline carried the troughs and swells of the music like waves across a broad sea. At first he floated on the crests and furrows of the sound, enjoying the fat warmth of the tones, the buoyant tilt of calypso that kept bubbling to the surface, keeping him riding high with the hot summer's day. But as he listened he began to fall deeper into the music and began to trace the subtle shifts in the patterns. The rhythms now were beaten on tabla, intricate raps and swoops blending into ragga as the bass dropped through the floor, before returning in metallic shards of chords, looped once again around the tabla's timpani, and then all the complexity stopped, leaving him hanging on a single crystal clear note, that then echoed to silence like dub reggae. Then all the elements returned, blending back with the fading echo, and the driving baseline of the beginning rose to the surface again.

X was so absorbed by the sounds that when Tanoop tapped him on the shoulder it came as a shock. He had crouched down in front of him to get his attention, and the first thing X saw were Tanoop's enlarged pupils inches from his face, which combined with his thick tufty black eyebrows and goatee, gave him the startling appearance of an Asian Groucho Marx. When he stepped back, X revised his opinion. Tanoop was probably handsome in a chiselled, bony way; tall and wiry, easy in his movements, and, at this moment, clearly quite blissed out.

"Beautiful!" said X.

"Absolutely!" Tanoop replied, "But you've got to take it a step further."

"I don't want to do any pills".

"No. No. No. Whatever you want." Tanoop dismissed the notion with a wave of his hand, "Freedom is freedom. No. What I meant", he went on, "Is that you have to get inside the music."

X didn't understand so Tanoop explained, "The sounds you just heard began with what I'm picking up from West London right now - then I hopped around the city a bit to give you a variety of voices. Did you get the Dagenham bit at the end with all the metal pressing and the mridangam?"

X understood some of Tanoop's words but he just couldn't seem to get it.

Seeing his puzzlement Tanoop cut to the chase, "OK. Short cut. We hook you up." He picked up a boxy black headset. "Put this on. You'll hear some simple sounds and rhythms. Relax completely into the sounds and let yourself float away with the ones you like most. After a while the pattern will coalesce into the harmonies that most satisfy you, and then settle into a stable pattern, creating a kind of signature if you like, completely unique to you. We record it, I mix it, and then we send it up with the rest of West London sound."

X put on the headset and did as he was instructed, letting himself float on whichever harmony he liked best. The tune would sometimes collapse completely into discord as a new rhythmic pattern upset the old order, and then it would settle into a new shape, each one more attuned to him than the one before.

"Got it!" cried Tanoop, and as he played back X's sound to his own headphones, he exclaimed again, "Wow! We'll have to keep an eye out for you! - Spikey!" He twisted a couple of dials on the controls, "Great. It's uploaded. Now put on the other headphones and I'll play you back the sound of West London you were listening to earlier."

X lay back on the couch and sipped at his beer. He could hear the same tunes that he had heard before, but they were slightly different, intermittently so, a half-octave, a tan shade altered, and as he listened deeper, he caught it; just for a second; his refrain, in the mix with all the other sounds, harmonious but distant. And then it was gone, swept up in the swell of the collective sound of the city.

He took off his headphones, moved. "I get it now."

"Great."

Suddenly he remembered Gary's rock-breaking. "What time is it?" he asked.

"You're asking me?" Tanoop laughed.

"I've got to go", X said, grabbing his rucksack, "Thanks Tanoop."

"You're welcome – see you at the party tonight – bring a friend!"

*

He ran through the fields, feeling the strength in his limbs with every stride, a poise and balance to his gait that allowed him to hurtle down the dust path at a half-sprint. He was scarcely out of breath by the time he reached White City.

Gary's shack had been completely dismantled, its scaffolding poles and tarpaulin now stacked neatly in the corner of what had been the furthest field. But since his last visit, Gary's foray into the concrete ocean had gained a new frontier, a further ten metres of ground, its grey soil now littered with angular chunks of concrete like glacial moraine. Gary and Levi were loading rubble into wheelbarrows and others could be seen in the far distance trundling empty barrows back from the entrance of an old warehouse. At the field's edge, Kate and two young men were working hard to turn the huge wheel of a piece of equipment that looked more like a medieval trebuchet than a JCB. The machine was a brutal thing of heavy wood and sharp steel bolted onto a wheeled platform. A system of pulleys raised a pillar as thick as a mature beech trunk high in the air and when it reached its highest point, the workers stood back, and an older man who had been fussing around with an oil can while the others laboured, pressed a lever, and the pillar crashed down into the concrete, breaking another chunk away from the mass like a rock fall from an eroded cliff edge.

"You're late!" shouted Gary.

"Sorry", he said, "I was at Tanoop's."

"Of course. No worries. Can you help Johnone and his boys with the crusher?"

JOHNONE. Visits often, mostly for long weekends with his two sons REUBEN and ANDY. Mechanical Engineer. Uses scavenged materials to build simple, effective machines.

For the rest of the morning they took turns at the wheel, sweating in the heat, shoulder to shoulder with Kate, Levi or the boys at the ropes, or trundling the rubble across the concrete in the shimmering heat. Relentlessly; the winch turned through the air, propelled upward by the sweat and sinews of their labour, the pillar rose and fell like Mjolnir and a lightening crash of sound would echo across the clearing, followed by the dull rumble of wheels as the machine advanced another yard, then the creaking of the pulley ropes and the shouts and grunts of the workers, and the whole process would repeat itself again. For the first few hours the barrelling was conducted with great spirit, impromptu races clattered across the stone, bets were laid and ironic fists pumped the air when the finishing line at the warehouse door was crossed. As the day wore on, the races ceased, and the labour developed a slower, steadier rhythm under the hot sun's rays. Gary tried to work twice as hard as anyone else, keeping the volunteers supplied with cool water and ferrying huge quantities in each barrel load. They played on his guilt, bursting into quick trots with their barrows whenever he looked in their direction, and theatrically staggering to the water barrel when they knew it was empty.

Halfway through the day, with the sun directly above them in the sky, they took a break, collapsing in the shade while Gary fed them, placing huge bowls of steaming stew in front of his guests. While the others dunked their black bread into the goulash and sucked away at the juices with relish, X found he had no appetite and only nibbled at the corners of his bread. He noticed that Johnone and his sons scarcely touched theirs either and felt a little better about leaving his food uneaten. While they ate, Johnone droned on about scavenging for materials and the construction of the crusher, explaining, at length, some of the ingenious engineering required to make it work. It was quite tedious, but given what his machine had enabled them to achieve, everyone listened politely. Eventually he left with his boys to get the blade sharpened for the afternoon's work and when he was out of earshot Gary said, "Means well, that John, but he can't tell a story to save his life."

"Tell us a better one then", challenged Kate good humouredly.

"Once upon a time..." Gary began. Everyone laughed. "Once upon a time, there was a world where people and metal moved about with great speed", he swept his arms across the still plain, "and the soil was poisoned, and the air was choked by their fumes..."

"You can't start there", Kate complained, "It'll take forever."

Gary raised an eyebrow and continued undeterred, "Then the bad days came..." Kate and Levi groaned in unison but Gary continued undeterred, "...and when those days had ended, the streets were full of cars, and there was very little petrol left in the city. Cars that had been smashed to pieces in the chaos were scattered like battle debris on bridges, buried in broken walls and gridlocked in frozen demolition derbies at crossroads. Some were still capable of running, but useless now with so little fuel. So all of them lay rusting, barricading the streets and clogging the fields..."

"Where is this going?" asked X.

"...and then word got around that they had got the furnaces up and running in Dagenham and would welcome the steel. Everyone was to work together to clear their area of cars. There was a special day, when all the cars would be cleared, everyone worked up to being ready on that day."

"The Cavalcade," announced Clara, who joined their circle at that moment, apologising for her late arrival, "Good name huh?"

"And Clara and I..." Gary nodded a bow to Clara, and she curtseyed in reply, "Rode in on the last moving car of the cavalcade."

"An Austin 1100", Clara added, "We found it in a garage in Chiswick. One lady owner, neat as a pin, and we had enough petrol to chug it all the way to East London. Every other car was being pushed or towed behind horses. We just kept on going. People stopped and waved as we puttered past them, it was very nice."

"Last one through the Gates!" declared Gary.

"Actually there were a couple behind us..." interjected Clara.

"Not moving under their own power", contested Gary, "and anyway, don't spoil a good story." They all laughed, and X acknowledged that while Gary had indeed told his story well, it was a better story than Joneone's and therefore he had an unfair advantage. "Ah", replied Gary, "But it's the same story. The tip of the crusher that has been chipping away the concrete from my field is metal from the Dagenham furnace."

"Cars into ploughshares", said X.

"Exactly."

Refreshed, they set about their work once again with renewed vigour. For a while Clara danced around them snapping shots of them straining at the ropes before setting her camera on a tripod and recording time-lapse photographs of their progress. X threw himself into his labours in order to impress her, and when he looked up she often seemed to be looking at him, a smile hovering at the edges of her lips. Before the work was completed, she got up to leave, applauding their efforts and saying that she had her whole family coming over and had to go. Before she left she walked over to X. "Listen. If you're on your way over to Tanoop's tonight, drop in at mine first. You'll have to meet the whole clan if you can stand the thought of it, but after they've gone we could stroll down the river to the party together if you like."

Of course he liked. He would come over early evening when he had finished up here.

When it was time to stop, they all helped themselves to a pitcher of Gary's beer and stood quietly contemplating the day's achievements. The concrete had retreated another hundred metres, leaving a block of hard-packed earth and rubble chip behind it. A field of battered earth, the size of a 5-a-side football pitch had been freed from its tomb.

X didn't linger, and waving goodbye to his neighbours, he returned to his shack to freshen up for the evening. While he showered, he dwelt on Clara's casual invitation to her home and the party afterward. What did it mean? She must at least be interested him. Why else would she have invited him over?

Dressed and ready to go, his body felt toned and strong from the day's exercise and he headed into the night filled with a sense of hopeful optimism.

34. CLARA

When he arrived at Clara's flat, it was clear that her family gathering was well underway. Bicycles of all shapes, sizes and colours were littered around the entrance of the modernist apartment block, shoppers, racing bikes, choppers and three-wheelers lay where they had been dropped like a collapsed peloton on the grass. Music spilled out of the open windows and the sounds of animated conversation, the clinking of glasses and bursts of laughter rose and fell in waves as the front door swung open and shut. A gaggle of excited kids raced down the steps as he approached, shrieking with delight and chasing each other round the building and down to the riverbank.

Entering, he stepped swiftly through the crush of bodies at the door, and looked around. He couldn't see Clara anywhere but the atmosphere in the room was so convivial that X felt comfortable drifting into stranger's conversations, and joined the group of middle-aged men who were standing nearest the door. They were all in hearty spirits, and when he declared himself to be a friend of Clara's, they all raised their glasses and cheered.

"Any friend of Clara's is a friend of ours", declared **JAMES. Clara's sister-in-law's son by second marriage.**

James was an affable, balding man in his mid-fifties with a broad, open face and iron grey tufts of hair sprouting up from behind his big fleshy ears. He welcomed X into the group, explaining that they had spent the day touring the North London vineyards and were now enjoying the fruit of their hunter-gathering.

ANDREW; Clara's second cousin on her uncle's side, cut in, swaying gently forward over his belly as he spoke, "For the most part", he bemoaned, "our wives and partners, declined to accompany us on our journey and went to some kind of, 'show', instead."

"Yes!" said James, "They thought we'd all just get pissed!"

There was a collective guffaw-cheer at James' words, and

glasses were raised again and quickly drained. James refilled their glasses from another bottle he had just uncorked. "Primrose Hill red. Merlot. South facing vines", he announced, passing a glass to X.

There was some discussion of the wine, "Hampstead, Primrose Hill, Richmond Park...", wondered **MARTIN. Clara's uncle's third son.** "...Funny how all the poshest places got all the vineyards."

HELENA, Clara's ex-brother-in-law's granddaughter, spoke up. The only woman in the group, she was heavy-set and hearty and her long brown hair was so matted with sweat and the dust that it resembled a rook's nest. She spoke with a booming bark like a Sargent-Major's on parade. "It's obvious lads. Access to sunlight has always been a commodity. No democratic distribution of the sun in your face back then."

Although Helena's point seemed valid, there was clearly no desire among the company to contemplate anything too seriously, and soon, a chubby, jovial man in his late fifties or early sixties, **SIMON, Clara's sister's niece's husband**, started to reminisce about a previous expedition and the great vintage bottle he'd acquired from Crystal Palace.

"Now the *South* London Vineyards", he began, but as soon as he started the sentence, his friends all echoed his words, chanting, "Now the *South* London Vineyards, in exactly the same tone.

"Stop me if you've heard this one before", said Simon.

They laughed again and raised another toast.

X slipped away before his glass was re-filled again, and headed out into the party looking for Clara. He caught sight of her heading toward him across the room, hotly pursued by a chain of small children. She gave X a quick wave and a bright smile, before pretending to be overwhelmed by her pursuers and, falling backwards over a sofa, threw her legs in the air, a pair of chunky training-shoes wobbling on slim ankles above her head. He watched as she organised the children into a game of 'wink murder', marshalling the kids into a circle, picking a po-faced little girl with a snotty nose as the detective, and choosing a giggling blond goblin of a boy as her murderer. When the murderer winked a big dewy eye in her direction, Clara died theatrically onto the carpet beside his other victims. When it was her turn to be the detective, she set about her investigation with due seriousness, failing somehow to identify the little dark-haired girl with fairy wings as the murderess, despite the child blinking like a shell-shocked angel to everyone in the circle at the same time.

With Clara occupied, X wandered further into the party. A middle aged man and his two children caught his eye. They were huddled together in one corner, excitedly discussing the contents of a map laid out in front of them. His curiosity piqued, he leant over their shoulders to have a look, and they ushered him into their circle enthusiastically, moving aside to make a space for him on the sofa. The father, **RAJ, Clara's brother's first wife's son**, introduced him to his children, Rebecca and Azim, and proudly explained how they were in the process of producing the first map of the greened city.

"We've been camping out at Heathrow, surveying the land by the dome's edge. You can see the barrier here", he began, pointing to a thick black line that arced across the map cutting off about a quarter of the page in the North West. On the far side of the black line the map was completely blank.

"What's it like at the barrier edge?" X asked.

"Weird", said Rebecca

"But amazing!" pointed out Azim.

Raj explained, "Close up it's like a white wall, totally opaque. Look straight at it and you can see nothing at all on the other side, yet rain falls through it and you can feel the breeze blowing from the other side. Sometimes you can smell things that you can't see, like …"

"Like shit", added Azim.

"Use dung", cautioned his father.

"So how does it work then?" asked X

"I've no idea", replied Raj, "but you can't get close to it. Don't even try! Anything within a metre of the wall gets instantly incinerated. Vaporised, as far as I can make out. Nothing left at all. There's a burnt strip of grass on edge of the pasture. It runs along the perimeter like a rind of bacon, but be careful, it's not always a reliable guide."

"Yea, and that's what we measured", said Azim, "We trundled a wheel all the way from here to here", he pointed proudly to the map.

"And it was scary", said Rebecca, "we strapped a two-metre long stick to the wheel to keep our distance from the barrier, but as we walked the tip of the stick would keep burning up inch by inch …."

"Yea", interrupted Azim, "So as the stick gets shorter you're slowly drifting towards the incineration line!"

"No room for day-dreamers!" he said, ruffling his son's hair.

They turned to look closer at Raj's meticulously–crafted, hand-drawn map. The flat lands that surrounded the old airport were shaded green, marking out a vast expanse of grassland with the outlines of the airport buildings at its centre. There were patches of marshland, moor and woodland South of the barrier and the course of the river Crane had been fully plotted, but much of the rest of the map remained blank.

"Work in progress", said Raj, clearly savouring the challenge of filling the uncharted territories on the family's map.

"We're in Hounslow Heath now", said Azim excitedly, drawing X's attention back from the photographs, "It's wild out there!"

His sister joined in, "It's very beautiful too – with the purple heather and yellow gorse…"

"But wild!" Azim argued, "The wind howls across and all the trees are bent, twisted and thorny. It's spooky."

"And there's that weird man", said Rebecca.

Her father pulled her up gently, "Not weird, my girl", he said, "just different."

"He is a bit weird", argued Azim.

"Be careful not to judge, children", admonished their father, and turning to X explained, "He is a hermit, lives alone and away from everyone else..."

"Mutters and shouts at himself", interjected Rebecca.

"But..." Raj continued, "he does no one any harm; he just wishes to live by himself. It is his prerogative to do so if he wishes after all."

"He smells", said Rebecca.

Raj nodded, "He does indeed, smell..."

X thanked them and moved further into the room, drifting into the orbit of a group of middle-aged women who had convened around the sofas in the sunken lounge. They made space for him after he had hovered a while, and he asked the woman next to him what her day had been like.

MAGDA, Clara's uncle's granddaughter, was clearly having fun, and was delighted to begin her version of the day amidst a chorus of cat-calls and exclamations from her friends. "Well", she began, "It was down at Turnham Green this, 'show'.

She made the inverted commas sign with her fingers at the word.

"Here she goes!" came a cry from the group.

Magda tossed back her chestnut hair, and looking into her eyes X realised he couldn't asses how old she was at all. She had all the presence and confidence of a mature woman, but her skin, hair and body looked much younger.

'Anyway", she continued, "The stands were rickety."

"She's off now", piped up someone, "The rickety stands!"

"But the stands were rickety", Magda insisted, 'You should have been down my end when that big woman sat down..."

"Fattist!" came a cry.

"So having endured the rickety stands", Magda continued, "It wasn't much of a show was it?" She raised her arms to implore the gathering to agree with her. "Fire-eaters, acrobats and jugglers? She paused, "Well I know it's all very skilled and a bit dangerous, but it's not really *entertaining* is it? Take juggling", she went on, "I know it's technically very difficult to juggle eight clubs at once whether they are on fire or not, but after about five minutes I want them to up the ante... I don't know, juggle with live badgers or something..."

"Live Badgers!" exclaimed the woman sitting next to her.

"Or whatever, it's a metaphor."

"A metaphor for what?'

Magda gave up trying to convince them of the aptness of her badger metaphor and collapsed back on the sofa smiling at the ceiling. When they'd finished laughing at her, the circle of women broke up into small groups who sat chatting amiably.

At that moment Clara came over and tapped him on the shoulder. "I've just escaped the kids", she said, 'come and make my break out complete by whisking me away to the balcony. The teenagers have commandeered it and they form an effective cordon against intrusion by small children. And adults too", she added, "But I suspect you and I together can brave it out."

Below the balcony, the river was lit blue-golden in the late afternoon sunlight, white gulls glided on the breeze above treetops the excited screams of kids leaping into the cold water cut the air. On the balcony itself, the teenagers were all peering down at the riverside below. Even the most elegantly bored of the girls had stood up, and one boy, a gangly, russet-haired lad, was leaning far out over the railings and shouting down the path. The boy was balanced perilously on the second bar of the railings, right on the tipping point of his centre of gravity, and gesticulating wildly at the receding backs of two figures making their way away from Clara's down the path.

"FUZZY YOU"RE A WANKER", he shouted.

Clara's arrival on the balcony had already been registered by its other occupants, and everyone else had gone quiet, but the boy was too wrapped in his rant to notice, shouting "WANKER", again, leaning out even further and making the accompanying gesture with both hands at the same time.

The boy suddenly became aware of the silence behind him and turned around.

"Oh shit", he said.

"What do you think you are doing?" Clara said in a cold, toneless voice.

"But Aunt Clara", the boy began to plead, "It's Fuzzy... And he is being a wanker...."

Clara said nothing, and fixed him with a look that brooked no argument.

The look broke his spirit of resistance completely, and he was instantly apologetic and desperate to explain what was happening, "Jag's dared Fuzzy to jump off Hammersmith Bridge with her, and you know what he's like, won't be beaten by a girl will he.... And you know Jag'll do it 'cos she's mental, and Fuzzy such a dickhead that if she does, he'll do it... So he *is* being a wanker isn't he Aunt Clara?"

"And sorry about the swearing", he added.

"Oh shit!" said Clara. "I'll talk to you later young man", she added sternly to the boy, and apologised to X. "Got to go! Rescue mission."

X stayed on the balcony to watch events unfold.

Less than a minute later he saw Clara, followed by a posse of parents and relatives, dash along the riverbank path in the direction the kids had gone earlier. Crowds of children followed in their wake hoping to see Jag and Fuzzy make the jump before Clara could stop them. Ten minutes later, X thought he heard a faint cheer floating down the river but the bridge was a long way off and he wasn't sure he hadn't merely imagined it, but sure enough, shortly after the phantom cheer, two bedraggled kids, clinging to the snouts of kayaks, were unloaded at the embankment below them. They had just long enough to take the balcony's applause before their parents arrived and they were dragged unceremoniously away.

The party began to break up, and Clara was busy hugging and kissing her guests as one by one they made their departures. The wine drinkers were the last to go and could be heard singing from the lane below until they were cut off abruptly mid-voice.

"Phoweee", said Clara, slumping on to the sofa, "Are you ready for another party?"

He was.

"A different kind of party", he said.

"A different kind of party indeed", she concurred, rising to her feet. "Let me freshen up for a minute and then we'll head off."

*

"Time to go!" declared Clara, stepping down from the steps with a flagon of cider and a backpack in her arms. She was dressed simply, wearing the same tight black jeans and sleeveless silk top she had worn earlier, adding only a black choker with a glittering silver clasp around her neck and applying dark lines of kohl under her eyes. But the subtle changes amplified her beauty in X's eyes, and the make-up seemed to deepen the intimacy of her gaze. X, scared that his desire would be exposed if he looked too directly at her was forced to avert his eyes.

Clara misunderstood him, "Don't worry about the cider", she said, "I'm not a drunk. It's the lazy farmer's choice. You can always trade cider. Collecting the apples is the only hard part, and I do it with a load of other poor farmers, ship it all by llama-train down to Mortlake and get it pressed there. Job done."

She swung the pack easily over her shoulder and they headed off together into the night.

35. PARTY TIME

They walked in silence, their footsteps making no sound on the dusty earth path along the riverbank. Only the sound of the water accompanied them as they walked, an ever changing pattern of licks and slaps against mud banks, its tempo shifting as tide and current battled for dominance. As they grew nearer their destination the music from Tanoop's party gradually became audible, occasional wind-blown notes and a dull, thudding bass, which blended with the lapping water and the ghost-hoots of owls as though it was the music of a city submerged beneath the water.

Some acoustic quirk meant that it was only as they rounded the final bend that the sound of the party hit them, and when it did it seemed to slap them in the face like a sudden blast of freezing air on a mountain crest. Tanoop's apartment was lit up by huge spotlights positioned on its roof and a huge silver windmill, spinning above the top floor, scattered rainbow colours up at the clouds. Electrical cables painted day-glo colours snaked across the lawn to turbines bobbing on the tide. Every level of Tanoop's home, from the top balcony to the courtyard, swarmed with people. Men and women, mostly young, and all dressed to kill, were dancing in swaying masses to music that permeated the air like liquid.

"Where do all these people come from?" X asked Clara, thinking of how quiet and peaceful the city seemed by day.

Clara shrugged, "Who knows?" she said, "Tanoop's happenings are always massive, people come from everywhere, party, and go home. And it is solstice-eve", she added, "big gathering."

The crowd looked different to the people he'd met so far. They were all younger, fitter and healthier. Many of the men clearly worked-out to the point of narcissism, and rippled under their cap-sleeved T-shirts and singlets. There were a lot of tight trousers. The women were uniformly sexy; Stepford babes, blond, brunette or redhead, all stacked, thin-waisted, and hard bodied. Dresses hugged curves and lots of soft flesh was on show, tiny mini-skirts and pierced belly buttons, spangly bras and halter-necks. Most danced in bare feet.

He caught sight of John, over in the far corner of the third tier of dancefloors above the courtyard. He was naked, of course, and dancing in a kind of upright strut like a robot peacock, his face a grin-grimace of pleasure, moving in short staccato bursts with no obvious connection with the rhythm of the music. Nobody was paying any attention to John's nudity, and in the group of dancers around him, two naked women swayed and jiggled between a squadron of bare-chested men in shorts, gurning as they pumped along to the beat.

On the highest tier, Tanoop's mixing desk sat like a cross between a grand piano and a throne set above the party, and X could see other, smaller consoles, laid out round the edges of each floor. He asked Clara what they were for.

"Inputting your 'signature', your 'sound-wave structure', your 'leit-motif' into the music", she replied.

X looked bewildered.

"How do I explain it? OK. Take the obvious fact that the DJ on the main consul is running the show, although only for now. In theory, anyone can have a go, but the crowd has high standards, so I wouldn't advise it"

He had no such intention.

"OK. So he or she is running the show, mixing the West London tunes. On the smaller mixing-desks, people are playing with their own sound, re-mixing it to fit the way they feel tonight." She pointed to a queue at the nearest desk, "It's mostly single people now, but they'll be more couples later. Look there's one!" She pointed to a platinum blond and a dark-haired Apollo of a man, "Those two will mix their signatures together until they get a blend that feels right to both of them. Then they pass it over to the DJ. "See!" she pointed at the dark-haired woman in a spangly mini-dress who had control of the main consul, "She's given a thumbs up to that skinny boy. When the moment's right, she'll drop his tune in the mix. Groups of friends do it sometimes" she went on, "It's fun – gets a bit tribal. Not tonight though, I don't think. Too many visitors."

And with that, Clara led X straight through the throng and into the middle of the dancefloor. Settling into the swelling sound and mass of moving bodies, he caught his own signature node in of the music began to dance within it, feeling his own rhythm flow easily through his limbs. As his shoulders dropped and his hips eased, he began to feel the collective heartbeat of the bass as a physical force, passing through his torso in rippling bands of power, strengthening his back and legs, rooting him in the crowd-forest. He felt whip-lithe, powerful and strong at his core, and yet he was light-footed when the music rose, dancing as though in reduced gravity, he floated upwards with the tune, and then was heavy and powerful when the bass pulled the crowd back down again.

He could only allow himself to look at Clara in snatches.

Each glance was a poem.

She moved so naturally and easily, sexy without guile, her eyes half-closed, dream-lost in the music, her arms rising slowly with the ascending tones, fingers and wrists gracefully poised like an Indian dancer's, then, when the beat dropped; straight on it, hot and funky, letting out a great whoop of delight.

Mind blowing.

He looked away, catching sight of Levi across the dance floor in the thick of the melee. On one, grinding it down on the deeper beats, moving in synchrony on a heavy pulse with the packed crowd around him. Top button and waistcoat still done up and somehow immaculate despite the sweat dripping off his brows. He stood out in his suit among the semi-naked revellers around him like a missionary priest leading the savage's to rebellion on a warrior charge. He somehow caught sight of X at the same time he was looking at him, and pumped a fist in the air before dropping back to the beat.

X looked at the young women dancing around him, allowing himself to freely enjoy their grace and beauty, watching them dance as he could watch a beautiful woman dance in a film without requirement to hide the pleasure and appreciation in his gaze. He made eye-contact with a dark-eyed brunette dancing beside him. There was no embarrassment, her eyes signalling a wordless permission for his gaze, comfortably accepting the compliment inherent in his regard. She smiled slowly and he felt her appraising his body, with the same unselfconscious ease and approval as he had given her. The exchange was erotic, but without desire as the predominant emotion, respectful; yet charged, sexy; but without invitation. She smiled and turned, dancing a step or two away, signalling an end to their moment, but also granting him full permission to watch her dance from behind. As he watched, she stretched her arms in the air and languidly moved the rhythm through her body, dropping snake-smooth into the sound. Her mini-skirt stretched taut as she dug into the bass, her buttocks pushing tight against the fabric as she rode the beat at the pace of a slow, deep, fuck.

X wondered if there hadn't been an invite there after all, and smiling, he turned back to Clara.

Time ceased to have reference point or meaning as he danced, ecstatic, deeply connected to the mass that moved as one to the sound of their collective unconscious, yet alone; lost altogether in the music with only the humming beacon of Clara's presence guiding him through the haze-light. At some unknown point in the dream-dance Clara pointed out Tanoop, ascending to the controls, bare foot and resplendent in his white shalwar kameez. He threw his arms back, assuming the posture of Christ crucified, took the cheers and then, nodding and smiling, set to work. He lifted them with a sweet soulful sound looped end to end, and when the crowd were in motion, he cranked the beat up a metallic ladder of rising tones, leaving them stranded on the top, floating on a single note before dropping into a grinding industrial drone, a sucker-punch to the sternum that forced the air from X's lungs. Tanoop kept them down there, squirming, until releasing them suddenly with something achingly sweet and pure that lifted them high in the night again. Tanoop's set had inspired John to break into a kind of Ska strut, cock and balls flailing, good spirited, but so out of rhythm as to disturb the dancing of others, and he was beginning to clear a section of the dancefloor around him. In a widening empty circle, he performed his own inimitable skank, utterly oblivious, completely content. Clara was giving it some too, the new tunes had woken her out of her dream-dance and she now seemed more fully alive than ever, her eyes flashing with delight as she looked up at him. He looked at her often, and every time her eyes were trained on his.

Later he saw Tanoop descending to the dancefloor, exultant, a blond on each arm, moving like a prince through his chamber, dispensing magnanimous smiles as benediction for his fawning courtiers. X caught Clara's eye, and nodded at Tanoop. She laughed and carried on dancing.

Then there was another shift in the music, a new, more alien sound began, tougher but warmer, the drumbeat somehow faster but slower, a fuzzy aggression hovering like mist over the greened textures. X had been looking Clara directly in the eyes when the new sound rose in the mix, he seemed to have glided forward until they were only inches apart, his stare drawn to her lips and then back to her eyes, then to the perfect arch of a solitary brow, the corners of the lips turning up in a grin, a further minute reduction in the distance between them. Then, something in the new music distracted her and she took a step back. For a second her face broke out in an expression of pure joy then just as quickly sadness, and she abruptly stopped dancing. She stood motionless, staring at the ground a boulder in the human wave.

"Sorry X, I've got to go", she mumbled, "I need to be on my own...sorry", and without looking up at him she pushed her way through the crowd and before he could react had disappeared from sight.

X was suddenly alone, bewildered.

What happened? Was is something he'd done? Could it have been something in the music?

He turned and asked a pretty boy who was dancing next to him what the music was.

"Manchester dearie, other city stuff; ROUGH beats...LOVE IT", he replied, shouting over the music. Not your girlfriend though...? he asked, gesturing in the direction that Clara had just left in.

"She's not my girlfriend", X shouted back.

"Oh, so if she's very definitely *not* your girlfriend, am I in with a chance then?"

X declined politely.

"You never know if you don't ask", the young man said before turning away, "That's my motto."

The direction Clara had fled in led back to the river, and he followed her path as best he could until he reached the bank, and stood standing, scanning the edges of the crowd and up and down the river path.

There was no sign of Clara.

He caught sight of Gary, lying down on a raised grassy bank with his head propped up on his backpack, surveying the party as though it were a stage set laid out before him. He was taking a toke of a large spliff as X joined him.

"I thought you said you only smoked when I was around."

"I knew I'd bump into you", he replied, passing the joint.

They sat and smoked for a while in silence, looking back at the party. It was still busy, but the crowd had thinned a little, the top floor was nearly empty and the remaining dancers moved now like drones in a hive, each on the same sympathetic metronome as each other. He wanted to ask about Clara, but wasn't sure he had the right, so he asked another question instead. "What surprises me", he began, suddenly wondering why he had started down this track, but continuing anyway now that he had begun, "is that this is the most sexually charged crowd I've ever seen, but nobody is actually having sex."

"What, on the dance floor?'

"Well, anywhere."

Gary laughed, "You got that one wrong X! The whole ground floor of Tanoop's place is made up of private rooms, some big, some small, places you can watch and be watched...whatever...Tanoop lays it all on, you just have to bring the sheets back laundered next time."

X grimaced. The whole thing suddenly seemed a bit sordid to him, like some kind of brothel.

Catching X's look, Gary interrupted his thoughts, "What was that expression for?" Mimicking John's voice he went on, "Were you suddenly appalled to discover that people enjoy sexual intercourse? Or perhaps you were unaware that human sexuality is complex and heterogeneous, and this has come as an awful shock to you? Or perhaps you were already aware of these things, but feel that any sexual behaviour that differs from *your* taste is necessarily wrong in some way." He paused before concluding, "John was right to pull you up the other day – You are a prude."

X raised his hands in submission.

It seemed as good a time as any to ask about Clara and he explained what had happened on the dance floor.

Gary thought a while, "Was it during the Manchester set?", he asked. "I think I understand", he said, "But I'm slightly hesitant if she hasn't told you herself." He was quiet a moment, and then coming to a decision that disclosure was acceptable, he began again, "It's about her sister. I never knew her, but they were very close. After a serious family row, apparently, her sister went to live in Manchester – so a temporary falling-out became a forever-unresolved schism. And what you've got to remember is that when she heard the Manchester sounds she's not merely reminded of her sister, she feels actually connected to her. And she's right, in a way, her sister's signature is up in the music the other city's putting out, and Clara can pick out her few notes from the rest of the mix. Clara believes that she's become so highly attuned to the tiniest shifts in her sister's sound that she can determine whether her sister is well or ill, happy or sad. It'll have stopped her in her tracks", he concluded, "and then she can't help but want to concentrate on her sister's 'message' as she sees it. Poor girl, the separation breaks her heart. Leave her alone, is my advice. If she wants to find you later, she will."

Clara didn't return, and Gary and X drifted away from the party before dawn had broken. They strode companionably home through the night, the sounds of the party fading behind them until the calls of night birds and the sound of their own voices were they only noise in the becalmed city. They talked of everything and nothing, in a natural, unthinking lazy rhythm. He had only to begin to form a question in his mind, and it would seem that Gary's thoughts had arrived, by some other, parallel and looping route, at the same juncture. Their succession of tangents, seemed woven into a purposeful common thread, some over-arching meta-argument that they would ultimately resolve without the expenditure of any effort whatsoever.

*

Alone in his bed, he thought about Clara, deeply moved by the sadness of her estrangement from her sister. The reaching out for someone she could never touch seemed so lonely a pain, that X felt an overwhelming sense of tenderness toward her. Tenderness then began to mingle with desire, and then faded again, and, thinking of her vulnerability, a sweet melancholia drifted over him. He thought back over Clara's gathering, thinking how he had felt so elated when he had left with her, not knowing that Clara, having given so much to everyone else, had hidden the secret pain of her sister's absence so well in front of the rest of her family. She had been so alive to the day itself, not allowing what could not be to destroy what was.

He was thinking of her as he closed his eyes.

36. THE FAVOUR

He woke early and set about weeding the potato rows, attacking the task with vigour and a practised hand. He was on the eighth row and well into his stride when he heard a shout and was surprised to see Clara leaning over the gatepost waving at him. He stood up and strode towards her, slapping the dust off his hands on his jeans as he walked.

She was smiling as he approached the gate, "Sorry about the, 'Vanishing woman', act last night", she began, "You know - family!"

He assured her there was no need to apologise.

"Good. I was going to pretend I'd dropped by to return your jacket, but actually I've come to ask you a favour. Do you remember Rollo?"

ROLLO. Clara's brother in law's step Grandson... He shook his head. He seemed to know the genealogy but not the man.

"He was the scraggy-haired kid on the balcony, the one that was shouting..."

X formed a mental image of the ginger haired boy and associated it with the data. He nodded.

Clara continued, "His parents claim to have reached their wit's end with him, and to cut a long story short, they've dumped him and Fazil -that's Fuzzy, the one that jumped off the bridge, on me for the day and I'm already all out of ideas of what to do with them." She laughed, "I thought I'd ask you- you were a teenage boy once, after all, I wasn't! Any suggestions?"

Delighted that she was here, and flattered that she was asking him for advice, he was surprised to find that he did, indeed, have an idea. He had got into a conversation about climbing with Johnone at the stone-breaking, and the man had generously offered to loan him his equipment whenever he wanted. It might work... "OK.", he declared, "I've just got to borrow some kit, I'll meet you back at your place in an hour."

"So commanding!" she laughed, "But you've not told me what we're doing."

"Having an adventure", grinned X. And with a backward wave he set off across the field.

*

Trudging down a narrow track with the boys in single-file behind them like prisoners in a chain gang, it no longer seemed like much of an adventure. A sudden rain shower had left them all drenched, and although the rain had now stopped, their shoulders brushed against the wheat lining the path, causing fat droplets of cold water to fall on them as though they were marching through a car wash. Beneath their feet the path had turned into an oozing squelch of mud the viscosity of potter's clay which clung to their shoes in heavy glutinous lumps and they advanced in slips and slides like trainee clowns.

Rollo had had enough. He had been going on about his trainers for some time. "Look at them! They're trashed!" he moaned, "There's fucking slime on the laces. Slime!" He went quiet for a moment and then started up again, "And look at my jeans", he whined, "I look like Wurzel Gummidge."

"Shut it Rollo!" shouted Fuzzy from behind him.

Clara turned and gave them both a stern look. "Come on Rollo", she said, "You really don't need to worry about clothes *here*, do you?"

"See. Like she says. Shut it Rollo", added Fuzzy helpfully.

"But what if somebody *saw* me?" Rollo muttered under his breath.

At last the sun broke through the clouds, and half an hour later the dank tunnel of wheat had been miraculously transformed into the walls of a golden corridor, roofed, high above, by a cloudless, electric blue sky. At the top of Shepherds Bush Road, the wheat gave way to a small wood, and they passed under the boughs of the plane trees that had once bordered Brook Green. Left untended, the old trees had stretched their limbs across the ghost-width of the old roadway, forming an arbour like a high vaulted cathedral. A family of lemurs made their way through the canopy above them, chittering to each other as they passed. To the left, the old green had been colonised by juniper bushes, and brambles had overwhelmed the tennis courts, creating an impenetrable thicket peppered by bright white flowers and red berries. The path took them out into Hammersmith Broadway. Here all the buildings had crumbled away, collapsing into the crater that had opened up over Hammersmith station, leaving a wide, flat plain covered with meadow grass. At the centre of the meadow, St Paul's church stood alone, surrounded by grazing sheep and tranquil pasture as it would have done in the middle ages.

X led them across the plain and into the green-gloom of vine-shrouded light under the Hammersmith overpass. Pushing through the curtain of vines they broke back into the sunlight, directly opposite Hammersmith Odeon. The abandoned building had been transformed by the green. Ivy running over its steps and twisting round the columns that framed its entrance, had given the old music hall façade the gravitas of a ruined Greek temple.

X led them round the back of the building to begin their ascent, marshalling them up a zig-zag course of fire escape stairwells. Traversing the rusting metalwork was like crossing a series of fraying rope bridges, slats missing or crumbling, bolts creaking under their weight, the tread of their feet kicking down a rain of iron dust on the climbers below. He saw Clara raise an eyebrow from time to time at the wisdom of X's plan, but they proceeded by careful co-operation, the boys exhilarated now, guiding each other across the gaps with no sign of their earlier rancour. At the summit, the boys raced off, clambering over the turrets and sliding down the vaulted arches of its Gormenghast rooftops whooping with delight.

X directed them across the building until they were back above the entrance and looking out over the raised roadway. He carefully unpacked his kit, selecting a grappling hook and firmly securing a line. Having estimated that the distance was about twenty-five metres, he loosed thirty metres of rope and began to swing the hook in a lazy circle around his head until he had sufficient momentum to fling the metal barb out into space. Releasing his grip at exactly the right moment, the hook flew true across the divide, its prongs clattering to the ground over the corrugated metal railing of the central divide. He carefully took up most of the slack, and then with a swift jerk, pulled the hook tight on to the railing, and, keeping the tension in the rope while he bound it tightly around one of the Odeon's turrets.

"Zip Wire!" he declared when he was done.

"Who's first?"

There were no volunteers. Although the drop to the motorway wasn't that steep, a fall to the ground from the wire would have serious consequences, legs and pelvis smashed at least, if you were lucky.

X had to go first.

He stepped off the edge of the theatre roof, wondering just for a second if he had really thought the whole scheme through well enough. He had. He soared across the gap and was soon jumping clear off the potholes in the tarmac on the other side. He signalled to the others to follow.

He saw Fuzzy hesitate, then throw himself off the roof, fear turning to joy on his face, howling with delight as he landed on the deck.

"Wicked!" He said, "Can I do it again?"

Clara crossed last. She stood for a long time with her eyes closed her on the brink, then stored her camera carefully away before gliding gracefully, legs extended and feet arched en pointe, across the void, landing lightly on the roadway beside him.

"That was dangerous stuff", she said, smiling.

X nodded at the boys by way of reply. The young men were

standing shoulder to shoulder looking back at what they had just done, pointing out details and laughing at each other's bullshit stories of bravery.

"OK", she relented, letting out a long breath before laughing, "What next?"

They abseiled down from the roadway under X's instruction, all of them now dropping to the ground with the surety of paratroopers.

X gathered them round to reveal the next stage of his plan. "Tarzan!" he exclaimed.

He was met with a wall of blank faces.

"Really! None of you have looked at those vines and thought 'I want to swing along there, leaping from vine to vine shouting owwwaaa-owaaahha'" He thumped his chest to accompany the king of the jungle's cry, but the kid's faces became more bewildered and Clara looked at him sceptically.

"I'm not sure that's going to work X", she cautioned.

He ignored her, certain that it would work out just as he envisioned it.

He took a running jump, and grabbing a bundle of vines in his arms at the highest point of his leap, swung back and forth using his bodyweight to gain momentum. After a few swings he let go, hurling himself forward along the wall of vines. He had just begun the jungle cry, "Owwa...", when he was cut off short, crashing, full-face into a woody vine stem a couple of metres further along the curtain wall. The air was instantly crushed out of his lungs and, unable to gain any kind of handhold, he slithered to the ground, landing flat-footed, his arms covered in scratches and his hair full of leaf debris. He had travelled no further than a long triple jump from where he'd started. He tried to brave it out. "There you go. The new World Record! Beat that if you can!"

"No", said Rollo, speaking for him and Fuzzy, who nodded his head in agreement as the other boy spoke, "It's a shit idea."

X refused to give up, and thinking he knew why he'd failed, gave it another crack. He'd decided that the problem had been he didn't have enough time in the air to pick his spot, but if he could get a longer swing...

He got a firm grip on a sturdy liana and shook it away from the weave as high up as he could. He repeated the action with two similar tendrils and bound the three together before running as hard as he could in the opposite direction before leaping up, and treating the vines like a rope swing, catapulted himself into space at the top of the second swing. With more time in the air he picked out a vine bunch sturdy enough to keep him aloft, and his momentum was sufficient to break it clear of the vine mass and send him swinging in a second arc.

He'd got the hang of it.

Then suddenly there were no vines to grab. A ten metre stretch of the vine wall had been completely cleared.

He hung in space for a second like a cartoon character above a cliff face, arms and legs flailing before he fell, hard, to the ground. As he landed, pain shot though his spine, there was a loud tearing sound, and something slimy splashed over his hips and buttocks. For a second he thought he'd ruptured his internal organs in the fall, and in his rising panic, was just on the point of screaming 'Flame On!" when he heard the sound of his companions laughing.

He couldn't be that badly hurt.

He looked down.

He had landed in a field of melons. The pulpy mass smearing his hands and wrists was merely burst watermelon, not his own intestines exploded out of his body on impact. His health had been conserved only at the cost of his dignity, and he was still struggling to his feet in the slippery mass when the others caught up with him.

Their laughter was cut short as an old man burst out of a shack across the field, shouting and waving a stick in their direction.

"Oi! You! Johnny-fucking-Weissmuller! What the hell do you think you're playing at?"

X felt deeply foolish. The man was clearly very old, bent almost double as he walked, white haired and with a face as wrinkled as a shrivelled prune. He had destroyed this old boy's carefully cultivated crops while doing something stupid. "I'm really Sorry", he began, "What can I give you in exchange for your..." He looked around, "four... No... five melons" His angle of entry had wiped out an entire row.

The old man was quickly placated. "I could do with some help weeding", he said, "My back..."

X readily agreed to help him, and the old man softened, "Ah don't worry about it, Let the boys eat them rather than let them go to waste, and if you promise me you won't try that bloody nonsense again, that'll satisfy me."

Just as events were reaching an amicable conclusion, the old man caught sight of Clara, who had been hanging back from the rest of the group. "Is that really you Clara?" he asked, but as he spoke it was clear he knew the answer, "You haven't changed", he added, his voice suddenly deadpan.

It took Clara longer for recognition to dawn. "...Arthur?" her voice sounded shocked, "You're..."

"I am how I am Clara", he interrupted, "The decisions we make eh!"

Clara remained silent, her eyes downcast.

X didn't understand why their brief exchange had seemed so charged. Clara had obviously known the old boy at some stage, and he seemed friendly enough. He'd certainly been very decent over the melons. Hoping to break the awkward atmosphere he spoke up, "I'll come back tomorrow and help you with your weeding", he said, reaching to shake the old man's hand, "I've promised the boys one more adventure and I assure you it has nothing at all to do with Tarzan." The old man looked away from Clara, gave X's hand a swift shake and waved them off with a resigned and dismissive gesture as if in the end they'd all disappointed him and he was only too glad to see the back of them.

Clara was a little on edge after the odd encounter, so X left her alone, and went ahead with the boys, leading them on his final destination, the Ark.

The Ark had once been no more than a gargantuan office block designed to look like a ship moored in the city. It had stood, drenched in petrol fumes and largely forgotten, in the triangle between a railway viaduct, a roundabout, and eight lanes of carriageway and up-ramps. Now, covered in a blanket of seaweed-green moss it was as though a galleon, sunk long ago and preserved intact in the alluvial silts of the ocean bed, had resurfaced in the heart of the city. The moss, hugging the outline of the building like a second skin, had enhanced the architect's nautical vision, flowing over the bow-curve of the hull above them, rendering it as proud and beautiful as an Elizabethan man-o-war.

The boys were sizing up the building. "So how are we going to climb it?" asked Rollo, looking up at the smooth walls of slippery moss and the looming overhang of the bow above, "It looks difficult."

He disappointed them with his reply, "We'll go up the stairs", taking a few steps back and pointing upward, "I fancy sitting right up there."

The boys followed the line of his finger, directing them to the crest of the building where, raised above the roof and connected by vine-covered gantries was a kind of crow's nest that looked out over the ship's prow. "We'll come down the outside", he added.

He led them up the leaf-litter strewn steps into a cleft in the building where he expected the door to be. Taking out a hunting knife he began hacking away at the tightly-bound moss, and when he had cleared enough to free it, gave the door a hard shove with his shoulder. It swung open expelling a whoosh of fetid air like the entrance to a sealed Egyptian tomb.

They stepped through the ripped curtain of moss into a huge atrium. A deep green light fell from high above them and the air was wretched with sour old age and thick with fungal spores. Under the blanket of moss, generations of fungi had lived out their lives, eventually digesting every scrap of office furniture before undertaking a fratricidal war for resources among each other's flesh, the evidence of their cannibalistic fight for survival written across the walls in multi-coloured blooms of long-dead hydrae. Higher up, bright white walkways crossed the vast atrium's chasm at odd angles and glass elevators hung stilled at various heights as though eternally waiting for the office workers to return from lunch. A crystal-shaped dome, suspended on a platform half way to the roof, added to the eerie atmosphere, as though they had stumbled into some kind of secret base for Alpha scientists, suddenly abandoned after the project went catastrophically wrong. They climbed swiftly through the lifeless building, their footsteps disturbing the dry dust and sending vertices of fungal spores billowing up and falling in slow graceful spirals behind them.

They were delighted to escape into the fresh air at the top of the climb, and, old hands now at crossing rickety gantries, were soon at the very crest of the building, legs swinging over the roof of the crow's nest and contemplating the view. X let the boys play at abseiling down the mossy surfaces while he and Clara relaxed on the summit. He watched them below him, tethered and carefully belaying each other, sliding back and forth across the Ark's prow, clearing huge swathes of moss from the glass like human windscreen wipers.

It was going to take forever to get that kit clean.

After a while, and when X was convinced that they were taking safety at least moderately seriously, he returned to Clara. They sat back to back, sometimes pointing out landmarks from opposite sides of the city and sometimes in silence, enjoying the illusion of steering the great galleon-building over a vast chick weed covered sea. As time passed, he became more and more aware of the delicious warmth of her back against his, and her breeze-blown hair, licking against the nape of his neck, sent an intoxicating musty odour that seemed to hover around him.

"Thanks X", she said, "Rollo and Fazil have had a great time. They were at each other's throats when we started if you remember, look at them now!"

"Don't thank me until we've got them back without serious injury", he said, and just as he spoke a cry of alarm burst out from Fuzzy below.

X stood up to peer over the edge.

The boys were traversing the cleft over the entrance and Fuzzy had merely given himself a fright when he slipped a few metres down the moss before regaining control of the rope. Rollo stood behind him, tied off against the wall with the safety ropes.

They seemed to have it under control

"No, don't thank me", he said as turned back to her, "It's been a perfect morning." And with those words, he kissed her.

In truth, it was no more than a moment's pressure on her lips, a kiss that could have been made to a sibling or an old friend after a long absence, but given the virginity of their lips, the moment was startling in its intensity.

He sat with his back to her again, his heart racing, sensing the muscles on her back unclench, relaxing into him again, and then her hand reaching behind her to put the tips of her fingers in his.

Her touch was accompanied by a more solemn voice than he had hoped for. "Take it slow X", she said, gently releasing his hand, "No need to rush anything here."

He felt mildly rebuked and sad, but she added, "Take it slow X", she repeated, "and everything will come to you."

It felt like a promise.

37. GAMES AND TING

That afternoon, while strolling with Gary along a rutted dirt track between hedged fields of broccoli, X had an episode of profound disorientation. As he'd raised one footstep from the dust of the track, a sharp pain suddenly erupted on one side of his head and when he placed his foot down again, it was somewhere else, somewhere where gravity no longer functioned and his leg moved without connection with him. It sent him stumbling in the dirt, pushing a wave of nausea, like motion sickness, curdling up from his stomach. And then, suddenly, he'd lost it completely.

*

He had parted from Clara at about midday having arranged to meet her later at a West London gathering that was taking place on Wormwood Scrubs that afternoon, and having freshened up, had swung by Gary's to have some company on the journey. All was well with the world. Everything was as it ever was. There was reliable Gary by his side, the powder blue sky above the dome, the green fields and the crumbling stone of the city he knew so well. Just by glancing at the shape of the fields, he could recall the most precise details about each farmstead, and had only to catch sight of a crop to know its Latin name and probable yield. They greeted everyone they passed with a smile and when Gary spoke their name a tumbling back-story of their lives would unfold in his mind. Everything around him was as utterly familiar as ever.

Then the sudden pain in his head and suddenly his sense of *always* knowing this world slipped, and the scene in front of his eyes flickered like a TV with a faulty connection. The sudden, urgent thought rushed into his mind. Who was Gary? He felt like a life-long friend but he had only just met him, hadn't he? How long had he been here?

He knew the answer. Three days.

How could that be?

And Clara?

The same paradoxes and impossibilities. He knew that the exquisite tenderness he felt toward her, the aching longing to reach across the few millimetres that separated them, the exhilaration that flooded his blood-stream like amphetamines whenever he thought of her, were the symptoms of new love, of courtship and beginnings. And yet, he also felt, with almost equal certainty, that he had known her a long time and loved her from a distance, untouchable and perfect, just out of reach; but not her, some essence of her…

The image of a beautiful blond woman with startling blue eyes flashed in front of him, burning an after-image on his retina like a subliminal advertisement.

Eva.

A name without data attached.

The pain in his head returned, and the girl disappeared, replaced, bizarrely, by the open door of an enormous fridge looming above him, a huge carton of orange juice laid open on its side, slowly emptying its contents from the top rack. He watched the sticky orange droplets forming a pool in the vegetable tray,

"That's going to be a hassle to clean up", he found himself thinking.

Then he was back, Gary's voice coming through the fog like a tranquilising balm. X could hear the concern in his voice before he felt the strong arm that helped him upright. As his vision returned, his first sight was the softness of the eyes in his friend's ravaged face, and it brought him back to the surface with a deep exhalation of breath.

"Are you all right?" Gary asked again.

"I'm fine", X stuttered, and, as he said the words, he realised he was, indeed, fine. The wave of sudden alienation had passed. The birds sang, the sun shone, and he was here, blissfully alive in this moment and this glorious day. "I just tripped", he said unnecessarily, and to avoid any further questions about himself, asked one instead. "Where exactly are we going again?

Gary explained that they were heading for the solstice gathering in the fields behind the old prison. "This is the biggest gathering of the year", he went on, "as it's midsummer, but we hold these meetings throughout the year, on a lunar cycle, the big day coinciding with the full moon. People come from all over the city", he continued, "but mostly from the western half. Some come a week early and set up the 'ting' – that's for want of a better word", he added, "no-one can agree on its name and it doesn't matter anyway...It's held in a tent, like a small big top with a hole in the roof", he made a sweeping circular gesture with his arms, "People come to talk and debate about issues of interest to all...or at least some", he laughed, giving up on already vague explanation, "...you drift in and out", he concluded, "You'll see."

So it's like a parliament?" asked X.

"You'd think so", Gary replied, "But no. There's no-one in charge, anyone can speak and there's no authority to enforce any decisions."

"Oh", was the best X could reply, wondering what the point of it was at all, but before he could ask, Gary had moved on.

"Of course, a market's grown up around the ting. It'll be busy, several hundred stalls I expect. More people come to barter and exchange, meet old friends, take part in the games, get drunk, that sort of thing, than get involved in the debates, like I said... You drift in and out." He looked up at the sun, "It's about two o'clock now", he went on, "so the market's entering its second phase. There'll be more interesting trades now and the atmosphere will be less frantic."

X asked what the first phase had been, and then instantly regretted asking the question.

Gary explained that the day started with producers exchanging foodstuffs until each had sufficient for their needs. "It's chaotic, but strangely ordered" he stated, "and remember X, it's all barter and were all farmers."

X felt none the wiser.

"OK", he continued, "When you have what you need in terms of food, you have choices. You can take your surplus and explore another part of the market, where you can exchange it for different kinds of goods...I don't know.... Pots and pans, crockery, alcohol, tools...that kind of thing. Or for services in kind of course", he added. "Or if you don't feel you need anything in particular, you can leave your surplus for someone else to use or trade. The soil's very fertile and you know how well these crops grow..."

X nodded.

"...but there's still plenty of reasons that can leave you turning up at market short of what you need, pests, bad decisions, misfortune of one kind or another...." He waived the bad news away with his hands, "Anyway, it's a surprisingly efficient system of distribution. There's very little waste."

They turned off Scrubs Lane shortly after the underpass, and pushing past a small flock of sheep, emerged on to the grassland of Wormwood Scrubs. In the distance the rainbow awning of the big top was clearly visible, raised above a jumble of wooden shacks piled like a shanty-town around its base. They passed the old prison on their left. A full grown ash had burst through the West wing, and stairwells and cells opened into thin air, their interiors exposed like Broadway stage sets. The East Wing was largely still intact, although a hole the size of a tube tunnel had been blasted through its walls as though the inmates had dynamited their way out in a final cataclysmic escape. A solitary dark-skinned figure in an ochre robe sat on the bars of a makeshift pen in the courtyard, watching half a dozen llama pulling mouthfuls of fresh hay from a bale at his feet.

As they strolled past, X asked what the prison was used for now.

"Not much", Gary replied, "Some of the cells were used as animal pens for a while, but they proved too cramped for the cattle and the sheep butted up against the walls and got nervous.

The obvious question occurred to X.

"What about criminals?" he asked, "What do you do with them?"

"The truth is", Gary started, "Is that I have no direct experience of it. Crime, that is. Not here. There's any number of explanations for why there's no crime", he continued, "but I'm happy to accept the view that when all the old hierarchies and their associated authority, power and control were gone, we drew a collective breath, looked at humankind anew, and no longer felt the need to cheat or steal or lie or possess." He smiled, pleased with the way he had expressed his case.

X pondered a moment, "But what if someone comes along without this ... enlightened mind set?" he asked, "What do you do then?"

"I've got no experience of this X", Gary was anxious to point out, "But there is a kind of solution – it leads to exile." He tried to explain, beginning, "It's a bit like the Anglo-Saxon tradition of declaring someone a *nithing*, a nothing, if you like. A collective decision that someone's actions have been so serious that their membership of society has been revoked. No one would trade with a nithing, but more importantly no one would converse with a nithing. They'd be able to scrabble around and get enough food to live, but the mental torment of being sent to perpetual Coventry would eventually drive them away, hopefully to another part of the city where they would build a better relationship with their fellow human beings. I suspect it's not a perfect solution, but as I say, I've never had to experience it."

They entered the market, making their way down the crowded dirt streets and wooden shacks that had formed a temporary village around the circus top. Winding quickly through the crowds, they passed stalls piled high with fruit and vegetables, agricultural implements, radio transmitters and wind turbines, some neatly housed on firm table tops under cowling, others no more than a collection of scavenged junk laid out on blankets on the ground. Gary guided him through the press with an old school deftness as though he was heading to the front of a sound system at Carnival. They entered a narrow street where sturdily-built shops with pennants bearing the symbol of their trade flew on long poles above each entrance. The anvil and hammer symbol of blacksmiths fluttered in the breeze next to the soldering iron of electronics and the beaming yellow sun of solar power. In another street revellers sat on benches with flagons of beer, stilt-walkers and fire-breathers weaved through the crowd, and spitted sheep turned slowly over open fires. With the smoke from the braziers, the smell of roasting mutton in the air, and the stall pennants fluttering in the breeze, the scene was like a ribald medieval fayre, but one without lords or castle. Gary guided them just as quickly though this section and into the central tent.

Stopping inside the canvas, X saw that hay bales had been stacked in tiers around a wide circle at the centre of the tent. About fifty people were sat on the bales listening to a speaker standing inside the centre circle. They scrambled over the bales and squeezed into the gap between a middle-aged couple and a young man with dark brows and a neatly trimmed goatee. The young man was listening earnestly to the speaker, leaning forward with his chin propped up on knee and elbow. He flinched at the disturbance as X and Gary settled in beside him. In the centre a tall thin woman with long dark hair was talking in a shrill voice and making expansive and slightly frantic hand gestures with her long thin fingers. Each digit was adorned by Celtic weaved silver bands, ankhs and moulded crystal jewellery, and three entwining jade necklaces chimed like a glockenspiel as she paced up and down.

"What's she talking about?" X asked the red-faced balding man sitting next to him.

"Potlach", he replied, "Some system they're trying in Camden she says". He continued, nodding toward the woman speaking, "You earn status in your community, apparently, by giving gifts greater in value than the gifts you receive."

The woman sitting next to him, who X took to be his partner, a blousy, chubby-faced woman with grey hair and bright, alert eyes, leant over, "But why would you be interested in status?" she asked, "I just don't get it."

"So why did you come then?" barked the young man with the goatee, his voice dripping with contempt.

The woman replied swiftly, but in an even and measured tone, explaining that that by attending she had, "given herself the opportunity, and the pleasant experience, of considering the political philosophy of a system known as 'potlach' that she had never encountered before, and, having considered its merits and disadvantages had become unconvinced of the soundness of its fundamental premise."

The young man was quiet after that.

Eventually the speaker ran out of energy and sat down and there was a waving of hands from the circle.

"At last", X's neighbour sighed, "That woman's a bloody nightmare."

As he spoke an old man on the other side of the circle with a sagging face and big bleary eyes had risen with difficulty to his feet. The expression on X's neighbour's face turned to dismay, "Blimey!" he exclaimed, "Not old George. That's it love, lets nip off for a drink. I'm not sitting through half an hour of potato yields." And with that, the couple climbed down off the bales and disappeared through the tent flap into the market.

The old man began speaking, but his voice was so frail that it failed to carry across the circle. "Speak up!" someone shouted, and when that didn't work, a chorus of "Get the boy up!" broke out. Eventually a sullen looking teenage boy was nudged to his feet and stood, grudgingly, next to his grandfather and began relaying the old man's words to the crowd by shouting out what the old man was mumbling with the intonation of a deaf translator. Despite this severe impediment to communication, it was clear that the old man had undertaken some meticulous research into the spacing of potato seedlings of various varieties and their subsequent yields. X found himself surprisingly interested, but the boy, unable to pronounce the plant's Latin names correctly, was constantly interrupted by his grandfather and the whole thing became completely incoherent.

There was a wave of impatient shuffling around the circle and a murmur of discontent began to rise. The old man came to an abrupt halt in his monologue and stood in silence, blinking owlishly at the crowd. A grey-haired matron, sitting behind the speaker, gave the young man a quick kick, and the boy took it as a cue to announce that anyone who wished to discuss his grandfather's experiments further should join him outside the circle. A few figures stepped down from the bales and followed the old man out of the circle.

A broad-shouldered, heavy-set man with a soft Welsh accent gained the floor after the old man's departure, ceded temporary authority by some unseen mechanism that seemed acceptable to all. Standing at ease in the circle, he spoke with a measured pace and with both clarity and some passion, about a plan to re-open part of the river Fleet, buried in the growth of Victorian London and disappearing completely from view in the 19th century. He explained that he didn't feel it was a *necessary* project – there seemed to be no serious issues with fresh water anywhere in Bakhuninland.

"As long as the pumping stations are maintained", shouted someone from the back.

The speaker acknowledged the comment, continuing to explain that for him it was a romantic vision really, the pleasure of liberating the old river from its centuries long concrete bondage seemed likely to create beauty, he hoped, and seemed symbolically apt for the age. He explained the section of the river's course he felt was the most promising to start with, but cautioned that it was entirely possible that the river's path had been diverted irrevocably into the deep cisterns and underground rivers of the tube network.

The speaker's subject was clearly of interest to many in the crowd and a debate involving twenty or so interested parties batted back and forth across the circle. There was a great deal of standing up and sitting down, the occasional loud voice and short bursts where everyone talked over each other, but the discussion was surprisingly ordered in other ways, each speaker allowed time to fully expand their point, and although this gave some license to give emphasis to some minor aspect of the issue and delay progress, after half an hour's debate, a broad strategy had been agreed. Seeming to reach some natural conclusion, the debaters stepped away from the circle en mass and took up a position in a big huddle at the far side of the tent.

Gary indicated to X that he intended to join them, leaving X alone on the bales.

X gave the next speaker, a young black woman who looked like a Caribbean Modesty Blaze, only the briefest of chances, and although he was sure water transport on the Thames was as important as the dazzling young woman was saying, he slipped of the bales and headed off in search of Clara.

*

They were lying on the grass by the running track.

He had bumped into her almost immediately he'd stepped outside the tent and they had strolled happily through the market together.

She was laughing at him about the coconut shy. X fought a rear guard action, trying to distract her with the same point he'd made ten times already, "It's their fault", he argued, "Your supposed to win the coconut you knock off at a coconut shy, but they're probably the last three mouldy examples left in London, so I was forced to make a choice."

"But you know you're missing the point X", Clara interrupted, still laughing, the question is, "Why would anyone in their right mind think that a stuffed badger was just the right prize to win a girl's heart?"

"It's kind of cute?" he ventured.

"In a dead animal kind of way." she replied, laughing again and, lying flat on her back she raised the stuffed mammal at arms-length above her chest and stared into its cold glass eyes. X leant over and grabbed the badger off her, clowning around and pretending it was attacking him, ending up with the badger in a half-nelson pinned beneath him in the grass.

"Idiot."

Gary, Tanoop, Levi, Kate and Rhiannon had wandered over, and lay scattered in the grass around them, chewing the ends of long-stalked grass and staring up into the sky. The sun had long passed its peak, but it was still a lazy summer's afternoon, full of peace and with only the scent of freshly mown grass hanging above them in the air.

Levi stood up, picked up the badger and raising it above his head on a single extended arm, announced, "Fellow Olympians- what events shall we test ourselves with today?"

"Oh Shit", said Clara, "I've signed on for the long distance,"

"Me too!" chimed in Rhiannon,

"When does it start?"

"You've got ten minutes", reassured Levi.

"I've put you down for the sprint with me X", Levi went on, "How many do you need for a tug-of-war?"

"Seven", said Kate.

Levi counted up. "Great that's us then."

Tanoop objected, "These hands are delicate things", he bemoaned, declaring them, "precious instruments", and holding his hands out in front of him with his fingers as though they were precious jewellery. He was collectively booed and shouted down by his friends, and their entry for the tug-of-war was settled.

"You try getting a decent manicure", moaned Tanoop.

Levi threw the badger at him.

"What about you Gary?" asked Levi.

Gary was lying on his back in the afternoon sun, supine, the only indication that he was alive was the twitching of the grass stick he was chewing, like a sheep mulling over the cud. "I'm the audience", he replied.

"I'm not having that!" declared Kate, and laughing, she dragged

Gary up from the grass, and, linking arms, she propelled Gary across the field like they were competitors in a three legged race.

Rhiannon and Clara slipped away to the start of their race, and X followed the others toward the frame at the far end of the field, that X had assumed was set up for pole vault. As they drew closer it was clear that it was designed for a far less sophisticated sport. A stocky, red-faced girl with long, blond hair, stood facing them with her back to the frame holding a pitchfork. She plunged it into a hay bale and raised it, testing its weight briefly on the prongs before flinging it over her shoulder, sending the bale up and over the rope-bar behind her.

There was a ripple of applause from the small crowd.

Kate dragged Gary into the fray, and so focussed were the two of them on beating each other, that all the other competitors were soon eliminated and it became a contest between just between the two of them. Gary, his tattooed skin sheathed in sweat and dust, groaned and shouted obscenities each time he hefted one over, and then quickly apologised to the crowd for his bad language. He was clearly a strong man but lacked any craft in his throws and X was fairly certain Kate had his measure. She strode up to each new height exuding confidence, spat quickly on her hands, rubbed them together and rolled up her sleeves before sending the bale high over the bar in one smooth motion of arm, thigh and shoulder.

He saw Clara and Rhiannon pass by on their long circuit around the scrubs, they were both jogging easily near the rear of the field, chatting away happily. She smiled and waved as she passed, and X returned the gesture, watching her run fluidly but without haste away from him, already re-absorbed in her conversation. He had the strongest sensation that this image, of Clara turning away from him with a smile, would merge with the sweet scent of the grass to form a few frames of cine-film memory that he would hold for life. The moment was nothing and somehow everything. Every innocent summer's day ever, the memory of the first glance of a young man's future bride across the village green, the same memory that would also be his last thought on the day he died.

He turned reluctantly back to the competition as she disappeared from view to hear a gargantuan cry of "FUUUUUUUUUCK", from Gary, but this time the bale crashed into, but not over, the bar. Kate, already clear at the height, began whooping with delight, and Gary, defeated and covered in scratches from the brittle hay, slumped to the ground at her feet. Kate celebrated by running around in small circles, punching the air in victory and hollering like a Sioux chief. She was pursued and eventually caught by the bushy-bearded and very fat man who had won last year, and grinning from ear to ear she knelt down and accepted the victor's wreath of bound rosemary on her head. Her friends formed an honour guard to clap Kate back into the group, cheering and slapping her on the back as she passed under. Kate was clearly quite moved now that the original exhilaration had passed, and they pretended not to see her tears as Rhiannon hugged her.

In contrast, they fell apart hopelessly in the tug-of-war.

On paper, the team had enough muscle, but Kate and Gary, were exhausted from the bale-toss, Gary barely able to stand, and Kate largely putting on a brave face, and although X put his back into it, Rhiannon could contribute little more than spirit. They might still have made it if they had not been fatally undermined by Tanoop's refusal to *actually* touch the rope for fear of inflicting burns on his delicate skin. His solution was to wrap his arms around the rope and hang from his elbows, contributing nothing to the pulling and adding his bodyweight to the burden borne by the rest of his team. They were dragged, slipping and stumbling over the line by a team of middle-aged accountants in cut-down chinos who didn't appear to have dropped a single bead of sweat on their unbuttoned shirts in pursuit of victory.

There wasn't much time to mock Tanoop before the start of the sprint, and as Levi and X hurried over to take up their positions, the DJ gave a lazy wave and drifted away with another crowd, a girl in hot-pants already glued to his arm.

Arriving just in time for the race they were ushered into line by naked John, who was officiating and, in some strange homage to the original Greek games, had chosen to anoint his entire body in oil. He glistened and dripped alarmingly on the start line like a giant hairy foetus. As X crouched, it occurred to him that the grass was long and he would get more traction barefoot, so he hastily kicked off his shoes. Levi was lined up to his right, still immaculate as ever, the creases in his white tailored shorts as sharp as blades, and with a high, round-collared, white singlet he looked every inch a priest superhero. The gun went and X was smoothly up from his crouch, arms pumping and knees high, he lifted his head, relaxed his shoulders, and drove forward in full stride. Twenty to thirty metres out and he was ahead of the pack, a cool wind on his face, the track laid out like a magic carpet in front of him, the other runner's falling away in formation behind him like trailing geese. Half way down the straight he hit maximum velocity, and knowing any further straining for speed would only harden his footfalls and slow him down, he concentrated on staying fluid and relaxed, each stride as smooth as the last, the tape drawing magnetically to his chest.

Levi passed him like a freight train.

It had taken him longer to get his greater bulk up to full speed, but now his sheer power propelled him past X as though he were standing still, breaking the tape a good metre and a half ahead of him.

X was second.

"Bollocks", he said, hands on knees, crouched over and gasping for breath.

Levi was leaping around, completing a back flip that looked positively suicidal for such a big man, and then kissing everyone, even greasy, naked John while he placed the rosemary wreath on his head. He placed a big smacker of a kiss on X's lips, embracing him and Clara in a big bear hug while ruffling their hair.

Clara was consoling, "Never mind", she said, "No one ever beats Levi. You're still my hero." And with that she linked her arms around the back of his neck and pulled him down into a long deep swoon of a kiss, her tongue deep in his mouth.

She broke away smiling and with raised eyebrows.

She took a step away, then reached back for his hand, towing him stunned and happy back to the group.

Everyone's spirits were high after the games, so Clara's suggestion that they record their exulted spirits and put it out into the day as a group was met with universal enthusiasm, and they headed back into the market to seek out a mixing booth.

Inside the booth Clara and X put on headphones and standing side by side connected themselves to each other and the mixing desk by umbilical wires. Clara, more familiar with the controls, took the lead, subtly altering the frequency and pattern of her tune until it wound itself through the peaks and troughs of his wave form, creating a pattern of less jagged rhythms, a smoother, deeper harmony in the mix. It was impossibly sexy, a blind blending of him and her in sound, and in the shell casings of their headphones they were as alone in their intimacy as on a desert island. But it wasn't quite right, thought X, and, fumbling, but gradually mastering the controls, he took some of the raw edges off his sound, making fatter beats that followed the same frequency, but were more apt for his feelings on this day, and he fed these back to Clara. She blended them again until his and her sounds were interwoven around each other's like the entangled limbs of lovers. The mix completed, X closed his eyes and let their music flow through him. He could feel her soft breath on his face and when he opened his eyes she was looking directly into his pupils, boldly, her face no more than a foot away. It was a look of such penetrative honesty and openness, that its passage not only bored its way directly into his soul, but flayed her of all protective covering, leaving her open, precious, nakedly-vulnerable in front of him. It only lasted a few seconds. Such a look could not have stood immobility long, it required consummation, an actual falling into each other that was impossible,

Here.

They were jolted sharply back into the world by the flat of Levi's long bony hands hand slapping on their shoulders. Ebullient and beaming, Levi embraced them both in a giant bear hug and began gesticulating wildly at them to take of their headphones, his lips moving as though he were shouting, but soundless to their muffled ears. They emerged back into the rush of the forgotten day like a train leaving a long tunnel, the rush of sound hurtling in all at once, the shouts in the street, the music bursting from the speakers, and Levi's laughter booming like a bass drum over it all.

"Come on love birds. Snap out of it and hand over the tune", he demanded.

Levi took control of the mixing desk and then began to blend the six of them together in the music, focussing on his task with great care and attention to detail.

Headphones on, they listened to Levi working the harmonies and rhythms. At first to X it felt like drowning, as the beautiful melody of his and Clara's fusion was submerged under the other's patterns. But as Levi worked, X could hear it re-surface, now blended with something truer to the wider day than merely X and Clara's story. The tune Levi created was a little ragged, but somehow included, the bright sunshine, Gary and Kate's battle, Levi's power in the sprint and the gentleness of Rhiannon's presence. They looked across at each other, deeply connected by the sound and the story it told of them. To complete the edit, Gary stepped out of the booth to collar Tanoop who was passing, surrounded by a gaggle of identikit Malaysian women with shiny hair and shiny mini-skirts. Dragging him away from the women, Gary drew Tanoop to the desk and fed him the collective tune.

"Now *you* want the use of these immaculate hands, it's a different story", he pointed out, before proceeding to make a few delicate adjustments to Levi's mix – and then they were up, out in the speakers above the shack with the rest of the London sound, distinct, upbeat, a new little score in the sound stream, friendship and new love floating in the summer breeze.

38. UNDERGROUND

They'd drifted back out of the market, and now lay again in the grass by the running track, listening to the city sounds on a small radio, and riding out the last phase of a triumphant day together as a group of friends. Although it was now well into the evening, it was midsummer's day, and the sun was both hot, and still high enough in the sky to cast shadows on the ground the same length as the figures crossing the grassland, liquid black shapes trailing behind them like flattened wraiths. X lay on his back looking up at the sky with the back of Clara's head propped against his chest. She turned to him, and something in her expression told him exactly what she was going to say before she said it.

"I know I freaked out last time", she began, "but it was so unexpected and... But today...I'd like to share a bit of my happiness with her... Hear how Manchester has responded to the solstice, pick up her part in it..." she trailed off. "I might get wistful X," she spoke up again, quietly, "But I won't be like last time. I promise!"

She turned the radio to the Manchester sounds.

It was instantly apparent that something was wrong.

Even to X's untutored ear the music sounded profoundly different; drunk, he thought at first and almost laughed. But it wasn't happy disarray; there was a queasy lurch to the music, a slurring of sound that felt like sickness rather than mirth. Ugly belches came in waves, coagulating around the healthy rhythms and pulling the flow of the music away, like audio-tape slipping on the reel.

Clara was instantly silent. He felt her body snap rigid against his side and her hand dropped from his like a dead weight.

X couldn't identify Clara's sister in the sound, Gary had explained that you had to know someone intimately to be able to separate their signature from the sound texture.

But Clara could.

She leapt to her feet and began pacing rapidly up and down, each gesture a stab of her panic, muttering to herself, "Sick. Really Sick" over and over again. "Oh God what can I do?" she cried out, her pacing now that of a caged animal, turning back and forth at the limits of invisible bars.

As she paced, X felt drawn into the cage with her, the dome seemed to press down on him from above, sealing him in; no longer a protective shield but what it really always had been, the walls of a jail.

At the furthest end of her pacing from him she suddenly stopped. "What can I do?" she screamed. She clutched fistfuls of her hair, "I've got to get out of here." Then she ran, sprinting across the field away from them, desperately trying to outrun her fear.

X stood to start off after her, but Gary grabbed him by the arm.

"Let her go X", he said, in a stern, almost fatherly voice, "It doesn't necessarily mean what Clara thinks it does X. All city sounds get sick sometimes.... And Clara isn't exactly...rational...about her sister", he added, "Let her calm down first."

"Not this time Gary." X shook off his friend's hand and set off in the direction Clara had gone.

"Don't do anything stupid X!" Gary shouted after him, "Remember there's nothing outside but heartache and bitterness."

His words seemed oddly cryptic to X, and he forgot them quickly as he jogged across the field after Clara.

*

He ran at an easy pace. Assuming that Clara was heading back to her apartment, he was content to let her get out of sight, and thought it would be better anyway if he gave her a few minutes to compose herself before he got there. She opened the door red-eyed and stony-faced, but as soon as she saw X, burst into gut-wrenching sobs, and burying her head in his chest, wept inconsolably.

She pulled away from him, blowing her streaming nose on a tissue, and wiping her eyes, she took a sequence of long breaths and regained control.

"I'm going to get out", she said, "I'm going to see her. I can't stand this anymore."

X didn't know what to say, despite her desperate desire to see her sister, he knew he had to remind her of the impenetrable barrier that made Manchester as distant as Mars,

"We can't get out of the domes, love", he finally said.

"But what if we can?"

*

Clara had two possible means of escape. When she outlined both options, X had felt they were both were equally implausible, so they had made the decision with a flip of a coin.

Heads for the river. Tails for Heathrow. It had come up tails.

Heathrow it was then.

In the weeks she had spent out at Heathrow with Raj, Azim and Rebecca, she explained, she had wandered down into the deserted station beneath the airport. At the time she had been too scared to do any more than flash a torch into the darkness, before the cavernous, rat-scuttling dark had caused her to race back up the stilled escalators into the daylight above. Even at the time she had found herself wondering what had happened to those tunnels that ran so close to the barrier.

"On most of the tube system", she explained, "by the time the network reached the barrier line the trains were already up and out of the ground, shuffling commuters back to the suburbs on raised embankments, but at the airport they had to lay the track deep underground to avoid undermining the runways above. And what's more", she added, "They were extending the line when the barrier went up. "It's just possible that the deep tunnels beyond Heathrow extend beyond the barrier itself. All we have to do is walk as far as we can and see what happens. I don't know, maybe there's a ventilation shaft or a maintenance access point that surfaces on the other side."

It seemed a slim chance to X, but safer than Clara's other option, so, equipped with camping gear, torches, a copy of her cousin's map and as much food as they could carry, they selected two sturdy looking mountain bikes from the mound still piled up outside Clara's steps and, swinging by Johnone's place on the way to borrow climbing gear for the second time, they had set off on the dusty road out of town. The path soon became a deeply rutted track that weaved its way through plots of farmland and then out into the wastes of Hounslow Heath, soon they were jumping potholes under the shade of wizened thorn trees. X led, enjoying himself and taking every opportunity to get both wheels airborne, standing on the pedals like he was riding a BMX. Clara kept up, riding more smoothly and just as fast, displaying the skill of a seasoned club cyclist. She had learnt fast. When she'd first sat on the bike, she'd tottered alarmingly, and had been able to make no more than a wobbling half-circle before slipping off the saddle. X had briefly wondered whether they would have to walk. But then she'd closed her eyes, and after meditating for no more than a few seconds, got back on the bike, took two deep breaths and rode away like a confident teenager. He had cheered.

The journey to the barrier had taken no more than a couple of hours and judging by the length of the shadows, the sun looked set to hang above the horizon for some time yet.

What time did it get dark on midsummer's day? He could never remember.

They'd had to lay down their bikes when the track petered out in the savannah of tall grass that began at Hatton's Cross. From that distance, the barrier; that had first appeared as a white smudge on the horizon, now looked like a light evening mist, skimming the surface of the broad flat land. As they grew closer, pushing their way through the long grass, it seemed a feature of the land itself, a vast bank of white chalk cliffs perhaps, or maybe a stretch of snow-covered Sugarloaf Mountain. There was a distinct moment, however, when it seemed to detach from the earth completely and become a feature of the sky, a razor straight line separating the air into two immiscible layers, like oil and vinegar, or a cocktail before stirring.

Close up it was nothing so poetic. Just prison bars.

The barrier loomed above him as a solid wall, sheer and completely smooth, a sheet of ice-white nothingness rising into the air. It flowed in a fluid, queasy undulation across the land, like some kind of giant blancmange mould, a softened sickly wave across the breadth of the horizon. Rising some thirty metres above him, the wall came to an abrupt halt, above which the dark, almost navy blue sky and wisps of fine cloud took over, like the decorative border on a blank canvas.

It chilled him to the core.

The walls of this prison were impregnable and somehow contemptuous at the same time. The soft texture the barrier seemed to possess made it seem like the kind of cage a nursery school pet would be kept in, a pressed-plastic bubble designed to keep the dumb animal safe, secure and utterly oblivious of the world beyond.

"Can we jump over it?" asked X, knowing that they couldn't.

"It does look you could reach the top doesn't it", said Clara, "But it's an optical illusion, something about the angle of the light, whatever height you look at it from its always opaque, and you can never reach the top. It's a rainbow's end. A few hot air balloons went up at one time, and they couldn't see any more than you, and one of them confirmed that it really is a dome the hard way. Sharp winds and disintegrating force fields, you can see why ballooning didn't become popular."

X picked up a stone and threw it towards the barrier. About ten metres out it flashed with light, emitting a small crackle like a firework spluttering, and disappeared, vaporised into nothingness. He threw another stone, this time flinging it as high as he could it hit the line of the barrier with blue sky behind, spark, crackled and was gone.

"Let's get underground", he said.

They stepped cautiously onto the escalators, their torches cutting out bright round circles in the pitch dark of the cavern below. Every surface was covered in a thick, even layer of dust that carpeted the platform with a fine down, the marks of Clara's footprints from her previous visit still visible in the dust like Armstrong's imprints on the surface of the moon. The immaculate velvet surface of the platforms was disrupted along their edges by smears and splatters of guano, shining as white as toothpaste in X's flashlight beam. The only sound in the darkness was their soft footfalls and the scuttling of rats disturbed by their passage. He swung the torch up to the high ceiling. Its light disturbed two hanging bats who fell and after one leathery-winged slap, glided across the vault silently, above him.

X shivered.

It was cold in the dark, but the shiver was of fear.

The changes in the world above were so familiar to him, and seemed largely both beautiful and benign, that he had forgotten all that had been lost in the transformation to this new London. In the stilled and silent station, it felt as though a neutron bomb had been detonated on the platform and the press of people had been obliterated in its blast, sweeping them away as they squeezed out of the narrow trains, their bones, disintegrating as they struggled to keep their kids together on the crowded platform. Ghost images flooded through his mind, saris and turbans, Bermuda shorts and sober business suits, immaculate air hostesses, heels clacking, wheeling luggage like poodles behind them, big shouting West African families unloading suitcases and microwaves, women wrapped in vivid green and gold as glamorous as royalty, tired warehousemen with stubble and cheap shoes, shop-workers with name tags, excited children and sniping couples.

All gone.

His torchlight picked out a frozen lost past, as obliterated as Herculaneum or Pompeii, lacking only the charred bodies.

Stepping off the escalator onto the dusty platform, its strangeness suddenly seemed familiar. He recalled the rush of a train through a deserted U-bahn station in Berlin, part of a loop left stranded on the Eastern side of another walled city. Its platform, also layered in dust, had been guarded by a young soldier with a rifle. As the train flashed through the dimly lit station, the soldier had raised his gun, levelling it directly at the windows of the passing train. At the sight of a rifle barrel pointed at his forehead, X had flinched and started to get out of his seat, but as the image of the soldier clattered down the windows in magic lantern frames, not a single West Berliner had raised as much as an eyebrow above their folded newspapers.

Would there be guards at this wall too?

They padded across the soft dust and with a silent nod to each other, jumped down from the platform on to the tracks, following the tunnel that headed west.

Their head torches lit only the few metres in front of them and outside the arc of the light's tepid beams, the darkness closed in around them, blind-black and absolute. As they walked on, X couldn't help trying to avoid standing on the third rail, and as the darkness filled the tunnel behind them, he became haunted by the feeling that, without a moment's notice, the rail would become live, a whoosh of air would begin to boom from the darkness, and a sudden blinding light would throw twin Giacometti shadows ahead of them for an instant before they were crushed under the screeching wheels of the ghost train bearing down on them.

In order that they didn't blunder across the barrier line in the dark, only discovering that the force-field was still active when they had both been vaporised, X walked carrying a long branch, which he held out in front of him and braced and under his armpit as though it were a wooden lance. Advancing from sleeper to sleeper in an awkward, jolting passage, strides either too long or too short for comfort, the branch would gradually droop to the ground until it snagged in the rails, tripping him. X led them on into the darkness with a hobbled, camel-like motion lance held aloft like a blindfold Don Quixote.

Clara reached for his arm and they stumbled forward along the tracks.

"I'm scared", she said, her voice ringing eerily clear and true, echoing like a bell off the tunnel walls.

Her words shook X from his own unquiet reverie and he gained courage from her fear. With her confession he remembered that he wasn't alone, and with the fear now shared it became only the background texture, not the whole story, of their great adventure. He pulled her close, putting down the stick and stretching his free arm around her shoulder. "It's only darkness", he said.

"It's not the darkness I'm scared of", her voice timid now, "It's what we're doing." She was quiet a moment and then went on, "I'm sorry X. Sorry to have dragged you into all this." She hushed him before he could object, "I got so hyped up I'd forgotten about Them."

"Them?"

"Them. The ones who built the domes." She laughed, a bitterness in her voice he hadn't heard before, "Morlocks, we used to call them. The ones that decided that most of humanity was merely a drain on the bottom line, and chose to seal us of like contaminants, leaving us to tear each other apart or rot or whatever they hoped would happen to us, Them! There still out there X.

X thought for a moment how very young she must have been when it all happened and how tough it must have been for her as kid.

"If we get out of here, we'll have to face them again. It's been a long time X. What will they have become after all these years?"

"Socialists?" he suggested.

*

They had walked in better spirits for a while, chatting lightly, but soon were dulled to silence by the monotony of their march. Along the tunnel walls the same cabling stretched forever into the darkness, the twin rails running to grey at the end of the torch beam, always coming together, never arriving, and each hobbled step from sleeper to sleeper the same as the last. The effect was hallucinatory. The blackness they walked through was absolute and all-encompassing, wiping out their existence behind them with each forward stumble. It became as though they were utterly detached from their surroundings in the endless dark, unsure if it was them advancing in their twin cones of light, or whether the walls were moving slowly past them, and they were merely treading water, holding station against the flow of rock. No sense of distance or time was possible. There were no reference points to hold on to. It seemed endless. It might have been no time at all.

Finally, the torchlight picked out the metallic hulk of an abandoned track-laying tender that marked the abrupt end of the rails. By the time they had squeezed around its suspended mechanical arm, frozen above them like some monster's claw, it was clear that they were entering an unfinished section of tunnel. Up to this point, the walls had been backed by huge concrete hoops corseted by steel bands, now the props were make-shift buttresses and joists, and the tunnel was sealed only by a thin concrete crust. Water seeped through the walls, sliding soupily into shallow puddles on the uneven mud floor. They had just got used to their new, slippery progress through the dark, when, passing under a ragged archway of cracked stone, the tunnel walls dropped suddenly away. Standing in a wall-less black void X was overwhelmed by vertigo, and fought for his balance as though finding his footing on a pitching deck at sea.

He raised his torch to the roof. The light flickered faintly on the roof of a vast vault some thirty to forty metres above them. He scanned the torch looking for a wall on the other side. Nothing.

The cavern they had entered was huge.

He shone his torch into the darkness ahead of him. Marking the path of some ancient watercourse, a glutinous smear of larvae-white stone, meandered into the cavern's depths. The dead river rippled across the cavern floor in stone-scallop waves, pearl-beads of bright-white calcite had formed in its eddies and stone flowers bloomed on its banks like mantelpiece porcelain.

Despite the eerie beauty of the cave, X found his thoughts surprisingly practical. Caving was part of his expertise as a rock climber, and looking at the frozen white river he recognised the rock formation immediately, **Floodstone**. Clear evidence of the crystallisation of Calcium Carbonate, its slow deposition... He shook his head. The railway had broken out into a network of limestone caverns.

Limestone?

At Heathrow?

How could that be?

They set off following the flooodstone river across the cavern, cutting across meanders and skirting ox-bow lakes. It wasn't the most direct route but it saved them wandering in circles in the dark. The stone was the worst kind of footing, rounded and slippery, and they had both fallen several times and were nursing grazed knees and bruised elbows by the time their torches picked out a great rock fall that filled the cavern in front of them.

"This is it isn't it?", Clara's voice was timorous in the darkness, "The line of the barrier."

He was sure Clara was right. Some enormous pressure applied from above had cracked the cavern roof like an eggshell, and the line of the rock fall was too straight to be natural. It had to be the barrier.

He advanced with his stick held out in front of him until its tip touched the rocks. There were no sparks. He breathed a sigh of relief. They must have gone deep enough to be out of its destructive range. But although they were safe from incineration, they were still trapped. The huge boulders towered above them, rising out of sight to the cavern roof, sealing them in as tightly as a cork in a bottle.

X stared at the barrier, a thought forming in his mind. Although it seemed like a dead end, the climb itself didn't look too difficult, and there was a good chance that there might be gaps near the top, perhaps even a channel through the rock if they were lucky. There was no way of telling without getting up there.

They had come this far after all. It was worth a try.

Clara agreed, but insisted they ate something before making the ascent. She opened her backpack and laid out a picnic on a flat-topped boulder; some bread, a hunk of cheese, three rosy red apples, and a jug of water. "I'm famished", she said, and began tucking into the bread and cheese with gusto.

While she ate X sorted out the kit he'd borrowed from Johnone, carefully laying out the coiled ropes, karabiners, jammers, harnesses and footloops on the rock and began rigging the rope for SRT. As he worked, he cursed himself under his breath. He hadn't brought the right equipment for caving. He should have brought ladders and poles and all sorts of other kit. And water. He hadn't prepared for water. There was always water in caves.

"Squeezes and siphons", he said out loud, "Fucking caves – give me mountains any time."

Clara laughed at him good spiritedly, "Curmudgeon", she said, "Stop pacing up and down and come and sit by me – Here, try one of these apples, they're delicious"

X took one and bit into it. It tasted like papier mache. He sucked the juice out of it, spitting out the pulp when Clara wasn't looking and carried on sorting out the gear.

In the silence Clara called out, "Can you hear that?"

He listened as hard as he could. Yes. It was water falling hard but a long way off, almost completely muffled by the rock.

Good news.

He explained to Clara, that where there was an underground river, there had to be an ingress and an egress – a sink, where the water came in, or a resurgence, a place where the water came out, a spring or a waterfall. Both ways might lead to exits but it was better to follow the water up, although it would get narrow and tricky and could end in a dead end, because down could lead you into a labyrinth of underground watercourses, where you could get lost completely.

She had looked up at him with complete confidence. He hoped it wasn't misplaced.

The climb was relatively easy, no more than two short pitches and the limestone rock was fresh fallen, full of easy handholds. and the rock was quite clean, needing very little gardening. In case he dislodged a chockstone, and sent rock crashing beneath his ascent, he ensured that Clara kept well away from him as he free-climbed, but even climbing in walking boots however, he dislodged only small stones that clattered to the cavern floor like coins in a penny falls. Fixing a piton and belaying from half-way up, Clara joined him rapidly on the ledge, climbing through his light with sure-footed grace, a fluid certainty in each easy motion up the face.

The second pitch was no harder, save for a short chimney, involving a little back and foot in the bridging and a small leap onto one face as it widened, but X had chosen the route partly for fun and they arrived at the cavern roof elated.

They edged along the shattered rock-face until they found a narrow channel between two giant slabs that was broad enough to enter standing, but, with just over a metre's clearance to the roof, too low to even stoop comfortably, and they entered hunched over like early hominids. The rock was rough-hewn and jagged and they caught their heads and elbows repeatedly against sharp outcrops. Ten minutes of this and the passage narrowed further. Now they were crawling, knees and elbows grazing on the rough stone. From then on each hard earned metre of advance into the darkness was met by a concomitant tightening of the walls and lowering of the ceiling until they were shuffling face down on the floor like lizards. Even laid flat on their faces, their backpacks were catching on the rocks and X stopped to sort it out, laboriously squeezing his pack past his body and attaching it to a rope line, before securing the line itself to his harness. He signalled to Clara to do the same. If they wanted to take their kit any further they would have to drag it behind them like pit ponies.

"We've passed the barrier, haven't we!" she called. "We're out."

X thought she was probably right, and lying on his back in the darkness he carried on attaching the bags to lines. Unable to raise his neck high enough to see down the length of his body, he concentrated on tying the knots by feel alone. He could see the vapour of his breath forming a cloud in the cold air, and float up to condense on the rock face six inches above his forehead. He had perhaps a foot of movement on either side of his shoulders.

"Here's to freedom", he said.

He turned on his stomach to let his head torch play down the length of the passage. A swirl of fear clenched at his gut. The shaft swept down and away from him, a chamber-tomb tunnel narrowing to coffin dimensions and then either taking a sharp turn to the right around a tight squeeze, or coming to an abrupt halt against a slab of stone. At this range he couldn't tell. It was downhill, so he should really enter feet first. A backwards retreat uphill would be hell. But turning round would require a long retreat, so he rejected the thought and pushing back the desperate need to piss that suddenly came over him, he committed himself. The crack narrowed rapidly to the contours of his body, and he could only advance by shuffling forward on his elbows, his legs trailing uselessly behind, relying on the traction gained by his shoulders and thighs to gain tiny fractions of advantage.

He was now lying completely flat, his face in the dust, half-blinded by the refracted light of his beam.

He reached the squeeze.

A protruding rock had halved the circumference of the tube, and required him to shuffle on to his side while he rounded the bend, his back pressed up against the sidewall, sliding like a worm in its casing, propelled only by his toes and fingertips, grappling round the L-bend in the rock, its point, centimetres from his chest, an immense stone axe pressed against his heart.

The rock opened out on the other side of the squeeze and he pulled himself clear; exultant, breathing freely again and calling for Clara to follow.

The sound of running water was louder, but still faint.

It was tall enough to stand upright, and they stood awhile, arching their backs and releasing the full length of their limbs, feeling the claustrophobic weight of the rock rise, at least a fraction, glorying in their momentary space and freedom.

The fissure that they had crawled through had broken out into a passage of the old cave network and once they had stretched to their satisfaction, and before their sweat set them shivering in the damp air, they set off again, making swift progress, skidding and slipping on the moonstone smeared floor. The passage make X feel faintly nauseous, the slippery rippled surfaces, the ghastly white of the rock in the torch beam, and their slip-sliding downward motion felt like they were descending a giant oesophagus, pushed ever downward in a peristaltic wave like a bolus of food heading for the gut.

There was one sharp drop, of no more than five metres, and X fitted a piton and they abseiled down. He left the rope behind, figuring they could prusak back up if they had to. He knew their chances of success were still slim, there was a good chance their channel would just come to a dead end in the rock, and although the sound of the water grew louder, they were still heading down.

There was a second squeeze.

There's always a second squeeze.

"Fucking caves." It was becoming a mantra.

The second squeeze was truly grim.

The floor had been rising to meet the roof ceiling for some time, forcing them to advance in a crouch. Here, at some ancient convolution in the fault, the glutinous layers of floodstone, flowing over each other in lazy waves for centuries, had piled up until they nearly filled the whole aperture of the cavity. The molten-wax stone floor rose to a plateau, just beneath the roof–ceiling, leaving a letter-box shaped slit, just deep enough for a flat-packed human torso to pass through.

Shining their torches into the gap revealed some five metres of flat-face-pressing squirm before the channel opened out beyond.

X went first.

Clara had protested, pointing out that she was slighter and more flexible and that she should therefore lead.

He had acknowledged that she was the better caver, but argued that was exactly why it was necessary that he went first. If he couldn't make it, it was game over anyway. She couldn't possibly carry on alone.

He stripped to his underwear, stretched and loosened his muscles, and stepped forward.

As he leant into the mother-of-pearl white rock, he felt it was like feeding himself into the jaws of a giant clam, the rock lips gradually swallowing his whole body in an act of ritual suicide for an unknown sea-god.

Arm. Shoulder. Head turned to the side. Cheek to the floor. He eased himself into the crevice as though he were squeezing himself out of a tube of toothpaste, keeping his breaths measured and shallow, and maintaining a constant, unhurried press into the rock. The stone at least, was butter-smooth and wet so there was no danger of injury. The moisture would act as a lubricant over his naked skin.

Under his stomach as he inched ahead, the smooth ripples of stone pushed upward on his gut, each crest as it passed a slow roll of stomach cramp across his abdomen.

Half-way into the squeeze, as far forward as he had already struggled, and with retreat backward inconceivably complex to execute, he reached the limits of his endurance. One bulbous crest of stone, raised no more than a millimetre or two higher than any other, pressed tight on his sternum, and took him over the edge. Unable to take a full breath, panic set his heart accelerating like a sprinter, and he began to gasp for air, involuntarily, like a dying fish on the dock. Each unmet craving for oxygen fed back into his rising panic. He was suffocating, drowning in the rock, the massive weight above him bearing down on his back, crushing his chest like an iron cloak. He lost control of his body, spasms running the full length of his torso set him twitching like an eel in the tube, and his fingernails dug into the rock, scrabbling, rat-desperate for grip.

He fought for control.

Concentrate only on his breath.

Become his breath.

Return to his centre.

Inhabit only his own body; as ever, even within this tomb.

Breath,

Only breath.

His body fought him. He could feel the crystals of adrenalin fizzing as they dissolved in his bloodstream, preparing his muscles for the sudden flight across the savannah and back into safety of the trees.

He fought to control the programmed response of millennia, the correct strategy for two hundred and fifty thousand years for a species with poor claws and teeth on the open plain.

Run.

Run to survive.

Here.

Still.

Still to survive.

Breath,

Only Breath.

Shallow breath

One shallow breath at a time.

Help me.

One breath

Two,

Oh God,

Three... four...five.

Enough.

Stretch fingers,

Grip, pull,

One breath, two breath, three,

Grip, pull,

Move on.

He flopped out the other side, sliding down over the lip of the smooth rock into a pool of tepid muddy water, face-first, and limp and gasping for breath he lay there, unmoving, utterly exhausted, waves of relief crashing over him.

His first shiver in the cold water roused him, and by the time Clara had come through he had forgotten about his exhaustion and was jumping about in the opened out passage-way flapping his arms about to keep warm.

Clara joined him, flush-faced and triumphant as she emerged from the press, her whole body glistening with water and sweat, her hair pressed to her head like a bathing cap, her eyes flashing with delight. She too had stripped to her underwear for the squeeze, and soaked through, her singlet had been rendered completely transparent. The thin fabric had stuck to her chest, outlining her large breasts and showing her erect nipples, haloed by huge dark aureoles like buttons, pressing hard against the cloth.

X felt his cock twitch and then laughed at himself. Even here!

They continued. The passage was wider now, and the sound of rushing water grew louder with every step. Then the shaft turned right, took a sudden drop of about a metre and was equally suddenly full of water. He jumped into the cold water, splashed forward as far as he could with his head above the surface and then ducked down. Johnone's lamp was watertight, and he thanked him for having such good kit, but still he could see almost nothing. His landing had caused a thin layer of sediment like duck-shit to floated up from the bottom and uncurl slowly in brown sticky clumps making the already murky water around him even more opaque. He came back to the surface.

Clara looked concerned, but he was confident he had the measure of this. They had no diving equipment so the limitations were clear; if the sump went on for more than ten metres then that was the end of it. You had to hold enough breath to ensure you could turn round and swim back to where you started. Push on any further and you were gambling with your life. He explained the situation as he saw it, and tying a rope round his waist, got ready to make the dive.

Clara was staring down at him, her eyes seemed magnified in size, beautiful and soul-sad.

"This might be it, you know", he said, "The end of the line."

She leant down and pulling his head to her, drew him into a deep kiss, only breaking eye-contact as their lips met. It was better without words. He felt it all in her kiss. The trust. The depth of her gratitude to him. He saw himself as she saw him, with her through the descent into the darkness, the clam-squeeze, her seeing his fear, his tenderness with hers.

Better than words. Unspoken truths passing from her lips to his.

This wasn't the end of any line.

There would be no wild risks here. It was worth being alive.

They broke apart and X took a series of deep breaths, then stood breathing normally for a while, before filling his lungs with air and sliding back into the water. In the flooded tunnel, it was too tight to make any kind of stoke and he had no flippers, so he turned over onto his back, reaching for handholds in the rock to pull himself along. Protecting his face as best he could, he scrabbled like a crab along the upper face of the flooded passage, sediment disturbed by his passage spiralling like miniature galaxies in the murky water and restricting his visibility to no more than the length of his arm. The warm, soupy water made it feel as though he were pushing his body through amniotic fluid and as he skidded on in the gloom he was strangely calm, almost peaceful.

He counted the seconds evenly as he swam.

Ten more now before turning.

Then.

The fingertips of his outstretched hand,

Cold.

He broke the surface, deafened by the roar after the silence underwater, and pulled on the rope to signal Clara to follow before he had even looked round.

Clara came through quickly after him, towing their packs behind her.

He helped her heave them out of the water.

"Ugh! Like soup!" she said, and then looked up.

Their journey was over.

They had found the underground river they had been seeking, but it offered no way out. High above them, a torrent of water, pouring over some unseen lip, sent a waterfall hurtling past them before disappearing down a vertical shaft with the deafening roar of a jet aircraft, heading for some deep underground lake far below, way beyond the range of the torch beam. An outcrop from the sheer walls below broke up the sheet of falling water, sending it crashing into the rock and hurling spray upward with the force of water cannon, lashing the walls of the shaft with layers of thick, churned-up spume. They had emerged from a small crevice in the face of a sheer wall of rock, the shaft dropping unbroken the length of the torchlight beam, and rising as far again above. They were poised on a small lip, hanging above the abyss, intermittently soaked by backdrafts of spray. Upward the climb was impossible. The face was near featureless, with only the tiniest of fissures scarcely cracking the surface of the rock. Some fine-edging and a lot of luck and it was E9 in the dry. In the wet it couldn't be done.

He looked across the span of the chasm. Thirty-five metres, he estimated. He couldn't throw that far with any accuracy, at least not with kind of grappling hook he'd have to jerry-rig. But even if he set up a line, they'd have to cross under the full force of the falls, and the chances were they'd be swept away into the abyss.

He pulled Clara to him as they sat, soaked to the skin and drenched in the spray, balanced above the drop on the narrow ledge, her head in his chest, her violent sobbing unheard in the roar of the falling water.

No way out.

38. THE RIVER

He floated in the river, breathing easily through the aqua-lung, watching the crude craft they had constructed float upstream on the rising tide. Lashed together from planks and half-filled cider containers, it was designed to float beneath the surface, the cider-raft the same density as the water around it, calibrated to maintain a steady height in the river flow.

Calibrated.

Designed.

It was clearly a shambolic, Heath-Robinson affair, not the first they had tried, and not, in all honesty any better than the last.

He watched its slow submarine passage upriver with the tide, floating low over the surface of the riverbed as they had hoped it would. Moving through the water with the grace of a bale of compressed garbage, it held steady for a few metres before beginning to spin, slowly, rotating turgidly in the fast flowing water. Tilting as it turned, one corner caught the edge of an unseen eddy in the current and the craft began to spin faster and rise in the water. It reached the barrier half a metre above the riverbed and two metres below the surface.

It was instantly incinerated in a blinding flash of light.

*

The return from the underworld had been less terrible than the descent, at least for X. Even the squeezes were easier than before as each centimetre gained through the crush was another fraction further out of the rock and back into the light, each breath and push upward through the guts of the earth; a reverse peristalsis this time, his body forcing a slow, remorseless regurgitation from the stone. It was harder for Clara, each step, crawl, press and climb undertaken, heavy-limbed with defeat, fighting the rock in her anger and despair, emerging bruised and scratched, her face streaked with tear-tracks. But as the passages opened out and the weight of the rock began to lift off them, the failed jailbreak began to feel like liberty, and spirits rising, their stride quickened as they ascended.

Eventually they surfaced, climbing the escalators out of the deserted station, re-treading their own prints in the dust on the abandoned platforms, erasing the evidence of their descent in the footfalls of their hasty retreat. Stepping into the morning sunlight, they were immediately blinded by its intensity and were forced to sit in the shade of the ruined station, eyelids open only as slits, blinking mole-like under the shade of their hands. When they were able, they crawled into the daylight on their hands and knees, and lay on their backs in the meadow, stunned and joyous in the light and space. A strong wind blew high, wispy clouds quickly across the sky, and they lay, spread-eagled in the long grass, pinned to the earth beneath the sun and waiting for the motion to stop before they could rise.

As soon as they could reliably stand upright without losing balance, they had set off again, moving at pace, heading back to the river and racing to put Clara's back up plan in motion before night fall. They had separated at Hammersmith, X heading off to find Levi and get hold of some diving equipment and Clara to rig up some means of testing how deep the barrier went into the water.

That was Plan B.

They would leave with the tide.

It was at least plausible. After all, the river breached the barrier easily enough and Clara had pointed out that the river was full of fish. Wouldn't they need to get to their spawning grounds up stream? The barrier *was* permeable then, at least to water, and perhaps its power weakened at greater depths allowing the fish to slip through?

They didn't know, but it at least seemed worthy of examination.

They'd had two choices of exit point. The most likely to succeed being where the Thames left London as a swollen behemoth of a river, ever widening and deepening as it merged with the sea beyond Rotherhithe. It was a magnificent sight, apparently, the barrier stretching across the estuary mouth, "Like a banked raceway for cartoon celestials", as Clara described it, but it was a long trek east, and if successful would have deposited them on the wrong side of London for Manchester. So instead, they had made the much shorter journey West toward Richmond, where the river entered the city, leaving them here, floating in the river, hoping on the full moon and the tide.

The destruction of the second raft had only told them what they already knew, that their best chance would come at high tide, if it came at all.

Surfacing at the same time as Clara, he clambered on board the rowing boat they had moored mid-stream causing it to list alarmingly and nearly capsize. Clara joined him and they struggled out of their harnesses, laughing at their clumsiness while the little skiff lurched around in the current. Unburdened, they lay on their backs, side by side in the sun on the wooden floor of the boat, looking up at the purpling sky and soaking up the last slanting orange rays of sunset. X trailed his hand in the cool water beside the boat, letting it run through his fingers. It reminded him of somewhere else... some other time...

Clara hooked an ankle over his foot as they lay on their backs, and the thought drifted away, all his attention focused on touch of her skin on his. She curled around him, laying her thigh across his and resting her head on his chest.

*

After they had separated, X had headed straight to Levi's and had caught him at home, tending to his tomato plants in the back yard.

Levi was impossibly well connected in Bakhuninland, and could normally be relied upon to secure anything that was available in the domed city, but as soon as he had found out what X wanted the diving equipment for, he'd become reluctant to help.

All he needed was some diving equipment. What was so hard about that?

"Look I'm not saying no..." Levi had prevaricated, shuffling awkwardly and scratching the back of his neck as he spoke, "...but you've done the hero thing...earned her love...or whatever man..."

X was starting it get irritated, "Are you going to help me get the stuff or not Levi", he interrupted bluntly.

"I can get the kit X, but really...as a friend..."

"Just get me the stuff Levi. Please."

"If this is what you really want …. But man..."

"Just get me the stuff Levi – we can sort out the trade later."

"It's not about the trade for fuck's sake!", exclaimed Levi, "It's just that you really are missing the point X."

"The kit Levi, please."

"OK, OK, You'll have it in an hour."

Levi was as good as his word, and in less than an hour had returned with a llama fully laden with diving equipment. He handed X the llama's lead and embraced him in a huge bear hug, holding him longer and tighter than X was comfortable with and then just as suddenly, releasing him.

Turning his back and waving, he used the same words as Gary had, "You're still missing the point X", he said, as he walked off, "There's nothing but heartache and bitterness out there."

His last words had been the same as Gary's.

*

When he'd arrived at the river bank, Clara was tying empty plastic canisters to planks of wood using lengths of climbing rope. She was hot and visibly frustrated, muttering to herself as she struggled to keep tension in the rope bindings. She waived away his offer of help brusquely.

He trotted the llama down the bank, untied its pack, and left it to graze while he took sight of the barrier at close quarters. As before, the queasy unnaturalness of the barrier was horribly apparent. Its gloppy plastic nothingness reducing the horizon to ten metres, its whiteness closing out the view like an attack of snow-blindness.

He found himself involuntarily shielding his eyes.

Up river, jagged shards of tarmac, piled up like burnt and blackened coral, marked the point where the barrier had guillotined the dual carriageway of the Chertsey Road, and, pitted with bushes and thick clumps of nettles, the roadway now made a pot-holed dash to nowhere. In contrast, the crystal clear water of the river poured into the city over an invisible weir, emerging from nothing as though the water was being alchemically created by the barrier itself. Like the fount of a magical spring, the river seemed to pull colour into the world dragging deep green algae along its bed like the hair of drowned mermaids, forcing up golden bulrushes up from the shallows, and throwing up stately guardian willows on its banks; their olive leaves casting shadows on the white parchment of the barrier like a finely sketched Japanese print.

X picked up a driftwood branch and threw it out into the river. It was carried away swiftly downstream, turning lazily in the current before disappearing out of sight.

Still a while before the tide turned then.

He turned and strolled back up the bank to Clara. She was standing back from her contraption with her hands on her hips, contemplating her work with a look of disdain.

"It's official", she said as he approached, "I'm really shit at this."

He kissed her quickly on the lips, but she batted him off, "Too sweaty!"

They stood and looked at the depth tester that Clara had built. It looked like something you might find bobbing about at the base of a weir.

"I'm sorry to inform you, Ms Duffer", Clara intoned, "but you have not been selected for further leadership training as you appear to be completely shit. Have you considered human resources?"

X laughed, but something about the joke made him seem queasy.

By the time they launched the Mark II, word must have got out that someone was trying to shoot the barrier and they had gathered something of a crowd. Families had set up picnics and barbeques on the banks, and the wind blew bursts of laughter, smoke and the smell of grilled fish across the water toward them. Two teenagers had swum around them while they made their underwater preparations, but X had shooed them away as high tide approached and the current, amplified by the full moon, grew stronger. The threat of being swept into the invisible barrier and incinerated was very real and he made sure he and Clara were always securely tethered whenever they entered the water.

But as he lay in the boat, the danger they faced seemed abstract and distant. This escape attempt had none of the desperation of the underground route, and not really expecting to succeed, they had laughed at each failure, meeting the sympathetic groans of the crowd on the banks with cheerful waves from mid-stream. The afternoon had passed in glorious splendour, the land's beauty flooding over him each time he broke the surface of the water and, wound round Clara's body in the skiff, it had felt as close to paradise as he had ever experienced.

His mood shifted abruptly as the sun began to dip over the horizon. He shivered. How many more sunsets would he see? Failure was so certain that he hadn't considered the consequences of success at all. Would he be killed the moment he stepped outside?

"What time is it?" asked Clara, waking from her doze and stretching out her arms.

It was ten minutes from high tide. Time to go.

They kitted up and slipped into the water. With the sun having set, only a dim moonlight penetrated the surface and the danger suddenly seemed much more real. Tethered, the tide swept them upstream, leaving them dangling like marionettes on the end of their strings only metres away from certain death at the barrier's edge. He was scared now. What were they doing?

He turned on his diving lamp. The white null of the barrier lit up five metres in front of him.

He turned to look at Clara. She was holding herself steady against the current by making minute, graceful strokes with her hands. staring intently at the barrier as though she was waiting for it to part in front of her like a magic curtain. He realised then that while he had been play-acting at escaping all day, she had remained in deadly earnest. He felt saddened, certain he would have to comfort her when this attempt, too, had failed.

He checked his watch. Five minutes before high tide.

Nothing was going to happen.

His lamp caught a flash of the white bellies of a school of fish turning and spinning in the current around him. There had been fish swimming around them all day but there seemed to be more of them now. He looked down. The river-bed was completely covered by a twisting, silvery mass of fish, an improbable shoal of different species spread like a shiny carpet over the mud. They seemed to be maintaining a precise distance from the barrier's edge, frantically holding station against the tide.

They too, like Clara, were waiting for something.

For a moment the barrier remained as opaque as ever, and then, as the water level rose to its peak, a ripple passed along its bottom edge. As though the barrier had begun to fray like an old curtain, parts of the hidden land beyond began poking through tears in the cloth. Suddenly, there was a disorientating extension of his field of vision - like being swept forward by a camera zoom, and a long expanse of riverbed strewn with small boulders and trailing electric green algae, rushed into view from nowhere.

The fish responded first.

Slithering over each other in one seething and boiling mass, they raced toward the breach, heading instinctively for the deepest part of the channel and in a twisting vortex of scales and fins began pouring under the barrier.

Exit.

He looked across. Clara had already untethered herself and was swimming down into the shoal of fish, arrowing herself like a torpedo into the narrow channel under the barrier, flanked on all sides by an honour guard of silver-bellied fish, escorted through the barrier like an Atalantian princess.

He dived after her.

39. OUTSIDE

Swimming as fast as he could after Clara, he followed her through the thrashing silver tunnel of fish, fighting to stay as low as possible in the water, skimming the surface of the riverbed, his chest catching on small sharp stones in a series of sharp jabs to the ribs, his lamp beam, pitching wildly with every stroke, revealing only the tips of Clara's flippers disappearing into the murk ahead of him. Then suddenly, the fish around them scattered upward and away, dispersing with a twist of fin and tail, rising up to reclaim the whole river again as of their natural right. They followed them up, breaking carelessly back into the moonlight world above, heads bobbing above the surface, treading water as the tide swept them slowly on.

X pulled off his breathing mask and filled his lungs with fresh air.

They were out.

The air was sweet.

He turned back to look at the city. It had gone, entirely obscured behind the featureless white wall of the barrier. The river materialised out of nothing and flowed serenely between banks of densely-packed alders that shielded the land beyond from view. The remains of the old road bridge crossed the stream, its footings reduced to small islands covered with osiers and tall marsh grass. On one, the moonlight picked out the white feathers of a swan settling down in its nest for the night. It was as peaceful outside as inside.

Strange. No screeching alarms, no uniforms, no guns.

And the distance they'd swum?

No more than ten metres.

In the end the barrier no thicker than a crusader castle's walls and easier to breach; its gate left open each time high tide coincided with a full moon. Ten metres. There had been no need for the aqualung and flippers at all, the distance less than the width of a swimming pool, an underwater swim a child could undertake on a single breath. It was as though they had merely ducked down in the deep end, and swum through a gap in the wave-machine bars to freedom.

No guards.

If it was this easy to get out why were there no guards?

His musing had let the tide swept him slowly upstream, and he caught sight of Clara signalling urgently at him. She pointed toward a patch of mud beach on the far side. If he didn't start swimming now he was in danger of being swept round the next bend. X concentrated on swimming as hard as he could, and made just enough progress to catch the mud-spit before he was swept past.

By the time he had struggled out of the water, Clara had already taken off her diving gear and greeted him by flinging her arms around his neck and hung there while she drew his head down into a deep kiss.

"Thought I'd get a bit of celebrating in first", she said, "It looks peaceful enough so far, but we've still got to look over there."

She pointed up the steep grassy bank to the top of the ridge where big tumps of tufted grass formed the horizon, shielding them, but also hiding the rest of the land from view.

They needed to know what was up there before they could relax.

The scrabbled together up the bank and crawling on their bellies like counterfeit commandos, they pulled apart tall stalks of grass, and peered through the gaps at the land beyond. Ahead of them close-cropped grass, turned white and smooth by the moonlight stretched away towards low-rising hills on the horizon like a vast ice sheet laid across the land. Just before it disappeared over the hills, the ice-grass came to an abrupt halt, slashed from East to West by a thin black line that X took to be a road. On the other side of the road the texture of the land was different, the white moonlight scattered across its surface in pointillist dots.

There were no buildings; no sign of any human habitation at all.

X and Clara were alone in the world.

"Where did the all people go?" she asked.

X tried to remember what had been here before. Twickenham? Hampton? Big houses close up to the river, semi-detached suburbs beyond, roundabouts and petrol stations, schools, the rugby stadium.

Gone.

X allowed himself a smile. It was a bleak and eerie landscape, as strangely lifeless as the surface of an unexplored asteroid, sure, but at least it wasn't threatening.

They were out and they were safe.

For now.

Clara stood, and looking out over the land, with her back to the barrier, she took a full breath of air and stretched her arms in a sun salute at the world on the other side of the cage bars. As she held the pose, the moonlight shone on her motionless body, its silver light turning her pose from a private moment of triumph into a statue, a memorial erected centuries ago for another warrior or goddess, a Hippolyta or Boudicca captured in stone at her moment of victory.

When she was done, she turned and smiled at X before heading off back into the alder wood and disappearing under the dark shade of the trees.

X quickly stripped out of his wet suit and put on a baggy sweatshirt and a pair of loose cotton tracksuit bottoms from his pack. He wondered if Clara might be hungry, and had set off down the bank to gather firewood, when he heard a sudden cry from Clara. He began sprinting up the bank and racing along the crest, only slowing when he heard muttered curses and then laughter floating across the air.

"This is really embarrassing", she said, her voice coming from just ahead of him, "But you're going to have to come and rescue me."

When he reached her, it was clear what had happened.

Struggling out of her wetsuit, Clara had taken an undignified tumble backwards into a furrow formed by the gap between two soft tussocks of grass. She lay on her back, her legs propped higher than her head over one tussock, and her neck and shoulders bent over the opposite hump. Her wetsuit was bunched around her knees like a rubber hobble and she was completely stuck, unable to either turnover in the groove or struggle upwards out of it.

"Don't just stand there X!", she commanded, propping herself up on her elbows as best she could, "Get this bloody thing off me!"

X dipped his knee and made a bow, and giving her a gallant courtier's wave, knelt at her feet and began working the wetsuit down her legs. The moonlight cut her ice white flesh from the shadowed grass like a finely crafted pen and ink drawing, and as he set about his task, she let her head fall back on the soft tump behind her lying before him in an attitude of complete surrender.

God, she was beautiful.

"Get on with it", she mumbled without looking up.

He returned to his task and as soon as Clara was freed she swung herself out of the furrow, and laughing headed toward the trees.

"I need a pee X. Wait here for me will you."

X stayed where he was, standing still until the sound of Clara's passage through the trees was drowned out by the rush of the river. Lost in his own thoughts he didn't hear her return.

He looked up.

She was naked.

She stepped lightly, barefoot into the furrow, and carefully laid herself in the soft grass, her body taking up exactly the same posture as before.

"Now. Where were we?" she asked.

This time she was a Caravaggio in front of him. Her skin, vivid-white and tender-beautiful, defiantly shining out against the overwhelming darkness behind her. He fell into her arms like a man returning from a long sea voyage, and they tumbled into the grass, entwined in each other, the moonlight shining so brightly off her body that her skin seemed as fluid as mercury and he could not tell if his hand flowed under or through the silk of her, nor where his skin ended and hers begun. Shadows passed over them and he saw everything only in moonlight flashes through gaps in the clouds. Fragments of skin in the silver-grey light; the fine, delicate hairs that ran the whole arch of her back as far as the cleft in her buttocks, each one crystallised in the white light. The sweep of her soft hair over his thighs as he touched the heart of her with the just very tip of his tongue. Her ghost-pale breasts, each cupped by soft sickle moon-shadows. Her eyes falling away from him, distant-lost in bliss, then surfacing again, x-ray intense, on him. Just him. Her body moving in sinew traces above him, passing in and out of the textured soft blackness that enveloped them. They tumbled deeper into the furrow, fingertips, hips, hands, soft shadow skin pressed nectar smooth around him. His final cry broke out of him with hers, echoing across the empty fields like the mating cries of wild animals.

40. THE FIELDS

When X opened his eyes, dawn had already broken, but it seemed only a moment since he had closed them. The whole night had passed, and the sun long-since risen, lifting the dew off the grass in which they lay. The air was already warm.

Clara lay next to him, curled under the blanket with her back to him. She had scrunched down in the night for warmth, and only the tousled hair at the top of her head was visible above the covers. She was still fast asleep, her eyes sheltered from the morning sun, and he woke her gently, peeling back the blankets edge and tracing a finger over an eyebrow and down her cheek. He watched her stretch, languorously; eyes still closed, pushing back the covers and letting the rising sun warm her skin. Before she had opened her eyes, a lazy smile had already formed on her sleep-softened lips, some memory of last night, perhaps, surfacing with her as she swam up to consciousness. She prised open her sleep-heavy eyelids a crack, and spied him through the curtain of her eyelashes, the smile now wide on her face.

She spread her arms and pulled him down toward her.

The day began perfectly.

*

Standing on the ridge, it was as though the world had been shot with an entirely different camera than the night before; the silvered monochrome reel replaced by one shot in blistering, vivid cinemascope. The grass was now a virulent lime green, and beyond the road a bright orange wasteland ran like a Martian desert to the horizon. It was a silent, stilled world, shorn of any distinguishing features and as rigidly ordered as a circuit board, a landscape where nature had been recreated as an exercise in colour by a minor abstract artist.

"We're not in Kansas anymore", Clara had said.

*

With the sun not yet high in the sky, they had set off cheerfully, holding hands and chatting idly as they walked, and had soon crossed the wide expanse of pasture. Where the grass ended there was no road, only another vast field, this one planted with some kind of grossly altered wheat. Huge ears, each as big as a man's head, held seeds as orange as hot embers which wobbled on the top of razor thin stalks like out-sized standard lamps. The plants marched to the horizon in regimented rows, bearing their flaming orange heads like silent soldiers in a vast torch-lit parade.

Their progress through the wheat was slower, and they trudged along the furrows in silence, step-stumbling over broken clods of earth, and with the sun bearing down mercilessly on their unprotected shoulders. The land undulated gently, and each shallow crest revealed only more ranks of blazing orange corn, military row after military row, stretching endlessly ahead of them. Finally, at the rise of one unmemorable crest after so many such unmemorable crests, there was a break in the monotony. In the distance, a deep green band cut East to West across the orange, like a border fence drawn up by colonial treaty, and, hazed in dust on a distant hill ridge, a flat silver machine moved slowly and silently along the wheat rows. Tethered by some kind of hose, a cigar-shaped dirigible floated behind the machine, creating the impression of a feeding insect dragging an engorged abdomen behind it by a thin stand of gut.

"Some kind of harvester?", Clara speculated.

It seemed a plausible guess. Behind the machine, a strip of brown earth was cut out of the orange creating a colour contrast as unnatural as a child's toffee bar.

As they neared the green strip, they heard birdsong for the first time, and only then realised how silent the land had been since they had left the city. Suddenly the air was full of the chirps and chirrups of small birds making short swooping darts into the field, and their cheerful trills rang out like an act of defiance in the empty land. The strip was merely a tall hedgerow, densely-packed with the thorny bushes, small trees and ivy. It was about seven-foot-high, and X had to jump and down to see over it. At the top of his leaps he could make out that it was about the width of a football pitch and gave way to brambles coiled like razor wire on the other side.

"Bollocks", he said. The hedge was taking them due west, but there was no way they could pass through it, they would have been cut to pieces before they'd got ten yards. They would have to follow its course and hope for a break.

Clara had sat down facing the fence, munching on an apple from her backpack. "It's amazing", she said, "all the time I've been walking, I've been looking at this relentless monoculture and wondering, 'How does it work?' I mean, how does it all stack up without the eco-system crashing? Can you strip out *everything* down to only the crops you want to eat without having untold catastrophic events up and down the chain? But that's what they've done isn't it", she said, gesturing towards the hedge, "They've put exactly the minimum in! Each strip – the trees by the river – the band of pasture – this wedge of hedge ...I bet its calculated to the nearest percentage point." She shook her head, "Look at this hedgerow... elder, alder...guelder rose, bramble...sloe, dog rose... It's like a medieval hedge, all the biodiversity they need packed into this one strip. And... Yes, I'd put money on it... They're also green corridors. They've been designed to allow all the insects, birds and small mammals they need to move from one zone to another, I bet they're all linked into a grid, My Go it's so..."

"Efficient", X interjected, remembering Gary's adage that you could always rely on *them* to ensure the minimal possible cost. It was all a piece with the machines they'd seen; automatic, solar-powered probably; the harvester trailing its dirigible all part of the same pattern - moving bulky produce by airship would require little energy and meant there was no need for the maintenance of any roads.

Clara laughed, "I was going to say soulless, but you're right it is clever too, clever and soulless, but soulless nonetheless. Oh God!" she exclaimed, "I wonder if they selected the birds?"

It was cheerful walking alongside the hedge even if they were going in the wrong direction. It provided no shade, but the small birds breaking into flight in front of them as they walked gave their progress a musical accompaniment and the air was enlivened by buzzing insects, full of frenzied energy in the heat, carving kamikaze passages through the thorn scrub. Clara wasn't sure what to make of the birds. "They all seem to be some type of chaffinch", she said, mostly to herself, "But all a bit different from each other... I'm not sure", she admitted, "I never was very good with birds... But there's certainly no sparrows, wrens or blue tits as far as can see..."

After several hours of Westward passage, they finally came to a break in the hedge. The grassed track that cut through was scoured by the distinctive markings of caterpillar tracks, but the soil was parched, and it was impossible to say how recently the vehicle had passed. X was delighted to be heading in the right direction once again, and after half-an-hour's walking, equally delighted that the wheat fields finally came to an end. The fields were now planted with some kind of monstrous beetroot, swollen to gargantuan proportions and pressed together in rows like livid sunburnt Buddhas. X stepped off the track and cut a slice off one of the plants with his knife, chopping it in half and passing a piece to Clara. She declared it to be starchy, sweet and not altogether unpleasant, but when he took a bite found it tough and largely tasteless. After gamely chewing for a while he spat it out.

The beet fields turned out to be worse than the wheat. The lurid purple colour made X nauseous, and as he walked the vivid purple lines began to detach from the soil, hovering hallucinogenically in a grid above the ground, forcing him to walk at times with his eyes closed, holding on to Clara's shoulders like a blind man. After two hour's slog, he was profoundly relieved when the beets were replaced by maize. His delight was short-lived. The maize, another forced evolution from the native plant, had huge clusters of blinding yellow cobs, wrapped in electric green papooses and guarded at their base by, thin, colourless leaf-blades, serrated and scimitar sharp like cacti. Unlike the wheat, the maize was tall, and towering above them, they walked for hours through a yellow tunnel glowing like the bars on an electric fire.

They didn't notice the approach of the airship until the tip of its bow cast a curved shadow across the path in front of them. When X looked up the zeppelin was almost upon them. There was no point in running, they were hopelessly exposed in the ocean of maize.

He wondered what they would do with them.

He remembered what Gary had said about the Morlocks, "Just imagine what the cheapest and most soulless way of acting in any given circumstances, and ten to one that's how they'll act every time.".

Shit, they'd just shoot him and leave his body in the field for fertiliser.

He ran.

He crashed into the field behind Clara, razor sharp leaf-blades lacerating his ankles as he plunged blindly down the rows. Even as he ran he knew it was pointless. There was no more cover in the fields than on the track. The game was up. But Clara kept going, so he followed her, and then, miraculously, there was something to aim for... a barn of some kind, hidden from the road by the maize, the first building of any kind they had seen since they left the city. He started to sprint, hurdling the spiny leaves like an Olympic athlete, but before he was a third of the way to the barn, the airship overtook him. As its shadow clipped his shoulder he involuntarily flinched, anticipating the bullet severing his spinal cord and then...

He was suddenly drenched.

A downpour of foul smelling liquid had poured from the blimp, falling in a curtain of syrup as the airship passed over him. The liquid slathered on to his hair in gloopy layers and slithered down his body, sticking in patches on his t-shirt like lumpy, rancid soup. Clara, ten metres ahead of him had also been caught by the stinking shower, her hair was plastered flat to her face, and as she held her hands aloft in dismay, streams of filth fell to the sodden earth beneath her feet. The stench was terrible.

It smelt like…?

Chicken shit.

It *was* chicken shit.

The airship passed serenely on ahead of them, fertilising the land with its chicken-shit spray, entirely unconcerned by the plight of its victims below.

"Hey Clara", X called out, wiping a smear from his forehead with the back of his hand as spoke, "That's what I call a welcome! First contact in decades and they literally shit on us from the sky."

It didn't raise a smile.

There was no means of getting the crap off them in the open fields, so, having picked the worst clumps out of each other's hair, they were forced to make an uncomfortable passage down the furrows toward the barn. Moving with the gait of double incontinents, they shuffled and squelched across the field, re-joining the road as it curved around to the barn. Sliding down the bank on a smear of chicken shit, they discovered that the path itself was guano-free, the blimp presumably programmed to avoid unnecessary waste on non-productive land.

If they hadn't run…….

The barn door was open and they entered cautiously. Much of the high-vaulted space was filled by two of the flat machines they had seen in the fields, one part-dismantled with its components neatly stacked on a metal-framed rack. On the opposite side, part of the barn had been partitioned to form a large workshop. Its glass door was ajar and X could make out a tall stool set in front over an over-sized bench with tools neatly arrayed on hooks running along the wall. A large ceramic sink sat at the far end, the basin as big as a bath, with a chunky metal tap set in the wall above it. Clara had spotted it too, "Ladies fucking first", she exclaimed, stripping off and heading straight for the sink. Thrusting her head under the tap, she shrieked as the cold water cascaded over her, only hesitating for a moment before clambering fully in, shivering and laughing as she sloughed the filth off her skin. When she was finished he took his turn, and then they did their best to scrub their clothes tolerably clean before lying outside in the sun to dry off.

*

They drowsed happily in the heat, Clara's head propped on his chest.

His repose was broken by Clara, "Can you hear that?" she asked.

At first he could hear nothing, but then he caught it, a low rumbling sound with a whiney edge. An electric motor. Standing up, he caught a flash of something red above the yellow maize, it disappeared for a moment and then came back into sight as the road rose over a crest.

It was heading down the path directly towards them.

They grabbed their damp clothes and ran back into the barn, hiding behind one of the racks of weeding machine parts, fervently hoping that the vehicle would pass them by. The sound of the electric motor whined louder, and then, when it was clear the vehicle was immediately outside the barn door, shuddered briefly and then stopped. They heard heavy footsteps and then the barn door swung open.

The thing that entered the barn was monstrous. At least seven-foot tall, its torso was covered by smooth, hairless, bright green skin like that of a frog. It's right arm was fleshy, but its left was entirely prosthetic; hydraulic shafts like metallic sinews ran from shoulder to elbow, and along the length of a forearm swollen in circumference like a sten-gun, knives, files, and screwdrivers lay in grooved slots. Its hand was a blunt-fingered metal claw.

They crouched lower in the darkness as the monster crossed the barn with a shambling, sailor's gait and entered the workshop opposite their hiding place. Turning on a desk lamp it heaved its bulk onto a stool, selected a tool from the rack and began carefully filing the teeth of a small cog, pausing to measure the depth with a feeler gauge every few strokes. Illuminated by the lamp, its face was at least human, if ugly. Heavy, fatty brow-ridges half-hid small beady eyes, and its big fleshy lips were pursed as though they had frozen in the act of blowing a kiss.

Hidden in the darkness, they watched him at work.

"Is it human?" whispered Clara.

X could only shrug.

The green man finished his filing and carefully placed the cog back on the bench in front of him. Levering himself out of the chair, he left the workshop and began crossing the floor directly towards them. There was no chance of making a dash for it without being seen and they instinctively crouched lower, hoping that the deep shade would be enough keep them hidden from view.

Although there was nothing about the creature's expression or behaviour that suggested violence, X was undeniably very scared. The thing that was approaching them was the stuff of nightmares, monster-coloured, stupid-looking and built like a gorilla, its prosthetic arm would clearly make an effective weapon as well as a toolkit, and X suspected that even a blow with a club hammer to the creature's temples would do little more than irritate it.

He hoped it couldn't run fast.

It stopped in front of the rack they were hiding behind. X caught the strong stench of its breath, a musty, peaty odour; not unpleasant, like the smell of a farmyard animal, a comforting smell in other circumstances, but here in the darkness of the barn it seemed to strip him of another slice of his humanity. No human had ever smelt so much like a cow.

The creature slowly raised its prosthetic arm, his metal hand reaching forward in the half-light toward X's face.

X held his breath and then, absurdly, closed his eyes.

When he opened them, he could see that the green man had

plucked a coil of hosing from the parts-rack and, having achieved his goal, had turned back to the workshop.

He let out an involuntary sigh of relief, the air whistling gently through the gap in his front teeth as he exhaled. His legs were suddenly like jelly and he had to grip the metal frame hard to stop himself from falling.

It rattled loudly in the silent shed.

The green man swung round and, peering into the darkness, fixed his gaze directly on X. For what seemed an interminable duration, it stood silently staring at him. As the time passed and the silence lengthened, X felt a gradual lessening of his fear until, despite the creature's frightening appearance, the situation began to feel more socially awkward than terrifying, as though they were stuck in the kitchen with a particularly dull party guest and a shortage of small talk.

"Hello", ventured X, his voice weak and tentative as he spoke up, extending his right hand forward in greeting and fixing what he hoped was an engaging smile on his face.

There was a long pause while the green man continued to stare silently at X and then he suddenly declared, in a thick West Country accent, raising his fleshy arm to his brow in a half-salute as he did so, "And a good morning to you Sir!" before falling silent again.

This pause was shorter, and before X could muster a reply the creature started up again, bursting out a pair of sentences in sharp succession in the same staccato manner as before. "Fair ye well then", was followed rapidly by "I must tend the machines". And with that, it turned away from them and strode back across the barn and into the workshop. They watched as the giant moved around the room, this time selecting a range of small components and laying them out carefully in front of him in ordered rows. Their presence in the barn appeared to have been completely forgotten.

"Well that was fucking weird", said X,

"What have they done to him?" Clara asked, "Each explanation I come up with doesn't fit. At first I thought he was retarded, lobotomised or something truly foul like that. But look at all the complicated work he's doing."

The green man had settled into his chair and was methodically fitting together the small components he had gathered, assembling some complex piece of machinery, whistling out of key as he worked.

"And why is he green?"

"To make him look like Frankenstein", ventured X, "Scared the shit out of me pretty effectively."

She laughed, "So what do we do now?"

Their decision was made for them by the green man. His task completed, he stopped whistling, picked up the now fully assembled component, closed up the workshop and headed out of the barn. They followed him out, scuttling behind him from shadow to shadow although it was clear there was no longer any need for concealment. When they emerged into the sunlight, he was just getting into the cab of the machine that had brought him here, settling down behind the steering wheel in front of a consul with large coloured buttons arranged along the dashboard in rows. He pressed one of the buttons and the engine whirred into life.

The green man's machine was a strange mixture of post office van, railway freight train and tank. It snaked down the green lane outside the barn in four linked segments behind the driver's cab, all painted bright pillar-box red and was stamped with the silhouette of a Chinese man's head, neatly bordered in gold leaf. The first carriage was an engine of some kind, mounted on caterpillar tracks and with exhaust outlets on its roof like the pipes of a big American roller and the rest clearly wagons, with large sliding doors set above rubbered wheels. The final carriage had a flat platform at the rear that jutted out like a dropped-down tailgate, above which sat a panel of big bright buttons similar to those in the driver's cab.

The green man pressed another button and the machine began to pull away, gathering speed surprisingly quickly.

X and Clara had the same thought at the same time, nodded to each other, and ran toward the departing truck, hauling themselves up easily on to the waist-high platform at the rear.

*

The journey through the day on the tail plate of the green man's charabanc was remarkably pleasant. They sunbathed on the rear platform as miles passed effortlessly underneath them, the breeze cooling their skin as they trundled through the fields. They sat, shoulder to shoulder, with their legs dangling over the platform's edge, as free as hobos crossing the prairie on a freight train. The green man stopped the machine from time to time, stepping down to clear clogged sections of a roadside ditch, or even out potholes on the path's surface. Each time, and with the same unhurried, methodical pace, he would carefully select the right tool for the task and scrape and shovel until the job was done. The truck also stopped whenever the crops changed, and the green man would carefully harvest the first few rows of beat, or maize, or violent orange carrot, stacking the produce in neat piles in the third carriage. On other occasions he would stop to collect chaff, presumably deposited by one of the automated weeding machines at the side of the path. These bales, too bulky for a normal man to lift alone, were hefted easily by the giant into inlets on the roof of the engine. Curiously, he also kept a significant portion for himself, depositing it on the seat next to him in the cab, periodically stuffing clumps into his mouth as though he was eating dried spaghetti.

X and Clara used the breaks to stretch their legs, at first cautious about revealing their status as stowaways, but it was quickly apparent that the green man had no interest whatsoever in his uninvited passengers. They passed the time as they rolled along, either in contented silence, rocked into reverie by the steady passage of the machine, or in a recurring and inconclusive debate about the nature of their driver.

"OK. How about this then", said Clara, returning to the theme, "What is the most cost-efficient way of generating energy for a living organism?"

"I don't know, what is the most cost-efficient way of generating energy for a living organism?" replied X as though the question required a punch line.

"Sunlight." She said.

X failed to follow her train of thought and said so.

Instead of explaining, she asked another question, "What do plants use to extract energy from sunlight?"

He knew this one, "Chlorophyll."

"And the colour of chlorophyll", she answered her own question before he could say it, "Green. That's why he's green, he's photosynthesising."

It the most plausible explanation either of them had come up with so far.

"So why he is eating all that grass?" asked X, "If he can extract energy from the sun why does he need the food?"

"Why not both? Energy from sunlight isn't enough to enable plants to move, so it's never going to animate a big beast like him. It's just a back-up system. No, the most interesting thing about the chaff is that he shouldn't be able to digest it at all, no human can, he'd need a second stomach like an ungulate to break down the cellulose."

They both had the same thought at the same time,

"Do you think…?"

"Ugh."

"That's really quite grim", said X unnecessarily," but at least it would justify the bad breath."

The truck had stopped again, and X lazily poked his head around the side to see what the driver was up to.

This stop was clearly quite different to all the rest.

41. THE SUBURBS

At first there was no indication that this halt would be any different than any of the other breaks on the journey. The green man, moving with the same expressionless economy of motion as ever, opened and then entered the third carriage. X stepped off the platform, yawning and stretching his limbs, assuming that their driver would emerge with a shovel or mattock or some other appropriate tool and would go about his tasks at his customary measured pace.

However, when the green man stepped out of the carriage he carried no implements, and was instead utterly transformed in appearance. He was now fully dressed, his shiny green torso hidden under a neat navy jacket with gold trim and shiny black buttons. Epaulettes at his shoulders were embroidered with the symbol of a tall skyscraper in gold thread, and he wore matching, sharply creased navy trousers, the gold thread running down each outer seam. Under the jacket he had on a crisp white shirt and blue tie, and his bald head was covered by a peaked cap with a gold crest on the brim.

He walked to the rear carriage, leant over to the consul above the tailgate, and pressed a bright blue button on the panel. A previously hidden slot slid open in the carriage side and when its aperture was a wide as a letter box, the green man pressed another button and the pitch of the engine shifted, altering from the familiar low rumbling into a high-pitched skittering note. The screeching ceased and then a rapid tapping sound began inside the machine, sounding to X like the cursor of an electric typewriter sweeping across a page, and sure enough, as the green man stood patiently by, the slot began to disgorge reams of printed-paper, falling and folding into a neat pile on the platform's surface.

X lent over to take a closer look at the product of the hidden printing press. It appeared to be generating something like a tabloid newspaper and a bold headline in letters four inches declared 'GYPSY SCUM TAKE OVER TOWN'. Beneath the lurid headline was a blurry photograph of a solitary youth with a headscarf, sitting on the kerb in an indistinguishable high street, his legs outstretched into the road. He was drinking from a can of full-strength lager, his head tipped back in the act of swallowing. Two more cans stood lined up next to him on the pavement, and a scraggy Jack Russell nestled its muzzle in the boy's lap.

As the last sheet flopped through the slot, the green man smoothed the surface of the top sheet with a sweep of his hand and hefted the newspapers onto his shoulder. He pressed another button and the slot began disgorging crisp sheets of A4 paper, each one folding into thirds as it fell; an address, complete with postcode stamped on its uppermost surface. Having stored the newspapers, he fired the engine up again, and Clara and X climbed back on to the empty platform, too bewildered to communicate in anything more than shrugs and raised eyebrows. The machine rose over a small crest and stopped, pulling up alongside a white picket fence where a tarmacked road joined the green path under the shade of a large spreading chestnut tree. The road ran perpendicular to the green path for two hundred metres or so before halting abruptly at the first furrow of the wheat fields beyond. Before it disappeared, however, the road formed the central street of a village, a pristine slice of suburbia appearing in the vast corn wastelands as though it had been dropped, intact, from outer space, its appearance as surreal as finding a roundabout in the middle of the Sahara desert.

Halfway along its length, the road split around a small village green, with neat borders of brightly coloured flowers and two dwarf cherry trees, their pink blossom in full bloom. There were only two buildings on the edge of the green itself, a plate-glass fronted café, with stainless steel chairs and tables corralled on a narrow pavement by a chain link barrier, and an old-fashioned village post office with mullioned windows, its produce displayed behind small oblong frames of thickened glass. On the opposite sides of the green, the only other two streets in the village branched off at right angles to the main road, each neatly ordered roadway forming a loop around its own small green, creating matching cul-de-sacs north and south of the main drag. The close to the north had the larger houses, perhaps twelve in total, semi-detached and mostly Mock Tudor in design. Each house was tidy and well-appointed, looking out on to clipped green lawns bordered by privet hedges or freshly creosoted wooden fences. Each garden was seemingly marked by a flamboyant signature plant; chrysanthemums in one, carved topiary in another, the hairy fronds of pampas grass dominating a third. The north close's green had a tall monkey-puzzle tree at its centre, twin green metal benches and a path cut through grass as short and smooth as a putting green. The south close's houses were smaller, more cottages than mansions, whitewashed or pebble-dashed and in a more mixed condition. A small terrace of squat dwellings like alms-houses, covered perhaps a third of the arc, and one house was completely sealed from view behind an impenetrable barrier of dense green Leylandii that topped out above the chimney pots. Some, but not all, of the gardens were well-tended; in the middle of the row an arbour of pink and orange roses sat next to one of dandelions, cracked paving and broken plastic garden furniture. The south side's green had a yew tree at its centre, and under the tree's deep shade the grass had died back to brown earth, and patches of moss grew in clumps in the shade. A weathered plastic slide sat next to an overturned barbeque set on the patchy grass. All around the village, hedgerow-less fields of wheat stretched to the horizon in every direction.

    They slipped off the platform and watched, peering round from behind the truck, as the green man, resplendent in his smart new uniform, stood placidly at the junction, the newspapers piled carefully on a two-wheeled trolley in front of him. Presently, an old lady in a gingham dress, her hair pulled into a tight, white bun on the top of her head, tottered down the road toward the waiting creature. She appeared to be a perfectly normal old lady, and was clearly unperturbed to be meeting the monstrous deliveryman in such circumstances. When she was still a metre or two short of him, he raised his peaked cap, revealing his ghastly green head in all its glory, and pronounced, in the same Devonian accent as before,

    "And a good morning to you, madam!"

    "Good morning Posty", the lady replied, her voice clipped and a little crackly, but loud enough in the silence for X to pick up every clearly enunciated syllable.

"And what a fine day it is", she said.

"It is that madam. How are you today?"

"As good as can be expected", she replied, "I trust you are well?"

"I am, thank you. I am pleased to hear you are well too."

Although the green man's accent was a softened country drawl, and his tone reassuringly humble, each sentence was preceded by a long hesitation, a pause that suggested he was choosing an answer from a list of possible replies, and it made the dialogue between them formal and abrupt, almost ritualistic in content.

"It is always a joy to arrive at your beautiful village", he started up again, the…" There was a long hesitation, "…the pansies are looking very pretty today."

"You are kind. We do our best. Someone has to keep up standards after all!"

The green man nodded in agreement.

"And how are things in the city?" she asked.

The green man shook his head, in what was presumably supposed to resemble sorrowful regret, but given the size of his cranium and speed of movement was more like watching a statue topple from its plinth. "Worse every day", he said, and then, after a pause, 'I don't know what has become of young people today."

The old lady nodded in solemn agreement, her arms folded under her ample sagging bosoms and they stood in silent communion for a moment, mutually appalled by the un-discussed developments in urban decay and the morals of youth.

"I will start unloading then", the green man started up, abruptly breaking the silence.

Assenting, the old lady and the giant green monstrosity walked side by side up the road and disappeared round the back of the village shop. A few moments later the green man appeared alone, returning to the truck and stacking crates of virulent purple beetroot onto his trolley, before wheeling it up the road to the shop again.

There were no other people visible in the village, but X sensed movement out of the corner of his eye as around the close net curtains twitched as though disturbed by a light breeze.

Behind the cover of the truck, Clara and X debated their next move.

It was clear that the green man would be unloading the contents of the carriage for some time, and they watched him ferry loads of maize, then wheat then cabbage across the short distance to the old lady's shop. As yet it was probable that no one in the village had noticed them, and Clara was in favour of remaining hidden and continuing their journey on foot, picking up the green man's truck on the other side of the village if it was still heading in the right direction.

X was, on the other hand, overwhelmed with curiosity. "This can't be *them*, Clara", he argued, "The terrifying corporation clones that sealed the cities", he argued, "If it wasn't completely bonkers it would be impossibly twee. Where's the threat? I can't see that little old lady holding us hostage."

Clara was no more than half-persuaded, but X was determined to scope out the village and he followed the green man up the road on his next delivery, Clara tagging reluctantly along behind him. Crossing the green, X had the sensation that he was being silently observed from behind the blank windows, and under this invisible scrutiny, found himself trying to look smarter and more respectable, smoothing down his messy hair, flicking dust of his sleeves and altering his pace from a stroll to a purposeful, upright gait, as though he had some important business to attend to in town.

Outside the old lady's shop, the newspapers with their alarming headlines were proudly displayed on a rack by the door and X peered through the milky glass-panelled windows. Inside, the white-haired old lady stood behind a ceramic counter, engaged in conversation with a grey-haired man in a tweed jacket. Above her, huge distended cobs of sweet corn hung like cured hams from the ceiling, and a behind the counter row of shelving were stacked with canned goods. On the right stood two wooden barrels filled with vegetables, one with potatoes the size of pumpkins and the other by stalks of sugar cane as thick as a man's leg. Displayed in the window were packets of flour, tea and sugar each neatly labelled and stamped with pictures of wheat sheaves, smiling Indian women in saris and roaring lions. A stack of purple jars labelled 'Old Ma Heggotty's traditional sliced beets' sat next to tall thin tubes of 'country-fresh sliced carrot', and jars of jam, each topped with a scrap of muslin and secured with a rubber band, offered raspberry, gooseberry and carrot flavours. One sequence of panes was covered in faded notices stuck to the window with browned sellotape and X read through them carefully. One was an appeal for a lost kitten, and offered gratitude, thanks and respect for the recovery of the little black and white pussy pictured underneath. Another advertised French lessons, giving a PO Box number as a contact address. X was reading a third notice, a strangely aggressive missive that demanded the return of a pair of garden sheers, 'THIEF! WE KNOW WHO YOU ARE!' it began, 'If the garden shears are returned we will say no more about the matter" and he had got as far as, "If not, 'I CANNOT BE RESPONSIBLE FOR MY ACTIONS!'" when the tinkle of the bell announced that the customer had left the shop.

    A dapper old gentleman in his mid-sixties stood in front of them. Under his tweed jacket he wore a crisp white shirt and regimental striped tie, his cuffs were joined by agate cufflinks and a folded handkerchief extended in a perfect triangle from his breast pocket. The old man's long straight nose had a prominent bump on its ridge and a thin pencil moustache above bloodless lips lent him a distinctly military air.

    He had actually taken a step backwards when he first saw them, but the flash of alarm on his face was quickly replaced by a look of wry amusement and, recovering his poise quickly, he extended his hand toward X in greeting. "Visitors! How remarkable!" he declared, shaking X's hand vigorously. "Excellent! You've come straight to the right man. Wing Commander Percival at your service", he announced,

"Call me commander, everyone else does. Retired now of course, but you never lose the stripes eh! And you are...."

"Michael", replied X, picking a name at random.

"And this is...?"

"Zara", said Clara, introducing herself and leaning past to shake the commander's hand.

"Marvellous! Marvellous!"

His moustache twitched on his upper lip and he smoothed it down with his hand as he spoke, part contemplatively and partly to supress his clearly apparent excitement. "You must come with me then, there's nothing else to it", he declared, and seeing the momentary flicker of alarm across their faces, added hastily, "Come and enjoy the hospitality of my home, meet the wife that sort of thing. One must always offer succour to strangers, mustn't one? It's what makes us better than Johnny Foreigner, eh! My wife will be delighted to meet you, she loves nothing better than..." the man hesitated, suddenly unsure of what it was his wife actually liked. "...Meeting people", he went on, "Asking questions, chatting, things like that...woman's stuff..." he petered out, addressing a slightly plaintive look at Clara as though, she, as a woman, would understand these things much better than him.

Clara nodded politely.

He brightened quickly "That's settled then – follow me. It's just across the road. Two minutes, and the lady of the house will have the kettle on."

And without further ado, the old gent tucked his crisply folded newspaper under his arm and gently guiding X by his elbow, began steering them toward the north side close.

In such a short journey, they gained a great deal of information on the commander's views on appropriate garden care. He expressed most of his opinions to Clara, under the assumption that gardening was women's work, including X only when he made disparaging noises about his neighbour's lawns. "Call that a lawn, eh Michael", he forwarded, pointing out a patch of green in a garden surrounded by beds of pale lemon gladioli, "Clover, daisies and dandelions", he reeled them off, "That's a Paki's carpet not an Englishman's glory, eh!"

"No offense", he added.

The commander announced each of his opinions in a loud declamatory voice as though he was giving his squadron a briefing, and his booming voice echoed down the silent suburban street. A rose arbour in one garden was, 'pretentious, green fly-ridden shit', and although he approved of a patch of carefully weeded bizzie-lizzie, he was lost for words at the sight of the giant feathered fronds of pampas grass in the garden next door, and kept touching his nose and muttering to himself until they had passed and was only shaken out of it when a low hedge of tightly-packed dark green leaves bearing small clusters of red berries angered him even more.

"Cotoneaster!" he exclaimed appalled, "Put it on a roundabout. Not in a garden!"

He seemed quite upset about the hedge and was almost shouting in the street now. "Not even good enough for South Close", he boomed.

"Not good enough for SOUTH CLOSE", he repeated, louder still.

Despite the string of negative invective, the commander was clearly enjoying himself hugely and he ushered them between the twin stone horse's heads and through his garden gate with a flamboyant gesture. His lawn was edge-clipped with the precision of nail-scissors, and the flower beds ran in rigid straight lines to the bay window. Potted hyacinths were arranged around the porch and a brass lion's head doorknocker rattled loudly as he struggled to undo the multiple locks on the door.

'Margaret dear. I've brought home some guests", he shouted up the stairs as they entered.

"If you've brought that old bitch Heggarty back again - I'm not doing it, no matter what she says. It's not natural", came a sharp voice from above, "I'll..." The voice stopped abruptly as a woman's head briefly appeared above the bannisters and caught sight of X and Clara standing awkwardly in the hallway.

The commander's wife seemed to lack some of her husband's polish, although she too seemed remarkably well attired for the middle of the day in a matching faun jacket and knee length skirt. Her accent was coarser, her hair brittle with hairspray and dyed an orange colour closest in tone to urine, and her features were pinched and mean, wrinkles around her mouth and nose suggesting a sneer was a more common resting expression than a smile. On catching sight of the pair of them, she touched her hand nervously to her hair, smoothed down her skirt and hastily kicking off a pair of fluffy slippers, descended the final steps in stockinged feet.

When she spoke again her voice was softened and treacly, "You should have told me we were having guests, darling", she cooed.

"I didn't know dearest", the commander explained, "This coloured chap, Michael wasn't it? and his charming wife..."

"Girlfriend", corrected Clara.

"Girlfriend", continued the commander, "Were just passing through so I thought...."

"Yes, Yes, of course", the commander's wife flapped, "You take them through to the lounge dear, I'll get myself ready and put the kettle on

Ushered into the lounge, the commander gestured for them to sit on the large brown sofa, while he sat on the matching chair opposite, its plastic covering crackling as it took his weight. No sooner had he settled then he was up again, in response to a call from the kitchen, and they could hear the exchanges of a muffled, half-whispered argument drifting in through the open door.

X looked around the room. The brown wallpaper was lightly flocked, the carpet beige and a little threadbare, a welsh dresser displayed willow pattern plate and a china dinner service, and a tall grandfather clock ticked loudly and dolefully in one corner. Everything was very clean and a smell of furniture polish mixed with pine-fresh disinfectant pervaded the room

Margaret replaced the commander in the room, entering carrying a tray laden down with china cups and saucers, a bowl of sliced lemons, half a sponge cake and a teapot in a knitted cosy. She placed the pot on a low table and spread out four doilies carefully on its surface. She had slipped on low heels, a pearl necklace and matching bracelet and added a layer of peach lipstick to her thin lips.

"You'll have to take it without milk, I'm afraid" she announced.

While she poured, X could hear the commander behind trying to not clatter the knives and forks as he hastily removed the silver and disappeared with it into the kitchen.

He returned empty handed, "Yes, shame about the milk. Supply isn't what it was. Not that anything is eh?" he snorted disdainfully.

"The only cow in the village is old Mr Swanson's", Margaret continued, "And his cow is as old as he is."

"And he's deaf as a post", the commander interjected.

"He can hear well enough when he wants to", she contested.

"And across the road, Barbara Jessop keeps goats, of course," the commander added helpfully.

"Hah", exclaimed Margaret, "Babs!" she sneered, "All fur coat and no knickers that one", she declared, her accent and decorum momentarily slipping in her spite, "Practically have to beg her for enough milk to make a cake."

"To be fair my dear, she always seems to come up with something when I go over."

"I'm sure she does", said his wife, fixing him with an expression of contempt as though her husband prostituted himself for a drop of milk in his morning cup of tea. She turned back to Clara and touching her arm gently explained in confidence that, "She lies, she does. Always seems to be enough for some. Favourites she has.

Favourites." She practically spat out the word.

"Have you thought of keeping goats yourself", asked X who had always been fond of the animals and felt he should make some contribution to the conversation.

Margaret looked at him as though he had just shat on her carpet.

She snorted angrily, barking at X, "I didn't endure, all I've had to endure to end up some kind of farm slut like Babs Jessop." She gathered herself, forcing some treacle back into her voice, "It's nasty filthy work looking after animals" she purred, "Best left to the lower orders don't you think?" She smiled and leant forward, putting one hand on Clara's knee, "like that Bar-ba-ba-ra", she bleated, laughing loudly at her own joke.

"So what's life like in your village?" asked Clara. "What do you do here?"

"Do!" exclaimed the wing commander, surprisingly put out by the question. "We've done our bit young lady. Retired now. Having some well-earned rest thank-you. We squirreled away a whole lifetime, didn't we dear, scrimping and saving so that we wouldn't have to *do anything* in our old age. You've got to keep your wits about you, young lady, work hard, make sound investments, keep your nose to the grindstone.... Otherwise...well, with the whole damn world gone to the dogs...."

"Don't swear dear", his wife admonished him.

"Quite right darling. Sorry", he continued, his voice rising as he spoke, "But what do these young people know about anything? You mark my words, young lady, once you've worked hard, miserably, every day of your life until retirement, then I'll take some notice of what you've got to say, but until then..."

Having made his closing statement, he sat back proudly in his chair.

"Jam sponge?" offered Margaret, and cut X, but not Clara, a thin slice. "Raspberry jam, from my very own raspberries" she declared proudly.

"I saw some in the shop", said X, hoping that the mood had lifted after the commander's brief tirade, 'Was that your jam?"

Somehow his innocuous question was another faux-pas, Margaret shrieking with scornful laughter at his words, "Oh goodness me no, you stupid boy. Why would I do that? It's that senile old biddy in South Close, Julie Bleasdale that makes the jam. Makes it by the gallon she does, until her fingers are boiled raw, puts it in fancy jars, sticks it in the window, and there it sits until Heggaty gets fed up with the files its attracting and makes her take it home again."

X looked confused.

"Everybody makes jam here. Why would you go to the shop and buy it?" she sneered.

"Why indeed?" inquired the commander.

"Ridiculous woman", Margaret repeated, "Ridiculous."

There was another uncomfortable pause, interrupted by the sound of the letterbox clattering in the hall. The commander apologised and went to collect the mail.

X could see the green man retreating down the garden path and carefully closing the gate between the horse's heads, his brown satchel swung over his shoulder.

The commander had returned to his seat, put on a pair of reading glasses and began pouring over the letter with great care.

"Don't be rude darling", his wife barked, snatching the sheet off him and commencing to read it herself.

"I don't know why we bother", bemoaned the commander, "All we get is junk mail these days, offers for things you don't need, competitions you don't want to enter; save a disabled donkey, give £10 to stop river-blindness", he went on, "All scams these appeals, and if the money you give doesn't go on expense accounts and free lunches for Guardian reading do-gooders this end, then the fuzzie-wuzzies steal it to buy Jacuzzis, Lear jets and chemical weapons at the other."

"No offense", he added.

Margaret put down the flier with a sigh and turning her attention back to the conversation, leant forward again, resting her hand on Clara's arm and, having arranged her face in an expression of concern, dropped the pitch of her voice back to syrupy and asked, "How *are* things in the city my dear? We try to keep informed, of course, but it just seems to get worse and worse, drugs, violence, prostitution, immigrants, sodomy. I don't know how you could hope to raise a child righteously in such filth..."

Clara was saved from having to make a reply by the sound of the green man's truck starting up in the lane. X jumped up, spilling his tea, apologising, and both of them made hastily for the door as quickly as they could despite their host's protestations.

"You mustn't go!" the commander called after them, "I forbid it."

But they were gone, fleeing as fast as they could out of the close, sprinting to catch the truck before it picked up speed. Bursting through the garden gate, X could see in his peripheral vision that the village was no longer deserted. As they ran under the monkey-puzzle and back to the road, people had emerged from their homes and stood standing, sentry-like, at their garden gates, immobile, every gaze directed at the fleeing pair.

They threw themselves on to the rear platform like drowning sailors hauling themselves on to a life raft and before they had caught their breath, the road had turned a corner and the village was lost from sight, disappearing like a desert mirage in the heat haze behind them, leaving only the endless orange fields covering the land once more.

42. THEM

As the truck settled in to its familiar jolting rhythm along the track, they lay back on the platform, letting the breeze blow the commander and his poisonous wife out of their minds. Clara was adamant that she didn't want to talk about their experience in the village. "They were so ugly X", she had said, "Ugly inside. Let's forget about that horrible, claustrophobic place. Please." She shivered with disgust as she spoke, as though she was trying to shake off the memories like dust from her sleeves.

"They hated everything and everybody didn't they?" X agreed, "And yet they seemed to be happy, smug even...."

Clara didn't respond and X let the subject drop, happy to let the swiftly moving truck put miles between them and the villagers.

They made faster progress now that the green man was no longer halting to harvest crops, and he seemed to have no need to repair this stretch of path either, stopping now only to load the bales of chaff needed to keep the engines running. X couldn't regain his earlier contentment however, Clara had withdrawn into herself, and he was perpetually troubled by three fat flies that had joined them at the village, and seemed to delight in making sorties at X's ears every time he began to slip into reverie. He slapped one away, but it simply retreated to hover a safe distance from his arms, buzzing like an unwanted thought demanding attention.

After an hour of monotonous passage through fields of sugar cane as tall as pines, it was clear that the track had begun to turn South West, and X began to wonder if the time hadn't come to jump ship. But the truck was travelling much faster now, and he suspected that jumping off a train moving this fast was a lot harder than the stunt men in the movies made it look. In addition, he dreaded the thought of toiling on foot through the baking-hot fields again, and he delayed the decision until the compass made it clear that the truck had turned due south and they were reversing the gains made earlier in the day. He was about to give Clara the bad news when the truck slowed gently to a halt.

While the green man dumped chaff into the engine vent, X showed the compass to Clara, and they slipped off the track, hefting their backpacks on to their shoulders and getting ready to undertake the next stage of their journey on foot. He felt surprisingly sad to be parting company with the green man. He may not have been the most entertaining of companions, X thought, but as a delivery man and mechanic his role in this world was at least productive and useful and his exchange with the postmistress on reflection seemed much like his own attempts at polite conversation in North Close.

He waved farewell to the departing truck. The green man did not wave back.

The red machine pulled away, quickly gathering speed and was soon no more than a red dot in the distance, moving through fields of cane stalks like a blood-filled louse through fine hair. X batted away a fly that mosquito-buzzed his ear and looked round at his surroundings. The truck had deposited them at a crossroads between two green grass paths. The route west passed over a small stream on a low metal bridge and disappeared into a copse of alder and willow. Thirsty, they scrambled down the bank, and finding the water to be fresh and clean, drank their fill before filling their water bottles and resuming their westward journey.

They saw it when they stepped out of the shade of the trees. A strange, milk white, egg-shaped building that seemed to have been dropped into the fields from the sky. Enhancing the illusion of a celestial origin, concentric rings of raked gravel ran around its circumference, the ripples in the earth like the seismic waves formed at the moment of its impact. The unblemished whiteness of the building's surface had the same eerie, blandness of the London barrier, and he laughed, briefly wondering if it was indeed a mini-dome; one built to encase a city of people no larger than ants.

X felt drawn to the strange building, and was immediately determined to investigate more closely, but Clara reacted with horror at the idea. "Please X", she implored, "The village was just horrible, but this... everything about it says *Them*. Please", she begged him, "point the compass in the right direction and let's just walk round it."

He paid her little attention. There would be miles of beetroot fields ahead. At least this was interesting. Then the thought occurred to him that perhaps it truly was a mini-dome, a hideous personalised prison where someone the Morlocks particularly detested was kept in perpetual solitary confinement. Certain now of the moral necessity to at least attempt to free the prisoner, Clara's desperate entreaties fell on deaf ears and he began walking the perimeter of the gravel rings, trying to see if there was any variation in its smooth surface that might indicate an entrance of some kind. After his first tour he could see no fault line in its walls but sunlight seemed to reflect differently off the very top panels.

Perhaps they were glass. Some kind of skylight?

He went back to the trees, broke off a branch, and returned, advancing straight across the gravel waves with it held out ahead of him. As he walked his feet broke the soft soil on the ridges, desecrating the purity of the circles with seaside footprints.

Only half way across did it occur to him it might be a minefield.

Clara tip-toed behind him in his footsteps.

There was no incinerating blast when his stick pressed against the building's wall. He wrapped his knuckles against a random stretch of the white featureless surface, half-expecting a hidden panel to slide silently open at his touch. Nothing happened, the material was hard and unyielding, and made no sound at all in response to his blow. He began circumnavigating the dome, trailing his hands along its surface as he walked. It felt as frictionless under his fingertips as a show-room polished car, and just when he had decided there was no variation in its billiard-ball smooth skin his fingertips felt something; a shallow indentation in the surface. He ran his fingers along it. The groove was a couple of inches deep and about two feet long. There was another above it.

Steps.

The same sickly-white colour as the building's walls, the steps were only visible thanks to faint shadows cast by the sun in their shallow grooves, but when he looked from the right angle he could just make out their imprints marching one above each other to the skylight on the dome's roof. He set about the climb straight away. At first he made no progress, the steps were so shallow that he was unable to squeeze his boots into the grooves and lacking the strength to climb only using his hands he kept slipping back down. He unlaced his walking boots and tried again. Climbing barefoot it was easier, but not much; he could gain purchase with his toes in the cracks, but his hands were soon slick with sweat and he had to jam his fingertips hard into the grooves to haul himself up onto each successive mini-ledge. He was breathing heavily by the time he cleared the concave lower walls and the roof began to level out. Wiping away the sweat on his T-shirt, he signalled down for Clara to follow, faking nonchalance at the ease of the climb.

Halting before the final step, he waited for Clara to join him, putting his arm around her to help her balance and feeling, once again, the soft warmth of her in the crook of his arm. He leant to kiss her gently, reassuringly, on the lips. She responded feverishly, kissing back with such intensity that he almost lost his balance. Steadying himself and smiling, he began a mock countdown before taking the final step.

"One,

Two,

Three",

They stepped up as one and peered down through the clear glass into the dome below. Below, a giant screen had been tilted upward toward them, as if it had been deliberately placed at an angle to be viewed from above the skylight. The screen was 3d, and from where he stood it was as though he was falling into the frenzied motion it depicted. A few seconds more, and the images on the screen began to cohere. The black circle in the foreground, shaking and shivering, but holding a steady position in the blurred rush of light around it, was the back of a crash-helmeted head, jittering and jerking as though buffeted by a hurricane wind. In front of the head, two hands, gloved in fireproof gauntlets, gripped a tiny steering wheel covered in complex switches and levers. The rest of the driver's body, hidden under the bodywork and truncated by the angle of the view, was wedged in the nose of a single-seater racing car being driven at impossible speed down a long circuit straight, its twin front endplates quivering in the violently turbulent air.

The viewpoint gave X feel the sensation that he was actually driving the car, and as the driver's plight seemed desperate, set his heart racing with fear. The momentum of the race-car was so great that the sides of the track were reduced to a flashing blur of light and shade, and ahead the barrier was rushing towards him at the speed of a punch in the face. The driver jerked the wheel hard to the left, piling on opposite lock as the car drifted beyond the apex, and, still struggling for traction, the car slid remorselessly toward the barrier. Just as X was bracing himself for the inevitable collision, the tyres gained purchase, pitching the car into violent oversteer, and with the driver wrestling it all the way through the turn, the barrier was missed by millimetres, the flat of the rear tire kissing the wall as the car snapped back into line. Before X could take a breath, he was diving down a dip as steep as a ski-slope, then howling up and out the other side, full-throttle into the next corner, the car bottoming out at the crest, sending showers of sparks spraying up from the track. The blue rear wing and fat tyres of the car in front were just visible, mounting the crest ahead in a similar shower of gold.

X was so absorbed in the action on the screen, that it was some time before he noticed the actual driver.

When he did, the disorientation was much deeper and long lasting; his whole sense of self sent swimming upward in a familiar-unfamiliar fracturing of his consciousness. Below him, facing the screen, but not apparent focussed on it, was the top of a man's head, un-helmeted, but completely covered in a blue-black mask with the rubberised texture of a wet suit. The man was lying in a suspensor chair, complexly articulated so that every bump and swerve of the on-screen racing car was reflected in balletic synchrony by the man himself. His hands, held out in front of him, mimicked the movements of the screen hands, but held nothing, clutching only at the thin air in front of him.

The scene below was something he knew, part of some other life he had once lived. He recalled a similar wetsuit, Craig? Charles? Karl! Giving him advice, another woman's face, not Clara's, flashing in front of his eyes. He shook his head violently from side to side to dispel the chaos, then pressed his face against the glass, breathing deeply as he gathered himself.

He looked at Clara, she was pale as a sheet. Was she crying?

Why?

He looked away from the man and back at the screen. The race was still under way, the car screaming down another long straight, now only inches from the blue machine in front, pressed tight under its rear wing, locked in the hole in the air made by the other car and poised to overtake.

X noticed for the first time that there were numbers in the top corner of the screen.

72/72. This was the last lap.

The driver was clearly very good and very brave. The straight was rapidly coming to an end and he remained locked underneath the blue car's gearbox, waiting for the last possible moment to dive out of the slip-stream and steal the lead. The driver left his breaking later than the car in front dared, squeezing down the inside of the corner through a gap no bigger than the car itself, but it was obvious he had carried way too much speed into the corner and was never going to control it enough to avoid a collision on the exit. X watched, unable to breathe, as the driver fought to keep his car stable under the banzai late-breaking. The rear snapped away from him, clouting the sidepod of the car alongside. X caught a glimpse of its driver, fist raised in anger, pushed wide and rattling over the curbing, and then they were through, the tank-slapping having shed enough speed to make the corner with inches to spare. X couldn't help but feel elated, as though he had achieved something himself, and then; only seconds after the moment of triumph, disaster.

Wisps of smoke were coming out of the engine, then they were pouring out in dirty black clouds. Small tongues of orange flame began to lick at the cockpit's side. It was all over. All that bravery had broken something vital in the car, a fuel line, probably, was now spraying petrol onto hot metal.He would have to park it up before the machine became a fireball.

X looked away from the screen at the driver himself. The body in the chair was wracked by convolutions as though he were writhing in agony, his mouth wide open in a silent scream of rage or pain, but despite his violently twitching limbs his hands maintained a firm grip on the imaginary wheel in front of him.

Up on the screen the car was now engulfed in smoke and flame, the driver sawing away at the wheel in a desperate attempt to keep it pointed in the right direction, skidding from right to left on a slick of its own burning oil. As it passed under the chequered flag, it was a ball of flame, components on its dashboard melting, the driver's gloves beginning to smoulder, and the man in the apparatus thrashing his side from side to side in agony.

A huge number one flashed on the screen and then went black.

The driver in the suspensor chair flung himself back, arms outstretched in victory, the chair spinning him in high speed circles like a fairground ride.

The chair stopped spinning.

The man tilted his head back, turning his masked face toward the skylight above. Two bloodshot orbs opened in the dark mask, their demonic gaze fixed directly on X. The man raised one finger in salute.

And then the world went black.

43. ENDGAME

"You should be able to hear me now."

X opened his eyes. He was sitting bolt upright inside the dome, bound to a chair like an inmate in the execution chamber. His legs had been shackled and his hands were cuffed so tightly he had to clench and unclench his fists to keep blood circulating to his fingers. A leather strap across his forehead clamped his head tightly to the chair's headrest. There was a strange sensation in his eyes. Able to move his head only the merest fraction, he could just make out Clara in his peripheral vision. She was tied to a chair in the same manner, her eyelids taped to her brows, her face ghost-pale and frightened. She was staring blankly ahead like a shell-shock victim, tears rolling unchecked down her cheeks.

He tried to call out to her, but although he could feel his tongue moving in his mouth and his jaw working, he was unable to make any kind of sound beyond a kind of breathy wheezing.

The giant 3d screen he had seen from the top of the dome had been swung round to face them and hung directly above the head of their captor, who sat with his back to them, waving his hands over a computer screen seemingly oblivious to their presence. The room itself was almost featureless, its milky-white walls running seamlessly into a rubberised floor of the same colour and lit by a cold, white light which seemed to emanate from the walls themselves.

Having completed his task, their captor spun his chair round and stepped down, standing in front of them with his legs spread and his hands on his hips, silently contemplating them with an expression of amused contempt. His stance was clearly intended to give maximum display to the rigid cod piece that rose from out of his groin like an upturned oven glove. He was very short, as slight as a twelve-year-old boy and with the grotesque protuberance extending in front of him appeared more like a Greek priapic statue than anything human. He had folded back his rubberised mask, exposing a large head, fine brown hair that receded at the temples, and skin so white that it was almost translucent, like that of a creature hauled up from the depths of an ocean trench. He was clean-shaven, and one of his checks bore the pockmarks of adolescent acne.

Having given them ample opportunity to observe his manhood, he threw his head back and laughed, a forced unnatural roar of triumph and contempt like that of a cartoon villain, a laugh that rose in pitch to a sort of squeak and then cut off instantly.

"You will regain the facility of speech in three to three and a half minutes", he informed them. "The paralysis you are experiencing now is only temporary and its duration proportional to your body mass. The necessary flexibility of your vocal chords will return slightly earlier for you", he said, directing his words to X, *"Michael"*, he sneered, "that was the name you gave the suburbians, I believe. I doubt it's your real name, but an aggravating glitch in the programme returned only the letter X when I looked up your data, so we'll stick with Michael."

He turned to stare at Clara, "and *Zara*. You really used your imagination there didn't you - Clara?" he continued, his voice dripping with contempt, "So what does that make you? Mick?"

"In contrast to your pathetic pseudonyms" he went on, "I feel no shame in my name, and have no desire to disguise who I truly am." He bent from the waist in a mocking bow, "Hayek Millstrom III, absolutely *not* at your service!"

He began to lecture his hostages, pacing up and down as he did so.

"Don't get too excited when your capacity for speech returns. I am not remotely interested in dialogue, and won't tolerate interruptions. These are absolutes. You need to remember that you are completely in my power - the chairs you are lying in are wired into my control panel, and with a wave of my fingers I can control your every sensation. I could" he said, his voice cold and emotionless, "make you both spontaneously defecate if I so wished. I won't, of course - my whole domicile would be contaminated. But then..." he mused, "Power is such pleasure is it not? It's not often one gets the opportunity to *truly* infantilise another human. I may decide not to deny myself the pleasure." He made a vague dismissive gesture with his wrist, waving the thought away like a bad odour. "Oh, and don't bother trying to activate the safe words you have embedded. Deleting the command words was my first action after I captured you. Don't look so shocked my dear", he directed his words to Clara, "Who do you think wrote the programme? I am a…. What did you call us? A Morlock! I do like that."

He stopped pacing. "Speech should be returning about now. Is that correct 'Michael'?"

X found he could speak. "Let us out of here you fucking bastard!" he spat out between half-paralysed lips and over a tongue as heavy as a slab of boiled meat.

"Tsh, Tsh, Tsh. That won't do at all Michael"

Hayek swept his arm over the consul and a stinging sensation spread down X's back as though he had fallen backwards into a patch of nettles.

"You see, Michael, I can keep the pain threshold just where I want it. Don't want to trigger the eject button prematurely do we? Let's keep it nice and polite eh?"

"Fuck off!"

Hayek shook his head sadly and made another small gesture over the consul. Needle sharp darts of pain stabbed the soles of X's feet, each one the sensation of standing on a drawing pin in bare feet. He cried out.

Hayek let the pain run a little longer, then suddenly cut it off.

"Nice and polite", he repeated.

X nodded.

"Now that's better, isn't it? Any questions?"

X fought back the impotent desire to leap forward and throttle their tormentor, calming himself just enough to articulate some of the thousands of questions that were rushing through his head. "Why have you done this to us? Why are you doing this?" he forced out through gritted teeth.

Hayek smiled down at X, his voice slow and patient as though he were spelling his words out carefully for an unruly child, "That's better. Although I will need your tone of voice to be more deferential, if you wish to speak again. Remember, 'Michael', you are addressing your social superior, and use language appropriate to such an occasion." He paused a moment before suggesting, "Perhaps it would be useful to imagine you are speaking to the headmaster at your school, or perhaps the governor at your borstal….?"

"You asked two questions. The first is very simple to answer. When you escaped, you broke the rules of our little game. You were trespassers, anomalies in the programme. You had to be detained. And look at the furore you created with the suburbians. Actual, honest-to-goodness riff-raff turning up in their village, dirty, dark-skinned unemployed vagrants loitering by the privet hedge! We can't have that! You had to be brought to heel. We allow you to play in your paradise of mediocrity as long as you don't disturb us. But you couldn't resist could you? Your plastic Pandora just had to have an adventure with her new beau? What did you expect? You would slip through undetected like ninjas?"

He moved his hands in chopping strokes to mimic karate moves.

"Pathetic! We picked you up when you were registered by one of our Mechanic-Gardener-Operatives. You were rumbled by the first Frankie you stumbled across. Couldn't even manage to avoid a lumbering monstrosity with the intelligence of a cow! Not very impressive!"

"The green man!" X burst out, "What did you bastards do to him?"

He was rewarded for his outburst with a gesture from Hayek and a flash of pain across his left cheek, a stinging sensation that lingered, as though he had been slapped with the back of an invisible hand.

"Manners!" Hayek reminded him.

"The green man?" Hayek continued, the pitch of his voice as steady as before, his use of pain clearly a casual act, no more significant to him than the swatting of a fly, "I'm not sure they have a gender in any meaningful sense of the word. And how typical of you people", he snorted, "full of assumptions in your ignorance, instantly up on your high horse before you know the first thing about it. They're terribly useful, the Frankies, aren't they? And very reliable, much cheaper than machines and more flexible, even if they are dumb as oxen."

His pace of delivery was once again slow, as though he were speaking to a child or a simpleton, "No cruelty there Michael. Before we transposed their consciousness into the cyborg-gardener constructs, the Frankies were all highly autistic, near-catatonic mental patients. We rescued them from a life lived entirely in asylum corridors as an act of mercy. We granted them work tailored to their temperaments; tasks that involved minute attention to detail and were embedded in a repetitive, unchanging routine, entirely lacking the troublesome social interaction that had so disturbed them. Tell me, did the post-mistress cause your MGO any distress when she spoke to it?" he waved his hand dismissively, continuing without waiting for an answer, "Wearing their smart uniforms they have been transformed into pillars of the community. We have given them that too. They volunteered, my boy!" He shrugged, "As much as they could. Not much of a life I'll admit, but better than no life at all, don't you agree? They are, at least, happy."

X was about to argue that it was impossible to tell if such a damaged thing was happy or not, when he recalled the green man whistling as he worked. He had, in all honesty, seemed at least content, if not actually happy.

"Cat got your tongue?"

Hayek's tone became cooing and solicitous, "I'm mildly curious as to why you'd want to break out", he began, "perhaps you got tired of being surrounded by underachievers? Did the sheer tedium get to you? The decay? Did the prospect of living in a world where the process of natural succession had miraculously preserved only the cutest of the charismatic mega-fauna finally just seem too childish and stupid?" He laughed. "No", he raised a hand, "Please don't tell. I suspect it was the big-breasted whore's idea wasn't it?"

X's jerked forward in his restraints in response to his insult to Clara, but instead of Hayek punishing him with pain, he leant toward X with a fake expression of concern on his face, "I know this fantasy stuff is terribly compelling", he whispered in X's ear, his voice creamy with patronage, "But you really mustn't forget where you actually *are*, dear boy. You haven't totally forgotten have you?"

He had.

Not now. But he had.

As soon as he had seen his captor's chair, he had remembered the other chair, remembered sliding into its embrace, the mask coalescing over his face, Karl's helpful advice, Svenbrenner's felicitations, her face; Eva. None of this was real, he knew that now, but he *had* forgotten, become completely lost in this electronic artificial world. The very 'Fantasy Role-Playing game', he had scoffed at, had swallowed him whole and was now a nightmare from which he couldn't wake. Then he remembered Karl saying he would be under for a fixed time, with or without the safe word. Twelve hours. That was the limit. But then he became confused again, certain once more that he'd been in Bakhuninland for ever. How long had Karl said it would feel like in the game?

The answer came to him.

Five days.

How long had he been here? He tried to count how many sunsets he'd seen but couldn't remember.

Four?

He thought so. Four. This was the end of the fifth day.

It couldn't be long now.

Then he panicked for a moment and had to struggle not to thrash around in his restraints. Had this monster over-ruled that part of the programme too? Would he be stuck here forever?

No. There would be some way of reviving him back at the facility.

His breathing calmed again.

Hayek had waited, apparently to allow X's internal struggle to run its course, and now continued insulting them, "In some ways", he expounded, "That's the most pitiful aspect of you people. Not only do you want to live in a cuddly little dream-world, where everyone's nice to each other, and nobody tries *too* hard just in case they upset someone, but you can't even face up to your own selves. Oh No! You have to be a super-hip DJ or a black man with enormous muscles. Look at you!" He pointed at X. "I strongly suspect you're not brown-skinned in the real world are you? You're some white boy, pretending to be a bit black because you think it makes you cool. Aren't you Michael? Some insecure little man ashamed even of his own race."

He hadn't got any of that right.

But Hayek had gone on, "And I'm absolutely certain you're not an Olympic standard athlete in the real are you? No low body-fat index for you, all dressed up here like a hero. I suspect it's all jowl, paunch and slippers back at home isn't it? Some fat stoner sitting in front of the computer screen in his mum's house."

Nor any of that.

"And as for you", he turned to Clara, shaking his head with contempt, "I'm glad *I* don't have to pretend to be a sexy young super-woman to feel alright about myself. You should be chastised for your lack of imagination if nothing else", he sneered, "I recognise the VXN9. Picked it off the shelf on your very first day, did you? Very old-fashioned design isn't it? How long did you say you'd been wearing it?"

"Please!" Clara exclaimed, her cry dragged out of her like that of a mother seeing her child run out into the road.

"He doesn't know!" Hayek barked a sudden sharp nasty laugh, "How rich, how perfect. Shall I tell him?"

X was hardly listening, concentrating on fighting down his impotent rage, unable to lift a finger while Hayek bullied his defenceless lover. He could only just make out Clara's face, and the sight was agony; she seemed to be begging Hayek with her eyes while streams of tears ran down her cheeks.

"Oh dear. I'm really tempted - A 'Seeker of Sweden' to boot! Tut, tut, tut, old girl, and your sort *dares* to accuse *us* of corruption." Hayek came to a decision, "No. He'll find out soon enough, and won't that be a nice surprise?"

He turned his attention back to X.

"In contrast to your *lifer* friend, the so-called Zara, I have maintained my physical being. I holiday up there every year. Take a six-week break in the spring, swim, work out in the gym, get my golf handicap down and pound round the exercise circuits until I'm lean and strong. I round off the vacation with a competitive half-marathon, come back as fit as a professional sportsman. I've probably put on a few pounds since then, but what you see is what you get."

He spun slowly round, his arms raised above his head and a gleeful expression on his face, giving them a complete tour of his scrawny body.

X hadn't been touched by Hayek's insults, but his words had made a devastating impact on Clara, seeming to wash away all her courage, leaving her a shaking, sobbing wreck. He yearned to hold her in his arms, tell her everything would be alright, but he couldn't move an inch or even meet her eyes.

Hayek droned on. "And as to your second question - Why am I doing this? The answer is that it pleases me, and after all that is the only consideration that truly matters; my pleasure. But it is also true that your pitiful journey here has been useful to me. You witnessed the motor race of course." He suddenly brightened at the recollection, "The timing was perfect, although I thought at one time that the bleating woman would make you miss it altogether. A fantastic victory, I'm sure you'll agree, painful, but what was ever gained without suffering?" He paused, then snorted, "Wrong audience. What would you know about achievement, with your green hippy fantasies and your cult of failure?"

"Fortunately, however", he continued, "The people that actually matter, did indeed appreciate its meaning, and combined with my elegant solution for your little transgression, the day has given me just the nudge upward I required. It has been an excellent day" he declared triumphantly, "Today's events have ensured my ascent to the Four Hundredth Floor!"

Hayek seemed to have briefly lost interest in them as he reflected on his own success, and when he resumed, he spoke in a patronising, declamatory voice, "That means nothing to you, of course, but let me assure you it is an achievement that only the smallest sliver of the elite ever attains, and would be far beyond your meagre abilities if you were given a million lifetimes to attempt the climb. I have afforded you the privilege of witnessing my triumph, but I must not be disturbed, hence your confinement" He made a dismissive gesture with his hands over them, content that his needs fully justified propping up human beings like tailor-shop dummies in his own private window display.

He stopped talking and the silence was filled by the Clara's wracking sobs. The sound enraged Hayek and he began shouting, his face pressed against hers, globules of his spit splattering her cheeks as he bellowed at her, "Be quiet you stupid bitch! If you don't stop sobbing this instant! I'll make you feel you've been lashed with barbed wire!"

X had to do something, "Leave her alone you bully!" he shouted.

"Nice and polite remember" Hayek warned X.

But he was too enraged, "Congratulations", X spat back, "You've had your fun, hurting and humiliating us. Is that your paradise, video games, bombast and cruelty?"

"Not polite enough, dear boy"

Hayek waved his hands and the sensation of a sharp blow to the testicles overwhelmed him, leaving him hanging in the straps like a rag doll, gasping for breath until the agony passed.

'You forget yourself Michael. Please don't do so again. I take no pleasure in cruelty, or very little, but I have no compunction about using pain for control. It is as natural as breathing for our species to use the whip. After all humanity rose by using pain to control the beasts of the field, and mastery of suffering has always been the mark of the Ubermensch has it not?"

Hayek reflected a moment, or at least appeared to do so. All of his actions had a theatrical quality, over-exaggerated gestures and expressions as though he was playing the male lead in a poor amateur production of Shakespeare. "As you are, absurdly, listed on your data as a 'Seeker of Sweden', I will spare you a few moments to explain", he continued, "Although how rutting in the fields with the first slut who batted her eyes at you qualifies you for that title is beyond me."

X bristled, but a look from Hayek and the memory of the pain silenced him.

Hayek then commenced a long oration as though he was delivering a soliloquy to a rapt audience, "Your misconceptions are so fundamental that I doubt you will even begin to understand my truth", he began, "You in the cities consider yourself free, yet you load yourselves down with responsibilities for each other and restrict your freedom so thoroughly you can no longer see the straight-jacket that binds you. I am free and you are not. I live alone. I live alone and therefore have no need to make a single compromise to satisfy the desires of another. No partner's bad breath or menstrual cycle to take into account, no children's shrill voices demanding endless attention, no afternoons at grandmamma's with only the smell of lavender and her faeces for company, no requirement to consider even the gardener's sensibilities. Utterly un-entangled from the snare of connection to others, I can do just what I want and only what I want, forever! Technology, Michael, has made a fairy tale of life. At the blink of an eye I can access a thousand genie's wishes whenever I chose. Spend a week in a harem of Arabian women, the only purpose of their existence to give you pleasure; track a tiger through the jungle for days and bring it down by a single rifle shot, feel the soft fur on your face, still warm from the kill… take the Cresta run, the ice tearing up at you hard as death. All these and many more have I done. I am free, free like only the gods have ever before been free."

"But that is only part of the story, and even if you could grasp the implications of that fully", he sneered, "You would still miss the deeper truth, that your adolescent version of freedom denies the most fundamental freedom of all. The freedom to dominate our own kind. Who hasn't enjoyed the pleasure of mastery of another? To deny that pleasure is to deny our full humanity. The notion, Michael, that we rose from the primordial slime by co-operation is poppycock. We are not evolved ants; we are a selfish, individualistic species. You only need to watch small children snatch and claw at each other over trifles to understand that. We slaughtered the Neanderthals, murdered the aborigines on two continents, and we have killed or enslaved the weak and stupid throughout history. We were never created equal. There have always been masters and slaves, kings and peasants and there always will be."

Hayek finally grew tired of his monologue, "I might as well lecture the cows in the fields", he concluded, turning his back on them once again and settling back into the suspensor chair, "I have business to attend to. You will stay and witness. You might conceivably learn something, but I strongly doubt it."

Left alone with his thoughts, X considered Hayek's words. They had a sort of nasty, twisted, logic, but in the end he really didn't give a shit. He just wished the whole ordeal was over and he could take Clara back in his arms.

But who was Clara?

The other woman; the one he'd desired for so long, Eva?

Was Clara Eva?

He'd thought so once, then he'd doubted it, then he'd forgotten altogether that there ever was a woman called Eva. When this ended, would he sweep Eva into his arms, sobbing and holding him tight after all they had been through?

If Clara wasn't Eva, who was she?

X took a breath. He would only know when they were back in the facility. One look in her eyes would be all he'd need.

All he could do was wait, try to ignore the ache of his unblinking eyes, the pain in his clamped wrists, Clara's despair. There would be more to endure here before he'd get any answers, whatever the next show on the big screen was to be, Hayek had gone to elaborate lengths to ensure that he and Clara had ringside seats.

Hayek lay back on the headrest and the suit resealed over his face. He made a few gestures in front of him, and then his repose was shattered, the small man's head thrashing in agony as it had during the racing car's immolation. Hayek gave out a cry of terrible pain, and then his whole body pitched forward and lay motionless in the chair.

Minutes passed. X began to wonder if the machine had malfunctioned, inadvertently killing its occupant. He felt no concern at the thought of his torturer's death, but the terrible thought arose that, with Hayek dead, there would be no-one to release them from their bonds. He and Clara would be forced to sit opposite his decomposing corpse until they too succumbed, dying by slow starvation, unable to move a muscle to save themselves.

The hiatus broke suddenly. Hayek raised himself upright in the chair, leaned back in to the head-rest and peeled back his mask. Fresh scar tissue covered his left check from eye to chin, the flesh strawberry-pink and raw, like that of a newly grown skin-graft.

He smiled at X, and pointing at his scars said, "Who I really am."

X's was inclined to disagree. The markings on his face were those of a burns victim who had endured months of skin grafts, painful surgery and recuperation. His face would still have been raw with blood and pus this soon after the race. He also noticed that the new pink flesh had conveniently covered up his old acne scars.

Hayek re-sealed his mask and turned away. The 3d screen flickered back into life, this time affording a view of Hayek's actions from a notional camera located above and behind his head. The picture showed their captor's diminutive frame, now attired in a dark pin-stripe suit, advancing toward a gleaming glass office block that rose hundreds of stories high into a bright blue cloudless sky. They walked with him through the sliding doors and across the floor of a huge atrium. In their peripheral vision, men and women could be seen bowing their heads deferentially, some approaching to shake his hand before retreating swiftly into the background. A beefy, red-faced man in a canary yellow suit, briefly held up their passage, faking a punch at Hayek's shoulder, then squaring up and raising his fists like a prize-fighter, before breaking into a grin embracing Hayek, and slapping him on the back as they moved on. At the mahogany desk at the far side of the floor, where immaculately made-up receptionists were pointing Hayek out to other immaculately made-up women at the counter, he was met by a brown-haired man with the perfectly regular features of a catalogue model. The man was tall and broad shouldered, and exuded a confident masculinity from every pore. He shook Hayek's hand firmly, and as he did so a data strip appeared in the top right hand corner of the screen stating: 'Roger Testament, 8th Vice President, external affairs'.

"Congratulations Hayek", the man was saying, "Remarkable. All in the same day, now that's some going old chap. You've caught everybody's attention I can tell you. We all thoroughly enjoyed the Grand Prix of course, but capturing the two Eloi at the same time. Well, well, well. Panache. That's the only word for it. Panache." He stood back, a manly smile crossing his manly features as he contemplated Hayek's scarred visage. "Not too painful, I hope?" He gestured at the damaged side of Hayek's face.

"Nothing that can't be mastered Roger", Hayek replied firmly.

"And the Eloi, are they still present?"

"Yes."

"Good, give them a little glimpse of glory but best advised not to let them linger longer than necessary. We must always remember to put out the trash at night or the kitchen will stink in the morning."

"Of course."

"Walk with me."

Shoulder to shoulder, the two men strode across the foyer, stoically ignoring the spontaneous applause that broke out around them as they passed. By the time they reached the clear glass elevator on the far side, an honour guard flanked them on both sides and the cheering was raucous.

The lift was marked 'Senior Executives Only'. Roger handed Hayek a swipe card. "All yours now", he said, and gripped the smaller man's hand firmly in his own. Both men held the poise, beaming with self-satisfaction while camera flashes lit the scene.

The lift's rapid ascent turned the people below first into ants, then dots, then nothing at all. Arriving on the 400th floor Roger, his hand on Hayek's elbow, guided him through a grand reception lined with abstract art, briefly acknowledging the dark-eyed receptionist, who curtseyed as they passed. He swept Hayek quickly around a swimming pool and through a well-equipped gym, pausing only to introduce him to his new personal trainer, Thor, a man with a passing resemblance to the Norse God himself, clad in spangly lycra, and who seemed positively orgasmic to meet Hayek. They passed through a room laid out like a Victorian gentleman's club, with high-backed leather chairs and waitresses in black and white maid's uniforms, and through a gleaming cocktail bar whose single-malt whiskeys and fine brandies where tended by liveried youth who bowed deferentially as they passed. From there they toured the offices themselves, each one fronted by a monogrammed smoked glass door, and each one opening out on a view of crystallised skyscrapers that could have been Manhattan, Tokyo or Rio de Janeiro, but was all and none of them at the same time. Each opened door revealed an executive, often an almost exact replica of Testament, seated behind a hardwood desk on a swivel chair, in rooms with soft carpeting and walls lined with leather-bound annals. Hands were shaken firmly, pleasantries gruffly exchanged and then Roger whisked him on; Hayek, the coming man, too important even for the denizens of the 400th floor.

They paused, briefly, before another smoked glass office door, this one monogrammed with HAYEK MILLSTROM III. Rather than enter, Roger, with one hand on his colleague's shoulder, turned him away, "Mustn't keep the board waiting", he said.

They entered a dimly-lit boardroom where twelve middle-aged men in sombre suits were arranged around a table that wouldn't have looked out of place in Versailles.

Testament guided Hayek directly to a tiny Asiatic man with a hard, immobile face and a poker player's dead red eyes sitting at the head of the table.

The label CHAIRMAN appeared in the top right-hand corner of the screen.

The chairman remained impassive as Hayek approached, and it was a Testament variant with grey hair who rose to greet him, shaking Hayek's hand vigorously while congratulating him on his victory in the race.

There was a moment's silence before the chairman himself spoke, "Dazzling victory", he confirmed, "But we are not much interested in games here."

"Quite", said a tall, nervy, man with strange bulging eyes seated two down on CEO's left.

"Will you keep the scarring?" asked the chairman.

It seemed a loaded question, and as though in answer to X's thought, the image on the screen panned out and he could see that the board was evenly balanced between Testament-clones and those with a more natural appearance. Four of the naturals had marks on their faces like duelling scars, and the skin of the one at the furthest end of the table was horribly mutilated. The view switched to a close up of the chairman's face. His left check was marked by faded lacerations as though he had once been repeatedly slashed across the face by a razor-blade.

"I will see how the scars fit my face as they heal", Hayek replied.

The chairman seemed satisfied with Hayek's response but his tone was still terse when he spoke again, "I'm more interested in the Eloi. And one of them a 'Seeker of Sweden' I gather. Quite a prize catch."

"Yes, although he is entirely unremarkable" replied Hayek.

"Let us see the events leading up to their capture", the chairman commanded.

Hayek nodded and a cube of video screens rose slowly upward form a hatch in the centre of the table, ensuring all the executives had a clear view "As you can see", Hayek began, "They first attempted to come out through the tunnels. I tracked back and found them on the infra-red camera" An arrow appeared on the screen, "You can see their outlines on the ledge to the left."

X did not need to be guided to the spot. He could easily pick out their bodies entwined together above the gorge, their fuzzy red outlines merging and unmerging as he had held her shaking body.

"They got no further that way?" The chairman asked.

"No Sir", replied Hayek, "They retreated back into the tunnels."

"There is a way out, though, isn't there", asked the chairman, making it clear that he knew the answer and was merely testing Hayek again.

"Yes sir" Hayek replied, and although he addressed the chairman, it was as though he was speaking directly to X, "If they had dropped a rope down from the ledge, there is an outcrop that leans out above the height of the fall. They could have flung a line across there reasonably easily. The climb up the other side is hard, but they were both set to 'expert' so they could have made it. But they failed at the final test. The last successful escape by that route was twelve years ago", he added.

"I remember", the chairman said. "What happened to him? A man with that amount of gumption should have gone far!"

"The 114th floor", piped up the Testament clone to his right.

"Twelve years", said the chairman, "The same length of time that'd you've been here Hayek, and even with all that spunk he isn't close to the 400th floor is he? Very impressive. We will have to watch out for you." It sounded like a warning. "What next with the Eloi?"

"They came out through the river of course", Hayek continued. We have no guards stationed there anymore and so didn't pick them up until they encountered a Mechanic-Gardener Operative about twenty miles Northwest. Although we missed them coming in, I did pick up some footage from just after, I'm afraid the camera angle's not perfect, but..."

The men around the board table chuckled to each other as the images unfolded on their glasses.

X was forced to watch as the laughing men shattered his and Clara's privacy and desecrated their beautiful moment on the riverbank. He strained to look at Clara out of the corner of his eye to tell her that it made no difference to his feelings for her or to the moment itself, that they could not be shamed by their act, that the only people demeaned here were their tormentors. But Clara was staring blindly at the screen, her face as expressionless as a coma patient. At that moment, X felt something change inside him. Instead of humiliation or even rage he found he no longer cared about the events unfolding in front of him. These people's scorn couldn't touch him. Whatever mattered to them didn't matter a damn to him. He had no choice but to watch, but the scene in front of him was distant now, as though he was watching characters in a nasty, dull play.

The thin executive two rows down had spoken up, his voice irritated and abrupt, "All very amusing I'm sure. But why are there no border guards in your sector. Do you let these vagrants run free across the land, fornicating like rabbits whenever they want to?"

Hayek took the verbal assault in his stride. "There have been eight breaches of the London perimeter in twelve years, ten if you count today's escapees. The cost of recovering those ten trespassers has been 512 yen-dollars in total. The cost of a guard over that time would have been a thousand-fold more expensive. Are you recommended the extra expense?"

Hayek had cut straight to the heart of the matter. Gary was right, X found himself calmly thinking, the words 'extra-expense', were powerful talismans here.

The thin exec was flustered, but stuck with the attack, 'Why not alarms then?"

Hayek was ready for this too. "We found that swans and badgers set them off too frequently. After too many false alarms operatives prioritised other objectives and stopped responding to alerts. When we identified this we removed the system, the alarms cost very little, but if you count in the productivity loses from false alarms..."

Hayek had won the round, giving him the right to move on with his story. I monitored them more closely after they reached the village", he started.

"There've been complaints!" someone from the far end of the table cried out.

"Excellent", said Hayek, his voice unwavering.

"Excellent!" came the voice of another executive around the table, the voice sneering at his words, "That's all you've got to say, excellent!"

Hayek stood his ground, "Yes excellent", he repeated, "Their appearance was perfectly judged. No damage was done and the suburbians were given an opportunity to be self-righteously livid. Nothing, I suspect, could have pleased them more."

There was a wave of laughter around the room.

"Nothing happened?" It was the same voice again.

"They had tea and ate some sponge cake, I believe", said Hayek.

There were roars of laughter round the room this time.

A new deeper voice weighed in from the far end of the table and X's view swung round to take him in. A grotesquely damaged face sat upon a heavy set body with powerful arms and shoulders. One half of his face was brown-skinned with lugubrious features, but the skin on the other half was as smooth and pink as a baby's bottom, and its features narrow and pinched, as though it belonged to a different person altogether. The effect was highly disconcerting.

X suspected he intended it to be so.

"You said you 'monitored them more closely'", the voice boomed, "When exactly did you get a chance to do this? When you were negotiating the Zantorini curves? Were you not more interested in wasting your energy on fripperies than attending to matters of security?"

Hayek paused. Apparently shaken by the accusation.

But when he began he spoke calmly and confidently, "Firstly, I had given my word to corporate bodies, companies and individuals that I would compete in the race. In my view a contract containing the word 'compete', is only fulfilled if you give everything right until the chequered flag. I had given my word. That means something to me." It was a good opening, and Hayek followed it up, "But the key question you have to ask", he started, "Is not, were my actions flippant? But were they *productive* and *economic*." He emphasised the words heavily. "Let me start by acknowledging that I was indeed unable to check on the Eloi's progress while sweeping through the Zantorini curve. But I will return to that later. I had earlier despatched three calliphora370 surveillance drones, a design that's styled to look like blue-bottle flies and imitates their form of flight to avoid detection."

The three fat flies. He should have known.

How could he have known?

"Cost!" someone shouted.

Hayek replied without hesitation, "Just under 0.5 yen-dollar per hour per drone device, for six hours. Nine yen-dollars in total", continuing, "Unable, as you say, to monitor their progress in the curves, I downloaded the required data each time I entered the back straight. I consider this approach 'efficient' rather than frivolous. I could show you the footage from the MGO's truck's tailgate but its monumentally dull, I assure you. After that", he continued, "It was simply a matter of programming the MGO to keep his vehicle moving fast enough to make dismounting dangerous, and directing him to deliver them right to my doorstep. I correctly assumed that the skylight would lure in the 'Seeker of Sweden'. He'd been reckless to enter the village, and I was certain he would be impetuous again. I merely remoulded the skin of the dome a little to create some tantalisingly hidden steps, knowing he would be drawn to climb them. Once I had lured them into making contact with the shell of my dwelling, they were, of course, connected to my systems, and I simply de-activated them, stripping out their escape coding as a precautionary measure. They arrived on my roof on the 69th lap, and as you know, I was very busy at that time, so I let them watch before getting the job done, and then paralysed them as my first action after victory had been secured."

Hayek paused for dramatic effect before continuing, "But the key issue we should be addressing is not what I do for sport, but was the capture conducted economically? You mentioned the Zantorini curves. The footage of my car rounding those very same curves in flames has received 12 million views so far across the six corporations. We have a 2% share in the associated advertising revenues. "In addition", he continued, "The bidding war for the on-car footage, whose rights we hold in entirety, has now reached seven figures."

"Your stake?" someone shouted.

"Forty-nine per cent", Hayek replied quickly, "I am a company man. Moreover", he went on, "Eight million of those views used the word 'Zantorini' in text or commentary, most associated with the word 'wow! The share value of the Zantorini Corporation, in which we own a 25% stake, has risen two percentage points since the race, taking it above the DNA games peak. If we chose to sell we'd be 120,000,000 YDs up, but I am also in a unique position to enhance their brand if we wish to hold. In answer to the fundamental questions of cost and efficiency then gentlemen", he concluded, "Taking into account the cost of re-routing the MGO, and some depreciation on the drones, it works out at twelve yen-dollars fifty. A conservative estimate of completing the two tasks simultaneously would be a profit of 119,999,88 YD, if you'll allow me to round down the decimal point."

His challenger was gracious in defeat, "Congratulations Hayek", he said, "You have earned your place on the 400th floor."

There were mutters of agreement around the room.

"The Eloi are still with us?" asked the chairman.

"Yes", Hayek replied, smiling, "But don't be concerned Sir, I'll dispense with the garbage soon. I'll make certain the kitchen doesn't stink tomorrow morning.'

Even the chairman seemed to chuckle at that one.

Hayek's debut was over and Testament escorted him swiftly out of the room and through the smoke glass door into his new office. He walked across the soft carpet and stood staring out at the other, lesser, skyscrapers falling away beneath him, the master of all he surveyed.

Testament had followed him into the office and perching on the edge of Hayek's desk he pressed a button on the intercom and started loosening his tie. A tiny woman, with long jet-black hair, big doleful eyes and enormous breasts entered the room. She was wearing a black micro mini-dress that hugged her figure like clingfilm. The dress stopped short, high up her upper thighs, revealing a band of pale white flesh above sheer black stockings and she tottered across the carpet on seven-inch stiletto heels. Even with her elevated footwear, the tip of her head was still no higher than Hayek's.

"Meet Nikki", said Testament, "She's working her way up from the 47th floor."

Both men laughed.

"I thought we'd share a perk or two", said Testament, "It's your day Hayek. What do you prefer, cunt or mouth?"

Hayek smiled. "As it's a special day", he said, "I think I'll start with arse if you don't mind."

"Of course not", Testament said affably, "I may well join you there later!'

The girl knelt on the floor in front of the desk and pulled her skirt over her hips.

She suddenly looked very young.

X couldn't turn away or even close his eyes. He was forced to continue staring as the two executives stripped and approached the woman from either end. As Hayek positioned himself in a crouch behind the kneeling girl's buttocks, the camera angle shifted again, rushing to a close up of his face. A bead of sweat ran down his forehead and trickled down the course of his scar, his mouth curled into a lascivious grin and Hayek raised his eyes to stare directly at X.

"Don't like what you see?" Hayek's eyes flashed briefly with rage, "Hypocrite", he spat out. Then his whole face stiffened before relaxing again, his mouth slack with pleasure. For a moment he was silent, his head jerking up and down rhythmically and his breathing coming in gasps before looking up at X under heavy lids, he smiled and said,

"Game over Michael. You lost."

Pain burst through X's body as though he had been electrocuted. Unbearable, searing agony in every muscle, his heart exploding in his chest, blood pounding at his temples as though they would burst.

Then the pain suddenly ceased and it was though he was falling down a dark well into nothingness.

44. THE FALL

Screaming, he opened his eyes.

The pain had gone.

It was silent in the room.

The ceiling had clean, white tiles.

He was lying flat on the chair, every muscle slackened to weakness in the shivering aftermath of the pain. His body felt like it had been systematically pounded with a baseball bat. His genitals felt bruised and tender and a headache of migraine intensity hammered around his brain.

There was a moment's absolute calm.

And then it all rushed in at once.

The pain and humiliation in the chair, Clara's desperate sobbing and Hayek's twisted, leering face his lips curling into a snarl of ecstasy and contempt, inches from his face. X closed his eyes to dispel the images, but Hayek's face continued to hum red under his eyelids like a retinal burn, slowly eviscerating itself like a Francis bacon portrait into a smear or orange and green.

Immobilised in the chair, he suddenly felt trapped, hideously, claustrophobically, trapped. The suit, its sweat-skin still meshed with his flesh, wrapped around him like a winding sheet, sealing off his nostrils suffocating him. Gasping for breath like a sprinter at the end of a race, he began tearing at the plasticised skin on his face, but his gloved hands could gain no purchase. Flailing his limp arms around helplessly, he toppled out of the chair, peeling away from its surface like detaching from liquorice, and crashed face-first onto the floor.

For an age, he lay on the cold tiles, fighting to control his breathing and lacking the strength to move, his head spinning, a tendon in his left leg twitching in involuntary spasms like a stopwatch counting off the seconds. He eventually struggled to his feet and staggered across the room, sweeping a row of bottles off a shelf with a trailing arm as he lurched toward the exit. Outside, he was immediately overwhelmed by vertigo. The white-walled corridors, stretching long and featureless in either direction, began pitching like a ship breaking heavy waves, and X lost his balance altogether. He crashed hard into something and the impact sent him tumbling to the floor.

"Whoah buddy!" a disembodied voice exclaimed, "Are you OK?"

X tried to focus on the figure in front of him, but his sight was blurred and losing grip of the horizontal axis of his vision, the man began to spin slowly round as though he were trapped in a tumble-dryer.

His sight cleared enough to make out a tall, muscular man with tousled black hair and a rolled towel draped over one shoulder leaning over him.

"Olaf?"

The man leant closer. It wasn't Olaf.

"Can I help?" his voice was full of concern.

"Get me out of this suit!" X gasped, his voice, high and pleading.

"OK buddy, stay calm. Deep breaths now."

The man made a few small movements around X's throat and the material covering his face relaxed and slid back over his head, flopping back like a hood over his shoulders. The body of the suit peeled away like Velcro from his skin, leaving him lying in the corridor in a floppy wetsuit that sagged at his knees and elbows.

The man helped him to his feet, talking to him in a reassuring voice, "Come up from a deep one, have you? Don't worry you'll be fine in a moment or two. Is this your room?"

X thought so.

"Pop in there then, ditch the suit and grab a towel, I'll take you down to the shower room. You'll feel a world better after a good soaking."

*

In the silent roar beneath the showerhead, his mind slowly began to clear.

It was all a game.

An immense wave of relief rolled over him. Just a game.

All the odd, ugly, foul things,

Unreal. Just the stuff of some programmer's fantasy.

Even the pain.

Unreal.

Clara! What had happened to Clara?

Oh God! Was she still trapped in the chair?

Then, Eva; all his memories of her unspooling like a cassette tape on fast forward, refilling him with all that was her.

He was lost again, utterly bewildered once more.

Was Clara Eva?

If not who was she?

From there the possibilities seemed to spiral away to madness.

Giddy with confusion, he let go of the wall, and blinded by the thundering water lost his footing for a moment on the wet tiles. There was a sudden sharp pain in his leg, just below his knee, as though somebody had kicked him, although he was completely alone in the shower, and he slipped further, nearly losing his balance altogether. As he fell, he instinctively reached out to protect himself, but instead of finding only air, his fingers pressed into something plastic and unyielding, as though the barrier had reformed in the facility. He thrashed at the invisible screen but just as he got enough purchase to get a tug on its slippery surface it disappeared, leaving him hoping about on one foot until the pain in his leg faded away.

When he finally willed himself out of the shower, he found that the man who had helped him earlier had hung around in the changing room to make sure he was OK. It was a very thoughtful gesture and X thanked him as whole-heartedly as he could.

The man was dismissive of X's thanks, "Really it's no trouble at all", he insisted, "That's why I don't do deep dives. Coming up's too rough for my taste! I bet you've been dashing about in the game, feeling fit and strong, starting each day fresh and full of energy. But actually you've been lying flat on your back in the chair for 24 hours or a week or whatever, as though you were laid up sick. The machine does all the work for you", he explained, "That's why your muscles are so slack and weak right now, they haven't done any real work in a long time. Hey!" he exclaimed, take a swim when you feel ready, it feels great, like your real body's coming back to you."

X nodded. He was slowly reviving, but still weak, and he was grateful for the man's company as he struggled to raise the strength to towel himself dry.

"I pop in for long weekends mostly", he continued, "It's like owning a beach house or a cottage in the country but without the maintenance!" He smiled at his comment and X managed a smile in response. "Got a little piece of virtual estate in Bakhuninland, down by the river ..." He paused noticing X's startled reaction, and asked him if he knew the game.

X confirmed that he did, managing to stutter out that he had just come from there.

The man took encouragement from their shared interest and went on. "It's a beautiful place isn't it", he said, "I love the quiet, slowed-down pace, the way everybody treats each other decently... I only *really* relax down there on my little plot. Always come back refreshed. My place is right down on the riverbank and the fishing is tremendous..." He shrugged, "Bit close to the barrier mind, but Hey! It's a long running game and I was late to join – that's the way it goes. The view *downstream* is lovely anyway."

X could feel it coming before he said it, and sat with his head in his hands as the man carried genially on. "Mind you", he continued, "It wasn't quiet this time! Two people swam the river tide out of the city! Crazy! As I said", he continued, "I'm close to the barrier, so the whole thing was right outside my doorstep, so to speak. A lot of people came by", he went on, "I got a barbeque going and we all cheered when they popped out of sight. Though goodness knows why we were cheering", he added, shaking his head, "It's like cheering a suicide on a ledge. Why would anyone want to do that? He shook his head again, "knew a girl once", he was saying, "Swam out under the barrier for a bet. Used to see her a lot before, but she only came back once or twice after that, said it wasn't the same for her anymore...."

X could understand that.

But nothing seemed to add up. Did everyone know you could swim the barrier at high tide? Did Clara know? Then why the caves? And if Clara wanted to see her sister so desperately – Why didn't she just leave the game?

*

When he got back his room Karl was waiting for him. He stopped inspecting the equipment and got up as soon as X entered, rising with a smile of relief on his face and enveloping X in a bear hug before stepping back and looking him over.

"You look OK", he said, "Are You?"

X managed a nod, he felt rubbery on his legs and exhausted, and his mind was crammed with conflicting emotions and ideas. He was dazed.

"Pain shock?" Karl asked.

X nodded, it probably was, at least partly.

The pain blast Hayek had given him had triggered his automatic exit from the game. "Set off all the alarms back here", Karl shook his head. "They'll all be here in a moment so I'd better check you out." He slipped a contact sheath over one of X's fingers to monitor his pulse, and took a blood sample while X sat half-slumped on the suspensor chair. "What happened?" Karl asked, "Did you fall off your bike. I knew I should have advised you against 'cyclist' as your specialist skill", he said, shaking his head with remorse, "Even set at 'expert' those potholes are lethal."

If only it had just been a bike accident.

He tried to explain what had happened, starting his account at his escape from the city with the words, "After we had got out of the dome..."

But Karl interrupted him straight away, a confused expression on his face, and made him repeat the sentence several times. When he was certain he hadn't misunderstood X's words he let him get on with his story, and stayed quiet and attentive from then on, letting him speak without interruption until his tale was told. When X had finished a shortened version of events, sparing Karl the most gruesome details, there was a prolonged silence.

"Wow!" Karl eventually exclaimed, letting go a huge lungful of air he appeared to have been holding on to for the full length of X's speech. "Wow X! That is the maddest story I have ever heard." He stood shaking his head awhile. "Shit X!", he exclaimed, "You broke *into* jail!"

X didn't understand what he meant and asked him to explain.

"Man", Karl replied, "You don't want me telling you this sort of stuff...as a Seeker of Sweden and everything... You'd be better off waiting for your anthropologists to get here, they'll to get here, they'll explain it much better..."

"Anthropologists?"

Karl blinked when X said the word, and speaking as though he were merely stating the obvious, went on, 'Yes, the two professors and the post-grad, the one that's studying you, the tall pretty one..."

Anthropologists? The post-graduate student who was studying him, the tall pretty one?

Eva.

Karl had gone silent, lost in his own thoughts and entirely oblivious of the punch in the guts he had just given X.

All that time.

It was so obvious and he was such a fool.

He'd known that Tasan and Erika were anthropology professors from that time in the room of African masks. And as Erika was Eva's tutor she was clearly studying anthropology too. If he'd thought about it at all before, it hadn't disturbed him, she rarely discussed her studies, and then only in very general terms.

Because she was studying him.

That was the hammer blow. All those times when he had thought that she had sought out his company because she liked him. Not so. She had met him to further the research project she was engaged in.

Pieces began to fit together in his mind. He remembered Erika's words in the university café, after she had given him his study schedule she had instructed Eva with the words, "Understand that I am expecting thorough, focused scholarship and reports written with appropriate rigour this time."

She had taken notes after he had left and discussed her subject's behaviour and response to stimuli in her weekly tutorial.

The sadness was achingly deep.

He clutched at straws. Being a Seeker of Sweden? That was an honour wasn't it?

No.

There was always a question mark after it, wasn't there?

What was a Seeker of Sweden?

He had taken it as a badge of merit, but now he thought that, after all, he had merely been a 'seeker' of some unstated and never-reached goal, and 'Sweden' the destination point at which their anthropological study would acknowledge his ascent from savage to civilised being. And what then? When he had reached their exalted standard and was considered good enough for Sweden? Would he be allowed to rise as high as the 114th floor like the dome escapee in Hayek's world?

That was the purpose of the journey by boat, he understood now. They were studying his responses to different cultures. No doubt sitting down for case conferences in the cabin after each of his visits.

'Bonobo-boy.' 'Gorilla-man.' 'Chee-chee'. 'He doesn't look like a chimp...' Xanthia's had been the most honest of all of them.

His mouth was dry. He felt sick.

No. There was friendship too. He was sure of it. She'd

batted away Erika on the university steps so that ... No that meant nothing, but she had introduced him to her friends...they had been through a lot together. Surely their experiences in Bakhuninland had changed their relationship for ever and whatever it had been in the beginning no longer mattered at all?

Only if Clara was Eva.

Karl broke his chain of confused thoughts. The technician had undergone a change of heart about his responsibilities. "Maybe its destiny", he declared, "That I'm the only one here to give you vital knowledge at a crucial time. Hey!" he exclaimed, "Perhaps I'm your accidental spirit-guide, the humble techie who somehow plays a pivotal and unknowing role in the 'Seeker of Sweden's' enlightenment. You know - like a humble page offering key advice to the valiant knight. Does it work that that?" he asked.

X could only shrug his shoulders. He had no idea.

Karl was undeterred, and entered into his task with due seriousness, speaking well and choosing his words thoughtfully. He began by saying, "As we see it, the society we've created is one where poverty has been eradicated, life expectancy vastly expanded; the entire, highly-educated populous is gainfully employed, and there is both plenty of leisure time and the means to pursue your private interests. A genuine utopia. This has been achieved, of course, by simply following the fundamental truth; that if we look after the interests of all equally; we all prosper. Wealth, capital or power concentrated in a few hands is immiscible with our egalitarian society, but who cares? The highest quality of life yet known to man is available to all, we believe, if we all focus on the collective good." Karl paused for breath, rightly pleased with his summary before beginning again, "But what if you are someone who cannot abide a world designed this way? Karl had warmed to his theme now, "All shades of grey", he continued, "But if we just deal with the two types you encountered...."

"One: Those who just love power more than anything else. From your common bully, to those who are never happy unless they are bossing someone else around, right through to the full-blown sociopath who can't, or won't, understand that other's emotions are as real as theirs, or do, but just don't care. What do you do with them?"

"And, Two: The misanthropes. Like the ones you met in the village who have weighed up humanity and found it wanting. Hang on...." Karl scratched his head. "Philosophy class – I can almost remember it... Jeremy Bentham... Nineteenth century? ...Eighteenth?" He reached for his glasses then thought better of it, aware that he was losing the thread of his argument. "Anyway, Bentham listed the pleasures of man - my philosophy tutor made a big thing of it, after amity; the pleasure of friendship, Bentham listed enmity, the pleasure of disliking others, the joy of holding grudges and looking down on people. What do you do with the people who hold the pleasure of enmity more dearly than that of amity?" he declaimed rhetorically, answering his own question "Our world would be torture. What would there be to complain about? Who to despise? Pity instead of respect in everybody's eyes."

"You can't force these people to agree with you X", Karl continued, "but if you let these two groups alone, the first will inevitably raise up a dictator to burn down your system and the others will dance in the ashes, knowing that they were proved right all along and everything really was going to the dogs. So we give them an alternative. If what you want is the spiteful little village; you can have it. Live there forever, delighting in the failings of others and hurting no one at all, existing only in the company of other miseries and misers, all equally happy in their mordant loathing of their fellow man. And the dangerous ones, like this Hayek you encountered", he went on, "the ones that want power that badly? We give them mighty towers to build in the virtual world, rivals they can trick or enslave, crystal-perfect tyrannies to raise from the dust. Those that want it red in tooth and claw can have their Darwinian struggle. No one is harmed in the real and only volunteers need play. The sadist finds his masochist and everybody's happy, so to speak." He shrugged. "I mean it's freedom, but it's jail really. I suspect a nasty one like Hayek isn't permitted to leave the facility grounds. But why would he? He has everything he needs here."

X felt he understood now, the madness made some kind of sense after all. Hayek had thought he lived in a utopia too, he'd told them as much, and if you were a misanthrope, even the poisonous village might seem like paradise.

"You breaking into jail is a weird one though", Karl went on, a puzzled expression on his face, "I assumed your handlers expected you to wander around in Bakhuninland, soak it all up, and come back with some perspective on anarchy as a political system, then pick your brains – see if you considered it to be 'Sweden' or not. But Hey! What do I know?" he laughed, "you're the first, 'Seeker of Sweden', I've met, maybe you were supposed to consider all the options.'

Was he? Did he care anymore if he did what he was *supposed* to do?

"I mean no disrespect or anything X", Karl added, "But you don't come across as some super-wise guy particularly. I mean, It's not like I feel I'm in the presence of Buddha or anything. How did you get the title anyway?"

X had no idea. Even if he had the title he didn't want it any more, it was irrevocably tainted.

The others returned into his life in swift succession.

Svenbrenner, who he had all but forgotten, was the first in the room. He entered with a sheen of sweat on his forehead and a shortness to his breath suggesting he had only stopped running down the corridor just outside the door. He curtly asked Karl about X's medical condition, dabbing his forehead with a white handkerchief as he spoke. Karl confirmed that he had run the necessary tests, and the 'Seeker of Sweden', was a little shaken up, but unharmed, needing nothing more than a sauna and a swim to restore him to full health. Svenbrenner expressed his delight in X's good health and then disappeared, sliding gracefully out of the room as Erika and Tasan crashed through the doors.

He had forgotten about them completely too.

Erika's angular face, flushed pink by the exertion of rushing to his side, was taught with concern and her eyes scanned across X like laser beams. Tasan, however, arrived slightly later, and was unmistakably smiling from ear to ear.

X suddenly realised that he didn't like Tasan. He understood now, that while the professor probably had some nominal oversight over the research, he was in practice on a grand holiday on the faculty's expenses, top quality seats at the DNA games and a long sea voyage. He was on a jolly. No wondered he smiled all the time. No harm there really, but Tasan seemed happiest when things went wrong, or it was all a bit ugly, or he could get one over on Erika. He'd never liked Erika, never liked the way she treated Eva, but at least she had the decency to look concerned, Tasan looked like he'd won a bet.

Then Eva arrived.

And he knew, as he must always have known, that Clara was not, and had never been, Eva.

One look into her eyes was enough.

The concern on her face was real, but she looked out from eyes that had not been assaulted by Hayek's defiling face, or marched across the endless fields with him, or lay with him in the moonlight on the bank of the river. They were clear, beautiful, ice-blue eyes, unblemished; remote from him. They were not Clara's eyes.

Who was Clara then?

What had he done?

He was obliged to tell his story once again. This time, he tried to soften the moment were he revealed that he had broken out of the dome, and so he started the tale even earlier, padding out his story with Tanoop, Gary and Levi, the ting and the races, but the room was still shocked to silence when he described shooting under the bridge with Clara. Time seemed to freeze; Erika's face, pulled taut now with anger, her jaw locked rigid with rage; Tasan, his head thrown back, making a short sharp cry that could have been surprise but sounded more like laughter; Eva with her hand raised in front of her mouth in shock.

Tasan broke the ensuing silence, his question slithering across the room to X, "And who is Clara?" he asked.

At that moment, he couldn't help but turn to Eva. Not that he had any doubt now that the two women were separate people; his look was merely a backward glance at a lost dream. But the moment was too charged for even the smallest of gestures to pass unnoticed. Eva start back a step in shock.

When she spoke it was it was to confirm what she thought his look implied, "Tell me X, what did this person look like?"

Before he had thought it through, he began, "Like you...."

He had so much more to say, how he meant to say like you *in spirit*, but different...But Erika talked over his attempts to expand his answer, almost spitting at him through pursed lips, as though she could only just conquer her rage enough to get the words out, "And did you have sex with this person?" she demanded to know.

Erika's question stripped X of his dignity, exposed him as though he had been caught wanking under the bed sheets by his mum, and forced to justify his actions in front of...

Eva.

He saw the expression of disgust break over her face, and understood. He had had sex with an avatar that looked like her. He had been caught masturbating with a love doll with her face on it. It was a violation by proxy, bringing a seedy, inappropriate infatuation to its inevitable sordid conclusion. But it wasn't seedy, he wanted to say, as tears began to form in his eyes. What he had with experienced with Clara, had been the most beautiful thing that had ever happened to him. Hadn't it?

With Clara. With who?

His eyes stayed fixed on Eva as she shut him out forever, a rushing away from him at telescopic pace, a journey never to be reversed. The retreat of her eyes from him paused just once, like the backward glance of an old lover leaving the room with someone else, a little sadness, disappointment, then disdain, and finally, just before the shutters closed down for good; pity.

Eva turned to face Erika directly. "That's it", she declared, "Finished. I'm declaring this project over."

Erika tried to splutter an objection, but Eva silenced her with a look.

She was beautiful, even now, full of controlled anger, indomitable. "The ethical basis of this project is open to serious question and I will be placing my concerns in front of the University Board. The rights of the subject have not been fully considered, and the primitive has been made vulnerable without his full consensual understanding."

The primitive.

"So *now*, you form an attachment to the subject", Erika spat out at Eva.

Again, she was silenced by Eva's stare, "And I", Eva continued, livid now, "will not continue to prostitute myself in the interests of however dazzling a research opportunity this was, if that was ever it's real purpose. It is finished Erika", she said with a sigh, "I will clean up the last of your mess and then we all go home. And you!" She looked over Erika's shoulder at Tasan, 'I don't know why you think you can stand there smirking like the cat who got the cream – In the end it makes you worse than her.

Get Out! Go. Both of you. Now!" she shouted. Then her voice altered, still determined, but softer, and faltering as she spoke, she added, 'I need to explain some things to ...to...to X. He has a right to know what has been done to him."

He loved her for that, not at the end of things, 'the primitive', she was terminating their association with the kiss of his name on her lips; not the genus she classified him under.

X was crying silently now, and as Erika and Tasan walked out of his life, he saw their leaving only through a haze of tears. Erika seemed humbled by Eva's words and shuffled out with her head bowed, but Tasan was uncowed, striding to the exit with a jaunty step and his head held high. At the doorway there was some kind of altercation between them, and seemingly in response to Tasan's goading, Erika took something from her pocket and stuffed it into his hands before pushing past him and out the door. Tasan paused before leaving the room and through his tears X watched him flick what appeared to be a gold coin high in the air, catching it mid-flight before tucking it smartly into his jacket pocket and having secured his prize, the old man danced a little jig on the spot, before hopping through the doorway and out of sight forever.

Karl had tried to slip away too, but Eva had stopped him in no uncertain terms "You are needed here", she commanded.

She led them wordlessly out of the room. Selecting a door off the main thoroughfare seemingly at random, she marched them down the sweep of one of the white-walled corridors that ran into the heart of the mountainside. They walked for a long time in silence with Karl and X struggling to keep up with her fierce pace.

Then suddenly she stopped.

X looked down the corridor. Ahead of them the sterile white walls ran into the far distance, every one of the thousands of doors along its length closed and every window shuttered, the only movement along its whole length a solitary service robot, its rotating brushes buffering the floor as it crawled slowly away from them. He looked over his shoulder. The corridor behind was a mirror image of the length in front, utterly empty and nearly featureless.

They had stopped nowhere.

There seemed no particular reason for Eva to have chosen this exact spot to deliver her final address. Perhaps she had simply walked far enough to work off her anger and was now sufficiently collected to say what she wanted to say.

She began by asking Karl to explain what an avatar was, and X recognised the tone of her voice. She had returned to the educative, dispassionate manner she had used so often when they first met; she was going to explain something to him now in measured steps, giving him a chance to reach his own conclusions.

X found it familiar and almost soothing to hear her talk this way, he imagined for a second that he was back in his early days on campus, and she and Pooja were explaining something to him in the long meadow grass by the stream.

But her voice was colder than that.

She spoke first to Karl, "Explain to X what an avatar is."

X felt he understood this already, but listened attentively to Karl's answer, still hoping he could somehow redeem himself in her eyes. "It's a form you occupy in the game world." Karl explained dutifully, "It doesn't have to look like you, of course", he added.

Eva pressed on, speaking to X directly for the first time, "The people you met in the game, can you name some of them?"

He stuttered them out in the order he'd met them, with only a small choke when he voiced Clara's name aloud.

"Who did you meet first?" Eva asked.

"Gary."

"Karl. What can you tell me about Gary?'

"I can't discuss individual members of the game", he waved his hands, "Really. I know you're angry, but its confidential, I can't give you that information. I'd lose my job, and I wouldn't anyway, it would be wrong"

Karl was clearly adamant so Eva tried a different track. "X, what was the first thing you knew about Gary?"

It popped straight into his head. "That he was a friend."

Eva turned back to Karl, "Now can you *generalise* a little about Gary...."

"OK. Some", Karl admitted, "Gary's probably a greeter. His job is to meet people new to the game and help them settle in. Greeters are chosen by recommendation from the other long-term game-players, who consider them to be residents with wise heads on broad shoulders so to speak."

That was Gary.

"Describe him to us", Eva commanded.

X obliged, and did so again when she asked him to describe Levi, sure he knew where she was taking him.

"Why do they look so different?" Eva asked Karl.

He explained, "There's two different ways you can represent yourself in the game. Actually there's millions of ways, but two basic main types. Either you chose an avatar that looks like yourself - you might age that avatar in real time- you might not. I'd suspect Gary is that type. He would probably have looked similar if you'd met him in the real world. Alternatively, you can choose some kind of fantasy figure – Your Levi sounds exactly like that. A black super-athlete without a hair out of place," he smiled, I've no idea want he looks like in real life but I very much doubt it's that."

He sounded like Hayek.

He hadn't been listening then. He was now. He knew what was coming. Hayek had as good as told him so...

"And Clara?" asked Eva, her voice almost sweet.

'The VXN9', Hayek had said, 'Picked it straight off the shelf on your first day, did you?"

He hadn't understood the mockery then.

VXN9.

The Vixen 9. He got it now. Clara was wearing a standard hot-chick body that Hayek had sneered at for being out of date. He had no idea what she looked like.

He thought about his own body within the game. Sure he'd been browner, a bit skinnier and maybe slightly taller, but he'd still looked like him, maybe Clara...he shuddered to a halt in the middle of the thought. He hadn't looked in a mirror the whole time he had been in Bakhuninland. He could have been looking out from anyone's face; he'd only *assumed* it was his. The thought made him feel sick.

Seeing the distress on his face Eva's was suddenly apologetic, 'I'm sorry X", she said, "I know this must seem cruel, but you need to know what has been done to you."

The same ominous words again. There was more to come then.

She began asking him questions about how long Gary and Clara had been in the game. X replied like a witness giving evidence in a court of law. Clara had indeed, often talked about the early days of the game as if she had been there, so had Gary.

She turned to Karl, "And how long has the game been running?"

"Thirty years."

But X knew it was more complicated than that, and on Eva's prompting Karl confirmed his thought, calculating the amount of time that had really elapsed, "OK if someone had been down there from the beginning...The game runs mostly at 'normal'", he flicked down his glasses, "No!" he exclaimed, raising his glasses again, "It ran at 'slow' for the first ten years while it was getting established - so real time. They've been there... about twenty years", he concluded.

He knew what Eva was trying to tell him now, that not only did he not know what Clara looked like, but that Cara was also old.

But he wasn't convinced. Say Clara's parents had taken her into the game when she was a teenager, say fifteen for an adventure, she'd be what, thirty-five. He'd have put her in her late twenties in the game, but it wasn't so much of a stretch.

He tried to work out her age.

All those relatives. He still had all the data stored in his memory. **James: Clara's sister-in-law's son by second marriage.** He was her brother's son by a younger wife. Lars had been a grey-haired man in his fifties. But her brother could have been much older.

Without a name he had no data.

He tried another. **Andrew: Clara's second cousin on her uncle's side.** Too complicated

Martin: Clara's uncles' third son. Didn't tell him much.

Helena: Clara's ex-brother-in-law's granddaughter. Helena had been a bull-necked woman in her mid-thirties. Grandaughter?

They were right. Clara was old.

He started aging his image of her in his mind. In her late forties, still trim and athletic but more Thai-chi than aerobics now; then grey-haired and elegant in her fifties, still able to turn a good heel. It didn't seem so bad.

Then the wizened old face of the pumpkin grower whose crop he'd destroyed loomed up at him. Karl's words suddenly made sense of the scene 'Some choose to age their avatars in real time....' The old man had recognised Clara, but she hadn't recognised him, at least not at first. No, it proved nothing, he could have been much older than her when he entered the game. Then Hayek's sneering face flashed in front of his eyes, Clara's desperate tears; had her age been the secret she was so scared he'd reveal? What had he said? 'He doesn't know does he? ...and your sort dare to accuse us of corruption....' Another face flashed up involuntarily in front of him, a toothless old lady lying on a bed in a filmy negligee, her ulcerous legs and swollen feet laid out across the bedspread.

He felt himself gagging.

No she didn't have to be that old. He couldn't really be sure. He took a long deep breath to calm himself. Did it matter if she was old? What he'd shared with Clara could still be beautiful couldn't it? The flesh in the game had been young after all and the feelings were true whatever the covering....

A Zimmer frame, a stair lift, the smell of full incontinence pads...

He gagged again.

But still, somehow, Eva was not yet done.

"I'm sorry X", she said, laying a hand on his shoulder. It no longer had the electric affect her touch used to have on him, but it was kind, and he had to fight to keep himself from breaking into sobs. "Karl", she asked, "What is the best indicator that someone has been in the game a long time?"

"If they eat, "he replied bluntly, and then expanded his answer, "I explained to X before he went in that it's a bad idea to eat in the game if you're a day-tripper – digestive juices etc. But if you intend to stay down a long time and don't want to leave the game to eat you can get an adaptation to the apparatus"

"Explain", commended Eva, stony-faced.

"Well the problem is", Karl began, "That if you want to eat on command you need to be digesting food with texture and nutritional value at least, and you're obviously going to have to be fed automatically. You can't inject straight into the stomach, because the lip, teeth and jaws are going to be working away in the game and they need something to chew on. So the solution is to seal off the whole mouth cavity, leaving breathing slots of course, and attach a feeder tube to a central vat. A lumpy nutrient solution slides down the tube and into the mouth whenever the player eats. It's just slops, of course, but we programme the sensors on the tongue to treat it as all manner of culinary delights. The tricky bit is that the seal around the mouths got to be tight, these systems aren't locally monitored…" he swept his arms along the walls of the corridor before continuing, "you can't have any leakage around the mouth, so as I said before, the adaptation is kind of surgical."

All the time Karl was talking X was wracking his brains to remember if he had seen Clara eating. He couldn't remember her having any stew round at Gary's. Gary, Levi, John, Kate and Rhiannon had all tucked in, but he could only remember her drinking cider. Nor the next day either, she'd only taken photos and left at the stone breaking she hadn't stopped for lunch.

Then he remembered.

By the rock fall, where the line of the barrier had crushed the cavern roof. He remembered the apple, pithy and tasteless to him, and Clara declaring, 'I'm famished' and working her way through her picnic with relish while he sorted out the kit. Clara had the surgical adaptation that to enabled her to eat food in the game. That was why she couldn't leave Bakhuninland to see her sister. She had been in the game, lying flat on her back, for twenty-years.

He looked down the endless sweep of the corridor into the mountain. In one of those shuttered silent rooms for twenty years.

What would she look like now?

And then it came to him, an image flashing into his mind in a single, searing, hyper-real vision. The second flat he had visited with Jorgund so long ago. The obscenely fat woman laid out on the chair as on a mortuary slab, folds of her ill-smelling flesh flopping over each other like slabs of tripe, the white feeding tube rising to the ceiling.

Jorgund's words, 'Immersers... They're mostly up in the mountains...'

Clara?

My love?

The white-walled corridor seemed to stretch, curl and rush away at the same time. Karl and Eva slid away from him as though on ice until they were indistinct stick figures in the distance, barely human at all, and then the whole passage began to be sucked into a spinning vortex, dragging his feet out from under him. He turned away and he opened his mouth to scream....

FLASHING RED LIGHT

He could hear nothing. Was he still screaming?

There was a sweet smelt in the air, the scent of coconut mixed with soap, of clean skin, and other, more rancid, odours drifting around in the background.

He was lying on his back on something soft and comfortable.

Sight returned in a blink, a white wallpapered ceiling with a familiar L-shaped crack appearing above him.

He sighed with relief.

He knew where he was. He was lying on his back in his own bed. He looked down his body, struggling to raise the strength in his neck muscles to lift his head. He was naked except for a soft white towel wrapped around his waist and his skin smelt fresh and clean as though he had just stepped out of the shower.

He seemed to be in decent shape.

And he hadn't left his flat.

Thank god for that. He had gone mad without ever leaving the room.

He checked himself. Was he mad now?

He felt terribly weak, physically battered, his muscles aching like a prize-fighter's after a bout, a throbbing pain banging away above his right temple, and a sharper, more localised pain, somewhere below his left knee, but he seemed OK.

But that wasn't answering the question.

He drew a breath and struggled to sit upright on the bed, his jelly-limbs scarcely following his commands.

He was fine. He had woken up from a nightmare in his own bed. Nothing had happened. How long had he been under this time?

He raised himself to look around his flat.

It was trashed.

His bedroom looked like it had been ransacked by burglars who had then had a fight among themselves. Two chairs lay splintered against the wall, the broken neck of a Jack Daniels bottle stuck out of a sofa cushion and shards of broken glass were sprinkled liberally across the carpet. The TV lay on its back, still plugged into the wall and beaming random patterns of static at the ceiling. His records seemed to have been skimmed across the room like Frisbees and a pile of shattered vinyl lay under the bookshelf like broken crockery at a Greek wedding. His books had been piled up in heaps, forming garbage-piles of torn covers and flapping pages as though they had been fly-tipped into the corners with a barrow.

Everything except him was filthy.

In his dream state he must have repetitively paced up and down like a caged tiger, and the marks of his pacing cut the room diagonally in half. A trail of sticky footsteps entered from the kitchen and marched in a straight line across the room, rising over a corner of the bed and terminating in a pile of books on the far side under the window.

That smell?

No.

It was unmistakable. At some stage he'd taken to pissing in that corner.

Great.

His throat was parched. He got up and staggered into the kitchen, gulping down glass after glass of cold water from the tap. The fridge door was wide open, and a carton of orange juice had spilled its entire contents onto the floor. A cluster of blue-backed flies were feasting happily on the congealed mess.

That was going to be a hassle to clean up.

The thought seemed familiar. He had a sudden flashback to the moment he'd stumbled on his way to the ting with Gary. He felt the side of his head. He must have fallen, slipped on the juice or something, and it had briefly jerked him out of the game.

He shook himself. No more of that nonsense.

He stepped into the bathroom. The shower rail was snapped and the curtain had been ripped off its hooks and lay scrunched up in the bath and the toilet was backed up with shit, but nothing worse. As he flushed the toilet the thought occurred to him that in real life he must have been mimicked the dream-shower he had taken at the facility. He remembered the slip and the filmy fabric he'd grabbed hold of as he stumbled. He looked down at his leg. There was a big purple bruise just below his left knee. He must have slipped in the shower in the real world and smacked his knee hard against the bath's rim. That had nearly jerked him out of the dream too.

He looked in the mirror above the sink.

He had lost a lot weight.

His body had slimmed down to a wiry, lean torso, all muscle and tendon, and his face was altered too, his eyes now deep-sunken, red-rimmed and weary, and his face was gaunt; the skin pulled taut over his cheekbones and forehead giving him a skull-like, intense appearance that was entirely new.

Gaunt.

Perhaps he could make it work for him.

How long had he been under?

He was starving hungry, and having set some pasta to boil on the stove, he set about tidying the flat as best he could, putting fresh sheets on the bed, mopping up the orange juice from the kitchen floor, and stuffing the piss-soaked books into black plastic bags and putting them outside the front door. The TV was bust and the chairs were done for, so he dragged them over into a corner and threw a blanket on top of the pile to hide it from view. It looked a bit shitty, but with the windows open at least it no longer smelt rank.

He sat down and begun wolfing down his spaghetti, pressing the blinking red button on his answerphone without thinking. He regretted it instantly, but once it had started he let the whole tape spool through. The first was from Mike Verne, his tone considerate, if not sympathetic, asking him to meet him at two that afternoon in his office. Verne took great pains to stress that it was imperative he attend. There was one from Toby asking him out for a drink, and a breezy message from Sara, asking about his trip and reminding him about their date that evening. The next message from the company was different in tone. It was from Mike Verne's PA, and explained that following the closure of New Television magazine, he needed to attend an appointment with the director that afternoon to discuss his future with the organisation. The third was from someone in human resources who he had never met, and contained the words, 'contractual duties' and 'severance pay'.

They didn't waste any time.

The corporate calls had been spaced out between messages from Sara. The earliest ones were full of concern; her voice sounding almost desperate by the third, "Jeanne's not answering her calls either – What the hell happened out there? Are you OK?" The later calls had a different tone, lacking in the earlier compassion, and rising in irritation. The penultimate message signed off demanding that he, "Stop feeling so fucking sorry for himself and have the fucking decency to at least call me back."

But it was her final message that got him starting out of his seat,

"Right X", Sara's voice began, "This is it. Ultimatum. I don't care how hard you've taken the mag folding anymore. Sulk as much as you want, I don't give a shit. But if you want to have the slimmest chance of still being considered my boyfriend, you need to be at the launch at 7.30 prompt tomorrow night, smiling and shaking hands and supporting me or I tell you X, we are done."

45. SHARK FIN IN A HEATED POOL

With the television bust, and not yet ready to leave the house, he was forced to listen to an interminably long play on Radio 4, where nothing happened and all the actors had the same middle-class accents except for the one who inconsistently faked a Canadian drawl, until they finally announced the time and date on the news. It was the day of Sara's launch. He had been gone for 5 days.

No wonder he had lost so much weight.

It was three o'clock in the afternoon. He had four hours to try and turn himself from a wreck into some kind of vaguely presentable shape.

The only suit left in his wardrobe was a black two-piece with thin lapels that he'd always felt looked dated and funeral. When he'd put it on, he'd managed to convince himself it didn't look so bad. With the weight he'd lost it fitted him better than before and looked almost stylish, even though wearing it meant attending a media launch dressed like a well-presented mourner.

*

The villa in Kent Sara had borrowed for the launch, had been built into the side of a small hill in a modernist, Scandinavian design. There was to be some kind of celebratory meal on the top floor for the most important guests, but when X arrived the room was still unoccupied. He was reasonably certain he hadn't missed the main event as behind its tall glass windows he could make out a long dining table laid still laden with food and festooned with flowers and fruits in colours designed to match the new company's logo. In contrast, the floor below was packed with guests. Its wide balcony had been turned into a terrace café by Sara's caterers and a crowd of women in cocktail dresses and men in their work-day suits with their ties at half-mast, were sipping at brightly coloured long drinks with parasols and curly straws.

Guests were climbing the cantilevered metal stairs that wound round the building to the balcony on the first floor, and X followed them up. As he trudged up the steps behind two PR girls in tight blue mini-dresses, he glanced down, catching sight of a sunken garden below, a flash of blue water visible in the dying rays of the sun; the corner of a swimming pool almost completely hidden from view under an arbour of fig and hibiscus trees. Half way up the steps he met the advertising manager of the Marketing magazine at his old company coming down. "Aye, aye X", he said as he passed, "You look dressed for a funeral. No bad news I hope?" laughing, he slapped X on the shoulder and carried on down the steps.

Sara was waiting for him at the top. She was beautiful of course, but dressed more soberly than he had expected, in a navy two-piece whose pencil skirt stopped just above the knee. Her jacket had wide lapels and padded shoulders and she wore a plain white blouse underneath. She looked business-like, serious and just sexy enough to make you want to rip all that tight tailoring off her and let the full woman out.

"Just in time, I see."

He checked his watch. It was 7.30 exactly.

"You look terrible."

"Thanks."

"Sorry. You can tell me everything later, and thanks for coming. But now, rise and shine! Get smiling and shaking hands and bigging me up please!"

X smiled. Maybe he could be of some use.

For the next hour he shook hands, smiled and said confident and uplifting things about Sara as a person and a businesswoman, but he couldn't shake off his fatigue and confusion. Clumsily side-stepping any questions about himself and what he'd been up to lately, every exchange stuttered awkwardly to a halt, and the effort of keeping the small-talk as inane as possible was exhausting. He was still dutifully holding station beside Sara when she spotted Ron Jeremy coming up the steps and ran down to greet him. The presence of the Essex boy-commercials-director-made-good-in-LA at her launch was a considerable coup, a sprinkling of stardust she had drawn back to London from her travels. She brought the great man over to meet him.

"Ron, this is my partner X", she said, "He used to head up New Television magazine."

"New Television!" he declared, "Crock of shit. Never read it."

X could see Sara looking at him, begging him to bite his tongue for her sake. He gritted his teeth, "You have excellent judgement", X said, "It closed this week."

"See! What did I tell you?" he exclaimed delightedly, happy that his instincts had proved prescient once again.

He slapped X on the back.

Sara gave him a wan smile of thanks and steered Ron on a regal passage around the room.

X took the opportunity to slip away, finding a quiet corner on the edge of the throng and stood nursing a beer, trying to calculate how soon he could leave without upsetting Sara. But the modest amount of alcohol he had drunk had an amplified effect on his emaciated body, and as it hit his bloodstream he found himself scarcely able to stand upright. The events of the past week began to whirl in front of his eyes and feeling like he was strapped into a demented roller-coaster he became disorientated, stumbling forward and bumping into someone. It was the boy who'd hassled him the night of Sara's party, the one whose name he could never remember and always thought he owed him an apology.

Perfect. Just what he needed.

"X! Wow!" he exclaimed loudly, "Great to see you!" The boy draped an arm around X's shoulder and waved to a group cuff-linked clones who were shouting and guffawing at each other a few yards away. "Hey lads this is X", he shouted, "*The* X! The real deal."

The men briefly raised hands in greeting, one shouting, "Yo! X", before returned to talking over each other again.

"So what are you doing now that New TV is over X?" asked the boy excitedly, "What's the next big project you're working on?"

He didn't know what to say. There was no next big project, but the boy's adulation required some kind of response in order not to appear rude. "I've mostly just been dreaming", he said.

At least it was true.

"Cool X. Dreaming - I like it. I understand, got to keep it all hush-hush", he tapped his nose, "But if there a chance for me to be in on the ground…"

X nodded. "I'll let you know."

'Really? Wow! That's great." The boy was genuinely thrilled. He looked furtively behind him and then pressed his mouth against X's ear, "And I can do you a favour too", he whispered, "It just so happens that I've got shed-loads of the finest quality Bolivian marching powder. I don't know how, the stuff I get is usually shit", he confessed, his arm on X's shoulder and his beery breath in his face, "But for some reason this stuff is the dog's bollocks, I'm not sure it's even cut at all. No idea how it got to me. But take it from me, it's the business." He slipped a wrap into X's hands and winking, gestured toward the toilets.

Why not?

"Don't forget!" the boy called after him, "You don't need much."

By the time he left the toilets the boy and his mates had disappeared. He had only chopped out a skinny line, but the boy had told the truth, it *was* really good shit. He was high as a kite. The coke transformed him, everything that had been wrong was now right; his body was trim and athletic, not scrawny; his suit simple and stylish not drab. From having nothing to say he became Oscar fucking Wilde. He couldn't put a foot wrong. Women flirted with him and men listened to his every anecdote with rapt attention. He found himself telling scandalous tales of MIPCOM to wildly amused audiences, impersonating Howard at his most absurdly ebullient, making them cry with laughter at his witty motivational speeches and mixed metaphors. He was hilarious.

He was a scream. When the euphoria started to wear off, he nipped into the toilets for another line.

Coming out of the toilets after the second line, he looked up at the balcony. Sara was on the top floor behind the glass windows, surrounded by bouquets of Bougainvillea, in full flight, articulating a point with an expansive sweep of her arms; vivacious, clearly funny, the group around her collapsing into laughter as he watched, their bodies rocking backwards and forwards like children's toys while she stood, smiling, her hands on her hips. She was magnificent.

He thought about joining her, certain he would cut a dash, but then he remembered the swimming pool he'd noticed on the way in.

Why not?

Excited at the thought and pumped up by the coke, he pushed his way through the crowd and leapt down the spiral staircase that led to the pool, jumping three steps at a time and ripping off his tie as he ran. The trees in the sunken garden shut out the noise of the party above him and he descended into the dim light beneath their bowers with only the clang of his footsteps echoing in the sudden hush. As he leapt off the last step he saw that the two PR girls he had noticed earlier had also made their way down to the pool and were hanging around the diving board at the far end. The women were still in their blue mini-dresses; one barefoot, standing with her toes over the edge and looking down into the water, the other sitting on the diving board, a wine glass and a packet of Rothmans next to her, puffing away as she talked to her friend.

He swaggered over to them, calling out a challenge as he approached, "Lovely evening for a swim, ladies. Care to join me?"

The one sitting on the diving board scoffed at his question, "Not on your life! It's bloody cold and we've got no towels.'

Her friend, however, disagreed. "Come on Lisa!" she argued, "How many times are we going to be at a party with a fancy pool like this?

X dipped his fingers into the pool. The water was cool, rather than cold. He expected that the heating had only been turned off a few hours ago. It would be chilly going in but fine after a few minutes.

'I'll go in if you go in", he said.

The one standing by the edge looked up at him, her hazel eyes blinking under heavily mascaraed lashes. She sized him up for a moment, clearly checking him out before she made a decision.

"OK then", she said, and, still looking directly at him, she unzipped her mini-dress and shuffled it down over her hips.

Stood on the poolside in front of him, she stared boldly into his eyes with her hands on her hips, defying him to follow suit. He met her stare, nonchalantly allowing his gaze to pass over her body. She had a round pretty face, framed by a bob cut of dark-brown hair, and stripped down to her underwear in front of him, her curves cut a more erotic picture than if had she been completely naked. Her blue silk brassiere cupped and pushed her full breasts upward like offerings, and the diamante pendant that dangled from her pierced belly-button pointed, enticingly, at the triangle of thin blue silk between her thighs.

She was Aphrodite-hot.

He quickly undressed, rejoicing that he had put on a clean pair of black boxer shorts before coming out and knowing that his slimmed down body looked good, gave her plenty of time to appraise his body as he had hers. Seeing the look of approval in her eyes, he smiled and pulling himself up to his full height prepared to dive.

Locking eyes with her chanted, "One… Two…Three."

They jumped together.

The water when he hit it felt like ice, just for a second, and then he was wildly invigorated by the cold, roaring to the surface and swimming two lengths of crawl before looking up. The girl was a couple of arm's lengths away, swimming a slow breast-stroke, concentrating on keeping her head out of the water and her make-up intact, "Great isn't it?" she called out, flipping over onto her back and floating lazily alongside him. He turned onto his back too, and they slowly drifted back to the shallow end together.

When they had hauled themselves out, she sat on the edge of the pool, shaking her head to get the water out of her wet hair as best she could. In the cool air she soon began shivering, and he handed her his shirt. Wearing it unbuttoned across her chest, it seemed more an act of undressing than covering up.

Her friend seemed to have disappeared.

He knew what had to happen now.

"By chance I got given some really good coke earlier tonight", he said, and knowing exactly what was implied by the words added, "Do you fancy a line?"

"Sure", she replied, a smile curling on her lips, "We can do it in my car. It's only just over there and I've got a warm top in the boot. I could give you your shirt back." He followed her out of the pool and down the steps into the car park, glancing briefly up at the lit balcony behind him.

*

He took her over the bonnet of her XR2. Bent over beneath him, he moved the strap of her thong so he could dig deeper into her flesh; real human flesh, not fantasy-freak-madness-dream girl flesh; the real thing, alive and yielding under him.

Even with the coke he wasn't going to last long, it was all the release he needed, her soft skin, the deep throated cries forced out of her by his passion, the warmth of her back under his hands. He heard voices and looked up. Two figures had wandered down to the roadway above him to wait for a taxi. He stopped thrusting for a second. No, they couldn't be seen, the car park was unlit and they were completely hidden in the darkness. He sank his fingers into the girl's hair, pushing her face down into the bonnet and began pounding into her again.

Then three things happened at exactly the same time.

X reached his climax; all his pent-up rage and frustration roaring out into the night as he came.

A taxi-driver, seeing customers hailing him from the road-side, turned on his lights before starting the engine of his car.

Sara turned her head in the direction of the cry from the carpark.

For a second, X was spot-lit in the beam of the taxi's headlights, his back arched, head held aloft, a naked girl pressed down beneath him. Only for a second, and then the taxi crawled forward, the angle of its beams altered, and he was hidden in darkness once again.

But it had been enough.

He watched Sara turn and walk away. At the foot of the steps she stumbled, stopped, shook herself and then, after a moment's pause with her hands on her hips, she picked up her stride and walked swiftly back to the party and out of his life forever.

"Hey!" the girl beneath him said. "If you're all done, can I get some clothes on? I'm getting cold here."

His flaccid cock flopped in his own semen between the girl's buttocks.

It was all over.

He had learnt nothing.

EPILOGUE
31.3.1990

And that was the end of it all.

End of Sara of course, and he'd effectively sacked himself from work by failing to turn up after the magazine failed, so that was the end of shiny suits and the Groucho Club as well. He could never have gone back anyway; not after Cannes. It was done in his mind too. Finished. They paid him off with three month's tax free salary as a settlement, so at least there wasn't any need to worry about money for a while.

It wasn't quite the end of the dreaming however. There was still one final visit to be endured.

He had sensed that it was going to happen the moment he lay down to sleep, and as soon as he'd closed his eyes he was back, standing by the tramway opposite the park where it had all begun. He stood in the gathering dusk as he had before, under trees weighed down with bright orange leaves. A stiff, cold breeze was blowing down the tracks. He crossed the road and entered the park heading for the brightly lit running track across the grass, thinking that perhaps Eva would be there and excited at the thought of seeing her again. Before he set foot on the grass a figure stepped out from under the shadows by the wrought iron bench.

"Hi X", said Sven.

He stood a yard or so away, hanging back by the bench as though he were purposefully keeping his distance from X. "Tasan said you'd be here at this time so…" His voice was tentative.

X recalled his last sight of Tasan, his obscene jig of delight at the doorway. He shuddered involuntarily. He didn't want to think about Tasan ever again.

"How's Eva?" he asked.

Sven rubbed the back of his neck and shuffled awkwardly, "She's

OK now, but it's taken a while..." he began, clearly struggling to find the right words, "she was quite... messed up by it all... and after you were gone it got worse...she made a formal complaint against Tasan and Erika, and all the preparation was constant stress, and, well, you know what Eva's like..."

Did he know what Eva was like? He wasn't sure if he ever really knew her at all.

"But then it all got very strange", Sven continued, "Just before the hearing was due, Tasan and Erika upped and disappeared. They didn't just leave town in disgrace, it was more like they had vanished into thin air. When they opened the door to Erika's apartment it was stripped completely bare and not only did the neighbours not witness her leaving, none of them could even remember her ever having lived there. It was the same for Tasan. It got even weirder when the university began looking into their backgrounds. None of their qualifications checked out, no-one knew where they'd come from, and no-one could recall how they'd got appointed in the first place. It was big news for a while although it's died down now, but you can imagine...the publicity was just more stress for Eva".

Sven paused, unable to look him in the eyes as he spoke, "She just wants to put it behind her X."

"Can I see her?" he pleaded, unsure of what he would say, but desperate to have one last chance to make amends.

"No X", Sven replied gently, "as I said, she just wants to forget about it and move on".

"She's here, isn't she?" X asked, "On the running track". He was certain of it.

Sven was firm in his response, "I'm not going to answer that, and you should respect her wishes – you at least owe her that".

So she was there. He could ignore Sven, run across the grass and say.... Say what?

Sven interrupted his thought. "You can't cross the grass without an escort".

"What!"

"Tasan told me." Sven shrugged. "It's the way it works apparently. He came to my flat just before he disappeared, told me you'd be here at this time and that you couldn't cross the grass alone."

"Will you take me across the grass then?" X asked.

"No. I'm sorry. I won't."

"Will you pass her a message from me at least?"

"No, I won't do that either."

X was suddenly angry, "If you won't pass a message and you won't take me across the grass, why did you come?"

"So there was someone to greet you, let you know what was happening; it didn't seem right to leave you standing on your own in the dark."

Sven was always the kindest of them. His thoughtfulness dissipated X's anger, now he just felt defeated and sad.

They were silent a moment.

"Does Eva know that you intended to meet me here?" X asked.

Sven nodded.

"Will you at least tell her I came?"

"No X, I won't. I don't want to lie to you, you've had enough of that, but I'll tell her I came to the bench and no-one showed up. I think it's better that way".

There was nothing more to say.

Sven stepped forward, "Goodbye X", he said and touched his forehead against X's brow. The gentle pressure somehow delivered a blow of such enormous force that it sent him hurtling back through the trees, out of the park, up over the tram tracks and high into the air above the city; his speed of ascent so fast it was as though he was being hurled not only into the sky but out of the very fabric of the world itself.

He had woken crying in his own bed, knowing that whatever it had been, it too, was now over.

*

Unemployed and with time on his hands, he thought deeply about what had happened to him for the first time.

After days sat in Hammersmith reference library poring over medical texts he became certain it hadn't been any form of epilepsy; none of the symptoms were right, and epilepsy was a lifelong condition, it didn't just come and go. Having satisfied himself that it wasn't a medical condition, he then hit on the most pathetic of explanations; the Harlesden doctor had been right, it had just been an inadequate young man's sad fantasy of lust. At first this explanation seemed to fit the facts. The dreaming had begun, after all, just after his first sighting of Sara, and he had certainly been chasing one woman or other in every single episode.

Eventually, he dismissed the thought. Surely the complexity of the dreamworlds were far too great and totally unnecessary to be have just been the background for some vapid masturbatory daydream.

Next he concluded that it had all been some sort of crisis of conscience. The moment he'd met Sara had also been the day when he'd committed to selling out his principles, to give up working with the needy and go all out for himself. Maybe his mind had invented better, more moral worlds for him to inhabit in recompense? All the worlds had clearly been utopias of some kind, so perhaps the whole fantasy was his mind desperately trying to send him a message that he had wandered off track.

In the end he rejected that explanation too, both because the dreams had themselves been too vivid, too real, too physical, to be merely musings of his own mind and, in all honesty, he hadn't paid much attention to their morality and social structure, only half-listening to Eva and Gary's patient explanations. It couldn't be possible to ignore your own crisis of conscience surely? But what did that leave him? That he'd really been transported into a parallel dimension? Some astral version of him passing through time and space to become a seeker of truth, ultimately failing to be guided to enlightenment by their occupants?

Perhaps he was mad after all.

Then one night he woke in a cold sweat with the realisation that Tasan was an anagram of Satan.

He was back in the library the next day, pouring over books in the occult section in a cold sweat. It all seemed to make perfect sense. He had made a Faustian pact on the day he delivered his manifesto of self-interest to Kevin. Tasan/Satan had delivered his part of the bargain to the letter, for all the good it had done him; the flat, the car, the girl, the job, right down to the finest quality cocaine. The more he thought about it the more it made sense. In this light, his conversation with Tasan on the big wheel read like a storybook tale of a meeting with the devil on the wheel of fortune; the DNA games had been a vision of hell where demon competitors fought it out in a sulphurous caldera, sex with Clara had been the fruit from the tree of knowledge that had got him expelled from Eden, and the gold coin that Erika had passed to Tasan right at the end of it all; it had been his very soul. No wonder the devil had been so delighted.

Then, just when he had convinced himself that he had inadvertently damned himself to hell eternal, it occurred to him that Tasan was also an anagram of Santa, and his laughter became so hysterical that he was asked to leave the library.

He gave up on trying to understand what had happened to him but couldn't shake the thought that there was some purpose to it all; that there was something he was supposed to learn.

The other worlds he had experienced had been better than this one, fairer, more compassionate, he had been a better person when he was in them. So he set about trying to be a better person. Who knows? Maybe he could still save his soul. He also started thinking about how the world he actually lived in could be made better, setting himself a program similar to the courses he'd taken at the dreamworld's university. He began with every utopia he could find in the library, working his way from Thomas More through William Morris to Aldous Huxley and Ursula Le Guin before grinding through textbooks on sociology and political theory. He began an evening class in Scandinavian culture and started a humanities module with the Open University.

While the search for enlightenment went on he still had to earn a living, and when the money ran out he went back to working in homelessness. It paid the rent and maybe earned his damned soul a few days off its tenure in purgatory, but the work was still no more than a sticking plaster on a festering sore and he felt certain he had to do something bigger; something that really changed things, but he didn't know what. In pursuit of being a better person he made up with Paul, was civil to Griff and even tried to earn Kevin's forgiveness, but too much damage had been done. He hung out with Alex and her crusty friends a fair bit, trying to listen to their Aquarian optimism with respect and even took a pill with them one night at a club in the East End. For an evening he loved them all, ending the night on a bench by the toilets cosmically connected to a geezer he had never met before who would have probably have been giving him a good kicking for looking at him funny if they hadn't both been chemically enhanced. He had beamed all the way from the taxi rank back to his flat, certain that if only they could get the world's leaders on pills it would all work out.

But with a pounding hangover at the kitchen table the next morning he knew he was done with that kind of dreaming.

It wasn't enough, he had concluded, just to dream up better worlds, he had to take action, and coming to this demonstration had been the first step. A tax that had the Duke of Westminster paying the same bill as an office cleaner was clearly so wrong that it had to be stopped, and given the numbers that had turned out in protest, he wasn't alone in the thought. He felt full of optimism. Perhaps people, like him, were finally waking up.

He'd planned to meet Paul at Tottenham Court Road station, but the crush was worse than carnival, and there wasn't the remotest chance of spotting him in the crowd. It had taken him an hour to get out of the station, and when he had finally reached the street it was chaos. Oxford Street had been blocked off by lines of riot police and smoke from burning cars floated in the air. The sound of glass smashing as bins were thrown through shop windows mixed with police sirens and the roars and chants of the mob. Swept along with the crowd he had been pushed further and further into the heart of the protest until he found himself in Trafalgar Square, sheltering behind the empty plinth in the shadow of the National Gallery.

Everything had gone crazy, the long deep sleep of England shattered by the pent up rage of its people whose roars, crashing like seismic waves across the square, were now met with the rhythmic drumming of truncheons on riot-shields and the clattering of horses' hooves. The plinth acted as an eddy in the surges of the mob and for the first time since he'd struggled out of the tube he could pause to take a breath. He stood, exalted but also a little scared, wiping the sweat of his brow with the back of his hand.

And there she was, crouching next to him, taking snaps of events in sudden darts around the side of the plinth like she was under sniper fire.

Her.

She turned away from the square and looked straight into his eyes

He stood stock still, unable to move or speak, the surface of his skin suddenly charged with static electricity as though he'd been struck by a lightning bolt. Time seemed to freeze around him and the cacophony in the square was suddenly stilled to silence

She continued to stare at him as though she too had been frozen in the instant.

And suddenly it made sense, all of it. All the mad wanderings and dreams of glory, all the lies and deceit and confusion, all of it leading inexorably to this moment, explicitly designed to ensure that he would be standing on this precise spot at this exact time.

Sara, Eva, Clara. She was all of those women and none.

He had thought he had learned from them only that he couldn't trust his own judgement and was unworthy of love. But now he understood, his betrayals, desperate misunderstandings, and humiliations hadn't been without purpose. They had made him ready for this instant, had armed him against making the same mistakes ever again.

In the frozen silence of the square he thanked each of them for what they had given him.

She stared back at him, equally transfixed.

Looking into her eyes X knew, as if it were the only thing in the world he knew, that with this woman, he would build something beautiful and true, something real and lasting, that they would be together, side by side until the very last breath of his life.

He spoke into their private bubble of silence, "What do we do now?" he asked.

She smiled, and X was certain that she knew the question was not merely what shall we do this instant, but what should they do for the rest of their lives.

"I don't know", she said, still smiling, "But right now, "help me get this camera up onto the plinth - I think the horses are about to charge".

ABOUT THE AUTHOR

David Christie has the kind of cv that is either evidence of an interesting life or proof of an inability to stick at anything. He was a market-stall tradesman, a fish-farmer in Devon and Africa and an advertising executive before spending ten years running projects for homeless people. He has since done other stuff. He has degrees in both Biology and History. *Sweden* is his first novel but may well be his life's work.

Printed in Great Britain
by Amazon